LIFE AFTER

THE COMPLETE SERIES

JULIE HALL

ISBN-13: 978-0-9989867-5-3 (paperback), 978-0-9989867-6-0 (hardback)

Julie Hall

www.JulieHallAuthor.com

Huntress, Warfare, and *Dominion* cover designs by Nathália Suellen.

Logan cover design by Christian Bentulan.

CONTENTS

HUNTRESS

WARFARE

LOGAN

DOMINION

AWARDS

FOR THE LIFE AFTER SERIES

ADVENTURES OF UNFAILING LOVE

Finalist, Speculative Fiction
Huntress
2018 ACFW Carol Awards

Young Adult Book of the Year
Huntress
2018 Christian Indie Awards

Gold Medal Winner
Huntress
2018 Illumination Awards

First Place Winner, Religion
Huntress
2018 IndieReader Discovery Awards

Christian Fiction Finalist
Huntress
2018 Next Generation Indie Book Awards

Alliance Award (Reader's Choice)
Warfare
2018 Realm Makers Awards

Parable Award, Finalist
Logan

2018 Realm Makers Awards

Gold Medal Winner
Huntress
2017 The Wishing Shelf Book Awards

Best Inspirational Novel
Huntress
2017 Ozarks Indie Book Festival

Best Debut Author
Julie Hall
2017 Ozarks Indie Book Festival

Second Place Winner
Huntress
2017 ReadFree.ly Indie Book of the Year

First Place Winner
Huntress
2012 Women of Faith Writing Contest

USA TODAY Bestselling Author
August 17, 2017 & June 21, 2018

PRAISE AND REVIEWS

The romance is sweet, mysterious, frustrating, and perfect. With fantastic world-building, Julie Hall has created an interesting and desirable afterlife. I love the unique take on angels, demons, and the life after death. Characters are relatable: Audrey, flawed and confused, but also filled with untapped strength; Logan, strong and swoon-worthy. Enough action and mystery to keep me flipping the pages.

Jaymin Eve
USA Today Bestselling author
of *The Walker Saga* and
Supernatural Prison series

The Life After series is wildly creative and packed with heart pounding adventure, plot twists that leave you reeling! You will not be disappointed.

Leia Stone
USA Today Bestselling author
of the *Fallen Academy* series

Julie Hall is destined to be one of the great fiction writers of our time. Not since Frank Peretti has an author had the writing genius to weave together spiritual and physical worlds into a believable epic journey. Her first work will keep young adults riveted, expanding their sense of wonder and challenging them to think about forces and powers beyond what they can see.

Rebecca Hagelin

columnist with *The Washington Times*;
author of *30 Ways in 30 Days to Save Your Family*

Huntress will have you holding your breath and falling in love. Beautifully creative! Julie Hall expertly weaves an action-packed plot and swoon-worthy romance with powerful, heartfelt themes of love, family, forgiveness, and redemption. I can't wait for the sequel!

Kelly Oram
author of *The Supernaturals* series
and the *Jamie Baker Trilogy*

Dominion is the perfect ending to a beautiful story. While Audrey questions her own existence, she remains fiercely loyal to the ones she loves, especially Logan. Gripping and emotional, it's filled with hope and unconditional love.

Cameo Renae
USA Today Bestselling author
of the *Hidden Wings* series

Julie has created a world so imaginative and exciting that I can't help but want to be there. In Audrey, Julie Hall has given readers a heroine who is strong, vulnerable, and relatable. This book creates a safe place to ask questions, but also shows us we will not always get the answers we want. The adventure is in moving ahead, in faith, even without them.

Catherine Parks
author of *A Christ-Centered Wedding*

Huntress is absolutely charming, imaginative, and sweet. It is a fast-paced, original, and intriguing story. I hope it's a series because I can't wait to see what happens next.

Susan Elllingburg
senior writer for Women Of Faith

DEATH WAS ONLY THE BEGINNING

HUNTRESS

LIFE AFTER
BOOK ONE

JULIE HALL

USA TODAY BESTSELLING AUTHOR

PROLOGUE

The chains rattled when he changed positions, grinding against both flesh and floor. Chains so familiar you'd think he'd be used to them by now. He wasn't. Whether standing in his tower, as he was now, or roaming grasslands and streets, his illusion of freedom was always only that—an illusion.

He ground his teeth in anger.

The misshapen messenger who'd interrupted his musings did not even bear looking at. His contempt for it and its companions was almost as strong as his contempt for *them*. The chosen ones. Those inferior beings created with limited sight and innumerable weaknesses. He was sick of watching them fumble around in the dark with the freedom he deserved.

"What is it?"

"We think we have something. Something new our spies have discovered." The creature's voice was thick and oily, with barely a wisp of its former cadence.

"What exactly would that be?"

"We think it may be what you've been waiting for."

His interest was piqued, if only marginally. Numerous false reports over time had dulled his curiosity.

"Go on."

"An ancient weapon has awakened—a double-edged sword that blazes to life at a touch. It's been witnessed to penetrate even to the division of the soul and spirit."

"The cherubim sword?"

"We believe so."

The creature had his full attention now. His shackles marred the ground as he walked briskly to look down over his domain.

"Who wields the weapon?"

"A mere girl."

He was surprised. Then his eyes narrowed. Why give that much power to someone so feeble? He would have to verify the findings himself. If the news was correct, this could be it—what he'd been searching for. Something this important couldn't be trusted to his slaves.

"Where is she now?"

The creature had the sense to look nervous. It shuffled its feet and brought its body lower. As if groveling could assure protection from his master's wrath.

"Sh—she's no longer here. She's been taken back up."

Red anger flashed in his eyes. Fools, all of them! The messenger scurried out of reach. He turned back to look over the expanse. The pathetic being wasn't worth the energy it would take to destroy it.

"You will tell me the moment she returns."

"Yes, of course."

The creature hadn't been dismissed, but it took the opportunity to quietly back away. He didn't notice or care. After all this time, could it be that a mere girl would be the key to his freedom? Oh, the irony.

He smiled to himself. Deceiving a girl had been the start of his imprisonment. Perhaps it would also be the end.

IN THE BEGINNING

"*Oof!*"

Air exploded from my lungs as I hit the ground and rolled. I wish I could say I saw my life flash before my eyes, but I didn't. In fact, my eyes were squeezed shut. My body jostled painfully with each lumpy impact. Through the noise I heard a name being yelled. A desperate sound. I wanted to respond, but I couldn't find my voice. My nostrils stung, and there was a metallic taste in my mouth. I tried to spit it out. Something warm dripped down my chin.

And as suddenly as it began, everything stopped. My body was no longer moving. The silence was deafening.

After forcing my eyes open, I immediately wished I hadn't. I stood in nothing. Startling white all around. Brilliant and soundless.

Without a sense of up or down I stumbled as I tried to take a step forward. Turning in a shaky circle, the breath in my chest hitched. I dropped to my knees, patting the space before me, and my hands began to sink—down and down until I pitched forward and my down was up. My arms stretched to their limits and I found myself reaching into the space above my head rather than below my feet.

Where was I? How had I gotten here? I was about to grasp something important, but with a sudden whoosh the memories were yanked from my mind. Tendrils of my consciousness reached out to haul them back, but returned with emptiness . . . a mirror of my surroundings.

One memory remained, standing out like a lone star in a black night. A jar of pickles on a black granite countertop. A memory that made something inside me prickle with anger even as I wondered why. But everything else was simply gone. Every other memory gone, as if it had never been there. As if *I had never been.*

I was about to lose it. Hysterics bubbling up inside, but before they broke free something caught my eye.

Squinting, I saw something, a dot. It was either very far away or extremely tiny. Without the luxury of surroundings to give it perspective, I wasn't sure which. I blinked—it was barely, but perceptibly, larger. I squeezed my eyes shut and opened them again. Suddenly, not only was there a dot, but the expanse around me had a line.

A horizon.

Relief washed over me. The dot continued to grow in size and began to take shape—a man, I realized. A man with his back to me and partially bent over, moving his arms and hands as if conducting a silent symphony. The more intently I stared, the closer he appeared to be.

His arm arched down in a curve and then back up, and a great crash came from behind me. Spinning around, I gasped.

A mighty sea had appeared, waves smashing against the break. I stood on a cliff, the sea churned below me in a kaleidoscope of blues, and the smell of salty water wafted up, tickling my nostrils until I sneezed.

As I took a step back, something brushed at my ankles. Glancing around my eyes widened. More splendor had sprung out of the nothing. Bright green grass—so lush I could feel its suppleness beneath my feet—covered the ground. I was filled with a sudden yearning to slip off my shoes and sink my toes into its cool softness.

But then the man was inexplicably closer. Close enough to see the color of his brown hair and the medium build of his body. His arms had stopped their quick pace and were instead swaying back and forth to a slower, unheard melody. Stretched out before him was a landscape with trees, fields, and rolling hills dotted with flowers, a pinwheel of colors displayed before my eyes. The salty air mingled with the sweet tang of fresh summer blooms.

My breath caught when I flicked my eyes up and a vivid blue sky burst from horizon to horizon. A magnificent red bird shot through the air with a sweet song, followed by a flock of brightly colored birds echoing the melody. They danced in the air before soaring away and disappearing from view. No sooner had they vanished than a brown streak shot through my peripheral vision. I glanced around in time to see a doe dart out from a cluster of trees and lope, carefree, through the pasture.

Twisting my neck, I peered over my shoulder at the man, who was now standing only an arm's length in front of me. He was focused on something hidden from my view, nodding to himself and humming a tune I couldn't place. I remained where I stood, uncertain; wanting to get his attention but unable to bring myself to move. The strangeness of the whole experience was too overwhelming. Unsure of what to do, I waited, convinced for some unknown reason that the man was also waiting for me.

At last, he straightened and turned to face me. He was just a man. A man with skin darkened from either birth or sun, dressed in dark washed jeans and a smudged white T-shirt. His fingers were tinged with what looked like powder or paint. He brushed one hand over the other and then rubbed them on his jeans. They came up clean. A soft smile of contentment lit his lips.

And then he spoke.

"We've been waiting for you." His baritone was as deep as it was soft.

"You have?" I replied, not even trying to hide my confusion.

He nodded.

"Do I know you or something?"

He shoved his hands in his pocks, smiled pleasantly, and nodded again. "I'm here to welcome you and to show you the way."

"Welcome me where?"

"Welcome you home." It was said simply and without irony. "So welcome home. You can call me Joe."

There was a familiarity in the man's voice that distracted me, but what he was trying to explain was more important. Concentrating hard, I pulled as much of my attention back as possible to reconcile the word 'home' with where I was now. I rolled the word around in my mind, slowly, deliberately. And strangely, I discovered a deep-rooted sense of truth buried inside of me.

"Home." I tested the weight of the word in my mouth. "And . . . you're Joe?"

He just nodded, affording me the time I needed to process what he'd said. His eyes, so dark brown it was hard to see the pupils, appeared young and sharp, even with the faint age lines that sprayed from the corners like rays of sunlight. As with his voice, there was something distracting about his eyes. Something familiar that danced on the edge of my subconscious. I desperately grabbed for it, but it slipped by like water through cracks.

I shook my head to clear my thoughts. Something wasn't clicking. I was unable to shake the feeling that there was truth to what he said, but this place felt completely alien.

"Have I been here before?" I asked.

"No, but this place has been prepared and waiting for you for a long time. From before you even learned the true meaning of home."

How could that be right? I had just watched this place be created from nothing.

"I'm not where I used to be?"

He smiled. "No, you're not," he said gently. "How about I show you around?"

"I suppose . . ." but I paused in apprehension. "But shouldn't I be somewhere else?"

Another gentle smile. "No, I promise you are exactly where you are supposed to be. Not a moment too soon, not a moment too late." He gestured forward. The air sweetened as we retreated from the ocean and through the lush greenery of the world he had just orchestrated.

The grass tickled my ankles as I stole glances at Joe. I had trouble concentrating on his features. I'd look at his hair to memorize the exact shade of brown only to look away a moment later and forget. His build seemed average at first, but with each new look I was convinced he'd grown taller or shrunk to a smaller size. Even his skin seemed to lighten or darken with each glimpse.

Most disorienting of all was the burning familiarity at the edge of my consciousness. Without a memory to search through, it was impossible to place him. Everything about him was so utterly nondescript—even racially ambiguous—it was possible I was trying to remember an entirely different person.

We walked over fields of grass freckled with delicate flowers and through forests of trees that reached impossible heights. We traveled for what might have been hours, or mere minutes, until we stood on the banks of a tranquil river.

"I thought you might be thirsty," he said.

Now that he said the words, I found I was parched. So much so I couldn't get a response out, only nod in agreement.

"Then drink as much as you please." He sat down on the ground and crossed his legs, keeping a watchful eye on me.

I dropped to my knees on the soft bank and cupped my hands to dip them into the water. My insatiable thirst was quenched in a moment. The water was so crisp and fresh I had the wild thought that I'd never be thirsty again—as if the river was flowing inside me. But what felt possible at the time seemed ridiculous when the moment passed.

After drinking my fill, the water calmed, turning into a glassy mirror. I leaned forward eagerly—but the face that rippled on the surface was utterly unfamiliar to me.

I brought a hand to my cheek, and the image in the water did the same. Large, dark brown eyes set in a petite, heart-shaped face, stared back wide-eyed. Equally dark straight hair poured over my shoulder as I leaned closer. It grazed the water's surface and mingled with the reflection, creating an artificial curl in the mirror image. Who was this girl looking back at me? I touched a finger lightly to the surface, and her face distorted from view.

"Would you like to tell me what you are wondering?"

I looked back at the stranger sitting next to me with that unwavering smile on his lips. Now that we weren't moving, his image was once again static. His hair, which hung almost to his shoulders, was a shade darker than my own. Stubble across his face aged what might have been a younger complexion. He appeared to be in his late twenties or thirties, but small physical contradictions prevented a more accurate guess. He was so normal, yet completely atypical at the same time.

"Joe," I once again tested his name on my tongue, "why don't I remember anything? Why don't I remember you if we've met before? Where am I? What happened?"

"Good questions, but perhaps not the right ones. You will remember your life again in time, but for now, you're meant to focus only on this new existence. It would be a distraction to have your memories before you settle into life in the ever after."

He leaned back, resting his weight on his arms. "You now have an eternity to experience."

It was then that I knew—I had died.

It was strange the way my mind and body accepted the fact peacefully, even as I knew I should be feeling something else. Frightened, perhaps? Sad? Angry even? Emotions I told myself to have, yet was incapable of feeling.

"Shall we continue?" Joe asked. He stood, never taking his eyes off me. "There is so much more waiting to be discovered."

I pushed to my feet and we continued along the river's edge. I split my attention between the man and the scenery until a mountain range cut a jagged path through the landscape in the distance. The mountains, with whitened tips, grew before my eyes at a much faster pace than they should have. I looked down to see the land speeding along underneath me with each step. The details of the ground blurred, as if we were traveling too fast for eyes to focus.

Giving up my attempts to make sense of it, I lifted my eyes to a radiant city that had suddenly come into view. Structures nestled snugly within a mass of piney trees at the feet of the mountains. Giant spiraling towers wove their way into the air. Glistening monuments reflected the light in every direction like crystals. Smaller buildings stood proudly at the feet of the others, refusing to be overshadowed, some with milky smooth façades and others with intricately carved corners and trim, all shining brightly.

Both awed and repelled I fumbled a step. Was this where we were headed, and if so, how was I supposed to find a home in a place so splendid, so perfect? Would my own imperfections corrupt its purity?

A chill ran down my spine as a breath caught in my throat. There was movement in the city. People dotted the ground around the magnificent buildings. That changed everything. Maybe someone there could help me understand. The beating in my chest picked up a notch, hammering in my ears. I knew the city was where I was supposed to be.

Below, the river had swelled to a powerful rush, and it stood in my way. I looked to the left and right but couldn't find a bridge in either direction. The water was too ferocious to cross without one.

I glanced at Joe, who was studying me silently.

"Can you help? I don't see a way across."

"And you're sure you want to go forward?"

"Yes, please. I want to see it up close."

He nodded. "Then that is where you shall go."

No sooner were the words out of his mouth than the water split in front of him, and a dry path formed on the riverbed. Not even a droplet of water remained.

He turned to motion me forward.

"Are you scared?" he asked, seeing my hesitation.

"Yes," I admitted. Afraid of not just walking through the waters, but also of what was ahead. The future I was taking a step toward, and the past I was leaving behind.

"You needn't be."

I believed him.

An unexpected thrill of excitement suddenly propelled me to act, curiosity alongside apprehension. Striding forward, I marveled at the dryness of the ground below my feet. The walls of water shot well above my head, yet stood as still as glass as we passed. I stopped to take note of a brightly colored fish, at least the size of my forearm, the O shape of his mouth opening and closing as he watched us in return.

Reaching a finger out, I touched the wall of water. The spooked fish vanished. The tip of my finger started a series of small ripples that caused the wall to undulate wildly.

I looked back at Joe in alarm.

"Not to worry, it'll hold," he said.

Joe stayed next to me during the short walk between waters but stopped just before the river's edge.

"We've traveled together as long as needed. You'll take the next steps on your own."

"But wait!" I was suddenly desperate to stay with the one person I knew. I couldn't navigate the city before me alone. "What will happen to me? Will I see you again?"

He stepped forward and wrapped me in his arms. He quietly said something in my hair—was it "I missed you"?—before he stepped back once again. It was the first time he'd touched me.

"Yes, most certainly you will, Little One. But now you have other things to do."

"But isn't this it? Is this how it ends?"

An easy smile crossed his face, almost as if I'd said something he found amusing. "No, Audrey, this is how it begins."

He reached down to me, touched a hand to my cheek, and in a blink was gone. But he'd left me with something I hadn't had before.

A name.

PROCESSED

"*A*udrey?"

I was shaken out of my reverie by that one simple word. The only thing I knew belonged to me.

I fixed my eyes where I thought the voice had come from, but there wasn't anyone there. Instead, across from me and to the right, an open doorway appeared where a smooth white wall had been a moment before.

When I'd taken my first step out of the dry riverbed, it hadn't been onto the soft green grass of the opposite bank as I expected. Instead, I stood alone in a room with four white walls and a glossy, unremarkable plastic chair. The first thing I did was tap the floor with my foot to ensure I was still on solid ground. As I moved the chair across the room, it scraped against the floor with a nails-on-the-chalkboard screech. The normalcy of the sound comforted me. A quick turn confirmed that the room didn't have any doors or windows

Glancing back down at the chair, a note on thick white parchment paper appeared. The marks on the paper were elegantly written in gold strokes. At first, the large swirls were illegible, but when I tilted the paper, my mind made sense of the characters.

> *Please take a seat.*
> *We shall be with you shortly for processing.*

"Processing," I mumbled under my breath. "What am I? A sheep?"

Without any other options, I folded the paper and put it in the pocket of my pants, before obediently taking a seat. I'd lost awareness of time while trying to get past the jar of pickles and the confusion in my memory, until someone had called my name and the doorway had appeared on the wall across from me.

"Okay, off to processing I go," I said under my breath with a false sense of bravado.

I pushed myself out of the chair and took a few tentative steps forward, just far enough to peer through the opening.

A pretty blonde woman sat behind an oversized mahogany desk with a boxy-looking gray machine mounted on top. Carvings on the panels and legs of the desk depicted battle scenes.

My eyes scanned the carvings as I hesitantly made my way through the doorway. Unfamiliar creatures were frozen in combat. Long and powerful wings spread behind some of them. Many brandished large swords, their faces oddly peaceful even in the midst of such turmoil. Others, with misshapen bodies bent over and twisted at impossible angles, extra appendages that often came to a sharp point, and faces utterly malformed, were sure to give me nightmares for days. That is, if I dreamed anymore. Did dead people dream?

I was still studying the images when the blonde woman cleared her throat. My head snapped up, and I found myself staring at her. She couldn't have been older than mid-thirties, with skin as luminous as porcelain. Her hair was carefully swept back into a loose bun at the nape of her neck. What appeared to be a forgotten pencil stuck out of it.

Blondie made another sound with her throat, and I realized I had missed something.

"Oh, I'm sorry," I said, forcing myself to pay attention to the words coming out of her mouth. Was she glowing?

"Don't worry about it, sugar. It happens all the time," she drawled with a Southern accent as smooth and sweet as honey. She smiled at me. "It's a big adjustment. Why don't you come all the way in and sit down for a moment while we get your assignment figured out?"

I didn't know what she was talking about, but I smiled and nodded anyway as I pulled out the only chair in front of her—an underwhelming black plastic one. "Um, I'm sorry. My assignment?"

"Yes, of course. What you learned about in orientation, dear." She smiled patiently back at me.

"Orientation?"

"Yes, orientation." A wrinkle of concern appeared between her brows. "You did come here from orientation, didn't you?"

I didn't like that she sounded so unsure. "No, I mean, I don't think so. I've been in the white room ever since I crossed the river."

Blondie's eyebrows shot up, and I could swear she glowed even brighter. I twisted my head up to see if a spotlight or something was adding to the effect.

"Really? Well, that is rather . . . unusual."

Her reaction gave me the urge to hop up on the desk and start demanding answers, but instead I sat rooted in place, patiently waiting to be herded to the next thing. Everything was so surreal.

Whatever was so "unusual," she recovered from it quicker than I did. The soothing tone returned to her voice. "We'll get this all figured out in a snap. But to give you the abridged version, this is where you come to get your working assignment for eternity."

One heartbeat, then another.

"I'm going to have the same job, like, forever? And I get *assigned . . .* as in, I don't get a choice?"

"Yes, of course you'll have the same job for eternity, but it's nothing to worry about. Everyone gets the right one." She said that as if it would make everything all better, and then continued without giving me the opportunity to respond.

"Let's move forward, shall we? Can I ask you your name, sugar?"

"Audrey."

"Can you tell me how old you were?"

I didn't know. I looked across the gleaming desk at the woman. She stared back at me patiently. Then suddenly there was a sound in my head like a cork being released from a bottle, and my brain supplied the information.

"Eighteen." That surprised me. I thought the reflection in the river had looked younger than that.

"And Audrey, dear, can you tell me how you died?"

Finally, the words struck me with emotion. I bit back tears, making a mental note that you could still cry when you're dead.

"I'm not sure," I whispered.

I didn't miss the softening of her eyes. "That's okay, sugar bear. Sometimes it takes some extra time to get caught up."

I nodded numbly, not knowing how to respond.

She reached forward to give my hand a reassuring squeeze. Her touch was more than just warm; it spread a feeling of goodwill throughout my body. It was both soothing and disconcerting at the same time. I pulled my hand back. I didn't want to feel either of those emotions.

Blondie gave me a small smile as if to say she understood before focusing her attention on the boxy object in front of her, which looked almost like a large, very outdated computer monitor. She worked for a few moments without looking up at me, her raised fingers moving quickly and silently over the screen. But that was the side I couldn't see, so I really didn't know what she was doing.

Finally she said, "Oh, here we go, it's coming up now."

Even though I had no idea what was going on, I held my breath in anticipation.

"Oh dear," she murmured.

I let the breath I had been holding escape in a loud rush. She looked more flustered than when she'd found out I'd skipped orientation. The nervous itch returned. What I read on her face was a mixture of concern and confusion. That couldn't be good.

She suddenly remembered I was still there and tried to wipe the look from her face, replacing it with a mask of calm assurance.

"Well, if you'll excuse me a moment, dear. I need to go get someone. I'll be back in no time."

I nodded since my throat had gone dry. Blondie gracefully lifted her willow frame from her chair and pressed her hand to the white wall behind her. A door swung open, one I hadn't even realized was there. It shut soundlessly behind her.

The slight nervousness that had started in the pit of my stomach spread and grew into a near panic as I waited for her. I looked around the room to get my mind off what was happening, but it was empty. All white walls, no pictures hung. Besides the desk, which stood like a monolith in the white drenched room, there was a gray table behind me and black chairs lining the walls. Ordinary office furniture. After a few minutes I gave up trying to distract myself and started gnawing on one of my fingernails. This was crazy. I mean, after you're dead, what kind of administrative mix-ups could there really be? Was I not supposed to have died? Could I have been sent to the wrong place somehow? If so, was I going to be sent back? And what was up with skipping orientation?

I was torturing myself with ideas of where I was *really* supposed to be when the door in the wall magically appeared again, admitting another woman, tall, with raven hair swept up in a high, tight bun and a no-nonsense look on her face. She moved briskly toward the desk. Blondie was on her heels, talking quickly as if I wasn't even there.

"It's just so *unusual* that I thought I should check with someone else before processing her."

The words "unusual" and "processing" stuck like knots in my stomach.

"I mean, I know mistakes in the assignments don't happen, but look at her."

Blondie gave me an apologetic smile. I couldn't help but feel a little offended even though I had no idea what she was talking about.

The second woman had her eyes glued to the machine and gave no indication she was listening to Blondie whatsoever.

She finally spoke. "I understand you wanting to verify, but He doesn't make mistakes. She's been assigned." She looked up from the machine to fix me squarely with a grim stare. Whatever the screen said, she wasn't too happy about it. "I'll take her from here, Celeste."

Blondie looked relieved. "Oh well, yes, that would probably be for the best." She glanced at me with worried eyes. "Don't worry, Audrey, you'll be in very good hands with Shannon."

Shannon smoothly rose from the chair. "Audrey, you can come with me now."

Her words might have made it sound as if I had a choice, but her tone confirmed that I did not. I took a deep breath and rose from the chair. I gave Celeste one last look before following Shannon out the door. I think she mouthed, "Good luck," but I couldn't be sure. My spirit fell even further when the door clicked shut behind me.

THE JOB ETERNAL

*T*en minutes later, Shannon held a door open for me as I stepped past her and into a room jammed full of people—and not just anyone. The room was packed wall-to-wall with huge, well-muscled guys! My stomach dropped. I'd been mistakenly drafted by the afterlife division of the NFL. This had to be a mistake.

Shannon placed a firm hand on my back and nudged me further into the room. I tried in vain not to gawk at the scene around me. Beefed-up guys sat conversing around twenty-five round tables. The atmosphere felt relaxed, almost like a break room. I couldn't pick up full conversations as we wove our way through the room, so my mind worked overtime inventing some of my own.

Hey man, what did you do today? the guy in the skintight purple T-shirt that said "I ROCK" on the front would say. And the dude on his left would answer in a deep, Schwarzenegger-esque accent, *I picked things up and put them down.*

We reached the other side without stopping to talk to anyone. Shannon placed her palm on the wall and produced another hidden door.

From my limited view behind Shannon's head, it appeared to be a gym of some kind. Not even the high-decibel manly noises coming from behind me drowned out the unmistakable sound of metal on metal. Shannon stepped to the side. That's when I saw, on the far end of the gym, two fighters locked in a death match. They were bearing down on each other so quickly I could hardly distinguish the movements. The source of the sound was the thick, heavy swords they were fighting with.

One of the fighters jumped high into the air and landed at least two body lengths from where he'd been standing, narrowly escaping a blow aimed at his shins. I gasped. A move like that wasn't humanly possible!

The fighters, wearing silvery, sleek body armor, didn't miss a beat as they bore down on each other with a series of quick blows. The movements blurred with their speed, the sound of the swords meeting deafening.

I gasped again when one of the opponents swung his sword in an arc and nearly took off the head of the other, who ducked and rolled just quickly enough to avoid decapitation. If this was a sparring session of some sort, it must have gotten out of hand. I looked up at Shannon anxiously. Surely someone should stop this!

Her face was a mask of calm, mixed perhaps with a bit of impatience. One of the fighters took advantage of an unsteady moment to get his opponent to one knee. He was just about to deliver a final blow when Shannon loudly cleared her throat. Both fighters froze. Shannon smiled coolly at them and said, "Logan, may I have a word with you?"

The fighter who had the advantage took a step back and lowered his sword.

"Sure, Shannon, just give me a sec," he said, not sounding nearly as out of breath as I thought he should. He reached an armored hand down to give his opponent a hand up. Not a bit of malice remained in their movements.

Logan shook the hand of his opponent, who was quite a bit bigger in both height and girth, and gave him a friendly pat on the back. They said something to each other I couldn't make out and chuckled before parting. The other guy gave Shannon a wave and a nod before pushing through a different set of doors.

As Logan moved toward us, his armor began to evaporate. First, his shin and shoe guards melted into the air, revealing brown sandals and dark-washed jeans. Then the metal covering his arms and hands disappeared, followed by his breastplate, uncovering a T-shirt that read "Hunters Rule, Demons Drool." He was leaner than the guys back in the break room, but still muscular. Last, his helmet evaporated. He looked younger than I expected . . . perhaps only a few years older than me. But who knew if age really meant anything here.

Shifting my weight I craned my neck to the left, trying to make sense of where his armor had just gone, peering around him as if it might magically appear somewhere behind him.

I was still gaping when he stopped a few feet short of Shannon and me. "Hey Shannon, what's up?"

He glanced my way with only a mildly curious look. I wasn't certain if I should be offended or relieved.

"Actually, I've brought you a new trainee."

Logan tilted his chin up to scan the area behind us. I turned my head as well to see who he was looking at.

"Oh yeah, that's great! Where is he?"

Shannon gave me a firm prod. Unprepared for the push and still gaping at Logan, I stumbled forward.

"Here *she* is," Shannon said with a smile.

Logan's eyes opened wider, and this time he *really* looked at me. He had dark blond hair, on the longer side and tousled, with wild highlights throughout, the type you get from too much time spent in the water and sun. His eyes started at my feet and slowly moved up my body until they locked with mine. Under the scrutiny, I registered that his eyes were a deep cobalt blue. It reminded me of the color of the ocean on a sunny day. The intensity of his stare embarrassed me. Heat rose to my face but was trapped in his gaze. I felt judged.

Without releasing my eyes, he addressed Shannon. His words came out deliberately, with an icy edge.

"You have got to be kidding me."

His tone sent a chill down my spine, which actually helped combat the warming of my cheeks. That was the final straw.

I broke his stare and pivoted on my heel. I'd had enough of all of this. Muttering to myself about how crazy this all was, I marched purposefully toward the door. I didn't care if there were a zillion muscle dudes on the other side, I just wanted out.

Before my fourth step, Shannon was in front of me. In fact, she appeared so quickly I walked right into her, bounced off, and landed on my butt. Dang, how'd she get there so fast? She appeared to be glowing but was no longer smiling. She looked over my head at Logan.

"You know we don't make mistakes about these things. There is a reason for this."

"She'll be eaten alive out there. Just look at her, Shannon."

Shannon glanced at me, sitting there on my butt, before looking back up at Logan. A shadow of doubt crossed her face but was gone almost as quickly as it had appeared. Eaten alive. How was that even possible when you were already dead?

"Logan, it is what it is. You've been chosen as her mentor. You need to train her as you would anyone else."

Neither of them spoke. I looked back and forth between the two. Then Logan asked with slightly narrowed eyes, "Is this because of what happened?"

Shannon's features softened perceptibly.

"No, Logan, this isn't some sort of punishment. You know things don't work like that here." Her voice was quiet but still strong when she continued, "What do you think they said about Romona when she first joined?"

Logan let out a deep sigh. There seemed to be some silent communication, a faceoff, going on between those two. Shannon must have won, because after a few minutes her calm, cool smile returned.

"Thank you, Logan. I'll leave her with you now. You know what to do." The words sunk in fast as she turned to go.

"Wh-what?" My speech was stuttered as I scrambled up to stop her. In my rush I lost my footing again and ended up half-running, half-crawling after her. When the door shut behind her, it occurred to me how pathetic I must look. I struggled to my feet and stared at the door.

Indecision about whether to run after her or turn around and face my fate, kept me rooted in place. I was equally torn between wanting to shout at someone or break down crying. What in the world was going on? Whatever I might have thought the afterlife would look like, it surely wasn't this.

I inhaled a deep breath to steady myself. There was no use getting too upset until I found out what sort of job I had been assigned to anyway. Could it really be that bad?

So far, Logan hadn't made any attempt to talk to me. For all I knew, he wasn't even still there. I squeezed my eyes shut and let the air escape my lungs. When I opened them and turned, Logan was exactly where he had been when I attempted to make my grand exit. He was either giving me time or didn't know what to say, so I took control of the moment. At the very least, I needed to try to pull back some of the dignity I'd already lost.

I plopped my hands on my hips and let out a breath. "Okay, so will you at least tell me what exactly it is that we do?"

Logan looked me straight in the eyes and said, "We kill demons."

I saw his eyes, heard the words, and then everything went black.

I had never fainted before in my whole life. At least, I was pretty sure I hadn't. But when I came to, I knew exactly what had happened—it wasn't like the movies when someone slowly wakes up, looks around, and asks "What happened?" in a calm and sleepy voice. Nope, I woke up into full awareness and total embarrassment. And it hurt! My left shoulder was throbbing, my arm was crossed in front of my chest at a weird angle, and my face was squished into the floor but didn't hurt. If I stayed like that much longer, my arm and face were likely to fall asleep.

I considered pretending I was still out cold. Maybe if I stayed on the floor long enough Logan would just go away, or better yet, I'd magically be back in the real world.

Deciding I couldn't just stay there, I rolled onto my back with a groan. Logan was standing directly above me looking down. He had a look on his face that might possibly be concern. And then he opened his mouth to speak, and I learned what really worried him.

"Do you do that often?"

Irritated, I sat up, ignoring the question. That was as much of a dignified stance as I could muster considering the circumstances. I needed a little more time before getting to my feet.

I took a moment to scrutinize the gym more closely. Logan's fight had completely monopolized my attention earlier, and I was beginning to notice all the details I'd missed. It was a small gym with high ceilings. Three of the walls were nondescript and gray. The left wall stood out, as it was lined floor to ceiling and end to end with more hand weapons than I had ever imagined even existed. Some I had never seen before. They had odd angles and sharp edges and looked menacing enough that I hoped to never touch them.

I didn't want to think about the weapons. I didn't want to think about what they were supposed to wound.

The floor beneath me was black and slightly squishy. I reached down to poke it with my index finger, which left an indentation for a moment before smoothing over. I spent a few more moments than was necessary poking at the spongy ground. It was time to stand and face the music, or in this case, Logan.

He was silent while I mentally and physically pulled myself together. I didn't have to wonder if he was still there; I felt his stare boring into my back. He didn't offer to help me up.

Stumbling at first, I managed to get to my feet and turned to face him. He was leaning against the wall with one foot crossed over the other, arms folded over his chest like he had all the time in the world. His hair was still tousled, but in just the right way to make you wonder if it was styled or just messy. His eyes were slightly narrowed, sizing me up, but the rest of his expression was closed off.

"Okay." He pushed himself off the wall, apparently having made up his mind about something. "I guess we should at least get you settled."

He walked straight toward me and then straight past me. He didn't say so, but I assumed I was supposed to follow him, so I did. Heading down a long gray hallway, we passed a number of doors with strange sounds emanating from most—swords clashing, maybe somebody practicing martial arts or just listening to a Bruce Lee movie really loudly. I scurried past one door that vibrated with the roaring noises coming from within. None of this fazed Logan, who forged ahead as if I wasn't there.

Logan stopped suddenly in front of a door and pushed it open. The light from the other side was so bright it stung my eyes. I blinked a few times. We were outside. It was beautiful.

We'd exited a building on the edge of the glistening city, but it was the mountain range before us that completely captured my attention. Tipped with white snow and rising from a base of lush green forest, the sight truly took my breath away. Moments passed before my gaze dipped lower. Laid out before me were streets and sidewalks to the left and green space to the right. There were people everywhere! Briskly zigzagging around each other to my left and relaxing, playing, and running in the fields and courts on my right. There were young people and old people and every age, shape, size, and nationality.

I followed Logan as he walked straight into the masses and headed for a sidewalk that appeared to skirt the city. At his brisk pace I had to pick up my own to keep up.

To the right was a small field with people playing a game I didn't recognize. A few shouted greetings to Logan. He nodded or gave short waves in response. Straight above us was a crystalline blue sky, free of any clouds or imperfections. It was so clear, in fact, that I noticed the absence of the sun, despite the overwhelming amount of light all around.

Apparently I stared up too long, because when my eyes lowered, I wasn't following Logan anymore. I turned in a quick circle and spotted him to the left. *Whoops! No time for sight seeing I guess. Time for a quick jog.* When I caught back up, he either didn't notice I had been missing or didn't care. Both possibilities irked me. It wouldn't kill him to be a little sensitive to my situation. But instead of saying anything, we walked along in silence. Him leading and me following behind like a little duckling.

"Quack."

"What's that?" Logan turned his head.

"Nothing." I hadn't meant to say that out loud. Logan didn't press it, just rolled his eyes and refocused his attention forward.

There was too much to take in to be annoyed at Logan for long. Leaving the sidewalk, we veered off on a stone pathway that led us toward the mountains and trees and past small meadows of brilliantly colored flowers, winding brooks with water as clear as glass, and familiar yet oddly misplaced things like ice skating rinks and sledding hills next to swimming pools and skateboard parks. As we walked, the tall spirals and buildings became smaller, and the forest before us captured my full attention.

Trees soared hundreds of feet in the air, wider than small skyscrapers. It was only when we reached the wooded edge that I realized just how enormous they really were. We were like grasshoppers standing next to them.

Logan put his hand to the trunk of a tree, and for a moment, it looked like the bark was melting off. Reds and browns merged together and streamed down to pool at Logan's feet. With a poof, the melting bark evaporated, and a shiny brown door appeared on the side of the tree.

Logan reached for the doorknob without hesitation. It registered with me that this should be completely insane, but after what had happened in only the past few hours, it wasn't the strangest thing by far. I considered staying outside longer just to see if he'd notice but decided against it. He most likely didn't care, and I was too curious about what was inside that massive tree to wait.

We entered a corridor. The walls were uneven and dark brown like dirt. It was slightly musty inside, and the humidity made the air feel sticky. Whatever they used for lighting wasn't working very well, because I had to wait for my eyes to adjust before I could see much.

About ten feet in front of me, Logan moved gracefully and quickly through the corridor. I reached my fingers out to lightly touch one of the walls. It felt soft and mossy. I held the fingers up to inspect them, but the tree wall had left no residue.

Still examining my fingers, I walked right into Logan's back. He barely budged, but I bounced off of him like a basketball and rebounded into the wall. Luckily the mossy texture had some cushion, so it didn't hurt as much as it could have. No words of concern from Logan, of course. He simply glanced over his shoulder and then held his hand up to the wall much the same way he'd done to the tree trunk. This time a white door materialized out of the brown. He stepped back and finally looked at me.

"Here it is," he said.

"Here *what* is?"

Logan shrugged. "You know, your room."

I stared at him incredulously. "You mean I live in a tree?"

One corner of his mouth quirked up in amusement. "Don't worry, it's not forever. And you'll get used to it after a while."

And with that, he turned and headed back the way we'd just come. No good-bye, no see ya later, no instructions or explanations. He just left. And despite the million questions I should have asked him, my mind had gone completely blank. I was too overwhelmed for a quick retort. I mean, was someone coming back to get me? Was I supposed to know what to do next? How long was I going to have to stay in this tree?

When I couldn't see Logan's retreating figure anymore, my body finally unfroze. I peered at the white door. It was so smooth. Could it be plastic rather than wood? How stupid would it be to live in a tree and have the door be made out of something other than wood? I gave myself a mental shake. *Pull it together girl!* Gripping the white handle I slowly opened the door.

The room was white. Utterly and completely white. So white it caused a bout of déjà vu, as if I stood in the nothingness once more. The walls were the same color as the floor, and it didn't look like there was anything else to the room. I was alone in a big white room . . . again. What the heck?

Taking slow and steady steps forward I hesitantly reached for one of the walls, afraid it might be padded like at an insane asylum. Something mechanical clicked at my touch. My feet tangled from my hasty retreat as a bed slid out from the wall. It was white too.

At least I now knew the dead still slept. Judging by the serene whiteness of the room, it must be true they even rested in peace. A little giggle escaped my lips. Okay, that wasn't an appropriate or even a good joke, but I was a little slaphappy at this point. I sat on the bed, unsure whether I wanted to touch another wall to see if anything else would pop out. The bed felt soft and luxurious, but how was anyone supposed to sleep with all this light?

The moment I thought it, the room went pitch black.

Okay, that was creepy, I thought. *I think I preferred the lights on.*

They came back on.

My brows furrowed. *Hmmm, let's try that again.*

I thought lights off, and the room darkened. I thought lights on, and they came on again. *Well, that is definitely cooler than The Clapper,* I thought with another chuckle.

I lay back on the bed, staring straight up at the white ceiling. How was it I could remember The Clapper but not anything about my life? I tried to catalog what I did know: The Clapper. That Logan's highlights came from time in the sun. I knew facts and details of things on Earth, I just couldn't pull up any personal memories. I remembered peanut butter but didn't know if I liked it, hated it, or was allergic to it. I remembered actors and movies and TV shows, but I didn't remember when I had seen them or whom I was with. I couldn't make sense of any of it.

Lying on the bed made me realize I was beyond exhausted. When had that come on? I curled up into the fetal position with my eyes still open. I tried in vain to feel bad about what I had left behind, but instead, I found myself aggravated that I couldn't remember what exactly that was. Exhaustion pulled at me, and I wasn't able to hold onto my frustration for long.

Just before I nodded off, I remembered to think *lights off,* and everything went dark.

TRAINING

I was awakened by a knock at the door. On the second knock, I sat up so hastily I almost tumbled out of bed. *Lights on*, I thought quickly, and the room was drenched in white. I shut my eyes against the sudden change. Another knock sounded at the door.

I rolled out of bed, free of bedding because I hadn't bothered to get under any. Was it Shannon or Logan? I hesitated a moment before reaching for the knob. I couldn't decide which option I preferred.

When I opened the door, a girl around my age but taller, with warm brown eyes and a wide, friendly smile stood on the other side. Some of my tension eased.

"Hi, I'm Romona." She waved, then reached out for a handshake.

When our hands met, I sucked in a sharp breath and immediately snatched mine back, protectively holding it to my chest as if injured. It had happened so quickly it was difficult to make sense of—as if a feeling of warmth, salted with pity and concern, had spread from our connected hands and through my body. I glared accusingly at Romona. Her dark brows furrowed, then smoothed a moment later.

"Oh, right, the empathy link. You must not know about that yet. Whenever our skin touches, we get an impression of the other person's emotions." She brought her hands together to demonstrate. "I know it's a little odd at first, but you'll get used to it after a while. Well, most people do at least."

I regarded her warily. "And what if you don't get used to it?"

She gave a slight shrug. "Then you just get used to not touching anyone, I suppose."

Ha, I thought, *just like that, huh?*

"Anyway," she went on, "I wanted to come introduce myself and see if you wanted any company on the way back to the training center today. I know it takes some time to get used to things around here, especially with all those guys." She rolled her eyes with a lopsided grin. "Logan was supposed to get you, but when I heard you were here, I asked if I could instead. I'm a little excited to have another girl in the ranks. And . . ." she swiftly bent to retrieve a small white bag at her feet and held it proudly out in front of her, "I brought you some breakfast!"

I was still trying to figure her out. "Are you a . . . um . . . you know, one of them?"

"A hunter? That's right! We few girls need to stick together!"

I released a breath I hadn't intended to hold. "I'm so glad I'm not the only girl."

"I'm getting the feeling they didn't explain much to you, did they?"

I could have cried with relief at being understood. "Everything has been pretty vague so far. I didn't even know what I was supposed to do when I woke up today. So I guess I should say thanks for coming to get me. And for breakfast too."

"Of course! Can I come in?"

"Oh yeah, sorry." I stepped aside to let her through the doorway.

She glided into the room, making a quick turn to take in all the whiteness. I wondered if the floor made her dizzy too. Within seconds the room filled with the pleasant aroma of whatever she had in her bag.

Romona sat on the end of the white bed. Her skin, the color of a light latte, stood out in contrast to the starkness of the room. Her hair, a shade of brown-black, was braided in a plait that fell over her shoulder and almost down to her waist. Her brown eyes sparkled with excitement. She was trying hard to keep herself in check as her folded hands, resting on her knees, bounced up and down with the jiggling of her legs.

Finally, she couldn't wait any longer. "So how long have you been here?"

"Oh, just a day. I got, uh, here yesterday. I think. Are there still days here?"

"Yep. And they already have you training? Gee whiz, that's fast."

"Really? How does it usually work?"

"There's not really a 'usually' about it. Everyone is different. But most of the time they give people time to adjust. I suppose there is a reason to throw you right in."

That wasn't reassuring. Sensing she'd said something wrong, her face fell. She continued quickly. "But that's better, because it means you get to acclimate yourself to being a hunter that much faster. And you'll get to meet people and train right away."

The smile on her face looked plastered on. It was obvious she was trying hard to make me feel better. I plastered on my own smile in return.

"Well, I guess that's a good thing then. So what am I supposed to be doing this morning?"

"Oh right!" She jumped up from the bed. "I'm supposed to be taking you to your first day of training. Would you like to change into your training clothes?"

I looked down at myself. I was wearing camel-colored flats, dark-washed skinny jeans, and a couple layers of purple-hued tank tops. I didn't know what was appropriate for training, but it was safe to assume this wasn't it. Romona, in tight-fitting Spandex and sporty shoes, looked ready for a five-mile run. I did not.

"Um, I guess so?"

Her eyes sparkled. "Let's get you ready for your first day of training!" She put her hands on one of the white walls, which split apart to reveal a wardrobe.

Only a few other people were at the training center early. I was pleased—I wanted a moment to get my bearings. I was grateful for Romona. Not only had she fed me and shown me the secret closet, but she'd given me a brief tour of the facility.

The training center was even larger than I had imagined. There were four main gyms for general use. Each was almost as large as a football field, with a wide array of machines, weights, and weapons. Never-ending hallways led to smaller individual training gyms.

Romona explained that a hunter is always either in training or training someone else. She was working with another new recruit, as she called him. I briefly wondered how he was handling being trained by a girl. Although the way Logan had shut up after the mention of her name yesterday, I imagined Romona had a reputation for holding her own.

Apparently, the first few weeks of training for a newbie were the most intense, something about shocking the body into becoming a fighting machine. Nothing about that appealed to me.

I now sat alone in the middle of the training gym waiting for Logan. Even with my workout clothes on, I felt incredibly out of place. My mind wandered to what I must have done to be assigned this type of occupation in the afterlife. Was it possible I was in a gang or something? If so, I would bet I had some crazy street moves buried somewhere in my memory. I glanced over at the weapons wall. Was I a championship fencer or archer? There had to be *some* special skill I possessed or they wouldn't have let me in here, right?

I chewed a fingernail as I let my eyes browse the room. Weights and punching bags. Slightly padded floor; no windows unless you counted the small ones at the top of the doors that let out into the hallway. Everything looked pretty normal, that is, except for that massive wall of weapons.

Wanting a closer look I pushed myself off the mat. The wall was without a doubt the most interesting part of the gym. There were swords and knives of all different shapes and sizes, bows and funny-looking arrows, and ninja-type weapons like nunchakus and fighting sticks. It was obvious all these weapons were fashioned for men. Most of them looked extremely heavy and sharp, and were larger than the width of my arm. I tried to visualize wielding one with confidence, but I couldn't imagine using them with any sort of ease. I was fascinated, but I didn't feel a stirring familiarity that would suggest I had been into any of this stuff when I was alive.

I stopped in front of the collection of swords. Unable to restrain myself, I tentatively picked up one of the heavier-looking blades, holding the handle in both hands. The sharp blade on this sword was slightly curved and wider than most of the others—wide enough to see my reflection.

Dark eyes stared back at me—eyes that should have been familiar but weren't. Brows slightly raised in surprise. They were delicate and evenly shaped, a few shades deeper than the dark brown hair pulled back in a pony-tail. The eyes were a rich brown color. Not dark enough to look black but not light enough to be hazel. More like a deep walnut. The nose was small with a slight slope and sat in the middle of a heart-shaped face that was completely nonthreatening. I tried to memorize the contours of the stranger's face in the reflection.

The sound of the gym door being thrown open made me jump. I dropped the sword and let out a short, high-pitched scream. I immediately clamped a hand to my mouth to stop the painfully girlie sound. The sword narrowly missed my foot, embedding itself in the soft floor of the gym.

Two sets of eyes watched me from the gym's entrance. Their faces telling. One friendly if not mildly curious, and the other annoyed.

Logan, the annoyed one, spoke first. "You shouldn't be touching those. You could hurt yourself."

In contrast, the guy standing next to him wore a wide grin. Tall, broad-shouldered, and Viking-like in appearance, he stuck out his hand. I extended mine and was slightly unnerved as his emotions rushed in. At least now I knew why he was grinning—it wasn't so much out of friendliness as amuse-ment. He gave my hand a good shake and then let go. His hand was so large it was like shaking hands with a bear. I had to crane my neck to look up at his face.

"Hi there, my name is Alrik. I didn't get the pleasure of introducing myself yesterday."

Yesterday? He must have been the one training with Logan. I took Alrik in again as he pulled the sword out of the mat and returned it to its place. Sandy blond hair fell to his shoulders. With a jolt, I realized that with a name like Alrik he might actually *be* a Viking. When he straightened, he turned toward Logan, who was tall but didn't come close to Alrik's semi-giant stature.

"See, no problem here, Logan. You don't have to pout over there like a baby."

Alrik turned back to me with a grin large enough to say he knew exactly which of Logan's buttons he was pushing. He bent closer to me and whispered, "Don't worry, Aud, Logan's really a big softy at heart. Don't let him push you around too much."

He straightened and gave me a wink before leaving. After a moment his voice boomed from down the hall. "Now try not to kill each other, you two. You know the expression is make love, not war." He was laughing at his own lame joke as the door swung shut.

I willed my face not to turn pink. Logan didn't say anything, but he was shaking his head as he walked over to a bench to set down his bag. Without a word, he pulled out a pair of shoes to replace the ones he was wearing. Self-conscious and itchy in my own skin, I shifted my weight from one leg to the other. Even though he had been pretty rude so far, it hadn't dampened my curiosity about him.

Some hair fell over Logan's face as he finished tying his laces, so I lost the opportunity to study it. So far, I'd only seen his moods range from stoic to annoyed and slightly angry. I hoped he had a broader range than that.

He looked up and caught my blatant stare. I turned in a futile attempt to cover my gawking and pretended to be extremely interested in a particularly menacing-looking weapon with multiple spikes attached to a large wooden handle.

"Okay, let's get started with some warm-ups. We'll see what kind of shape you were in when you died."

Another pit formed over the seemingly permanent one in my stomach. I was willing to bet that working out could be added to the list of things that weren't familiar to me in life.

Forty-five minutes later, I was throwing up into a garbage can in the corner of the gym. Logan had apparently been using the term "warm-up" loosely. He started by running me through twenty-five minutes of calisthenics, which left me struggling for breath. He followed that up with what he called a light run around the gym. When we finally stopped, I started dry heaving and gagging. Logan rolled his eyes and pointed to a trash can in the corner of the room. I barely made it there before my breakfast came back up. There was no way I was ever eating eggs with cheese again. When it finally felt as if my entire meal was out and my breathing and heartbeat had slowed, I straightened.

Logan was standing just a few feet away with a paper cup in his hand.

"Here," he said, extending the cup toward me. I was careful not to touch his fingers when I took it. I didn't want to know what he was feeling.

"You'll want to swish and spit. Then fill it up over there." He jerked his head to the left to indicate a drinking fountain. "You can get dehydrated fast when you throw up." His mouth turned down at the corners. "You're more out of shape than I thought."

I took a gulp of the water, swished, and spit it into the can. *So disgusting.*

"You're going to have to work on building up your endurance outside of training," Logan went on. "I won't be able to do much with you if you're throwing up before we even get to skills training."

My blood boiled at the flippant insults. Before I realized it, my mouth was moving again. "Well, I'm really sorry I didn't get in better shape before I *died*. Had I known I'd be working with a bunch of meatheads for eternity, I'm sure I would have prepared a little better."

Shaken, I pitched the empty cup and turned to get fresh water from the drinking fountain without waiting for Logan to respond. He was silent as I took a few glorious gulps of cold water.

When I finished and turned back to the gym, Logan threw something at me. I was so caught off guard that one smacked me in the shoulder and the other bounced off my stomach.

"Put those on."

"Huh?" I looked down. Boxing gloves. He had thrown boxing gloves at me. He had to be kidding.

"Don't I get a break?"

"You just did." He moved a large punching bag into position.

I grudgingly pulled the gloves on. I fiddled with the Velcro straps, trying to figure out how to tighten them with so little mobility in my thumbs, until Logan finally came over to adjust them for me. He pulled the straps around my wrists tight enough to cut off circulation.

Suddenly, I had the worst itch on my nose, impossible to scratch with these oversized oven mitts on my hands. I lifted my arm to try to scratch it on my sleeve when I noticed Logan staring at me. He waited by the punching bag with his arms crossed over his chest.

"Are you done?" His voice was even as usual.

I slowly lowered my arm and willed myself to ignore the itch as I shuffled over to him.

Logan didn't wear gloves as he demonstrated a few basic punches for me. He moved slowly to demonstrate the correct stance and form, but the bag still swung violently when he connected.

When he felt satisfied with his instruction, he let me take my turn. I wound up for my first punch and put as much power as possible into the hit. The bag barely groaned. My hand started to throb.

"Oww! You didn't tell me that was going to hurt!" I shook my hand out to alleviate the pain.

His brows furrowed. "It's not supposed to. That's why you have the gloves on."

"Well, it totally did."

"That means you're not doing it right."

I didn't have a comeback. He was probably right.

"Okay, then what am I doing wrong?"

"Hmmm." He took a moment to think about it. "Pretty much everything."

"Well, that was extremely helpful."

"It's obvious you didn't listen to anything I was saying."

"That's so not true. I did exactly what you told me to."

He rolled his eyes. "Well, let's see. Your stance was off, your arm was in the wrong position, and you didn't have any follow-through."

"Wow, is that all?"

"No." Logan didn't elaborate, but it looked as if he wanted to. His blue eyes blazed.

We stared at each other in silence. I knew it was stupid, but something about him made me bristle.

We were interrupted by another loud bang of the doors.

"Oh, isn't this cute? Staring deeply into each other's eyes."

I flushed a few shades darker. Alrik was leaning one shoulder against the doorframe, grinning.

"That is so not—" I sputtered.

"Not a good time, Alrik," Logan spoke up behind me.

"Yeah, I can tell." He barked out a laugh. "So, did she?"

Logan was silent for a moment. "Yeah, right after the run."

"Ha!" Alrik looked extremely pleased with himself. "You can settle up with me later."

I gasped. "Excuse me? Am I hearing you right? Did you actually bet on whether I would throw up today?"

Logan wouldn't quite meet my gaze, but Alrik appeared to be having a dandy day. "Not quite *if,* hon, but *when.*"

My blood pressure spiked. "Seriously?"

Logan still refused to look me in the face—suddenly, repositioning the punching bag was really important to him. "I thought you'd last until at least after kickboxing."

Using my teeth to tug off my oven mitt of a boxing glove I chucked it at Logan's head. To my utter annoyance, he caught it easily before it smashed into his face. I ripped the other one off and threw it at him too. He caught it just as effortlessly.

"Oh, hey there, hon, don't be so upset. We all do on our first day. It's nothing personal," Alrik said from the doorway.

"Do you guys even care that I died, like, literally yesterday?"

Finally Alrik, with shoulders hunched and downcast eyes, had the decency to look a little convicted.

"We're just trying to make you feel like part of the team." He pushed himself away from the door frame. "Okay, okay, I can tell when I'm not wanted. I'll let you guys finish whatever it was that I walked in on and get back to work. Don't worry, Aud, the first day's always the worst."

Then he looked over my head to address Logan. "Good luck with this one. She's got some spunk!"

When the doors shut behind him, I was determined to do a better job. I couldn't be *that* bad at all of this.

"Okay, give me the gloves back."

Logan gently handed them to me. I flinched away when he tried to help me and stubbornly tightened them with my teeth instead, way past caring how I looked. I was going to get the bag to swing or die trying.

CELESTIAL HEIGHTS

"*I*s this a joke?"

I stood next to Romona inside her favorite restaurant, staring straight up. Giant cotton balls floated aimlessly through the air in twenty stories of open space above our heads. The white puffs, which reminded me of clouds, were about the size of small cars. People lounged on them as if sitting on oversized floating bean bags.

Romona had insisted on bringing me here to celebrate my first day of training. I couldn't stop staring. The waitstaff buzzed around the cavernous room with small bronze wings fastened to their backs. They flitted through the air with the grace of ballet dancers, trays brimming with all sorts of foods and drinks.

"Pretty neat, huh?"

I tore my eyes from the scene above. Romona was grinning from ear to ear.

"Yeah, I guess. I mean, is this for real? Do we really eat on those?" The height was making my stomach flutter in nervousness.

"Yes, it's a lot of fun."

"How do we even get up there?"

"Using those." She pointed to the right where a row of bronze wings hung on pegs.

"You're not kidding, are you?"

"Nope. You're going to love it. Flying is amazing!"

She tugged me over to the wings. The hostess appeared and demonstrated how to fasten and operate them properly. We were assigned a cloud—that's actually what they called them—toward the top of the room. Romona took off and glided through the air with ease. I was told flying was like swimming, but without having to kick to be propelled forward. Taking a deep breath, I bent my knees and pushed off the ground.

She was right: flying was amazing. I enjoyed it for all of five seconds before smacking my shoulder on the floating crystal chandelier. I dipped hard to the right and plummet down, then bounced off the side of a cloud. The people seated on it gasped as they were shoved into a wall. Fortunately the clouds were as soft as they looked, so it didn't hurt much to ricochet off one. Unfortunately, the hit literally dumped me in the middle of someone's dinner.

The couple in front of me was covered in food. I'd hit their table at an angle, causing everything that wasn't on me to catapult onto them. The man and woman stared at me with matching looks of shock as I tried to get right side up. In an instant Romona gracefully landed on the edge of their cloud.

"Oh my goodness! Are you okay?"

I didn't know if she was asking me or the couple I'd just baptized in aqua-colored gravy.

Alrik's familiar voice boomed from somewhere above. "Hey, Aud, that was amazing! I'm giving it a 9.5! Would have been a 10 if the landing had been a little cleaner, but extra points for dramatics!"

I looked up and instantly regretted it. Not only was Alrik beaming down at me from twenty feet above, but he wasn't alone. Logan and a boy named Kevin who I'd met at lunch were leaning over the edge of their cloud as well. What were the chances they'd be at this same restaurant? I looked at Romona with the question on my face.

She cringed. "Sorry, I may have mentioned to Alrik that we were headed here tonight."

I ignored the boys to deal with the problem at hand. The couple I'd crashed into were mopping food off of themselves and their seats.

"I am *so* sorry! I can't believe I did that. I've never tried this flying thing before. That chandelier just popped out of nowhere." I laughed nervously.

"Is there anything we can do to help?" Romona asked.

The woman stopped cleaning and looked up. An unexpected smile blossomed on her lips. I was startled by the agelessness of her face. If I had to guess, I would say she was frozen in the age between motherhood and her golden years. Her beautiful silver hair refracted the light when she moved, and the slender wrinkle lines on her face didn't make her appear old but rather accentuated the interest of her appearance. Her eyes of blended browns and greens sparked with life.

"Oh please, this is nothing to fret about. It was a simple accident." Her smile reached her eyes. "And besides, we welcome unplanned interruptions in our lives. Don't we?"

She playfully poked her companion in the side to get his attention. He was handing a batch of soiled napkins to the server and receiving clean ones in return.

"Pardon?" With a head of thick salt-and-pepper hair and dark brown eyes, the man possessed the same ageless splendor as the woman. "Oh yes, no harm done. You just took us by surprise, that's all. Things like this keep us sharp in our old age. My name is Lapidoth, but please, you call me LD. Most people find Lapidoth quite a mouthful."

"Are you injured?" The woman's slight frown did nothing to diminish her timeless beauty.

I did a quick assessment of all my appendages. Everything seemed to be working properly. Only a few sore spots, but those could have been from training. "I don't think so. Thanks for being so gracious. I feel so bad."

"It is a small price to pay to meet new friends. Would the two of you care to join us?"

"Oh, ah," I looked to Romona for guidance. She smiled at the pair.

"Yes, thank you. That would be nice. My name is Romona, and this is Audrey."

"My name is Deborah, and LD is my husband. Please do take a seat."

She indicated a hand toward the soft bench on the other side of the table. "Now, I hope I'm not being too presumptuous, but by any chance are you new, Audrey?"

I smiled at her. "Not presumptuous, just insightful. I've only been here a short while. This is my second day, in fact."

I snuck a glance up at the guys' table, but they'd gone back to eating their dinner.

"Should we order some more food to replace what we ruined for you two?" Romona offered.

"You read my mind!" LD said.

Romona's smile broadened. "We'll let you order then. I like most things." She left out the part about me not knowing what I liked.

"That is most kind," LD said and then waved over one of the servers.

I took the opportunity to sneak glances around the restaurant while he ordered. Mercifully, no one appeared to be watching us anymore. Maybe crashes were a regular occurrence.

After taking our order, the server politely cleared what was left of the mess on the table. I watched as he expertly zipped through the air.

"So, Romona, Audrey, what brings you out to Celestial Heights tonight?"

"This is one of my favorite places." Romona answered. "I wanted to show it to Audrey. Although I'm afraid she's no longer going to trust my picks."

Romona glanced my way for confirmation. I lifted my eyebrows at her as if to say, "You've got that right." Romona laughed back good-naturedly.

"Oh no, you mustn't be turned off to things so easily. Some things just need practice and perhaps a little bit of patience," Deborah said.

"I suppose you're right." I conceded.

"So Audrey," LD interrupted. "What has been your favorite thing so far? Or perhaps the most surprising? I love to hear from the new arrivals what they think."

I thought about it for a moment but couldn't come up with much. Everything had been a surprise, and I hadn't been here long enough for favorites.

"I'm not really sure. I haven't actually seen very much yet. I think I'd love to go hiking and explore the mountain range, though. Are we allowed to do that?"

"Of course! I would suggest going with someone who knows the lay of the land before venturing out on your own," LD said.

"I'd love to take you sometime if you'd like," Romona quickly offered.

"That would be amazing! There just seems to be something out there calling to me." No one spoke. "Sorry, that probably sounded kind of weird."

"Not at all. It's completely understandable." Deborah leaned forward to pat my hand. I got a wave of good intentions from her. It felt like being wrapped in a warm fuzzy blanket on a chilly night.

She, on the other hand, quietly gasped and jerked her hand back a few inches. Her clear eyes widened, and her gaze seemed far away. The next moment she leaned back, and the smile returned to her face. I looked over to check if Romona had caught what had just happened. From the look on her face, she had.

Deborah changed the subject without addressing her odd behavior. "So do you two know each other well?"

"We just met, actually. We're kind of the only girls in our jobs."

"Ah! You must be huntresses, then?" LD's eyes lit up with interest.

"That must be extremely exciting."

I looked at Deborah doubtfully. She laughed. "I have a feeling you are in for quite a ride." I didn't miss the pointed look she gave her husband.

LD took Deborah's hand. "My wife is usually right about these things."

That's when our dinner arrived. The food was a beautiful array of colors and smells that effectively distracted me from our new friends' strange comments. It took three servers to bring it all. It couldn't be possible for us to eat everything. Some of the dishes were so perfect they could be mini works of art. The smells were equally captivating. My stomach rumbled loudly in expectation.

LD picked up a plate of something purple, about the size of a small potato, and encouraged me to try one. I tried not to appear skeptical.

"Sometimes looks can be deceiving," he said with mischief in his eyes.

With a forced smile I reached for the object. It had a soft texture and felt like it would pop if I squeezed hard enough. That thought almost turned me off. I took a small bite, which broke off easily like a soft roll. My eyes widen as I chewed. It reminded me of a dense cake doughnut with fresh fruit inside. *Mmmm, delicious.* It was just the right amount of sweetness without being overpowering. The second bite was even better than the first.

"Wow, this is great," I said between chews.

LD sat back proudly.

Deborah pointed to a pureed dish, red with green seeds throughout.

Christmas colors. I spooned some on my plate and added a few other suggested dishes. Everything was incredibly tasty.

Deborah and LD were wonderful dinner companions. LD shared about the first time he came to Celestial Heights and how, after forgetting to put the wings back on, he almost fell off the cloud after the meal. We all laughed. I appreciated his sincere attempt to put me at ease. Before I knew it, we had finished everything in front of us. I stared at the empty serving dishes in amazement. My stomach was full beyond belief.

"This was so much fun! I'm glad I crashed into you two," I admitted.

"We would welcome the intrusion anytime." Deborah said with a smile.

As if on cue, a familiar voice boomed to the right of our table. "Hey, you girls want to join us for dessert?" The guys' table had drifted down next to ours.

Even if I weren't utterly stuffed, I wouldn't have wanted to join them.

"Thanks for the invite, but we're not done here, Alrik."

"Oh don't be silly, of course you can join your friends. We've already taken up enough of your time," Deborah jumped in.

"No, no really—"

"Great, and Aud, look, you can just walk over nice and easy so you don't cover us in food too." He wore a wicked grin. He was having way too much fun with this.

Romona turned to our dinner partners. "It was truly wonderful to meet you."

"Oh I assure you, the pleasure was all ours. We wish you both nothing but the best." LD waved good-bye. He was already standing and adjusting the wing's straps on his shoulders. He picked up Deborah's once his were in place to assist her.

She rewarded him with a smile and accepted the wings. "Why don't I meet you at the door? I'd like a moment with Audrey if you don't mind."

There was a knowing look in LD's eyes. "Of course, I'll see you shortly." He turned and gave Romona and me a small bow of respect before rising and disappearing below the cloud.

Romona stepped easily over to the guys' table, taking both of our wings with her. She immediately launched into a story, purposefully capturing their attention.

I turned to face Deborah, curious and a little apprehensive. What could she possibly want?

She didn't bother to ease into her topic. "Audrey, it's important for you to know that you do have a purpose."

"Oh, okay." I didn't know how to respond.

"When things look the darkest, I hope you remember that. There is always a plan, a bigger picture, even if you don't understand at first. Despite how it might appear, how you might even feel, you are never alone, not for one single moment."

Okay, that sounded creepy. A chill ran down my spine like someone had just walked over my grave, but even so, her words resonated within me, causing my heartbeat to pick up its pace. Something inside was telling me to pay attention.

"Thanks. I'll try to keep that in mind."

"I hope you will. I realize this may not make much sense now, but I believe that someday it will." She hesitated, pursing her lips as if considering whether she should continue. "Also, be careful to trust the right people. Learning to correctly discern motives is going to be important for you."

Without warning, she hugged me tightly. I was wooden in her embrace. Her words stirred something inside that equally scared and thrilled me. For a wild moment it felt as if she spoke a deep wisdom that my soul recognized. But mostly, I was weirded out.

Over her shoulder, Logan considered us carefully. When she pulled back, she gave my arms a final squeeze, shooting a bolt of fearlessness through me before releasing them to gracefully slip on her wings.

She turned to the table across from us before leaving. "Enjoy your evening." She waved and then addressed Logan: "It's nice to see you again."

Logan smiled and inclined his head in a friendly gesture.

"I take it you are still figuring things out?"

"That I am," he answered.

"There's nothing wrong with that. I have faith you will work it out."

"I appreciate the confidence."

"I think you know I have more than that."

Logan smiled. "That I do. Please pass my respects along to Lapidoth."

"I will." And with that, she rose into the air and descended to her husband.

What was all that about? My mind reeled with what she'd said. Was there something she knew that I didn't? Could Logan help make sense of it? I was hesitant to share her words with him. What if I sounded silly or even arrogant? I was frozen in place while I considered it all.

"Audrey!" Romona shouted. The sharp tone in her voice shook me out of my musings. "You need to come over now."

The clouds had drifted further apart. I groaned. I'd have to make a jump for it. Romona had taken my wings with her. Alrik was moving the table out of the way for me.

"It's now or never, Princess."

I took a deep breath and jumped. I landed without taking anyone, or anything, out.

"Ha!" I shouted in glee.

Alrik looked disappointed as he moved down so I could take the seat next to him.

"Expecting another show, huh?"

"Well, you have to admit, it was a pretty safe bet."

"Don't listen to him, Audrey, it was a very graceful leap," Kevin came to my defense.

"Thank you, Kevin, that's very nice of you to say."

I gave Alrik another smug look before turning my attention to the desserts on the table. They looked delicious. I was still full, but I started calculating how many of the brightly displayed treats I could stuff down before having to be literally rolled back to my room.

The remainder of the evening was unexpectedly enjoyable and blessedly incident free. Kevin and Romona went out of their way to bring me into the conversation, especially since most of their talk went far over my head. Alrik kept us entertained with outrageous stories of his adventures in the afterlife, most of which I had a hard time believing. I insisted on meeting his pet polar bear if he truly had one.

Logan was pleasant enough. He did a decent job giving off an air of relaxation, participating in the conversation, laughing, or chiming in at the appropriate times—but more than once I caught a remote look in his eyes. That seemed to be the trick with Logan. He could expertly mask the rest of his face, but the eyes were his tell. I couldn't stop myself from casting curious glances his way when I thought no one was paying attention. He was too deep in his own mind to notice, although I think Alrik might have caught me once.

After that I only turned Logan's way if he was addressing everyone, but my mind wandered to him and Deborah. It wasn't long before I caved.

"So Logan," I began when the other three were preoccupied, "you know Deborah and LD?"

"Not well," he answered, barely looking in my direction.

"That's odd," I said, "you sounded pretty acquainted. You must have made an impression?"

Logan causally turned toward me. He sounded blasé but took the opportunity to capture my gaze with his steely blue eyes. "I would guess she remembers all of her prophecies."

There was a pause the span of exactly three heartbeats before I could answer.

"Her what?"

"Prophecies," he repeated. "Deborah is a prophetess."

I was stunned into silence as my brain raced to digest the news and jogged over her words again. Purpose . . . plans . . . things looking the darkest . . . trusting the right people. Could her words have carried more importance than just friendly advice?

Logan's eyes were clear and intense as he waited for my response.

"Prophetess—like a fortune-teller?" I squeaked out.

He shook his head. "Not even close, although I can see why you might think that. The title has gotten distorted over time. Prophetess was more of a title for a leader in her time. But she's gifted to see some of our destinies as well."

"So she *is* like a fortune-teller."

It was disturbing how conversational Logan was being about this subject. Almost flippant.

"No, she's not. The fortune-tellers like you are thinking of are either frauds or getting their information from a dangerous source. If the latter, whether they've spoken truth or not, I can promise you their words are not for our benefit. It's extremely unwise to mess with fortune-tellers. The things pulling their strings are motivated only to mislead."

"What 'things' are pulling their strings?"

"Demons."

"Why would they want to do that?" My throat was suddenly dry.

He answered with a level gaze and deliberate words. "Because they're looking to destroy humans. They hate us."

His words hung in the air for a time.

"We're the recipients of God's unconditional love, not them. It's part of what happened to turn them into demons in the first place. With how flawed we are, they didn't think we deserved that love. They became angry and bitter at God for giving His love to such unworthy beings. So to get back at Him, they've devoted their existence to destroying as many of us as possible."

I swallowed past the dryness coating my throat. "How could what happens to ordinary people get back at God?"

"Destroyed lives, denying His existence, hurting each other, all that pain people endure yet still refuse to turn to Him for help—it all hurts Him. He cares. It was never intended to be like that. And someday it won't be anymore, but this is what we deal with now. That's the small part that we hunters play. We go back to Earth to protect people from the demon's influence. There's a battle raging that most aren't even aware of. A battle for souls."

"But what about free will? Aren't people just going to do what they want anyway?"

"Of course, but by keeping demons away from people, we're protecting their minds from influence. Anyone hell-bent on doing wrong is going to find a way to do it." Some dark emotion flashed across Logan's eyes. "Demons don't have the power to force anyone to do anything."

"If they don't have the power to force anyone to do what they want, then why are we interfering at all?"

"You're underestimating the power of suggestion. Just because they can't force someone to do what they want doesn't mean they aren't *very* effective at manipulation and deception. And I'm not even talking about the people who purposefully invite them in." Logan let out a strong, low whistle. "Those demons are buried in so deep it's like trying to dig out a tick."

The idea was repulsive. "Why would anyone ever do that willingly?"

Logan held up his hand and started to count reasons off with his fingers. "Power, greed, selfishness, loneliness, acceptance, or because they simply don't realize what they've opened themselves to. Pick one. It happens all the time for many different foolish and selfish reasons." There was a bitter bite to Logan's words. They chilled me. I wanted to get back on topic.

"So Deborah told me my destiny?"

Logan shrugged a shoulder like he was done with this conversation. "How should I know? I don't know what she said to you."

"Hey lovebirds!" Alrik shouted. "What ya chirpin' about over there?"

Logan rolled his eyes. "Nothing interesting."

Ouch.

The conversation digressed from there, and I pretended to listen to the others as I wondered about the repercussions of tonight's revelations. Demons, angels, prophetesses. I didn't think the afterlife could get any weirder, but I was wrong.

OVER THE RIVER AND THROUGH THE WOODS

"Wow, he's out for blood today," Romona said as I joined her outside the gym. Inside, Logan glared at me. I ignored him. He'd called it quits for the afternoon in exasperation after I spent a good portion of the time picking myself off the padded floor.

"You've been here a while?" I guessed.

"Not too long. Hard day today?"

"Ha, you don't know the half of it. I'm starved. Want to grab something to eat? We skipped lunch."

"You skipped a meal?" Romona's brows furrowed in concern, and she cast a dark look at the gym door. Logan was throwing knives at the wall for target practice. He needed to get a life. Or at least an afterlife. He spent too much time in that gym.

"Yeah. I accidentally slept in this morning, and a grueling workout paired with no lunch was Logan's way of getting back at me. At least, that was the second half of his evil master plan. The first involved getting woken up by a pitcher of water. I thought I was drowning."

"What? Logan went to your room and poured water on you?" She seemed genuinely appalled.

"Yep. Speaking of, is there any way I can get a lock put on my door?"

In the three last weeks, I'd gotten a little stronger and gained a bit more endurance. I had to—Logan was making every day a meat grinder. Our relationship had a few ups and downs but generally hadn't gotten any friendlier, and my skills were nowhere close to what he wanted. The other hunters and trainees weren't too bad, and I had made a few friends. But I still hated it here. The feeling that I didn't belong with this group hadn't dissipated. Whenever I mentioned it to Logan he would bark platitudes about everyone's assigned jobs, sometimes even while complaining about my progress.

Romona was still fixated on the water incident. "I can't believe he did that. Logan's too disciplined to pull something like that."

A snort escaped me.

"And there's really no excuse for not letting you eat lunch. That's not safe." She glanced back at the gym door, her face a mix of concern and calculation.

"Hey, well, I'm okay now. Let's just go get something to eat." I grabbed her arm and tugged her down the hallway. I didn't need Romona fighting my battles. Especially not with Logan, who I expected would be twice as hard on me for it. I considered heading to the locker room to clean up but was too famished to bother. Romona would just have to put up with my stink.

Romona and I were practically inseparable by now. I couldn't pinpoint exactly how it had happened. She simply seemed to be there all the time, and I certainly didn't mind the company. She had a quiet strength about her. And as an added perk, she knew everyone. I'd probably met half the other hunters during our lunch breaks alone. She had a way about her that made you feel she truly cared. That was a deeper comfort to me than I would admit.

There were times when I felt a black hole of bitterness welling up deep inside me. I wasn't even sure where it came from, but its intensity scared me. Romona always seemed to be able to sense it, and she would offer wise and calming words. Perhaps it should have been intimidating to be around someone who always appeared so peaceful and put together, but it was a soothing balm to my soul.

To see her agitated over something as small as a skipped meal was new.

"So what's up?" I prodded to regain her attention.

"Oh." She gave herself a visible shake and offered an apologetic smile. "Sorry about that. I was waiting to ask you about your day off tomorrow."

"Huh?" My plate was already loaded with food, its aroma teasing me. Now I was the one having difficulty paying attention.

"You know, our day off training."

"We get days off?"

She laughed. "Of course we do. We get them off whenever we need them, and usually one every seven days. I noticed how hard Logan's been training you." She let out a huff. "Let me guess. That's something else he forgot to mention?"

"I think he was more focused on the retribution he was going to dish up today. That's great, though. I could use a day off."

"That's what I was thinking. I wondered if you might want to go hiking? You've mentioned that before."

I looked up. Windows ran from floor to ceiling in the cafeteria where most hunters ate, letting in a plethora of light and a view of the distant mountains. She was right. The need to explore was strong. An innate part of me knew there was something out there worth searching for.

"Yeah, that'd be great," I said around mouthfuls of food.

"Perfect! Leave everything up to me. I know just the spot."

I woke the next morning thrilled to be going somewhere other than the training center. I'd been dead for weeks now and had hardly seen anything past the bland walls of the training center and gym. Romona had said it was good to ease into some things, but that obviously didn't include training. Logan had pitched me in the deep end immediately.

This morning was different. Today I wasn't going to get bumped and bruised by my own mentor. Today I wasn't going to throw on ugly workout clothes and sweat through them within the first hour. Today I wasn't going to feel like the task I was undertaking was too big, too hard, and too impossible to handle. Today the black hole wasn't going to get me. Something bubbled inside my chest that said today anything was possible.

I started my morning routine with a bounce in my step. My only moment of hesitancy was when I stood in front of my closet, unsure of what to wear. I finally pulled out some jean shorts and a light blue T-shirt, plus a pair of brown and blue sneakers. My first instinct was to pull my hair up in a ponytail, but I decided against it since I was always forced to wear it back in training. I left it cascading down my back and shoulders instead. It was likely to make me hot if the hike was strenuous, so I stretched a ponytail holder over my wrist just in case. With that I was out the door.

I was supposed to meet Romona near the ice skating rink. I watched as snowflakes appeared about twenty feet above the skaters and floated lazily down to the icy surface. People materialized hats, gloves, coats, and scarves as they stepped on the ice. A group of kids skated together in a swarm with their heads tilted up and mouths open as they tried to capture snowflakes on their tongues.

"I'll bet you loved skating." I hadn't heard Romona join me.

"How do you figure?"

"By the look on your face. I think this is the most peaceful I've seen you."

"Hmmm." It was something to consider, but until I got my memories back there was no way to truly know. "So what do you have there?" I asked, pointing to the two bulging backpacks placed at her feet. She handed one to me with a smile.

"I'm making you work for your food today!"

"I wouldn't want it any other way. Which way are we headed?"

"That way." Romona lifted a hand and pointed toward the mountain range. My smile grew. I'd wanted a closer look at those mountains since the first time I laid eyes on them.

"I thought you might like that. They're even more beautiful up close."

"I'm looking forward to seeing that for myself."

Romona motioned with her head. "Great, let's go!"

We left the rink and headed toward the forest in the other direction from where I lived. Here the trees were denser, but not nearly as large. I imagined Hansel and Gretel picking their way over the vine-and-moss-covered ground, leaving breadcrumbs to find their way home. With no clear path to follow, I had the urge to start dropping markers ourselves. I was glad for Romona's experienced company. I could easily have become lost for lifetimes in those trees.

The deeper we traveled, the heavier my feet felt as they stuck to the soggy forest floor, making suctioning sounds with every step. The smell of rotting leaves and dank mushrooms permeated the air. On a few occasions I heard scampering in the thick canopy above our heads, but there was never anything there when I looked up. I followed close behind Romona, not wanting to lose her in the low light.

"Man, this is intense." We hadn't spoken much since entering the tight foliage.

"Yes, I know. It's what's on the other side that makes it worth picking through this mess."

I cast a weary glance up at the tangle upon tangle of branches above us. "It's going to have to be pretty amazing to warrant enduring this."

"Well, I guess you can tell me for yourself . . . I think we're finally through."

I'd missed the growing brightness in front of us while I concentrated on the underbrush that constantly snagged my feet. As if on cue, my foot caught on a root and my body jostled forward the moment I tried to make out what lay beyond the tree line. I braced myself on a moist trunk to keep from falling. My hands came away with brown and green mossy residue. *Yuck*. I scrubbed them against my shorts before moving forward.

It was a few more slow-moving minutes before we broke free from the forest to stand on the edge of a rolling meadow of vibrant red and yellow flowers. I blinked against the sudden brilliance, and the sweet fragrance of the flowers swept away the smell of decay behind us.

"Wow."

"That was pretty much my first reaction as well. It is beautiful, isn't it? They're tulips. They bloom all the time here. They aren't the most fragrant of flowers, but where there are so many of them like this, the smell is lovely. We're not stopping, though, just headed through to the foothills beyond."

From where we stood, the slight undulation of the meadow cut off whatever lay beyond and made it appear that the tulips continued indefinitely.

Free of the narrow forest path, we could finally walk side by side. I cautiously treaded through the radiant plants. Romona giggled beside me.

"What exactly are you doing?" she asked. "Trying out a new walking technique?"

"No, the flowers are so pretty I'm trying not to step on any of them," I answered with a knee in the air and arms spread out for balance. "But it's hard because they're so close together."

She laughed again. "It's really okay. Look." She stepped in front of me and crushed a few soft tulips under her foot.

"Oh, come on, I was trying really hard not to do that!"

"No, wait, watch this." She lifted her foot, and the flowers sprang proudly back up. "You can step on them. It won't hurt them at all."

"Oh, I see." I felt a bit foolish for my high-stepping. "I just didn't want to ruin them or anything. They seem so perfect."

"I shouldn't have laughed. You just reminded me of a little kid playing hopscotch or something."

Still hesitant, I forced myself to take a step forward without looking down. The tulips made a soft ground covering, but I snuck a quick look behind us as we moved on to make sure Romona was right. Satisfied that I wasn't leaving trampled flowers in my wake, I focused ahead just as we crested the first hill.

From here, we saw a glassy stream cutting a natural barrier between the two-toned meadow and the mountain's foothills beyond. The water was full of blue and green river rocks and tiny purple creatures that darted through the water like aquatic hummingbirds.

We walked along the bank until the water was low enough for us to jump on protruding rocks to the other side. The purple creatures, which at a closer look appeared to be starfish with large, flat tails, followed along with us until we set our feet on the opposite bank. Then they splashed away in a blink.

"Those don't look familiar. What are they called?"

"I'm not sure. Perhaps they haven't been named yet."

"Is that even possible?"

"Sure. There are lots of different species of plants and animals here that didn't exist on Earth. God's always creating new things for us to see and experience. Whoever sees them first gets to name them."

This wasn't the first time someone had mentioned the big "G" by name. There were also lots of mysterious, "Hims" and "Hes" thrown around that I assumed meant God, but not a lot of elaboration. I didn't remember going to church, conversations about God, or ever praying, but as I dug internally I found facts about God embedded in my mind. Much like the knowledge I had of things like the process of osmosis and how to do long division by hand. I must have been taught about it all at some point, but I didn't remember anything that gave me a personal connection to such a powerful being.

I turned my attention back to the starfish. "How do we know if we're the first to see them?"

"Give them a name; then we'll check the living museum when we get back.

There's a record of every named plant and animal there. If you're the first to name them, we'll be able to look them up under the name you've given them."

"This is weird. You want me to name a new type of fish?"

"Sure, why not?"

I didn't really know—naming just seemed like a big deal. "Don't you have to have credentials to do that? And what would I even name them?"

"Well, what did they look like to you?"

"Star shooter . . . thingies." I was instantly embarrassed. "That's totally lame, right?"

"No, no, not at all. I think it's a cute name. Star shooters. We'll have to check out the museum when we get back. Let's keep going. I want to get a little further before we have lunch."

The foothills in front of us were frost covered but also dotted with plants in full summer bloom. I could hardly comprehend how so many diverse terrains and climates could exist in one place. The breeze that blew my hair was kissed with warmth even as icy grass crunched beneath my shoes.

My feet had just started to protest when we reached the top of the third foothill and Romona suggested we stop and enjoy the picnic. My stomach growled its approval as we bent down to fish the contents out of our backpacks. The frozen water on the patch of grass in a ten-foot circle around us began to melt and then evaporated into the air, leaving us a warm, dry place to set out our picnic.

"That's incredible! Did you do that?"

"Nope, it happened because we stopped. Neat, right? The ground was only frosted because no one has been here for a while. It'll frost back over sometime after we leave."

My pack contained several large loaves of bread. Romona's contained the heavier bounty. After materializing a blanket, she removed a feast of meats, cheeses, breads, fruits, and even delicately decorated desserts. I'd learned food was one of the few things you couldn't just materialize here. It had to be grown in order to be digested; something materialized would just dematerialize again as soon as you started chewing.

One of the contents of her pack caught my attention. I picked up a red cylindrical roll and gave her a questioning look.

"Just thought you might like that," she said.

"A fruit roll-up? Seriously?"

She shrugged and went back to emptying her pack. Romona had probably packed too much food, but I was famished.

I settled on the blanket, and my gaze turned toward the mountains. I'd been so preoccupied with all the wonders at, or below, eye level that I hadn't looked that high during our hike. The mighty cliffs appeared to emerge from the ground in front of us, even though we were still some distance away. Green vegetation and snowy peaks dotted the mountain face, bare patches beneath them exposing rich mineral veins. But everything paled in comparison to the structure perched on the highest peak of the tallest mountain. My jaw dropped.

There above us, stretched so high it reached into the clouds, sat a blazing fortress of gold.

The golden light was blinding, like trying to look directly at the sun. My eyes teared as I tried to make out the form of the fortress. Little by little, I picked out more of the details. It was made out of translucent material: rather than simply reflecting the light, the blazing golden radiance flowed in undulating waves from the structure itself. It literally took my breath away.

I tore my gaze away to question Romona. Her back was to me as she arranged food on the blanket.

"Romona, what is that?" I asked, awed. "Oh my gosh! Are those angels flying around it?"

The great winged beings suspended in air were humanoid in their features. Their white-garbed bodies glowed like the moon next to the radiance of the structure. I took an unsteady step back as understanding blossomed. Celeste and Shannon must be angels—they emanated the same white luster as these creatures. Brightness from the fortress sparkled off their wings. Romona looked over her shoulder, then turned to give me a perplexed look. She seemed uncomfortable.

"You can see that?"

"Of course! It's so bright I can't believe it took me so long to notice!"

"It's just that most people can't see it until after their memories return. So I assumed you couldn't." She tilted her head. "It's a little odd that you can."

Well, that was nothing new. "Chalk it up to the oddity that is me. But hey, at least I'm overachieving in one area. So what is it?"

"Well, technically it's the tabernacle. But in layman's terms it's God's home. That light is what gives us our daylight."

Questions flooded through my mind so fast I tried spitting them out all at once. "Really? God has a home? Like a normal person? He's just hanging around here like the rest of us? Have you ever seen Him?"

"Whoa there!" Romona floundered for a moment before regaining her composure. "First of all, God is not a normal person, but yes, He does have a home. But not like what I think you are imagining. More like a holy dwelling, but that's completely confusing. Yes, of course He's here, and yes, I have seen Him. I think that covers all the questions, right?"

"So I may just randomly bump into Him one day?"

"No, it doesn't *exactly* work that way. I'm sure you'll meet Him, but it won't be until after you remember. You have to remember *Him,* remember your relationship with Him first. When you do, He'll reveal himself to you. It's part of the process we all have to go through."

What in the world was that supposed to mean? Relationship with God? Was that like having an imaginary friend or something? Wasn't God just there to *be God*? To set things in motion and then watch everything play out?

I peeled through the layers in my mind for what I knew about God: Creator of the universe, been around forever, angels do His bidding. I hit a wall, though, whenever I tried to make a personal connection. Just like what happened anytime I tried to pull up a memory.

Romona squeezed my forearm and offered an apologetic look. Her uneasiness rushed through the empathy link as strongly as her encouragement. She knew I didn't like her explanation.

"Don't look so worried. It's different for everyone. It'll come back when the timing's right."

My frustration suddenly threatened to come out in tears. "I don't think I understand what that means. Romona, why can't I remember my life? No one seems able to really explain that to me."

She paused. "I can't tell you. And I mean that. Not that I *won't*, but that I truly *can't*. It's different for everyone. It has something to do with dealing with the grief of losing your former life, but it's also a lot about learning what your new life, your eternal life, will be like. It's a fresh start, but the memories always do come back. Who you are today is still about who you were on Earth. There are just some things you need to take in without the distractions for a while. You have to have faith that there's a purpose."

"Faith in what, though?" I blinked away the new tears.

"Faith that the Creator of the universe knows what He's doing."

I looked back up at the gleaming fortress. Angels circled the structure as if in continuous orbit around the sun. Romona wanted me to believe God cared. But what if that was exactly what I doubted? When I searched my heart, I wasn't sure I truly believed He cared about me. So far, my life in the ever after felt like one giant mistake, not like a celestial fairy godfather was taking care of me. How could things be going according to His plan when I felt so alone?

Romona brushed her fingertips on my elbow and gave me an encouraging smile. "Maybe you can see the tabernacle because He wanted you to know He's actually here?" There was a hopeful note to her voice.

"Just like the great and powerful Oz. The man behind the curtain."

"No, Audrey, he's nothing like that. A man didn't become a wizard to deceive us. Instead the wizard became a man to save us."

I was less enchanted by the scenery on the hike back and even quieter than before. Romona, cognizant of the fact that I needed to process, gave me time alone with my thoughts.

I couldn't stop wondering about the life I no longer remembered. Everything led back to that. My gratefulness for Romona caused me to wonder about my pre-death friendships. What if there were people who depended on me but I wasn't there for them anymore? It was sad to think that I couldn't remember the people who were mourning me. It seemed unfair that they had to go through that pain when my slate was wiped clean. I simply didn't understand the point of it all.

I turned my head to get another glimpse of the fiery sanctuary high up on the mountaintop before we ducked into the shadowed forest. It was just a speck sparkling in the distance.

Who was this God who ran the realms in this way? If He couldn't even bother to see me right now, how important could I really be to Him? Why couldn't He just explain all of this to me Himself rather than force me to bumble around in the dark?

I struggled to feel anything other than anger and frustration toward Him. The heavy darkness and mucky topography of the forest appropriately reflected my mood for the rest of the hike.

DUMPED

*a*gain," Logan barked from across the room.

I kept my eyes squeezed shut and concentrated on making sure all my limbs still moved properly. There was a dull ache on the left side of my head where a golf-ball-sized bump was growing. Since my arms were, in fact, still working, I lifted a hand to gingerly probe the spot. *So not fair that you can still get hurt after you die.*

"Audrey, get up. We're going at this again."

Logan was clearly annoyed, but I had no interest in jumping up for another beating. He had thrown me across the room and into the padded wall for probably the fifth time that day. I was supposed to be practicing defensive techniques, but like everything else so far, I was failing miserably. And my body hurt everywhere.

I lay corpse-still and prayed Logan would believe I was dead—if it was even possible to die after you'd died—and leave me alone. Logan stomped over as I calculated the severity of the injury I'd have to sustain for him to ease up. I stubbornly refused to open my eyes. Stubborn was one thing I had probably been fairly good at in life.

"Audrey, you can stop faking it. I know you didn't faint, and you certainly aren't dead."

I let what I hoped sounded like a pitiful moan out of my throat. The next instant, Logan hauled me sharply to my feet. But I wasn't done making my point. As soon as he dragged me up, I simply let my legs go limp and landed on my butt in a heap on the ground. At that moment, maturity seemed highly overrated.

"Audrey, this isn't a joke."

I looked up and stuck my tongue out. I suspected it was the only muscle in my body that wasn't going to be screaming in pain later. Logan's eyes narrowed, and his facial muscles hardened.

"Fine, if that's the way you want to play this."

In a blur of motion, he bent down and heaved me up and over his shoulder.

"Hey wait, what the heck are you doing?"

I used the remainder of my strength to pound his back while attempting to squirm off his shoulder. I twisted to the left and felt myself slip, but he simply compensated. I found myself hanging upside down even further, with his hold tightened to steel. The blood rush to my head was beginning to make me dizzy.

I craned my head to the side to see where he was taking me. With a small shock, I realized we were already out of our gym and walking through the training center, past startled bodybuilders giving us weird looks. I thought I spotted Romona practicing on a punching bag, but Logan moved so quickly I couldn't be sure it was her. We were swiftly past before I thought to call out for help. Some part of me was probably too mulish to ask for it anyway.

"Okay, Logan, you had your fun, you can let me down now. If I knew most of these people, this would be pretty embarrassing." I was breathless. It was hard to talk while dangling upside down.

No answer from Logan as he continued parading me through the training center.

"Logan, come on, I'm starting to get really lightheaded."

No answer.

"Logan!"

This time I balled my hand into a fist and tried a reverse punch on his back. He didn't even flinch. *Man, I really do stink at this hand-to-hand combat stuff.*

Logan pushed through the front doors of the training center and carried me into the light of day like a sack of potatoes. Shocked faces seeped into my peripheral vision. This was definitely getting embarrassing. I was almost happy the blood was already pooled in my head, or else the blush of humiliation would have shown through.

I was gearing up to launch a verbal assault when Logan halted. *Finally!* But my relief was premature, for the next instant I was flying through the air, arms and legs flailing. I let out a huge scream that was muffled by a frozen blanket and a big lung full of water. It took a moment to figure out which way was up, but I eventually came sputtering to the surface coughing and hacking.

Logan had thrown me into a lake. Or rather, a fishing pond. Surprised strangers all around weren't even hiding their stares. Logan had managed to toss me at least sixty feet. It was too deep for me to touch bottom, so I noisily struggled to the shoreline and then hacked up a couple lungfuls of nasty fish water. I looked up to see Logan push through the training center doors without glancing back.

By the time I'd reached land, most of the people had resumed fishing and were politely pretending not to stare. A few were not very discreetly covering smiles, and those closest to me came over to make sure I was okay. I should have been happy that at least someone cared, but at that moment I was beyond furious. I couldn't imagine I'd ever been so mad in my entire life. Who did he think he was? He hadn't even stuck around to make sure I could swim! He'd tossed and left! I choked down my anger long enough to assure the small crowd around me that I was in fact okay, even as I sporadically coughed up water.

As the crowd dissipated, Romona burst out of the training center. She surveyed the shore of the pond before spotting me and sprinting over, her face radiating concern. Fully dressed in workout gear, she didn't appear the least bit winded.

"Audrey, oh my goodness, are you okay?"

I was not okay; I was furious. I took another moment to empty my lungs and shakily rose to my feet, setting my sights on the training center doors. If the murderous look on my face didn't give away my intentions, Romona was assuredly tipped off when she grasped my arm to help steady me.

"Whoa, Audrey, you shouldn't go back in there just yet. Logan's not in the best mood. I know you must be angry, but trust me, you don't want to get into it with him right now."

I was already purposefully striding toward the door by the time she finished her last sentence.

Oh yeah? Not get into it with him? He *doesn't want to get into it with* me *right now!*

I shoved the front door open with enough force to draw attention. The puddle at my feet grew as I searched for the first muscle-built guy who would look me in the eye.

"Where is he?" I ground out.

His eyebrows shot up, but he gave a quick jerk of his head, indicating a set of doors behind him. I stalked across the room and busted through both doors. My anger had tripled since I'd entered the center, and I was ready to do some serious damage.

Logan was alone in the room. He'd done his own serious damage to a practice dummy, which was now slumped over with multiple broken appendages. The startled look on his face was short-lived. After a quick sweep of me from head to toe, a corner of his mouth quirked up in amusement.

With that, something in me broke free. I snatched the closest weapon I could find and ran straight toward Logan with a banshee scream. Romona yelled a warning behind me, but I wasn't sure if it was meant for Logan or me. I was both out of control and completely focused. Time seemed to slow, and I was able to calculate things I'd never thought possible—such as the weight of the object in my hand, which I finally recognized as a fighting staff, and how far until I was in striking range.

I took a premeditated swing at Logan, which he narrowly deflected with a staff that instantly appeared in his hands. Using his surprise to my advantage, I twisted fast enough to catch him in the stomach with a back kick that sent him stumbling a few feet. I followed up with a roundhouse kick straight to his shoulder, swinging my staff around and then immediately up, disarming him.

Before I could savor my victory, Logan dropped low to swipe my feet out from under me, and I landed hard on my back. Even disarmed, Logan was faster, stronger, and more skilled than me. Before I could regroup, he kicked my rod out of my hands and held the blunt end of my own weapon to my throat. He stood above me, breathing as heavily as I. Whether from exertion or anger, I didn't know.

Everything happened over a short few seconds, but it felt as if we were locked in that stance for ages. Eventually the rest of the world leaked into my consciousness and I realized we were being watched, but I couldn't break from Logan's blue gaze. Our breathing slowed, but neither of us moved an inch.

"Looks like you have your hands full with that one, Logan," someone laughed from the newly gathered crowd.

The laughter broke the tension, and chuckles, followed by a few jokes, were thrown our way. The atmosphere felt noticeably lighter. Logan looked away as he lowered the weapon. He turned to head across the room, picking up his staff on the way. I propped myself up on my elbows to see we'd managed to attract a few dozen people—filing out of the room since the show was clearly over. I was surprised to find that my anger had dissolved. It must have burned off in the fight, and now that it was over, I was exhausted to the bone.

Romona hunched down to my level, a slight frown on her face.

"You okay?" she quietly asked.

"Yeah." I rolled my right shoulder and instantly regretted it. "I just feel like I've been through a cement mixer today."

Her features softened, and she gave me a small, comforting smile. I guessed she still didn't approve of what I'd done. Logan might have dumped me in a pond, but I wasn't exactly blameless. "It will get better."

I looked at her skeptically.

"I promise," she continued. "Let me help you up."

She stood up and reached a hand down. I grasped it. Even with her help, I struggled to stand.

"Wow, you are tired, aren't you?"

I gave her a half-smile since it was all I could muster. Her brows furrowed in heightened concern.

"Seriously, can you even make it back to your room?"

I shrugged a shoulder and turned toward the door. "I'm fine."

"Romona, can you give us a minute?"

The sound of Logan's voice jolted me. After my fury burned itself out, I'd actually forgotten he was still there.

Romona only paused for a moment before she nodded. I watched her go. She sent me an encouraging smile before closing the door firmly behind her, blocking out prying eyes. The small burst of energy from hearing Logan speak evaporated, and I was left incredibly weary, so much so that I had a hard time staying on my feet as I turned to face him.

Standing at a distance, Logan looked somewhat weary himself. Of course, he'd hardly broken a sweat, but his eyes betrayed him. If he wanted to talk, fine, I would let him start.

He took a big breath of air and ran a hand through his hair before saying anything. "Can we at least call a truce?"

I gave him what I intended to be a skeptical look. He laughed. A true, genuine, hearty laugh—something I'd not heard from him before now. It was a rich sound that actually eased some of the tension from my shoulders. Man, I was tired.

"Here." He materialized a metal folding chair behind me. "Sit down; it looks like you are going to fall over . . . or maybe faint for real?"

I was a little jealous he could do that so easily.

"I told you I don't faint," I grumbled under my breath, but I didn't argue as I slid into the metal chair. I was convinced I might fall over at any moment. Part of me was already fantasizing about my bed. If we were going to have this talk, I wanted to channel as much energy as possible into talking rather than staying upright.

Logan materialized a chair for himself and sat down about an arm's length away. His motions were deliberate, like someone approaching a spooked animal. He waited a second before speaking. When he'd chosen his first words, his eyes focused and locked with mine. "It seems you retained at least a little of what I've been trying to teach you."

A pause. I didn't know how I wanted to respond to that.

"I mean, your form was sloppy, but you did get in a few solid hits before I disarmed you."

I was too tired to be offended and more than a little surprised at being given any sort of praise, even if it was weak. It must have shown on my face.

"Audrey, I'm not here to antagonize you, you know." The weariness in his eyes returned as he lifted a hand to run through his hair. "I think we made our points today, probably the wrong way on both sides, but we do need to find a way to work with each other."

I was struggling to comprehend. This was the first time Logan had initiated a conversation with me that wasn't tactical or related directly to a new fighting skill or technique. I could only nod in agreement. No argument from me. What we'd been doing wasn't working.

He continued, "You know it's my job, my responsibility, to make you a fighter. You can't imagine what you will face out there. You need to be able to defend yourself as well as others. This is only a small fraction of what you will need to ultimately learn. You have no idea the amount of things I need to teach you in a short time."

Rather than his usual threats, this sounded more like a plea.

"Is there going to be a test on this stuff that I don't know about?" The question may have come out flippant, but I was at least half-serious.

"There's no test, Audrey. You go straight from training to the field, where you won't have the luxury of making mistakes. Any errors or miscalculations will directly affect those you are trying to protect."

"What exactly does that mean?"

"That means that if you screw up, if you forget how to use a weapon or where to deliver the most effective punches, or you run out of energy on a chase, then someone on Earth gets hurt. That could mean yourself or someone on your team as well."

This was the most information I'd gotten about being a demon hunter so far. I was intrigued. I wondered if I'd be able to contact anyone I knew on Earth, my family perhaps, if I even had one.

"We need to find a way for you to tap into your fighting instinct and skills when you aren't angry."

Against my will, I smiled. And because I couldn't help myself, I said, "Oh, you noticed that, huh?"

His mouth turned into a smile that didn't quite reach his eyes.

"Yeah, you're a mean fighter when you're mad."

We sat in a comfortable silence for a moment as we contemplated our options. For once, Logan was treating me like an equal. I wanted to be careful with my next words.

"I think," I finally began, "that I might do better if it wasn't so serious all the time."

I went on quickly because I imagined he was already starting to reject the idea. "I mean, if it didn't feel so much like a class all the time or if we were friendlier with each other, I would enjoy training a little more, and maybe I'd start to do better."

I shrugged and looked to my left, unsure of myself. When I looked back at Logan, he was staring at the wall above my head with what appeared to be a thoughtful look on his face. He didn't say anything for a while. Finally, he gave himself a small nod and looked me in the eyes. The full effect of his blue stare was always somewhat startling. Despite myself, my stomach did a little flip before settling again.

"Okay, Audrey, I hear what you're saying. I have a few ideas. Will you give me another chance to try this out?"

His face had taken on an intensity that was overwhelming. I was still slightly leery of his methods, but that he was *asking* me for anything, rather than demanding, was a change. And right now I was so tired, I probably would have agreed to anything. It felt a little like defeat, but I slowly nodded.

"But only if you agree not to dump me in any more ponds."

His face lightened, and he barked out a short laugh. "Well, I can agree to that. I'm sure I can think of more creative ways to get you motivated in the future. And if not, there are always pools and lakes around here as well."

I frowned. He laughed even louder.

"Don't look so worried!"

I wasn't so sure, but I was beginning to get tunnel vision, so I only nodded and focused on the floor in front of me.

"Audrey, are you okay?" Logan asked.

I nodded again without answering. If I could just get to my room, I'd be fine. I shook my head to clear my vision. Logan put a hand on my shoulder, careful not to make any contact with my skin. He may have said my name again, before giving me a little shake. I tried to shrug off his hand. I'd been manhandled enough that day.

"I just need to get some sleep," I mumbled and attempted to stand.

I'd spoken the truth, but my body demanded sleep sooner than I had intended. My legs gave out on the first step, and my tunnel vision narrowed to near blackness. Logan lunged forward to catch me before I hit the ground.

I must have caught him unawares, because he forgot to materialize protection between our skin. There was a moment of contact when I could almost grasp what he was feeling, but it was swept away with blackness.

CHANGES

"Oh no!" I sat up with a start. I was back in my room. Romona perched comfortably on the corner of my bed, her darker complexion striking against the monochrome white of the room. The last thing I remembered was talking with Logan in the training center.

"Is Logan here?" My words rushed out in a breathless huff.

"Nope. He brought you around the back of the training center. I don't think anyone saw you guys. He asked me to check in on you. We both think it was a case of overexhaustion."

I rolled my eyes. She ducked her head to hide her expression. My eyes narrowed.

"You think this is funny!"

She coughed and stood up, turning her back on me to walk across the room. "Would Sleeping Beauty like some water?" Even with her face obscured from view I heard the smile in her voice.

Traitor.

Romona knelt down and pushed some points on the white wall as I mulled over the fact that Logan had seen me faint . . . again. How badly was he going to hold that over my head?

A small door swung open in front of Romona, catching my attention. *Where did that come from?* Craning my neck, I glimpsed a few bottles of something before she grabbed two clear ones and shut the door, which instantly blended back in with the wall.

"What in the world?"

I popped out of bed far too quickly and wobbled my first step. I took another step and a half before regaining my footing. Dropping to the floor in front of Romona, I ran my fingers over the flat white surface. Smooth like seamless plastic. "It's gotta be here somewhere," I mumbled. I barely registered Romona's bemusement.

"Um, Audrey, what exactly are you doing?"

I lifted my gaze. Romona stood with a bottle in each hand and a look that said I'd grown an extra head. I was on all fours with my face only inches from the wall.

"How'd you do that with the door? Where did those bottles come from?" I rocked back on my heels.

"Here, drink this. It's only water."

After I reached up to accept the gift, she motioned toward the wall.

"It's your room fridge," she said. "You just need to push here and here." She indicated two invisible spots on the wall, then deftly punched them with her fingers. Two spots glowed red momentarily, then a panel swung open and gently bumped into my knee.

I peered inside at the treasure. Nestled within were five rows and six columns of different colored bottles. I bent my head to look deeper; the bottles appeared to go on infinitely. Already, the clear bottles Romona had taken had been replenished. I giggled. This room was amazing!

"Shut up!"

"What? I didn't say anything."

With my head still in the fridge, I said, "Oh no, not you . . . I was just making an exclamation."

"Oh, well, I know the variety isn't that extensive, but once you move out of here, you'll have a wider selection."

I gawked. I couldn't even name as many different types of cold drinks as were in that fridge.

Romona startled me out of my musing with an irritated snort. "No one's told you much about your room, have they?"

I shook my head. "What 'they'? Logan just dumped me here the first night, and that was it. There hasn't been any other 'they' to tell me anything. Just you about the closet."

Romona let out another perturbed burst of air as I scrambled to my feet and said "boys" under her breath.

"That explains why this place still looks like a padded cell in an insane asylum." She crinkled her nose. "Come over here. I'm going to give you a real lesson. This room is a blank canvas. It's up to you to paint the picture. I think we need to begin with something simple."

She drummed her fingers on her bottom lip, considering. "How about we start with the wall color? What color would you like your room to be?"

Logan's distinct blue eyes popped into my head.

"Maybe blue?" I answered hesitantly, turning my face to cover a slight blush.

"Okay. Can you think of the shade of blue? Exactly what it looks like?"

"I think so."

"Close your eyes and really imagine the color. Feel the shade of it. If you can imagine where you've seen that shade before, get a mental picture in your head. Then imagine the color splashed on these walls."

She gave me a moment to produce the image in my head. Rather than cobalt eyes, I imagined a bright blue sky with big, fluffy clouds floating in it. We sat in silence for a few minutes until Romona started to laugh lightly.

"What?" I asked, lids still pressed together to concentrate on keeping the picture.

"Let me guess—you're picturing a sky?"

I took in a quick breath of surprise. "Hey, how'd you . . ." My lips stayed puckered on the word "you" because I opened my eyes and my room *was* the sky. Not just any sky, but the exact sky I had pictured! The precise shade of startling blue dotted with fluffy marshmallow clouds. And the two-dimensional picture was more than just a mural—the clouds drifted slowly as if a slight breeze nudged them lazily through a summer sky. Staring at the floor, which was also moving sky, had a slightly dizzying effect. I gave my head a good shake to free myself from the vertigo.

"How in the world did I do that?" I whispered in amazement.

"I still can't believe he didn't tell you *anything*. I would have done this ages ago if I'd known." She rolled her eyes and crossed her legs as she settled herself on the bed, launching into teaching mode. "This room is attached to you. Specifically to your imagination. This should be the spot where you feel most comfortable. In many ways it can be whatever you want it to be, whatever you can imagine it to be . . . within some limitations, of course."

Throughout the next hour, Romona showed me wonder upon wonder hidden in my four walls. In fact, I learned my room didn't have to have four walls. It could be almost any shape I wanted. In addition to the mini fridge, I also had a built-in snack bar with everything from potato chips to fresh fruit and even fruit roll-ups. She said the room knew what my favorites were and automatically stocked the selection. I was both grateful and jealous that the room knew my favorites when I didn't.

We tweaked the color of my room a bit because the movement of the clouds was disorienting, and I settled on a lighter and more muted shade of motionless silvery-blue. Romona also helped me materialize some furniture, since I still wasn't very good at that. I tried and only managed to bring up some loose stuffing. She thought materializing would get easier for me when my memories returned.

When we were done, I was extremely pleased with the result. My bed had been changed into a four-poster bed of dark mahogany wood, delicately carved with damask designs and scrolling. The bed covers and pillows had been transformed into a pretty shade of lavender with a light damask pattern to match the posts. With just a push of a thought, the bed was still able to magically fold up and disappear into the wall. We created a seating area as well, with comfortable sofa chairs and a low coffee table. I was envisioning a coffeehouse feel, where people could come in and chat and enjoy a few of my super delicious snacks. That is, when I finally made a few more friends.

I shook my head. What a big bad huntress I was going to make with tea parties in my room. I wondered again what in the world they were thinking, making me a hunter. I couldn't brush off the suspicion that one day someone would admit a huge mistake had been made and assign me to something more appropriate. Maybe party planning or dress designing?

Perhaps that was wishful thinking.

Romona interrupted my thoughts. "What are you thinking about? You have a strange look on your face."

I shook my head and smiled ruefully. "Oh, just that it's obvious someone made a colossal mistake. Look at this place. It's definitely more pretty-pretty princess than bloodthirsty demon hunter."

Romona frowned. She looked hurt, which puzzled me. I hoped I hadn't offended her. She was the only person who had truly taken the time to get to know me, and I would hate to have said something to make her unhappy.

"No, Audrey. Mistakes like that don't happen here. Ever," she said. Her eyes avoided mine. "Being a huntress doesn't mean you're not feminine anymore. It does mean, however, that you have something valuable to bring to the table. It means you were specifically created for the job. You might not see it now, but I believe you will eventually. Not everything about being a hunter relies on brute strength and agility."

"But it sure doesn't hurt."

One side on her mouth turned up in a smile that didn't quite reach her eyes. "I'll give you that one."

Romona gave herself a visible shake. "Let's get out tonight. It's not good for you to spend all of your time in this room or the training center. The afterlife is so much more than that. I think you need a little fun after the day you've had."

"That is the best idea I've heard all day." I headed toward my magic closet, determined to end the day well. It was time to change more than just my room.

Romona knew exactly what to do to get my mind off of training, fights with Logan, and my ongoing string of embarrassments. We had dinner with a couple of her friends at a place that resembled a 1950s diner. We sat in red vinyl booths and were served by waitresses on roller skates with foot-high beehive hairdos. But far more interesting than the venue were Romona's friends.

One was a petite, redheaded girl with a great sense of humor, named Sarah. She looked even younger than me, but she said she had been here a while. She didn't elaborate, but the way she said "a while," I assumed she was older than me despite her appearance. She worked as a historian in the great library, which I didn't even know existed. That alone proved I needed to get out more.

The great library not only housed all the books of the world but also the accurate histories of the ages. Sarah explained that she spent time making sure all the events on Earth were cataloged and recorded properly so everyone here could keep up with what was going on there. Most of the information was relayed to the historians through the angels, who frequently traveled between the two realms, but she also admitted there was another source she wasn't allowed to talk about. She remained pretty tight-lipped about it, laughing good-naturedly at my unveiled attempts to pry more details from her. I made it my secret mission to get more information out of her the next time we met.

The other of Romona's friends, Gary, was an equally interesting character in a completely different way. Gary was a black man who grew up in Georgia and actually lived through the American Civil War. He looked about forty years old. Gary's Southern accent was thick, and he was quick to laugh at my "Yankee" accent, immediately making me feel comfortable. His work here had something to do with agriculture. He said it wasn't exactly farming, but close. The next time I had a day off, he'd show me where he worked.

I stayed up late talking and laughing with Romona and her friends and woke up regretting it. Lethargy weighted my limbs as I dragged my feet through the training center hallways. But it wasn't only the lack of sleep that had me moving slowly this morning. Logan had left a note on my door with special instructions for the day. Included was a list of needed items. Considering he'd chucked me in the pond the day before, I thought it was a joke—a bad one. Towel, swimsuit, sandals, and bag lunch. Luckily for Logan, Romona had stopped me from hunting him down to tell him exactly where he could put his list. She somehow even managed to convince me to bring everything he requested.

Logan was doing pull-ups with his back to me when I entered the gym. I didn't bother to stop the door from banging shut behind me. The sound echoed loudly through the room, but it didn't interrupt the rhythm of his reps. I waited for him to acknowledge me. The muscles in his shoulders and arms flexed as he smoothly pulled himself up and down. I was both jealous and impressed at the ease of his movements. I had struggled with just a few pull-ups the day before. He made it look effortless.

Logan finished his set before hopping down and bending over to grab his water bottle. From the state of the room, he must have been there for a while. The practice dummy was once again missing a limb that lay about seven feet away from the rest of the body. A pair of boxing wraps were unraveled next to the punching bag, and the room smelled. *Eww.*

Logan put down his water bottle, wiped his forehead with a towel, and finally jogged over to me. Apparently he did sweat. Kicking my butt must not be much of a workout for him. That prickled my already heightened annoyance. I was prepared to walk straight out of the gym if he said one word about my fainting episode.

"You know, if you've already had your workout, I'm happy to call it a day and come back tomorrow."

"Ha, you should be so lucky. This was just my warm-up"

"Lovely."

"Glad to see you're in another one of your good moods, Sunshine." He eyed my bag. "Did you bring all the things on the list?"

"Yes."

"Good," was all he said.

I let the shoulder strap slide, and the stuffed bag thumped to the floor. "So, speaking of, what do you have planned today?"

"It's a fun surprise. I can tell you one thing, though."

"What's that?"

"We're going down today."

"Down? Down where?" He'd lost me. There was only one floor to the training center. Maybe there was a basement I didn't know about.

"Down down . . . down to Earth down." He motioned and said the words slowly, as if he were speaking to a child. That was annoying, but I was too caught off guard to care much.

"Really? I mean, we can do that?"

"Of course. Where do you think we fight demons, anyway?"

Holy cow! "We're going to fight demons today? That's what you consider *fun?*" This guy was certifiably crazy.

"Nope, something better." He read concern on my face, and his mouth split into a grin. "Oh come on, don't you trust me?"

"No," I answered flatly.

"Well, fair enough. I did dump you in a pond yesterday."

"Yes, you did."

"But didn't we have a good conversation afterward? Didn't you say that you would trust me?" He took a step closer, and I had to tilt my head back to look at his face. He was trying to manipulate me.

"Yes, but . . ."

"And didn't we agree that you needed to be trained properly?"

I glared at him. I had serious reservations about going back to Earth, even if I wasn't sure why.

"So we can go back, just like that?"

"Yep, just like that."

"We don't need a permission slip or something?"

"Nope."

I met his eyes and tried to look serious. "Are you sure this isn't your evil plot to get rid of me once and for all? Go to Earth and leave me there to wander for the rest of eternity?"

"No, Audrey. I promise." He had the serious face down better than I did. All the earlier teasing was put aside now.

I chewed on my lower lip. Thinking of going back to Earth caused a knot to lodge in my stomach. And maybe I did know why. Going back would mean I would have to admit to myself that this was all real. Was I really ready to start moving forward? So far everything had been new and weird and different, but it certainly didn't feel like *real* life—or rather, *real* death. More like a really long and weird dream.

"Oh, come on, Audrey." He was close enough there was no need to speak loudly. It felt like a whispered dare. "What are you so afraid of?"

His stare was so intense I wanted to squirm. I suppressed the urge and swallowed my remaining reservations.

"Okay, then. How does this work?"

The words escaped my lips as a chill slid down my spine. I didn't have to be a prophetess to see change coming. It encircled and tugged me forward like a rope tied at my waist. The way I saw it, my only options were to either concede to the change and walk upright toward it or plant my feet and be dragged. Either way, change was coming.

RIDING THE WAVES

*L*ogan led me across the training center to a room that must have been based on stolen blueprints for the *Star Trek* transporter room. Focused technicians stood behind counter-height panels punching buttons, barely sparing us a glance. In front of them and to our right was a raised, rounded platform with lighted pads just large enough for a human to stand on. I swallowed a giggle.

Logan told me to hang tight while he spoke with the technicians. When he returned, he gave me a few short instructions. After stepping onto one of the pads, I simply had to close my eyes and empty my thoughts.

I stepped up. Clearing my thoughts was harder than expected. Nervous fingers of apprehension skimmed over my body. I'd been told not to talk, so I was left in the blackness to silently wonder what was next.

"She's a little worked up, but it shouldn't be a problem. You're a go for transportation whenever you are ready, Logan." Suddenly a blast of warm air hit me from all sides, then began to swirl like a tornado, blowing my hair in all directions and muffling my surroundings. I experienced a moment of weightlessness right before the whirlwind stopped.

I squinted against the sudden brightness behind my lids. Tears welled in the corners of my eyes as I forced them open and the world slowly came back into focus. I smelled the salt in the air and heard the rhythmic sounds of the tide flowing in and out before my eyes adjusted enough to see a strip of beach stretched out on either side of me.

Seagulls were calling above, and I smiled. In that moment I discovered something else about myself. I *loved* the beach. I loved the feel of the sand beneath my feet and between my toes, the warmth of the sun on my skin, and the coolness of the water. I loved the weightless feeling of the tide sweeping the sand from beneath your feet as the waters recede back into the ocean.

With a laugh, I stripped off my shoes and ran into the surf. It was as cool and refreshing as I had hoped it would be. I waited with my toes buried in the wet sand to feel the pull of the tide and lifted my face to the sky to soak in the warmth. Inhaling a deep breath I absorbed the peace of my surroundings. There was nowhere else I wanted to be.

And then I was attacked.

I shrieked in surprise when a large, wet, and furry being jumped on me. I lost my balance and landed butt-first in the sand with the creature on top of me. My hands came up in defense as the thing goobered me with its tongue. The sun was so bright and I was so startled that it took me a moment to recognize that a very large dog was on top of me, licking my face as if his life depended on it. Some demon fighter I was! Rendered useless by a family pet.

Realizing I wasn't in any immediate danger, I started to laugh again. The dog licked me with increased fervor. In my defense, the thing must have weighed at least a ton. I struggled to get him off me between mouthfuls of laughter. Why is it always harder to move when you're laughing?

Mercifully, someone yelled, "Peanut! Come here, baby, what are you digging at over there?" The girl calling from down the beach was a petite brunette who didn't look at all as if she could handle an animal his size. "Come here, boy, I've got a treat."

At the word "treat," the dog lifted and turned his head toward the voice, his overgrown apricot coat blowing in the breeze. He sniffed the air as if it testing the validity of his owner's promises.

"Come on, boy, let's go home."

With that, the dog stepped on my throat before bounding off after his owner. I was left on the ground covered in sand, seawater, and dog saliva, but it was the happiest I'd been since I'd woken up dead.

"Some animals can see us, but the people here won't."

Logan's voice jerked me out of the moment. I bent my head back to see him standing a few feet behind me with a relaxed smile on his face, looking off in the direction of my furry friend. "His owner probably just saw him pawing at the sand."

"Yeah, well, I appreciate the chivalrous rescue." I couldn't sound too serious with the big grin on my face.

Logan certainly didn't look offended. "And stop the love fest that dog was giving you? Never!"

He gracefully seated himself on the sand next to me. I was intrigued by the information he'd just given. "So none of them can see us, huh?"

"Nope. They just see currents in the water or wind blowing the sand."

"So will they, like, just go through us like ghosts? Because I'm going to say right now that I think that would be a major violation of my personal space."

"Well, first of all, there's no such thing as ghosts, but to answer your question, no. When we're on Earth, the people living here have a sixth sense to avoid running into us. Watch this."

He pointed off to the right, where a family of six was walking along the beach with arms full of beach gear. Mom and Dad were trying to corral three young boys and a girl right toward us. When they got within about five feet, the mom pointed at a spot on the beach near the water, and the whole lot of them veered off before stepping right on Logan.

"So what happens if we bump into them?" I asked.

"They trip."

The family was busy setting up their beach chairs and cooler. "So what else should I know about being back on Earth? To actually hunt and fight demons, this is where we need to be, right?"

"Yep, this is the battleground. We usually come down in rotations. We do most of our training back in our realm and then spend time down here protecting, patrolling, and sometimes following up on leads. But we don't stay down here for too long. The longer we're on Earth, the weaker we get—both mentally and physically. We're not made for this realm anymore, so it takes a toll on us. It can be pretty dangerous if we're here for too long."

"How long is too long?" I asked.

Logan shrugged his shoulders. "Don't know exactly. We usually try not to stay for more than a few days at a time. Even that is hard. You'll see what I mean."

He picked up a shell in the sand and threw it side-handed into the ocean. I watched it skip across the water before pressing him.

"But what happens if we stay longer?"

Logan's silence was telling. Apparently he wasn't ready to have that conversation yet.

"There are other interesting things about being back on Earth," he told me. Without warning, he picked my hand up from the sand and held it between both of his. I was so taken aback that he was holding my hand that I didn't notice the point he was trying to make. Logan was always so careful to avoid touching my skin.

My hand was so small between both of his. His fingers were long and graceful, more like a painter's than a fighter's. They were a lot softer than I would have imagined them to be as well. Not that I'd ever imagined them to be anything! With that thought, my cheeks started to heat up. Thank goodness for the warmth of the sun.

"Pretty cool, huh?"

Was he talking about holding my hand being pretty cool?

It was only after he dropped mine and went on talking that it registered that I hadn't felt anything from the empathy link. I had been feeling too much of my own stuff to realize I wasn't getting anything from him. That thought made me shift uncomfortably on the sand, putting a few extra inches between us.

"None of us have the empathy link with each other here. It feels the same as when we were alive. But more importantly, you need to know that we can link with the demons." The muscles in his shoulders tightened, and he sat up straighter. The talk was getting serious.

I finally found my voice. "The demons?"

Logan nodded gravely.

"But why would we want an empathy link with a demon?"

"Exactly. We don't. But *they* do."

As usual, I wasn't following. My brows came together in confusion. "You see, the demons are filled with everything dark in the world—all the hate, wrath, lust, greed, jealousy, and just plain blackness out there. If they get hold of one of us, it's as if we absorb what they are feeling, and it's incapacitating. Not only that, they feed off our emotions. It's similar to the myths of vampires sucking blood from their victims."

I jerked another inch away, creeped out by the thought. "Eww, you have got to be kidding me. That is nasty!"

"Afraid not. Of course, they can't ever *really* suck what's good in us away unless we let them, but it's something I hope you never have to experience."

It was on the tip of my tongue to ask him if *he'd* ever experienced it, but the way he talked about it, it felt too personal a question to ask.

"Demons grow stronger by destroying the people here on Earth. They latch onto people and encourage them to do all sorts of things that ultimately hurt them in the end. The more lives the demons ruin, the greater they grow, but their hunger doesn't stop with the living. If the lives of the living are food to them, then we're a drug. Sometimes they even seek us out because of it . . . like an addict looking for his next fix. It makes some demons very unpredictable and even more dangerous."

That sent a chill down my spine. "I hadn't heard that before."

"There's a lot you still don't know." Logan stared at the waves. A faraway look had captured his eyes. I felt comfortable studying his silhouette because he was so focused on the unseen. "That's why it's so important for you to get all you can out of this training. We try to work in units as much as possible, but you need to be able to defend yourself alone if it ever comes to that. What we do is important to the people we are protecting, but it's also dangerous to ourselves—perhaps even more so for you because they might see you as weak."

I would have been offended by that last comment if he hadn't said it so matter-of-factly. And it wasn't like I could disagree. I'd already admitted more than once that I was a pretty pathetic hunter.

We were both quiet for a few more minutes. I couldn't feel the sun warming me anymore. It felt as if a ball of ice had lodged itself in my throat, preventing me from swallowing. I had to break the tension somehow.

"So did you bring me out here to teach me to swim or something? Because you know, I already figured out that I can swim thanks to the pond you dumped me in yesterday."

The corner of his mouth went up. Now that we weren't in the heat of the moment anymore, even I acknowledged the humor of our fight.

"No, as a matter of fact, I brought you here to teach you to do that."

He pointed. I brought a hand up to my brow to block the sun and spotted a person on a bright blue-and-green board gracefully riding a wave. He agilely cut the board to the left and right to stay on the wave and rode it back to shallower waters.

Immediately, anything demon related was forgotten as I jumped to my feet in excitement.

"Now *that's* what I'm talking about! Where do we start?"

Logan took his time getting to his feet, brushing the loose sand off.

"I'm glad I found something you can be enthusiastic about."

He reached down to the duffel bag he'd brought with him and fished out two wetsuits. I eyed them skeptically. They didn't look particularly comfortable or fashionable. He tossed one at me. I managed to grab the suit before getting slapped in the face with it.

"First, you need to get your bathing suit and that on." He nodded at the black bundle in my hand.

"Why aren't you just materializing yours?"

"Ah, that's another thing about Earth. It takes a *lot* of skill and time to learn to do that here. It's a handy trick to have back home, but it probably won't do you very much good here. You have to bring all your supplies with you. Only what you bring with you will remain invisible to the people here. We can't just pick up a weapon off the ground. We need to use one we've brought with us so people don't see a crowbar or baseball bat floating in the air. But don't worry; we stash weapons from home around so that anyone who needs them can find them in a pinch."

I picked up on probably the most unimportant part of the explanation.

"So you're telling me other people can do something you can't."

Logan, smart enough to realize I was trying to bait him, just rolled his eyes and pointed a finger behind me.

"Girls' bathroom is that way."

I rolled my eyes back at him and headed in the direction he'd pointed.

After getting changed, I rushed back to the beach. The wetsuit, a rather thick unitard, was not as uncomfortable as I'd imagined. Unfortunately, it was twice as unattractive. I shouldn't have worried since Logan was the only one who could see me, but I was still pretty self-conscious about how ridiculous I looked.

Logan was down the beach a little way waxing up one of the boards. The other lay flat in the sand. I was slightly disappointed that he didn't look half as silly as I felt wearing a wetsuit. But his didn't cover everything from his wrists to his ankles like mine. It was T-shirt style and only went down to his knees.

It clung to him like a second skin and showed off all of his lean muscles. More than that, for once he truly looked relaxed.

He stopped working on the board when I walked up.

"Great, you're ready. Have you ever been surfing before?"

I gave him what I hoped was a scolding look.

He winced. "Whoops, sorry about that. I forgot you wouldn't remember. I think we should assume we're starting from square one. The most important thing about surfing is balance. That's why I think this will be a great training exercise for you: if you can learn better balance on a surfboard, it'll help with your balance when fighting."

"Hey, what's wrong with my balance?" I put my hands on my hips in mock annoyance.

Logan shot me a bland look before continuing. "So as I was saying, balance is the first building block you need to become a good fighter. You need to be in control of your body at all times. Surfing will help you get a feel for your core so that, when there are variables on the outside that are changing, you are still in control."

"All right, I'm ready. Let's go." I grabbed the board he wasn't working on, hefted it under my arm, and turned toward the surf. Before I could get two steps, Logan grabbed my arm to stop me.

"Hold on there. The lesson starts on land."

The water called to me. I stuck my lower lip out in a pout and set the board back down as I gave the ocean a longing look.

Logan laughed. "Oh come on, don't look like that. You look like a puppy that just got his favorite toy taken away."

I put a hand on my hip. "You know it's an incredible tease to be this close and not be able to enjoy it. You just had to find a way to torture me, didn't you?"

Logan laughed harder. "Yes, that's it, Audrey. I'm here solely to make you miserable."

I had to laugh too, despite my annoyance. "Just as I thought. At least you've finally admitted it. And I don't really appreciate being compared to a dog."

He got in another short laugh. "Duly noted. Now let's get started. The faster you catch on, the quicker we can get in the water."

That was motivation enough for me.

THE GREAT ESCAPE

*W*hen Logan finally gave me the okay to pick up the board and paddle out into the surf, the water felt as amazing as I'd thought it would. We had spent an hour on the beach as he proceeded to teach me every idiosyncrasy of surfing—including its history. The lengthy wait in my black wetsuit made getting in the water as refreshing as a long drink of iced lemonade on a hot summer's day. I used my arms to paddle out past the breakwater. Although breathing heavily when I finally made the distance, the peaceful surroundings engulfed me. Sitting upright on the board and letting my feet dangle on either side in the water, I took in the vastness of the ocean in front of me.

Logan paddled up beside me.

"It's beautiful, isn't it?"

I just nodded. With all the wonders in the afterlife, seeing the ocean sparkling in the sunlight still took my breath away.

"It's hard to imagine that people would deny a Creator with all the beauty around them. This doesn't just happen by chance. His fingerprints are all over this world."

I took a deep breath to process his words. There was a lot of wisdom in what he said. "Did you enjoy the ocean this much when you were alive?"

It was the first time I'd ever asked Logan anything about his life on Earth. It was the first time I'd ever cared enough to ask. I turned my head to study him while I waited for a response.

His eyes stayed on the horizon, his expression unreadable. His stoic face safely locked in place. "Yeah, I used to come here a lot. My family owned a home not too far down the beach. This used to be one of my favorite spots."

Here? Logan used to live *here?* I was equally surprised that he was comfortable bringing me to this spot. I looked toward the shore and tried to imagine Logan as a kid running along the beach. It was difficult to envision him so carefree.

"Let's get started," he said, interrupting my thoughts. And with that, Teacher Logan was back. He launched into another lecture on surfing that I was forced to wait out until trying the real thing.

Three hours later, I lay in the sand exhausted. I didn't even care that my hair was covered in sand or that there was a beach crab getting dangerously close to my foot. I was wet, tired, and happy. The surfing had been harder than I anticipated, but I thought I'd done okay. There were times when it felt as if I was flying along the surface like a bird. Eventually my body just gave out on me, and I started making stupid mistakes. Logan picked up on it and called it a day. We both rode a wave toward the shore. I'd pulled my board up onto the sand and collapsed. Logan had taken a moment to look out at the water before setting his board carefully in the sand and taking a seat next to me. As usual, he hardly looked winded. I was too content to care.

"That was fun! Definitely my kind of workout!"

"I'm glad you enjoyed it. It's good to see that when you're properly motivated you're not so much of a klutz."

The backhanded compliment warmed something inside me, and I smiled.

Logan reached up and unzipped the back of his wetsuit, peeling it off to his waist. I almost gasped in surprise at the angry scar that ran diagonally from his left shoulder blade down to his ribs on the right. It looked as if the flesh had been torn from his back. What could make a wound that large? It was the first scar or deformity of any kind I'd seen since entering the afterlife.

I resisted the urge to reach out a hand and trace the scar. Logan looked back at me. If he guessed at what I had been staring at, he didn't let on.

"You ready to get back? I think it's probably about time we got going."

I let out a deep sigh. "If we have to."

The beach was almost deserted. From the position of the sun, I guessed we had an hour of daylight left, if that. I pushed myself up to a sitting position and tried not to stare at Logan's bare chest. I had to admit it was pretty distracting. *My gosh, the boy probably doesn't even realize what effect he could have on girls because he's cooped up in the gym all day.*

I tore my eyes from Logan to stand. Now that we were out of the water, I was equally eager to get my wetsuit off. I reached up to pull the zipper down my back and started to peel the wetsuit from my upper body.

"What are you doing?" Logan sounded startled.

I stopped in the middle of peeling off the right arm. "What?" I looked down at myself and then around at the beach. What was the big deal?

"Don't you want to go to the bathroom or something to do that?"

Huh? "I'm just taking off the wetsuit. I've got my bathing suit on underneath." I didn't know why, but I became a little defensive. "I'll get all my clean stuff nasty if I don't take it off here. It's not as if you've never seen anyone in a bathing suit before." And because I couldn't keep my mouth shut yet again, I added, "Besides, you look practically naked in that thing yourself."

I gestured to his upper torso as I continued to peel the wet material from my skin. Geez, I was even wearing a one-piece. Would his head have exploded if I'd worn a bikini? The thought made me chuckle and lightened my mood.

Although he tried to hide it, Logan looked anything but relaxed. He sat rigidly in the sand with his face trained on the ocean. He might have been a shade or two redder than normal. I was enjoying the idea of making him uncomfortable. Served him right.

All of a sudden he made a huffing sound and pushed himself gruffly to his feet. "Whatever. I'm going to put these boards back. I'll see you back here when you finish getting changed."

Logan grabbed my board as I struggled to get the suit off my legs and stomped up the beach. Seriously, what was his problem?

In a moment I was free of the wetsuit and feeling very sandy and salty. I'd seen showers in the bathroom and decided I deserved the extra time to wash off the grit. I didn't see Logan anywhere. *Oh well*, I thought, and made my way to the bathrooms.

The shower felt heavenly. I wasn't sure what the people there were seeing —probably just a broken shower steaming up the bathroom—but at that moment, there was nothing nicer than the feeling of clean water washing away the sand and salt from my body.

When I got out, I pulled the towel from my bag, dried off, and quickly put my clothes back on. I sent a silent thanks to Romona for convincing me to bring the bag of extra things. She must have known what we were going to do. I spent a few extra moments working knots out of my long hair, especially happy I'd thought to put a brush in my bag. With my hair down so it could air-dry, I exited the bathroom carrying my bathing and wet suits in my hand.

More time had passed than I realized. The sun was already setting over the water as I traversed the cooling sand. *Huh, guess that means we must be on the west coast somewhere. My money's on California.*

The sky was a mixture of purples and pinks that faded to orange and gold toward the horizon where the sun made its final farewell for the day. As breathtaking as it was, I didn't take too much time to admire it. Logan was likely impatient for my return. In my mind's eye I saw him leaning up against a post with his arms crossed against his chest in frustration. I swiveled my head to find him, but the beach was almost empty. I couldn't see him anywhere.

Suddenly, a bad feeling clenched my chest. It was as if I smelled something wrong in the air. But it wasn't a smell at all. It was something icky trying to burrow its way into my brain. I looked around frantically to locate the source. I could have sworn there was a pressure against my head, but when I turned there was no one there. My breathing picked up as my mind went wild with possible explanations.

Out of nowhere Logan appeared, grabbed my hand, and jerked me into a run. It was difficult to sprint across the sand, especially carrying a bundle of wet things and a pack, but I somehow managed to keep up. When we reached the road and rounded a corner, I was finally able to yank my hand free.

"What in the world was that all about?"

Logan looked at me with the familiar annoyed look. "Keep walking."

"Logan, what's going on?"

He refused to look at me as his eyes scanned the area. He spoke more to himself than me. "I know there's a boardwalk around here, not too far away. We just need to get there."

"Logan!" I shouted this time. "What was that back there?"

I slowed down, forcing him to look back at me. He finally did.

"It was a demon. We have to keep moving."

I stumbled on nothing when he said "demon" and took a few quick steps to steady myself. This wasn't the time for questions, but I had a million of them. A cord of dread grew thicker in my gut. Logan looked concerned, and if he was concerned, I was sure there was cause to be.

"Did it see us? Does it know we're here?" I took a quick look around us, suddenly convinced we were going to be attacked at any minute. My imagination was running ahead of me, but I didn't know how to stop it.

"I'm not sure. If we get to a group of people, we should be able to blend in. Usually, the only way they can distinguish us—when we aren't in body armor —is that we can see them. If we blend in naturally, there's a chance the demon won't realize we're here."

We were still walking at a fast clip. Logan continued, "Getting back isn't as easy as getting down to Earth. We have to get a lift back from an angel. One was scheduled to get us on the beach, but we can't wait for her there anymore. We'll have to go to the backup location after we've lost the demon."

My mind was spinning. There was so much I didn't know.

"Don't you want to, maybe, stay and fight it or something?"

Although that was the last thing *I* wanted to do, I wondered why we were running. Weren't we supposed to be fighting? Wasn't that what we were, demon hunters?

Logan's eyes flicked toward me for a moment before scanning the area.

"We aren't prepared, Audrey. We don't have any weapons, we have no armor. You're almost completely untrained. This isn't a time we want to meet a demon."

He suddenly grabbed my hand again. "Quick, it's this way, I'm sure."

We made a sharp turn to the left around a small dune, and sure enough, there was a bustling little boardwalk up ahead. The lights were just coming on with the darkening sky, and it was filled with people. It was exactly what we needed to blend in. I started to get giddy with renewed hope, but a moment later, I sensed the demon again: the smell that wasn't a smell, the dark pressure on me. It pushed against me from behind.

"Logan . . ." Something in the tone of my voice made him turn to me. "I can feel it coming."

Logan looked less worried and more determined and gave my hand a quick squeeze as he pulled me forward.

"We're almost there." It was all he said, as if getting somewhere would mean we were safe.

And he was right. We stepped onto the planks of the boardwalk and were swallowed into the crowd. I was relieved for about two seconds until I realized the crowd was parting around us, just like Logan had said they would. There was something wrong with this. We were still too conspicuous to hide, and I felt the demon behind, stalking us from the beach. We needed to go somewhere more private but still busy, somewhere where it wouldn't look weird to have people avoiding us.

Logan must have been thinking the same thing, because he quickly pulled us toward the opposite side of the boardwalk where it was slightly less crowded. It took all my willpower not to look behind us. The fine hairs on the back of my neck stood up, and the non-smell was getting worse.

We walked by some of the less popular stands on the boardwalk. Logan kept me moving at a quick pace. I dug in my heels all of a sudden and tugged on Logan's hand to get him to look at me.

"Logan, we have to stop running. It just makes us look more obvious."

It went against every instinct I had not to break out at a full run in the opposite direction of the demon, but I knew I was right. Logan looked at me doubtfully but stopped, and together, we started again at a slower pace. What could we possibly do to blend in with normal living humans? And then a thought came to me.

To our left there was a space between two stands that was slightly dark but still partially lit by the boardwalk's bright lights. Impulse took over, and I went for it. I caught Logan by surprise enough to drag him in after me.

"What the . . ." was all Logan was able to get out before I crushed his mouth with my lips. My face heated with embarrassment, but I willed him to understand what I was doing. No such luck. He was an unmovable statue, with his arms tense to his sides and his feet rooted to the ground. He obviously wasn't catching on. This wasn't going to work if he couldn't play along.

I pulled back enough from the fake kiss to urgently whisper, "Put your arms around me." When he didn't immediately comply, I whispered the command more forcefully, "NOW!" and stomped on his foot for emphasis.

Something finally roused in him. His arms obediently slid around my waist, and he pulled me closer. I reached a hand around the back of his neck to bring his mouth back down toward mine and kissed him like my life depended on it.

As Logan suppressed his surprise and regained control of himself, he also captured control of the kiss and softened it. As his lips molded to mine, I tried hard not to think about how soft they were. When he tilted his head to change the pressure, I tried hard not to notice that he tasted like peppermint and that my lips were now tingling a little. With a mind of its own, my hand moved up the back of his neck to bury in his thick hair. One of Logan's hands slid up my arm to cup the side of my face, leaving goosebumps in its wake. His other tightened around my waist to pull me even closer. He tilted his mouth to deepen the kiss as his thumb slid under my chin to stroke the sensitive skin there.

With a sigh, my body melted into his hard chest. The quickening of my pulse now had nothing to do with the demon stalking us, and I forgot why we were kissing. A moment later, when Logan pulled back slightly, I found myself stunned, and a small sound of protest slipped out of my throat. He looked down at me with lidded eyes. Like always, his steel-blue gaze held me prisoner. We were both breathing far too quickly.

"I think it worked," he said huskily. I was close enough to feel the words vibrate in his chest.

The sound of his voice snapped me out of my daze. Right! The demon! The kiss was to throw the demon off us, and it had been my idea. My earlier embarrassment flooded back. One of my hands rested on his chest and the other was still buried in his thick, soft hair. I felt his heart beating through his shirt, almost as fast as mine.

With a small gasp, I yanked my hand out of his hair and pushed against his chest to free myself. But his hold on me tightened, and I found I couldn't move. He tilted his head down to bring his mouth close to my ear. His breath caressed my neck, and his thumb was now making lazy circles on my cheek.

"Hold still. It's still out there."

My body immediately tensed, and he felt it. "It's okay. I just want to get a little more distance between us."

Logan held me close, trapped between his arms and chest, for what seemed to be a few more minutes. My heart beat wildly, and my whole body remained tense. What had just happened?

Finally, Logan used the hand under my chin to force me to look up at him.

"Are you all right?"

His blue stare captured me. He should not be allowed to be dead with those eyes.

It took me a second to find my voice. "Yeah," was all I could squeak out.

"That was pretty quick thinking."

I did not want to talk about that kiss, especially since we were still in a "fake" embrace. I put pressure on Logan's chest again, and this time he released me. I took a few shaky steps back and looked anywhere but at him. The air felt hotter than it had under the midday sun. My mind grasped for a way to escape the discomfort.

"So where do we go from here?"

Logan took a moment before answering. When he did, there was a change in his voice. He was all business again. "We have to find the backup extraction point. I don't want to go back to the beach tonight. I think I know of another one in the area, though."

"How do we know we won't be followed?"

"I'll be more careful this time. I should have seen the last one coming from a mile away. I was distracted."

I snuck a look at Logan. He wasn't looking at me. He had a shoulder leaned against the wall of the stand and was scanning the crowd behind me. He looked both casual and alert.

Where *had* Logan been when I got to the beach? I was about to ask when he straightened and quickly brushed past me.

"Come on," he said as he passed.

He stopped at the boardwalk to wait for me. Serious Logan was back, and for once, I was glad of it. I bent over to grab my discarded items. I must have dumped them on the ground when I attacked Logan. He didn't grab my hand this time when he stepped out into the crowd. I was glad about that too.

We walked along the boardwalk in silence. Not close enough to touch, but close enough to still make it appear that we were together. It was probably the most awkward moment of my life. Or so I would guess, since I couldn't remember any of the other moments.

Shaking my head in chagrin, I realized I had been right about one thing: change had definitely arrived.

THE DAY AFTER

*I*s there a word stronger than "awkward"? If so, multiplying that by twenty would describe what it was like to be in the training gym with Logan the day after our trip to Earth.

We'd returned the evening before and were immediately directed to fill out a report on "the incident." I'd mumbled through some answers before finally claiming a headache, hiding from Logan as much as from the questions. Logan stayed to finish the report while I fled. I cringed to think of what he'd revealed.

I lay awake half the night thinking of other ways we could have escaped the demon. We could have hidden behind a building, pretended to be in line for cotton candy, taken an empty seat on one of the rides, or jumped off a high bridge into shallow water. *So* many attractive options. Why couldn't I have thought of one of those?

Hunters swarmed our training gym in the morning, wanting to know all the details. I wished we'd come up with something clever to tell people other than that we'd made out. And that it was my idea.

"Hey Audrey, I hear you *knew* the demon was coming or something? That you could feel it? What's the deal with that?"

The curious question came from someone to my right. This was a safe topic. Some of the murmur died down.

"Yeah, well, it's hard to explain, but I just kind of knew it was gaining on us and generally where it was. It felt like a pressure. Or maybe a smell, but it was a smell that wasn't a smell, ya know?"

Apparently the articulate part of my brain was in the off position.

The guy, most likely trying to help by changing the subject, veered to a topic that caused my stomach to jump to my throat.

"Well, what did you guys do to shake it? I'd love to hear how you gave it the slip when it was already on to you."

Heavy silence hung in the air as they waited for an answer, hoping to discover a secret for bluffing a demon. A sea of faces full of anticipation. My cheeks heated and my mind buzzed. My "technique" could not be duplicated —not by this bunch of meatheads, anyway. I couldn't think of what to say.

An unexpected rescue came from across the room. "Audrey pulled us between two of the stands."

"And it didn't see you guys? That didn't look suspicious?"

"We tried very hard to look inconspicuous."

The way Logan said it gave finality to the answer. There was a disappointed murmur throughout the crowd, evidence that the muscle-bound hunters didn't understand the logic. "Sorry it's not more exciting. We were lucky to have gotten out of there unscathed. And if you guys don't mind, we've got to get back to training so the next time we won't have to do so much hiding."

There were a few chuckles from the crowd at the not-too-subtle dismissal, but they got the point and dispersed.

My feeling of relief was short-lived. It was only after the last person left and the doors slammed shut that I reluctantly turned in Logan's direction. Taking a deep breath, I looked him in the eyes. His clear gaze stared back, and his familiar stoic expression was in place. That, in a way, was oddly comforting.

"Do we need to talk about this?" His voice was flat and to the point.

"Nope," I answered just as directly.

"You sure?

"Yep."

"Okay then, let's get back to work."

And with that, the matter appeared to be closed. But I couldn't shake the awkwardness of simply being around him.

Before yesterday, I'd spent a good amount of time imagining Logan getting his butt kicked by one of the other hunters or losing his balance and falling on his face. I'd be lying if I didn't admit he'd always had unquestionable good looks going for him, but he drove me so crazy I never cared. He yelled at me, pushed me past my limits, made me train when I didn't want to, and remained a constant reminder of every strength I didn't possess.

Now, what I thought of Logan was all jumbled up, and I didn't like that. I'd even arrived a few minutes late this morning because I couldn't decide what to wear.

The change in my behavior was not welcome. How could one stupid fake kiss change so much so quickly? I was resolved to get back to where we'd been before, even if that meant being at each other's throats. At least that made sense to me.

Only I wasn't sure how to make that happen.

Logan was characteristically quiet as he went across the room. I tracked his movements as he bent over and pulled something metallic out of his bag. He brought it to me, stopping with a gulf of space between us. He tossed the object. I snatched it from the air before it collided with my face. Perhaps my reflexes were improving.

Pinching a section, I rubbed it back and forth between my fingers. It was some sort of fabric or bendable metal, incredibly smooth and slick, almost like reptile skin. I held one end up and let the rest drop to the floor—a garment. It made a faint clinking noise as it fell.

"It's your body armor."

Oh.

"It's what we wear for hunting. It creates a barrier so the demons can't create an empathy link with us, and it protects us from getting physically hurt. It's very difficult to cut through."

I took my eyes from the material and looked up at him.

"You were wearing this the first day we met, weren't you? When you sparred with Alrik?"

That had been the first time I'd seen anyone dematerialize anything. The sight of the armor melting off Logan had been shocking. That day seemed lifetimes ago.

"I was. Sometimes we wear it when sparring—it's good to be accustomed to it. It's incredibly strong. You know chain mail, right?"

"Huh? Like a spam e-mail you're supposed to pass on to everyone you know?" I couldn't see how that had anything to do with the bundle in my hands.

A small smile snuck its way onto Logan's lips before they flat-lined again. "I believe you are thinking of chain letters. Chain *mail* is a type of armor. They used it in the Middle Ages. It's made from metal linked together." He linked his fingers together to demonstrate.

"Oh right, that." I ducked my head in embarrassment.

"Well, this material is similar except the links are unimaginably small. And it's made from a metal that's not found on Earth. That's what makes it so light but still strong and protective."

"That's pretty cool, actually." I brought the material up to my eyes. Despite closing one eye and squinting at the armor, I couldn't discern the weave. It looked completely smooth, like a flat sheet of metal.

"Anyway," Logan continued, "I figured since our adventure yesterday, it's time for you to start learning about our fighting gear. It's what you'll be wearing the next time you face a demon. So you need to go and get that on."

"It goes right over my clothes?"

"Yes. It will form to whatever you're wearing and create shields for extra protection on vulnerable areas of your body."

Logan materialized his own armor covering. Shadows clung to his form, and an instant later solidified into a full body covering.

As I remembered it, his suit was made of closely fitting metal armor. His shins and thighs were covered with extra plates, the ones on his shins stretching low enough to cover his ankles as well. A belt encircled his hips, complete with a scabbard encasing his sword. A breastplate protected his chest, and similar plates of metal shielded his arms. From the neck down, whatever parts of him weren't fortified by a metal plate were covered with metallic material, including his hands and feet.

The armor made him look like a cross between a medieval warrior and Batman. Logan wore it as if he were born to do so.

I really did need to learn how to materialize things better. It was going to save me tons of time. I looked down, doubtful that what I had in my hands was the same thing Logan had just materialized. I grimaced at my mental picture of myself in the armor.

"Okay, Show-Off," I said lightly enough so he would know I was kidding, "I'll go put mine on."

Logan didn't crack a smile, but his jaw twitched—as if he was clenching his teeth to keep his mouth shut. He really was in rare form; as if he couldn't decide what his mood should be.

I pushed through the training gym's doors, forcing Logan and his moods out of my mind, and walked toward the girl's locker room. Empty. I turned the fabric over in my hands, trying to find an opening to insert a limb. I was baffled. The armor rolled through my fingers like slippery seaweed as I searched for a seam or some kind of shape.

"It's easier to put on if you hold it right-side up."

Startled, I dropped the material. It landed on the ground with hardly a sound. I spun.

Resting a shoulder against one of the lockers was a girl dressed in black-and-pink workout clothes. She was tall and lean with honey-tanned skin. Her long blonde hair was pulled back into a high ponytail that brushed her right shoulder. My hair never looked that good in the sporty do, but it both fit and complimented her features perfectly. She reminded me of a beach volleyball player—not overly muscled like the guys, but well-toned.

And gorgeous.

I gaped as she continued talking, repeating herself as if I hadn't under-stood the first time. "You know, the armor." She gestured toward the heap on the floor. "You need to hold it the right way to get it on." She was smiling, but I wondered if it was really a smirk.

"Oh, well, that's news to me," I answered with bite to my words. Why hadn't Logan explained that?

"Whoa there." She pushed her shoulder off the locker and put her hands up in front of her in an "I mean no harm" manner. Two perfect eyebrows rose. "Listen, it just looked like you needed some help."

"Sorry." I blew out a frustrated breath and forced a smile. "I've just been a little stressed lately. I didn't mean to be rude. It's one of those days, you know?" I looked down at the material at my feet and bent to pick it up.

She nodded as if she understood, her smile still in place. I couldn't shake the suspicion she was laughing at me.

"So, ah, could you tell me which side is right-side up?"

"Here, do you mind?" She plucked it from my hands. "You see this?" She showed me an almost indistinguishable bulge in the material. "You need to hold it there."

When she demonstrated, the armor magically took form. There was clear definition between the top and the bottom as well as where your limbs were supposed to go.

She continued, "Then you see there's a seam here that acts kind of like a zipper. You slide it down in order to step into it."

She handed the bundle back to me right side up. I quickly found the seam she was talking about. I lifted my head to say "thanks" only to catch a glimpse of her back as she exited the locker room.

Now that was weird. Who was she? Another hunter? There were other female hunters, but besides Romona, I hadn't seen any, and frankly, I'd hardly given them much thought.

But if I had done so, that girl was what I would have imagined. Nothing like me. Whereas her limbs were long and toned, mine felt short and weak. Her posture oozed confidence; mine usually radiated clumsiness.

The new feelings bubbling up inside were ugly. I shoved them down.

Giving my head a shake, I forced my mind back to the task at hand, which was getting into this ridiculous outfit. Twenty minutes later, I achieved victory.

I was taken aback when I faced the mirror. Mine was obviously a girl version of the suit. The metal plates that covered my legs, chest, and arms were less pronounced and more delicate. The armor fit like a second skin, as much as it did Logan. I looked like some sort of futuristic, comic-book warrior queen. All I needed now was dark, smudgy makeup and a few purple highlights. Perhaps looking the part would help with my training?

I threw a few practice kicks and punches at the air in front of the mirror. The suit still felt slightly cumbersome despite its sleekness. It was going to take some getting used to . . . but I was willing to put the work in. I definitely looked more hardcore now.

I was in a decisively good mood as I marched down the hallway back to the training gym. I received some curious stares and someone even whistled at me, which in a weird way helped increase my confidence as much as it tinted my face. I was giving myself a silent pep talk when light, singsong laughter wafted out from our training gym. I stood on tiptoes to peer through one of the door's high windows. It was a precarious position to say the least, but it offered a view of the whole gym.

Logan was standing in the middle with the girl from the locker room, facing her with an easy smile on his face. He said something, and the girl tilted her head back to laugh, flipping her ponytail over her shoulder at the same time. She leaned in closer and put a hand on his armored bicep, whispering something in his ear. Logan smiled and nodded at her when she pulled back.

That same ugliness gurgled in my chest once again. It nettled me immensely that she had touched him so familiarly, and even more so that he didn't seem to mind.

A hand on my back scared me so much I yelped and pitched forward, smashing through the gym doors with a crash and landing sunny-side down on the floor. I somehow managed to elbow myself in the stomach on impact, knocking the wind from my lungs. I gasped for breath on the ground, my face squished to the padded floor. I *seriously* needed to get better at reacting to the unexpected.

Logan and the girl looked up from their conversation with matching expressions. My attacker quickly stepped forward and offered me a hand up.

"Oh man, sorry about that, Audrey. I didn't mean to scare you."

I craned my neck to look up. It was Kevin. Tall and lankier than most of the warriors, Kevin was nevertheless imposing. He glanced down at me and then at Logan and the girl, and then back at me again. The look on his face said he realized what an awkward situation this was.

"Ah, yeah, it's no problem," I mumbled hastily and accepted his offered hand. He practically dislocated my shoulder jerking me to my feet.

"Whoa there, sorry! You're a lot lighter than you look." His face turned from his normal latte color to a deeper coffee hue when he caught his mistake. "I mean, just that, you know, you ah . . . I mean, it's not that you look heavy or anything. Really, you're super short and all; it's just that you're really light."

He was digging himself into a deeper hole with every word and finally gave up. There was a moment of uncomfortable silence. Logan and the girl continued to stare at us as I rubbed the feeling back into my left shoulder.

Kevin broke the silence first. "Well, anyway, I'll let you get back to it." He backpedaled out of the gym. "Your armor looks great, by the way, Aud. Fits you really well. Not that I was noticing how it fit you or anything, but ah, yeah. Well, ah, I'll see you around then."

With a quick wave, Kevin turned and fled. The doors swung shut behind him.

It was painfully quiet after he left. Logan and the girl remained rooted in the same spot, their faces turned toward me. The silence stretched for a few heartbeats.

The girl let out a nervous laugh. "Well, I helped you figure out how to get the armor on, but I'm afraid I can't help much with your coordination."

To my extreme embarrassment, Logan laughed with her. My face turned colors, but there wasn't much I could do. I'd just been caught eavesdropping and proved to be the biggest klutz alive. I still didn't appreciate the jab at my expense.

"Kaitlin, as you've probably already guessed, this is Audrey."

The girl, Kaitlin, stepped forward and extended her hand, practically daring me with the empathy link. I was prepared to step up to the challenge but remembered as she grasped my hand that my armor prevented me from getting an emotional read. I was covered from fingertips to toes. I twisted my mouth in disappointment. I really wanted to know if she was purposefully trying to make me look stupid or not.

"We met a little while ago in the locker room," Kaitlin told Logan. "Audrey needed some help getting her armor on."

I felt like the third wheel in the gym even though, technically, *she* was the intruder. This training time was supposed to be for me.

"I guess that was fortunate," Logan answered. He finally addressed me. "Kaitlin and I go way back. She's stationed with another group of hunters in a different part of the realm, but she's over here helping out with a special project. We were just talking about her training with us sometime while she's here to give you some pointers. She's got some great moves."

My eyes narrowed. "Sure."

Kaitlin laid her hand on Logan's arm again. Could she stop touching him already?

"Well, I should probably get going. It was great to get a minute to catch up, Logan. I'm sure I'll see you soon."

"Yeah, definitely." Logan offered her one of the easy smiles I so rarely received.

She walked past me as she left. "It was nice to meet you, Audrey. I'm hoping to see you around too. It's always nice to have another female hunter in the mix."

The smile she gave me seemed genuine enough, but I couldn't muster the emotion to return it. She looked unsure for a moment and her smile slipped fractionally, but she stepped gracefully through the door without another word.

I waited for the door to shut fully before turning back to Logan. He was watching me rather than the door. I felt myself go hot, then cold. His face quickly changed, and he turned toward the weapons wall.

That was odd.

Logan came back toward me with a sword in his hands, his training face back on. "We'll train without the helmet at first until you get used to the rest of the armor."

He extended the hilt of the sword to me. As always, it seemed a little too heavy.

"All right, let's get started."

We barely said two words to each other the rest of the day. Mostly just Logan's short commands to correct my form or tell me to try harder. There was none of the warmth or carefree spirit I'd seen a day earlier. There was no light banter. Logan kept his distance, and I trained on practice dummies the entire day. It was as if, with that one kiss, we'd erased any positive progress we'd made—even taken a step back. There was a cold tension that hadn't been there.

I was exhausted when I left the training center later that day. I didn't notice that I was mumbling to myself until someone answered me.

"What was awkward?"

Romona's voice made me jump, and I put a hand to my chest to calm my beating heart. Why was everyone startling me today?

"Oh my gosh, sneak up on people much?" I snapped.

Romona didn't deserve my sarcasm, but I was in a testy mood. The look on her face said I'd hurt her feelings.

"Oh geez, I'm really sorry, Romona. I'm just kind of out of sorts today." I smiled meekly at her. "Yesterday shook me up a bit."

Always quick to forgive and comfort, she moved to put a sympathetic hand on my arm. I quickly jerked out of reach, not sure which of my jumbled emotions the empathy link would reveal. Her eyes widened as she regarded me suspiciously.

We stood in silence. Without a plausible excuse for pulling away, I froze.

"All right then, when you want to talk about it, let me know." She briskly turned and walked away.

I felt incredibly alone watching her retreating figure, but I didn't have the nerve to chase after her. I wasn't ready to talk about it. Besides, it was just a kiss—a fake kiss at that—so things would surely go back to normal in a few days. I hoped.

With a resigned sigh and an overwhelmed heart, I headed toward my tree, feeling as if I missed a best friend I'd never had. Or perhaps I had, but I'd forgotten her along with the rest of my life. The thought depressed me further.

Once back in my room, I flopped onto my bed, curling my knees and hugging them to my chest. Something warm and wet rolled down my cheek and absorbed into the pillow under my head. I squeezed my eyes shut to stop feeling so much. Fresh tears leaked out of the corners anyway. A flood I couldn't dam crashed down on me. And as the salty water continued to flow, it revealed a cavern inside. An emptiness I had ignored that had been growing steadily every day since I arrived, fed by hopelessness I didn't know how to overcome. Unchecked, I feared it would leave me as a hollow shell—only a husk of a person.

I was suddenly very angry at the God I hadn't met and didn't remember. I sat up and punched the pillow that collected my tears. I'd forgotten my past, and my future was uncertain at best. I didn't have a family to mourn or even a God to turn to. I was utterly alone and completely abandoned. What kind of God would plan for this? Would take away everything only to replace it with nothing? Giving me a task that was so beyond my abilities was an extra punch in the gut.

I held my breath and waited for something catastrophic to happen. Wasn't being angry with God cause for expulsion from this place? Wasn't that why I hadn't been honest with myself until now—hadn't been willing to admit how angry I really was?

I continued to wait as the tears dried on my face and nothing happened. The longer I sat in silence, the better I felt. I hadn't thought I'd be allowed to be mad at Him without repercussions.

An unexpected emotion stirred in the empty hole of my heart. God was giving me the freedom to be angry without turning His back on me. It didn't make sense, but in that moment, alone in my room, without saying a word, I experienced something that felt an awful lot like comfort.

More tears welled in my eyes, but these were born of a different emotion. One strong enough to soften my hardened heart.

I jumped up off my bed, wanting immediately to share the revelation with Romona, but then I remembered our parting. I deflated a little.

With my hand on the doorknob, I considered my options. I did need to apologize, but I wasn't ready to tell her what had happened between Logan and me.

My feet were moving before I realized the decision was made. I at least needed to make things right with her.

Finding her, though, might be somewhat tricky. I chastised myself for never taking the time to find out where she lived as I hurried though the damp hallways and then out into the dwindling light of early evening.

APOLOGIES

"*H*ey, Audrey, wait up!"

After exiting the forest I skirted the city on the sidewalk, heading back to the training center to look for Romona. I was so buried in thoughts I hadn't noticed the familiar face I passed. I jerked my head to the left to see Kevin jogging to catch up.

I wasn't angry at Kevin for today's embarrassment, but his wasn't the friendly face for which I was searching. I stopped anyway. Someone just knowing me well enough to want to talk made me feel better.

"Hey, Kevin, what's up?"

He wore his easy smile. "Nothing much. I was just hanging out with some guys." He waved his hand over to a group playing basketball on the court I'd walked right by. The players not currently in the game nodded their heads or waved back.

I looked back up at Kevin. His height and lanky limbs made me wonder—I could imagine him effortlessly finding a home on an NBA court or some other professional sport. Someday when I knew him better, I'd ask about that.

"You kicking any non-hunter butt over there?" I asked instead, returning the smile he'd offered.

"Ha, more like learning from the best. Some of those guys were all-stars down on Earth." He leaned a little closer and lowered his voice a little. "Although I did win a wicked game of HORSE a few minutes ago. Hunter jumping skills may have given me an advantage." He looked so proud of himself I couldn't help but laugh with him.

"So where are you off to anyway? You look like a girl on a mission. Had to yell your name a few times to get your attention."

Man, was I that dense sometimes? "I was looking for Romona. I'm not exactly sure how to find her. I wish we had cell phones here. Or a sixth sense to know where anyone is at any given moment."

"That would be kind of weird."

"Yeah, I guess so. I wouldn't want to know every time someone went to the bathroom or anything."

He gave me a strange look before continuing. "Well, maybe I can help out. She lives in the same building I do. She might still be there if she hasn't left to get dinner. I could show you where it is."

"That would really be wonderful."

Kevin jogged back to tell his friends he'd be back in a few and returned in no time.

"So where do you guys live anyway? I'm assuming we all don't live in trees."

"You live back in the redwoods?" He seemed genuinely surprised.

"Yeah, is that bad?"

"Oh no, that's pretty cool actually. It's a little further away, but not very many people get assigned out there. You're kind of on the fringe." He didn't have to tell me that. Although beautiful, the giant trees did always feel a little removed. On the fringe—that was a good way to describe how I always felt here.

As Kevin forged ahead, I quickened my pace to keep up with his leggy strides.

"We live over there."

His outstretched finger pointed to a group of shining buildings not far from the training center. I'd taken notice of them several times because of their unique design. The buildings were shaped like an open book, with windows everywhere. It looked like they were floating in the air, but they were actually supported by some sort of clear, crystal-like material. A gigantic escalator brought people up and down from the ground to the first floor, which looked to be over a hundred feet up.

"Do you like it there?" I asked as we approached.

"Sure. It's temporary housing. The same as you're in right now."

"Temporary? What's that mean?"

"It just means we haven't all picked a permanent home yet. That's typical of people who still have family living on Earth."

"Really? Why's that?"

"Because usually you want to wait to settle somewhere near the people you loved when you were alive. A lot of us are just holding tight until that happens, ya know?"

I looked up at Kevin's content face as we approached the bright building.

"May I ask how long you've been there?"

"A while."

"Is it hard to wait?"

He didn't make me clarify. "At times. But I want them to finish out their lives on Earth. If they aren't here, it's because they still have things to accomplish there."

"But even if they have stuff to accomplish, a purpose for still being there, how does that make it easier to not be with them? Just because your head knows something doesn't mean your heart will follow."

Kevin nodded. "That's true—there's a difference when something penetrates your heart as well as your head. I suppose I'm okay because I believe in here," he patted his chest to indicate his heart, "that it's for the best, and I know I'll see them again."

Kevin's comment was surprisingly insightful. I was humbled to think I hadn't considered him very deep. There was more to him than just the sports fanatic I'd seen around the lunch room. I smiled to think I counted him a friend.

"Well, here we are! I hope you don't mind if I head back. I promised the guys a rematch."

I nodded before looking up at the structure before us. The escalator brought people up and down. We were right in front of the building, and I could make out its belly, which was just as see-through as the crystal pillars. People, looking tiny from here, walked back and forth on that first floor. It made my stomach flip simply looking at it.

"I appreciated the company. Do you happen to know which room she's in?"

"Just take the escalator up to the front desk, and they'll direct you the rest of the way. They're really nice."

"Thanks, Kevin!"

I gave him a quick hug for all the kindness he'd shown me. He backed away a few steps after I released him, uncomfortable. "Don't mention it. You're good people, Audrey."

I watched him jog off, then took my time getting to the escalator. Making amends with Romona wasn't going to be as easy as talking to Kevin. Some of my nerve was pinched away when I stepped onto the rising steps.

The escalator was also slightly translucent. Reluctant to look down, I surveyed the view. The city sprawled out before me in brilliant white. It contrasted with the green woods and brilliant sky surrounding it, yet city and nature were each just as beautiful in their own way. Each building had uniqueness about it. Close by, a tall spiral building high enough to pierce the clouds was circled by many shorter square buildings with pointed roofs and etched stones on each corner. The skyscraper beyond plunged and rose in a seemingly random pattern that was still pleasing to the eye. I wasn't thrilled with heights and was relieved to make it to the top without falling over the edge.

I stepped off the escalator and into a world of light. The ground twinkled with inlaid colored diamonds; crystal end tables supported jeweled vases full of vibrant flowers reflecting sparkling light. Even my arms appeared to have picked up a luminescent quality. I looked down to see a distorted landscape below, then jerked my gaze up.

"Is there something I can help you with, Little One?"

The voice had come from behind the large mirrored front desk to my left. The large man standing behind it had a deep voice, filled with warmth. He made me think of Christmas—of Santa Claus, complete with the rosy cheeks and white beard that glowed in the strangely lit room.

"I hope so. I'm looking for a friend. Her name is Romona . . ." How was it possible I didn't know her last name? Come to think of it, I didn't know anyone's last name.

"Romona the hunter?"

"That's the one," I said, relieved.

"She's a very sweet girl, isn't she?"

"Yes sir, she is." It was another reminder of how horrible I'd been to her that day.

He spent a few short moments punching something up on the clear monitor in front of him. "Here we are." The Santa smile lit up his rosy face. "She's up on the fourteenth floor. Room 733."

"Thank you. Is it okay if I just go up?"

"Yes, of course. Have you been here before?"

I shook my head.

"Just take the elevator over there. Straight up to the fourteenth floor and follow the signs in the right direction."

"Thank you, sir."

The elevator, constructed of completely see-through material, was more than a little unnerving. I squeezed my eyes shut so I didn't have to watch the ground getting further and further away and concentrated instead on the soft harp music. A chime sounded before the doors slid open.

To my immense relief, the floor was not transparent. Shiny as plastic lacquer and illuminated from below, but not translucent.

Squinting against the near blinding whiteness of the ending hallway, I found a plaque opposite me.

Rooms 1–500 to the left, and 501–1000 to the right. A thousand rooms on this floor alone? Romona's room couldn't be larger than a shoebox.

I started off to the right. Sparkling white diamond doors butted up next to each other. Twice I spotted people exit their rooms and tried to get an inconspicuous look as I passed. Were they crammed into a long, narrow corridor of space? Both times I missed a peek as they closed their doors behind them.

When I finally reached room 733, I looked down at a floral mat with the word "Welcome" spelled out. I certainly hope so.

With a deep breath, I lifted my hand and knocked. It was several moments before the door gently opened. When it did, Romona just stood there and stared. I stared back. A few awkward seconds ticked by.

"I didn't realize you knew where I lived." Her tone wasn't harsh, but it was slightly guarded, confirming her hurt.

"I ran into Kevin, and he showed me. Otherwise I would have been aimlessly searching the food district all night."

"Oh."

My uncertainty over coming to see her started to grow. I told myself again this was the right thing to do.

"So, um, would you mind if I come in? I actually wanted to apologize for earlier this evening. You know, after I was leaving the training center. And I was wondering if you wouldn't mind talking a bit. I just have some stuff on my mind I was hoping I could talk about."

I stared down at the mat, feeling rather dejected as she left me hanging outside. And then Romona's hand came to rest on the same shoulder I'd shrugged her off earlier. With relief, I sensed through the empathy link that I was already forgiven. She gave me a reassuring squeeze before letting go.

"Of course. Come on in so we can talk." She held the door open for me.

My jaw dropped as I walked through the door. Romona lived in a ballroom. Domed ceilings soared at least thirty feet in the air, meeting at a point in the middle where a crystal chandelier dropped down like a pendant to light the room. The walls were draped with rich velvet fabrics and adorned with gilded mirrors. Intricately inlaid wood covered the large square floor from one end to the other. And a wall of glass held a breathtaking view of the distant mountain range.

"What do you think?" she asked

"It's empty," was the first thing out of my mouth. "I mean it's incredibly beautiful, but you don't have any furniture." And then as an afterthought, "And how did this all fit behind your door? There's another door not a foot away from yours!"

She lifted her eyebrows. "I would have thought after we finished your room, you'd realize spatial rules don't really apply anymore." She shook her head, a small smile playing at the corners of her mouth. "And I do have furniture, I just put it away sometimes. I like the peace of the empty room. It keeps me from getting distracted."

She circled the room, pushing points on the velvet walls and inlayed floors. Within a matter of moments, the area was transformed. Thick rugs appeared, expertly placed beneath lounging chairs and couches. A wood-burning fireplace popped out of the far wall opposite a lavish dining room table with eight seats.

"I swap the bed with the table in the evenings," she offered before I even realized it was missing.

"This is so . . ." I couldn't finish. I was entranced.

"It's home for now. But you said you wanted to talk?"

"Yeah, ah, that would be nice."

I took my time getting settled in a peacock-blue wingback chair. Romona sat perpendicular to me on a tufted brown leather couch. She remained silent while I collected my thoughts, but I didn't get the sense that she was angry . . . just waiting.

"I really am sorry for how I acted earlier today."

"Thank you, but it's already forgotten. We all have our bad days."

"But that's just it. You've been nothing but nice to me. I shouldn't have snapped at you. I feel extremely bad for repaying your kindness with sharpness."

"Audrey, none of us are perfect." When I tried to object, she held up a hand to silence me. "We all have our breaking points, and while I was hurt, you've come to make amends, and that's really all that matters. Don't you agree? Our friendship goes deeper than one sharp exchange. We're kindred. There's nothing to have lingering guilt about. But there's more you'd like to discuss, isn't there?"

I nodded. Of course she was wise enough to realize something had set me off. The lightness I'd felt at her declaration of friendship was weighted down by the reminder of my troubles.

"Yeah, that. I had a pretty hard workout today. All the attention we got from being on Earth was awkward. And I met a new hunter today, which threw me for a little bit of a loop." All true.

"Well, the last part at least sounds like good news. You need to meet some more people. It will make you feel more part of the team."

"Yeah, I guess so."

She folded her hands and leaned forward a little. "There's something I'm missing, isn't there? You've had rough training days before. Who exactly did you meet today?"

"I mean, it probably shouldn't matter, but it was another girl. Her name was Kaitlin. I don't think she's from around here. But she knew Logan pretty well."

Romona looked thoughtful for a moment.

"Kaitlin. Hmmm, yes, I've met her. Logan introduced us a while back. If I'm not mistaken, I think they knew each other back on Earth."

That rocked me. But what did I care if Logan had history with a very blonde and leggy friend? I shouldn't, as long as it didn't interfere with my training. The uncomfortable and confusing knot in my stomach refused to be convinced.

"Oh, well, that explains why they were so friendly." I tried to sound nonchalant instead of unnerved. "I supposed I'm just not used to seeing other girls around the training center. Do you think she'll be around for long?"

Was I really doing this? Pumping a friend for information.

Romona shrugged her shoulders in indifference. "I suppose it depends on what she's doing here in the first place. If it's just for a social visit, then probably not. But she could be here on assignment. In that case, there's no telling how long she's going to be around. She might even have a permanent transfer for all we know."

I tried hard not to show my panic. Seriously, why did I even care? Why were my insides churning? Shouldn't having another girl be around be a good thing? Yes, it was a good thing. I could use another girl to relate to. And why not Kaitlin?

The ugly answer rose in my gut faster than I could ignore. Jealousy. That's why. I was jealous of Kaitlin without knowing much more about her than her perfect ponytail. Disgusted by my own weakness, I sighed heavily.

"What is it?"

"Nothing. It would be good to have another girl around."

"That isn't what that sigh sounded like." Romona eyed me carefully.

I sighed again. "Okay, truthfully I was a little intimidated by her."

Romona only nodded to let me know I could go on, as if she knew there was a deeper core to the matter.

"You're going to make me say it, aren't you?"

She shook her head gently. "Not if you don't want to. But I think you may feel better if you do."

"It's just . . ." I struggled to get the feelings out without betraying any connection to Logan. "She seems to be everything I'm not. I'm not picking this up quickly, Romona. I'm horrible at it. I know I sound like a broken record, but sometimes I think I'm actually getting worse. And if nothing else, Kaitlin seems to fit in so easily. She reminds me of what I'm not. And it puts me on edge."

Romona's brows creased deeper as I spoke. When it was quiet, she spoke up.

"I don't think you're giving yourself enough credit."

"Ha! I don't think Logan would agree with you." I kicked myself as soon as the words were out—I wasn't supposed to be bringing him into this conversation.

"I think he would. That's the impression I got from talking to him about yesterday."

My heart skipped a beat. "You talked to Logan about yesterday?"

"Yes. After you snapped at me, I was worried something worse had happened than what I'd heard. He said it was your quick thinking that got both of you out of the jam. He also mentioned you weren't completely horrible at surfing, which I'm guessing is pretty high praise from him."

A smile played at the corners of her lips. And she was right— "not completely horrible" was just about the highest praise I'd received from him. My heart still beat erratically. I couldn't imagine Logan telling her we'd kissed, but the knowledge that they'd talked about yesterday made me nervous.

"Well, anyway, that's just how I felt today. Kaitlin reminds me of my weaknesses."

"Your differences from the other hunters are not weaknesses, Audrey. You have no idea yet what you are capable of. What special gifts the Lord has given you. You've hardly even begun to figure them out. Kaitlin is absolutely going to excel in some things you don't, but that doesn't mean you are any less important, any less gifted than she is. We're not supposed to be looking to the right or left to see how we measure up."

Even delivered gently, the reproach in her words was loud and clear. I found myself both humbled and hoping it was true. Humbled because of how I'd treated Kaitlin and hoping that I was special—uniquely created for a purpose.

"Do you really believe there's something special about me?" I asked quietly.

"Absolutely! I have no doubt about that at all."

I smiled. "Thanks, Romona. I needed to hear that."

She smiled back and squeezed my hand. This time I didn't even flinch. I welcomed the compassion she always offered so freely.

"Here, let's have something to drink. I think it'll make you feel better."

She reached under the coffee table and pushed a button. A panel slid back, and a polished silver tray holding a teapot, two teacups, cream, sugar, and a few small round cookies rose in the middle of the table. I went for the cookie first as she poured tea.

"So, ah, what's the deal with people falling in love here anyway?" I asked around a mouthful of cookie.

Romona choked on her tea but managed to gracefully regain composure.

"Never mind. Forget I said anything."

Why had I asked that? It had just slipped out. I picked up a delicate cup and took a sip, refusing to look anywhere but out the window. Romona's room faced the outdoor rec area, and a smudge on the glass was suddenly very interesting.

"What made you think of that?" Romona's tone was soothing and nonthreatening, as if she was trying to coax the truth out of me.

I shrugged, still staring intently at the smudge. "Nothing, it just randomly popped into my head. I'm always curious as to what the rules are here. Having missed orientation and all."

Romona stayed quiet just long enough to make me believe she was going to let the topic slide.

"Yes."

"Huh?"

"Yes, you can still fall in love," she answered.

"Oh." I should have left it at that. "So, have you like . . . you know . . . met anyone or anything?" My face warmed as I spoke. I snuck a quick glance at Romona. There was a wistful smile on her face.

"I've already met the love of my life." She took a deep breath and let it out. She was remembering something, perhaps even savoring a memory. She pegged me with clear eyes after the moment passed. "I'm waiting for him here."

"So you mean he hasn't died yet?" I crinkled my nose. "Won't he be kind of old when he gets here?"

Romona burst out laughing even as I literally clamped my hand over my mouth. She laughed so hard she had to put her teacup down to keep from spilling. It took her several minutes to calm down, but she'd started to hiccup. I stared at her with raised eyebrows.

"Well . . . *hiccup* . . . I guess you can just say . . . *hiccup* . . . I like older men."

Ew. I was doubly sorry I'd asked.

A SECOND CHANCE

*W*hen I arrived at our training gym the next day, I found a note waiting for me in Logan's distinct handwriting.

There are some things I need to tend to today. You're on your own. You can use our gym or find another to continue training.

Under the brief message was a list of exercises and drills. There was no signature.

Holding the message in my hand, I contemplated the likelihood of being able to blow off training without being caught. As soon as the plot started to form, I dismissed it, sighing heavily. Regardless of whether he'd find out, using his absence to skip didn't sit well with me. And besides, I was unexpectedly enticed by the idea of training for a day without a mentor. It sounded almost peaceful.

I surveyed the familiar gym. No, if today was going to be different, even special, I needed a change of scenery. Someplace that didn't remind me of Logan so much. Grabbing my bag and shoving Logan's note into one of the side pockets, I set off to find an empty gym.

Craving solitude, I walked to the remote reaches of the training center, assuming a gym this far on the fringe would be vacant. Without thought I shouldered the doors and barged in on someone. Surprising us both.

"Oh, geez, Kaitlin, hey. Sorry, I didn't know you were in here. I'll ah, get going. Good luck." I mumbled the hasty apology while backpedaling out the door.

"Hey Audrey, wait up a second."

I froze with my left leg over the threshold, facing the freedom of the hallway. I'd almost made it out. I let out a quiet breath of frustration before slowly turning, all the while silently reminding myself that she really hadn't done anything to deserve my scorn.

"Sure. What's up?" I plastered what I hoped was a pleasant smile on my face. It might have worked, because she relaxed and smiled back in return.

"You can come back in. I was hoping to find an opportunity to talk to you anyway."

I reluctantly stepped back into the gym. The door swung shut loudly behind me. I wished it stood as a barrier between us rather than confining us together.

Kaitlin brushed a strand of blonde hair out of her eyes. "Listen, I think we may have gotten off on the wrong foot yesterday. I was hoping for a fresh start. I think we could be friends, maybe even good friends. I know yesterday didn't go that wonderfully. I want you to know I really was only trying to be helpful. Well, that and I was trying to be funny, but I see now it fell flat and I just ended up embarrassing you in front of Logan. I really—"

I cut her off. "You didn't embarrass me in front of Logan. I mean, it doesn't make any difference to me what Logan thinks. He's just my mentor. Why would you think I cared?"

I wanted to slap a hand over my mouth again. I could imagine the gears working in Kaitlin's brain to make sense of my outburst. Before she could think about it too much, I continued, "But anyway, yeah, I'm sure we could be friends. Why not, right? And you know, don't worry about yesterday. It was just kind of an off day for me in general."

She twirled a piece of her ponytail as she considered my words. I knew she wasn't buying it.

"Well, I should get going. Lots of fun workout stuff to do today." I took a step backward and searched blindly for the door with my hand.

"Are you sure, Audrey? You seemed a little upset with me yesterday. I would really like to make amends."

My fingers found the door handle. "Yeah, I'm sure. It wasn't you. Like I said, it was just an off day."

"I guess I can understand that. Especially considering what had happened on Earth the day before. Logan seemed a little off as well," Kaitlin said, still twirling her hair and scrunching her perfectly shaped brows together thoughtfully.

It took an extreme effort to keep my features schooled. "Yeah? Not so sure about that. I'll let you get back to it. Have a good workout."

With a quick turn of the handle and a step backward, I was breathing in the free air of the hallway. I took off to the left but slowed to a stop after a few hurried steps. Touching my forehead to the wall, I sucked in a huge breath. What was wrong with me? Was I just a naturally nasty and distrustful person? Is that what I had to look forward to when I reclaimed my memories? Kaitlin had been perfectly nice, and I basically ran out of the room in a panic. Why did I have to react negatively to everything? Why was I incapable of giving Kaitlin a fair chance?

I knew the answers to all my questions. It was because I felt threatened by her. Her very existence made me insecure. It didn't have anything to do with Logan—or at least it didn't *need* to have anything to do with him. I needed to get over this. And quickly.

Before I could consider what I was about to do, I marched a few purposeful steps back to Kaitlin's gym and pushed open the door again. She was in the middle of a series of kicks on the punching bag. She stopped and gave me a quizzical look.

"Hey, I'm sorry to bother you again. I wanted to let you know I really do want to try to be friends. I'm just in kind of a weird place here. This," I used my hand to indicate the gym we were in, "is a little more difficult for me than I think for everyone else. A little less . . . natural. I'm still getting my footing. For some reason, seeing you yesterday threw me off. If you really meant it, and if you can get over my weirdness from yesterday and today, I would like to try again."

Yikes! It wasn't my intention to share that much, but there it was. I was taking a leap of faith that Kaitlin was sincere. I hoped I hadn't made a mistake.

Kaitlin's eyes softened considerably. "Thank you," she finally said. "Thanks for trusting me with all of that."

It was a relief that she understood the risk I'd just taken. "I didn't give you a fair chance. And I'm trying to be . . . better, I guess."

"I understand."

"I hope you aren't offended that I find that hard to believe." My words were free of their usual acid this time—I was being sincere.

She nodded. "I know what it's like to feel like you are alone in all of this."

"Really?"

"Yes . . . I didn't settle into all of this as easily as you might think. I had a learning curve too. And there were lots of things I needed to come to terms with as well. I figured there might be some things you wanted to talk about. I know you have Romona, but I hope you know I'm here as well if you ever need another ear. The guys here are all great, but well, there are just some things they won't get." She finished with a lopsided smile.

"Ha, that's for sure." My barriers were starting to crumble and with it the tightness I carried around inside, loosen a notch.

"Anyway, I know the chance you were taking by coming back in here, and I want you to know I don't take that lightly. And I've got a good feeling about you."

I wasn't sure what that meant. I gave her a look that said as much.

She laughed. "Don't look so scared! It's a good thing. I'm just saying I think you have some amazing things ahead of you. I'd like to do what I can to help you reach them."

Now she was confusing me. "But why would you do that?"

"Why wouldn't I? There's great joy in being able to be a part of each other's victories. And in caring for one another."

"I'm embarrassed to say I haven't given that much thought since I arrived."

She smiled. "Don't be. I know it might not seem like it, but the time you have now, before your memories come back, can be a gift. You have the opportunity to take an unencumbered view of everything. Decide who you want to be, then make it so."

"That easy, huh?"

"No . . . that hard."

I nodded and smiled back, happy she got it too. I'd simply wanted to make amends for my bad behavior—I didn't really expect Kaitlin to turn into a friend. Today was full of surprises.

"So that's about as deep as I can get for one day. Want to train in here with me for the rest of the afternoon?" she asked.

"That's really nice of you to offer, but . . ."

"You like the solitude, right?"

"Yes, I do."

She nodded knowingly. "I get it. It helps me get things sorted out myself sometimes. There's another gym at the end of the hall that's probably available. This far from the center, most of these gyms are probably covered in cobwebs."

"As long as the spiders are long gone, I can handle that. Thanks again."

"Anytime."

The sky was already changing color when I left the training center, which surprised me. It didn't feel like I'd been there all day. Between running drills, I'd been going over all that had happened in the last few days. Calculating moves, distances, and speed while processing conversations, body language, and motives. But instead of being exhausted, I was rejuvenated. I didn't have anything figured out per se, but the freedom to soak everything in on my own seemed to have helped. And something about the actual workout was encouraging as well. For the first time, I felt in sync. Without the pressure of being critiqued, I fell into a rhythm, and my usual awkwardness and clumsiness melted away.

It was quiet on my walk back. The sky was a kaleidoscope—breathtakingly beautiful. I had an overwhelming sense that it was a gift just for me, but of course that was a silly thought.

On impulse I stopped and closed my eyes, taking a deep breath of fresh air, and wished I could freeze the moment to enjoy later. When I opened them, a blur of movement to my left distracted me.

I turned my head in time to see Logan disappear into the forest. In the low light, he vanished so quickly he appeared to be swallowed by the darkness.

My curiosity took control, and I jogged to the edge of the tree line. I could just make out his silhouette moving further away. Maybe if I was very careful, I could follow him without being detected. There was so much about Logan I didn't know, I couldn't seem to help myself.

When I stepped under the cover of the trees, I too was instantly swallowed by darkness. The thick forest canopy completely blocked out the vibrant colors of the dying day. I didn't wait for my eyes to adjust to the low light. I had to start moving now or I'd lose sight of Logan completely.

It was a mixed blessing that I was so far behind him. Despite my best effort, I still made a lot of noise as I picked my way through the foliage. Eventually, my eyes adjusted and I started to see more details in the early night.

I didn't wonder if Logan would be mad at me for following him. Instead, I forced myself to concentrate on keeping up. A breeze picked up and tossed my hair behind me. The cool nip to the air sent a chill down my spine. Logan's form was barely discernible—despite his unhurried gait, he was getting further away from me at every step—I could lose him at any moment. A bolt of fear shot though my body. I was suddenly desperate to get closer. The idea of losing him in the dense darkness scared me.

Another gust of night air blew, and mist coiled around my feet with a strong chill. I yelped despite myself and took off in a run. My heart beat violently, and I looked back to see the mist hugging the ground, spreading toward me. I had the wild thought that it was chasing me and picked up my speed, surprising myself by dodging roots and low-growing plants with relative ease. There seemed to be light coming through a break in the trees ahead. If I could just get there, I'd be safe.

I came to a halt a few trees short of the break.

Logan was kneeling on the ground in what might be called a clearing. It was closer to a crack in the canopy that allowed a wide beam of silvery light to break through and illuminate a patch of grass.

His back was to me, his head bent, shoulders slumped, like they carried the weight of the world. The odd silvery light created a glow all around him. With his head bowed and hunched over his knees, the deep rumblings of his baritone voice filtered to my ears. His words weren't loud enough for me to discern, but they were filled with emotion. And something about what I was seeing, even if I didn't understand it, moved me. I stared at Logan with an equal mix of awe and wonder, the mist all but forgotten.

After a time, he heaved a big sigh and said, "You can come out now. I know you're there."

There was no use pretending. This close, knowing Logan, he could probably hear me breathe. I stepped out from behind the trees at the same time Logan stood and turned.

"Well, I suppose it would be you." He tilted his head back with a humorless laugh. "Thanks."

"You're welcome?" I said.

He gave me a look I couldn't interpret. "I wasn't talking to you, but never mind. What are you doing out here anyway?"

"I saw you walk into the forest on my way back from training and wanted to make sure you were okay."

"And what exactly did you think would happen to me out here?" He sounded amused.

I wracked my brain for an answer that didn't seem incredibly lame. Then something close to the truth hit me.

"That weird mist stuff?"

Logan's brows knit. "Say what?"

"That creepy mist. You didn't see it?" I took a quick look at my feet to make sure none of it was hiding under my shoes.

Logan shook his head and continued to regard me with a look that said he didn't believe a word coming out of my mouth.

"Well, whatever." I shrugged. "Now that I see you're fine, I guess I'll just get going."

I glanced around the forest and realized I had no idea where we were. I chewed on my lower lip while I considered which direction to go. How large could the woods be, anyway? Maybe if I wandered in them long enough, I'd end up in another part of the realm around people I didn't constantly embarrass myself in front of. I was just about to take a step forward when Logan spoke up.

"You know, I think the *truly* implausible thing is that you expect me to believe you spent the entire day training without me there to make you."

I whirled around to face him. "Hey," was as far as I got in my defense. Logan had taken a few steps closer to me, and when I turned we were practically on top of each other. The silvery light had disappeared, so we stood together in relative darkness. The look on Logan's face was obscured by shadows as he peered down on me. I grasped to remember what we were talking about. It was floating close enough to the fringe of my thoughts that it came back to me.

"I really did train all day. You can check the log if you don't believe me." My words sounded breathless. The fire I'd intended to put into them was nowhere to be found.

"Well, that's surprising." Logan sounded annoyingly thoughtful—and not the least bit affected by me as I was by him. That bruised my ego enough to give me the frame of mind to step back and rekindle the fire.

"Well, it shouldn't be. If you'd try to focus on some of my more attractive qualities you might learn to develop a measure of faith in me." I spun in the other direction, determined to get away from him.

Logan huffed out a breath behind me and mumbled something that sounded like, "I'm trying quite hard to do the exact opposite."

I didn't have time to ponder that. He grabbed my arm, halting my retreat. I turned only my head in his direction. "It's this way," he said, nodding to the left.

"Oh."

"Mind if I walk back with you? You know, just in case the mist comes back. I'll need someone to protect me."

I rolled my eyes and grunted in response. Truce, then. We fell in step with each other and walked in silence for a while before Logan said anything.

"Audrey . . ." He paused a moment before going on. I looked over to see him staring straight ahead with a serious look on his face. I had an intuition that I wasn't going to like whatever was going to come out of his mouth next. "I think we should talk about what happened."

My stomach instantly knotted up, and my heart started to beat wildly. Why was he bringing this up now? Hadn't we already agreed it wasn't something we were going to talk about, ever?

"Audrey, did you hear me? I think it's important that we at least talk about what happened."

My feet propelled me forward even as I felt paralyzed on the inside. It was eerily quiet as Logan waited for me to say something. Where was that creepy mist when I needed it?

Logan sighed after a few long moments. "Listen, I know this isn't something you *want* to discuss, but as much as we would like to, I don't think we can just pretend it didn't happen. There are things . . . rules . . . you don't know about that you should."

He sounded tired. I didn't dare try to read his face. Instead, I busied myself with taking extra care to pick my way along the nonexistent path through the trees.

"I would like to have more than a one-way conversation."

"Well, that's a first."

I could practically feel Logan's walls go up. I'd hit my mark. Rather than being happy he'd stopped talking, I regretted my words. I snuck a look at Logan out of the corner of my eye. His profile was as hard as stone. I'd done that.

It occurred to me only then that Logan was trying to be vulnerable with me, and I'd just thrown it back in his face. I couldn't think of a way to make it right again. Maybe if I swallowed my fear and just talked about the stupid kiss, it would right things between us.

I'd almost worked up the courage to do so when we broke through the trees.

"I'll see you tomorrow," Logan said before turning in the opposite direction.

"Logan, wait!" I yelled after him. I jogged to catch back up. It was only when I did that he stopped to face me again, the wintry look still on his face.

"It's just that, I don't really know . . ." I wasn't exactly sure what I was going to say, but it didn't matter because that's all I got out before we were interrupted.

"Did you guys just come out of there?" Romona stood a few feet away, looking confused. Her eyes darted back and forth between Logan and me. "It's kind of late to be training out in the woods, don't you think?"

I wasn't sure if she was asking me or Logan. He saved me by replying, but his eyes remained glued to me. "We weren't training. I found Audrey roaming around and helped her find her way back."

It was the one version of the truth that made me appear incredibly incompetent. Between his comment and the intense way he was still staring at me, my emotions teetered between aggravated and uncomfortable.

"Audrey, what were you doing wandering out in the woods by yourself?"

I broke the stare-down. "I thought I saw something out there, and then I got turned around. I kind of stumbled across Logan."

Romona turned everything over in her head. She was clearly having a hard time adding it up.

"I'm going to get going," Logan said. "It's been a long day. I'll see you tomorrow." His voice was less harsh than before, but he didn't wait for us to reply before taking off. By the time I could open my mouth to answer, he was already jogging off.

I stared after his retreating form with a frown, trying to make sense of everything that had happened that evening. What exactly was Logan doing out in the woods? And what was up with that silver light and mist? And perhaps the question I was most curious about—What would have happened if we'd had the talk he wanted? A small part of me was disappointed that I'd missed the opportunity to talk with him.

I almost forgot Romona was there until she laid a soft hand on my shoulder.

"Everything okay?" she gently asked.

"Oh, yeah, sure." I chewed my lower lip in concern. Romona was kind enough to change the subject. "How'd your day go? Did you get the chance to talk to Kaitlin?"

I gave her a genuine smile. "Yes, we did actually get to talk. It went okay. She was nice."

"See!" Romona's smile was from ear to ear. "I told you it wouldn't be that bad!"

"You were right. I'm glad we got the opportunity to clear the air. We decided to try to start over."

"That's really great, Audrey. I'm glad that isn't weighing on you anymore." She linked her arm through mine and propelled me in the direction of my tree. "Now, on to more important things! Let's get you cleaned up. I was hoping you'd want to hit the town with me tonight."

A few hours later, pampered and beautified, we looked at our made-up, nail-polished, and blow-dried reflections in a salon mirror. She looked beautiful. So did I. It was the last thing I'd expected to do that evening, but I couldn't believe how much it lifted my spirits. And the night was still young—Romona had plans to hit a restaurant afterward. She stood behind me with a soft smile on her face as she looked at my reflection. I took in hers in return.

Romona's hair looked awesome. Her hair was a bit darker than mine and free of my unexpected highlights, but the texture was the same silky thickness. Her skin, slightly darker than mine, held a hint of the same olive shade. Our eyes matched perfectly. It was weird that I hadn't noticed that before. I suppose I wasn't familiar enough with my own reflection to notice the resemblance. Brown seemed like such a boring color I hadn't thought there was much variation. But our eyes were a rich warm mahogany color, not light enough to be considered hazel but not too dark to hide the variety of brown hues.

"Look, we have the same eyes."

Romona's face in the mirror reflected surprise. "Really, you think so?" She took a tentative step toward the mirror to verify my statement.

"Yeah, definitely! I mean, brown is brown, but if they weren't on your face I would swear they were mine."

Romona smiled at that. "Well, that's funny. I guess we're eye twins, then."

"Ha! Yeah, I guess so. Who knew?"

The smile remained on Romona's face even if it didn't quite reach her eyes.

"Feel any better?" she asked.

"Actually, I do."

"Thought so. You looked like you needed some serious pampering."

"In that case, I'm glad you can read me so well, because I would never have guessed this was what I needed."

"Well, it always made you feel better before, so I just figured."

"Huh? What do you mean by that?"

Romona's face fell. "I only meant that you seem more relaxed with some girlie stuff every now and then. Like your room, right?"

I was still frowning. "Yeah, I guess you're right."

By the time I made it back to my bed, I was tired but happy, and I fell asleep instantly. The good of the day far outweighed the bad.

Even so, that night I dreamt dark dreams of running from mist.

14

FIGHT

*L*oud crashes and the sound of colliding metal assaulted my ears. I picked up the pace and rushed down the hallway, bursting through our gym doors with a loud bang. The room was in shambles. Weapons lay strewn throughout the gym. Practice dummies were destroyed, various equipment was overturned, and in the middle of the room two fighters were locked in furious battle.

Even covered from head to toe in body armor, Logan couldn't be mistaken. Kaitlin's long, lean body and ash-blonde ponytail made her hard to mistake as well. I stood in awe of what I was seeing. Blades crashed in blurred movements. Attacks were diverted and sidestepped with unbelievable precision. It was like watching two powerful animals fight, each matched with speed and agility. It was both beautiful and intimidating.

Watching the two of them spar made me realize how lightly Logan was going on me during training. A bit of familiar jealously towards Kaitlin rose to my throat. Even though Logan outmatched her in weight, her movements looked effortless in their quickness and balance. I swallowed down the envy.

In a blur of movement Logan managed to disarm Kaitlin. She quickly threw her body to the side and rolled out of the way, putting herself within arm's reach of the weapons wall. She grabbed a weapon and immediately threw a fighting star at Logan. I gasped. Logan just used the side of his blade to deflect the metal, as if swatting a fly away. But Kaitlin had used the attack to divert Logan's attention and get into a stance to disarm him. The ploy worked, and within seconds Logan's weapon was also lying on the ground. With a warrior's cry Kaitlin launched herself at Logan, taking them both to the ground.

"Yeah, Kaitlin! Kick his butt!" someone yelled behind me. Another voice gave an encouraging hoot to the fighters. I turned my head to see that a small crowd had formed.

Logan and Kaitlin ignored the ruckus. With a series of roundhouse kicks Kaitlin pushed Logan back toward the corner. It was a smart move, leaving Logan with fewer options to retaliate.

Just as it seemed Kaitlin had Logan where she wanted, he quickly turned and ran straight at the wall that was boxing him in. Without hesitation he ran a few steps up the wall, pushed off, and flipped backwards over Kaitlin's head, landing safely on the other side of her. That garnered a round of cheers and shouts from the crowd. Logan swept Kaitlin's feet out from under her. She landed hard on her back with the wind knocked out of her. Logan was over Kaitlin immediately with his recovered blade, and with a blink it was all over.

Logan's facemask melted away to reveal a huge grin as he leaned over to give Kaitlin a hand up. When she took his hand she made a great show of trying to take him down with her. Logan laughed and effortlessly hauled Kaitlin to her feet. Her mask disappeared to reveal a matching grin.

Alrik stepped forward to give Logan a hug-slap on the back. His voice boomed loudly. "Well, Logan, you need to stay a little sharper. She almost had you there."

"I would have had him if he played by the rules. He didn't get the memo to go easy on girls." And then she spotted me. "Right, Audrey?"

"I don't know about that one. I hate to admit it, but after watching the two of you it's obvious Logan's been giving me more slack than I realized."

"Oh come on, Audrey, I don't believe that. I've heard that you've disarmed him before."

My cheeks warmed. That was *not* my favorite memory. Sure, it was probably the best I'd ever fought, but I hadn't been able to duplicate it with controlled emotions.

"Well, anyway," I said, "from the looks of it I don't think he should be cutting you much of anything. That was really impressive." I was proud of myself for being objective. Her fighting did kick some butt, and it wasn't my place to withhold praise when it was due.

Kaitlin's face lit up, and her grin widened. "No need to worry, then. With my help you'll have him flat on his back in no time."

The unintended double meaning in her phrase drained the color and smile from my face. There was an awkward moment when people expected me to say something back. My tongue was frozen in my mouth. I looked at Logan to see his reaction. His eyes snapped up and found mine in an instant. He looked stricken as well. A breath caught in my throat.

He recovered quicker than I. "If that's the case, maybe I shouldn't encourage you guys to train together." He broke our stare and smiled lightly at the group. A few people around the room chuckled. My eyes swept the crowd. I caught Alrik suspiciously eyeing us, his gaze switching between Logan and me.

"Okay, guys, the free show is over. You'll have to catch the next one." People started to file out around me. A few here and there stopped to praise both Logan and Kaitlin.

Before he left, Alrik bent down to say something to Logan. Logan shook his head once and wouldn't look at him, and a muscle in his jaw jumped. Alrik gave a hearty chuckle and slapped Logan on the back before heading toward the door. He winked and smiled at me before leaving. I was dying to know what he'd said.

When the last person left, Kaitlin slid to the mat with her feet planted, knees up, and arms stretched out on either side of her. The rest of her armor melted away.

"Sheesh, I thought they'd never leave."

Even Logan sat on the floor. He nodded his head in agreement as his armor dissolved. "Yeah, that was a pretty intense sparring session. I didn't realize we'd attracted so much attention."

They seemed to have forgotten me again, which was an annoying habit of theirs. I cleared my throat. Kaitlin's head came slightly off the mat.

"Hey Aud, I'd forgotten you were there." Typical.

Logan just gave me his usual soulful stare. The intensity made me want to fidget. I shifted my weight from one leg to the other. It was my training time, but they looked pretty comfortable together. How did I become the intruder? I began to backpedal slowly towards the door.

"I guess I'll just be going then and let you guys, do, ah, whatever it is you need to do."

My face was on fire. I couldn't make my escape fast enough. Unfortunately, the sole of my shoe caught the mat and I lost my footing. There was a mortified moment of clarity when I knew I was going down. I squeezed my eyes shut and waited for the familiar impact of back and butt on mat, but it never came. Instead, my fall was cushioned by gentle hands. They braced my back so that the whole upper half of my body was lying horizontal to the floor. I slowly cracked open one of my eyes.

Logan's face was a breath away. He'd somehow managed to get from his spot on the floor to me before I hit the ground. How could he have moved that fast? And more importantly, why? He'd never tried to stop one of my falls before. In fact, most of the times my back or butt had collided with the mat were pointedly because of him. I opened the other eye.

Logan searched my face like he was trying to figure something out. His brows were drawn together in what might have been concentration. I didn't dare move a muscle. Logan leaned in further, and his bare arm brushed mine. An electric zing shot through my body, and something intense rushed at me. Before I could gasp, I slammed into the mat. The wind was knocked from my lungs. I shook my head to clear it and looked up at Logan. He'd straightened again and was staring down at me.

"What the . . ." I started, but the look on his face brought me up short. Was he upset?

I looked at Kaitlin. She was staring at us with her eyebrows lifted. "Wow, Logan. That was really an ungallant rescue there."

Logan's stone face returned, and he shrugged. Kaitlin seemed like she wanted to say more, but didn't. Instead, she turned her head to where I was sprawled.

"All right, Audrey, time to get up. You're mine today." She gave me a wicked grin as she rubbed her hands together.

"What do you mean I'm yours?" I asked suspiciously.

"We're going to train together today. I'm going to share some of the super-secret tricks reserved for only the coolest hunters."

She glanced over at Logan when she said the last part, intending to bait him, but he acted like he hadn't even heard her. A shadow of concern crossed Kaitlin's face before it turned to a look of excitement—one that looked forced to me.

"So what do you say? Are you in?"

I appreciated that she was making it seem like I had a choice, even though I knew I didn't. Maybe Kaitlin would have some advice that would step up my game. I forced my own chipper smile as I pushed myself to my feet.

"A day away from the boys? I'm always in."

"Great! Let's get started. We just need to get rid of Logan." Her voice trailed off at the end because Logan had already left. The gym doors were swinging shut behind him.

"Wow, someone's a little moody today," Kaitlin said.

I didn't respond, just stared at the door Logan had pushed through with vexation. Between yesterday and today, I agreed that something was definitely up with him, and I had a bad feeling I knew exactly what it was. I changed the subject.

"Okay, Super-Cool Hunter, where do we start?"

Training with Kaitlin was a lot more fun than I expected. Getting a girl's perspective was insightful. She showed me new kickboxing moves that used my lower body rather than my arms and shoulders. She explained that most of a girl's strength was in our legs, where guys relied more on their upper body. It was important to learn to utilize the whole body for fighting, but learning to channel extra energy to our strongest areas was a big advantage in a pinch.

She also showed me how to use my size to my advantage. Since Kaitlin was almost as tall as most of the guys, I was impressed that she knew some tricks for the vertically challenged. The more I trained with her, the more I found myself wanting to like her, even though there was still a part of me that insisted on keeping her at arm's length. I didn't think I'd ever feel as close to her as Romona, but a genuine friendship was blooming. The training flew by quickly. It almost felt too soon when Kaitlin called it quits.

"That was really great, Audrey. I think you're going to make an amazing hunter."

I felt a measure of pride at the compliment. Kaitlin pulled off a boxing glove before extending a hand. I hesitated before clasping it. I wasn't as wary as some of the empathy link, but I still hadn't gotten used to being so exposed to people. Kaitlin waited patiently. I took a silent breath before extending my hand and steeled myself against her emotions.

Kaitlin's smile widened. I'd always gotten the impression that she was silently laughing at me, but the emotions I absorbed through the link surprised to me. Amusement was definitely present, but respect and accep-tance were the stronger sentiments. It was as if Kaitlin had developed a sisterly affection for me despite my behavior. I think all she was getting from me was shock and perhaps a small dose of distrust, but she didn't seem to mind.

After helping me to my feet, she let my hand drop with an ever-wider smile. Delight danced behind her eyes, as if she knew something I didn't that allowed her to overlook my distrust.

"So, are you excited about the celebration?"

"The what?"

"You know, the celebration!"

Her tone left no question as to whether she was excited. I still didn't have the faintest idea what she was talking about.

"What celebration? What are we celebrating?"

"Oh, Audrey, you are in for a treat! It's basically the biggest and coolest party you've ever been to."

"Who will be there?"

"Everybody!" she answered.

"As in all the hunters?"

"No, as in everybody, everybody. Everybody from the realm is going to be there."

My brain couldn't wrap itself around those numbers.

"But what are we all celebrating?"

I mentally ran through some of the holidays we might be celebrating. But since I didn't remember when I had died, I didn't even know what time of year it was. I was guessing it wasn't something lame like Columbus Day, though.

"We celebrate everything."

"Such as . . .?" I prompted.

"We celebrate everything that has to do with being here. That we are here, how we got here, what we're doing now. It's just a big celebration where everyone can get together and, well, celebrate."

"Okay then, so I guess this is something I should be looking forward to."

She laughed. "Definitely!"

"Well then yes, I guess I am excited." I answered with a laugh even though I wasn't sure I really meant it. Something twisted within the familiar pit at the bottom of my stomach. It signaled my growing anxiety. If I could, I would punt that emotion right out of me.

It was then that Logan decided to grace us with his presence. "So, have you turned her into a fighting machine?"

Kaitlin gave me a quick wink before turning to answer him. "You bet! You'd better watch your back. I've given her all my super-secret tricks."

Logan's face split into a grin that held a playful glint. "Is that so?"

"Yep! Just you wait, you're going to be sparring one of these days and BAM," she clapped her hands loudly, "you're not even going to know what hit you."

Kaitlin was talking me up a little too much, but Logan wasn't taking her seriously. I half listened to their banter while the rest of my mind strayed. It was hard to ignore my jealousy at the effortless way they conversed. If only Logan and I had had that ease in the beginning, we wouldn't be struggling right now. I couldn't deny the part I'd played in building the wall between us. I'd done a good job putting it together brick by brick, but for his part, I'd rarely seen Logan let down his guard. There were only rare moments here and there when I saw through the façade. But his stoic mask always slammed back on eventually. I sighed when I thought of the opportunity I'd missed the night before.

With Kaitlin and Logan still talking, I decided to slip away. There was a twinge of sadness at how easily it was done without notice, but hunching my shoulders, I headed away from them with a heart torn in two.

15

THE CELEBRATION

$\mathcal{A}$fter so many days of wearing workout gear or T-shirts and jeans, it felt good to get all done up for the celebration. I twisted in front of the mirror in my cobalt blue dress. It looked really nice against my olive skin and dark hair. The bodice of the dress was fitted, ruched, and cinched low on the waist. There was a piece of braided material that went over one shoulder to create an asymmetrical neckline. The skirt dropped from my waist to a few inches above my knees. It was a soft silk that looked and felt almost liquid when I moved.

The closet had stubbornly spit out a handful of awful dresses before finally relinquishing this one, but it was worth the wait. I felt absolutely myself when I put it on, both feminine and confident. Some anxiety about the celebration disappeared because I just knew that the dress was me. It was the first time I knew with absolute certainty that I would have liked this dress in life.

Romona had performed true magic on my hair. She curled the straight locks and pulled up the front in an intricate weave of braids and twists. The light caught highlights I didn't know existed. The curls she'd manipulated fell in soft waves down my back. Besides being a genius with my hair, Romona helped materialize some makeup for me as well. I used a touch of eye shadow, black eyeliner, and mascara to give my eyes a slight smoky effect. I was surprised at how rich my eyes appeared with just a bit of work. I brushed on some blush and shine to my cheekbones. When I looked in the mirror, I finally saw someone familiar looking back at me. Someone not as painfully average as I had been feeling these past weeks.

A small smile touched my lips, and I released a breath I didn't realize I had been holding. This was the girl I was comfortable in.

Romona came up in the mirror next to me. She looked lovely. She'd picked a knee-length dress as well, but that was the only similarity. It was delicate and vintage, lacy and frilly and a perfect fit for both her body and her personality.

Romona had managed to make a masterpiece of her hair as well. She had piled it all on the top of her head with a few tendrils hanging loose here and there. And even though her makeup was lighter to match her soft pink dress, there was no mistaking that we had the same eyes.

"All right, I think we're ready. Want to get going?" she asked.

I took a final look at myself. Something seemed to be missing. What could it be? A wild thought appeared in my head. Was it even something I could do? I wasn't sure, but I wanted to try.

I closed my eyes and concentrated very hard. When Romona gasped a moment later, I knew something had happened. I opened my eyes to watch a thick lock of my dark hair turning from brown to purple. Romona's eyes widened beside me as color slowly spread from root to tip. I beamed triumphantly at my success and had the urge to do a short victory dance. Instead, I turned my head to the side to get a better look at my work in the mirror. *Ha!* I might not be able to master the art of making something from nothing just yet, but this new trick was pretty cool. How many people could turn their hair colors with their mind? Actually, I had no idea.

Romona tentatively picked up the end of my purple lock. "Wow, that is neat!" She looked meticulously through the strands of hair, but then she brought a hand to her mouth and sucked in a quick breath of air. "Oh no, do you think it's permanent?"

I laughed at the stricken look on her face. I could think of a few more horrifying things than having a chunk of my hair a different color for eternity. Still laughing, I shrugged a shoulder.

"Let's hope it wasn't a single flash of genius so I can get it back to brown later." A wave of giddiness started to bubble up inside. "But you're right, let's go. We can worry about this later."

I grabbed Romona's hand to pull her out the door. When our hands connected, I stifled another laugh at how genuinely worried she was. What a silly thing to be concerned about. I wondered what I'd look like with a head full of fuchsia hair?

Outside the celebration tent, people were dressed in almost anything and everything imaginable. Multiple decades and even centuries of formal and casual wear were represented.

"Hey guys!" Kaitlin weaved her way through the crowd. She was stunning. Her hair was pulled back in an elegant French twist. She wore a simple, but chic, pale yellow dress that accentuated her tanned skin and flowed to the ground. She must have had some serious heels on underneath that thing, because she was at least four inches taller than usual. She towered over me now.

"Kaitlin, you have to show me what shoes you're wearing."

She smiled knowingly and lifted the hem of her skirt. The thin spikes she was standing on were nothing short of scary. At least six inches high with an extra inch of platform.

"I know, they're crazy, right?" She hunched down to my level and lowered her voice. "Super high shoes are my guilty pleasure." She wore a sheepish expression. There was nothing to do but laugh.

"Don't worry, there's no judging here. I think they're fabulous!"

"What's fabulous?" came a deep voice from behind.

My body flushed involuntarily as I turned toward the voice. Logan stood casually a few feet away. His blue eyes were electric and his hair expertly styled to look unstyled. His laidback attire for the evening was a white linen shirt rolled partway up his arms and light khakis with brown sandals. He looked every bit the California beach boy he'd once been. I couldn't imagine anything else looking as good on him.

"Oh, um, Kaitlin's shoes. I think they could double as weapons." I answered hurriedly.

"Oh really?" Logan's easy smile was surprisingly soothing. "Okay, Kaitlin, let's see these things." He indicated with a hand that she pull up her hem.

Kaitlin appeared slightly embarrassed as she lifted the bottom of her dress again. Logan barked out a laugh. It was a rich sound. "Well, that explains why I suddenly feel as if I've shrunk a few inches."

Kaitlin dropped her skirt and laughed back. She was almost as tall as Logan now. I stepped back and noticed what a handsome pair the two of them made. Unwanted sadness seeped through the cracks in my heart as the two of them shared a moment. Turning my head away, I caught Romona staring at me with what may have been a concerned look.

Out of the corner of my eye, I recognized a familiar face and gestured to Romona to say I would be right back. I didn't wait to see if she understood before fleeing. It was cowardly, but I wanted to be someplace else at that moment.

I quickly dipped into the throng. Swiveling my head, I caught another glimpse of Kevin in front of me and to the left and set out in that direction. The thickening mass forced me to maneuver carefully so not to brush up against anyone. I wasn't used to having this much of my skin exposed.

Between chasing Kevin and artfully weaving through the masses, I almost missed the large white tent until it was practically upon me. It stood shiny white, with poles like a circus tent stretching high into the sky. I stopped and gawked.

The trance was broken when someone bumped into me, forcing me to take a shaky step forward. I quickly scanned for Kevin, worried I'd lost him in the horde. Moving in the direction I'd last seen him, I glimpsed his back just as he rounded a corner of the tent. I broke free of the denser crowd to follow, half-jogging, half-speed-walking to catch up.

When I rounded the corner, I smashed right into someone and stumbled. Warm hands shot out to steady me. With a rush, I was ambushed by foreign emotions and sucked in a harsh breath. Surprise, followed by curiosity and a measure of concern. Then the arms dropped away, leaving me alone with my own emotions.

"Hey there! Sorry about that—I just wanted to make sure you didn't fall."

I gave myself a mental shake and glanced up. My near collision was with a handsome prince. Literally, the stranger was dressed like a prince. He caught me staring at his outfit and shifted uncomfortably.

"Oh yeah, this, it's actually kind of a joke."

When my eyes reached his face, I found my voice. "So you're saying you don't dress up like royalty on a regular basis?"

I cocked an eyebrow, a small smile forming.

When he realized I was poking fun at him, he seemed more at ease and matched my smile.

"Only for very special occasions."

"Oh, I see. Well, at least your friends will be able to find you in a crowd." I turned my head and did a quick scan of all the crazy get-ups. "On second thought, maybe not."

He laughed along with me.

"Seriously though, sorry about running into you. I thought I saw a friend head this way." I peeked my head around his side, but no Kevin. *That's so bizarre. How could I have lost him?*

"Yeah, no problem, it was an interesting way to meet. And speaking of . . . Hello, new friend, my name's Jonathon."

"I'm Audrey."

"It's nice to meet you, Audrey. And may I say that color of blue looks very lovely on you."

I willed my cheeks not to change color and smiled politely. With sandy brown hair and eyes to match, he was certainly nice looking. It didn't hurt that he was playing the role of Prince Charming.

"Yes, it does." Logan's deep voice was unmistakable.

He placed a hand possessively on the small of my back. I failed at keeping my cheeks from coloring this time. Jonathon's eyebrows shot up a fraction as he regarded Logan, a sociable smile still in place. Logan wore his usual stoic mask, neither angry nor happy.

"So this must be who you were trying to find?" Jonathon asked.

"Oh no, it was someone else. Jonathon, this is Logan. Logan, Jonathon."

Jonathon immediately extended his hand toward Logan in the traditional greeting. Logan, however, just nodded his head. Jonathon let his hand drop.

I was acutely aware that Logan's hand hadn't left my back and that he stood much closer than necessary. I didn't want Jonathon to get the wrong idea. Heck, *I* was starting to get the wrong idea.

"Jonathon, Logan's my mentor."

Jonathon's eyebrows shot up. "Whoa, so that means you're a huntress? Wow, you are an extremely rare creature. I haven't met a female hunter before." The typical response. His smile broadened. "I guess that means I may be seeing more of you in the future."

"What do you mean?"

"I'm a healer." My blank stare prompted him to continue. "Almost like a doctor. You guys come to us to get patched up. Most of our patients are hunters. They seem to get themselves banged up on a regular basis."

"Oh." I gestured back to his outfit to change the subject. "So are you going to tell me what the joke is?"

He dipped his head, and his voice dropped in volume. His nearness felt somewhat intimate to me, but I didn't have anywhere to go with Logan's hand boxing me in on the back and Jonathon's broad frame on the front.

"I'll have to tell you about that another time. I think Cinderella is late for the ball and has a few of her mice waiting for her." He shifted his eyes to the side conspiratorially. Following his gaze, I found Romona, Kaitlin, and Kevin all staring at us. How in the world did Kevin get over there?

Jonathon stepped back, took my hand and brought it to his lips for a chaste kiss. There was more heat in that kiss than he showed on his face, and I blushed when he released my hand. Logan moved a bit closer and tensed up.

"Now that I know where to find you, I'm sure we'll bump into each other again. It was very nice to meet you, Audrey." And then, as an afterthought, he included a nod of his head. "Logan."

With a wave, he stepped around us and disappeared into the multitude. Logan's hand dropped from my back the instant the crowd swallowed Jonathon. I found Romona looking between Logan and me thoughtfully, Kaitlin literally doubled over in laughter, and Kevin's eyes as big as saucers. I felt extremely exposed and kind of upset about inadvertently being made a spectacle. Regrettably, I did next what came most naturally. I turned on Logan.

"What was that all about?"

After removing his hand from my back, he'd taken a few steps away. The look on his face was detached.

"What do you mean?"

My eyes narrowed. "You know what I mean. What was up with the possessive act?" I gestured with my chin toward the bulky mass of people.

He shrugged carelessly. "I really don't know what you're talking about." Was that really how he was going to play this?

A strange sound caught my attention. Kaitlin had finally straightened and was wiping tears between giggles and hiccups with a yellow handkerchief that matched her dress perfectly.

"Oh, never mind." I rejoined our friends, giving Kaitlin a scolding glare for good measure.

"Oh, Audrey, I'm really sorry, that was just too much!"

I rolled my eyes and pretended to ignore her, for once not regretting the dark thoughts directed at her. Kevin looked like he'd swallowed his tongue, so I turned to Romona. Her eyes were still thoughtful.

"Well, now that we've found you again, should we go inside?"

No longer in the mood to celebrate anything, I shrugged. The excitement of the night had waned with the weirdness that had just ensued. Was the whole evening going to feel like an emotional roller coaster? Following behind my friends I huffed. It better not.

My jaw literally dropped when I stepped into the tent. I'd been distracted by the emotions of others as we bumped and jostled our way through the sea of people around us, but just one step inside, everything else was shoved from my mind.

The first thing that registered was the magnitude of the interior of the tent. From the outside it appeared to be approximately the diameter of a city block and the height of a ten-story building. By contrast, the inside space had been stretched and pulled to accommodate a city rather than a mere building. It was as if we'd been transported to a whole new world.

Just as I was about to swim against the crowd to double-check the exterior size of the tent, someone interpreted my bewilderment.

"Gateways to all the other parts of the realm have been opened so we can celebrate together. Most of the realm is here right now, so it needs to be big enough to fit everyone," Kaitlin informed me as she searched the crowd. "I may be able to track down some of my friends from home."

I nodded even as my eyes flew over the flocks of people. The music that drifted to my ears was like nothing I had ever heard. The perfect melody was created, sounding as if the wind was playing woodwinds and running water the strings. It was peaceful, exhilarating, and mesmerizing all at the same time. And it was also oddly fast-paced, with a catchy beat. Something you could really dance to.

As we made our way deeper into the tent, the sights took my breath away. Lights hung suspended in the air and twinkled like stars. Colors more numerous than I could count emanated from the crowd and wafted upward, mingling with a multitude of shimmering angels flying gracefully above. I realized with a start that the colors were somehow coming from the people dancing.

My eyes scanned for my friends, who had started to blend into the crowds. I spotted Kaitlin dancing first. Shimmering golden yellow dust floated around her like a halo before being sent up as she twirled with her hands in the air.

Romona smiled at me wildly and grabbed my arm to join the group. A pale blue hue illuminated her and pulsed like a heartbeat. Kevin was dancing out of sync with Kaitlin, but she didn't seem to mind. A bright sunset-orange aura surrounded him, and he sent up sparks every time his feet stomped the ground. I laughed in spite of myself. The atmosphere was infectious.

"It's the colors," Romona was saying in my ear.

"What?" I yelled back above the noise.

"It's the colors," she repeated. "It's like the empathy link, but you don't have to be touching. In here, everything good gets mixed together and shared with each other."

My eyes widened. "Really? That's so . . . so strange."

Romona laughed. "I know! But isn't it amazing too?"

And it was. How was it possible to be so happy, peaceful, and excited all at the same time? It made everything bad go away and just made me, well, want to dance.

And so I did. I closed my eyes and danced like I never knew I could, free of insecurities, and it was amazing.

Time ceased to matter anymore, and when I finally opened my eyes it was to discover that the world was bathed in purple. I caught my breath. My arms and legs were covered in a lattice of glowing lavender. I ran a hand down my arm, and the markings swirled like mist before slowly settling again on my skin like a blanket of intricate snowflakes. It was mesmerizing.

"We were wondering when we might see you again."

It was only after their cloud of mixed teals and greys thinned that I recognized Deborah and LD. Their arms were linked. Deborah's lustrous hair was piled on top of her head in an expertly styled tangle of braids. Her regal, one-shouldered emerald green gown with gold embellishments had an empire waist and flowed to the ground, allowing the tips of her golden Roman sandals to peak out. LD was dressed in a black tux complete with vest and tie. He reminded me of a wiser and more mature version of James Bond.

"It's you!" I exclaimed, slightly breathless. Even though Deborah's strange parting words at Celestial Heights had left me equal parts anxious and eager to meet again, I now felt only excitement from the infectious atmosphere.

"It's us!" Deborah laughed. "We saw you from afar and wanted to see what you thought of the celebration."

"It's kind of unreal." I admitted. "No one really warned me it would be like this."

"It's one of those things that's easier experienced than explained, isn't it?" LD asked.

"I was told that several times over the last week. I can see their point, but I would have preferred to be a little more prepared"

"Well we can't always be one hundred percent prepared for every situation." Deborah pointedly said. Before she'd spoken to me of purpose, plans, and wise decision-making. She now spoke of preparedness.

"Agreed. I'm continually being challenged by that truth." I laughed. "Some days more than others."

"Life, and even the afterlife, is a dance between being prepared and letting go. The wisdom is in knowing how to prepare and when it's time to let go."

She'd lost me again. Was this another riddle of wisdom or a fortune-cookie insight?

LD laid a hand on his wife's shoulder. With an affectionate look and a small nod, she turned her ageless eyes toward me.

"We're sure you are well on your way to figuring out these things on your own."

"You have our every confidence, Audrey," LD chimed in. "Now, what *I* want to know is have you had your first adventure as a huntress yet?" There was mischief in his eyes.

"Oh, I suppose you could say that I have," I hedged.

"That's grand! See, you've already broken the ice!"

"And are things going well with Logan?" Deborah asked.

"Some days are smoother than others," I answered honestly, if vaguely.

"I see." A small smile played at the corners of her lips.

"Romona is here somewhere." I did a half-turn to look for her. "I'll bet she'd like to say hello as well."

"We will keep a lookout for her."

LD shook my hand warmly and then looked at Deborah with playfulness in his eyes. "Audrey, it was such a pleasure to see you again, but I need to steal my beloved away for another dance."

"How could anyone refuse such a man?" she replied.

"My point exactly! Audrey, we are waiting in anticipation for your adventures to play out."

Ha! More like misfortunes. "I'll make the effort to search you out when I have a story worth telling."

"Excellent! Now enjoy the rest of your evening."

As they walked away, still linked arm in arm, their cloud of colors began to grow again, so tangled they existed as one instead of two.

"Wild, isn't it?" Kaitlin had twirled her way over. Her golden yellow haze sparkled, making her hair and skin shimmer.

"You're telling me! This really is unbelievable. Why didn't you guys warn me about this?" I poked at one of Kaitlin's sparkles before it disappeared.

"You have to admit this is kind of hard to explain. How would you have taken it if we told you space would bend over on itself to create more space and that when you danced you would change colors?" She shrugged. "We couldn't have told you what your color would look like anyway, and that's the best part."

"Do the colors mean anything?"

"Of course they do! They're a reflection of who we are. Everyone's is different because we're all unique. It's a manifestation of your spirit. Now that you've seen yours, there is something you know about yourself that you didn't before."

"That my spirit is purple?"

"Haha, exactly! And look!" She pointed her finger and lifted her face upward. Above us, all the different colors and textures were mingling. Beautiful was too mild a word to describe it. It was like a fireworks display, a sunset, and a rainbow all at once.

Despite the brilliance of the sight above, something vivid from the corner of my eye stole my attention. My eyes followed and settled on Logan.

Through the crowd, I caught glimpses of him dancing with Romona. He was laughing as he spun her around. His light was an intense silver that shone brightly as if a spotlight were on him. He was too far away to detect any details in the color, but even from where I was standing, he was spellbinding.

I yelped at a sudden hand on my back. "I did say I'd see you again." Jonathon's voice was close enough to my ear that he didn't have to yell.

Kaitlin quickly covered the startled look on her face with an easy smile. "Aren't you going to introduce me to your new friend, Audrey?"

Jonathon stepped to my side but didn't drop the hand on my back. That was a little forward, and since Logan wasn't around to box me in this time, I took a casual step to my left, allowing Kaitlin into a circle.

"This is Jonathon. I just met him." And to Jonathon I said, "Kaitlin's a huntress."

"Really! Another female hunter?"

"We like to roam in packs."

Jonathon flashed Kaitlin a smile. "Kaitlin, it's a pleasure to meet you as well." He extended a hand.

Kaitlin lifted an eyebrow before taking it. "Should I perhaps be giving you a curtsy instead?"

Jonathon seemed uncomfortable with the comment. "Oh, this." He looked down at his outfit. "It's kind of a joke with the people I work with."

The smile Kaitlin gave Jonathon could only be described as conspiratorial. "That wasn't what I was referring to."

The side of Jonathon's mouth quirked up. "Oh, please. You know that doesn't mean anything here. Besides, that was a lifetime ago."

"And modest at that. Hmmm, interesting."

Jonathon just shook his head.

I glanced back and forth between the two of them. They continued their conversation almost as if I wasn't there. That habit of Kaitlin's was getting old fast.

Finally Jonathon said, "Well, I was hoping to borrow my new friend here if you didn't mind."

"Oh, *I* don't mind." The way she stressed the "I" made it obvious she thought someone else would.

"Oh yeah," Jonathon turned his head to look toward the crowd. "Do you think your boyfriend would mind?"

"Huh?" I started to choke on nothing. Kaitlin gave my back a few hard hits before I got my breath back. "I don't have a boyfriend!"

Jonathon smiled broadly enough to show most of his white teeth. "Perfect! Then let's go!"

Without waiting for an answer, he grabbed my hand and pulled me in the opposite direction. I could barely wave "good-bye" to Kaitlin. The last I saw of her, she winked and turned to weave back through the crowd.

Jonathon pulled me through the crowd. "Hey, I can't feel anything." I lifted our joined hands to demonstrate, slowing our progression.

He smiled patiently at me. "It's because we're all sharing emotions in here, so the link doesn't work the same way. Too much stuff floating around to pick up on just one person."

"That's interesting."

"Let's keep going. I want to show you something."

I didn't resist as he pulled me forward and we dodged through the sea of bodies. Before I knew it I was outside, fresh air filing my lungs. But a sense of disappointment left me bereft, and I tugged my hand free of his, whirling around to return to my friends.

"Hey, wait a second!" he called.

Confused, I turned to glance at him, my hand on the flap of the tent.

"Will you trust me?"

Though friendly, Jonathon's smile made my stomach knot. I'd just met this guy, why should I trust him? And I really did want to get back to the celebration.

As if reading my mind, Jonathon continued. "I'll have you back in plenty of time to enjoy the rest of the celebration. I promise no one will even miss you."

With that comment, something ached in my chest. I thought about my friends having fun and enjoying themselves without me. I imagined Kaitlin and Logan's laughing faces as they danced. He was right, no one would miss me.

I gave Jonathon what I hoped was a normal smile and dropped the piece of tent.

"All right then, what's this amazing thing I just have to see?"

Jonathon's grin widened, making him look younger. There was a twinkle in his eye that seemed almost childlike, making my unease from a moment ago disappear.

We walked away from the tented celebration and toward the darkened forest. While we talked the music faded, and the sounds of the evening became the louder melody. Crickets sang a sweet lullaby that made me want to feel the tickle of the grass on my feet. I resisted the temptation and continued to follow Jonathon as he picked a path into the forest where the trees remained sparse. The denser woods could be easily seen through the foliage.

"Okay, so it's not far from here. He should be around here somewhere."

"He?"

"Yep!"

What "he" was he talking about? Was it possible he could mean the big "He?"

Jonathon grabbed my hand and swiftly placed me in front of him. He settled a hand on my bare shoulder and used the other to direct my line of site. The abruptness of the empathy link startled me. Jonathon was all excitement, and it was hard not to get swept away in his feelings.

"Do you see it? He's right there."

When I detangled my emotions from the ones being thrust upon me, I focused in the direction Jonathon was pointing. My breath caught.

There, through the trees, was a fairy tale come to life. His front legs bent in a low bow as he faced our direction. His eyes closed as if savoring the faint music emanating from the tent. His coat was the purest white, and my hands itched to stroke his flanks. I imagined it would feel like the smoothest velvet. Touching the ground was his shimmering pearlescent horn.

I'd forgotten Jonathon was there, let alone still attached to my shoulder. His words whispered in my ear. "They come out when we are all preoccupied during the celebration to pay their homage."

"He's magnificent," I whispered breathlessly.

"Yes. That's why they weren't around Earth for very long."

Sensing my confusion in the empathy link, Jonathon supplied additional information. "People had started to revere them as gods because of their beauty, so they were destroyed in the flood so we wouldn't confuse the creature with the Creator."

Standing there watching the magnificent being, I could understand how people might have been misled.

The sight of him urged me closer. Making a small movement forward, I accidentally stepped on a dry stick, which cracked loudly. I glanced down at the offensive stick, then up, but all I caught was a blur of silvery white disappearing into the forest.

"Oh, I'm so sorry. I just wanted a closer look."

Jonathon's hand had slid off my shoulder, but I was taken aback by how close he was.

"Don't worry about it. They spook really easily. That's why they're so hard to spot."

"Why did you bring me to see this?"

Jonathon's eyebrows shot up. He looked over my head and shrugged.

"I don't know. I guess I just figured this was probably something you hadn't seen before, you know, being new and all. And when you ran right into me," he gave me a wicked smile, which dropped off his face after only a moment, "I don't know, I guess I felt there was just something . . ." He let the rest of his sentence drop.

The moment hung in the air.

"Audrey, do you know how beautiful your eyes are?"

My mind startled at the abrupt change of subject. "But they're just brown."

"A rich brown."

He was leaning in, and I just froze. In another moment his lips would be close enough to touch mine. An alarm was going off in my head that shouted *too soon, too soon, too soon* over and over again, but my body stayed immobile, unable to obey.

BY THE LAKE

"*W*hat are you guys doing out here?"

Romona's voice broke my paralysis so suddenly that I jumped away from Jonathon. "Ouch!" Bark bit into my bare back.

"I was showing Audrey the unicorns." Jonathon responded without a hint of defensiveness in his voice. I, on the other hand, immediately felt guilty, so I started to ramble.

"Oh, Romona, it was amazing. I never knew there were animals so beautiful. And it was here one second, then I stepped on a stupid branch and scared it away. But I think it would have stayed if it didn't know we were here, so I'm pretty bummed I stepped on the branch, but I just wanted to get a closer look because it's not like you see one of those every day or anything."

I was out of breath by the time I finished my wordy account. Romona frowned.

"You shouldn't have left the celebration."

"That was my fault. I wanted her to have this experience. I'm sure you know how hard they are to spot."

Romona glared at him with a look I'd never seen cross her face. It appeared to be a mixture of disappointment and annoyance, with a solid measure of anger. Those weren't emotions she usually gave in to.

"Yes, I know they are rare, but showing her a unicorn didn't appear to be the *only* reason you brought her out here," she said with a sharp edge to her voice.

Jonathon held his hands up. "Okay okay, I get the picture. Not the smartest thing to do. I was just a little caught up in the moment. But everybody is okay; nothing happened."

Romona plopped her hands on her hips. "And what if the damage had already been done?"

Her accusing tone seemed to bounce off Jonathon as he flashed a dazzling smile. "Well, we've already established that's not something we have to worry about, now is it?"

"No thanks to you."

I gaped at how rude she was being. Yes, parts of their conversation were going over my head, but what could he have possibly done to make her this upset in just the short time we were away? Especially since, as far as I knew, Romona didn't know Jonathon from Adam. The way she behaved was practically parental.

"Romona!"

Jonathon's tone grew more sincere. "No, don't worry, Audrey, she's just being a good friend. I was out of line. I'll go and let the two of you walk back together."

Before I could argue, he'd picked my hand up and gently kissed the back. He was feeling a little wistful. His level of comfort with physical contact with me was just plain unnerving.

"I'm sure I'll see you around again." Without waiting for my good-bye, he walked away.

I turned on Romona with astonishment.

"What was that all about?"

Romona watched Jonathon's retreating form with eyes slightly narrowed. "I just thought he was taking advantage of the situation."

"Well yeah, I could have guessed that, but care to explain to me how?"

"Specifically regarding your lack of knowledge about some things here."

"What, you mean with the unicorn? How is that harmful?"

With a deep sigh, she angled her face toward me. And skirted the question. "You just have to trust me on this one. Some things mean more than you think."

"Like what things?"

She took a deep breath and deflected my question once again. "I'm not saying that Jonathon is a bad guy, Audrey."

"Well, why don't you explain to me exactly what you are saying so I can make my own assessment?" I shot back.

"Well, for one thing, he would be a big distraction right now."

I lifted an eyebrow as if to say "so what?"

"I think he might take your mind off what's really important."

Something I would consider a plus. Romona was trying to be helpful, but what was the harm she was alluding to? Jonathon seemed to be a decent guy. Not to mention pretty cute and paying some serious attention to me. And who was she to police who I could or couldn't hang out with?

"What are you, like my mom or something?"

The question gave her a visible start. "Hardly. But there are things I know more about than you do right now. It's up to you to trust that I'm telling you the truth. Even in this realm, there are consequences to your actions."

More riddles. I was suddenly very tired. What had promised to be an enchanted night had turned ugly fast. Sad to have lost the joy for the evening, my gut instinct was to pull away. I was inclined to give in.

"I think I'd like to be alone right now, if you don't mind."

"I'm not sure—" Romona started and then stopped herself, giving me a quick nod. "Okay, I understand."

She turned to follow the path Jonathon had taken. Part of me ached to follow her and rejoin the celebration, but I squashed that feeling and headed in the opposite direction.

I walked lost in my own thoughts for a while before stumbling through a break in the trees that opened to a small, pebbly beach on the shore of a still lake. The lake was embraced by forest on all sides and offered a view of the mountains in the distance. Water soundlessly licked the pebbles on the shoreline. This small oasis in the middle of the trees was calming. My heels sank into the stones as I walked clumsily closer to the water's edge. I closed my eyes and took a deep breath of the fresh air. On exhale, it felt as if I had released some of the ugliness toward my friend. The simple act was refreshing to my soul.

"I hear you want to be alone."

I opened my eyes to Logan sitting on a large rock a few feet away. I was certain he hadn't been there a moment before. His forearms rested on his knees as he stared across the lake.

The mountain peaks glowed in the odd night lighting and the lake shimmered and sparkled like millions of faraway stars. The air stirred lazily, causing strands of my hair to float over my shoulder and the hem of my dress to tickle my legs. The slight breeze was refreshing without being cold.

"I just needed to think."

Logan nodded in understanding.

"Mind if I sit down?" I asked.

Logan moved down the rock to make room. There was plenty of space for us both to sit without being in any danger of touching. I stretched my legs in front of me and crossed my ankles. From this position, I had a view of both Logan and the scenery. I took a few moments to study him in silence.

Being with Logan when we weren't at each other's throats was turning out to be oddly soothing. I was reminded of the other beach we'd sat on when I'd thought things were finally getting better between us. I stared out across the water and faintly heard the sweet music coming from the celebration. It was a while before either of us said anything.

"What did you think of tonight?" The soft timber of Logan's voice blended well with the night.

"It was incredible. I never would have imagined something could be so . . ." I struggled for a word to describe it . . . "magical."

Logan softly chuckled.

"I can see why you would describe it that way. There's something quite magical about it. Except the ironic thing is that's what life was supposed to be like. This is really what we were created for, what we'd been missing all along. When we were walking around on Earth, we had a veil covering our eyes, and now that veil has been lifted. If people just understood . . ." He didn't finish his thought, but his voice had turned passionate.

I turned my head. Logan was staring at me intently. I was a prisoner to those intense eyes.

"What is it you are trying to tell me, Logan?" Unconsciously, I moved forward a fraction, lessening the space between us.

Logan released a deep breath and pulled back, breaking eye contact. He ran a hand through his hair, a move I was quite familiar with. He did it frequently when annoyed.

"Nothing you won't learn soon enough."

I let out a small breath of frustration. We were back to that again.

"But not something you will explain to me."

I leaned away, tired of everyone edging around topics and treating me like a child. I just wanted someone to be completely honest with me. I didn't want to have to find everything out on my own. It was like trying to navigate without a map or even a final destination. Completely and utterly impossible.

"I'm sorry, Audrey, I'm sure this is wearisome. When you get your memories back, more things are going to fall into place. Unfortunately, some things can't be explained. There are choices you have to make."

His words rubbed a sore that was already sensitive. I pushed off the rock to walk the few feet to the water's edge. The slight tide rolled up mere inches from my toes, only to recede back a moment later. If I moved forward even a little, I would be able to feel the coolness myself. I remained rooted in place.

"Yes, those elusive memories I don't have anymore. You mean once I remember who I once was, everything will make sense? Ha! But what if it's the opposite, Logan? What if I remember who I was and all of this makes even less sense? What then?"

"It's not who you *were*, Audrey, it's who you *are*, who you've always been all along. You are still you, even though you don't remember the details."

I stared at the water, watching my reflection ripple in the shoreline. I ran a hand down the side of my dress and clasped some of the material in my fingers, feeling its softness.

"Then how does it make sense that I feel more myself in a dress than training gear? How is that supposed to make sense with what I am now? I don't see the two reconciling."

Logan pushed off from the rock, and his reflection in the water appeared behind me. When he finally spoke, his warm breath fanned my shoulder.

"I have to admit, you did seem more comfortable in your own skin tonight. Perhaps you were a pageant girl?"

I heard the smile in his voice as he said it. That idea was absurd for a number of reasons. I had a sudden image of me wearing my fighting armor with a tiara and doing a pageant wave down a runway. It was ridiculous enough to force a smile and a rebellious laugh to escape.

"I don't want to take credit for changing your mood, so can I ask what's so funny?"

I explained the mental picture I'd just had. The corner of his mouth turned up in my peripheral vision as well as in the hazy water reflection below. He took a step forward.

"That may be more of an accurate description of yourself then you realize."

"Ha! Yeah, right!" I scoffed.

Logan's distorted reflection in the water turned ever so slightly toward me. Just as I was studying him in the water, he was studying me. I couldn't make out the look on his face through the clouded image.

"So, is purple hair the new thing?"

I smiled. "Something I was trying out. I didn't think you'd noticed."

"Hmmm," Logan said thoughtfully but didn't expound. My breath caught when he reached a hand up toward my hair, only to drop it to his side a moment later.

"I'll let you be alone now." His voice was still soft but hollow.

I tried not to let myself feel disappointed. I nodded. Logan left as soundlessly as he had appeared.

My reflection mocked me. Each gentle wave distorted the image just as it was beginning to settle. The image of a girl I still didn't know. Who was she? I could count everything I knew about her on my two small hands.

I let out a harsh breath in exasperation and used the toe of my shoe to kick a pebble into the water. The stone slapped the face of the girl looking back at me and sent wild ripples out into the placid lake. Each ripple produced a sweet note of song, eventually fading into the stillness. I didn't want to feel so alone anymore.

As if the wind knew my thoughts, a soft breeze blew from behind, bringing with it the faint sounds of celebration. Involuntarily, something inside me responded yet again. A nudge told me I wasn't alone, I hadn't been forgotten, I did have people who cared about me.

In my mind's eye, I saw friends. Romona with her peaceful and gentle spirit, Kevin with his good and kind heart, joyous Alrik, patient and beautiful Kaitlin, and Logan with his steadfastness.

My heart's desire was to soften, but a ball of bitterness tightened around it instead. Wouldn't a God who truly loved me want to comfort me Himself? Why would He make me go through this alone? Why would He give me a task that was so obviously beyond my skills?

The sweet music from the dance still tugged at my soul, but I turned instead and walked the other direction, away from my friends, away from the comfort, and headed back to my empty tree to be alone.

ROMONA'S APOLOGY

"*H*i, can we talk?"

I rubbed my eyes to wipe the sleep from them, leaving a black smear across the back of my hand. *Shoot, I must have smudged mascara all over my face.*

My hazy brain took a moment to register that Romona was standing in my open doorway.

"Oh, ah, yeah, come on in."

She looked at me strangely.

It took me a second to realize how awful I must look in the crumpled dress with my hair all over the place, and a mess of black mascara and eye shadow smeared across my face. "Oh right, give me a second to get this off, will you?"

Romona sat gingerly on a sofa chair and patiently waited for me to pull myself together. Although silent, her face still projected that strange look. *I must look really bad.*

Standing in front of the mirror, I splashed water on my face. My reflection shocked me fully awake. It wasn't just the makeup smear or the disheveled clothes that had Romona transfixed—it was my hair. The wavy mass that wildly protruded from my head had been transformed to jet black and fire-engine red.

I looked like a madwoman.

I started taking in and expelling air at an ever-quickening pace. Each breath in and out was shorter than the last until I was panting like a dog on a hot day.

"Did you do that on purpose?" came a gentle voice.

I shook my head. There was a soft rustle as Romona joined me.

"Here, let's get you cleaned up first, and then we can deal with the hair."

She handed me a bar of soap. I bent to scrub the makeup from my face. Once I didn't look quite as frightening, Romona was waiting with a handful of bedclothes.

"Here you go."

I quickly changed and faced the mirror again to deal with my hair. I concentrated on relaxing and returning it to a normal shade of chocolate brown. Once my breathing was controlled, the black and red started to bleed from my hair. I sighed in relief. "That was really weird." Romona nodded in agreement.

"So what are you doing here so late?"

She took a deep, steadying breath before speaking.

"I wanted to apologize for what happened in the woods tonight. I overreacted, and also . . . I'd like to explain a little more. I think there's something you should know, even if it's intended for you to find out on your own." Sincerity shone in her eyes.

I'd never had reason to doubt Romona's motives. Yet I'd distrusted her this evening and lashed out in anger. The weight of the injustices I'd committed against her was heavy.

"Oh, Romona, no. It's really not your fault. I keep getting frustrated because there's so much I still don't know. You were only worried because I was out there alone with Jonathon. I see how that could be a little sketchy. Especially since I'd just met him. I should never have left the celebration to begin with."

Feeling my cheeks redden, I looked away. Going off with him was a stupid move.

She was shaking her head. "But, Audrey, that's what I want to explain. It's not only that. I don't care how it looked. Remember tonight when I was talking about consequences for your actions?"

"Yeah."

"Well, there are consequences in this realm for things you might not consider a big deal. We saw the way Jonathon looked at you tonight." I wanted to ask who the "we" was, but she rushed forward. "I was worried you might do something you couldn't take back later."

"Geez, Romona, what do you think we would have done? I just meet the guy! The worse that could have happened was a kiss. You don't honestly think I'd have gone further than that?"

Her eyes grew unnaturally large. "See, that's just it—a kiss is so much more than you think it is."

My heart skipped a beat. Thoughts of Jonathon slid from my mind, replaced by someone else.

"What do you mean?" My voice was flat.

"A kiss is more than a kiss now . . . here." She looked up at the ceiling to piece together words. I got the distinct impression she was getting ready to launch into a lecture on the birds and the bees. "A kiss here is more like a promise. It creates a bond. I was worried that Jonathon might take advantage of you not knowing that."

I only nodded for her to go on. I had to know what type of mess I'd gotten myself into.

"At the risk of sounding melodramatic, I didn't want you to get stuck with the wrong person for all of eternity just because you didn't know any better."

"What! If I kiss him, I would have to be with him *forever?"*

Romona held up her hands for me to slow down. "No, sorry, that's not exactly what I meant. When the bond is created, it intensifies any feelings you have for that person. It draws you to them and them to you. We weren't intended to have more than one soul mate, so when you pick your mate here, it's for keeps. Jonathon could have started that bond with you tonight without your consent, so to speak."

"So the first person I kiss here I'm picking as my soul mate? The person I have to spend the rest of eternity with?"

"No."

"No?"

"No, you still have a choice. What you are doing, though, is taking a step in that direction. You're making a decision to be pulled closer to that person on a soul level. And breaking the bond you create can be very difficult."

My heart beat so loud I wondered if she heard. The blood rushing through my head made it hard for me to concentrate. *My gosh, why in the world didn't I get the instruction manual on this stuff when I arrived?*

"Was this something I would have learned in orientation?"

"Probably."

"Why didn't anyone tell me then?"

"Skipping orientation is very rare, so we don't really know how much to tell you or what you're supposed to discover on your own."

I went to my bed, landed face first, and groaned.

"There are some things that seriously need to be told sooner rather than later."

"This wasn't really something I thought about telling you until this evening."

With the risk of giving myself away, I had to ask: "So when you're talking about all this kissing and bonding and junk, do you mean here in this realm or now that we've passed on in general?"

Romona stared at me quizzically. "I'm not following."

I had to know if I'd accidentally done something to Logan and me without meaning to. I chewed my lip in indecision.

"I mean, is this something that happens now because we are dead or is it just *here?"* I paused before completely spelling it out. "Does it like, count the same if it happens on Earth?"

As expected, Romona sucked in a quick breath. Of course she was smart enough to know something was up. It was visible on her face when all the pieces clicked together. Neither one of us spoke for a full sixty-five seconds.

I counted.

Then Romona asked me the question I'd dreaded and dodged for days. "Audrey, what really happened with you and Logan when you went to Earth?"

The question came out as a whisper. Almost as if she didn't dare ask it for fear she already knew. I chewed on my lower lip some more, my brows furrowed.

When I didn't answer, she asked the more direct version of the question. "Did he kiss you?"

"No."

Romona let out a deep breath, and her whole body relaxed. "Oh good, because . . ."

"I kissed him." I admitted hurriedly. It felt like ripping off a stubborn Band-Aid. Extremely painful.

Romona gasped, and she brought a hand up to her mouth. "I thought you guys could hardly stand each other!"

"Well, that's true most days."

"Then how did this happen?"

"It was an accident. Remember how we said we escaped the demon by blending into the crowd that day?"

She nodded.

"Well, that was true, but we never told you guys *exactly how* we blended in. I basically attacked Logan and made him kiss me so it didn't look like we were running from the demon."

"Oh, Audrey, you didn't!" The horrified look on her face said everything she didn't.

I slowly nodded my head in shame.

"The boardwalk was so busy, and the crowd was parting for us, which was a complete giveaway, and it was all I could come up with to get us away from the crowd and still make it look like we belonged there. I didn't think it through as well as I should have." I looked down at my hands.

With her hand to her mouth, Romona let out a small giggle.

"This is *not* funny, Romona."

"Oh, I know, but it's so unbelievable. And poor Logan, I'll bet he didn't even know what hit him."

I remembered Logan's reaction. If you excluded my complete mortification both then and now, it was kind of funny. I fought the lifting of the corners of my mouth.

"Yeah, he never saw it coming. He just stood there like a statue. I had to step on his foot to get him to snap out of it."

Romona let out a real laugh. "Oh my goodness, seriously?"

I nodded solemnly, but I hoped Romona's laugh and lightened attitude meant I wasn't in any real trouble.

"Okay, so how bad is it? It wasn't even a real kiss, so it shouldn't count. Is there a free pass or something since we were on Earth? Not to mention I was *completely* unaware of that rule!"

Romona sobered a bit.

"I'm afraid that little technicality doesn't matter. You know, now that I think about it, things make so much more sense. There's been something off between the two of you. And especially the way he acted tonight. He must really be fighting it."

I found that to be a little insulting. But Romona didn't mean anything by it.

"Okay, you need to tell me what sort of trouble I've gotten myself into. Am I stuck with Logan forever now?" The idea of being stuck with someone who aggravated me so much was suddenly very serious and a touch scary.

She was thoughtful a moment before answering. "Well, one big problem is that Logan's not really available right now."

Then it was as I expected. There *was* something going on with Kaitlin. I just knew it. Despite having always suspected it, the confirmation still pierced me.

"I see."

"No, I don't think you do, but it's not my place to tell you, it's Logan's. You guys are just going to have to work through this one. To be blunt, you inadvertently tied yourself to Logan whether you meant to," she lifted an eyebrow at me, "or wanted to. Whatever your emotions toward each other might have been, you just prematurely turned it all up a notch."

"Why didn't Logan tell me any of this?"

She shrugged her shoulders. "Can't say for sure. Maybe so he wouldn't freak you out. Maybe he thought it was too much for you to handle. Or maybe he doesn't want to admit it himself."

"So what you are saying is that anything . . . romantic I feel for Logan right now is just because I kissed him?"

"Oh no, that's not what I'm saying. The kiss doesn't fabricate feelings for someone else. It intensifies them. You're really only supposed to kiss the person you stay with, you know, forever. Imagine a seal on an envelope. The kiss is supposed to seal those emotions. That's why it's so important to be careful."

"Great, so I've doomed both of us?" My shoulders slumped in defeat.

"No, not necessarily. I didn't say it couldn't be broken, just that it was difficult. Or, if there really weren't any feelings between the two of you to begin with, then nothing should come of it." She watched my reaction closely.

"Really? So it could possibly mean nothing?" I bounced happily to my knees.

"Yes, but that's only if you can honestly say you don't feel anything romantic toward Logan and he the same." She arched an eyebrow at me that said she had my number. "Are you really going to try to tell me that's the case?"

I huffed. "Okay, then tell me what else I need to do to break the stupid bond!"

She nodded. "You need to let him go."

"Great, done." I brushed my hands together like I was brushing off the whole thing. "That sounds easy."

"It may sound that way, but it won't be."

Determined to hear only what I wanted to hear, I plowed on. "Okay, let's do this thing. Do I need to say some magic words? Burn a picture of him with some incense?"

"Audrey." Romona's look and tone said she didn't think I was taking this seriously.

"No really, let's get this over with. I want to get back to the way it used to be. Or at least should have been. I don't really want to go back to getting thrown into the water, but I'm sure there's got to be something better than this. What we have going on now is . . . distracting. So what should I do?"

"I'm sorry, I can't tell you that."

"What?"

"I can't tell you because I don't know. You have to figure out how to let go of him in your heart. There are no magic words or any rituals to fix this."

"Can't I simply choose to let him go?"

"Sure, in your head you can, but your heart's a little trickier. You've got him hidden in there somewhere."

"Oh come on, it's Logan we're talking about here. Hidden in my heart somewhere? Pa-leeeasse!" I rolled my eyes.

Romona shook her head. "You can deny it all you want, Audrey, but he's there. The faster you come to terms with that, the quicker you can work through it."

She gave me a sad look. One that said she understood how hard this was going to be much better than I did. It concerned me.

"I wonder . . ." She started but stopped with a shake of her head. "You know, a good place to start is to have an honest conversation with Logan."

I looked at her like she was crazy and told her as much. "I never want to discuss this with Logan, ever. It's bad enough talking about it at all, but talking to him would be sheer torture. Embarrassment taken to a new level."

"I see. Well, it's something I hope you'll think about."

Like there was anything else I would be thinking about now. My only promise was a nod.

She sighed. "All right, I should get going. It's extremely late, and tomorrow brings its own worries."

"What does that mean?"

"You'll see in the morning."

"Romona!" I groaned.

She laughed lightly. "Don't worry, this isn't a secret. Logan will explain tomorrow."

Romona gracefully rose from the sofa chair. I followed her to the door to say good night. Before leaving, she gave me a hug that folded me in a cushion of love. I hoped some of my gratitude made it back to her.

With all the thoughts swirling in my head, I assumed it would take me a while to settle down, but when my head hit my pillow, I was already half-asleep.

18

MEETING THE ARCHANGEL

I kept expecting something important to happen the next day at training, but it turned out to be an unexpectedly normal day. Logan was neither more nor less talkative than he had been of late. We ran through the usual training drills and sparring lessons. We started and finished the day at roughly the same time as had become customary. There was no talk about whatever Romona had hinted at the night before. All things considered, the day was anticlimactic at best.

I pushed through the locker room doors in a restless haze.

Kaitlin was finishing getting dressed, her hair still wet from the shower. The sight of her sent a sharp stabbing pain into my chest. Romona's words from the night before replayed in my head. *Logan's not really available right now.*

"Hey." I nodded in her direction, not allowing our eyes to connect.

It was difficult. On the one hand I was starting to like Kaitlin. She was confident, friendly, and nice with a sharp sense of humor and a wicked roundhouse kick. There was something magnetic about her. As if she were a bright light we were all drawn to like flies. And that was exactly what kept me wary of her. It was too easy, too effortless for her.

"So I didn't see you again last night after you took off with Jonathon." She purposefully let the statement float in the air.

I shrugged.

"Did you ever make it back to the celebration? I was hoping to introduce you to a few friends."

"No, I took the opportunity to spend some time on my own. It was really peaceful."

"I see." She nodded. "Did Logan ever find you then?"

"What do you mean?" I asked.

"Last night. When I told him you'd left, he took off after you. I just wanted to know if he ever found you."

"Yes, he did . . . eventually."

"That's good. He seemed rather . . . um . . . agitated."

Had Kaitlin told him in order to point out I was preoccupied with someone else? And if so, shouldn't she be upset that he'd gone to look for me? Nothing was making sense right now.

The doors behind me swooshed open and Romona came in, mopping her brow with a small towel.

"Hey girls," she said breathlessly.

"Let me guess," Kaitlin said, "the gauntlet?"

"You got it! Man, it really kicked my butt!"

"What's a gauntlet?" I asked.

"It's a training exercise. It's an obstacle course, but after every obstacle you have to defeat an opponent and then move on to the next. It's intense!"

"And really long," Kaitlin piped in. "Sometimes it takes hours to get through."

"Eww, I don't want to hear either one of you mentioning it to Logan."

"Ha," Kaitlin laughed, "too late; he already ran it this morning before he started training with you."

I shook my head in awe. And I thought *I* needed to get out more. He must have been at the training center for sixteen hours already.

"So why haven't I heard of this thing before?" I asked.

"Probably because they only break it out before big missions, when they are planning on sending a larger group of hunters down to Earth. It's like a qualifier to make sure everyone is still on their game."

"Oh." I looked at Romona. "So you're headed down for a mission soon?"

She looked perplexed. "Um yeah, but . . ."

"What?"

"Nothing, I guess." She turned to Kaitlin, who simply shrugged, before changing the subject. "Let's have a girls' night tonight!"

Their misdirection came to light as we were all leaving the locker room.

"So, Aud, you ready for tomorrow?" Alrik's voiced boomed from down the hallway.

I frowned at him. "What's so special about tomorrow?"

"What? Don't tell me they haven't told you yet," he continued after a moment of silence from me. "Well, that's a surprise. Tomorrow's your first mission."

I glanced at Logan who was in conversation with Kevin a little further down the hall.

If what Alrik said was true, why hadn't Logan said something to me? You don't spring this on someone last minute! I looked at Alrik in disbelief. He must have it wrong. I told him as much.

"I don't know, Aud, I heard it from up the chain. You've created quite a stir. A number of people are interested to see how your first official mission goes considering the adventure from your last trip to Earth."

I still blushed every time someone brought that up. This time especially since Alrik might know more about that fateful day than he let on. The twinkle in his eye whenever he brought it up said as much. Rather than stand there and argue with him, it was better to go to the source and get some answers. I brushed past him to get to Logan, who was still in conversation with Kevin.

The casual and friendly air Logan had with Kevin vanished when I faced them. I watched him slip on his mask of indifference. I sighed internally. Was it always going to be this way?

"What's this about my first mission being tomorrow?" I pointed a thumb behind me toward Alrik. "He's got it wrong, right?"

"Aren't you hanging out with the girls tonight?"

"Logan, come on, is there something you're not telling me? If it's true, I would have appreciated a little more heads-up, and to have heard it from you."

"There's nothing to give you the heads-up about. You're not going."

He actually had the nerve to turn back to Kevin as if I wasn't even there. Did he think I was a child he could dismiss with a wave of a hand?

Peeved, I did the unthinkable and grabbed Logan's forearm to get his attention. It was barely a fraction of a second before he snatched his arm away from me, but it did the trick. I had his full attention. It only took that moment of contact to realize the indifference he'd tightly cloaked himself in was far from genuine. I was taken aback at the strong emotions churning inside him. He was more worked up about this than I had perceived. There was some satisfaction in that.

Logan glared back as if I'd committed some giant violation of his privacy. Which I guess I had—he was the most anti-empathy link person I knew—but I was beyond caring.

"What do you mean I'm not going?" I asked.

He stepped out of my reach, making it abundantly clear that he didn't want me to touch him again. *Pfft.* As if I'd even want to. "I contested the decision. You're not ready." He said it matter-of-factly.

"Excuse me! You contested the decision? What gave you the right?" Unlike Logan, my emotions were on display for everyone to see.

"The fact that I'm your mentor and I don't think you're ready."

I flinched as if I had been slapped. I knew Logan wasn't one hundred percent pleased with my progress so far, but I'd thought I was getting better. To contest an order meant he really doubted my abilities. When I recoiled I might have seen something soften in his eyes, but it was gone in an instant.

"Hey man, that was kind of harsh." It was Alrik who spoken up in my defense.

The way Logan's eyes never left mine you'd think he hadn't heard him, but a moment later he addressed Alrik in a way I'd never heard him speak to his friend. "This isn't your business."

"Maybe not, but you know you're not playing by the rules. She's right, you don't have the authority to make that decision even if you are her mentor. If it was a direct order, only Audrey can contest it."

I turned my head to gawk at Alrik. Could he be right? When Logan didn't respond, it verified that Alrik spoke true.

Man, I could have kissed Alrik! Figuratively speaking, of course. Victory was within my grasp! I smiled brightly back at Logan, ready to end the issue right there and enjoy the rest of my evening. But Logan wasn't ready to concede defeat. He stared coolly at Alrik.

"You don't know what you're talking about. You weren't there the first time we went down. It was almost a catastrophe."

"Hey, I'd hardly call that fair!" I clenched my teeth. "If you remember, I was the one who finally got us out of trouble."

Logan's eyes widened and then narrowed again as if he were picking up the unspoken gauntlet I'd just thrown down.

"I had everything under control," he said. "Besides, it's not as if your *methods* would really come in handy in another situation."

"At least I know how to think on my feet," I shot back.

I was extremely glad we were in a poorly lit section of hallway, because I was certain both our faces were on fire. Luckily, no one except Romona really knew what we were talking about.

I was so wound up I almost jumped out of my skin when Alrik laid a steady hand between my shoulder blades.

"Listen, you two, let's just bring it down a notch. Logan can contest, but I've never heard of the council changing a decision because of a mentor's suggestion. Aud, if you want to go tomorrow, you should be able to."

Logan shot Alrik another annoyed look. When in the world had Alrik become the levelheaded one? I knew I was being handled, but considering Logan and I had publicly stumbled upon a very personal topic, it was probably best to listen. Suddenly I didn't feel like a girl's night anymore.

When I opened my eyes in the stillness of my room the next morning, I was assaulted by the nervousness I'd held at bay last night. I'd worn a brave face in front of my friends, but now, listening to the rapid beating of my heart, I was a bundle of doubts.

I closed my eyes and remembered what it felt like being stalked by an unseen demon. A shudder ran through my body. I had been so scared, desperate even.

Sitting up, I threw off my comforter, hoping to also throw off the apprehension that had my insides twisted. It didn't work, and although the temperature in the room was perfect as usual, an uncontrollable shiver ran through my body. I walked to the sink and surveyed myself in the mirror. My hair stuck up at weird angles and tangled its way down my back. My eyes looked darker than usual and my skin paler. *Am I crazy or just plain stupid?*

Perhaps I should have swallowed my pride and listened to Logan. If he didn't think I was ready, what chance did I really have?

I brought my hands to my face and rubbed the sleep from my eyes, taking a deep breath to steady myself. I wished for the hundredth time that I knew a little more about my life. Maybe there was a past experience I could draw on to gain confidence. Instead, all I had was a short history of poor performance and rash decisions.

"Come on, God, if you're out there, I could use a bit of encouragement and reassurance right about now."

I held my breath and waited in silence. For what, I wasn't sure, but I hoped for something.

Exhaling harshly, I shook my head. *What was I expecting to happen, anyway?*

A loud knock sounded at my door and I almost jumped out of my skin. Frozen in place, my heart raced fast and loud. Was there a chance God had actually heard me and was literally knocking on my door?

Another loud rap was followed by a voice. "Audrey, are you in there? It's me, Kaitlin."

My heart deflated. I took a quick moment to compose myself, then grabbed an elastic to wrap my hair in a bun. Kaitlin always looked so perfect. *Oh well.*

I opened the door. She stood with a big, if somewhat strained, smile on her face.

"Hey," I said.

"Hi! Romona told me where you lived."

Awkward silence followed. What was she doing here, anyway?

"Oh."

"I, ah, could we talk for a sec?"

It was bizarre to see Kaitlin so unsure of herself. She fidgeted with some bracelets on her right hand and shifted her weight. I was equally curious and cautious.

I invited her in. Relieved, she gave me a smile that lit up her whole face. She studied my room with interest.

"Cool chairs," she finally said.

"Thanks."

"So would you like to sit down?"

"Yeah, that would be great, thanks."

We settled into the overstuffed chairs. The strained smile on Kaitlin's face faltered.

"I know you aren't ready to start confiding in me like you do Romona, but

I wanted to let you know I'm supporting your decision to go on this mission today."

Kaitlin's arrival had temporarily pushed that from my thoughts. But the cool fingers of trepidation crept back up my spine.

"Logan wouldn't agree with you."

She smiled sympathetically. "You know, Logan does have his reasons for not wanting you to go, but you shouldn't think they all have to do with your ability. I've seen you fight, remember—I've trained with you. You're going to be fine."

I sat back. "You really think so? Logan was pretty specific about his reasons last night."

"Yeah, well, sometimes we don't always say what we know to be true. And Logan has some fears of his own he's still working through. Scars that have absolutely nothing to do with you. I think they have more to do with his reaction to your mission than you realize."

"What scars?"

Kaitlin had the sense to squirm uncomfortably. When she answered, it was apologetically.

"It's not really my place to say. You'll have to take it up with Logan. But I do want you to know that *I* think you're ready. And I'm not the only one, or else they wouldn't have assigned you."

It was disappointing to have hit another wall where Logan was concerned. Kaitlin had dangled a piece of the puzzle in front of my face only to snatch it away again.

She took my silence as an invitation to continue. "And besides, you'll have a lot of people with you."

I gave myself a mental shake to get back on topic. "Really? Do you know who will be there? Are you going?"

"No, I won't be there. This is something for your region only. But Romona should be there. Maybe even Kevin or Alrik."

Kaitlin's support was a balm for my raw emotions. Despite myself, I was getting closer to her.

"Thanks, Kaitlin. You've actually made me feel a lot better."

She smiled knowingly. "I thought you might be a little anxious about today. I didn't think the bravado from last night was one hundred percent genuine."

Her words left me feeling exposed, but I didn't mind. I found myself wanting to open up to her.

"Yeah, I guess you're right about that. I think the adrenaline was talking last night. And there's another reason I'm glad that you came this morning."

"Really, what's that?"

"Well, Kevin mentioned we weren't supposed to wear our armor today, and I think you are the perfect person to help me figure out what to wear instead!"

Kaitlin gave me one of her megawatt movie-star smiles.

"You've got that right! Time to check out your closet." She jumped up and faced my closet. "Hey there, Hot Stuff," she said to the door, "it's time to see what you've really got."

Not only was Kaitlin the ideal person to help me figure out what to wear, but she also had me ready in record time, which was why I found myself waiting alone in the training gym before anyone else arrived. As I sat in silence, my mind drifted to my first day of training. I was almost as nervous and unsure now as I had been then.

I glanced at the weapons wall and pushed off the mat to browse the now familiar objects, silently reciting the names and uses of each. My slow progression stopped when I reached the broad-bladed sword I'd first picked up. I grabbed it with confidence this time and brought the blade up to inspect, catching my reflection in it once more. This time the girl staring back was more familiar. Still mysterious, but certainly recognizable.

"You shouldn't be touching those. You could hurt yourself."

There was no bang of the door to announce Logan's entrance this time, and I kept a firm grasp on the hilt. Rather than chilling flatness, there was a warmth in Logan's voice that made me smile despite myself. I wasn't the only one being nostalgic this morning.

I carefully returned the blade to its spot. Logan was standing on the opposite side of the room, the doors still softly swinging shut behind him. I had expected round two of our argument from last night.

"You think so? Or are you worried I could hurt *you* with it this time?"

Logan smiled. "Part of me is always worried you could hurt me."

So rarely were his smiles directed at me that I mentally saved this one. It made him appear younger. I appreciated the softness I wasn't often privy to but purposefully ignored the slight hitch to my breathing that it caused.

It seemed silly to be talking across the expanse of the room, so I forced myself to confidently stride toward him. When I was halfway there Logan made the decision to meet me in the middle. We stopped our customary distance from each other. Neither one of us invading the other's bubble.

"How are you feeling today?"

I shrugged. "Fine, I guess."

He nodded as if I had said something more important. "That's good."

But I couldn't leave well enough alone. "So how'd your appeal go?"

"I decided to retract it." Logan studied my face.

I was stunned. "Why?"

Logan smiled. "I was given some good advice that I finally listened to."

Huh? Advice? Was Kaitlin the one who had changed his mind? Despite her encouraging words this morning, I realized how desperately I needed to hear some from Logan as well.

I knew how vulnerable I sounded, but I had to ask. "So does that mean you think I'm ready for this?"

Logan blew out a quick breath and ran a hand through his unruly locks before answering me, not quite meeting my gaze. "Oh, Audrey, I'm not sure I'm the best person to be assessing that anymore."

He said it with a half-laugh as if he considered himself the butt of a joke. Unexpectedly, he took a few steps closer, breaking the invisible barrier we'd been keeping. Something on the inside heated up as I looked up into Logan's deep blue eyes.

He was as serious as I'd ever seen. "But Audrey, I promise, I'll be there the whole time. Nothing is going to happen to you."

His gaze intensified. "Nothing."

His voice wasn't loud, but it vibrated in my head as if shouted. My heart thudded inside my chest loud enough to be heard. Any words I might have spoken died in my throat. My only response was to nod and hope he knew I understood.

The door flew open with a bang as a joking, laughing group of others arrived. I jumped away from Logan guiltily. I hadn't thought my heart could beat any louder than before, but I was wrong. It took a moment for the erratic beating to subside, and that was only after I realized no one was giving us much notice.

I glanced at Logan, but he didn't appear concerned. He strode over to the group to say hello. Man, he could change gears fast enough to give a girl whiplash.

Romona broke free of the small group. As always, I was grateful for her support. I wondered if I'd had friends as loyal and supportive as her when I was alive. I hoped so. She met me with her familiar friendly smile and a tight hug. I didn't need to feel her encouragement through the empathy link because her face revealed it clearly enough.

"Hey, so how are you feeling about this?" Direct and to the point. I both liked and disliked that about her.

"Good, I think."

"Don't worry, we'll all be there with you."

The group atmosphere was unexpectedly chill and relaxed. Any nervous energy in the room was mine alone. The others chatted lightly. Even Logan appeared at ease, trading jokes about demons with Kevin.

There were fifteen of us total. All of the hunters were familiar, even if I didn't remember their names.

"No, I've got a better one," I caught Kevin saying. "What do you call a demon that's having a bad hair day?"

He didn't get to finish because Shannon walked in just then, and all chatter ceased. Taking time to scan our faces, her gaze stopped on mine for an extended moment before traveling on to the next.

"Thanks for being on time. As you know, I'm here to give you a further rundown of your assignment. I expect you all know at least the preliminary details."

I inconspicuously scanned the other hunters. Their faces only showed focused attention. No one betrayed any inclination of confusion. Logan had done a poor job of preparing me—again. I heaved a sigh of frustration.

"You have something to say, Audrey?"

"What? No, thanks. I mean, sorry, I'm good."

The look on Shannon's face wasn't exactly disapproving, but I wouldn't call it benevolent either. After a pregnant pause, she nodded and resumed her speech.

"Your primary objective today is simple. You are going to be doing some reconnaissance work."

Some muffled groans wafted up from the group.

"I know this is a little basic for most of you. But it's still necessary. It will also be good for those of you without much ground experience to cut your teeth on something more supervised."

I knew whom she was talking about.

"There has been some out-of-the-ordinary demon activity in the section we are sending you today. You are to split into groups and check out the area, then report back on any findings. You are intended to blend in today, which is why you aren't in your body armor for this trip."

She gave us all a hard stare. "Under no circumstances are you to engage a demon. We have angels standing by to provide extractions should anything dangerous arise, but they are positioned far enough away not to raise suspicion. I need to make sure this point is clear and understood."

We nodded obediently.

Shannon was quick to dismiss us and make her exit. That's when Logan took over, making quick work of giving us a few basic details.

We arrived in an abandoned warehouse on Earth with as little fanfare as possible. I was in the first group to be sent down and watched the other hunters arrive, shimmering into being. One moment there was empty air, the next a twinkling, and then a person appearing. I giggled. It looked remarkably like the grainy TV image of Star Trek characters being beamed all over the galaxy—so much so that it hardly seemed coincidental. But how could the creators of a TV show know anything about the afterlife?

Romona lifted her eyebrows questioningly. I shook my head, not sure she would share my amusement.

The warehouse was large, poorly lit through a few dirty windows, musty and damp. I didn't like it. Too many dark places.

Logan's small group of hunters was the last to arrive. When he solidified, he immediately scanned the area until his eyes found mine. They only held for a few seconds before he turned businesslike.

"All right, we'll split into a few groups of two to do surveillance."

I did the quick math—our group of fifteen didn't split evenly. Logan quickly rattled off the names of people who were to form groups. There was no discussion or disagreement; people just moved around to stand with their partners. That just left Logan, myself, and an extra-large hunter named Dean. Dean was easily the largest guy there. Figures; Logan didn't consider me as a real hunter yet and as such had assigned an extra babysitter. The familiar twinge of annoyance prickled inside my chest.

Romona was paired with Kevin. She looked over and offered an apologetic smile as if she knew exactly how the extra person in my group made me feel. Subpar. I schooled my features so it wasn't so obvious.

I was about to move toward Logan when an impossibly bright light appeared directly behind him. I wondered later why it didn't frighten me. Instead, my eyes remained fixed on Logan, silhouetted by the light with his hair lit up like a halo. The brightness forced my eyes shut and seared the inside of my eyelids. Then, as suddenly as the brightness appeared, it disappeared, leaving me blinking rapidly to adjust to the low light in the warehouse. Splotches danced in my vision. I pressed the heel of my palms to my eyes and rubbed to relieve the sting.

Whatever that was had been beyond conspicuous. What had happened to lying low and staying out of site?

I looked up, and standing behind Logan was the largest and most intimidating angel I'd ever seen. My eyes grew larger.

"Who is that?" I whispered in Romona's ear. I'd subconsciously moved behind her, putting a physical barrier between myself and the majestic being. I had a hard time imagining how he could ever be mistaken for a human.

The angel had the form of a man but stood at least eight feet tall. He was dressed in white linen, with a thick belt of what might have been solid gold around his waist. His body looked as hard and smooth as a yellow gem, his face glowed like lightning, his eyes were like flaming torches, and his arms and legs gleamed like polished bronze. A sword hung loosely in a scabbard attached to his belt, easily twice the length of the ones I was used to wielding. Looking at him directly caused my knees to weaken.

Romona bent her head to whisper, "He's one of the combat angels. He fights the *really* bad guys."

I shivered. "What do you mean? Aren't they all bad?"

"Some are worse than others." As we spoke in hushed tones, Logan turned to address the angel with a surprising amount of ease. I couldn't quiet the tremor running throughout my body, but Logan looked like he was chatting with an old friend. My mind buzzed with fresh questions.

"Wait, so you're telling me there are different types of demons?"

"Of course there are. Demons were angels who turned against God and were cast out of their home and down to Earth. Since there are different levels of angels, there are different types of demons as well."

"Do demons look like angels then?"

"No."

"Why not?"

"It's because of the curse. When they were thrown out of our realm and led man astray, God put a curse on them. The weight of the curse has misshapen their bodies into a reflection of their innermost being—all twisted, black, and unrecognizable. When they lost their glory and splendor, their bodies became a reminder of how far from grace they had fallen."

Romona inclined her chin toward the angel Logan was speaking to.

"He's an archangel, and he fights the warrior angels who were hurled to Earth. The ones trained in battle strategy, with the strength of numerous men. We're not equipped to take on that type of force. At least not alone. I, for one, am thankful he's around. The fallen archangels are really nasty."

"Archangels. That sounds familiar." I searched my mind. "Do you mean like Michael and stuff?"

She nodded. "But don't forget, Audrey, every demon is dangerous in its own right. Don't be deceived into thinking that one demon is more dangerous than another just because of his size. A seed of jealousy, lust, or greed planted by a sly demon can be as destructive as a tornado."

Logan called my name. I looked up sharply. He was motioning me over. I swallowed. Even with my eyes averted, I felt the heat of the mighty angel's gaze boring into me. Romona gave my arm a slight squeeze and a subtle push forward. For once, I wished the empathy link still worked on Earth. Her emotions were always encouraging.

Squaring my shoulders, I walked toward them. My mistake was letting my eyes drift to the angel's face. I had the wild urge to fall to my face before him, and I faltered a step and diverted my eyes. The warehouse had become conspicuously quiet.

Logan made the introduction. "Audrey, this is Gabriel."

I choked on nothing. My eyes widened. The angel, Gabriel, bowed deeply.

"Gabriel. Like the Gabriel who helped Daniel with his visions in the Bible?" I blurted out before I could filter myself. How in the world did I know that?

Logan appeared surprised as well. Out of the corner of my eye I caught the barely susceptible lift of his eyebrows.

The angel simply bowed again. "My lady."

My head was spinning. "Huh?"

"Audrey, Gabriel is simply showing you the respect your position warrants."

"My position?"

Logan's voice was crisp with frustration. "Yes, as a human. As a child of God."

How did that make any sense? Gabriel was a majestic creature. Who was I to be given the respect?

"Oh, well, that's not really necessary. I'm not really that important."

Logan looked upward and took a deep breath. Yep, I was definitely testing his patience. The mighty angel managed to look both dismayed and understanding at the same time.

"My lady, that is not true. You were fearfully and wonderfully made at the hand of the Creator. It is my honor to show you respect."

Even the angel's voice was imposing. When he spoke, it was as if the rush of many voices escaped his lips, each harmonizing with the next to create one perfect and powerful sound.

I was at a loss. What was so fearful or wonderful about *me*? Certainly *he* was the one that was wonderfully made. I tried to look him in the face but shied away again—it was like staring at the sun in the middle of an eclipse. Possible, but still too bright for human eyes.

"Audrey, Gabriel is here as your personal escort. You're not to go anywhere without him while we are all here."

"Are you kidding? They sent me a celestial babysitter?" I realized how insulting that sounded only after it escaped my lips. I hastily addressed the angel. "I'm really sorry, I didn't mean it that way. It's just, you know," I lowered my voice, "kind of embarrassing."

"Not at all, Little One. I assure you it is a great honor. And I'm not only here for your protection, but also to deliver a message."

"Really?"

"Yes." Gabriel looked at Logan and the rest of our group. "I ask that you go ahead of us. We will catch up shortly. I have some things that need to be said to young Audrey here. Alone."

Logan looked like he might argue, but he gave a quick nod and led everyone from the warehouse, saying they'd wait down the block. Romona was the last to exit. She gave me a warm smile over her shoulder before disappearing with the rest.

"Is it hard for you to look upon me?" the angel asked.

The question startled me. "Yes, in a way. I guess I just don't see how I can be more special than you. I'm just so . . . ordinary."

"You do not yet understand because you do not yet believe. Your faith is surely small."

Ouch. "Maybe it's small because no one has ever explained to me why any of this has happened to me," I shot back.

"Do you really think you are in a position to question God?" He said it matter-of-factly, yet his statement humbled me to my core. I hung my head.

"There is much, Little One, that God has concealed of His own wisdom and understanding and power and might. He has even hidden secrets of the universe. It is said that it is the glory of God to conceal a thing, yet to search out a matter is the glory of kings. Perhaps you are searching for the wrong thing. Perhaps you are searching for answers rather than searching for the One who has concealed the matter?"

I didn't know what to say to that. The only consistent things I'd done since the day my existence changed forever was question, demand, doubt, and deny God, but had I ever searched for him? Would that have made a difference?

The angel waited patiently for me. When I turned my face toward him again, he smiled back for a moment before going suddenly as still as a statue.

A sudden yet familiar fear knotted my stomach, and the stench branded my brain a split second before the angel pulled his sword from the scabbard and charged me. I blinked, and he leapt over my head, collided with something invisible midair, and came crashing down in a heap behind me. I spun around. The angel kicked at something solid to free himself and stood like a barrier of bronze before me. His body coiled, ready for another attack.

Darker than midnight, with burnt, blackened flesh, I had mistaken the demon for shadows, but next to the shining radiance of the angel I now distinguished its features. It snarled and snapped at the angel with a misshapen mouth full of jagged teeth. Its hands, if you could even call them that anymore, were elongated by sharp talons on the end of each fingertip. It crouched low to the ground like a rabid animal, shuffling back and forth as it panted. Dark spittle dripped from its jowls and smoked like acid as it hit the dust-covered ground.

I screamed.

19

THE FIERY SWORD

*G*abriel's head snapped toward me at the sound of my scream, and with a sickening shriek the demon plowed into the angel, catching him off guard. The sword flew out of his hand and went soaring in an arch off to the left. Angel and demon went down hard. The warehouse shook. Brittle pieces of the building's frame snapped off and fell to the floor.

Paralyzed by fear, I hadn't moved an inch. Where were Logan and the others? They had to have heard the commotion! The mighty angel needed help, and there wasn't much of that I could give.

The demon bore down on Gabriel even as he was trying to get to his feet. A swipe of the beast's tail sent them both down and rolling across the cement floor. The glow of the angel was slowly being swallowed by the shadows of the demon.

The glint of Gabriel's sword caught the corner of my eye. It lay on the ground several feet from where the supernatural forces tangled, far from where my own feet remained glued to the floor. The demon fought with its fanged teeth and jagged claws. There was little Gabriel could do without his weapon but stay on the defense. The demon knew this and was keeping its body positioned in front of the large blade.

Gabriel leapt high to overcome the mangled beast and reach his sword but was once again smashed by darkness. I yelped, eyes riveted to the scene.

My gosh, where's Logan?

Battling against my own fear, I forced my body to move, scrambling up some boxes to skirt the fight. One was viciously knocked to the floor, and the world shook beneath me. I silently thanked Logan for all the emphasis on balance during training. Otherwise, I was sure to be lying in a broken mess on the floor.

Another box was knocked away, and again I kept my balance. It was slow going, but I finally managed to place myself on the other side of the warehouse. The huge sword was almost within reach. Was I even strong enough to carry it? I forced thoughts of failure from my mind. I had to try.

The demon and angel grappled with each other on the floor, but the instant I lunged for the weapon, the demon's head snaked up and spotted me. My movements had given away my intent, and with a horrible shriek, the beast dislodged himself from the fight to advance on me.

Without a moment to think, I reached my hand out to the sword.

The creature was mere strides away, but when my hand closed around the hilt, it was as if a hundred watts of energy shot through me. The weight of the sword melted away, and it blazed like the sun. The demon cried out in shock as I arced the blade though the air with an instinct I wasn't aware I had. I smelled the demon's dark flesh burning as the fire from the sword sliced into its shoulder. It roared in anger and lunged for me again.

I fell to a knee and rolled to the left to avoid the collision. The demon crashed into some boxes but quickly regained its footing, nails scraping against the concrete before it charged me again. I was barely on my feet but still managed to slash the sword up with strength I knew I didn't possess.

The severed head of the demon rolled back and fell to the ground before its body smashed into me, knocking me to the floor. My head snapped back and cracked on hard cement. I was smothered under the creature's weight before its flesh dissolved into smoke and ash. The sword remained clutched in my hand.

The building was eerily quiet except for the buzzing in my ears. I took a long, steadying breath before pushing myself up on an elbow. There was a small audience standing in a semicircle around me. Gabriel stood on the left next to Romona, then a few of the fighters I didn't take the time to recognize as I scanned for Logan, all the way on the right. Every single one of them wore the same stunned look. My rapid breathing was loud, even to my own ears. I didn't know what to say—I could barely believe what had just happened myself. And they were all staring at me so strangely.

Finally Romona took the first steps toward me—approaching me like someone would a feral animal.

"Audrey, are you okay?"

"I think so."

I took a quick survey of my body. Everything seemed to be all right. No blood, and nothing was throbbing besides my head. The sword in my hand, still blazing with its strange fire, had shrunk to a more manageable size.

I gasped, quickly releasing the weapon. It clanged to the ground and extinguished itself. The warehouse dimmed considerably.

Romona set a comforting and gentle hand on my shoulder.

"Do you think you can get up?"

"Yeah, I think so."

She extended a hand and helped me to my feet. My head pounded furiously with the movement. Romona threw her arms around me and hugged tightly. "I've never seen anything like that."

She pulled back to look into my eyes. "Are you sure you're all right? I've never seen anyone go up against a greater demon on their own. It was . . ." her voice trailed off. I got the feeling she was more horrified than impressed. The events of the last few minutes started to sink in, and a slight tremor shook my body.

"I wasn't trying to be brave or anything. I was just trying to get the sword back to Gabriel. When that thing came at me I reacted out of self-defense."

Behind Romona, Gabriel and the other hunters stayed where they were. I don't think I fully understood the implications of my actions. Killing a demon was obviously hard, especially a greater demon, but there was a serious amount of tension in the room. Only Romona seemed impervious to it.

"I knew you were special!" she said, squeezing my shoulders.

I backed up a step and out of her grasp. "Wh-what? I was just trying to protect my butt. I didn't do anything special."

"No . . . it was the *sword*, Audrey."

"Oh, right!" I reached down to grab the Gabriel's weapon, hoping it would grow in size again once returned to the warrior. "Gabriel, I'm sorry. I know this belongs to you."

As soon as my hand closed around the hilt, it flamed back to life. I immediately dropped it again. "Sheesh! That's distracting." I looked at Gabriel for an explanation. "Does it do that a lot?"

The angel met my gaze with awe, seemingly incapable of words. This was really starting to freak me out.

"What? What's going on, guys?"

No one made a move. I looked to Logan for help. His usual stoic mask was firmly back in place. At least something was normal.

"Logan, what's going on?"

His eyes connected with mine, and although he appeared to have his feelings in check, there was emotion swirling in his eyes. Even he hesitated before speaking.

"The sword's never done that before, Audrey."

I just stared at him for a minute. "O-kay, well, sorry, I didn't do anything on purpose. What's the big deal?"

"It *is* a big deal."

"Why?" I looked around at all of them.

I didn't want it to be a big deal. I was tired of everything being a big deal!

There was another long pause before Logan continued. "Because the only other swords like that were given to the Cherubim who are guarding the gates of the Garden of Eden. God's never given a blazing sword to anyone else."

"Well, he didn't give it to me either. It's Gabriel's sword."

I bent to pick it up, and again the fire took over the instant I touched it. As I turned to Gabriel, he began to back up.

"Here, it's yours." I stretched out my arm and took another step forward.

Gabriel shook his head. "No, Little One, that weapon was obviously meant for you. It is no longer mine."

My heart in my throat, I burst out, "Well, I don't want it! You have to take it back!"

The angel bowed low.

"That sword is now yours. It is a gift from the Father. You'll gain understanding of its importance in time."

He wouldn't take it back. What was I supposed to do with it? I didn't want the thing! I stood lamely with the sword still in my outstretched hand.

Romona gently rested a hand on my shoulder.

"Come on, Audrey, we've got to get back now. We have to report what happened."

She looked up at Gabriel. "Can you take a few of us back? The rest can stay and finish."

"Of course."

He spread his wings so we had a spot to grasp. Romona was the only one who would come within a three-foot radius of me. I felt a little silly with the fiery sword in my hand, but I didn't know what other choice I had. After touching the soft angel wing, we were back in an instant.

Word spread just as quickly as it had when Logan and I escaped the demon. Except this time, rather than mobbing me, no one wanted to talk to me. Hunters gave me a wide berth and avoided my eyes as I trekked through the training center. It was bizarre.

The sword's fire had blessedly gone out the moment we returned to our realm. And it was a good thing, too, because I may have singed some of Gabriel's wing on the way back. If he noticed he didn't say, and I was too embarrassed to ask.

I'd left the sword in my room this morning in hopes the atmosphere would return to normal. Seeing the averted glances and whispers that trailed me, I knew it had not.

It was actually Logan's reaction the night before that was the most worrisome. Both of my trips to Earth thus far had been eventful. But this second trip had Logan more shaken up than the first, and that was saying something.

At dinner with Romona and a few of our friends, I spent most of the time pushing food around my plate and sneaking glances at Logan as if he were a barometer. I was around him so much I was beginning to pick up subtle changes in his guarded expression. And he looked worried—so that made me worry.

This morning I'd woken up with another stomach full of knots. As reluctant as I was, I needed to know more about that sword.

I pushed open the gym doors to find Logan staring at the weapons wall. Everything about his stance was rigid. He was running his hands over the hilts of different swords and didn't acknowledge my presence. Heading to the bench, I dropped my bag.

"You know we're going to have to step up your sword training now."

I figured that.

"At least it's not my worst skill. Fiery nunchakus would have been a problem."

He half-turned with a slight smile on his face. Fencing and swordplay did come somewhat easier to me than some of the other weapons. Unfortunately, that wasn't saying much.

"Logan, we need to talk."

"Is that so?" One eyebrow rose. The rest of his face was the same as always. Emotionless.

I crossed the distance to him in a few purposeful steps, for once able to match his serious expression. I made sure to keep our customary distance. After discovering the potential damage from our shared kiss, I was only too happy to keep the tradition going.

"You need to tell me what's going on."

His eyes roamed my face without settling. Worry crept into his eyes before he captured my own with his steely gaze.

"Would you believe me if I told you I wasn't sure?"

There was a time I wouldn't have, but now I did. "Yes."

He quietly released the air from his lungs.

"But that doesn't mean you can't tell me what you do know, or at least what you think you might know."

Logan regarded me before answering. "I suppose that's only fair."

I was slightly taken aback at the ease with which he acquiesced. I had been prepared for another battle.

He turned from me to grab a sword from the wall. It was a large, sturdy blade, probably twice the girth and length of the Cherubim sword safely tucked in my room. Studying it, he continued, "I think we should take this lesson out of the training center today. A little bit of fresh air might be good."

He turned his gaze back to me. "Let's pick that sword of yours up on the way."

Thirty minutes later I was using the already infamous sword to cut a path through the forest. Logan had picked a trail where the foliage was so incredibly dense I could hardly take a step without getting tangled. The topography resembled a jungle more than forest.

Logan navigated with ease. He only had to slash with his sword every now and then to maneuver forward, where I had to hack everything in my way to do the same. Glaring at his back, I'd just begun to grumble when I tripped on a vine. I yelped and threw my free arm out to try to catch myself. Logan did a quick turn, and I fell face-first into his chest. He tried to steady me, but instead we both went crashing into the underbrush.

I landed square on top of Logan and heard the air whoosh out of his chest when he absorbed the impact of both the ground and me. We were a tangle of arms and legs. I squirmed to get off of him and realized the offensive vine was still securely wrapped around my ankle.

Logan was a statue beneath me. My face was squished into his chest. He smelled like fresh laundry and wooded pine. I tried to roll off, but we were wedged rather tightly between thick thorny vines, roots, and underbrush. My movement only managed to get us more snared.

"Will you just give me a second?" Logan's voice rumbled in his chest.

"My gosh, Logan, I'm so sorry. I think I tripped on a vine or something, and I'm still caught. Oh no . . . I dropped the sword." I tried to swivel my head even though it was still squished to his chest. "It has to be around here somewhere."

I took my hand off his chest to brace myself on the ground and push off him. As soon as my hand connected to the ground, pain shot into my palm.

"Ouch!" I quickly yanked it back to discover I'd impaled it on a thorn. A small droplet of blood was starting to form.

"How bad is it?"

I glanced up from my hand to see Logan mere inches from my face. Or rather, I was mere inches from him. He was staring at my hand.

When I didn't answer, his eyes made their way back to my face. A physical awareness skated down my spine when our eyes locked. Despite the low light, the blue in his eyes was electrifyingly bright. My pulse picked up speed. Neither of us said anything. I licked my lips and inadvertently drew Logan's attention from my eyes. My forearms were being used to prop myself only slightly off his chest.

Logan's arms moved gently to my lower back. Then one slid up to apply the faintest amount of pressure, bringing me ever so slightly closer to him. My eyes started to slide shut as Logan's breath tickled my cheeks. I smelled peppermint, just as I remembered. Without a coherent thought in my head I leaned in closer, and then . . .

"Audrey, you need to get off of me now."

It was like being doused with a bucket full of ice water. My eyes snapped open. Logan wasn't looking at me any longer. Instead, his eyes were staring at the canopy above my head. His arms had melted from my back, or had never been there at all, and were instead pressed firmly against the forest floor. His face was hidden in the shadows.

I sucked in a quick breath of air and frantically searched for the fastest way to get off him. I pulled again at my leg and found that the vine had magically unwrapped itself from my ankle. "I just, uh, need to figure out where to put my foot." The urge to ramble bore down on me.

Please let my hair be a normal shade.

"You should be able to put one on either side of my left leg and use the saplings around us to pull yourself up." He was still staring straight up, and his voice was succinct and to the point.

"Oh right, yeah." I struggled to rock back on my feet with the least amount of physical contact possible, taking care not to knee him anywhere important. When I steadied myself on my knees, Logan wasted no time scooting out from underneath me and righting himself. In fact, he was so fast about it he was standing before I straightened myself. Taking a cue from Logan, I looked anywhere but at him.

"My sword has to be around here somewhere. I dropped it when I tripped." Something reflected the sun to my left. I took a few careful steps and located the weapon lying in a small patch of sunlight among some mushrooms.

"Whoops!" Picking it up I brushed off dirt and mushroom grime, being careful not to cut myself. "Doesn't look too much worse for the wear."

"Okay then, let's get going. We're almost there."

Logan had retrieved his sword as well and was waiting for me, facing the other direction. His pace was slower than before, and he took more care to clear a path for me.

I tried to concentrate on the cleared path rather than what had just happened, but it was difficult. What *had* just happened? Had Logan almost kissed me? Had I almost kissed him? Did I have a hallucination and then Logan got too uncomfortable with me invading his personal space? I almost wished I had brushed some of his skin to get a read on what he was thinking. Then I cringed at the thought, because it meant Logan would have picked up on my emotions as well.

I was so absorbed in my own thoughts that the break in the forest took me by surprise. I stumbled into a clearing. Everything was bathed in gold. I put my hand up to my brow and opened my eyes further, looking first at my feet. I was standing on something soft. The breath in my throat caught as I extended my gaze from the ground up.

The clearing, although not large, was covered in hundreds—perhaps thousands—of small golden flowers. They were so densely grown that it looked like a carpet of gold had been laid out for us. I inhaled the sweetest smell imaginable, the essence of everything sugary, warm, and cozy. I don't know how a smell can be cozy, but this one was. The scent filled my lungs.

I lowered my hand and took in the beauty before us. I had the urge to run into the middle and create a snow angel in the flowers. A soft breeze blew my ponytail over my shoulder, and a soothing wave of calm enveloped me.

I had a vague recollection that Logan was here somewhere, but it was barely a concern. Inexplicably, in that moment I felt loved, cherished, and protected. All feelings I craved.

Logan wasn't looking at me. He had closed his eyes and was breathing in the same air I was. "This is the place I come when I want to be alone with God." *What, God's around here somewhere?* I quickly looked around, but it was just the two of us in the field of gold. I was inexplicitly disappointed.

"Does it only work if you are by yourself? You know, being alone with God." I blushed. *Stupid question. Of course you can only be alone with God if you are actually alone.*

But Logan just smiled. "It's not like that. It's more like a still, small voice right here." He laid his hand on his chest. "And a feeling of well-being despite whatever else is happening. Getting alone and away from everything is important. Sometimes He speaks in the silence."

I let Logan's words sink in. "I think I might know what you mean."

Logan was describing what was happening to me, minus the voice in his head, or chest, or whatever. An overwhelming sense of peace settled on me even as I continued to breathe the sweet air. I wondered if it was specific to this exact place. Was there a part of God manifested in this field? Was that even possible? Was this what Gabriel meant when he talked about seeking out God?

"I think it's time we talk more about this sword." Logan broke my train of thought. I'd almost forgotten about the heavy weight in my hand. "Come on, let's sit down over here."

He walked to a small knoll and sat. He looked relaxed. It reminded me of when we were on the beach. He spread his legs out in front of him and leaned back against his arms, bending his head back to soak in the warmth. I came to a seat a few feet away and carefully laid the sword between the two of us.

Logan seemed content to sit in silence. Perhaps having a silent conversation with himself. A pleasant one, because with his eyes closed and his face raised, he smiled. Time stretched on.

I waited until I couldn't wait anymore and cleared my throat. The sense that he was having a conversation was so intense that I felt awkward barging into his thoughts.

"Okay, Audrey, I know you're still there." He languidly opened his eyes and took another deep breath before adjusting his body so that he faced me.

"So, the sword. What questions do you have?"

I almost didn't know where to start. *Why are people treating me differently now? What does the sword do? What does it mean about me? Why me?* I had to start somewhere. "Tell me more about the Cherubim."

Logan appeared relieved that I'd started with something so easy.

"Cherubim are a type of angel. Like most angels, they have wings, but they aren't as humanoid as most angels. They have many eyes and many wings. There aren't very many of them, and they protect things that are very important."

"You mentioned something about the garden of Eden before."

"Right. God placed Cherubim at the entrance of the Garden of Eden to make sure no man could enter it again while the curse was still on the world."

He'd lost me. "Huh?"

"Okay, let's start a little further back. Do you know about Adam and Eve?"

I remembered that Adam and Eve were the first man and woman and had been tempted by a serpent to eat fruit from a tree that God told them not to. Then they were thrown out of Eden, and something about being naked. I relayed as much to Logan, who laughed lightly.

"So you seem to have the nuts and bolts down. God created man to have fellowship with him. When Adam and Eve willingly disobeyed God, they allowed sin into the world. The Garden of Eden was a place where we could be in perfect communication and live with God. Since Adam and Eve opened Pandora's box, so to speak, and let sin into their lives, they weren't able to live in the garden anymore. Since we are all sons and daughters of Adam and Eve we all inherited that sin nature, so we also can't be let into the garden." He looked over at me to make sure I was following. "You still with me?"

I nodded.

"So God put his most trusted protectors, the Cherubim, at the entrance of the garden of Eden to make sure no one could enter. Cherubim also guarded the ark of the covenant." I must have had a blank look on my face then, because Logan rushed to explain. "The ark was where the Law, also called the Ten Commandments, were held. For centuries, the Lord only manifested himself to men above the ark. So it needed to be heavily protected as well. God even told the people making the ark to include Cherubim into the design so they would remember how important it was."

"Okay, so Cherubim are like God's secret service."

He chuckled. "I guess you can look at it that way."

"Okay, but what does that have to do with the sword catching fire when I touch it?"

"That takes us back to the garden of Eden. That was the only time we know of when God gave anyone a flaming sword. It was the weapon the Cherubim were given to protect the entrance to the garden."

"So what does that have to do with me?"

Logan paused for a moment before answering.

"To be honest Audrey, I'm not sure. The only thing we know for sure is that the only other flaming swords in the universe are guarding the Garden of Eden. And they are wielded by some pretty powerful angels."

"So why in the world would it start on fire when *I* touch it? I'm not an angel."

He looked at me with sadness in his eyes, this time clearly wishing he had an answer for me. "I'm really not sure, but I know it must be something important. These things don't just happen by chance. There is a purpose."

"But you're telling me you don't know what that purpose is?"

Logan shook his head.

"I'm willing to bet you have a guess."

"A guess, a theory, is not an answer."

I scooted just a tad closer, still keeping the sword between us. "I'd like to hear what you think."

"I'm not sure that would be very beneficial to you."

"Why don't you let me be the judge of that for once?"

I could see that Logan was fighting an internal battle. His jaw set when he'd made up his mind. "No. There are too many options. Too many possibilities. I can't pretend to know the heart of God. You are meant to figure this out on your own."

I wanted to explode. More riddles. More things to figure out. More things to wait on. When was I going to get any answers around here? "Seriously? You're not even going to *try* to help me figure it out? We're just going to add it to my growing pile of mysteries? One more thing that doesn't make sense in my life anymore. Or death, or whatever."

"Audrey, you know it's not like that. I am helping you. I'm giving you the knowledge you don't have. I can't tell you what it means because I don't know, but I'm trying to tell you as much as I know for sure. You need to look to God for the answers, not me, not Romona, not anyone else." Logan's voice held an exasperated edge.

He had a point, one that echoed Gabriel's sentiments as well, but I wasn't in the mood to be reasonable. It felt like another blow. Like someone was playing a game with my life and having a grand old time doing it.

I stubbornly refused to look at Logan. Part of me wanted him to be as miserable as I was at the moment. I closed my eyes and leaned back into the blanket of flowers. They tickled my forehead as they swayed in the breeze. Fabric rustled and shifted as Logan moved. A soft ringing echoed from the blade as he touched it, followed by a series of scraping sounds as he pulled the blade toward him. I honestly didn't care. He could have the thing if he wanted it.

He continued talking even though it was obvious I was trying to ignore him. "Audrey, you need to look at this like a gift rather than a curse."

I snorted. If you counted suffering, confusion, anger, and misery a gift, then sure, it was a gift.

But then some things rebelliously leaked into my consciousness. My friendship with Romona, the joy of the celebration, naming new creatures, the beauty all around me, even the sword saving me from the demon.

Neither of us spoke for several minutes. With eyes shut, I imagined Logan inspecting the weapon like he had a hundred different swords before, with great precision and care. It got me thinking about something.

"Logan?"

"Yes."

"Why do we do this?"

He paused for a few heartbeats. His voice was unexpectedly quiet. "What do you mean?"

My heart was heavy. I needed to know that we had a clear purpose. Not a hidden one we didn't know about, but a real, solid, concrete reason for what we were training to do. And I needed to know that it was good.

"Why are we called to protect people, to fight off demons, to fight off evil? What is it about us that got us chosen for this job? Why does God need us at all?"

I opened my eyes and propped myself up on an elbow to watch him. His face was a bit melancholy. Again with the weight of the world on his shoulders.

Logan put the sword carefully back down before speaking. "I think," he began, and then paused to inhale and exhale, "I think for each of us the answer to that question is different."

Too vague. I was looking for someone to make sense of things. Of at least *one* thing. I needed to be assured there was a reason we were all here.

"Do you know what the answer is for you?"

Logan closed his eyes and took a deep breath. I thought for a moment he wouldn't answer. "I assumed there would come a day when you asked me that." When he opened his eyes, he turned his head to look at me. There was a storm brewing in his blue depths. "For me, I believe it is about redemption."

What did that mean? Logan continued without my prodding, but he turned his head away to surveying the clearing as he spoke.

"I lived my life like I was out of control. There was always something new to chase. A new sensation, a new high. And I was very creative at finding new experiences. My life was lived without regard for others. It was only at the end that I realized the damage I'd caused to those who loved me and how little I'd actually given to anyone."

Logan's face, even though I was only privy to his profile, was as closed off as I'd ever seen it. His expression was a blatant contradiction to the vulnerability of his words.

I wondered if he thought revealing some of the more unsavory details of his life would make me think differently of him . . . less of him. I wondered if regret over the way he'd lived his life was what caused his pendulum to swing so far in the other direction. He was so disciplined, even rigid at times. It made sense that he might believe one extreme would balance out his sins. But there had to be another reason for the distance he kept—the wall he erected to shield himself. I was getting a glimpse, but not the full picture.

"So you're trying to work off the deeds of your life?"

"No. I know it might sound like that. Real redemption, salvation, is a gift, not a penance to be worked off. There's no way for any of us to work off our regrets. No amount of good deeds could cover the bad ones in our lives, in any of our lives. There's only one way to cover those sins, and it has nothing to do with what works we do here in eternity. But even so, my spoiled life did have an effect on me after death. I believe I was chosen for this job, this duty, because of what I was supposed to have accomplished on Earth. I believe the plan for my life was greater than what I lived out. I think I've been given the second chance to live that purpose. And to realize that no matter how many good things I do, there is only one covering for my sin."

I turned Logan's words over in my head. They forced me to look introspectively. Did my afterlife fit into any plan? Could I expect to have a great purpose? I secretly feared waking one day to be reacquainted with a person I wished had stayed forgotten. A person full of hate and ugliness. What if that reality became true? It sounded like for Logan, it had. How would that change me now?

"Logan, how long did it take you to remember?"

"Not long. I remembered my life almost right away. It was important that I remembered so soon."

"Why was that?"

"Before I died, my heart had started to change. Things were different, but by then it was too late to make a real difference. When I woke up here, I needed to remember what had happened for the change to be complete. It only furthered my desire to serve the living, to help protect them. But it's been a journey to realize where true redemption comes from. I'm still making the journey. I understand here," he pointed to his head, "but I'm still working on believing it here." He pointed to his heart.

I couldn't stop the questions from falling out of my mouth. "What changed you then?"

Logan reached down and plucked one of the small golden flowers from the ground. He brought it closer to his face to inspect it with a small smile on his lips.

"I met someone."

Something in my stomach dropped. I didn't want to hear anything about Logan's romantic relationships on Earth. Seeing him with Kaitlin was hard enough. To break the bond I needed to let go of him, but that was getting harder as we grew closer.

"It was the most important, life-altering relationship I've ever had," Logan continued, oblivious to my inner turmoil. "I was loved for being me and accepted unconditionally, even with all the black marks in my past. When I started to truly see the mess I'd made of my life, it was hard to think that anyone could love me like that. Realizing someone would accept me in that state, well, that will change a person. I only wish I'd discovered it sooner."

My heart continued to drop. How do you compete with something like that? And did I even want to? There was a physical ache in my chest I wanted to ignore.

"It was a relationship that convinced me I was worth something. That my life was worth something. That everything ugly I'd done would be forgotten and it was possible to leave my old life in the past."

A stillness hung in the air, and Logan's next words were very gentle, almost a whisper.

"Audrey, I think you know this person as well."

And that's when I knew he'd really lost it. I sharply swiveled my head to find him staring back. There was a depth to his eyes that I couldn't begin to understand.

He might have gone on, and I might have questioned him further, but instead something came crashing through the trees.

ANGELIC ENCOUNTERS

I was on my feet an instant after Kevin loudly stumbled into our clearing. He was out of breath and a bit scratched up.

"You guys gotta come quick." He paused to swallow another gulp of air. "We've been called in for duty." He looked at Logan. "Level One combat."

Logan's jaw set, and he nodded once before scooping up both our weapons. He handed me the sword. I caught Kevin taking an apprehensive look at the weapon before I sheathed it.

Logan headed for the trees without a word, and I took after him at a jog. The idea of another mission so soon sent a bolt of something through me—whether fear, apprehension, or even excitement, I wasn't sure.

"Kevin, what's going on?" I asked.

"Some sort of crisis. They called a bunch of us in to help. Some hunters have already headed down to start the attack. Or perhaps prevent one."

Logan's head swung around. "Who's down already?"

Kevin looked nervous. "Alrik and Romona. And some of the hunters from the northern region, including Kaitlin. I would have gone too, but they wanted me to find you guys first. They want us to meet up with them at the safe house as soon as possible."

"This is something we're working on with another region?"

Kevin nodded once.

At that, Logan faced forward and continued his fast trek through the foliage.

"Kevin," I tried not to let my voice carry too far, "is there something wrong with that? What's the big deal with working with another region?"

Kevin dipped his voice as well.

"It's just unusual. We have enough hunters here that we don't usually need to work together. It only happens when something big is going on."

We were through the trees and walking into the training center in record time. I bent over with my hands on my knees to catch my breath, and pinched my side where a stitch had formed. Logan went to get the details of our mission and returned almost immediately. "Kevin was right; a group of hunters has already been dispatched. We're to meet up with them on Earth to get the full rundown. We need to get into our gear and leave immediately."

He looked at me pointedly. "Make sure to bring that sword of yours."

I nodded once as my stomach flopped. He thought we were going to be in a situation where I would need it. Since one touch of the sword seemed to slice through demons like a knife through warm butter, they most likely hoped I would be an asset.

"Audrey, do you have body armor here?"

My heart dropped. "It's in my bedroom."

"Use this, then."

Logan closed his eyes in concentration, and a moment later a puddle of liquid material formed in his upturned hands. He tossed the fabric to me. I caught it midair and shook my head.

"How do you even know my size?"

Logan simply lifted his eyebrows, looked me up and down quickly, and gave me a wicked smile. After that, he turned on his heel and headed down the hallway, his own armor quickly melding to his body. I was left staring after him, speechless and flushed. If I didn't know better, I would say that had been rather flirty.

Halfway down the hall, he threw an order over his shoulder. "We'll meet you in five minutes in the gym. Get that sword strapped to your back so you don't accidentally set someone on fire."

Kevin jogged down the hall after Logan with a small smile for me. I hurried to the girl's locker room. This time I didn't stop to admire myself in front of the mirror. I only spared a moment to make sure I'd put the armor on correctly before shoving through the doors to meet Logan and Kevin.

Minutes later we were standing in an alley on Earth. I was so jumpy that my hand itched to grab the sword from its sheath on my back. I willed it to stay. I'd draw attention the moment it roared to life. Attention we were looking to avoid.

"Audrey, stay here." Logan's voice made me jump from the tension, though I wasn't tense enough to instantly comply.

"What do you mean? Why can't I go with you guys?"

"We're going to make sure the coast is clear and figure out where we're meeting the other hunters. It must be somewhere close by. You'll be safer here."

The alley dead-ended not far to the right.

"Oh come on! You've got to be kidding!"

The look he shot me said he wasn't. I changed tactics and appealed to the easier target.

"Kevin, come on, this is silly."

Kevin shifted nervously from one foot to the other, his eyes moving between the two of us. "Sorry, Audrey. Logan's your mentor, it's up to him."

I leaned against the wall. "Fine, go off and do your thing. I'll just follow after you've rounded the corner. I'm getting a little tired of the overprotective act."

Part of me meant that. Another part was scared out of my mind and secretly fearful of being left alone. I firmly put a lid on the latter emotion and concentrated on the annoyance.

Logan forced my attention. "Audrey, you know I'm not asking for permission." His voice sounded menacing. He was trying to further intimidate me by trapping me against the brick wall. I stiffened my neck. "Kevin, would you mind giving Audrey and me a minute? I'll catch up with you in a moment." He didn't take his eyes off me when he spoke.

Kevin's footsteps retreated. Logan was using his eyes to their full advantage. I was reasonably certain that this time he knew exactly what he was doing.

"Audrey, we've talked about this before, and you need to promise to do everything I say today. I can't have you challenging every order, not here, not with the reality of these stakes. We're not in the training center anymore. This isn't a game or a joke or even a battle of wills."

My throat was so dry I couldn't find my voice. Logan took a half-step forward to take hold of my shoulders. I sucked in a quick breath. He was always so careful not to touch me, so when he did, even without the empathy link, it was a shock to my system. Standing here like this in the dimly lit alley, it was very hard not to remember the last time the two of us had been in a similar location.

Logan's mind wasn't in the same place as mine.

"Audrey, do you understand what I'm saying? I need to know that you'll listen to me. That you'll get yourself to safety if I tell you to." There was an edge of desperation in Logan's voice. It was his vulnerability that finally broke through my pride.

I was only able to nod once as Logan's eyes searched my face. When they lingered on my lips a moment longer than they should have, I flushed. Perhaps he *was* remembering the same thing.

He dropped his hands. Still standing close, it seemed he wanted to say more, but with only a nod, he abruptly turned and followed Kevin out of the alley. I couldn't move until Logan had disappeared around the side of the building. I kicked an empty can out of frustration, and it ricocheted off the opposite wall loudly before bouncing to rest not far from where it had first been. Why were things with Logan always so confusing? I had an answer for that almost as quickly as I thought it. That stupid kiss. And I had a suspicion that Logan had just effectively used it to manipulate me.

When this was over, I was really going to have to figure out what to do about the bond. In the meantime, the innocent Coke can received another kick for good measure.

I wasn't sure if it bounced back to the same spot because what happened next blasted me off my feet.

The powerful bright light sent me sailing, ending with a bone-shattering butt landing. For a few horrible moments, the world was nothing more than a burst of red and yellow behind closed lids. And then with a blink, the world returned to normal, and I was on the pavement with a very sore backside. My body armor had saved me from scrapes along my hands and arms. I shook my head once to clear the fuzz.

"I seem to have startled you." The strong voice echoed off the walls of the alley and again through my head, rattling painfully even after he stopped speaking.

I put a hand to my ear before looking up to see who had spoken. My eyes widened.

Lounging against a brick wall in the single ray of sunlight that had defiantly snuck between the buildings was the most beautiful angel I'd ever seen. In fact, the most beautiful *being* I'd ever seen.

His skin, smooth like polished stone, sparkled in the light, reflecting a myriad of colors. He wasn't looking at me, but was instead inspecting a speck on the knife he held. He turned it this way and that, letting the sunlight glance off the weapon as he moved it, blinding me occasionally. I was truly stunned speechless.

Without looking up, he addressed me again.

"You seem to have lost your way." It was an observation, not a question.

"Ah, not exactly."

"Is that so?" Still looking at the knife, he arched a brow.

"I was just waiting. Is there something I can do for you?"

That seemed to amuse the angel. He smiled.

"Perhaps. But it's a little too soon for that."

His words befuddled me. Something in his voice caused the thoughts in my head to jumble whenever he spoke—like talking in a dream, where things made sense without making sense. Something inside nagged at me that I should do something, but I only sat and stared.

The angel continued, almost as if he was speaking to himself.

"It is strange he would pick one such as yourself. Burdened by weakness and easily controlled by your passions. I would have thought a bigger challenge was in store, but it appears that is not the case. Disappointing even."

His words cut sharp and deep. Just like the knife in his hand was capable of doing.

"I suppose if he really cared, he'd have picked a more worthy opponent—

but then again, he has always enjoyed sending a sheep to the slaughter."

The words became like ice in my gut as I struggled to understand the angel's strange musings. Struggled to do anything but sit there and stare.

"Nevertheless, it is what it is, so I suppose we shall play another round."

The angel heaved a sigh. Was he bored? Frustrated?

"So what is it exactly that you have there?"

Without my permission, my hand inched toward my sword. My fingers were just about to wrap around the hilt when a flash of white and gold landed in front of me, shaking the ground.

Gabriel.

His appearance halted my hand. He stood between me and the other angel, who hadn't even looked up at the intrusion.

"What do you want?" Gabriel's words, booming in my ears, were surprisingly harsh.

"Nothing, dear *brother*. It was just a bout of curiosity. It appears to have been a waste of my time."

"I doubt it was only that."

The angel shrugged—he didn't care what Gabriel thought. He was still fixated on that knife, casually turning it over in his hands again and again.

"This one is under my protection for now." Gabriel took another step to shield me with his body.

"Hmmm, for *now*, you say. I was once a guardian myself. I wonder how long you will be in the position."

Gabriel began to glow. His hands clenched into fists and heat radiated off him, growing hotter every moment. Sweat started to trickle down the back of my neck.

"It would be good of you to remember whose domain you are in now, brother," the angel said.

"It would be good of you to remember how long that will remain true," Gabriel retorted.

A small clench of the jaw was the only thing that gave away the mysterious angel's anger. He covered it quickly with a slow smile as he shrugged again. "Perhaps."

Finally sheathing the knife in a holster on his belt, he turned in my direction. I gasped. Where his eyes should have been, there were none. Instead was just blackness, a fathomless abyss. Even with no eyes, I knew he was staring straight at me, perhaps straight into my soul—the real me who I didn't even know. Enthralled as well as repulsed, I had the sensation of falling into empty space before he broke eye contact to stretch his arms above his head. A pair of wings, made of shadows that spanned the height of a man in either direction, unfurled from behind him.

"There are more pressing matters to attend. Enjoy your babysitting while it lasts."

With a fluid motion, he coiled his body and leapt into the sky, dark wings barely flapping as he shot straight into the air. A strange, faded shadow trailed behind him as if tethering him to the earth. I craned my neck, watching him until he was barely a speck.

I was still sitting on the ground when the archangel turned to me.

"Who was that?" I asked, finally able to find my voice.

"He goes by several names," he replied wearily.

"Care to try one out on me?"

"He comes as the angel of light he once was, but now he is Abaddon."

"Huh?"

"Destruction."

I lifted my eyebrows. Scary, but I'd never heard that name before. "How about if you try out a few more on me?"

Gabriel said them like curses. "Accuser, Adversary, Deceiver, Leviathan, King of Babylon."

I swallowed. "Those all sound pretty bad. How is he still an angel then?"

"I said that he *comes* as an angel of light, not that he is one."

"I'm missing something ridiculously obvious, aren't I?"

The angel nodded his head.

"I think the name she knows him by is Satan."

I jerked my body around to see Logan walking briskly up the alley.

"Did you just say what I think you did?"

"Yes."

"Oh my gosh! Oh my gosh!" I started to hyperventilate, "You guys left me alone in an alley with the devil! Are you insane?" I stumble-crawled to my feet. "And what the heck is he doing looking all angelic? Well, except for his crazy wings and missing eyes. Shouldn't he be all shriveled and black with red pointy horns or something?" I used my hands atop my head to demonstrate the horn and skewed my face into a snarl. I was all over the place.

"Well that's obviously a misguided stereotype," Logan answered.

I stared at him incredulously. "You left me alone . . . in an alley . . . with the devil!" I punched his arm for emphasis. He only gave the spot a passing glance, but hurt flashed across his face and I knew it wasn't from the punch. It was gone when he looked up.

"Yes, and now you've lived to tell another tale."

"You're making a joke out of this?"

"No."

I let out a perturbed huff.

"Listen, I know we're supposed to be getting along better and that I should be following your lead, but I hope you realize the next time you try to leave me alone in a dark alley, or dark warehouse, or—"

"Gabriel was with you in the warehouse," Logan interrupted.

"Or dark wherever," I continued, "I'm *so* not having it!"

Gabriel interrupted our argument as if we hadn't had it at all.

"Satan is the great deceiver. He can appear in a number of different forms.

For whatever reason, that was the form he wanted you to see. Do not be tricked into thinking his true form is anything more beautiful than any other demon. His is the most misshaped and deformed of all. He simply does a better job of covering that up."

"Have you ever seen him before?" I addressed Logan after the span of a few heartbeats.

A muscle in his jaw moved. "Yes."

"Is that normal? Do all new hunters get a special visit from him? Like a 'welcome to the club, lookin' forward to sending my evil minions after you' type of thing?" I was more than half-serious.

There was a long pause before Logan continued. "No. Unlike God, he is not omnipresent. Meaning he can only be in one place at a time. He has a lot of ground to cover, which means he's generally not concerned with a few hunters here and there. He usually leaves us to his demons."

"So what does it mean that he sought me out?" There was a touch of desperation in my voice.

"Perhaps nothing to be concerned about, but regardless, we'll have to deal with this particular issue later. You're going to have to try to put it out of your mind for now. We have a job to do today," Logan answered.

"Right, like this is going to be an easy thing to forget."

Logan rolled his eyes. I looked back at the spot the fallen angel had been only moments before and shivered when I considered what might have happened if Gabriel hadn't appeared. I shared as much.

"He could not have touched you." Gabriel answered, his voice booming with authority. "He uses words and manipulation to lead people astray. He personally could not have physically harmed you. Not without permission. That is part of his sentence."

"Permission? Permission from whom?" I asked.

"God."

Permission from God to hurt me? What?

"What was his interaction with you before I arrived?" Gabriel inquired.

I explained as much of the conversation as I remembered. Already some of the details were muddled. When I finished, the looks on their faces weren't comforting. To someone who didn't know him better, Logan's expression might have passed for indifferent, but there was a hardness in his eyes that scared me. The silence stretched.

"Will somebody please say something?"

Gabriel's attitude changed immediately. "Let's get you to the safe house, Little One. Logan's right, we'll have to deal with this later."

Logan's posture hadn't changed, and that had me profoundly concerned. He turned his face toward the spot where the dark angel had stood. I took a step closer and laid a hand on his forearm. He looked down at my touch and then up at me. I willed myself not to be intimidated.

"Logan, what is it?" Something very real, very strange, was going on with

Logan. As if he was drowning in his own mind. What was happening?

The angel looked on in silence.

I slowly moved my hand down his arm and twined my fingers with his stiff ones, all the while returning his stare, and gave his hand a squeeze, hoping to give him something substantial to grasp, even if it was physical rather than mental. His gloved hand was warm and his pulse pounded rapidly.

"Logan," I whispered.

A barely discernable shudder ran through Logan's body, and when it reached our joined hands, it was as if a bolt of electricity burned through me. It was so sudden and sharp that I gasped and jumped back, releasing Logan's hand. Logan remained rooted in place, but the look on his face confirmed that he'd felt the electricity too. His eyes were wide with surprise.

"Did I hurt you?" He took a step forward, and out of reflex I flinched away, holding my hand protectively against my chest.

"What was that?" I accused.

The steel flooded back into Logan's schooled features.

"What was what?"

"You've got to be kidding me, right?"

"I just squeezed your hand too tight. I'd forgotten you were holding it." It was a lie—we both knew it.

"We need to leave now." Gabriel's commanding voice ended our standoff. Logan's attention jerked toward the angel. He probably welcomed the interruption.

Did he truly think that would be the end of it? Whatever had happened in that moment was not normal, and in the aftermath, Logan's unveiled expression had proven he knew that as well. I wasn't about to pretend nothing had happened. But I did agree with Gabriel: we needed to get going. Being out in the open gave me the willies.

I paused beside Logan. "We *will* talk about this later," I said. There were a lot of other things we should have talked about that we'd buried instead. I was finally ready to get my big-girl panties on and dive into everything, no matter how uncomfortable.

I let Gabriel and Logan usher me out of the alley, Gabriel in the lead and Logan protecting my back. We met up with Kevin at the mouth of the alley.

"Man, what was keeping you guys?"

He didn't look mad, only jumpy—probably anxious to meet up with the other hunters. The only reason he wasn't already with them was that he'd been sent to find us first. What plans were moving forward without us?

Kevin absorbed the serious looks on our faces but didn't press for an answer. I didn't relish the notion of rehashing the past thirty minutes with anyone. Too much had happened. And it would only give people another reason to stare at the strange girl hunter.

We started forward in silence.

21

THE GAME PLAN

*G*etting to the safe house was taking a lot longer than I expected. Without another option, we set off on foot. Our drop-in point had been on the opposite side of town. Kevin explained that everyone dropped in at different sites around town so we wouldn't give away the location of the safe house. Hunters were arriving in intervals so as not to be overtly obvious that we were traveling to the same place. We were taking a roundabout way to be extra careful not to be followed.

After meeting the devil, that last point only made me more paranoid. Convinced there were hidden eyes tracking our progress, I twisted my head side to side, sure I would see a shape stalking us from the shadows, only to end up searching the darkness in vain. There was a solid chance it was only nerves, but something felt off.

No one spoke as we walked through mostly deserted streets and alleys. Logan's shoulders were tense as he carried his sword free of the scabbard. Kevin and Gabriel followed behind Logan and on either side of me. A nervous giggle threatened to bubble up at the thought of having two dead and one celestial bodyguard. This was silly because sometime today we were going to be in a battle. A battle where I was going to be a fighter, not a ward.

While I was busy searching every shadow, I somehow missed the turn we took to the residential part of town. We passed modest but well-kept homes with green lawns and flowerboxes. We passed groups of kids coloring with chalk on driveways or playing in sprinklers on the front lawn, laughing and squealing. Even though leaves were beginning to turn red and gold, people were taking advantage of the warm day.

Something about the neighborhood felt inviting and slowly began to soothe my anxiety. A quick look at my companions showed I was the only one affected by the ambiance. Gabriel, Logan, and Kevin were all still on high alert. Muscles tense, eyes surveying the area with single-minded focus.

Growing more relaxed, I slipped into daydreaming. Popsicles and bike rides . . . the feeling of jumping into cool water on a hot, humid day and warm breezes ruffling my hair. With a start I realized these were memories and tried to hold on to them, but they were elusive. I groaned quietly. Logan cocked his head slightly to address me. "We're almost there now. The safe house is just up ahead."

"Oh, that's not what I . . ."

The explanation died on my lips. The house we were headed toward looked like it was hosting a party and had invited every demon hunter in the region. A two-story white house at the end of a cul-de-sac, it had blue shutters and a plantation-style wraparound porch. The sun, which was high in the sky by now, gleamed off the metallic body armor of the hunters and bronzed bodies of angels.

"Try not to stare," Kevin whispered. "If anything's following us, you don't want it to guess where we're going."

"Are you kidding? How could I not?" I hissed back at him. "Besides, they're just hanging out there in broad daylight."

"Demons can't see them. It's a safe house, remember? Once we walk over the border of the property, we'll be invisible to them as well."

"You think we're being followed?" I scanned the area frantically, my fear renewed.

"No, but we want to be careful."

"Why is it that they can't see us when we cross the border?"

Kevin, focused on the territory behind us, barely registered my question. "It's because the house and its property are cloaked in the prayers of the residents."

"I'm not following you."

"Shhhhh." A sharp command from Logan.

I scowled at his back. We *were* being quiet. I shot Kevin an apologetic look. He looked slightly dejected and moved far enough away that I couldn't rope him into another conversation.

Logan wasn't leading us directly to the house. Instead he guided us to a neighbor's backyard, and we weaved our way under the cover of the trees. A few houses away, he stopped.

"You think we're clear?" he asked Gabriel.

Gabriel nodded solemnly. "Okay, you two," speaking to Kevin and me, "we're going to take it at a run from here. Try to keep yourselves hidden in the tree cover. Got it?"

He looked at Kevin, who gave a short nod, before turning his blue stare on me. We were so close to the safe house that the high drama for these last few feet seemed seriously overplayed. Logan knew me well enough to interpret the look on my face.

"I'm serious, Audrey. If we *are* being followed, it's in this last leg that they'll attack."

"If everyone is invisible, then a demon doesn't know where the last few feet *are*." Pleased with my logic, I gave Logan a self-satisfied smile.

"That's assuming they haven't already figured out where we are congregating. They could have spotted another group entering and are waiting for the next one."

"Oh." I sighed. "I'll follow your lead."

Logan pressed his lips together, then turned and took off in a dead run.

Unable to keep a short exclamation from escaping my lips at his sudden departure, I scrambled to follow. Kevin and Gabriel, acting as guards, matched my pace.

The backyard was even more packed than the front. No one seemed particularly concerned about three hunters and an angel sprinting toward them. In a matter of moments we were there. Logan stopped short just past the boundary line. I collided with him.

"Oof!" The wind knocked out of me, and I landed on the soft grass. Logan merely took a step forward to steady himself.

"Oh jeez." I lay there for a moment while the world came back into focus. "You gotta warn a girl if you're going to put the brakes on that quickly."

Logan looked down on me. I spied the amused glint in his eye.

"You need to be more aware of your surroundings. A demon won't give you the heads-up."

"Thank you, Obi-Wan Kenobi, for another enlightening Jedi pep talk."

"You're comparing me to a Jedi master?" He appeared to like that idea.

I pushed myself to my elbows and then to my feet. "Boys."

"There you guys are."

The look on Romona's face was serious.

"Yeah, sorry," Logan answered cautiously. "We had a little incident that held us up."

Romona looked troubled, glancing between the two of us. Logan wasn't aware that Romona knew about our little bonding issue, so he couldn't read her face correctly, but I did. I needed to stop her line of questioning. We didn't need any more spikes in the awkward factor.

"Romona, can we chat for a minute . . . like alone?"

"Sure." She gave me a puzzled look, then turned toward the guys. "They're meeting about strategy in the front yard. Once you're briefed you can fill in Audrey after we, ah, chat."

We waited for the guys to leave. "So, out with it," Romona said with her hands planted on her hips. "What was the *distraction* Logan was talking about?"

"Not what you think it is."

She raised her eyebrows in interest.

"We kind of got interrupted when we arrived."

She nodded for me to go on. I worried the truth would freak her out. Besides, how exactly do you tell someone you met the prince of darkness himself and for reasons unknown, he's taken a personal interest in you? I tried to stop, but the words popped out anyway.

"Logan left me alone in an alley with the devil." I clapped my hands to my mouth.

As soon as "devil" left my mouth, Romona's features blanked. I expected gasps or a female overreaction. But nothing. When she spoke, it was as if to herself.

"I suppose I should have expected something like this to happen. I don't know why I didn't. What have I done?" The last question was barely a whisper. Her eyes stared through me. Instead of freaking out, she was freaking me out.

"Romona, what are you talking about?"

"Nothing, I'm sorry, just forget it. Are you okay? What'd he want?" Her face transformed into that of a concerned friend. Why was everyone reacting so peculiarly? First Logan, now Romona.

Before I could answer, someone hollered my name. "Yo, Audrey!"

I turned my head. "Kevin, I'm right here."

He jogged over to us. "Hey, hate to interrupt, but Logan needs to talk to you."

I sighed. "Okay then, well I'd better find him." Before I turned to leave, Romona gently caught me by the arm.

"You will tell me about it later though, right?" There was genuine concern in her eyes.

"Sure. How about after we get this craziness settled?"

She nodded and released my arm.

I shoved my way through the multitude in search of my mentor before spotting him in a corner of the yard by himself. When I reached him, there was a serious intensity to his stare. His casual stance against the tree was at odds with his face. His eyes held strange fire in them. Logan regarded me silently for a few more seconds than necessary. I wondered what was turning through his brain. He shoved away from the tree, eyes never leaving mine.

"What we're dealing with today is serious."

I fought the desire to roll my eyes and say, "No duh!"

"A boy has brought a gun into his school. There's already a battle going on between the angels and demons, but the angels have been unable to get into the school. The angels don't want any more demons in the school to feed the panic or hysteria, and the demons don't want any angels around to stop the massacre. We're going to distract the demons so we can infiltrate the school. The hunters will be able to slip into the school easier than the angels. We don't have the same power, so the hope is the demons will stay occupied with battling the angels. We're assigned to find and fight the demon that's influencing the boy. The hunters stationed outside the school will be acting to divert the demons' attention so the angels can fight them more effectively. Hopefully a few angels will be able to slip in with us. With their addiction to hunters' emotions, we'll be very distracting to the demons."

The magnitude of the situation pressed heavily on my chest. I couldn't begin to imagine the horror that awaited us. Logan took my silence as a cue to continue.

"The demon's been influencing the boy for a long time. Years perhaps. Our goal is to free the boy of the demon and to protect as many of the students and teachers in the school as possible. And if the boy is resolute about his path after the demon's detached, then we're going to try to minimize the damage until the authorities can take over."

"What do you mean if the boy is resolute? Won't the crisis be over after we get the demon? Won't the boy just stop? Surely it's the demon making him do this."

Logan shook his head. "That's not how it works. The demon can't make him do anything. He's been guiding the boy with lies and deceit, but the boy made a choice. He chose to bring a gun into school with him with his own free will. We're just hoping that if we can stop the influence of the demon, the boy's mind will be clear enough to make the right choice in the end. The demons have surrounded the school to keep us away from him. They know that free of the demon's influence, there's a chance a major tragedy can be stopped."

This was a lot to wrap my brain around. "But why weren't we just sent to the boy sooner? Why wait until it's escalated this much?"

"I can't answer that for you, Audrey. I don't know the answers to everything; I'm not God. Perhaps the boy never asked for help, perhaps we tried and he turned it down."

"But if God knew this would happen, why would He let it?"

"He's sending us now. Without us it would be a massacre."

I wasn't convinced. "Even if no one is hurt, this kid's life is going to be over after today. The minute he whips out that gun, his life is never going to be normal again."

"You don't know that."

"What do you mean I don't know that? Of course I do! Do you know how serious it is to bring a gun into school? Without even causing a single injury, that kid is never going to have a normal life. How could God turn a blind eye to that?"

"Audrey, you're not listening to me. God's not turning a blind eye. He knows the full picture. We don't. Yes, we have to live with the consequences of our decisions, but there's always hope. There is always the chance to turn things around. I can attest to that as well as any of us."

That shut me up. Our conversation in the meadow flashed through my mind. I think Logan was talking just as much about his life on Earth as his new beginning in the afterlife.

Logan took advantage of my silence, getting more heated himself.

"Life is so much bigger than what we see of it. And yeah, bad stuff does happen here, and that's because people aren't perfect. That kid is making a choice today. That is what we've always had—free will. God uses all situations for good in the end, but we have the freedom to royally screw up. In fact, sometimes it's those screw-ups that lead us back to God. So no, I can't explain to you the whys of today. I can only say that I trust that God's got a much better handle on this situation than you are giving Him credit for."

The last comment felt like a slap on the face, and I flinched when he said it. His words definitely left a mark, but on my heart, not my cheek. It all came down to trust. Why was I having such a hard time trusting God? The answer came to me quickly. Because it was a hard thing to do. It was hard to trust a God when I didn't have any proof of His trustworthiness. I stared at Logan in silence, not sure if he was aware of the battle raging inside of me.

"Okay, it sounds like we should get going then." I started to turn when Logan grabbed my arm, halting my movement.

"That's not all I wanted to talk to you about."

I averted my eyes.

"I want your word that you won't do anything without asking me first, and when I say something, you'll do it immediately and without question."

"Haven't we already had this conversation?" I asked in defeat.

"Audrey, I am beyond serious about this. The moment I have an inkling you aren't going to listen to me, I'll pull you out, do you understand me? I'll personally drag you out by your purple hair if I have to. Because if you can't agree to these terms, we can end this right now. I'll leave you tied to this tree."

His words were firm and harsh, but his eyes pleaded, almost as if he was scared . . . scared for me. This wasn't serious Logan who always had to get his way—this was another Logan all together. What I read in his eyes that hadn't passed his lips was that he would do anything to keep me safe. This was a Logan I couldn't refuse.

"Yes. I understand. You have my word."

"Thank you."

I nodded my head, eyes still averted. I was suddenly ashamed that he had to work so hard to garner my cooperation. Was I being difficult just for the sake of being difficult? If that were true, the frustration and fatigue in Logan's eyes made that much more sense. I was going to do better, to be better!

I took a deep breath and told myself to hold it together. I just needed to get through this day. One step at a time. There was a boy and a school full of kids that needed our help. Everything else could be dealt with later.

22

TO BATTLE

*A*s we approached the school, what at first appeared to be a low-hanging lightning cloud quickly proved to be something else. A myriad of angels and demons flew through the air, locked in combat. The enormous swarm of bodies was so dense that not even a ray of sunlight penetrated. The mass moved as if a single being rather than a mixture of opposing forces. Its energy was palpable, pulsating and wafting over the school campus.

Yet the creepiest part wasn't what my eyes were seeing, but rather what my ears *weren't* hearing. It was as if someone had pushed a cosmic mute button on the battle raging in the sky. Noisy cars drove on the road, students laughed and chatted in between periods, and even the wind rushed by my ears, but not a single sound from the conflict above. It made everything that much more surreal.

I looked to the hunters on my left and right to gauge their reactions. Determination was etched on each of their faces. Romona's face, usually soft and kind, was hard with concentration. Logan's customary stoic mask was sterner. Even Alrik, whom I'd yet to see attack any situation without an air of humor, looked resolute. Only I broke form—less stern and more bewildered.

"They're keeping each other out." Romona reiterated what Logan had told me.

"Why can we see the fight but not hear it?"

"We're being protected. The sound of that battle is more horrific than you can imagine. An angel is casting a protective shield. Once a demon breaks the barrier, we'll be able to hear plenty."

If the sound I'd heard coming from that one demon in the warehouse with Gabriel could be multiplied by a hundred or a thousand, my guess was we'd all be incapacitated in a very short time by the sound.

"So what are we waiting for?" I asked.

"Them to attack us," she answered.

I remembered the part about the demon's addiction to emotions. The thought that demons would attack us to get a fix was just plain scary. Some of us were essentially going to be demon bait.

"Why? Why don't we just slip into the school now while they aren't looking?"

"We need a few angels to be freed up first to help with transporting us back." She seemed reluctant to go on but did after a short pause. "For those of us who get seriously hurt and need to get back for medical attention quickly. We can't move forward until we know there are at least a few angels on hand for our wounded."

Romona turned to face me fully. Her eyes remained hard and serious.

"Audrey, please do your best to stay with Logan. You need to do exactly what he says. I can't stress how important that is." She was pleading with me, much like Logan had.

"Romona, is there something specific I should know about this mission?"

Her stillness confirmed my suspicions.

"What is it? Why am I here?"

"This is a serious fight, and they wouldn't usually allow someone as new as you to be here. But for some reason they have. I don't like it. I do know that . . ."

She was cut off by an unwelcome sound. The high-pitched shrill of a demon. I looked up as the "unsmell" burrowed into my brain. One of the beasts had broken away from the pack and was diving at an angle straight for us.

Before I knew what was happening, Logan had shoved me behind him. I was about to object when I remembered my promise. Even with the demon coming straight at us, the horde of hunters surrounding me made me feel safe.

The closer the demon got, the larger it appeared to be. Its wingspan alone must have been the length of two humans, its body the width of a large tree. Its flesh was the consistency of blackened bark.

The hunters around me held their ground, eyes glued to the shrieking beast. In mere seconds the demon would be on top of us. I started to shout a warning when a sharp command came from the ranks, and quicker than I could process, a line of hunters pulled bows from their backs, aimed, and fired arrows that crackled like fireworks as they sailed through the air.

The demon tried in vain to change its course, its wings flapping furiously as the first volley of arrows connected with their target. I covered my ears against its scream. Black ooze poured from the wounds and melted into shadows, but even so it still came at us. A second command was yelled, and another round of arrows shot into the free-falling beast.

Spurred by a sudden bad feeling in my gut, I glanced behind us. The other hunters' attention was so drawn to the injured demon that they had missed the silent approach of one from behind.

Instinctively, I grabbed the knife from the sheath at my thigh and threw it at the demon, yelling a warning to the hunters around me. The blade connected with the target, imbedding itself in the creature's blackened flesh. A number of quickly drawn arrows swiftly joined my knife. The crowd of hunters parted where the demon crashed to the ground.

On the other side, the first demon was still fighting a group of hunters on the ground. Even wounded, it was far from defeated. The creature had two tails of reflecting scales that went invisible at times, wreaking havoc on the hunters working to take it down. My body was moving even before I'd made up my mind to help. On the third step, someone jerked me off my feet.

"NO!"

I went limp. Fighting off Logan wasn't going to leave me much energy for much else. And again, there was that promise. Logan released his hold.

"We're headed over there." He pointed to the side of the school. "We're going around the building to slip in the side door. There's still time to catch the boy before he does something stupid."

I didn't bother with words, just nodded my understanding. Logan took off without looking back, trusting for once that I would follow.

I made the mistake of looking up as we made our break for the side entrance. More demons had broken off from the cluster and were headed toward the group of hunters we'd just broken away from. Including Romona. A few angels swooped down in a failed attempt to intercept them.

The pressure in my head built with every demon that broke through the barrier. I stumbled but caught myself before I fell. Logan disappeared around the corner. Focused on catching up, I sprinted to the point where he'd vanished.

I rounded the corner without any intention of slowing down, and the next thing I knew my stomach collided with a metal bat—or at least, that's how it felt when the tail of a demon swatted me in the midsection and threw me into the air. I landed on a soft patch of grass. I blinked to clear the stars and gasped for breath. My fear compounded as the demon approached, reaching near-hysteria levels as I coughed and hacked and struggled to get to my feet. Just behind the demon, I caught sight of Logan's shocked face as he ran back toward us. The demon must have dropped between us when we separated.

It felt as if I was drowning with air all around me. I still couldn't get in a breath, and my vision was starting to blur. I got to one knee and willed myself to get up. Logan wasn't going to get here in time. I was going to have to fight off the demon myself, and I could barely even get to my feet.

The demon shrieked and jumped for me. I dropped back to the ground and freed my blazing sword to defend myself. It was going to take me down with a fiery sword in its gut.

I could almost feel the tearing of the creature's claws when a blur of light slammed into it from behind and sent it sailing over me. Finally able to take in a breath, I scrambled to my feet to see Gabriel take down the demon with one mighty blow, severing its body with a downward sweep of his sword.

Someone grabbed my shoulders and roughly turned me around.

"Are you okay?" Logan's face was strained.

"Yeah," I croaked, and then bent over to cough before going on, "I'm okay. I just got the wind knocked out of me."

"Logan, get her out of here."

We turned our heads toward Gabriel, who gave Logan a stern look and waited for him to nod back before shooting into the air.

"You need to stay closer to me."

"No kidding."

"Audrey, I'm not joking."

"Neither am I."

It must have been the scared-to-death look in my eyes that convinced him. He nodded once. "Okay. Are you sure you can keep going?"

I wanted to say yes, but I had a suspicion if I opened my mouth that's not what would have come out. I just nodded. This time when he turned toward the school, he kept my hand firmly in his.

I was breathless with exertion and adrenaline when we burst through the side doors. A half-dozen other hunters were already there, scanning the empty hallways. It must have been in the middle of a period.

Logan dropped my hand the moment we crossed over the threshold. "How much time do we have?"

A large guy with fire-red hair and a full red beard answered him back. "Not much. We're running on borrowed time. If we don't find the boy soon, there'll be a riot on our hands." Logan's mouth was pressed into a straight line. "We have a scout team already moving through the school. We were getting ready to sweep this wing." The red-headed guy paused for a moment and looked straight at me.

"Is this the new one? The one we've heard about?"

"Yes," Logan answered.

Big Red nodded back, eyes burning a hole in my forehead.

"You can come with us. But put out that fire for now. I don't want any of my team singed."

The sword.

I'd almost forgotten it was still blazing. I sheathed it quickly as Big Red waved his team forward. The sounds from outside were getting louder. We jogged past classrooms full of people completely ignorant of the commotion outside. Angels, demons, and hunters battled outside the windows of the classrooms, yet the students inside were completely unaware—taking notes, whispering when they didn't think the teacher was looking, even cheating on tests. One part of my mind was focused on keeping up with the other hunters, but there was another detached half that was with the students of this school.

I wondered if this was what my life had been like. What did it feel like to sit in a classroom? To have friends to pass notes to? What subjects had I liked and disliked? Did I have many friends—a boyfriend? Did I play sports? An instrument? As inopportune a moment as it was, I couldn't stop question after question from assaulting my brain.

I didn't realize how unfocused I'd become until Logan had to call my name twice to get my attention.

My face must have reflected my guilt. There were more important things going on right now. Logan narrowed his eyes, suspicion forming. He opened his mouth to say something when the first gunshot rang out.

23

A SINGLE JAR OF PICKLES

*A*n eerie silence followed that first shot. The noise ricocheted off the locker-lined halls as all eight of us stood still. On the second shot, all hell broke loose.

Screams started from down the hall—human screams and the pounding of footsteps as a stampede headed our way. Within moments, we were mobbed by a sea of bodies that divided like the Red Sea when it hit our knot of hunters. The hysterics caused people to push into us, but most ended up falling, which caused others to stumble on their fellow classmates and teachers.

"Split up!" shouted Big Red. And we did.

Hunters dispersed into the crowd and worked their way against the current. Most stayed toward the sides to help the flow and prevent any further accidents. But I was still frozen in the middle of the hallway with people funneling around and right into me. My brain told my feet to move. But the shock that we'd been too late, that a shot had been fired, that this was actually happening, was too much.

It was the quietest of whimpers that broke my daze. A girl huddled on the linoleum floor to my right. She lay on her side with knees drawn to her chest and her arms wrapped around her head.

And she was being trampled. Someone stepped on her leg in their haste. She screamed out in fear or pain, maybe both. My feet finally in action, I ran the short distance, determined to throw myself on top of her if necessary to keep her safe.

I was only a half-step away when I was pulled off my feet from behind.

"Let me go! She's hurt!"

"No, Audrey, that's not why we're here."

I struggled futilely against Logan. "But she's hurt. They're *stepping* on her!"

As I said it, another person tripped on her, this time kicking her in the head. I heard her muffled sobs. She was too scared or too hurt to get up and move on. I understood. I struggled more furiously against Logan.

"Let me go!"

Logan only tightened his hold, restraining me within arms of steel. I struck out blindly and scratched his cheek with my nails, drawing blood.

"Audrey, stop, look!" He shook me once, hard. Down the hallway, an angel soared above the crowd toward us.

"We're not here to protect them, but *they* are. She'll be fine." I stopped struggling even as the angel settled over the girl, spreading its wings above her.

"If we want to stay in this fight, we've got to go." Logan's voice was even, but there was urgency beneath the calm.

Logan was difficult to keep up with. Even though theoretically I could have run forward unhindered, I couldn't stop the reflex to dodge people, and I kept ramming myself into the walls to avoid them. Whenever I glanced forward, Logan seemed further away. I rushed to catch up, but it was slow going.

An all-too-familiar screech rang out, higher-pitched and louder than what was coming from the scared kids around us. And then, in front of us, a hunter was thrown through the air and collided with a locker. He hit it with a dull thud and slumped to the ground. A few more hunters rushed to his aid. Logan stopped to assess the scene. My heart rate picked up. The boy and his demon were just around the corner.

"Get out of here, Lyons!" a strained voice shouted.

"Man, you don't have to do this."

Someone was trying to reason with the shooter. Someone young.

The only people around me were hunters. I hoped that was because all the teachers and students had made it out of the school unharmed. That is, except for the two boys around the corner. The two I could hear but not yet see.

"I mean it, you're not like them, but I'm warning you, that doesn't mean I won't do it," the shooter's voice said.

It was silent for a moment. The tension froze my forward momentum.

A loud bang reverberated down the passage, filling my ears and searing into my heart.

I started violently at the sound of the shot.

"I said get out of here!" screamed the shooter.

My heart beat wildly. Was there going to be a dead boy around the next turn? Would I be able to deal with that?

Not waiting any longer, Logan rounded the corner not more than twenty feet in front of me. I started to follow but heard the skidding footsteps too late and collided with someone at the bend in the hallway. I stumbled back at the force. A boy lay at my feet, knocked on his back by the collision.

He cast hasty looks around as he frantically scrambled back up, and for a split second, he glanced up and looked right at me. I blinked and the moment passed—and so did he. The boy who had been talking to the shooter. He was okay.

But on the heels of that thought, I fell straight to my knees in the middle of the hall, in the middle of the chase. It was all there in an instant.

Every memory from my life, back where it always should have been.

I remembered my parents, Judy and Dean. I remembered my siblings. My sisters Jessica and Lainie, and my little brother, James. James Lyons.

The same little brother who had just rushed by to get away from the gunfire I was running toward.

The same precious little brother I'd stepped in front of and pushed out of the way of the car.

I put my hands on my ears and pressed down, hoping to block out some of the memories that were flashing through my mind.

It was too painful, too hurtful to remember now.

I wasn't ready, wasn't prepared to deal with them.

This timing was all wrong.

I cried out in anguish, and it sounded as if my voice came from somewhere far away.

I had something to do, I knew I did, but my mind couldn't push past the memories of all I'd lost.

I may have heard my name being shouted, but it barely registered.

I remembered the pickles again.

Those stupid pickles.

They were the last thing I'd fought with my brother about. I'd found them left out in the morning and thrown the whole jar away. He said it was fine to leave them out, and I said that once they'd been in the refrigerator they had to stay there.

I didn't even *like* pickles, but I was still lecturing him for leaving them on the counter all night when the car came screeching around the corner—headed right for James, who was frozen in shock in the middle of the crosswalk.

It was as if I was there again. I felt my body start into motion with the ball of fear in my chest. I screamed at him to get out of the way, but he wouldn't move.

Why wouldn't he move?

I made it there in time to give him a shove strong enough to push him out of the way but ended up smashing into the vehicle myself.

In my mind I felt bones breaking, my body scraping across the ground after I'd been flipped over the car, and finally the blinding pain before the complete blackness as my head smashed into the pavement.

With a gasp I opened my eyes and was back in the school hallway. My heart would surely beat out of my chest as I gasped for air. I was having a panic attack, or else I was in shock.

My name was being yelled and I found the strength to lift my head. Logan, shouting for me to get up. I caught his blue eyes, the urgency in them. He needed me. They all did.

Down the hall, a demon's claws were deeply imbedded in a boy no older than my brother.

A sophomore at most.

I didn't remember his name—he would have been two grades below me—but I remembered his face. I'd seen him sitting alone in the lunchroom and walking through the halls with his head down, hood up, shoulders hunched.

He was small for his age. I didn't remember having ever talked with him, but I also didn't remember him looking this bad. His hair was matted and disheveled. His clothes were hanging loosely off his boney frame, and his eyes were glazed and vacant.

The demon snapped at the dozen or so fighters closing in but refused to relinquish its hold on the child. Logan and I stood several feet outside the shrinking circle of hunters. I had to do this. No matter what was going on in my head right now, I had to push it aside and get up.

I mentally shouted at my body to obey me, and for once it actually listened. A tear slipped down my cheek as I took a step toward the fight. I was ripping pieces of my heart out with every step, ordering myself not to turn around and look for James. I caught up to Logan, who grabbed my shoulders and gave me a shake.

"Audrey, what's going on? Are you all right?"

He looked rattled, torn between the demon and making sure I was okay. Although my mind was full, I suddenly felt very hollow. I didn't know how to answer him. I looked him straight in the eyes, which was probably a mistake because it showed what a mess I was.

He nodded once, his lips drawn into a straight line. "Okay, we have to get you out of here. You're not ready for this."

I shook my head—I couldn't leave now.

Another shot rang out. An angel appeared from who knows where and deflected the bullet intended for the fleeing students who had just burst out of a classroom. The chem lab, if I remembered correctly. Mr. Elliott's class.

I flinched. There were more screams, but they seemed very far away. I looked frantically around to see if anyone had been injured. It didn't appear that anyone was hit. I think the bullet had slammed into a locker.

Impulse took over. I shoved Logan's hands off my shoulders and hurled myself toward the boy and the demon attached to his body.

The demon wasn't the largest one I'd seen by far, but it was doing an effective job of keeping the other hunters at bay with its long, scaled tail, whipping it back and forth so quickly that no one could get close enough to pry the monster off the boy's back. At this point the boy's eyes were glassy. The demon had taken so much of his essence that he was barely a shell now.

I willed the boy to hang on.

Not stopping when I reached the other hunters, I pulled my sword from its sheath, and it instantly blazed to life. The demon shrieked at me. With a clean swipe, I severed its tail from its body. The tail turned to shadow, then disappeared.

I advanced on the beast. Its talons dug deeper into the boy, and the child's arm rose one more time, although this time he bent his wrist toward himself.

We were almost out of time.

Without a thought I brought my arm up and threw the blazing sword right at the demon's head.

The sword missed its intended target but sank deeply into the creature's shoulder. With an agonized scream, it finally pulled its claws from the boy and fell to the ground.

The demon pawed at the sword, trying to dislodge it.

The sword held its mark.

The flesh around the wound started to char and crumble away like overused coal.

I jerked my head up to locate Logan when the warning was shouted but couldn't react fast enough. The demon coiled its decaying body and sprang at me, bringing us both to the ground.

We slid across the floor until I slammed into a row of lockers. The air was violently expelled from my lungs. I was suffocating with the demon right on top of me.

It gave a horrid scream, then sank its three rows of teeth into my right shoulder.

After that, I may have screamed myself.

The beast was tearing at the very fabric of my soul as well as the soft shoulder flesh. With the empathy connection made, I knew exactly what it wanted to do—what it craved doing. To rip my body to shreds and feast on my soul.

It hated me. Hated me with the purest hatred there was.

It lived only to see my destruction.

It was all rot and death and evil. And in that moment, it was all I felt and what I had become as well.

It offered a black hole to swallow me whole. Soon I was unable to feel fear because the creature's vile blackness was consuming everything.

And then the hatred was ripped off of me.

I gasped for air, and my back arched off the ground. My vision was still black as I swam in the vile sensations and passions of the beast.

Someone put pressure on my shoulder, and I screamed in pain, my whole body arching away.

"Hold still!" someone yelled in my ear.

Out of instinct, I obeyed. It was Logan.

He knelt on my left, his shirt pressed against my shoulder. Naked from the waist up, he must have stripped off the top half of his body armor in order to use his shirt as a pressure bandage.

I would have made a joke if I didn't hurt so badly and if my mind didn't feel so fractured and violated.

The waves of pain were relentless. I held still out of sheer willpower to obey. Logan's cheek and one of his arms were stained, or rather coated, with fresh blood. I panicked.

"Oh my gosh, you're bleeding!"

I tried to sit up, but he pushed me roughly back.

"Don't move. That's your blood, not mine. Except for that scratch you gave me earlier."

Oh. An angry ocean churned in blue eyes that wouldn't meet my own.

A voice behind my head said, "It's taken care of. The hunters are tending to the boy until an angel can arrive."

Without turning from me, Logan nodded once. "I'm going to get her out of here. She needs to be treated. Send word that I'm taking her to the extraction point outside."

"Yes, sir."

And with that, Logan lifted my right hand and pressed it against the shirt covering my wound. He finally looked me in the eye. "I don't care how much it hurts, press down on this hard."

I'd seen Logan mad before, but I wasn't sure I'd ever seen him this worked up. Blackness still tinged the edges of my consciousness, but at this moment he scared me more. I nodded in agreement. The pain was truly dizzying, but I managed to keep pressure where he instructed.

He slid an arm underneath my knees and another under my back and lifted me from the ground. I bit my cheek to keep from crying out and tasted blood from biting down too hard.

Logan's long strides took us to a courtyard in the middle of the school in a matter of moments. There were still some hysterics going on outside, but through the hurt it all seemed far away. I grasped at anything to take my mind off my injury.

"You know, Logan, if you wanted to get me in your arms again, all you had to do was ask."

My lame attempt at a joke fell very flat. A muscle in Logan's jaw twitched as if he was gritting his teeth, and he didn't look down on me. A small knot of panic formed in my gut. Had I finally pushed him too far?

After a few long, silent moments, an angel appeared. He enveloped us in his wings, and in an instant we were gone.

We were taken straight to the healing center, the afterlife's equivalent of a hospital. Logan pushed through a set of doors that led to what looked like an operating room. He briskly but gently set me on the flat bed and put his hand over mine to add pressure to my wound.

The empathy link between us sprang to life, and I was assaulted by Logan's anger. I gasped at its intensity. He was furious.

He must have thought I gasped at the pressure, because he immediately let up a little, and in that moment I detected something hidden under the thick layer of anger. Logan was deeply concerned. So much so that he was trying to bury it under his anger. This was the first time Logan had ever purposefully touched me in this realm, and despite the pain, I found myself desperate to understand what he was feeling.

My eyes widened as I searched deeper, unable to get as far as I wanted. If I could have reached for his feelings with my fingers, I would have just grazed what he felt for me. I wanted to snatch it and bring it closer to get a better look, but it was buried too deep. But what I *could* brush felt strong and pure and had me panting for breath.

Was this what it meant to be bonded?

Logan stared down at me with one hand still applying pressure to my wound and the other pressed to the bed adjacent to my shoulder. His head blocked the light in the room, and his face was partly shadowed by his hair as he leaned over me. It reminded me of the first time I had fainted shortly after meeting him. Perhaps he was searching as deeply into my feelings now as I was into his.

The tricky thing about the empathy link was that if you weren't completely sure of your feelings, they could easily get confused with those of the person you were touching. When I looked up at Logan, I wasn't entirely sure whose emotions I felt. Something was blossoming in my chest, and I sucked in a quick breath.

"Why didn't you wait?" he asked.

"What?" I couldn't piece together what he wanted.

"What happened to you out there? Why didn't you wait for us? Why didn't you listen to me like you promised? Do you have any idea what could have actually happened to you?"

His voice wasn't harsh, but it wasn't gentle either.

"You mean something worse than this?"

Logan pressed his lips together in a thin line. "Yes, something worse than this."

"It's not like I could have been killed. I'm already dead."

I let out a humorless laugh, but it caused my shoulder to move, and another bolt of pain shot through my body. I bit my lip to keep from gasping.

So quietly I almost couldn't hear, Logan answered, eyes averted once again. "There are some things worse than death."

I felt a bolt of dread shoot through Logan's anger. He had a point. What in the world had I been thinking, attacking the demon like that? It was stupid and reckless, and I'd suffered because of it.

With a start, it all came crashing back. The memories. The pain, the sadness, the loss. Logan felt the moment it happened with the same intensity as I. He sucked in a breath of air so quickly it sounded like a hiss. He cradled my cheek with his free hand, capturing my eyes with his own.

My eyes pooled with tears, and the breath escaped my mouth in short gasps. Logan's face began to blur, but I heard his voice and felt his gentle touch.

"Audrey, what's going on here? What's happening to you?"

I couldn't get the words out. The anger in Logan's core evaporated and was replaced with deep concern that bordered on panic. Closing my eyes, I blocked out the world. I didn't even want Logan's touch right now, and I struggled to get out of his grasp.

"Audrey, stop, stay with me. What's going on?"

In that instant, the doors of the room flung open. The sound of people arguing filtered through to me, but I was in too much physical and emotional pain to comprehend. After a moment Logan's hands left my body, and I was left to deal with only my own pain. Then, a soft familiar voice spoke in my ear, telling me to relax, and the next moment it was black.

24

GOD

Golden warmth pressed itself against my closed eyelids. I floated on a cloud, every part of my body perfectly relaxed and tranquil. I breathed in air so fresh I could have sworn it had begun to circulate through my body, energizing everything from fingertips to toes.

I brought my arms above my head and stretched languidly. I'd never felt so alive yet so peaceful. I could rest here forever. Wherever I was, it felt like heaven.

I pressed my fingers to the cloud beneath me and was startled by the frosty bite of cold. I sucked in a crisp breath of air, and my eyelids fluttered against the brightness.

The world slowly began to take shape. The golden glow suspended above me morphed into blue skies. A brisk gust of wind forced my eyelids shut once again and blew strands of hair across my face, tickling my cheeks.

It didn't take long for the cold beneath my fingers to seep in, causing a chill to run up my arms and down my back to my feet. I opened my eyes with more clarity this time. I had been wrong. I wasn't resting in a cloud but was instead sprawled face-up on a brittle bed of snow. I pushed the weight of my half-frozen body to a sitting position and then to a stand, crystallized snow crunching underneath as I moved.

Hand to brow, I surveyed the world around me. I stood on the summit of a snow-covered peak, high up and looking down at the sparkling city beneath. Buildings and structures I'd first considered cold, sterile, and untouchable, I now knew pulsated with life. I imagined a warm glow palpitating from the white marble. Another gust of wind, noticeably colder than the last, added ice to my blood, reminding me just how far away I was from the sanctuary below.

I took a more discerning look at my immediate surroundings. The area was completely covered in a blanket of pristine white snow. It was flat for a twenty-foot radius around me, but beyond that was a straight drop. I was as trapped as if I'd been buried in the ground.

How had I been plucked from the valley and set up here? The mountain was far too steep to hike. My last recollection was of lying on a stiff bed with a bloody wound, Logan's concerned face floating above me. And me, a bundle of emotions too painful to explore. But that wasn't where I was anymore, and the pain, both physical and emotional, was absent.

I jerked my head to the left to check my injured shoulder, but I couldn't inspect the gash because I was covered from neck to wrist in white. The unfamiliar dress was tightened at my waist and flowed down to my feet. A few of my toes, still painted bright pink from my salon day with Romona, poked out the bottom. I took the material just above my knee and rubbed it between my fingers. It felt like soft linen. Lifting the hem, I found I was wearing white leather sandals, the style at odds with the cold snap of the snow at my feet.

Still bewildered, I had a sudden urge to look straight up and saw a small, dense cloud descending. Strange because it was the only cloud in a cloudless sky. Strange because it was moving vertically instead of horizontally. Strange because it was changing altitude at a rapid pace. I stood with eyes transfixed on the mass above until its white brightness enveloped me.

The first few moments in the midst of the cloud were eerily quiet. I held my breath in anticipation, realizing something was coming but not knowing what. I may have been standing on the edge of the cliff, only a small nudge from plummeting into the nothing.

A crack of thunder directly on the heels of a blinding lightning bolt broke the tension in a terrifying way. I jerked and gasped in shock, breathing rapidly. The wind picked up, and a tiny piece of hail, no larger than a mustard seed, hit my hand. I was pelted on my left shoulder by two more, this time the size of small pebbles. The hail increased, mixed with snow in an aggressive wind.

With another flash of lightning, a violent storm erupted, and the force of it sent me to my knees. My very breath was pulled from my lungs as wind, hail, and snow whipped, wailed, and whirled around me in an angry tornado. Fear, as icy as my surroundings, gripped my insides.

Thunder vibrated deep in my chest until my entire being trembled with aftershocks. I was in the presence of a power so enormous I could do nothing but cower before it.

I buried my head and clasped my arms around my knees, pulling myself into as small a ball as possible. This was more frightening than looking into a swarm of battling demons. In desperation, I cried out for help to the only being I was certain could hear. The one I'd been running from since the beginning. The torrent raging around me instantly swallowed my voice.

And then the thunder formed words that spoke to the very core of me.

"Audrey, do not be afraid. I have redeemed you. I have called you by name; you are mine."

Despite my turmoil, my trembling stopped, and I lifted my eyes in search of the one who had spoken my name.

He was walking toward me. My lips formed words that were stolen by the wind. This was the Lord. This was my God.

He appeared brighter than the whiteness all around, His features obscured by the light emitting from Him. The closer He got the brighter He became, until the brightness was so intense that I could no longer look at Him and was forced to shade my eyes.

When I looked away, the world was silenced. The only sound was the hitch in my breath. The wind evaporated, leaving only the cold in its place. I shivered.

A hand settled on my shoulder, and liquid warmth spread from the spot outward, replacing the icy bite of the snow and air. It wasn't a moment before I was encased in a heated bubble even as I remained crouched on the frozen precipice.

It was then that I became ashamed to look up at the God I'd forgotten along with the rest of my life. What could I possibly say or offer to Him that would be good enough? I bowed my head low to the ground, pressing my forehead to the snow. I had nothing more than humility to offer.

The snow crunched beneath Him as He stepped even closer. His hand had left my shoulder, but the warmth He'd given remained.

"Why do you hide yourself from me?" His voice was now a whisper in my ear. A loving caress to my soul. But despite the affection in His voice, I remained bowed at His feet. Like a servant to her master.

I forced my mouth to move, the words barely a breath from my lips. "You are El Shaddai—God Almighty." I spoke it as if it were an answer to His question.

"But am I not also Abba Father? You did not receive a spirit that makes you a fearful slave, but rather you received My Spirit and have been adopted as My own. You sought me in life and so have been given the right to be a child of Mine."

He paused while I remained paralyzed at His feet.

"I created your inmost being and knit you together in your mother's womb. My eyes saw your unformed body, and all your days have been written in My book before even one of them came to be. Shall I continue, dear Audrey, to tell you how great My love is for you? Shall I tell you how I have always known the plans I have for you, plans to prosper and not harm you, plans to give you a hope and a future? Shall I remind you how you came and prayed to Me and how I listened? How you found Me because you sought Me with your whole heart?"

Words I had once known came up from a deep place within my heart: *How great the love the Father has lavished upon us, that we should be called children of God.*

With those words, I knew that what He said was truth. I knew that He was love and that He loved me. And His love had been made complete in me so that I could approach Him with confidence.

My face lifted. Unshed tears blurred His image hovering above, with arms open wide, waiting . . . waiting for me.

With a cry, I half-stood, half-stumbled toward Him and was caught in His embrace. He lovingly wiped the tears from my eyes, and I took refuge in the shelter of His arms, awed that the Creator of the universe truly cared for me.

Eventually my tears dissipated enough for me to absorb the suspended world around me. Intricate ice crystals and water particles hung in the air as if attached by string to the sky itself. Twisters of snow stood frozen mid-turn. An encircling mist so thick it was tangible shielded us from whatever reality lay beyond. I held my breath in wonder.

"Are you feeling better, Dear One?" He asked.

"What's happened?" I whispered.

"I have stopped everything to show you how important you are to Me."

"I didn't even know that was possible."

He smiled. "But of course. For Me a day is like a thousand years, and a thousand years are like a day."

"So nothing else is moving forward in time except us?"

"You need only know that I'm here to be with you. And to answer a few of those questions you've been throwing at Me like darts these past few weeks."

With those words, I hung my head and stepped out of His embrace.

A soft sigh emanated from Him. "Always pulling away from me." In my mind's eye, I saw Him shaking His head sadly. "When will you learn to stop hiding behind fears and realize the depth of My care for you? It is not your questions I'm disappointed in, but rather the doubt of Me reflected in them. I cherish a heart bent toward understanding. But you must learn to stand firm on the truth as well."

"But I forgot the truth with the rest of my life," I protested.

"No, it was always there with you. More a part of you than those memories you missed so much. There was nothing in the Heavens or on Earth that could separate you from the truth. Nothing that could separate you from Me."

"I don't know what you mean," I sobbed, despair and shame leaking into my heart.

"Audrey, what is the first truth you learned about Me?"

I experienced a moment of panic before I realized I knew exactly what it was. *God is love.* That was the first verse I'd ever memorized. The first memory I had of my Creator.

Without me having uttered a word, He knew I'd captured the memory.

"And what has happened to make you doubt that?" He asked simply.

My head lifted even as my eyes struggled to remain downturned. Some hesitancy lingered in my soul up until the moment I looked at His face.

His eyes, set in a wrinkle-free face, spoke love. From forehead to chin, He radiated strength but also compassion. It was an ageless face full of grace and mercy. A human face, but somehow different, eternal, powerful. Beauty personified.

"This is what you look like?" My voice was hardly above a whisper. I'd surprised myself by getting anything out at all.

"This is how I choose to appear to you. This isn't the time to reveal My full glory to you. It's safe to say that would be a little overwhelming right now."

"So you look different? I mean on a normal day or whatever?"

He smiled down at me. A smile that spoke of both amusement and patience.

"I have as many different faces and shapes as are possible to imagine. Each one reflects a different part of who I am. I can manifest for you in whatever way I want, yet My form in its true glory is not able to be looked upon. For now, this is how I choose to appear. In time you'll learn to recognize My other faces as well."

That sounded like more riddles to me.

He chuckled warmly.

"They are not riddles, Dear One, meant to confuse or deceive you, but rather mysteries that are best unraveled over time. Discoveries are intended to be searched for. It makes the prize that much more precious. But I am here now to set some things straight and ease your mind. Come sit with me by the fire so we can talk."

I didn't have a chance to ask what fire before I spotted the flames to my left. The burning wood crackled and popped loudly as if carrying on its own conversation. The air twinkled with frozen water still suspended in place. Snowflakes felt like butterfly wings brushing my cheeks as I moved through them. We settled on white pillows positioned on the snow. The snow no longer held the chill it had before He arrived. He wore a robe much like my dress, but with a golden sash tied around his middle. His sandaled feet stuck out as he sat cross-legged facing me. The experience was normal and surreal at the same time.

"Is this real?" I asked.

"More real than anything you have ever experienced" was His answer. I believed him.

"Shall we finally talk about some of the things that have been on your mind?"

I teared up at the question, and my mouth spoke the words my heart had been crying. "Where have you been?"

He leaned closer yet made no move to touch me. "I've been here all along. Here with you from the moment you arrived. I never once left you. You have been too blind to see."

I was taken aback. Yet, I thought I understood. I remembered the moment by the lake when I'd felt His tug on my heart yet had denied it. I thought of the time I lay crying into my pillow and was comforted. And then I realized that if He'd been there all along, He knew all the times I had lashed out in anger.

Once again knowing my mind, He spoke. "As I said before, you were wrong to doubt Me, Audrey, but not to question. I want you to question things, to find deeper meaning in circumstances. To seek My will with all your heart. But through ups or downs, you should never doubt who I am. You should never doubt that I'm going to do what I say I will do."

I chewed on that a moment, debating whether to speak. But when I considered who He was, and that He already knew what I was thinking, I didn't see a point in holding back.

"I'm so sorry," I began, "but how am I to know that? How am I to believe that? I just feel so much fear sometimes, and I don't understand what You're doing."

"Believing those things is a choice, not a feeling. True faith is believing in Me even when you don't understand. Believing in Me even when you can't see the evidence with your own eyes. For there are times when your eyes will be deceived, and you will need to rely on the truth buried in your heart to overcome."

I was both overwhelmed and unsure.

He gestured toward the fire. "I have some things to show you. For us to watch together."

The crackling had subsided, and embers started to swirl at the base. I squinted and cocked my head. If I looked just right, it almost appeared as if I could see something other than the fire-eaten wood within its depths. And then, like a movie screen brought to life, the flames snapped into a flat line, and images sprang from the embers.

We sat together and watched moments of my life. Moments I had lived on Earth but now saw with the veil removed. He showed me the times in my life I had cried out for Him, and that He was there. He showed me the places I was too weak to go and He had carried me. He showed me the protection given to me by a multitude of angels and hunters. He showed me the things He'd protected me from. I was ashamed when time and time again that He went unthanked—that the blessings He gave me went unappreciated and the opportunities I had to love others passed me by.

When it felt like I was in the pit of self-loathing, He stopped the images, His attention fully on me.

"Audrey, I'm not here to bury you in guilt, but rather to set you free. You cannot do a single thing to make Me love you more or less than I do. My love for you is unconditional and everlasting. Its depth surpasses knowledge. It is not based on anything you may or may not accomplish."

I tried to grasp what He was saying, but it was simply too big, too overwhelming for me to process. I had a family on Earth, and I knew they loved me. In fact, they loved me a great deal, but the love He described was altogether different.

"I know this is something you will grapple with, but remember the words I just spoke to you. My love is not given by the measure of works you complete. In truth, you could never do anything good enough to earn it. It's given without regard to accomplishments when you became a child of mine."

Dare I believe something so radical, something so unbalanced as that? A part of my heart clung to the old feeling that I needed to do something to be good enough for Him despite what He said.

He sighed and shook his head, assuredly knowing what thoughts were bouncing around in my brain. "Just remember My words. There will inevitably be times you will be challenged and need them. Now, let me show you a few more of My favorites."

The images in the fire blazed back to life.

I didn't know how long we stayed together like that, watching the moments of my life in the burning fire. I was mesmerized. He'd lifted the veil and opened my eyes to what my life on Earth had really been like.

"You have got to be kidding!" I burst out as one of my chubby toddler moments appeared in the flames. We were having a family picnic, and I'd followed a butter-colored butterfly into the woods until it flitted over a stream. Wanting to follow it yet scared of the water, I danced a foot in and out of the riverbank. To my shock, I now saw that a sinister demon lurked in the water, silently teasing me forward.

A flash of light blinded me, and the demon was gone. An angel disguised as a human appeared on the path behind me. He explained to my toddler self how badly my family was missing me, and we agreed that a pretty butterfly was less important that my loving family. He pointed me in the right direction, then was gone.

It was my grandmother on my mother's side who found me as I waddled down the path the angel set me on. Her long hair, twisted into a braid, was dark mahogany with only a few grey streaks running through it. Even in her elder years she had remained beautiful. She picked me up and squeezed me tight, then pulled back to look me in the eye.

I gasped. The slight wrinkles and sags were not what I was most familiar with now, but her youthfulness shone through them anyway.

"You have mighty deeds to do in the future, little girl," she told me. "Things the Lord has prepared for you. I don't believe getting lost and scaring your family half to death is one of them. Let's get you back where you belong."

I'd grabbed her braid with my chubby hand and tried to tell her about the shiny man who'd said to return to them. She smiled and whispered in my ear that I must have a guardian angel watching over me. I giggled and squealed when she tickled a rib. But no one else believed me about the man. It was our secret forever after that. Whenever I was scared or discouraged, my grandmother would remind me that my angel was there looking out for me.

But I was trying to process what I now knew. "Romona's my grandmother!"

He chuckled at my reaction. "Yes. So much of who you are is because of her. She asked for you, you know."

"What do you mean?"

"She asked for a legacy, that a great warrior would be placed in her family. A person of integrity who would be used as a light in My kingdom. Her prayers for you and for the generations to come were frequent and heartfelt. It was because of her faithfulness to Me that you were placed in her family. You, my dear one, are the fulfillment of a promise I made to her."

Fulfillment of a promise? That sounded serious. The magnitude hit me hard.

"But how can that be true?"

"Just like all my creations, you have a great destiny."

I had a hard time swallowing that, and I told Him as much. "But what of real value did I ever do in life? I didn't live long enough to fulfill any type of great destiny!"

"Your destiny is far greater than what you accomplish on Earth. You forget there's an eternity to think of."

"But . . . look at me." I waved a hand to indicate my whole 5'3" frame. "What great feat could someone like me possibly accomplish?"

His eyes softened, and His voice took on a gentler note. "I am looking, Audrey, but I don't see as man sees. Man looks at the outward appearance, but I look at the heart. I've chosen you to carry my light. You were created with a specific mission in mind, on Earth as well as throughout eternity. You have the passion, truth of spirit, and character to be the one person to take on this task. You have my noble strength."

The words were inspiring, but something about them still bothered me. "Are you saying I'm just a robot created as a means to an end?"

I worried for a moment that I'd overstepped, but instead laughter rolled up from his gut. It shook the ground beneath us as well.

"Oh Audrey, so blunt, so perfectly you. Yes, you were created with a purpose in mind, but the decision has always been up to you. Just as you decided to give your life for your little brother. You have always had free will —the freedom to make up your own mind. You can choose what I have to offer or you can reject it. Just the same as when you lived on Earth."

I chewed my lip nervously. "So will I get kicked out of here or something if I don't want to be a hunter?"

His smile was gentle. "No, you won't get kicked out. You are here to stay as long as you want. You'll just be reassigned somewhere else. You'll simply be choosing a different path for yourself."

"But won't you need someone to do what I'm doing here?"

"You won't need to worry about that. The ends will be the same, but the means may be different. I've got a pretty good handle on things." He surprised me with a wink.

I chewed on my fingernail absently as familiar doubts rose to the surface.

"Tell me your fears."

"Don't you already know them?" I asked.

He smiled warmly at me. "I'd like to hear them from you, if you don't mind."

I bit my lip, embarrassed by the truth. "Well, what if I can't do this? What if I fail at it? What if someone gets hurt because of me? It's not like my first couple of missions have gone well."

"On your own, you will fail, My precious child."

My heart sank. That wasn't what I wanted to hear.

"This task isn't meant to fall on your shoulders. This isn't something you do yourself. Instead, you will need to rely on Me, and I will give you what you need to accomplish it. It's not by might or power you will prevail, but by My Spirit. My light will go with you and give you victory."

"There just seem to be so many people more capable than I am. My own *grandmother* is better at this than me. I'm nothing special. It doesn't make sense that you would choose me."

"Do you know how many miracles I've carried out through those you would consider ordinary? The people you read about in My Word, the saints living on Earth, they are all just ordinary people. But they are ordinary people with an extraordinary God. They are people who have given up on trying to live an extraordinary life on their own merits. They are people who understand that the only way to do great things is to rest on their faith and believe I am who I say I am and I can do what I say I can do. I will be the One who goes with you to fight against the enemy and give you victory. That's the confidence you should have moving forward."

"Confidence?"

"Yes, confidence in Me, in my power through you. Not confidence in yourself. That will always fail you."

"And you think I have the ability to do that?"

"Not think, I know. Did you just see the moments we watched? The girl you are?"

It was hard to argue with that. Despite the failures, in life I had been fearless. Perfect, no, but confident in my God and His plan for me.

The trouble was, I hadn't been that girl since getting hit by that car. I was someone different. Someone with doubts, with insecurities. Someone who'd crumbled and been crippled by the hit she'd taken.

"Am I still her anymore? I feel . . ." I had to pause before going on. "I feel broken." I cast my eyes down in shame. I had always thought I would handle the hard times with strength through my faith, yet I had not.

His hand settled gently on mine. "Everyone falls. You have the opportunity to be built up even stronger than before. I'd like to show you one more thing. Look over there."

I turned my head where he pointed and found myself in a familiar place. It was my family's lake house. I stood and turned in a circle to get my bearings.

I was in the living room. The sun pouring into the western windows indicated it was late in the day. There was a commotion outside, and the front door was thrown open. I nearly cried out when my dad step into the room followed by a miniature version of myself. I remembered this day.

Little Me squealed in delight and clapped her hands together as she followed Dad into the kitchen. I followed not far from their heels.

"Yay, Daddy!" Little Me cheered and did a happy dance, one that suspiciously resembled the pee-pee dance. "We did it! You said that we could, and we did."

"That's right, Audrey." My dad bent down to Little Me's level and tweaked her nose.

"And I was so brave, Daddy, wasn't I?"

"You most certainly were! The bravest little girl ever."

"Did that fishy almost get away?" Little Me's face changed from delight to little-girl seriousness.

My dad's face attempted to mirror the same, but he didn't quite manage it. "Yes, he almost got away, but we didn't let him, did we?"

Little Me shook her head fiercely. "No, Daddy, I wouldn't let it get away. It was caught fair and square. I helped get the fishy."

"Of course you did, Audrey. Remember, you're Daddy's little helper. I wouldn't have wanted to catch that fishy for dinner any other way."

Little Me's face brightened with Dad's praises. Her smile got impossibly larger, and she threw herself in Dad's arms. He scooped her up in a hug and rocked her back and forth as he planted kisses on the top of her head.

A tear slid down my cheek, but before it could land on the ground, I was looking into the smoke around our fire.

"That was one of my favorite days."

"Yes, I know."

"Thank you."

"I didn't just show you that for nostalgia's sake. I wanted to remind you of that day for a reason."

I brought my hand to my face to wipe the wetness away.

"Do you think your earthly father needed you in order to catch those fish?"

I shook my head. "Of course not." Looking back now, if anything, I must have been a hindrance.

"But at the time, what did you think?"

I took a moment to bring back the memory. It was one of my first, so if it hadn't been shown to me, I wasn't sure I could have recalled the details. I was only four at the time.

"I really thought I was my dad's helper that day. I thought we'd brought those fish in together. I remember thinking he probably couldn't have gotten as many without me. I was even a little smug about it." I chuckled a little at the thought.

"But what was the truth about that day?"

"That Dad would have done just fine without me. That he let me help him because it was fun for me and he could teach me how to fish, not because he needed me there. He wanted me there for companionship . . . because he loved me."

"Exactly, Audrey. Things are not so different today."

He gave me long moments for the implications to sink in, for the knowledge and the assurance to reach my head and heart. I was still meditating on it when He spoke again.

"You and Logan are not bonded like you believe."

It was said bluntly and so off topic I was shocked into continued silence.

"I know you were wondering about that but wouldn't ask."

I suppose my reaction was silly, but I couldn't help but be embarrassed. Embarrassed about the situation, embarrassed that He knew all about it, and embarrassed that I was really curious about what that meant for Logan and me.

"How is that possible?" I asked. "I mean, we did that thing that I didn't know we weren't supposed to do that makes you bonded." Oh gosh, I couldn't even say "kiss." There was a decent chance I was now sporting a head full of pink hair.

"It's still a choice, my dear Audrey. A conscious decision. A covenant, if you will, that you have to make with a person. One kiss was never meant to unknowingly seal you for eternity. It is not the kiss that does it, it's the covenant—the promise to one another. That is something you and Logan have not given to one another. But I'd be careful about the next time."

"Oh." I frankly couldn't think of what else to say. This whole time it had never seriously occurred to me that it wouldn't count. I was perplexed as to whether or not I thought it was good news. And what did that mean for how I felt about Logan? I knew I felt *something*. I'd just never taken the time to figure out what that something was. In all honesty, I'd always been scared to search too deeply.

"Wait, what? Next time?" My voice had a super attractive shriek-squeak thing going on. "There's going to be a next time?"

He only smiled broadly and shrugged.

"But what am I supposed to do now . . . about Logan?" I gazed at Him with wide eyes. Desperately hoping He would just tell me what to do but fearing He wouldn't.

"You know, Audrey, I created you with both a heart and a head. And the reason for that was for you to use both. When you try to follow one without considering the other, you will make bad decisions. This especially pertains to relationships. You need to evaluate where you are with Logan by using both of those important parts. I think once you do, the answer will be fairly clear."

I blew out an exasperated breath, not trying to hide my frustration; He already knew how I was feeling, so there wasn't a point to that.

"Audrey, what do you think your life would be like if I took away all your decisions? Took away your ability to decide what was right and wrong. Just marched you forward with a personalized life map, something you knew from birth that said 'You will like these subjects and dislike these. You will have this job, and on this day you will marry this person.'"

I took a moment to really think about that. On the one hand, it would mean I would never make any mistakes, never run into any problems. My map would force me to steer clear of them. On the other hand, there would never be any adventures or mysteries. Never any excitement or real need to use my brain. That didn't seem very fun either.

Still, there were some things I'd rather have an answer about right away. The messiness with Logan was one of those things. I looked at Him hopefully.

He shook His head. "You have a journey to discover. One that I've planned with infinite care and consideration. As my beloved child, I won't take that away from you."

"But I don't know what to do." There was a hint of whine in my voice.

"You will need to figure it out."

I chewed on the tip of another finger. The manicure I'd gotten with Romona was long past saving.

"But what if I do something wrong? What if I make the wrong decision?"

"If you trust in Me, I'll give you a gentle nudge back in the right direction."

"But you know who I will be with someday?"

"Yes."

"And you won't tell me if it's Logan or not."

Another smile. "No, I won't take your love story away from you by revealing its end."

"Love story?"

"I am the Creator of love in each of its forms. Learn what pure love should be, and it will lead you to the love of your life. Be watchful of what love is not, and discernment will steer you away from what is false."

"That easy, huh?"

"It is for those who earnestly seek Me."

"Ha. Okay, so I'll give up the life map, but I think the after-death orientation would have helped me out a bit these last few weeks. Why didn't I get that like everybody else?"

He smiled. "Let's just say you are more of a 'learn through experience' type of girl."

I wrinkled my nose. There were more than a few situations that would have gone down differently had I attended orientation. Namely kissing Logan. Was that the point? Was I supposed to kiss Logan—so that I would think we were bonded, or just as a way to escape the demon? Or did that situation have no bearing on missing orientation one way or another? I looked to Him for an answer.

"Not telling." He seemed immensely amused by this situation.

I buried my face in my hands.

"Audrey, I have one more thing for you before you go."

I uncovered my face and was pushed over by a very large, very warm, and very furry body. His laughter vibrated over the mountainside as my face was covered in slobbery dog kisses. I could actually feel the emotions rolling off the animal as he tried to reach over my head to chew my ponytail—all love and joy and excitement and happiness. It almost sounded like the animal was saying *I missed you* over and over again in my head. My eyes started to fill instantly.

"Bear! I missed you so much, boy!"

The slobbering continued as I struggled to get to a sitting position. My 110-pound golden retriever wasn't done saying hello. I grabbed the dog's head to look into his eyes.

"He's been waiting for you for some time."

I hugged Bear tightly and looked past his head to see Him beaming down at the two of us.

"I thought I'd never see him again. He died a few years ago. It was so sad. We'd gotten him as a puppy, and he slept in my room every day of his life. I didn't even know he *could* be here."

"Yes, the bond between some animals and humans is very strong. They were created with a purpose as well."

"Does that mean I get to keep him?" I asked.

He only smiled and said, "I think you'll find your old friend here will be a great help to you."

My eyes welled up with tears once again. I buried my face in the soft coat of my precious friend and let it dry some of the wetness from my face. What thanks could I offer? What payment could I give?

When I looked up to attempt to give thanks, Bear and I were alone. The cloud had dissipated, and the air was clear. It was as if He'd never been there at all.

"Thank You," I whispered into the breeze. I knew He heard and was glad.

25

AWAKE

*W*hen I woke, the world was no longer bathed in gold. Instead, I was indoors and staring at a white ceiling. It was a moment before I realized I wasn't in my room in the tree, reverted back to a blank slate. I tilted my head to the side and looked through an open window to the mountains in the distance. The white peaks glistened.

I sucked in a deep breath of the fresh air that had drifted in from the opening. Windows were hard to come by when you lived underground in a tree, but not in the city. It was clear I was tucked safely in a bed in the healing center.

I was taking my change in location rather well until I spotted the figure asleep in a chair at the end of my bed. Logan was stretched out with eyes closed in a sofa chair. Hospital chairs didn't look any more comfortable here than back on Earth—the barely padded seat looked as if it would squeak and squeal with even the smallest of movements.

With his long legs extended and arms folded across his chest, his only movements were the barely perceptible rise and fall of his chest. Logan looked as relaxed and peaceful as ever.

I took the moment to secretly soak in the sight of him, memorizing every-thing from head to toe. When my gaze had traveled the length of him and then back up to his face, striking blue eyes stared straight back at me. My breath caught.

He hadn't moved a muscle, but sometime during my unabashed ogle of his sleeping form he'd woken up. I blushed, seeing a piece of my hair slowly turn a rose color as well. Who knew how much of my appraisal he'd observed? It was difficult to pretend I was doing anything other than checking him out.

I tried a lame cover-up as I struggled into a sitting position and willed my hair to turn brown. A dull ache from my injured shoulder protested the movement. "I was just, ah, wondering if you were dead."

His mouth quirked up in a half-smile. "So who's this guy anyway? He just showed up sometime last night. Trotted right in here as if he owned the place, actually. I wasn't about to argue with him."

Logan pointed to something on the floor. I followed his finger to a pile of fluff on the ground. Bear was fast asleep on the cool tile floor, sprawled out on his back, tummy up, back legs spread, front legs bent and crossed as if praying, mouth open. There was a small pool of drool where his tongue lolled from his jowls.

I smiled broadly and ignored Logan for a moment to savor the simple act of remembering. My memories had been missing for so long it was now a precious gift to be able to search them, even the painful ones.

I had numerous such presents still waiting to be unwrapped, but now was not the time to relish them. I gave silent thanks to my Creator for the return of my companion as well as the other gifts He'd bestowed on me on that mountaintop. Perhaps to others it looked as if I hadn't left this bed, but I knew better.

Logan's eyes watched me, patiently waiting for an answer.

"This is Bear."

"He certainly could be one," Logan commented.

I smiled at that. The dog was huge. "He was a Christmas gift when I was four. He stayed smaller than me for about four months, and then I never caught back up. He died a few years back. Didn't think I'd ever see him again. I'm glad I was wrong."

The memory of losing him, even knowing that he was there with me now, caused my throat to constrict. I coughed to hide the sudden emotional rush. I was going to be having a lot of those in the coming days.

"So what happened at the school?" I asked.

I glanced at Logan. Concern wrinkled his brow.

"You mean you don't remember anything?"

"I meant what happened after this?" I gingerly touched a hand to my sore shoulder, avoiding his eyes as I did so.

"Oh." It was a heartbeat before he continued. "No one was hurt, including the shooter. He's in police custody now. We'll be sending groups down to keep an eye on him to make sure the demon can't reattach itself, but considering everything—"

"Wait," I interrupted, "you mean the demon got away? Even after I cut up half its body?"

"Yes." Logan's voice turned to ice. "After I pulled it off you, it barreled through the other hunters and got away."

I was suddenly unsure whether the hardness in his voice was directed at me or the demon, and I was too cowardly to meet his eyes and see. Silence stretched between us.

As if on cue, someone knocked on the frame of the open door. I looked up to see Romona standing outside the room, looking unsure. Nervous even. I absorbed the sight of her. How could I have spent so much time with her and not put together the pieces?

As she stood before me now, her face aged in my mind's eye. Wrinkles were added, extra laugh lines. Her hair turned grey but still remained vibrant. She'd had a scar on her left eyebrow where her sunglasses had cut her when she was playing catch with my younger brother and one of his throws went a little wild. I remembered how bad James had felt, but she'd just told him it would make her look more distinguished and get her some much-deserved respect.

And then I took in her eyes. They were always the same. Timeless. Beautiful, soulful, and rich. *My eyes,* I finally remembered. Everyone had always said I'd gotten my eyes from her. It was one feature I'd always been proud of. How amazing that now she stood before me, her body transformed back to youthfulness. Somehow she was still as much the Grandma, and the Romona, I knew and loved.

Logan cleared his throat stood. I had no idea if he knew who Romona really was, but he knew enough to know that we needed a few minutes alone. He didn't say anything when he left, just nodded to Romona on the way out. She took hold of his arm to stop him from brushing by and whispered something to him. My eyes widened because she'd grasped his bare arm just underneath the edge of his sleeve. Logan stiffened a little but didn't pull away.

"I mean it," she said softly, but with authority.

He gave a small, tight smile and another nod of his head. Romona released his arm, and he disappeared through the door and out into the hallway.

I couldn't hold back my curiosity when she turned to face me.

"What was that all about?"

"I was just thanking him. He has a hard time taking gratitude." Her eyes looked worried. "Are you okay? You've been out of it for a while."

I now understood just how deep her concern for me went. Man, how could I have missed it for so long?

A tear leaked from my right eye and clung its way down my cheek. It held onto my chin for a few stubborn moments before relinquishing its hold and plummeting to the blanket below.

"I missed you." My voice was barely a whisper, small and childlike, but I knew she heard me.

She made a noise that sounded like a half-sob and brought a hand up to cover her mouth. Matching wet trails ran down both her cheeks.

When she finally spoke, her words were as soft as my own. "You aren't upset with me?" she asked hesitantly.

At first all I could do was shake my head. When I found my voice it still shook a bit.

"No. If you had told me before I remembered myself, it probably would have weirded me out." I took a big breath to steady myself. Then suddenly another connection clicked into place, and I slapped a hand to my forehead. "Of course! Grandpa's the old guy!"

Her face split into a grin. "Oh, how I wish you could have seen your face! You were so appalled at the idea of me being with an elderly man. I almost completely lost it that day."

I was laughing so hard my eyes started to tear up again. I only got out a few words between laughs. "That makes," I paused while I tried to suck in some air, "so much sense now!"

It took effort, but I eventually gained control of my giggles. "But wait, how is it you aren't old anymore? There are people of all different ages here. Why aren't you the age you were when you died?"

"That's mostly thanks to the job. I needed a body that was a little more nimble. Age isn't really an issue here, so a lot of people look different than when they died. Your body is a reflection of the perfect age that you need to be."

I silently sent up a prayer of gratitude that I hadn't known that before. I would have made myself crazy simply wondering how old I was when I died. But as soon as I thought it, my mind went into overdrive trying to guess how old everyone else was when they died. There was just no way to tell. Besides a few very subtle tips, I would never in a million years have guessed Romona had been well into her eighties.

With all the noise we were making, we finally managed to disturb the other resident of my room. Bear's head poked up unexpectedly, and he rested his chin on the side of my bed, seemingly waiting for something.

"Hey there, buddy, are you confused too?"

"Is that Bear?" Romona had been standing in the threshold this entire time, but she finally entered the room to greet the dog. His tail wagged so hard his backside moved back and forth with the motion. Romona dropped to her knees to take the furry dog's face in her hands and look in his eyes.

"Well I'll be. It *is* Bear. It's good to see you, old boy."

Bear answered by breaking free from her grasp and planting a sloppy kiss on her left cheek and eye.

"Oh yuck. I'd forgotten about that. He's a chronic kisser."

Romona gave the dog another affectionate scratch behind the ear, expertly dodging his second attempt at a kiss before straightening and coming to sit on the edge of my bed.

Unable to hold back any longer, I launched myself at her for a hug, just like I used to. She absorbed my weight with a grunt, but her arms tightened around me. I closed my eyes and remembered the last time I'd given her a hug like this. It had been too many years ago. I'd been only in middle school. Her death was the first I'd ever had to deal with, and it felt as if she'd taken a big chunk of me with her. I sobered when I imagined how my family was dealing with losing me right now.

Giving her a final squeeze, I pulled back to sit cross-legged, facing her. Bear's head appeared on the side of the bed between the two of us.

"I miss them already."

Romona didn't pretend to misunderstand me. She put a comforting hand on my shoulder.

"I know."

"Do you know how they're doing?"

She paused before answering. I watched her face. The maturity in her gaze now made sense. "They are . . ." she took another short break to find the right word, "coping right now."

"Is there anything we can do to help?" I expected what came next, but my heart still sank.

"No, I'm afraid not. We all have to deal with loss at one point or another. They have to learn to cling to the truths they know. We're not the ones intended to offer comfort right now."

"But if they just knew that I was okay, that I was safe, I'm sure that would—"

Romona cut me off with a look and a hand in the air.

"That's not how it works. They need to learn to move on, on their own. It's a test of their faith, and they need to push through it without us."

"But if . . ."

"I promise you, Audrey." She took my cheeks in her hands and forced me to look her in the eyes. "They have everything they need to make it through right now. No one is ever promised a life free of pain. Far from it, in fact, but they have all the comfort and support they will ever need. That and more. Your parents and siblings are well looked after right now. It's going to test your faith to believe that as well."

My heart was breaking into a million pieces, but deep down, I knew her words were true. The moisture had returned to my eyes and was spilling over before I had the opportunity to stop it. Romona pulled me toward her, and I buried my face in her shoulder and sobbed. She rubbed my back and murmured in my ears.

I don't know how long we stayed like that, but finally my sobs subsided into small hiccups. There was still an ache in my chest, but I could manage it. Something about a good cry seemed to wash my insides clean.

A wet nose pushed between us. I looked with puffy eyes to see Bear's front paws on the side of the bed. Through his heavy pants, he was letting slobber from the tip of his tongue drop to the bedding below.

We always did have trouble keeping him off the furniture. "Bear!" I gave him a halfhearted and ineffective shove. Instead of budging, he gave my cheek a lick and discovered he liked the taste of my salty tears. He attacked me to lap up the remains. With a squeal, I tried to escape by burying my head under my pillow and yelling for help. Romona laughed.

"Looks like I picked the right time to make my rounds. Damsels in distress happen to be my specialty."

Surprised to hear Jonathan's voice, I made the mistake of lifting my pillow-slash-shield and was promptly slimed by a hot wet tongue.

"Oh yuck! Bear, down!"

Having completed his mission, Bear happily planted himself back on the ground and padded over to the now unoccupied chair, made a short jump up, turned in two circles, and settled into a comfortable position. I shook my head at him as I wiped the saliva from my face.

With a friendly smile on his face, Jonathan watched Bear make himself at home. Jonathon wore a long white coat that made him look very much like a doctor. It came back to me in a flash that he'd told me he worked as a healer of some sort. I had a vague remembrance of hearing Logan argue with someone in the operating room before I'd passed out, but couldn't be sure if that had been him or not.

"So how's my new patient doing?" Jonathan was all smiles and confidence. Romona had quietly relinquished her spot on the bed for a seat across the room.

"Oh, hi. I mean, I'm good I guess."

I was suddenly embarrassed by the state he'd discovered me in. I was sure my hair was standing up at funny angles. My face still felt puffy, and I thought with a sudden horror that I hadn't even taken note of what I was wearing. I quickly looked down to see I was in a white tank top and hot pink scrub bottoms.

Kinda cute actually.

I self-consciously attempted to smooth my hair and snuck a peak at a few strands to make sure it was still brown. I breathed easier when I found that it was.

Jonathan's smile didn't change, and he went on unfazed by my disheveled appearance.

"Great. I came by to see if you'd woken up yet. Mind if I take a look at your shoulder while I'm here?"

Suddenly mute, I shook my head. Jonathon took a seat on my bed and moved the strap of my tank top slightly toward my neck to fully expose the bandage beneath. His expert hands found the edges and slowly peeled it away.

"You doing okay?" he asked without checking my face.

I nodded before realizing he wasn't looking and let a quiet "yes" squeak out. His fingers probed different spots on my shoulder, some more sensitive than others.

"Can you move it all right?"

Without thinking I shrugged as if to say "I guess so."

"That's good. Any residual soreness?"

"Some, but it isn't that bad."

His smile returned, and his fingers left my arm. It wasn't until they'd left that I realized I didn't feel anything from the empathy link. I remarked as much.

He nodded in confirmation. "Yes, our empathy link is kind of in the 'off' position here so we don't upset the patients."

"That makes sense."

I snuck a glance at my shoulder and sucked in a breath when I saw what was peeking out from either side of my strap. The skin had been knitted back together expertly, but there was still visible evidence of my attack.

"You okay, Audrey?" Jonathan laid his hand on my good shoulder.

"I just wasn't expecting to have scars."

Jonathan nodded, as if understanding my confusion. "Demon scars are like emotional scars you can see. They'll disappear when you've worked through the emotion. Until then, they'll stay on your skin as a reminder of what you still need to address."

The deep scars that latticed Logan's back sprang to mind. So that's most likely where he'd gotten them. There must be something he was hanging on to as well.

Jonathan was still talking with his hand familiarly on my shoulder, and he leaned in close, but I wasn't really hearing the words he was saying as I thought about Logan.

"Hmm, I'm surprised Logan hasn't come back." Romona mused loudly.

Jonathan moved back to a safe distance in response to her words.

That *was* strange. Had Logan not come back because of Jonathan? That didn't sound like something he'd do—if anything, Jonathan's presence seemed to make him overly protective, borderline possessive. Maybe since I was okay he didn't want to stick around anymore?

Jonathon cleared his throat, pulling me out of my musing. His demeanor had changed. He seemed a little nervous and unsure of himself, which weren't traits that I'd picked up on before. His eyes wouldn't meet mine and he was fidgety. It was curious behavior for him.

"Audrey, there was something else I wanted to talk to you about. I realize that I came on a little strong at first, but I truly would like the opportunity to get to know you better." His eyes shifted to Romona for a moment before finally landing on me. "I'd like to take you out sometime, if that's something you might be open to." There was a hint of hopefulness in his voice.

It took me a moment to comprehend what was going on. Jonathan was asking me out. Here, in front of my grandma-slash-best friend.

I snuck a desperate look at Romona, who was staring wide eyed at Jonathan as if she hadn't seen this one coming either. She glanced at me and offered a small shrug as if to say, "you're on your own with this one."

"Ah, well, yeah, I guess that would be okay." I fumbled through my response.

Heat was coming off of my face in massive waves. Pink hair for sure.

Jonathon smiled broadly, looking as if he'd just won the lottery. That was kind of sweet, but the sentiment was overshadowed by my embarrassment.

"That's great! I already have something special in mind. I know you'll love it."

"Ah, okay." I sat on my hands to keep from chewing a fingernail. These types of interactions always made me uncomfortable. Unsure if he was waiting for me to say something else, I just stared at him. He stared back.

It was a few more awkward heartbeats before Jonathan broke the silence. "Looks like you'll probably get out of here today now that you're awake." He smiled and winked. "But don't worry, I know where to find you." He bent down to kiss my cheek and then turned to leave. I was left gaping in his wake.

It was only a fraction of a moment longer before I remembered Romona was still there, watching me with wise and thoughtful eyes.

"What color's my hair?"

"Do you really want to know?"

I groaned loudly. Maybe I should just turn my hair pink permanently and then no one would know when I was really humiliated. I closed my eyes for a moment to change it back.

"So have you decided what you are going to do?" Romona asked.

"About what?"

Romona wore a sly smile. "I remember when you were 8 years old and two little boys from your class had a crush on you. You got so freaked out you punched one in the nose and were so mean to the other you made him cry. I wonder how much you've matured since then?"

I'd completely forgotten about poor Rob and Peter. There were a few more details to that story, but she'd gotten the basic structure of it right. I'd gotten in a heap of trouble for punching Rob, even though I told my parents he was trying to give me cooties. Totally valid reason to defend myself. The poor kid went home with a shiner that day, but to his credit he didn't cry. Peter, on the other hand, was reduced to a pile of tears with only a few choice words. He never did look me in the eye again after that, even when we entered high school.

"Oh whatever," I batted my hand in the air as if I was brushing the whole thing away, "I was just doing my part to harden both of them up a bit. I was probably instrumental in helping them deal with an inevitable future heartbreak. Any boy who cried just because someone called him a booger-eater needs a little toughening up anyway." Seriously, who didn't eat their boogers at that age?

"Hmm, I wonder if they would look at it the same way?"

I had no idea what either of them thought about it. Rob had moved away the next year and I never talked to Peter again. I shrugged as if I didn't care, but something about her insinuating that there was a comparison to my present day events bothered me. Maybe it was being likened to an eight year old me that irked me. Maybe it was something else. Either way, I found myself squirming uncomfortably in my bed. Desperate to change the subject, I cleared my throat then moved on.

"So, I'm a little unsure what I should call you now. 'Grandma' sounds a little funny to me. What do you think?"

Romona just shook her head with a soft smile that told me she knew exactly why I'd changed the subject, but she obliged me anyway. "I see the dilemma. I'm honestly happy with whatever you feel most comfortable calling me now. What do you think that is?"

Looking at her sitting there, I could once again see my grandmother. But in the short time I'd been here I'd gotten to know a completely new dimension of her that was fully Romona, my good friend. My head was starting to hurt as I tried to reconcile the two.

"Maybe we should stick with Romona since that's what I've been calling you since I got here. Besides, it might be strange to other people if I start calling you Grandma now."

Romona smiled and nodded in agreement.

Romona stayed with me throughout the afternoon. We shared some of our favorite memories. Sometimes laughing with each other, sometimes letting some tears fall freely. But it was a good time of remembrance. Cleansing even. And I was thankful to have someone to share it with.

Bear never left the chair he'd taken over after Logan left, and Logan never returned to reclaim it. Neither of us brought him up again, but he was never far from my thoughts. A decision was forming in my head that I wasn't ready to talk over with her.

If Romona had an inkling of what was on my mind, she never let on. For that, I was thankful. I had an overwhelming number of things to chew over, and now wasn't the time to talk them all out. I had a feeling she understood that.

Before night had a chance to fall, a pretty brunette entered the room. Glowing slightly in the familiar way I'd come to expect of angels, she cheerfully informed me that I was free to return to all my normal activities. Within a matter of minutes I was up and changed into clothes, which, after a good amount of concentrated effort, I was able to materialize all on my own. There were no discharge papers like there would have been on Earth, no pushing me out in a wheelchair or hoopla of any sort. I left as if I had been a visitor rather than a patient.

Romona started to head in the direction of my tree when I stopped her. I explained in as few words as possible that I needed to do something first. The corners of her mouth tweaked ever-so-slightly downward, but with a hug and a quick scratch for Bear she let me go, promising she'd meet me at the training center for breakfast the next day.

After watching her leave, I let out a low whistle for Bear to follow and headed in the opposite direction, knowing I'd made the right decision but already slightly regretting it. But I knew the regrets were for the wrong reasons, so I picked up my step and walked resolutely toward my fate.

26

GOOD-BYE

"*Y*ou know he was there the whole time?"

Early the next morning I stood in the hallway outside our training gym—Logan's and mine . . . ours—silently watching Logan train. The voice behind me was so soft I wasn't startled.

Lost in his routine, Logan wasn't aware I was there. It felt voyeuristic, but I figured it was only fair. Who knew how long he'd watched me in the healing center before I woke up?

"What do you mean?" My eyes stayed on Logan when I answered. I was determined to drink in as much of him as possible while it lasted.

"He was there when you were recovering. Practically every minute. I think he even slept in the chair a few nights."

I let the implications sink in. Romona, my grandmother, wouldn't be telling me this without a reason. I shook my head lightly. In the end, what did it matter? I'd already made my decision, and a few minor details weren't going to change my mind. There was a saying for that. Too little too late.

"Doesn't matter anyway," I replied.

"Do you truly mean that?"

I nodded because the words were caught in my throat. I hoped she didn't notice.

"This will change things, you know."

Another nod. Of that I was sure.

I didn't understand how she knew what was going on, but I took her continued silence as acceptance. Perhaps she'd already been notified through the chain of command. Or perhaps she just knew me that well.

She crouched down to run her hand over Bear's back. He was spread on the ground like a bearskin rug, limbs out in each direction. He closed his eyes and purred like a cat as she continued her strokes. What a weirdo. What dog actually purred? I smiled at the thought.

Her next words were laced with love and support.

"Whatever you want to do, I'm behind you. And I'm always here to talk." She stood back up and gave my shoulder a gentle squeeze.

From behind my eyes, tears threatened to break free. She reminded me so much of my mom at that moment. My constant support and sounding board. The wisdom of the generations had certainly passed through Romona to her daughter. I silently prayed some of it had also trickled down to me.

As quietly as she had appeared, she left. I stole a few more greedy moments alone before making my presence known.

Logan was really working something out on that practice dummy, delivering a series of blows so strong it rocked back on its stand again and again. I expected its head or an appendage to come flying off at any moment.

He stopped and placed his forearms on the mannequin, limply draping a hand over each shoulder as if he were fatigued and needed the support. His head hung forward, causing the longer hair to fall forward.

It was only then that I spoke up.

"Gym was my least favorite class." It wasn't what I'd intended to say, but it was what came out.

The only acknowledgement that my presence surprised him was a sudden tenseness in his shoulders, which relaxed a moment later.

As usual, Logan didn't miss a beat. "I think I could have guessed that." I heard the smile in his voice even though he was facing the opposite direction.

"I needed four gym credits to graduate, and I put them all off until the last semester. I would have had two hours of gym classes every day if I'd lived long enough. Do you have any idea how wonderful just two hours of gym sounds these days?"

He chuckled. The richness of the sound comforted my frayed emotions. "Knowing you, yes."

"I suppose someone else is getting the last laugh now."

"Well, now you know there's truth to that saying."

"Which one?"

"About God having a sense of humor."

The corners of my mouth snuck up. He did have a point. "Yes, I suppose so."

This whole time he'd remained facing his practice dummy. When he finally turned, he lifted an arm to wipe the sweat from his forehead. He'd really been going at it hard today. Despite all the training I'd done with Logan, I'd rarely seen him sweat.

"So what was your favorite then?" he asked.

"What?" Embarrassingly enough, I'd completely forgotten what we were talking about the instant he turned and captured my gaze. His blue eyes were as mesmerizing as ever.

"Classes . . . which one was your favorite?"

"Oh." I thought about it for a second. Although everything was safely back in my brain where it belonged, there were still things I had to search through the memory catalog to find. I smiled when I found the answer I was looking for.

"Art."

"Mine too," he answered without pause.

I lifted my eyebrows in slight disbelief. Not only was I skeptical that we had something in common, but art wasn't a subject I could easily imagine Logan enjoying, let alone taking at all. But then I remembered thinking that his hands were those of an artist when we were on the beach. It was the first time he'd ever touched my skin. I was so caught off guard by the contact that I'd missed the point he was trying to make completely. The memory warmed my cheeks.

"Really?"

He nodded his head. "I liked to draw. I thought one day I might be an architect."

Now that was something I could believe. I imagined you'd have to be very precise and have a lot of patience for a career like that. As much patience as it had taken to train me.

I smiled. "I liked to draw as well, but I always imagined myself growing into a profession less practical and more whimsical. Maybe a fashion designer or makeup artist." The smile widened on my face. The irony of where I'd ended up was too thick to ignore.

Logan smiled back and shook his head as if he were thinking the same thing. After a moment his face turned more serious.

"So is everything back then?"

I sobered as well. "Yes."

"How are you doing?" he asked gently.

I shrugged and finally looked away. How should I answer that? Everything was . . . different now.

"Okay, I guess."

"That's not a real answer."

I huffed.

What was he looking for? I looked at my existence here in a whole new light now. How was I supposed to explain that to him? That no matter how much he thought I was the same, no matter how often he'd told me I would be, I wasn't.

I saw the ugliness in me so much more clearly now in light of who I was and who I wanted to be. And even though I had friends and Romona here, I grieved for a lost family. A family I was sick to think was also hurting because of me.

And it was painful.

On top of all that, I was also grieving the loss of my own life. Yes, I had an eternal life, but my plans, hopes, and dreams for the future on Earth had died with me that day. And now new ones needed to be born. It wasn't something I was going to come to terms with in a single day.

"What do you want me to say, Logan?"

He remained silent, staring at me so intently I fought the familiar urge to squirm. I wasn't sure if he was waiting for me to give him a better answer or trying to determine what to say next. It seemed as if he was working something out in his head, but I never was completely sure with him. Eventually his mouth turned down.

"I had hoped it would be better for you once you remembered. Is that not the case?"

His words surprised me. They shouldn't have. Logan was always one to cut through the layers of superficiality. Oddly enough, despite the contention it had caused between us in the past, it was one of the things I appreciated the most about him.

I answered as honestly as I dared. "Better, but different."

He nodded slowly as if he understood.

"But I'm thankful to at least have my grandma back now," I added, trying to lighten the mood.

Logan tilted his head and lifted an eyebrow in a silent question.

"You do know that Romona is my grandmother?" I asked. His eyebrows jumped up in another rare moment of being caught unawares.

"No, I can't actually say I saw that one coming," he said thoughtfully. As he began to put the pieces together, his face changed to a look of chagrin. "I suppose if I'd been paying better attention, I might have caught on. She did a good job of keeping the secret."

"Yes, from even me," I said.

"Well, I'm happy for you. To have someone here to help bridge the gap. That has to be a comfort."

I detected a hint of sadness in him. I longed to know the cause and absently took a few steps closer to him. He remained rooted in front of the practice dummy, and I was just barely over the threshold. The physical distance between us was vast considering the intimacy of our conversation, and as if pulled by a cord, I shortened the distance.

I came to my senses when I reached our customary distance and Logan hadn't made an attempt to meet me halfway. It was like hitting an invisible force field that stopped me short.

Logan regarded me with hooded eyes. I had no idea what he was thinking, but that was true of most of the time. I should have left it alone, but Romona's words swam in my head. *You know he was there the whole time.* Was it possible that meant more than I'd given it credit for? Before moving forward, I needed to know. I needed to hear it from him. No more guessing.

"Romona said you stayed at the healing center with me until I woke up. She said you even slept there."

Logan's eyes remained veiled, his gaze not quite meeting mine.

"I wanted to make sure you were all right. When I brought you back and they started to heal you, I felt . . . " He paused as if searching for the words. I held my breath, anticipating what he would say next.

". . . responsible for what happened to you out there. If I'd trained you better it wouldn't have gone down like that. You would never have rushed into the fight like that."

His hands fisted at his sides. My heart deflated along with my lungs. I wasn't sure exactly what I'd been secretly hoping he would say, but that wasn't it. Not only that, but the way he said it made me feel bad about everything, like I'd done something wrong. Like I'd failed. Failed *him*.

I now knew I'd been mistaken about what I had sensed through the empathy link before I passed out in the healing center. The strong emotion had only been something fleeting after all.

"So that's why you left when I woke up. Because you were disappointed that I didn't follow directions better." It was more of a statement than a question. I already had as much of an answer as my heart could take.

Rather than replying, Logan took a step toward me, and I took one back. Confusion flickered in his eyes and perhaps hurt as well. The look was unfamiliar to me. I steeled my resolve. He was about to say something, but I went on quickly before he had a chance.

"I've asked for a different mentor."

I'd shocked him twice today. His eyebrows shot up, his eyes grew larger, and his whole body froze as if he'd been hit by a stun gun. We stood in silence for several heartbeats.

"Why?"

The one question I knew he would ask—the one I'd been dreading. He deserved an honest answer, but I wasn't ready to be that vulnerable with him.

"I don't think this," I broke eye contact, "whatever it is that we are doing, is healthy for either of us."

"Audrey, I know there are times when we frustrate each other, but I don't think—"

He wasn't getting the right idea, so I blurted the one thing I didn't want to talk about the most. "And we're not bonded."

One, two, three . . . was that Logan's heart I heard jump into his throat, or my own?

I could have once again slapped a hand right over my mouth. My whole body flushed from the tips of my toes up to the roots of my hair. I caught something out of the corner of my eye that I was fairly certain was the beginning of hot pink highlights. I couldn't worry about that now.

"What are you talking about?"

Was he seriously going to make me spell it out? That was so not fair. Sometimes things with Logan were so difficult.

I forced myself to look straight at him when I spoke. As uncomfortable as it was, this conversation was long overdue.

"When we kissed, when we were hiding from the demon, it didn't count. We didn't accidentally bond to each other."

The room was once again silent while what I'd said sunk in. An eternity seemed to pass as Logan's eyes sought to determine my truthfulness.

"Are you sure?" His voice had gone flat again. Emotionless.

I nodded my head. "Yes, we got a 'get out of jail free' card. I didn't know any better because I missed that part in orientation." And because I couldn't say the next thing while still looking at him, I dropped my gaze and stared at an invisible spot on the ground, my voice a notch softer than before. "And you, of course, didn't know I was going to attack you like that. We didn't *mean* to form a bond, so no bond was formed."

"That's not a loophole I've heard of before. Who told you that?"

"Who do you think?" I started a little at the slight note of bitterness in my own voice. The pit of embarrassment I was wallowing in was deep. I tried not to, but I snuck a peek at Logan to study his reaction. I knew it was going to be bad, but I couldn't look away.

After a moment, the implications of my words finally penetrated. I told myself the emotion I read on him shouldn't surprise me, but it did. The tension that always seemed bundled tightly around him slowly dissipated. His body relaxed as if a heavy weight had been lifted. His eyes widened slightly in awe, and his facial features softened. His lips moved in soundless words as if he was sending up a prayer. He closed his eyes for a quick moment and let out a breath of air.

His whole persona radiated relief.

That was what he felt about us not being bonded.

Relieved.

More than anything else that had happened between us, this moment hurt the worst.

When he caught me watching him, he quickly changed his expression to indifference. He waved a hand in the air as if brushing the whole thing off as no big deal. "Well, if that's the case, then I don't see the complication with us continuing to train."

The pieces snapped together for me. He'd probably never told me about being bonded because he couldn't figure out why he felt nothing for me. Now he could move forward without that enigma nagging at him.

You stupid head, I wanted to shout. *Just because you weren't affected by that kiss doesn't mean I wasn't!*

I marveled for a moment at my ability to tuck the hurt into a hardened corner of my heart. Hurt that was teetering on the edge of anger and weariness. Uncharacteristically, the scales were tipping to the latter. I didn't want to obsess over what I thought of Logan anymore.

I was tired of it.

I didn't want to spend eternity next to someone who didn't want me back. I was fatigued from wondering what he thought of me and who else he was spending his time with, and always making sure I knew where he was in a crowd. Our relationship might just be peachy for him, but it was unhealthy for me.

I needed to move on. *I* needed to deal with mourning the loss of my family and working on who I was created to be.

I'd done what God said to do and tried to think about our relationship with my head and my heart, and this was what I now realized. I was finally able to be honest enough with myself to realize Logan was occupying way too much of my brain power. And I wanted it back for more important things.

Gosh, I could have hit him right then and there for his self-centeredness.

My next words escaped a few degrees colder than I had intended. "You don't need to understand, just to accept. The decision's already been made. I talked with administration yesterday after leaving the healing center. They're going to assign someone else to continue training me right away."

I turned to leave. I wanted to be anywhere but there right now.

I hadn't gotten two steps before Logan stopped me. He grabbed my bare arm and turned me to face him. His emotions slammed into me hard. I sucked in a breath of air. He was angry, and confused, and above all, very hurt. Some of those emotions mirrored my own at the moment, but surely for different reasons.

He released my arm as suddenly as he'd taken it. I looked up to see a blue fire blazing in his eyes. His stoic mask had melted completely, and I was reminded of how he'd looked at me after I'd been wounded by the demon. I couldn't understand how this situation was similar.

"Do you not care what I think about this?" In contrast to his face, his words were spoken softly and without emotion.

"Logan, I'm just . . ." I didn't know what to say to him to make him understand. "Tired. I'm just tired." It was the closest to the truth I could bear to admit.

He went on as if I hadn't spoken. "Because this doesn't make sense to me. I can't understand why this won't work. We had already started to make it work. Why can't we just be friends and move forward?"

I shook my head sadly. I couldn't make myself meet his eyes anymore. "I'm sorry, Logan, I'm not going to be able to do that."

"Why not?" The words were spoken as chillingly softly as before, but with a tinge of vulnerability that coaxed my eyes to his face. There, I discovered a question. A need for understanding that I couldn't, wouldn't, fully give him.

I thought back to the moments of jealousy I'd felt around Kaitlin and the times we'd fought over nothing. I thought back to all the moments of longing and the confusion they brought with them. I wasn't going to sentence myself to an eternity of that.

With a sudden clarity, I realized that Logan and I had never been friends, and even if feigning friendship were a way to keep him close, we would never be that to each other. And that was something he needed to hear.

"We were never friends, Logan. We can't go back to something we never were."

"I don't believe that. I don't accept that." His voice was beginning to take on an intensity that matched his face.

I shook my head. I wasn't going to bare my heart fully to him. I took a step back to create more physical distance between us. A move I'd learned from him. I needed that space to stand my ground.

"You're going to have to accept that. I'm not willing to do this anymore." This wasn't some battle of wills we were going to have to fight out. He needed to realize that.

Logan was tense all over. "I'm not going to pretend to know exactly how you got to this point, but it seems to me you are running away, and that can't be the answer. Why aren't you willing to fight through this, whatever it is? Because that's what I'm willing to do."

The blaze in his eyes smoldered. Anger still shimmered there, but also a bit of desperation. I stood firm and tried to hold the pieces of my heart together. I wasn't about to share my feelings for him when it wasn't something he was capable of returning. I knew that something better was intended, and that this, whatever it was, had to change. We were meant for so much more, and if that couldn't be realized between us, then we weren't meant to be anything to each other.

"I'm not running away. I'm running to something. Something new."

Logan turned into a block of cold steel. His posture went from intense and focused to distant and guarded, and the life in his eyes dulled.

"Something new," he repeated. "And you're telling me I'd just be in the way?"

Well no, that was not exactly what I meant. I mean, yes it was, but an uneasiness coiled in my gut, as if he was going down the wrong rabbit hole. Something I'd said had stung him on a personal level, and he'd retreated behind his mask. The one he put on to protect himself. My heart wanted to reach out and rip the disguise off. My resolve was shaken.

But all I had to say was *yes*, and it would be done. I'd be free. Logan would let me go without grilling me for more information, without trying to force my hand.

"Maybe." I stopped.

What was I going to say? Maybe it would be okay if he remained my mentor? Maybe in time we could be friends? Maybe someday things would all work out and we'd be able to laugh at how messed up I'd thought this was?

But I couldn't say that. I wasn't willing to take a chance on those maybes.

"Maybe I'll see you around."

Turning my back on him, I headed for the exit with a heavy heart, no longer sure I'd done the right thing. I walked briskly out of the training gym, forcing my legs to move at an even pace, hearing Bear's feet padding along behind me after I crossed the threshold.

I counted the steps as I moved away from Logan. Ten, then fifteen, then thirty-five. How many more steps would I have to hold off the tide before I got back to the safety of my room? Before I could tend to the internal wounds that had just been inflicted?

Too many was the answer, and I ducked inside the girls locker room before I completely lost it. I ran to the first steam shower and turned it on full blast, stepping in with my clothes fully on and letting the hot water wash away the tears already running down my face.

MENTORS

"*O*h, sorry. I thought this was my new training gym."

The man in the middle of the room was so frail I had no idea what he could be doing in the training center, let alone my gym. He leaned heavily on a cane as he slowly turned toward me, his back bent at the shoulders.

"I'm sorry, but can I help you find something? Are you lost or anything?"

Clear grey eyes stared back at me before crinkling heavily at the corners when he smiled. He nodded his head, and I was momentarily distracted by the poof of white poodle-like hair that bobbed along with it.

"Why, yes you can. I'm looking for Audrey Lyons."

"That's me, actually." But I was drawing a blank as to why this old man was looking for me.

"Why, so it is. Audrey, it's nice to finally meet you. I'm your new mentor."

My eyes widened, and my mouth fell open.

"You're a hunter?" I bluntly asked.

Would there ever be a time I handled the unexpected gracefully?

The smile on the old man's face widened, creating even more wrinkles and divots. "I'm actually more of a jack of all trades. We thought you could use me during your next phase of training."

So now my new trainer wasn't even a real hunter. What was going on?

"I don't mean to be rude, sir, but what does that mean? New phase?"

"I'm sure you'll see soon enough. But let me at least properly introduce myself." He took a few moments to shuffle over to me and held out his gnarled hand, which looked as if it had been ravaged not only by time but also by arthritis. "You can call me Hugo. I believe we are going to make a great team."

My mind was a skeptical mess as I reached for his feeble hand. But when my palm connected with his, a blast of power shot through his surprisingly sturdy handshake. My head jerked up, and I fastened on his sharp eyes. Whoever this man was, what he appeared to be on the outside wasn't all there was to him.

A genuine smile grew on my face. Maybe one day people would say the same about me?

I had the sudden premonition that the future was going to take some interesting turns, starting with this one. Anticipation bloomed in my chest. The afterlife had proven to be a bucket full of the unexpected, so why should Hugo be any different? I was no longer certain about my happily-ever-after ending, but if this was my journey, it was about time I started looking forward to the ride.

"Where do we begin?"

EPILOGUE

"*S*he is the one!" the creature hissed. It was curled in on itself in the corner, writhing and barely able to speak. Its barbed tail had been sliced off, along with a good portion of its left front flank. The hunk of charred meat, for that was all he considered the creature to be, still lived only for verification. Verification of what he already knew to be true, for he'd seen it for himself.

He smiled. She was vulnerable. Throwing herself into a fight she wasn't ready for. Whether from pride or sheer ignorance he didn't know, nor did he care. Either weakness was as deadly as the other, exploitable and leading easily to ruin. He'd been using them for as long as the feeble humans had roamed the Earth.

She was the key to his freedom. By her hand he would be freed to finish the task he'd set out to accomplish so many millennia ago. He'd reign over the Heavens and the Earth and any other realms there were to be ruled.

A pain-filled screech from the thrashing beast in the corner only stirred annoyance in him. With eyes narrowed in irritation, he turned to it. His jaws opened and disjointed like a snake's.

"No!" the creature screamed its plea right before the liquid fire burst from his open mouth, engulfing it. It took longer than he liked for the shrieks to subside and the beast's body to crumble completely. He didn't bother giving the remains another look as he walked into the adjoining room, slipping on his human skin as he did.

When the door clicked shut behind him, the human seated carelessly in front of the fire looked up with one dark brow cocked.

"A mercy, I assure you." He smoothly answered the unasked question.

"Of course." The human replied with a half-smile on his face, seemingly unconvinced.

"I have the confirmation I need. What else do we know?"

The human stood as he answered. "We received a report that she's not training with Logan anymore."

He raised an eyebrow of his own, feeling the fake flesh stretch and bunch on his face. That was interesting. He'd seen the result of Logan's training firsthand—they both had. The boy had worked miracles in a short time. Losing Logan as a trainer was most likely to their benefit. But that depended entirely on the replacement.

"Do you know who has been reassigned to her?"

"Our sources weren't sure but said that would be confirmed on the next report." As if knowing the significance of his next words, the human paused. An arrogant smile played across his features. "The reassignment was at her request."

Another surprise, but this time it didn't show on his face. Letting her decide to leave Logan was a bold move.

He dismissed the human with a flick of his hand, resisting the familiar urge to swat. This one, in particular, was useful. Misguided to think they would ever truly be allies, but useful nonetheless.

The manipulation was already forming in his head as the fallen human bowed and exited the room. He was too close to what he wanted for anything to stand in his way.

Thank you for reading *Huntress*!

If you loved this book, please write review on Amazon and/or Goodreads. I'd like to know what you think, and so will many others.

Reviews are the lifeblood of authors and your review will help others decide to read my books. If you want to see more from me, please leave a review. Thank you!

Please review *Huntress*:
http://review.HuntressBook.com

Keep reading to see what happens to Audrey and Logan in *Warfare (Life After Book 2)* →

THE BATTLE IS FAR FROM OVER

WARFARE

LIFE AFTER
BOOK TWO

JULIE HALL

USA TODAY BESTSELLING AUTHOR

THE TRIALS

*M*y heart beat as if it was trying to build up speed and erupt from my chest. I thrust my sword up in a defensive stance as I checked my surroundings, keeping my breathing shallow and silent. On the off-chance my enemy hadn't already discovered my position, I didn't want to give it up.

I weaved my way between cargo containers and shipping crates piled along the harbor. My feet moved soundlessly on the smooth concrete, a skill I'd been training hard to accomplish. The brackish smell of stagnant water cloaked the docks, infiltrating my nostrils and coating my throat. It tasted of decaying waste.

My stomach rolled.

Sweat dripped down my face, stinging my eyes and blurring my vision, but I couldn't risk moving to wipe it away. Wisps of fog played hide-and-seek around the crates. Between the darkness and the fog, visibility was low to non-existent. An attack from above was a real concern.

Fear scrambled for a foothold I refused to give.

My arms shook with the strain of the sword's weight. I'd finally built up the muscle to wield it fluidly, but the exertion and adrenaline of hours of fighting, chasing, and being chased was beginning to show.

"Don't lock up your muscles, even if you're so tired you think there's no other way to remain standing. Stay fluid and light on your feet, Audrey. Always."

Hugo's voice echoed in my head as clearly as if he stood right next to me. It was a lesson he often reminded me of. I tried to do exactly what he had instructed, but I was getting to the point where perhaps locked muscles *were* the only way to remain standing.

A sound drifted toward me—flesh sliding across the concrete. I cocked my head and strained to hear more, but only the breeze tickled my ears.

Three sharp clicks were my only warning before the creature sprang at me, talons, jaws, and an abundance of spikes extended toward me as it flew through the air. Without a moment to think, I threw myself straight at it, ducking into a roll at the last second while its tail's razor edge sailed over my head, landing in the very spot I'd so recently occupied.

This one was smaller than most of the others, but what it lacked in girth, it made up in, well . . . pointy sharp things all over its body. This was a beast I wanted to keep out of my personal space.

Someone had gotten creative with this fellow.

I seriously wanted to throat punch whoever that was.

The demon lunged at me with its claws, followed by a whip of its tail and a snap of its jaws. The assaults came in such quick succession that only the gusts of air from its movements alerted me to each consecutive attack. The demon herded me to a dead end, with containers blocking off all escape routes. I quickly wiped the sweat from my eyes.

Enough messing around.

I had to defeat this thing *now*. Only an offensive attack would bring it down.

I threw extra force into the next defensive block, just barely enough to throw the creature's equilibrium off for a millisecond. That was all I needed. I turned and sprinted toward the container and then took two clanging steps up its metal side before flipping backward. With a battle cry, I aimed my sword down, straight at the creature's spinal cord. I saw everything as if time itself had slowed, I saw my aim was true and I would hit my mark.

There was a single, solitary moment of victory before I was jerked to a sudden and painful stop.

The world went white.

I looked around in confusion. "What?" I yelled into the nothingness, still suspended awkwardly in the air. The harnesses that wrapped around my legs and abdomen pinched. There'd be bruises for sure. "I was perfect." The restraints disappeared and I dropped onto my belly as abruptly as I'd been frozen mid-strike. "Oof."

A huge screen materialized in front of me, playing back the last few moments. I watched myself deflect the creature, its balance shaken as I whirled around, reached the shipping container, and in a perfect maneuver propelled myself airborne and back toward the demon. I was right, my blade had been in perfect position. It was the tail—and the two-foot jagged spike attached to it—about to impale me, that I'd missed.

I sagged in defeat and thumped my head against the now-padded ground. Groaning loudly, I flipped onto my back.

"So not fair," I mumbled.

"That was the best one yet," a disgustingly cheerful voice said.

I groaned again. A horn blared, the sound ripping up my eardrums and I flinched. The voices of the technicians monitoring the gauntlet once again became discernible. The white around me transformed into a gym, one of many within the training center.

This one was typical. Floors padded with thick blue mats and windowless, bland walls. The only noteworthy differences were the absence of a weapons-wall and an observation deck situated high in the back, giving an overview of the action to observers and the technicians who monitored and ran the trials.

I cracked one eye open and craned my neck to watch Hugo's approach. "I am not convinced the other hunters run the same gauntlets as me. If they did, there wouldn't be any active hunters. This trial is freakin' impossible. If I'm not going to be skewered by a berserker hybrid demon—which doesn't even exist in real life by the way—then I'm being decapitated, drowned, slimed, or . . . wait for it, it's my personal favorite . . . squished by a fat demon who literally moves too fast for the laws of physics."

Hugo beamed down at me, patiently amused as I continued my rant.

"I stand by my previous statement. We should not have to fight things that don't actually exist. And," I ticked a finger in the air, "I should be able to use fire during these trials. In real life, my sword blazes, remember? Not having my weapon makes these challenges completely unrealistic."

"What an exciting gauntlet," Hugo said as he offered a hand to help me stand.

A jolt of power shot up my arm as our hands connected. I've never gotten a read on his emotions through the empathy link, only a strange shock of energy. He still pretended not to know what I was talking about when I asked about it, often changing the subject immediately, but the gleam in his eye told me he knew exactly what happened. I'd long since given up trying to figure it out.

I received a pat on the back when I got to my feet. "You're so close," he continued with a genuine smile on his face. "I'm so proud of the progress you've made in these short few months."

Even disgruntled, my heart warmed under his regard. With effort, I dematerialized my body armor and wiped the remaining sweat from my face with the sleeve of the fitted cotton shirt I wore underneath.

"That was the hardest one yet."

"Yet it was your best one so far," he countered.

The look I shot him had him chuckling again. My mentor's moods shifted only from calm to serious or happy. His ability to keep his cool in every situation was truly a gift I did not possess. It was as if, regardless of the situation, he was simply happy to be there with me.

An enigma for sure.

And very, very different from my last mentor. My heart twisted and I swiped a hand down my face to cover a wince.

"Another failed gauntlet," I said. "What are we up to now, lucky number thirteen? I should have known this one would be a bust."

Hugo laid a hand on my shoulder in a fatherly gesture of comfort. His eyes were kind. "You will get there, I promise. Sometimes—"

"Great work today, Audrey," Rhett, one of the technicians, interrupted. "You were almost there. We were all rooting for you. I'm sure you'll get through it next time. After you pass the initial trial, the gauntlets get shorter. You only run them to make sure you're still on your game."

I nodded my thanks, even though his interruption was kind of rude. It seemed like people constantly interrupted Hugo. You'd think his aged appearance alone would earn more respect.

Anyway, Rhett's words were nothing I didn't already know. Life since I had died almost six months ago, was a whole lot of getting on the game, staying on the game, and making sure I wasn't off the game. Nobody back on Earth had any idea how busy the afterlife could be.

I forced a kind smile before he turned and went about his business.

Then I turned to Hugo. "Sorry," I said. "I don't know why that happens so often. Some people need a serious etiquette refresher."

Hugo waved it off, smiling that secretive smile of his. He gestured toward the exit and we fell in step with each other. Well, kind of. Hugo shuffled and leaned heavily on his cane. His white hair bobbed along with him.

I slowed my steps to match his gait, more of a stroll than a true walk. It was refreshing in a place where everything operated at such a fast pace. Like stopping to smell the roses and all that junk.

Hugo was a walking—or shuffling—dichotomy. A frail teacher one moment and a fierce warrior the next. Serious and poignant, yet with a sparkle of humor often shining from his eyes.

Each cloak donned and discarded at a moment's notice.

He interrupted my musings. "Why don't you take a short break before we continue training?"

I groaned dramatically. "You mean we're not done?"

"Afraid not. We have a couple more hours of torture—oh, forgive me, *training*—before the day is finished," he grinned. "Here we are, the girls' locker room. Get some water and change into fresh workout clothes, and I'll see you in our gym in a bit."

I pouted even as I capitulated. "Fine, but I'm not going to be any fun."

"Deal."

I hadn't realized we were negotiating, or I'd have tried harder. He left me standing there, his poufy hair bobbing as he shuffled down the hall and around the corner.

I blinked once. "What a nut."

Back in the gym twenty minutes later, the door slammed with a bang. For a moment, my former programming kicked in and I spun around with a pounding heart and then an unacceptable sadness. Hugo hobbled toward me with a fatherly smile.

"Expecting someone else, my dear?" He always knew when my thoughts were elsewhere and didn't hesitate to call me on it.

It was as embarrassing as it was startling.

"Not especially," I answered truthfully. "For a second there I just thought . . ."

My brain snagged on the memory of my first day of training. Seemingly forever ago. Logan plowing through the door, the noise that followed, the dropped sword.

I shook my head to clear it. "Never mind, it was nothing." I forced a smile around the fractures in my heart. "What adventures are to be had this afternoon?"

It was a joke of ours. Hugo was all about learning through repetition, so the reality was that training was as far from adventurous as possible. Similar to Logan's style—my insides pinged again—but with a gentler touch.

Hugo always insisted I learn to use other weapons in conjunction with, and even instead of, my sword. Since I had a sword that burst into holy flames and charred the flesh off my enemies on contact, I kind of didn't see the point, but he held firm.

He said I needed to be a well-rounded fighter and shortcuts wouldn't do me any favors. I hardly ever argued with him. I simply didn't have the heart.

It would have been a reminder of my former mentor. The one I tried desperately to stop thinking about.

Logan and I had parted ways amicably enough . . . I supposed. There had hardly been a word between us since. If I were truthful with myself, I would admit it hurt.

But I prided myself on being deceptive only with myself these days, so the truth was deeply buried. Our mutual friends recognized the tension, and like the children of divorce, they took turns eating at our separate tables and spending the evenings with one and then the other.

I didn't like that, or most of the other changes since I'd switched mentors, yet I still thought it was for the best. Spending a lot of time with Logan was not healthy for me.

His cold demeanor, on the other hand, most likely came from wounded pride. People didn't know my real reasons for asking for a different mentor, so it reflected poorly on him.

And then there was Kaitlin.

There *had* to be something between them, but for the life of me I couldn't see it. It was as confusing as it was annoying.

Romona, my grandmother—and now my best friend—was my saving grace these days. She was my anchor to this realm and the earthly one as well.

She shared in the grief I'd been plagued with since getting my memories back and softened the blow of losing my family on Earth. She kept my mind on better things and reminded me of the Father who loved me.

I'd yet to see God since my time with Him on the snowy peak, but I felt His presence daily. The hole within filled in a little more every day, even as new fractures appeared in my heart. But, I reasoned, a heart could break and a person still remain whole.

I was banking on it.

I looked up at Hugo, realizing I'd become lost in my thoughts once again. He stood waiting, leaning heavily on his cane with both hands.

"I'm sorry, you should have said something. My mind wanders more often than it should."

His gentle smiled appeared. "Sometimes there is a reason for the wandering. A reason for the searching. If you never stop to be silent, you won't hear the nudging of the Lord."

"Nudging of the Lord?"

"Yes, that quiet voice inside that is trying to guide you. If you constantly fill your mind and never stop and be silent, how will you ever receive your answer? When you ask for guidance you must not merely ask, but believe. One who doubts is like a wave in the sea, blown and tossed by the wind."

I barked out a short laugh. "My silence isn't usually productive. More like obsessive. You'll have to teach me some better meditation skills."

"Do you have your book?"

I didn't need to ask which one. Hugo had been on me to read the ancient Scriptures since day one. But something kept me distant from my loving Creator's Word. I shrugged and turned to walk toward the practice dummy in the corner, busying myself with preparing it.

"The more you know of Him, the more you will be able to see the way He does, and the more you will be able to hear His voice above the throngs."

Hear His voice?

"Yes, hear His voice. The gentle whispering of His truth in your ears and heart, comes with knowing Him."

I turned to him with furrowed brow. Had I spoken out loud? "But I've only heard Him the one time up on the mountaintop."

"Oh, I'm sure that is not true, but it sounds like you need to add *listening* to your list of things to practice. Sometimes you need to be still and quiet before you can hear His voice."

Hugo's words gave me a spark of hope. Could I really hear from God on a regular basis? "Will He sound like He did on the mountaintop?"

"Not always." He flashed a cheeky smile. "There will be times He will sound like me."

"Yeah, right. I'm sure that's what all the mentors say to their trainees. So, what you're saying is I need to go into my room and close my eyes until I hear your voice whispering in my ear."

"Something along those lines." His toothy grin was familiar. It meant he was either making fun of me, or laughing silently at a joke I didn't understand.

Both regular occurrences.

I chewed my lip, taking his words to heart. As I turned away, Hugo's hand settled on my shoulder, startling me.

"It will come with time and practice, as do most things. Just like a baby taking her first steps. They are shaky at first, but become stable and sure with repetition."

"You know how I love being compared to a baby," I deadpanned.

The shrug of his ancient shoulders told me the analogy was appropriate. I humbly swallowed the pill. I would have jumped down Logan's throat for saying such a thing, but this wasn't Logan, and I was tired.

Humility was a hard lesson for me.

Hugo's words had constantly challenged me over the last few months. A few words from him could hit my brain and travel straight to my heart, leaving a burning impression in both places.

I would lie awake at night battling over them. It was as if my heart knew they were true, but my head fought them out of a defiance I didn't understand.

If my head would just yield to my heart, I might find peace, but night after night, day after day, my head fought on.

Weariness settled over me.

"You have your answer in front of you, Audrey—that which will quiet your tumultuous heart. It's yours for the taking."

Before I could think it over, he clapped his hands loud and hard. I jumped.

"Now, let's begin this afternoon's adventure. How about we work on swords for a bit? That should cheer your spirits."

He was right. I bounced on the balls of my feet and shook out my arms and legs, imagining the melancholy being shaken from my mind at the same time as the stiffness from my limbs.

"Let's do this thing."

THE GIFT

I inhaled a deep breath of fresh, woody air. It was just as clean in the city, but the way each lungful in my beloved redwood forest energized my system and cleared my thoughts tricked me into believing different. The giant trees that soared to impossible heights would dwarf their counterparts on Earth. Rays of light filtered through the generously-spaced behemoths, allowing ferns and vines to grow without overtaking the woods.

I paused a moment to pluck a lovely deep blue wildflower, its fruity scent as appealing as its appearance. I tucked it behind my ear to capture its beauty and fragrance for myself and continued on my way. The trek home was familiar enough that I closed my eyes for a moment to enjoy a songbird's melody from somewhere in the canopy above.

I'd been given the opportunity to move into the city—closer to the training center—closer to Romona—but I'd turned it down. The redwood trees simply felt like home.

Perhaps someday I would change my mind, maybe even move into an apartment with Romona, but for now I appreciated the solitude.

It mirrored the emptiness I carried inside.

The underbrush to my left shook slightly. I laid a warning hand on Bear's head to keep him from terrorizing whatever poor creature rustled around in there.

My golden retriever accompanied me to and from the training center every day. What he did during my long hours of training was a mystery. My furry friend was a boon granted to me from the Creator—a loyal presence I would forever be grateful for. I ran my fingers along the rough trunk of my redwood tree. The bark melted away to reveal a door.

Inside, the dank walls and low lighting of the corridor were no longer depressing and sad, but magical. The lights let off a humming glow, reminding me of candlelight. I could imagine I lived within the walls of an ancient castle rather than encased in a living tree.

I drifted through the hall with my gown trailing behind me. With Hugo's help, I was getting better at materializing what I needed.

When alone, I often practiced by changing my clothing into long, flowing gowns fit for royalty. Today I wanted to feel like a princess rather than a warrior.

The sword still strapped to my side, made it hard to believe the illusion, so to compensate, the long dress was extra whimsical. The light green material floated behind me like the train on a fairy's wedding gown, long and light, and moving on a current of air that was barely there.

I'd seen something like it once on the cover of a fantasy novel, and the design had stuck with me. Today, for a few moments, the dress was not just in my head but covered my body as I made my way home.

My fingers grazed walls covered in a layer of soft moss. I hummed softly as I glided along, remembering a nursery rhyme my mom used to sing. Melancholy still tinged each of my days. The loss of my family was not really a loss—after all, I would see them again—but it still felt like one.

As if sensing my mood, Bear stuck his wet nose into my palm and nuzzled it. My eyes remained transfixed on the bumpy wall as I flattened my hand and ran it over his soft fur. He leaned into the touch, even while matching his steps with my own.

Reaching my door, I grasped the smooth knob and heaved a heavy sigh before turning it, already lamenting the loss of my beautifully impractical gown, along with its wonderfully unrealistic dreams of fairies, princesses, and knights in shining armor.

I pushed open the door, but before my garb melted away, I was assaulted by the awful sounds of screaming and shouting.

"Ahh!" I stumbled and flashed into my body armor, reaching down to unsheathe my sword, simultaneously falling into a fighting stance.

There were a few gasps and a delayed "Surprise!" Belatedly, I recognized that my room had been transformed into party central.

Purple streamers hung from every foot of the ceiling above the thirty or so people who stood gaping at me. My furniture had been stowed somewhere in the walls or floors, leaving space to walk.

A long, narrow table draped with a lace tablecloth, stood along the right wall, food weighing it down from end to end. Adjacent to it stood a similar table, brightly wrapped packages piled haphazardly on top.

"Way to go, Aud. Still keeping up your tradition of grand entrances."

My heartbeat—which started to calm slightly—picked up at Alrik's jest. The faces of the people in front of me held as much surprise as my own. I was still in fighting stance with my sword at ready—up and to the right, almost as if I held a baseball bat. I slowly angled the blade down and slid it back in its scabbard.

"Um . . . surprise?" Romona repeated, offering a sheepish smile as she gently pushed her way forward. "Aren't you, you know, surprised?" Her smile closely resembled a grimace.

I answered her with a smile-grimace of my own. "I guess? What's going on here?"

"It's a surprise party," she said with fake cheer.

"I gathered as much, but for what?"

"Your birthday! You're nineteen now! Surprise," she repeated, apparently unsure of what else to say.

My voice lowered and I bent to whisper in her ear. "But I'm not nineteen yet. My birthday isn't for another five months."

She whispered back from the side of her mouth, "I know, but I thought you needed some cheer. Just go with it." Her eyes pleaded with me.

I huffed and rolled my own.

Another voice interrupted. "If I wasn't impressed with you before, I have to say I am now. Perhaps pulling a sword on your party guests was a little extreme, but it was kind of awesome too."

Jonathon half-lifted me off the ground in an exuberant hug. The look Romona shot him was half-relieved, half-peeved.

"I don't really startle well," I told him.

"That, little Aud, is quite the understatement. But I always appreciate your antics for their pure entertainment value."

I'd almost forgotten Alrik. Once Jonathon let go, I turned to the big Viking with a scathing look, which he laughed off as he used one of his giant paws to mess up my hair.

"Hey, come on," I complained as I stepped out of his reach. "Insult to injury here."

"What, me?" He feigned hurt. "I was just trying to tactfully remind you what your hair looks like when you get scared."

I groaned loudly and looked around. Thankfully, most people had gone back to conversing among themselves and hadn't noticed my instant dye job.

Kaitlin chose that moment to arrive. Decked out in black skinny jeans, a silver-sequined tank and dripping in silver jewelry, she reminded me of a disco ball, attracting attention wherever she went. Her blonde hair was pulled back in a slick, high ponytail with a few small braids dispersed throughout its length. Her matching makeup highlighted all the right features.

She was gorgeous.

I was jealous.

"What did I miss? Whoa there—it must have been something good. What does silver mean again, Audrey?"

"It means if I wasn't already dead, this little scene might have sent me to an early grave."

"Audrey, heart attacks at nineteen are highly unlikely," Romona cut in.

I rolled my eyes. "Are they more common at *eighteen*? Just give me a sec to take care of myself." I turned to flee.

"Mind if I join you?" Romona asked.

"No. Come on." I waved her forward. A moment of privacy with her would get me some answers.

Once in the hallway, Romona closed the door behind her, instantly muffling the sounds from the room beyond. She waited in silence while I willed my hair back to monochromatic brown, only a shade lighter than her own.

"Okay." I fully faced her. "I'm ready to hear the reason behind my near cardiac arrest."

"Audrey," Romona sighed, "you didn't almost have a heart attack."

"Tell that to my still erratically beating heart, because I'd love for it to chill out."

"Hey there." Romona leaned over and tapped a finger to my chest. "You can calm down now. You're giving my granddaughter a complex."

I gaped at her. I was still getting used to the fact that my best friend, who totally looked my age, was actually my grandma. "Cute."

She smiled broadly. "See, much better, right?"

Running both hands down my face, I resisted the urge to scream into them. "I know you love me, but what's up with the room full of screaming people? Especially when it's not even my birthday."

"I told you, we're celebrating your nineteenth birthday."

"But it's not my birthday. And besides, no one celebrates birthdays here. It's kind of pointless."

She shrugged. "So what? People still want to celebrate *you*. I thought it might help push you out of your funk."

I crossed my arms. "I'm not in a funk."

The look she gave me said she wasn't picking up what I was putting down. "Audrey, I know you miss our family . . . your family back on Earth. I thought, after remembering everything, you would start to heal, but instead it seems like your sadness is growing."

I raised my eyebrows at her. I thought I'd been doing a good job of acting like a person on the mend. Apparently I was wrong.

"So a birthday party is supposed to fix everything?"

Her face fell. "No, of course it isn't supposed to fix everything, but I wanted to prove you are still around people who love you. You have a family here as well."

People who love me? What about Logan?

The thought cut through my mind like the blade of a knife, traveling south and sticking in my heart. My wince was small but noticeable to Romona. She laid her hand on my uncovered arm, flinching when she experienced my emotions. Her sympathy was swallowed by my pain.

"Won't you talk to me about it?"

No.

Even if she knew what *it* was, I couldn't talk until I'd forced him out of my head and heart. I was convinced sheer force of will would work, yet so far, I'd gained little ground.

"I'm fine." It was only a half-lie. I took a deep breath, steeling myself. "This was a really sweet idea, even if it did almost kill me . . . again." I cocked a partial smile. "I guess I should go in and mingle with everyone. Especially since I'm the guest of honor and all that stuff."

"You don't have to if you don't want to. I can send everyone away."

"That would *almost* be weirder than me turning into a crazy huntress about to slay my party guests when they yelled 'surprise.' Man, I'm glad that didn't actually happen, right?"

She snickered. "If you had actually killed them, you wouldn't have to go back in there."

"Truth. Now, let's do this thing."

When we entered the room, one would almost guess the party had nothing to do with me, for all the attention we garnered.

But I was glad for it.

A loud crash startled me. Directly to my left, where a wall usually stood, ran two long, polished lanes with pins set up at the ends. People were lined up to take turns hurling a ball.

My jaw dropped.

A bowling alley? I was a horrible bowler. I'd broken my finger bowling. It wasn't a cherished memory. I slowly turned my neck until I scowled at Romona. "That," I jerked my thumb over my shoulder, "is not funny."

She stared back, wide-eyed. "*I* didn't do it."

"Nope, that would be my doing. Romona let your broken finger story slip, and I wanted to see if you'd improved with age." The smile on Alrik's face said he hoped I hadn't.

Why did he keep popping up? Was he everywhere?

"You," I jabbed a finger into Alrik's expansive chest, "are in big trouble, mister."

Alrik merely rumbled with laughter. "Oh little Aud, I'm game for a rumble with you whenever that new trainer of yours lets you rejoin the world."

I patted the scabbard still strapped to my leg. "You are so very lucky my sword only catches fire when I'm on Earth."

His answer was a wicked smile and a gleam. He enjoyed baiting me, but I also enjoyed rising to the challenge.

Kaitlin's voice stopped our verbal battle. "It's kind of like watching a Chihuahua go after a pit bull, don't you think?"

I laughed. "Hey, whose birthday is it, anyway? You guys are brutal! A Chihuahua? Really? I'd like to believe at the very least I'm a fierce-looking

Maltese, on a good day a miniature pinscher. Maybe one of those mixed breeds, both ferocious and fashionable."

Kaitlin's smile grew. "You're right, how could I have been so . . ."

"Insensitive, rude, tactless."

"Inaccurate."

"There's that as well."

Kaitlin threaded her arm through mine, the empathy link proving she was amused by our exchange, and pulled me through the crowd. "So now that *you* are finally here and *I* am finally here, we can get this party started!"

Kaitlin waved her hand toward the corner of the room, flicking an imaginary magic wand, and a DJ booth appeared complete with turntables and speakers.

Music began to play, despite the absence of a DJ. Enthusiastic partygoers sent up a few cheers and cleared a space in the middle of the room for dancing. A vinyl checkered dance floor materialized.

How retro.

This party was taking a decidedly eclectic turn. Bowling, lace, and a checkered dance floor. Romona was probably irritated.

We reached my closet just as someone stepped right out of it.

"Whoa, what? Who's in my closet?"

Kaitlin laughed. "It's actually how we all got here without tipping you off. There's a temporary portal between your closet and Romona's. People are showing up at her place in order to get here."

"Temporary portal? Since when is that a thing? And seriously, my *closet?*" I battled between annoyed and embarrassed. I hoped Romona had cleaned my closet before turning it into a transportation center. I'd left it pretty messy this morning. In fact, I'd left the whole room a small disaster.

"You have to get permission to create a portal. You fill out a few forms and voilà, here it is. But enough about that. I want to find something a little more stylish for you to wear. You look fierce in your armor, but maybe we can find something more appropriate for a party?"

I managed a weak smile. "Yeah."

"You're the guest of honor. You've got to step it up. You know, make the boys think they need to work a little harder."

"What boys?"

She offered a wicked smile. "Just boys in general."

I rolled my eyes while she riffled through my clothes, sidestepping every now and then when someone new arrived.

Kaitlin had asked to be reassigned to our part of the realm, and I'd come to realize she was a force to be reckoned with. She wasn't anything like I'd first assumed. Back then I'd been clouded by insecurities and a good dose of jealousy, so through my green, envy-filled eyes I'd written her off as snooty, aloof, and untrustworthy.

I'd nailed the mischievous part of her correctly—she frequently had something hidden up her sleeve—but where I'd seen it as malicious, she was usually hiding something harmless, often a poorly-executed attempt at do-gooding.

Once I got over myself, I'd come to learn Kaitlin had a really good heart, was funny and fun to be around, and kind. If I were honest with myself—which I habitually wasn't—I'd admit it was only my suspicions about her relationship with Logan that held me back from allowing our friendship to truly cement.

A sharp pain beneath my sternum reminded me of the certain someone I was most definitely not supposed to be thinking about.

"Ah-ha," Kaitlin's hand, clutched around a white bundle, shot into the air triumphantly, "this is perfect. Here." She shoved the material into my chest. "Let's go try this one on. I have the perfect idea for your hair as well. Seriously, I've spent hours staring in the mirror trying to get mine to change color at will. I'm so jealous of your skills."

"It's kind of overrated, actually."

She tilted her head. "Yeah, well, I guess it going hypercolor on you would be a little annoying." She shrugged. "Okay, let's get you dressed. Oh, wait."

Getting down on all fours, she dug around at the bottom of the closet, popping back up again moments later—but not before almost being stepped on by another late partygoer. "I almost forgot these."

She dangled a pair of three-inch-heeled silver sandals in front of my face before nudging me in the direction of the bathroom.

The white dress Kaitlin had picked out was both cute and comfortable. It fit snugly around my upper body and flared out at the hips, ending a few inches above my knees.

The white showcased my skin, naturally tanned due to the touches of Native American and Italian DNA running through my blood. The silver heels fancied up the outfit, while giving me some much-needed height.

While I dressed, Kaitlin found some chunky purple and silver jewelry to add to the ensemble. At her insistence, I streaked one small portion of my hair the same purple tone it had been at the realm wide celebration several months ago. That was the first time I'd changed any of my hair a different color.

The skill turned out to be more of a bother than a blessing, since it went haywire when I got emotional.

Kaitlin used an iron to add some volume and a gentle curl to my normally straight hair and then pushed me out of the bathroom. My room had expanded again, along with the growing number of people crowding the space.

The bowling alley, which I had no intention of going near, had added a few lanes. Kaitlin's dance party was a hit in the center of the room, and bright lights flashed in a very disco-esque way.

"Kaitlin." I leaned over to speak to her. "I only recognize about half of these people."

"Yeah, isn't it great? Word really got around."

I scanned the room until I found Romona. Her face said she wasn't too pleased her surprise had gotten out of hand.

I laughed to myself. She didn't stand a chance with Kaitlin and Alrik around. I motioned to Kaitlin that I was going to mingle, and she gave me a wink before turning toward the dance floor.

"All right, folks," her voice carried as she moved away, "let me show you how this thing is really done." Then the crowd swallowed her.

Before I reached Romona, an arm slipped around my waist, halting me.

"You look beautiful," Jonathon murmured. His soft breath on my ear caused an involuntary shiver.

"Oh, hi." I turned slightly and found myself fully in an embrace. I cleared my throat and returned the hug nervously. "Um, thanks."

Ever since my stint in the Healing Center where he worked, Jonathon had made good on his promise to stay in my life. His interest in me was clear. He'd even gone so far as to take me out on a few dates—which admittedly had been fun.

There hadn't been a repeat kiss attempt since the celebration, thankfully. But his insistence on always finding an excuse to touch me was uncomfortable.

It wasn't his fault exactly. I was still wary of the empathy link in general. He was usually good about not touching my skin, but the thought of an accidental brush put me on edge.

Especially since my feelings for him were so confused.

I wiggled out of his arms. He frowned slightly but didn't comment.

"I was looking for Romona," I said with more confidence. "Want to help me find her?"

"I'd like nothing more." He offered me his shirt-covered elbow. The gesture was so formal, I paused before slipping my hand in the crook. He seemed pleased with my response.

We found Romona in the far corner of the room giving it to Alrik. "The bowling alley is not funny, Alrik! You know how she feels about bowling, and that's—"

"Well hey, little Aud, looks like you draw quite a crowd," Alrik cut in before Romona could finish her sentence.

"I think we both know I wasn't the draw this evening."

"Whatever could you mean?"

"I mean this," I said with a wicked grin. Letting go of Jonathon, I grabbed the first person to brush past me. "Hey," I said to the surprised partygoer, a guy with red hair who looked to be in his mid-twenties. "Do you know who I am?"

He answered with a puzzled expression and obvious discomfort, "Um, should I?"

"Nope, just checking. Mind telling me how you found out about the party?"

"Well . . ." He shifted his feet, obviously wanting to get away from the weird girl gripping his arm. "My friend Trisha said this was the place to be tonight, so we all showed up."

"Okay, thanks."

Once off the hook, the guy took his cue and disappeared into the throng.

"Hmm." I tapped my finger on my lips, pretending to think really hard. "I wonder how word got around? Let's see, who do I know who would try to turn my private birthday surprise into the party of the century?"

As expected, Alrik only continued to smile. "Well, whoever it was, I'm sure he had your best interests in mind. Perhaps it was someone who was looking for an excuse to loosen you up a little. For your own good, of course."

"Well, of course."

"So does that mean you're up for a little bowling action?"

I swatted at him. "Not even if your life depended on it. Just make sure my room goes back to normal once this is all done. Shellacked wood planks are not part of my motif."

Alrik barked a laugh. "No worries there. My handiwork disappears when I do."

"Good to know."

Alrik slapped Jonathon on the back. "Well, Jonathon, at least I know you're good for a game."

"I'm not sure." He looked my way. "I don't want to leave Audrey alone."

"No, go ahead, have fun," I said hastily. "I'm good. I'm sure there's at least one or two other people I actually know here."

"Come on, let her have some girl time." Alrik practically forced Jonathon toward the alley. With a forlorn look Jonathon relented and allowed himself to be herded away.

I watched for a moment in concern. Why was I so quick to ditch him? He'd been nothing but nice and attentive to me. He was handsome and up front with his feelings for me, which I liked.

But something was missing. Some elusive connection I believed would appear . . . eventually.

"You know you're horribly bad at this." Romona's words pulled my focus to her.

"What?"

Her eyes were sad. She waved a limp hand in the direction of the boys. "That. Figuring things out with Jonathon. Guys in general."

I could have been offended, but I didn't disagree. "I know."

She forced a smile. "Hey, come on, let's get your mind off it for a night. This isn't exactly what I planned, but it's not all bad. Let's go play some games."

She pointed to where a row of arcade games had appeared behind me. I smiled. We were miles away from the lace theme by now. Looked like someone else had decided to take the liberty of redecorating my room. At least it wouldn't be permanent. "Sure, let's give it a go."

Hours later, I cast Kaitlin a bleary-eyed glance from my position on the couch as she handed me a present from the pile. Bear lay on the other end in a dead sleep, covering my legs along with the rest of the couch. I was unsure where he'd disappeared to during the party, but by the size of his enlarged belly, I could take an educated guess.

"Kaitlin, you are crazy if you think I have enough energy to get through that mound tonight. No way. I'm officially calling the party."

There wasn't much left to call—Romona was wandering around, cleaning up, and Kevin and Jonathon were talking. "Does anyone have the time?" I yelled. "I'm calling it!"

"Oh, come on." Kaitlin pouted prettily and I spotted Kevin eyeing her.

Was something going on there? My mood soured. If Kaitlin was with Logan, it would only lead to heartache for Kevin. I had firsthand experience with that.

I folded my arms across my chest in an I'm-not-changing-my-mind stance.

"Well, at least open one. Just one before the night is out, and I won't bug you about the rest."

"Fine, I can do one. Just hand it over. I think my feet are broken."

Kaitlin rolled her eyes at me and put a square box about the size of a cantaloupe in my hands. It was wrapped simply in white with a sky-blue ribbon tied around the center. I tore the paper off and opened the box.

Sitting inside was a perfect pearlescent conch shell. I gently lifted it out of the box, and a small piece of paper fluttered to the ground. Something about the gift made my heart skip a beat and then pick up.

Suddenly I didn't feel so tired anymore.

Romona stepped next to me as I picked up the note. It wasn't addressed to anyone, nor was there any salutation, but I knew the handwriting.

So you can experience a part of the ocean whenever you want.

I pinned Romona with my eyes and kept my voice low so it didn't carry. "You invited Logan?"

Her answer was revealed in her widened eyes.

"Yeah, that was actually me." Kaitlin's lowered voiced reached me. "I just thought there might be a small part of you that wanted him here. And I know he still cares, it's just—"

"So what'd you get?" Jonathon's voice stopped Kaitlin's next words. Words I secretly and desperately wanted to hear.

I faced him with a plastered smile, lifting the beautiful shell in their direction. "Someone must know how much I like the ocean. They didn't leave a name with the gift." I got a reprimanding look from Romona for purposefully misleading Jonathon, but I wasn't about to open Pandora's box.

Romona clapped her hands once. "Well, I think we should call it a night. Let's get out of here and let Audrey get some rest."

With effort, I stood to show them out. "Hey, guys," Faces turned my way, "Thanks for making this night special. I, um . . ." I floundered as I tried to put my feelings into words.

"You're welcome," Romona answered with a smile. "We'll see you later."

When the door clicked shut, I sagged to the floor with Logan's gift still clutched in my hands. I ran my fingers over the cool ridges before bringing it up to my ear to listen to its sweet melody.

Uninvited images of our day at the beach flooded my mind. His smile as he looked over the Creator's work, the churning and sparkling kaleidoscope of water laid out in front of us. The laughter in his eyes as I surfaced from a particularly spectacular wipeout. The shocked expression on his face when I stripped off my wet suit on the beach. His intensity as we fled the unseen evil that stalked us. And finally the memory I'd tried the hardest to bury.

The kiss.

I could no longer tell myself it had been a fake, just a necessary ploy to distract our enemies. He had returned my affections and turned it from something necessary to something gentle and sensual and beautiful I would never forget. And then there was the care he'd taken with me in the moments that followed.

The kiss had started it all. The axis of our relationship had shifted and remained tilted ever since.

I opened my eyes, not realizing I'd closed them in the first place. My fingers rested lightly on my lips, as if they still experienced the tingling sensation his had left behind.

Was that what he had intended with his gift? To remind me of that day? And if so, to what end? What was he trying to tell me?

Did he think of that day? Perhaps as often as I tried not to?

Or did it mean nothing at all?

"Agh." I threw the shell across the room in frustration. It hit the back cushion of the couch and bounced once on the seat before falling safely to the floor. Bear, shocked out of his slumber, tumbled to the ground. Getting to his feet, he shook himself vigorously, glared his disapproval, and lumbered off to jump on the bed, taking up as much space as possible in revenge.

But I didn't care.

I was too disgusted with myself. I'd turned what was most likely meant to be a fun gift into a declaration of feelings. I couldn't blame Logan for my agitation.

The blame lay at my own feet. My own inability to shake him from my heart. That door had been closed. Shut tightly, and I was moving on. I had Jonathon, who was great. Seemingly even perfect at times. My own Prince Charming.

Perhaps a little too perfect, but really, could that be counted against him?

No, it most definitely could not. *Too perfect*, in fact, was going on the top of the list of things I would force myself to find desirable. Yes, I'd start working on that.

Tomorrow.

I chewed my lip. Tonight, and just tonight, perhaps I'd allow my heart to feel what it was aching to feel.

A STRANGE STATE OF MIND

*M*y sword sailed through the air in a perfect arc, hacking clean through the practice dummy I'd already stabbed with daggers and throwing stars. Everything above its lifelike shoulders toppled to the ground with a thud. Its unseeing eyes stared unblinkingly at the ceiling. This one had a short mop of black hair sprouting from its head. I twisted my neck to get a better look at its unchanging facial features.

"Is there a reason the practice dummies look like humans instead of things with distorted limbs and long, spiked tails, or whatever a demon usually looks like?"

"Yes," Hugo answered calmly from the other side of the room. He fiddled around with the weapons along the wall, picking one up and inspecting it before replacing it somewhere new. I didn't see much rhyme or reason to his task, but that was Hugo for you. I'd learned to roll with it.

I waited for an answer I apparently would not receive. He hadn't bothered to spare me a glance.

"O-kay. So, do you *know* the reason why we practice with human dummies instead of demon dummies?"

"Yes." He picked up a new weapon and brought it close to his face squinting at the wide blade of the cutlass.

"Care to share?"

"No." He returned the sword to a different spot on the wall.

What in the world was he doing that for? Was it some OCD thing? Maybe he was arranging everything by size or alphabetical?

Focus Audrey. Completely not the point.

"Fabulous. Well, I'll just continue to learn to decapitate humans then. You realize I'm having flashbacks of my previous trainer because of your lack of elaboration."

Hugo turned and flashed his teeth in an amused grin. He hobbled over to me until he invaded my personal space. With only inches separating us, his eyes studied my face, missing nothing. "Perhaps you haven't given your previous trainer enough credit."

A whole slew of snappy responses nipped at my lips, but I choked them down. The way Hugo stared at me, albeit full of amusement, was significant. Like he wasn't just suggesting I hadn't given Logan enough credit, but was telling me so—in earnest. I lowered my sword, which suddenly weighed more than lead in my hand.

Hugo tilted his head, his smile widening. Satisfied with himself, he turned and teetered off to the other side of the room.

"You know you have this creepy Yoda-like thing going on sometimes," I called after him when I finally found my voice.

"Where do you think Yoda learned it from?"

"Har, har. Very funny, Master."

"Yes, I know. I basically invented funny. You know," he nodded toward the decapitated dummy, "that's the fourth one this morning. Although I appreciate the vigor with which you are attacking training, I detect you might be pulling motivation from the wrong place. Hmm?"

I tended to be a better fighter when I was angry. Something we were working on changing. Anger was not only a bad motivator, it was a dangerous one. It opened hunters up to sloppiness and had the potential to cause harm to our fellow fighters, as well as one's self.

I wiped the sweat from my brow with my sword arm. "I don't know. Maybe. Probably. I guess."

He waited for me to go on.

"The thing is I'm not sure why, or even who I'm angry with. Maybe my friends, maybe just myself. I don't know." I heaved a sigh in frustration. "Things just got a little . . . weird for me last night. I can't seem to shake it this morning."

"Angry at your friends for throwing you a birthday party? Or were the gifts not to your liking?"

"You knew about the party?" Dumbstruck, I blinked several times, then eyed him suspiciously. What did he know about the gifts? I wasn't about to touch that one with a ten-foot pole.

"But of course, I knew. Who didn't?" He gave a knowing chuckle.

I arched my brows. If my reclusive mentor had found out about the party, Alrik and Kaitlin had been *thorough*.

"Seriously? Why didn't you come then?"

"Oh, I'm far too ancient. I would have made all the youngsters nervous."

"I doubt you would have even been the oldest one there. Appearances can be very deceiving."

"That they can be. A very important lesson for sure. But just as important is learning to discern the truth behind the façade. Do you think you've mastered that yet?"

His question reminded me of Deborah. On our first meeting, she'd cautioned me to trust the right people and told me that learning to correctly discern motives was going to be important for me. I still hadn't unraveled that mystery.

Even though Hugo's tone was light, I detected a serious intent behind his smiles. I gave his question some thought rather than glibly throwing out a joke. And the answer I came up with was unsettling.

"No, I don't think I have. In fact, the times when I'm most sure I know the truth of a matter have been those when I've been the most incorrect." In a moment of sincerity, I continued, "It's frustrating, you know? To constantly feel flipped upside down and sideways. I think there are probably very few things I know for sure."

His expression was gentle. "And what are they?"

"The love of family and friends, I suppose."

"And what happens when they fail you as well?"

My heart balked at his words. If I couldn't rely on my friends, what did I have left? "That won't ever truly happen." There was a sharp note in my voice, even though I said it to convince myself as much as Hugo.

"But of course, it will. People, even those close to the throne, are not perfect. If you hold your trust and faith in them alone, you can be certain each one will eventually fail you."

"And you know this because . . . ?" I asked, irritated. His words started an internal earthquake, shaking the only solid foundation I had left. I wanted to tell him to stop talking, but my open-ended question gave him permission to barrel on.

"Because it is written plainly in Scripture. There is only One you will ever be able to solely put your trust in. The Scriptures tell us not to put our trust in human beings but instead to trust in the Lord with all our heart and lean not on our own understanding. You are to submit all your ways to Him, and He will make your paths straight. And I'm afraid until you allow these truths to be buried in your heart, you will find yourself lost and confused, with growing anger festering inside until it begins to rot."

I surprised myself with how vehemently I responded. "Oh my gosh. You make it sound like God's going to lay a curse on me until I believe it." Forget internal earthquakes, I was headed toward a straight-up freak-out. *Is it hot in here, or is it just me about to have a meltdown?*

"Not a curse, little one, but discipline from the One who loves you most. Your heart need not be broken over and over if you learn the truth. When you know the teachings in Scripture, you will know the truth and the truth will set you free. Putting your trust solely in the Creator will sort out your issues with discernment."

"How so?" I looked away from Hugo and kicked a piece of the practice dummy still lying at my feet. An arm. I left the shoulders and head alone—those unseeing eyes creeped me out.

"Because you will be walking in His will and not your own. He will be your guide, and you'll learn to discern through His filter. God uses all things for good. It doesn't mean there won't be trials, but with Him all things are possible. Don't you realize He's in the business of mending the broken?"

The question hit me unexpectedly hard. I felt my brokenness about Logan all over again, like jagged edges sticking into my soul. Did I really believe God could mend me?

"The lessons we learn and the growth we experience in our hearts and minds are just as important as the physical training I'm putting you through. In truth, they are even more important, because as you become a better fighter, you will have to fight against your nature, which will tell you that through your own merits you can achieve your goals. But the glory for your victories is not yours to capture. There is One far greater than yourself who has equipped you with everything you need to be successful. The glory should be His alone. And when you surrender to Him, you'll feel the freedom, peace, and fulfillment you are looking for now."

I stared at Hugo in awe. His little speech had the potential to completely change my life, but my skeptical nature reared its head. Control of my life was a lot to gamble, and not only that, what he asked of me was hard. It seemed impossible. I didn't even know where to start.

"It's a lot to take in, Audrey. It's okay to be confused. Overwhelmed even. But you aren't alone. Remember, you are not alone . . . ever."

I heaved a sigh and gave a slight nod. Hugo returned the gesture, but without his signature smile of approval—almost as if he knew something I didn't that disturbed him. Like he knew I would take the harder road.

He probably just felt bad that I was such a slow learner.

"I think that's it for the day."

"Are you sure?" I asked. By my count we should have at least an hour more of training before I was dismissed.

"Yes, that will do for today." He turned back toward the weapons wall with a smile on his face. "I believe I spied a gentleman waiting for you out in the hallway. I think we've let him wait long enough."

Logan. I took in a quick breath of air but almost instantaneously swatted the thought from my mind. Of course, it wasn't him. We hadn't spoken in weeks, and sightings at the training center were rare. Mostly a back or profile at long distance during lunch, or an awkward, hurried brush past, heads down to pretend we didn't see each other. No, it couldn't be Logan.

Jonathon never came to the training center. It was probably Alrik or Kevin wanting to touch base about training.

I headed to the weapons wall to help Hugo put things away. His bent form and slow movements compelled me to lend an extra hand.

"I know what you are doing," he said as I lifted a sword into place. "You know I'm capable of setting these things right, and I've already dismissed you for the day. If I don't hear the door shutting behind you in under a minute I'm going to be sore with you."

His voice held authority, and his large gray eyebrows scrunched together, but his serious demeanor was just a ruse to get me moving. "All right, all right, you win. I'm leaving now."

He nodded and turned back to the wall.

Before exiting, I splashed some water on my face and threw on a hoodie. I'd long since quit caring what I looked like after training, so I didn't give my appearance any extra thought before leaving.

I opened the gym door slowly and stole a peek down the hall. Jonathon casually leaned against the wall with a single red rose in his hands. I'd always had time to primp for our dates. Seeing two of my worlds collide was strange.

Now I definitely cared what I looked like.

I stole a moment to appraise him while his eyes were trained on the ceiling. With his crisp clothes, clean sandy-brown hair, and warm eyes, he didn't fit in with the hunter riffraff walking about—tall, sweaty bodybuilder types who, given the proper motivation, could break you in two. Mind you, I did get the impression that under his ironed shirts and formal demeanor, Jonathon would be a worthy opponent if pressed.

I let the door swing shut loudly behind me, and he turned my way with a smile as cute as apple pie. I returned it as he walked my way, then swept me into a large bear hug.

"What are you doing here?" I asked when he set me back down, a little relieved to break contact.

"Do I need an excuse for wanting to see you? This," he said, producing the long red rose, "is for you. It reminded me of you. A classic beauty who can stand on her own without the frills other flowers may need."

Blushing, I ducked my head and minded my hair so it didn't turn a weird shade at the flattery. "Well, I'm not sure I accept your assessment of me, but I will accept the flower. Thank you."

Jonathon handed me the flower without touching my fingers.

I smelled the wonderful scent of the beautiful rose. "So, is this flower the only reason you've been loitering outside my gym?"

"I was hoping you might grace me with your presence for dinner tonight." Jonathon swept into an over-the-top, joking bow. I'd learned, much to my surprise, that Jonathon was in fact a prince when he was alive—a minor prince of Luxembourg in the 1700s, not set to inherit the throne, but a prince nonetheless.

That had been a jarring discovery. We'd been on our second date when he broke the news. Remembering that conversation always brought an uncomfortable twinge to my gut. His jesting caused the memory to bulldoze my mind.

"So," Jonathon seemed uncharacteristically nervous. "There's something I need to tell you, and I'll admit I probably should have said something sooner. It's really not a big deal though."

His sudden nervousness didn't trigger any alarms because dang, this risotto was delectable. I listened with only half an ear and shoveled another forkful of delicious-ness in my mouth. It was several beats before it registered he was waiting for me to respond.

"Oh, right, sorry. What is it you want to tell me?"

"Well you see," he started. I snuck another bite of my meal while he talked. "You know how people are always making prince jokes around me?"

"Mmhmm." I nodded because my mouth was full.

"It's because I am actually a prince. Or rather, was a prince because we don't really keep our titles here." His words came out in a rush, as if saying it quickly would lessen their impact.

Gagging noises erupted from my throat as I choked on the food I'd just swallowed.

Jonathon's eyes widened as I beat on my chest until most of the risotto slid all the way down. I coughed up what went down the wrong tube into my napkin.

I did not just spit up food in front of a flippin' prince?

This was not happening.

But who springs that announcement on a girl while she's eating?

"What?" I finally managed to croak out.

The remainder of the date had been a semi-disaster. I hadn't taken the news well. Jonathon had gone on to explain he didn't tell me sooner because he was worried it would freak me out—and it kind of had.

In fairytales, sure, dating a prince sounded amazing. In reality, it was a lot of pressure.

Jonathon had spent the rest of the date trying to convince me he was just a regular guy who I shouldn't think of any differently. The rest of my scrumptious meal went untouched while I processed his elevated Earthly status.

I found out later that my friends had already known.

Benedict Arnolds, every one of them.

They all thought it was hilarious when I told them the story at lunch the following day. Kevin even shot mashed potatoes out of his nose because he had laughed so hard.

I restrained myself from rolling my eyes at the memory alone.

Jonathon and I had quite the age difference, but I tried to keep an open mind about it. No one seemed to take age into consideration here. And it wasn't like he looked or acted three hundred years old. He rarely talked about that portion of his life, and then only in jest. He worked hard so I wouldn't be intimidated to date him. It didn't always work.

My mock curtsey followed. "Why yes, I believe after I freshen up a bit I may be able to acquiesce."

"Great," he said, bringing our royal exchange to an end. "May I walk you to the locker room? I can pick you up at your tree later this evening. Say seven thirty?"

"Sounds good to me. The locker rooms are this way. I have to say I'm surprised you figured your way through this maze. Do I need to draw you directions to get out?"

His smile was warm. "Naw, I'm good. I can find my way out."

Just like a guy to refuse a map.

"Well, when you don't show up on time this evening, at least I'll know where to find . . ."

The rest of the words stuck in my throat as a figure approached from way down the hall. I shouldn't have been able to identify him so quickly, but something in me just knew.

As the distance between us closed, my throat tightened around a lump. Would Logan just nod or pretend I wasn't there, as he had the few other times we'd passed, or would something different happen since Jonathon was here?

Jonathon was oddly quiet beside me as we continued down the corridor. He didn't press me to finish my sentence. We were about five feet apart when Logan finally acknowledged our existence by making eye contact with me. No nod this time. He passed us. I was prepared to keep walking when Jonathon stopped me with a gentle touch on my arm, and called out to Logan.

"Hey man, how are you doing?"

There was a slight tightness in Logan's shoulders right before he turned back with a lazy smile on his face. The smile didn't reach his eyes and he avoided looking directly at me. "Been pretty good, actually. Lots of action going on these days, which always keeps things interesting."

"Really?" I asked without thinking. "No one has mentioned any action to me."

Logan angled toward me to answer, but his gaze was directed over my right shoulder. "There's always stuff brewing down on Earth. When you aren't training anyone, you get the opportunity to jump into things more often."

I wanted to ask more, but Jonathon beat me to it. "So, that's why we haven't seen much of you lately?"

"Something like that," Logan answered. "I should get going. I'm getting ready to take another trip down." His eyes shifted slightly to where Jonathon held my upper arm, making me want to squirm out of the prince's grasp. "And I'm sure you guys have your own plans."

Jonathon's widening smile confirmed Logan's statement. "Well man," he said, "we'd love to see you around more often. Just because you're not training with Audrey doesn't mean you've been blacklisted. Your friends miss seeing you."

Logan smiled back politely. "Yeah, thanks for the reminder." With a quick chin nod, he turned and continued down the hall.

Jonathon's hand dropped from my arm. Why hadn't he let go sooner? Did he think I was going to run away or something?

We continued walking. After a moment Jonathon spoke. "You know, it seems really weird with Logan. How so much changed after you asked for a new mentor. Not just with him, but you too. Do you think you'll ever feel comfortable enough to tell me what really went down between you?"

My internal alarms blared, screaming at me to evade and run. Jonathon wasn't stupid, but the last thing I wanted to do was discuss Logan with him. Or vice versa, for that matter.

Jonathon waited patiently for me to speak. My throat went dry.

"Truthfully?"

He nodded.

"I don't think so."

"Oh." Jonathon was visibly disappointed. He forced a smile. "Maybe one day you'll change your mind."

"Well, this is me." I pointed to the locker room sign. "Thanks for the company. I'll see you in a few hours."

The reminder of our dinner date put a genuine smile back on his face. "Looking forward to it."

As per usual, he took my hand and placed a gentle kiss on the back before turning to leave. I considered telling him he was going the wrong direction, but I dismissed it. He'd figure it out on his own.

And if he never made it to the tree by seven thirty, I wasn't sure I'd be sorry.

I looked at myself in the mirror, taking stock of the girl staring back with distracted eyes. I was almost exactly the same as the day I'd appeared in the afterlife. Same straight, long, dark brown hair with subtle highlights. Same mahogany eyes set in a petite, heart-shaped face. Same short stature. The only apparent change was a more toned physique from the hours spent training.

But something was different. It was hidden in the way I held myself. The image in front of me projected strength but was also jaded.

My brows furrowed and I pushed melancholy thoughts from my mind. I forced myself to look only at the surface, the paper in which the package was wrapped.

The dress I'd picked for my date was flirtier than my mood. I enjoyed the excuse to dress up when Jonathon took me on his usual formal dates, but with Logan on my brain, my heart wasn't in it tonight. The fabric was a glossy gray and muted yellow gingham check. It was short, with pockets—I loved pockets in dresses. The top part consisted of crisscrossed fabric with an off-center bow resting on my hip. I'd paired it with killer four-inch yellow wedges I'd materialized for myself.

Bear trotted over and pushed his head under my hand in a silent request for attention. He'd stayed in my room all day, sleeping off the activities from the night before. I wished I had that luxury.

I was due for a two-day break the day after tomorrow, thank goodness. The gang had planned a skiing and snowboarding trip on the south mountain. The thought of it made me smile. I loved snowboarding, which was probably why I'd picked up the basics of surfing relatively easily. Logan might even show for this trip since, from what I'd been told, he was an amazing boarder.

My smile dropped. Should I still go? I couldn't imagine spending time with him, but eventually we had to get past this, for the sake of our friends if for no other reason. When was the right time to work on normalizing our relationship? I heaved a heavy sigh.

A knock sounded. My eyes slid to the door. It was too early to be Jonathon, but my dispirited disposition stole my curiosity.

"Come in," I shouted.

A delicate arm appeared, followed by a waterfall of blonde hair.

Kaitlin.

Her gaze swept the room before her eyes landed on me.

"Hey," I said.

"Hey back, you." Her smile was cheerful. "You're lookin' hot. Where are you going tonight?"

I shrugged. "I'm not sure. Jonathon is taking me out."

"And you look thrilled." Sarcasm more than tinged her words.

Another shrug.

She pulled up a chair and sat facing me. "All right, girlie, spill."

Still facing the mirror, I focused on her reflection. "Spill what?"

"Why you're dating Jonathon when you're clearly in love with Logan."

I choked on nothing. She now had my undivided attention. Out of all the things I could have said, all I managed was, "*What?*"

"I knew it. You just confirmed it," she answered with a self-satisfied smirked.

"What are you talking about?" I didn't love Logan. Logan was just . . . well, I didn't know exactly what he was, but we weren't even talking right now. And why wasn't she acting like a crazy jealous person if that was truly what she thought?

"Oh, please. We both know you've been pining for him for months now. And he's been doing the same. I'm tempted to lock you both in a room until you admit your feelings to each other."

"Kaitlin." I turned on her, horrified. "Why are you even saying this? Logan's *your* boyfriend."

"What!" It was her turn to look horrified. Her eyes opened unnaturally wide, and her mouth gaped repeatedly, mimicking a fish out of water. "Logan is *not* my boyfriend! That would be so, so weird. We practically grew up together. It would be like dating my brother. Oh my gosh, why would you even think that?" She screwed up her face as if the idea grossed her out.

It was my turn to gape.

Wait. They *weren't* together? Could it be true?

"Well . . ." I cleared my throat, trying to pull my thoughts together. Why *had* I thought Logan and Kaitlin were an item? No one had ever said so. "It's just you guys always seem so close. He's so comfortable around you. Happier, it seems. And . . ." I paused. Should I tell her everything? Oh, what the heck! The wind left my sails as I finished. "Romona said he was unavailable, so I just assumed it was because of you."

Kaitlin held her hands to her darkening cheeks. "You mean to tell me this whole time you thought Logan and I were an item?"

I nodded.

"But," she stuttered, "why didn't you just ask?"

"I didn't think I needed to. And I didn't want to seem, you know, interested in him or something." It was my cheeks' turn to darken.

Kaitlin rolled her eyes. "Well, that would have been the most subtle of your tells. The longing glances you guys keep giving each other when you think no one is looking are a big fat giveaway. And believe me, we're looking. Even your bickering is charged, if you know what I mean." She wiggled her eyebrows suggestively, then gasped, "Oh, Audrey, please tell me this isn't the reason you asked for a new mentor."

I waved her off. "No, of course not. It's a much more confusing situation."

I tried to hide it, but my mind was being blown right now. I resisted the urge to look behind me to see if brain matter was splattered across the wall.

She leaned forward. "Okay, then, I'm ready to finally hear it."

I eyed her. "What has Logan told you?"

She huffed and leaned back again. "Nothing much. I hate to see him hurting right now."

One of the cracks in my heart started to bleed a little. "Why is he hurting?" I asked in a small voice.

"That is exactly what I'm trying to find out. We've all had enough of you two sulking around each other."

"Who exactly is 'we'?" I asked warily.

She lifted one perfect brow. "Do you really want to know the answer?"

I groaned and put my face in my hands. "No, I guess I don't."

"So, since we agree you are in fact in love with Logan—"

"Kaitlin, I never said that."

She plowed forward, regardless. "Back to my original question. Why in the world are you continuing to date Jonathon?"

This question at least I had answers to. I started to tick them off with my fingers. "First, Logan is *not* interested in me. No, stop," I said when she tried to interrupt. "I can promise you he made that more than clear." I cringed.

Kaitlin hadn't been there the day I told him we weren't bonded. She didn't see the relief permeate not just his eyes, but his entire body.

She crossed her arms with a frown, but let me continue.

"Second, there is nothing wrong with Jonathon. He's a great guy. He's smart and funny and has made it perfectly clear he *is* interested in me. And third, why wouldn't I give a guy like that a chance?"

She didn't look convinced. "Wow, Audrey, I never would have taken you as someone impressed by a title and a pretty face."

I gasped. "How can you say that?"

She shrugged a shoulder and threw an annoyed look in my direction. "I'm just saying what everyone is thinking."

"That's awful. Jonathon deserves so much more credit than you're giving him. He'd be hurt if he thought you meant that, which I doubt. He's really a great guy." All true. I didn't need to confess to my own conflicted feelings about dating him.

She had the decency to look ashamed. "You're right, I take it back. It was a horrible thing to say. But Audrey, let's pretend for a minute Logan isn't interested in you, which he *is*," it was her turn to silence me with a look, "Even if that were true, anyone can tell you're not really into Jonathon. Why continue the charade?"

"It's not a charade," I insisted. "Am I head-over-heels for him? Well, no. But sometimes things develop over time. I am somewhat attracted to him. Come on, Kaitlin, you know he's gorgeous."

"But you're not nearly as attracted to him as you are to Logan."

I gave her a scathing look. This had gone far enough. I really didn't need Kaitlin rubbing my face in what I couldn't have. "Listen, Kaitlin, I appreciate your concern. For both Logan and me. But even though you're not dating him, it's simply not meant to be." I shrugged. "Do you really begrudge me moving on?"

I thought I sounded pretty convincing—but did I even believe what I was saying right now? My mind hadn't had time to wrap around the fact that there was not, and never had been, anything romantic between Kaitlin and Logan. When I had a moment to really let it sink in, I was going to feel awfully sorry for myself. I was currently speaking on autopilot, and I knew it.

"Audrey, of course I don't. I just think you're headed toward settling for something that isn't what's best for you."

I shot her a weary glance. Logan's actions still spoke volumes. There was no way around that. He had never pursued me. Had never given any indication he was going to. Yeah, we'd had a few . . . moments, but when it came down to it, what did that really matter?

I almost wished Kaitlin *was* dating Logan, because now his rejection stung even worse. It was more personal than before.

That hurt.

I had a half-hour before my date with a different guy. Not enough time to process anything—especially in front of an audience.

"Uh, Audrey?"

"Yeah?"

"You've got a hair thing going on right now."

Of course, I did. "Didn't I tell you it was overrated?" A look in the mirror confirmed a gray-blue tone tinted my whole head. I closed my eyes to turn it back. I brought my fingers to my temple and rubbed in vain to stop the oncoming headache. "You know what I could use right now is a little support," I said before opening my eyes.

Kaitlin looked at me with compassion. "Okay, Audrey, if that's what you need, I'll lay off about Logan." Then came the pointed stare. "For now."

"Really?" I held back a sigh of relief.

"Yes." Her voice became almost timid. "You and I have become important to each other, right?"

I nodded and was surprised at the truth of her words.

"I want to be here for you. You need someone else to talk to besides Romona. And I hope you'll do the same for me."

I smiled. "Of course."

"Then I'll support your decision to date Jonathon." She threw her shoulders back as if readying for battle. "But I want it noted that I think you're wrong. I think you and Logan have strong feelings for each other that you're both too scared to admit or act on. I believe you'll have your chance someday. Maybe the timing's not right."

I didn't feel like I could process that possibility right now either. "In the meantime, don't you think I owe it to myself to see if there's something else out there for me?"

She nodded reluctantly. "But not if you are using Jonathon as a rebound or a shield. You'll only hurt yourself and him in the process."

Oh shoot, was that what I was doing? I didn't know.

She stood. "Here, let me fix your hair for your date. I can do an updo with braids if you like. I think it would look really pretty."

I met her eyes in the mirror. "Thanks."

I meant it for more than the hair. I think she knew that, too.

BOYFRIENDS

*J*onathon face-planted in the snow for the hundredth time. I struggled not to laugh. He'd been rolling down the hill since yesterday. His hair, white from the accumulation of snow, stuck up at weird angles. I rode up next to where he sat—looking shocked and shook up—and joined him in a drift. We rested in silence for a moment as we watched one of his skis slide the rest of the way down the mountain.

"You do know skiing wasn't invented until the 1800s, right?" he said gruffly.

I smiled and looked away so he wouldn't think I was laughing at him. "I wasn't aware. Want to try boarding instead?"

He looked at me incredulously. "Are you crazy? You're carving down the mountain on nothing less than a death plank. I've watched boarders wipeout. I'm content to take my beating on skis."

Unable to hold it back any longer, I started laughing. Tears appeared in my eyes while Jonathon looked on. "I'm really sorry, but it is kind of funny."

"For you, maybe," he grudgingly agreed.

"Okay, truth?"

He nodded. I patted his shoulder with a thick-gloved hand, whisking away chunks of snow in the process. "When I learned how to ride, I spent three whole days sliding down the mountain on every part of me other than the board. That is, when I didn't catch an edge and face-plant or land so hard on my backside I thought I'd broken my butt."

He cracked a smile, my intent.

"If you really want to learn, you should probably take some lessons next time. I learned how to ski before riding, but it's been so long that I'm not the best teacher."

"I thought about it, but then I wouldn't have been able to spend time with you." He pouted, lifting puppy-dog eyes to mine.

I lifted an eyebrow. "Is it fun for you to have me watch you tumble down the mountain all day?"

He cringed. "No."

"Didn't think so. Let's call it a day. Next trip you can take lessons, and it'll be a lot more fun."

"Yeah, okay."

Just then Alrik skied up, covering us both with a wave of powder. "Hey, you two. Taking another break I see." His eyes lit with mischief. Kaitlin and Kevin appeared and expertly slowed their boards to a stop so they could sit with us. Romona skied up without spraying us with snow.

"I think we're going to call it a day," I announced.

"What?" Alrik boomed. "There are still *hours* of light left."

I laughed. How to bow out without embarrassing Jonathon? "Um . . ."

He spared me the need. "She's only saying that for me. I think I've had enough. I may take a lesson if we ever come again. I didn't realize how difficult this was. I'm going to find a sport from my century, though, to get back at all of you." There was a challenge in his smile. "Audrey," he said focusing on me, "I want you to stay and enjoy the rest of the day. I'll be in the lodge thawing and will join everyone for dinner tonight like we planned."

"Are you sure?" I bit my lip. Jonathon really was wonderful. He'd hardly complained about his day, only giving in on this last fall. But I hadn't seen much of my friends this weekend because I'd been following in his wake, ensuring he didn't hurt himself. After several hours we'd only made it down a few runs, yesterday even fewer. I had been secretly disappointed, but didn't want it to show. Jonathon, always gracious, recognized my predicament.

"Of course." He picked up my gloved hand. "I want you to enjoy your day, and I'm only spoiling it for you."

"No, you're not."

The corner of his mouth quirked. "Liar."

I laughed once again. "Okay, truthfully I would like to get some good runs in before the trip's over. If you really don't mind." He nodded. "Then that would be great. Thanks."

"All right, then." He stood and unhooked his remaining ski. "I'm just going to safely walk down and retrieve my other ski. I'll see you later."

His eyes never left mine. I squirmed under the attention. My friends' silence burned the back of my neck. I watched Jonathon trudge down the hill until he was safely out of earshot before turning to them.

They all looked at me curiously.

"What?" I asked.

"Nothing," Romona answered quickly.

Alrik spoke up. "You know, we should have listened to Logan and never—"

"Really, nothing." Romona cut Alrik off with a glare. "Let's go, Audrey. I'd love to see you ride without having to stop every hundred feet. I was really starting to feel for you."

What was Alrik about to say? "It was all right. Jonathon's a trouper. But let's go. I'm looking forward to getting some windburn." With that, I took off and shot down the mountain, passing Jonathon with a wave and easily beating everyone else to the chairlift, where a small crowd of other skiers and boarders were already on their way up.

As I arrived at the lift, I smiled triumphantly and wiggled in my version of a victory dance.

Big mistake.

My board slid to the side and then caught an edge. I plowed face-first into someone, taking us both down. Jeers came from the crowd around us. My face was squished into a hard chest, and my feet—still attached to my board—were tangled with someone else's.

"You okay?"

No. Way.

I lifted my chin, and the tendril of hair hanging in my face turned bright pink.

"Audrey, are you okay?" Logan asked again.

The hair darkened to magenta. I gaped at him. "You're not supposed to be here." I winced at the bluntness of my words, wishing I could shove them back down my throat.

He looked away for a moment before answering, "Yeah, I know. My assignment was cut short, so I thought I'd catch the tail end of the trip. It's been a while since I've been boarding."

I was told yesterday that Logan wouldn't join us because he'd gone to Earth.

Shock dumbed my brain.

I did nothing but stare, which was awkward for us both since I kept him trapped against the cold snow, but I couldn't seem to help myself. His dark blond hair was tousled either on purpose or from our collision. A few day's worth of scruff covered his face—unusual. Was it due to neglect, or on purpose?

I was still staring at the perfect proportions of his face when someone finally jolted me to my senses.

"Audrey?" Jonathon jogged up to us, then helped pull me to my feet, keeping a tight hold so I wouldn't fall again. It's surprisingly hard to just stand on a snowboard. That's why boarders usually sit when we aren't moving.

I winced. Why couldn't he be back at the lodge already? "Caught that, did ya?"

Jonathon's smile bloomed. "Yeah, me and about half the mountain."

I looked over. Logan brushed the loose snow off himself. "I didn't hurt you, did I?" I asked him.

He looked up as if surprised I spoke to him. "No."

For the first time in months he looked straight into my eyes with those gorgeous cobalt eyes of his own. Their effect on me hadn't worn off. I had to crane my neck to meet his gaze because of his over six-foot height.

"Oh, ah, good."

Awesome. Way to sound super intelligent, Audrey.

Alrik chose that moment to enter the conversation. "You know what they say, Aud, pride cometh before a fall. It never gets old. I just have to wait long enough, and you're sure to take a spectacular spill and take out someone with you. Brings a smile to my face every time."

I stuck my tongue out at him. He was too much like the annoying older brother I'd never asked for.

"You're not hurt, are you?" Romona asked.

I checked myself—I wasn't. "Just my pride."

"Well, good." Alrik boomed. "Now that Logan's here, we can have some real fun."

"Alrik," I scolded and snuck a look at Jonathon, afraid he'd be offended.

He just rolled his eyes. "I'm going inside now." He leaned down and gave me an innocent peck on the cheek which revealed he was only mildly annoyed. All the while Logan's gaze seared into my back. "I'll see you later?"

"Of course." I forced a smile as Jonathon walked away, leaving me with the gang—and Logan. "So, I guess we should get going then."

Kaitlin caught my eye and gestured to my hair.

Right. Sigh.

I closed my eyes to fix it, and when I opened them, everyone was getting on the lift except for Logan, who'd waited for me.

Awkward.

Alrik turned around in his chair and winked at me. I put my fingers to the bridge of my nose and pinched my eyes close.

"You sure you're all right?" Logan inquired with a quirked brow.

"Yeah, yeah. Let's get going." I unhooked a boot and dragged myself forward.

Logan and I were the only two on the chair, seated on opposite ends with a space large enough for three between us. Gusts whistled through the evergreens as we ascended the mountain. I pretended to be interested in the skiers. This was the first time we'd been alone since Logan ceased to be my mentor. I heaved a sigh. Maybe it was time to try to start to normalize things.

"Thanks for the birthday present," I said quietly, half-hoping he wouldn't hear. For a while he didn't say anything, so I assumed he hadn't.

"You're welcome. The ocean . . ." He paused, not quite meeting my gaze. "It reminds me of you now."

"Oh."

"Did you enjoy your party?"

"Somewhat," I confessed. The wind blew harshly, swinging the chair back and forth. I ventured a look at him. "You know it wasn't really my birthday, right?"

He smiled. "Yeah. I thought that was strange, but I didn't tell anyone else. I suppose it didn't really matter."

I nodded. The chair jerked to a stop and swung more violently.

"Figures," I mumbled.

"Yeah," he replied.

I looked at him. A moment passed, and then I burst out laughing. Some of the hysterics were from frayed nerves, but what else was there to do? After a surprised moment, he joined me. By the time we'd calmed down the chair was moving again.

I was wiping a tear from my eye when Logan spoke. "So, Jonathon's your boyfriend, then?"

Thank goodness for safety bars. Without one I would have plummeted to the mountain floor. I mean, yeah, I guess I could see why he would think that, but I'd never thought he'd ask.

"Whoa there." He reached forward as if to steady me but stopped short. Apparently, I *looked* ready to pitch out of the lift. "Didn't mean to catch you off guard."

"No," I said.

"I didn't catch you off guard?" His brows pulled together.

"No, I mean Jonathon's not my boyfriend."

His look spoke disbelief. "Does he know that?"

"Of course!" My voice echoed off the mountain. I checked myself. "I mean, we have been on some dates." I scowled at him. "But we're not like *together* together, like an official item or anything."

He looked strangely satisfied with my answer and leaned back with his arms laid across the back of the chair and a small smile in place.

Gosh, he's attractive. The thought slipped out without permission. How annoying.

"Good," Logan said. "I never liked him anyway."

Wait, hold up. "What? I mean, why?"

He jutted his chin out while lifting the safety bar. "We're here."

He dismounted.

I scrambled to follow.

Everyone waited for us.

I gawked at Logan, still trying to process that last zinger. Kaitlin looked at me pointedly and a bit smugly. Alrik clapped Logan on the back, causing him to teeter slightly on his board before righting himself.

Kevin lifted his voice. "First one to the bottom gets bragging rights." And then he took off. I hurried to fasten my bindings and quickly followed.

The last few hours of the day were amazing. I flew, cut, and carved my way down the mountain with ease. Spending carefree time with my friends was refreshing. Logan remained in the back of my mind as well as in my peripheral vision, leading to a couple of spectacular wipeouts on my part. Alrik was always quick to laugh, Romona was quick to make sure I was unharmed, and everyone else's reactions fell somewhere in between. I carefully planned each lift so I never rode with Logan again. Even so, it was easier to be around him than I would have expected.

I was leaning over to unlace my boots at the end of the day when I was lifted into a hug from behind. I squeaked out my surprise.

"The rest of the day dragged on without you," Jonathon admitted.

Logan gave me a pointed stare before focusing back on removing his own gear. I wiggled out of Jonathon's embrace. Was he being more affectionate than usual, or was Logan's presence just making me more aware of it?

"So, babe, you work up an appetite for dinner?"

"Babe?" In fact, my appetite was getting smaller with every word and action. Multiple pairs of eyes watched our exchange.

"Yeah, I thought I'd try it on for size. Not your thing?"

"Definitely not my thing."

Jonathon shrugged. "Oh well, I'll find another that fits."

"Another what?"

"Nickname."

I shifted my feet. "Er, do you have to?"

He frowned slightly. "I guess I just like the idea of calling you something no one else does."

"Oh, ah . . ."

So uncomfortable.

So inappropriate.

Both Kaitlin and Logan's warnings about Jonathon's expectations slammed into me. What had I gotten myself into? And did I want to be here or didn't I?

Kaitlin saved the moment. "All right, peeps, I'm starved. Let's get our dinner on."

With our snow gear stowed and extra outerwear shed, we were ready to go. Jonathon laid a hand on my back to lead me forward, and I couldn't think of a good reason not to let him. A few moments passed before I noticed we were missing a person. I swiveled my head but didn't see Logan anywhere.

Kaitlin came up and matched my steps. "He's not joining us. Said he had to get back to Earth."

I didn't pretend not to know what she was talking about. She gave me a sad smile before moving ahead to talk to Kevin.

I refused to admit I was disappointed.

If I'd known it would be several weeks before I laid eyes on Logan again, I would have admitted it—at least to myself.

THE DEFEATED WARRIOR

I rubbed my arms. The training center hallways were unusually cold this evening. Despite it being the fastest route, I generally avoided this particular path through the center as much as possible. All these halls tended to look the same to me, but this one was different. Not in shade or shape, but in memories.

Perhaps it was the length of time I'd gone without catching a glimpse of him? *Three weeks and four days, but who's counting?* Perhaps I battled with a moment of nostalgia? Maybe it was simple recklessness? Whatever the reason, today I found myself standing outside my old training gym.

Our gym, Logan's and mine.

It was as silent as the evening was late. The facility was long since deserted. My palm lay flat on the door as if I hoped to feel something pulsating inside. I went up on my toes to silently peer through the tiny window. Just one quick look. One fraction of a moment to take it in, and then I'd go home. At least that's what I told myself.

But someone was there.

A lone figure sat on a bench in the semidarkness, dressed fully in body armor except for the discarded helmet at his feet. His body arched forward, forearms on his knees and fingers buried deeply in his hair, supporting his head. He sat motionless. My fingers reached to touch the glass next to my face. The emotion of the scene swallowed my surprise at seeing him there. So sad, and I didn't know why.

A gust of wind blew from behind me, swirling my hair in my face and shoving me violently forward as if I'd been pushed by a hand. My reflexes had improved, so rather than landing sprawled out over the floor as the door flew open before me, I dipped into a roll and came up to a knee. Thank goodness

Hugo was teaching me parkour. Where in the world had a gust of wind come from in the middle of the training center?

Logan's head simply tipped at the interruption. Dragging in a ragged breath of air, he forced his hands from his hair and rested his elbows on his knees before finally lifting his face.

We stayed like that. Just looking at each other.

When my eyes adjusted to the dimmed light, my heart skipped a beat. There was a growing smattering of blood beneath Logan's left leg, a slow drip adding spots to the floor. Multiple scratches on his face, a split lip, and a swollen cheekbone became visible as well.

Shoving down a gasp, I quickly rose to my feet. His eyes tracked my movement.

"What happened?" My words were so quiet they barely floated to Logan's ear.

The blanket of silence stretched even further—both of us statues, except Logan trickled red to the ground every few moments.

It sank in that something was really wrong, and the surrealness of the moment disappeared in urgency. I spied some towels folded neatly in the corner and ordered my feet to move. I grabbed one, wet it in the sink and returned to where he sat. The only part of Logan that moved were his eyes. They followed me.

I took a deep breath for courage and—without permission—started cleaning the scratches on his face. The dripping wound on his leg was certainly the more urgent injury, but I didn't have the nerve to face it quite yet.

"What happened? Did something go wrong on a mission?" I asked.

Instead of an answer, he studied me closely. My cheeks heated. I used what was left of my concentration to keep my hair from changing colors. I only half-succeeded. A pale pink lock fell in my face. Placing it behind my ear, I continued to clean the dried blood from Logan's forehead.

When that task was done I grabbed another towel and wet it under the coldest water I could get. Squeezing it out, I intended to put it on Logan's cheek to help with the swelling. Standing in front of him, I moved my hand toward him again. Before I could make contact, one of his gloved hands snaked out and grabbed my wrist. I looked Logan in the eyes as the towel began to drip water that mixed with the blood on the floor.

"Why are you here?" he rasped.

Both his grip on my wrist and the look in his eyes were demanding. If he could rip an answer from me, I believed he would. And yet only the thin layer of his glove kept him from doing so.

"I, ah, figured everyone would be gone by now. We ran late in our training today."

His eyes narrowed slightly as if he knew my game, then his hand abruptly released my wrist and his head rolled forward.

Alarmed, I dropped the wet towel to the floor.

For a moment I'd thought he'd lost consciousness, but to my relief, he spoke again. "Yes, but why did you come here?" Exhaustion, disappointment, and defeat all warred in his voice. He wanted the full truth without having to drag it out of me piece by piece.

"I'm not sure," I started cautiously. "I didn't even know I was headed here until I was standing outside. I usually take a different way around the center's hallways now."

He let out a humorless laugh. "Yes, I know that already."

What was that supposed to mean?

He continued. "So, it was a slip of the mind. Force of habit." A statement rather than a question.

Perhaps it was. I didn't know. But he offered me an easy way out, and I didn't intend to waste it. "Yes, that must have been it," I breathed out shallowly.

"Audrey, this isn't your concern. Go back to your boyfriend."

He said it gently and with his head still bowed, but it pierced and pinched at a buried spot inside. Logan was right. He was perfectly capable of taking care of himself. But he was wrong too. He needed help.

Right now, he needed me.

Maybe it was my old stubbornness around him resurfacing, because his dismissal only spurred me on.

"I already told you, he's not my boyfriend. And I'm not leaving until you hold this to your cheek and let me take a look at whatever is leaking blood all over the floor." I picked up the fallen towel and slapped it in his right hand. It was still wet but more lukewarm than cold, now.

He leaned back into the seat, staring up at me as he stretched out his leg and allowed me to probe for the wound.

Starting from the ankle up, I gently searched for the tear in his armor, desperately hoping I would find the wound before I reached his knee. Thankfully I spied a rip on the outside area of his calf. I pulled apart the body armor as much as possible for a better look. Something was still imbedded in Logan's leg. My stomach turned.

"I'd like to hear what you plan to do about that," he said, laughing without humor.

"Doesn't it need to be taken out?"

"Of course."

"Logan, why haven't you gone to the healing center already? This looks incredibly painful."

"Sometimes there are more pressing things to be dealt with than physical pain."

"But—"

With blurred speed, he captured my head with his hands, forcing my vision to fill with him and him alone. My eyes skated over the sharp planes of his face before getting snared in his cerulean gaze. He spoke more slowly this time.

"Audrey, this isn't your concern. Go back to your Jonathon."

His gloved fingers brushed my skin so tenderly I was swept back to another time, when his thumb had cast lazy circles on my cheek and his body was there to protect me from danger. Dumbfounded at how we'd found ourselves here, I could only stare at him.

"I thought you didn't like Jonathon," I whispered.

He let out a gentle sigh. "Audrey, do I need to spell this out to you?"

One part of my brain yelled, *Well yeah, I suppose you do!* The other part whispered, *Please don't.*

I couldn't stand to be rejected by him again.

I pulled away from Logan by willpower alone. Standing at my full height I was only slightly taller than his seated form. It had been stupid to come here. It had been better not to see him these past weeks.

But as I walked from the room, I couldn't stop myself from wondering if you could truly avoid someone when he had already taken hold of a piece of your heart?

I cornered Kevin the next day. After some consideration, I'd decided he was my easiest prey.

Something was going on that no one would tell me about. My friends had been tiptoeing around me for some time now. I'd interrupted enough conversations where the subject was quickly changed to know I wasn't being paranoid. All of my hunter friends had been on numerous rotations to Earth, yet no one would give me a straight answer as to what they were up to.

After last night and my strange interaction with Logan, I had to know the answer to the mystery.

I set my tray down and took a seat next to Kevin. He greeted me with a broad smile.

"Hey, Audrey. What's been going on? Feels like I haven't seen you in ages."

"You know, Kevin," I answered, "that's so true. It does feel like it's been a while. What's been going on with *you?*"

My first indication that I was really on to something was his pause before answering, and then the vagueness of his answer. "Oh, you know. The same old same old. Just busy with regular hunter stuff." He shrugged. Kevin's dark complexion may hide the evidence of a blush, but he had so many other tells it hardly mattered.

"Is that so?" I narrowed my eyes slightly. Kevin fidgeted in his seat. "It's so weird," I continued, "because everyone seems to be really busy these days, yet I haven't heard a thing about what's going on. Usually you are all a little more

... talkative about your assignments. I miss the stories." I plopped my chin on my hand and gave him a pointed look.

"Well, maybe there hasn't been much worth talking about?"

"Hmm . . . ," I tapped a finger to my lips. "I find that hard to believe. I happened to stumble across Logan last night . . . "

I let the statement hang in the air as I gauged his reaction. Kevin's eyes grew, and he choked on a fry. I helped by hitting his back until it dislodged. I'm a good friend like that.

"You were on Earth yesterday too, weren't you?"

Kevin just nodded—probably not trusting himself to speak.

"It was an interesting interaction, to say the least. Enough that I have a hard time believing last night was nothing worth talking about."

Kevin swallowed loudly. I smiled like a cat that had cornered a mouse.

I so had him.

"So, I was thinking it's about time you all let me in on what's been going on."

"What's been going on?" Kaitlin asked as she plopped into the seat across from me.

I didn't care. She was too late. "Oh, nothing much," I said. "Kevin's just been explaining to me the secret you've all been keeping about what you've been doing on Earth."

"Wha . . . what? No, that's—" Kevin started.

"Kevin!" Kaitlin shrieked. "You told her about her family? Kevin, she's not supposed to—"

"What!" I yelled so loudly most of the cafeteria turned to look. I pinned Kaitlin with my eyes. "What is going on with my family?"

"But . . . but . . . you said Kevin . . . I thought he already . . ." She looked to him for help.

Kevin's gaze was sympathetic. For Kaitlin or me, I didn't know. "I tried to tell you. I didn't say anything to her."

"Who cares who said what?" My body was going into panic mode. What was going on with my family? My friends were hunters—was my family under attack? Were they in some kind of danger? Had Logan's wounds last night come from trying to help them? What if he hadn't succeeded? "Somebody better start talking, and fast. And after you've explained, we'll have another talk about you keeping things from me about my family."

I all but growled the last part. A soft hand landed on my forearm. Empathy washed through me—sadness and also love. I swatted Romona's hand away before turning accusing eyes on her as well. "What have you done?"

"Come on," she said gently. "Let's go talk."

I restrained myself long enough to make it out to a picnic table overlooking the soccer field that butted up to the training center.

"Tell me," I demanded.

Romona took a deep breath before speaking. "The general rules are when someone's immediate family is under attack, they aren't to know about it."

I tried to interrupt, but she silenced me with a look. Not just a look, but *the* look. I chewed on my bottom lip.

"It's not a form of punishment, just an issue of judgment on the hunter's behalf. We aren't apt to think rationally when people we love are threatened by demons."

"Think rationally? What's there to think rationally about? They're demons! You kill them!"

"That's exactly what I mean." She heaved a burdened breath. "There's strategy involved. There are times when you must show restraint. When a family is targeted, like yours is, like *ours* is, there's something else going on. It's not random, Audrey. We're working very hard to figure out what it is and to keep them protected."

"We?" I spat. "They're your family as well. Why are you in the loop?"

"I've been here much longer than you have. Headquarters made an exception. Yes, they are my family, and I love them dearly, but you are still new to this existence, and frankly you have a history of acting before thinking."

"I—"

"You know you do." She pinned me with a stare.

I struggled with the conflicting urges—to hang my head in shame or pound on the table to demand more answers. I tried to calm down before giving what I thought was a rational response.

Take a deep breath.

The fresh air helped a bit. "Well, now that I know, I want to help." Perfectly rational. Delivered calmly.

"You can't."

"I'm helping." My nostrils flared as I attempted to keep my annoyance in check.

"You're not."

"Wanna bet?" Rational was officially overrated.

I stood up to leave. I had a mentor to talk to.

"Audrey?" Romona's kind voice stopped me. I averted my gaze, unable to hide the hurt in my eyes. "We all love you. We only want what's best for you. You have a family here you can trust."

"Trust? That's a joke." I gruffly shoved out a humorless laugh and trudged back to the training center.

By the time I reached the gym, tears threatened to pour from my eyes. Hugo took one look at me and folded me in a hug, rubbing my back while I pulled myself together. After the tears dried I stepped back, looking him straight in the eye.

"Tell me, please," I begged.

"Yes, it's time you know." The smile on his lips was a sad one. "Your family is special, Audrey. In truth, all families are special, but yours in a very unique way. Their callings in life will make a significant impact for the kingdom. The ripples they create will reach the entire globe. We believe the enemy has somehow become aware of this, and because of that, they've been targeted. So far, the activity has been localized to your old house, meaning it's only affected your parents and brother. Your sisters have been left alone. The hunters who have been dispatched to Earth, your friends included, are either there to collect intel or act as sentries and protectors for your family. They're doing a good job." He paused and took my hands in his. Power flooded my system. "Audrey, no one has been harmed. You need to trust they are being cared for by the Creator."

I wanted to. I desperately wanted to. But he was talking about *my* family. My parents and brother. How could he ask me to just let it go?

I slipped my hands from his. "I want to help."

"I've already told you they are being helped."

"But *I* want to help."

His brows pulled together in disappointment. "What can you do that is not already being done? Where is your faith?"

Ouch. Low blow. "Don't ask me to walk away from this," I pleaded.

"I'm asking you to have faith."

My shoulders sagged in defeat. I had faith. Faith in God, but also faith in myself. I wasn't built to sit back and do nothing when people I loved were in danger.

I wouldn't get any help from Hugo, so I'd have to help myself.

BREAKING AND ENTERING

I'd never been in the training center at this hour. Even when I worked out extremely early or late into the evening, someone was always milling around. At just after two in the morning, it was as if the air itself settled in for the night.

I didn't necessarily believe the bustling center was indeed empty. Not as if demons took time for a snuggly sleep during the night, so why wouldn't there be a late shift manning the room I intended breaking into?

I checked to make sure I had everything in place. My sword was secured in its specially-made baldric. The belt worn over my shoulder reached down to the opposite hip. It allowed me to carry my weapon on my back rather than strapped to my hip, giving me more flexibility for battle. My helmet was secured to my belt, along with a small pack with a change of clothes and some food and water.

I took a deep breath to settle my heart. I reasoned that I wasn't actually breaking in. The training center was unlocked at all hours—we were in heaven, for goodness' sake. It wasn't like we had to guard against criminals. So, there would be no actual breaking, only entering. Even though what I was about to do wasn't sanctioned, per se, didn't mean it wasn't the right thing to do.

Yeah, you keep telling yourself that, my inner voice mocked.

I reached the transportation hub, the section of the center I was least acquainted with. I only had a few dusty memories to guide me to the room I needed. If I found it, I still had to figure out how to get myself beamed down to Earth without any help.

Maybe I wouldn't pull this off, but I had to try. My family in danger. *My* family under attack.

An ugly fist of anger clutched my insides. My friends hid the truth from me for weeks, dancing and dodging questions while I was none the wiser. Out of all of them, Romona's deception hurt the most. My grandmother should have told me. She should have believed I had a right to know what was going on, regardless of 'the rules'.

My hand reached for a doorknob while I mused and fumed. My heartbeat picked up when the door swung soundlessly open. Even darkened, the room was unmistakable. The pad to the left still reminded me of something out of a *Star Trek* movie. The rows of desks and panels sat quietly to the right.

My feet had led me to this place as if on autopilot from years of practice. I furrowed my brow. It shouldn't be so easy. As I looked around the unlit room I realized I was wrong; nothing about this was easy. All the intimidating, futuristic machines I remembered were still here, and I had no idea how to turn them on, let alone use them. Typically, there were at least five people manning the equipment. Was it even possible to send myself down to Earth?

I took a deep breath. I wouldn't know until I tried.

I tiptoed over to the first desk. The smooth white surface was completely blank. I ran my fingers along the top and it immediately lit and started to rhythmically beep like medical equipment. I squeaked and jumped back.

Oh yeah, look at me, the big bad demon huntress . . . scared by a light panel.

I huffed in frustration and approached the panel, which was bright enough to illuminate half the room. I tentatively touched the screen again, and the rest of the room shook off its vestiges of slumber. With clicking noises the lights came on around the room, one at a time. Machines hummed and the transportation pad glowed softly as if it beckoned me closer while also mocking my lack of knowledge on how to use it properly.

My eyes skimmed the equipment, hoping to find something that would show me how to operate this monstrosity. A button that said, 'Push here to send self to desired location' would be nice. I scanned the boards for the *easy* button, but my search came up empty. There wasn't so much as a label on the equipment.

I moved to the next machine. Giving in to discouragement was not an option.

I chewed my bottom lip. This one had a series of symbols I didn't understand. I would never figure this out.

Of their own volition, my shoulders hunched. I frowned and gave myself a swift shake. No. I was getting down there if I had to knock out an engineer and drag him in here to send me. And it was happening tonight. Too much time had already passed. My family needed me. I needed to fight for them.

I slammed a fist down on the surface panel. Next to it landed a fat tear.

"What did that poor piece of equipment ever do to you?"

I jumped back and swung around, my heart beating out of my chest. Wild excuses flashed through my mind.

"Joe?"

To see the man who'd welcomed me into this realm after such a long time was confusing. His arms were crossed and he leaned against the frame of the open door. He wore the same worn jeans and white T-shirt I remembered. I stared at him wide-eyed.

"Wh-what are you doing here?"

He smiled warmly. He ignored my question. "It seems to me you're having a little difficulty." He gestured to the boards in front of me.

"Oh, um, yeah. I don't really know how to work this exactly." Heaviness settled in my chest, threatening to spread throughout my body. My immediate need to get to my family was overwhelming. "I need to, no, *I have to*, get down there."

A look of sympathy fell over his face. "Is this really the choice you want to make? Taking an unsanctioned trip to Earth will have some very real consequences attached to it."

How did he know the details of what I was doing? Was he a hunter? I'd never seen him in the training center, or anywhere else for that matter. This was just kind of . . . weird.

"I have to," I repeated in a small voice.

He'd moved soundlessly from the door and stood in front of me. I raised my eyes.

"Who is it you don't trust?" he asked.

I suppressed the urge to stomp my foot. Why was everyone making this about trust? This was about my family, plain and simple.

"If you feel you need to take matters into your own hands, there must be someone you don't trust to take care of your family," Joe went on.

Had I mentioned my family? I must have—how else would he know?

"This is not about trust," I told him. "My family is in need, and I have to be there for them. I'm trained to fight the evil that's attacking them right now. I don't understand why no one seems to get that! I need to be there. I *have* to be there. It's killing me to sit up here when I should be helping take care of them. Why would anyone want to prevent me from helping?"

Joe casually leaned against the machine I had taken my anger out on and studied me. His eyes didn't leave me after a minute . . . two . . . then three. I started to squirm. Who looks at anyone that long?

Awkward.

"You don't believe we know what's best." It was a statement, not a question, so I didn't bother to reply. "You have free will, even here, so if you want so badly to go down, I will allow it."

Allow it? Who was this guy to act like he had authority over what I did or didn't do? Another trainer here? Someone in hunter leadership?

My musings were cut short by his next jarring words. "But know you are going against God Himself in this decision. This is a direct violation of His trust."

Yikes! *Feel free to tell me what you really think.*

I set my jaw, no longer concerned with this man's position. "Look," I said, "I trust God. But I'm sure He has much bigger things going on. I think maybe He's not paying attention to my specific issue right now. I mean, come on, if He were to like pop in here right now and tell me Himself not to do this, of course I wouldn't." I spread my arms wide. "But where is He? We're supposed to help people. I'm not doing anything wrong."

Joe's eyes narrowed and my confidence withered.

"O ye of little faith." He whispered the words, but he might as well have shouted them in my face. I flinched.

He moved toward one of the monitors and started to type something. The sounds and lights brought forth by the motions of his fingers reminded me of a practiced orchestra. Gone was the methodical beeping and humming that made me think of a hospital. Instead, each time he pressed a point on the panel, a sweet chord rang out. I squinted. It sounded different when the technicians worked the machines. Lights around the room pulsed in time with the notes, as if he worked all the desks at once instead of a single machine. Finally, the lights on the transportation pad grew in brightness and pulsated with life.

"Wait, what? You're helping me?"

"These are your decisions to make," he answered, head bent and brows furrowed. Without looking up he asked, "Who else knows what you intended to do this evening?"

"No one," I answered meekly.

He shook his head as if astonished. Once his fingers stopped furiously going over the equipment, his head snapped up. His eyes pierced me as through the heart.

"I will help you with this, but I won't conceal what I've done. Your mentor will know, and so will the Creator. The consequences and their reactions to your decisions will be solely on your shoulders."

Tendrils of apprehension attached themselves to my heart.

"Won't you get in trouble, too?"

"I didn't say trouble. I said consequences and reactions. Get on the lit pad and I'll send you down."

He hadn't really answered my question, but the surge of adrenaline at being told I could go down to Earth pushed everything else aside.

I double-checked my gear. Everything was in place. Despite the feeling of unease Joe had planted in my heart, he helped me accomplish what I'd been determined to do. So yes, I was ready.

I stepped onto the pad.

"One more chance to change your mind."

I placed my hands on my hips, resolute despite the consequences. My loved ones needed me. "I'm not changing my mind."

The sad look flitting across his face tugged at my heart and caused unexpected tears to threaten my eyes. I didn't even know who this guy was, but he had a way about him that just got to me.

"Then you've chosen the hard way to learn this lesson. I'm sorry for that, Audrey."

Before I could respond, he hit a button and I was hurled through space.

ALLIES AND ENEMIES

I stood in the street in front of my old home and took in the fragrance of my mother's beloved hyacinths. I knew what they'd look like without even turning to see them—small clusters of blooms creating a bulbous effect at the top of each stalk. Mom planted all different types of flowers, so it always looked like a candy store had sprouted from the ground in front of our house in the spring.

The smell of flowers shouldn't have been the first thing I noticed when a battle raged on either side of me, but it was, and the moment of disorientation cost me. A sharp tail caught my midsection and sent me sailing into the neighbor's tree.

I couldn't breathe.

I hunched over, clutching my sides. There wasn't any blood, but I straight-up couldn't breathe. Panicked, I struggled to take in air. Spots formed in my vision. Right before I was sure to pass out, my back was forcefully slapped.

Sweet air, the true elixir of life, entered my lungs. I straightened, then quickly bent over and threw up.

"What are you doing here?" an angry voice asked.

I looked up. Alrik's brows where low and pinched. His nose was scrunched up in disgust and his free hand was balled into a fist. He practically vibrated with fury.

Whoa!

I was used to the playful and jovial version of Alrik, never this enraged beast of a man. He was covered in blood, his own and demon. The mixture of red and black created a macabre picture. Combined with his harden features, for the first time, he actually scared me.

"I'm here to help," I managed to squeeze out of my lungs and vomit-coated throat.

He barked out a harsh laugh. "Help? Once the demons realize who you are, they're going to swarm you, and that, little one, is something I know you aren't ready for. Magic weapon or not."

I reached back and brushed my hand over the hilt of my sword, its flicker a silent reminder of what my *magic weapon* could do. Anger rose in me, responding to his verbal attack.

"I'm not unprotected," I challenged him, "and those are my family members." I jutted my chin toward the house. "Those are the people I love most in the world. And I'm here to protect them."

Alrik shoved me to the ground as another blackened hunk of flesh swung my way. I watched him fight off the creature from the ground while taking stock of the scene playing out around me.

There were about twenty demons engaged with at least double that number of hunters in various spots around my family's home. They fought in the streets, on our neighbors' lawns, and even on a couple of rooftops. My internal demon-radar that no one seemed to understand—the smell that wasn't a smell—flared, but I'd become somewhat calloused to it.

It wasn't like I needed it to tell me we had our hands full at the moment.

Although demons didn't fight with traditional weapons like we did, their bodies were made of sharp edges and pointed appendages they used as weapons. It sounded like metal meeting metal when the hunters' weapons clashed with the impenetrable parts of the demons' bodies. Only my sword could slice through certain armor-like parts of a demon's anatomy. The rest of the hunters were left searching for the vulnerable spots to inflict injury or make a kill. Whatever anyone might say, I was needed.

Alrik landed a wounding blow to the demon he fought as I scrambled to my feet. The creature let out a piercing screech before stumbling away from us.

Alrik squinted at me while tracking the fury around us. "You know the rules. This isn't where you belong."

Angry tears stung my eyes. "I don't care. I'm here, I have my sword, and I'm ready to fight." I slipped my helmet on and reached for my weapon.

"Don't do this, little Aud," Alrik warned. "This isn't the place for you right now, and once those demons see that sword, they'll be after more than just your blood."

Tired of listening to him, I shoved past him. No one had the right to say this wasn't my fight. I pulled the sword from its casing and it ignited immediately. Red and blue flames hungrily licked the blade as if telling me it was ready for battle. I tightened my grip on the hilt. The holy fire's heat was intense, but it didn't burn me. The area around me brightened in the early morning light.

It was as if time stopped. The sounds of fighting quieted momentarily as the warriors from each side fixated on me. And then time sped up and snapped back into place. The demons—every single one—charged me.

Alrik yelled before the first monster reached me, then there were only inhuman screeches that ripped viciously at my eardrums.

The first demon was easily twice my size, yet small for its kind. Completely blackened flesh made it hard to distinguish its features. I adjusted the position of my sword to use its light to my advantage. The brightness reflected off the sharp parts of the misshaped body, letting me know where all the demon's concealed weapons lay.

It swung at me with a hand—if it could really be called a hand, tipped with serrated claw-like fingers. I ducked and shoved my sword up in a quick motion that brought it straight into the creature's skull.

The demon ripped at its own head before turning into a pile of ash, but before it even fell away, another was there to replace it. The second and third demons went down similarly and in short order, but my arms began to shake. I couldn't keep this up.

It was the fourth demon that tackled me to the ground. I managed to drive the blade into the creature's midsection, but as it screamed, crumbled, and ashed around me causing me to choke on demon remains—*gross*—I knew I was in trouble.

My fellow hunters blades' sang a gory tune as they hacked their way through the horde to reach me, but it was too late.

Snapping jaws and drooling jowls surrounded me from every angle. The demons were so frantic to reach me that they hindered each other from doing so. That wouldn't last.

In that moment, I was pulled back to my last demon encounter. I'd been sent to Earth with a large number of other hunters to help protect a school full of teachers and students from a boy who had fallen under the influence of a demon. The boy had brought a gun to school, with the intent to do damage. My part in the battle had ended with me lying beneath the oppressive weight of a beast while its teeth sank into the soft flesh of my shoulder. The physical pain was bad enough, but the mental anguish of being fed on was beyond excruciating.

I'd been warned about it, but I don't think it's something you can fully comprehend unless it happens to you. Everything dark, evil, and sinister from the being latched on to you is shoved into your psyche while it simultane-ously feels like your soul is being sucked from your body.

The physical scars from a demon feeding were nothing compared to the mental ones. The demons got a high from feasting on a hunter, which was what kept them coming back for more despite the danger. Right now, they were like sharks fighting over chum.

I was the chum.

I pushed through my fear and swung my blazing sword at whatever was closest to me. The real probability of getting bit again triggered my panic button and caused my aim to be wild and frantic.

Why hadn't I listened to Alrik?

A jaw snapped at my foot and I kicked out. A claw raked across my armor-clad stomach, causing an involuntary scream to leave my lips. I looked down expecting to see a bloody mess, but the armor had protected me from the claw. The look cost me.

A spiked tail hit me in the head, hard enough to knock my helmet loose and rattle my brain. Black spots danced in my vision.

A horn sounded, loud enough to be heard through the demon screeches and hunters' shouts. The demons mysteriously, or maybe miraculously, backed away, creating a circle around me. Through the black spots and pain in my head I caught glimpses of the hunters trying to penetrate the circle, but the demons would not be moved. Some turned toward the hunters to fight against them, while others remained fixated on me. When one fell, another stood in its place.

I lay there and waited for the ringing to stop and the hallucination of the demons creating a barrier around me to disappear. Even from the ground I kicked and slashed at the creatures probably still trying to eat me alive. Once the fog in my brain cleared, I was convinced I'd be met with the same scene I'd been battling before.

"Put your sword away!" someone yelled from a distance.

Huh?

"I can't get to you if your sword isn't sheathed. You'll burn through us all!"

Double huh?

I blinked at the air above me. Was there actually a red-scaled fairy-tale dragon hovering above me with a really attractive guy on it yelling down at me?

"I can get you away from all this if you'll just put your sword away and stand up," he yelled over the sounds of continued battle.

I quickly—too quickly—sprang up and looked around. A wave of dizziness hit and I struggled to stay on my feet. The lower the dragon hovered, the wider the circle of demons became. They hissed and snarled at both the hunters and my would-be rescuer.

The dragon and its rider landed within the circle. The demons kept at bay. The man, or rather boy—he couldn't be older than twenty—ran toward me. He took my shoulders in his hands none too gently and gave me a rough shake.

"Sheathe it so I can fly you away!"

The other hunters yelled, but I couldn't make out what they said. Was this guy a friend or foe? He was a human, so he had to be a friend, right?

A crazed look gleamed in his eye as he frantically scanned the circle, checking the demons with his eyes. They still kept their distance, but some of them seemed to creep closer—getting bolder.

"Our appearance alone won't keep them away for much longer. We've got to go."

"Our?"

"Yeah. Mostly I mean him." He jerked his chin toward the dragon. "Come on."

The young man took my elbow and dragged me toward his beast. The dragon reared up on its hind legs when we approached. "See, you have to put that thing away." He gestured toward my sword. "It makes him nervous."

I sheathed my sword, extinguishing the flame in an instant, and the young man heaved a relieved sigh.

"Now up you go."

The dragon flattened its body as close to the ground as possible. The young man pushed me up on its back and then followed, seating himself directly behind me. He reached around and grabbed golden reins on either side of me, the position more intimate than I expected. I scooted forward to put some space between our bodies, but I was thrown back into his hard chest with the first powerful stroke of the dragon's red-scaled wings. That one flap lifted us off the ground unexpectedly fast.

I looked back in time to catch Alrik's frantic gestures, but I couldn't decipher what they meant. I was just glad to be away from the horde and out of reach of their poison-filled jaws.

The demons on the ground closed the circle under us, shrieking at the sky. The ones that could fly gave chase while many of the others were cut down by hunters. Like dark shadows ascending from the earth, leathery wings unfolded as the demons shot into the air behind us. They looked like harmless figurines a child might play with until they started to gain on us and grow in size. With each flap of their wings, I made out more of their grotesque and distorted features.

I gasped, and my rescuer shouted a curt command to the dragon in a language I didn't recognize. The dragon turned mid-flight, causing me to yelp as I was almost unseated by the sudden move, but the young man's arms kept me on the beast. As the demons approached, the dragon opened his jaws and spit a flame at them with an earsplitting roar.

The demons dodged the flame without trouble, but they dropped altitude as they did so, appearing to give up. It was a strange thing to watch. Demons weren't known for retreating out of fear. They usually attacked with single-minded focus despite the danger. What was this thing I rode that it could cause such a reaction? And if it fought for good, why didn't we have more of them?

I didn't let myself dwell on the alternative—that this beast didn't fight for good and wasn't on my side at all.

The dragon changed its trajectory for our original course. The cage of the man's arms once again kept me in place. The flapping of the giant wings became more rapid, and the ground beneath sped by so quickly I lost track of my bearings. The more distance we put between us and the demons, the less my internal demon-radar detected.

"Where are we going?" I yelled over my shoulder.

"Someplace safe," was his answer.

Trying to have a conversation over the rushing of the wind was fruitless, but my anxiety spiked at his answer. I was already having trust issues, and the vagueness of his answer didn't help.

Only minutes later, he leaned forward to say in my ear, "We're almost there."

Even as he said it, we were slowing down. The ground, which was once again discernible, was completely unfamiliar to me. We flew over a rural setting with splotches of small towns scattered here and there. For all I knew, we could be in a different state by now.

Finally, the dragon started his spiraling descent and I closed my eyes tightly from dizziness. I felt, rather than heard, the deep chuckle behind me.

"It takes some getting used to," the young man said into my ear right before the impact of landing.

I pried my eyes open one at a time and took in our surroundings. Fields of gold stretched for miles around us, broken up only by lone trees sprinkled here and there. "Are we in Kansas or something?"

"Does that mean you're feeling like Dorothy?" he asked with another chuckle.

"A little right now. Although I wouldn't consider this thing Toto."

The dragon snorted, causing its rider to lean forward and bark a command I didn't understand. Its jarring irises—slit into two equal halves like a serpent—narrowed further and it shot out a flame too close for comfort. I wondered if that was the creature's way of putting the rider in his place.

A look of unease flitted across the young man's face before he turned his back on the beast. The look reminded me to stay on guard.

"I'd like to make the first introduction. I'm Morgan." He bent low at the waist in way of a greeting.

Much like the dragon, I narrowed my eyes at him. I waited a beat before responding, "I'm Audrey." I stuck out my hand to shake. I might like to dress like a princess now and then, but I wasn't the curtseying type.

Rather than shake my hand, he bent low to kiss the top before I could stop him. I yanked my hand back in response. One guy who insisted on hand-kissing was quite enough for me.

"Okay, I appreciate the help back there and all, but I'm not really comfort-able with that type of physical contact. I have a, ah, a . . ." What was I about to insinuate? "A person who wouldn't really appreciate your touchy-feely stuff."

Morgan tilted his head. "That is extraordinary."

Well, that was highly offensive. "What, I'm not pretty enough or some-thing to have a, ah, person? Who are you to talk, bud?"

That was a lame comeback. Insulting his looks would get me nowhere. He was beyond gorgeous. And I would bet he knew it. Tousled black hair, chocolate-colored eyes framed in sooty lashes, and chiseled features. So, I insulted his company instead. "Your best friend is a giant lizard. I'll bet that has all the ladies flocking your way."

Of course, I wouldn't be surprised to hear he *was* drowning in interested women. Giant lizard or not.

He looked confused for a split-second, then some sort of understanding dawned on him. "I wasn't speaking of your physical beauty, Audrey. I'm sure you well know you are the height of lovely."

Oh, well, that was better. What was his "extraordinary" comment about then?

"I was speaking rather of your changing hair color."

Oh . . . that made a little more sense.

"It was black and fiery red when I picked you up, but it seems to be changing to pink as we speak." There was laugher in his voice his face refused to show. "I believe it's what would be considered 'hot pink' right now, and getting brighter as I speak."

Well, of course it was pink. I was beyond embarrassed.

"Can I have a moment?" It came out like a question, but I wasn't really asking. I twirled my finger to indicate he should turn around.

He shrugged and obliged.

I concentrated, and my normal shade of brown returned. "Thanks."

He turned back. "Ah, and there's the real you. Even lovelier."

My gosh, what was up with being dead? Guys never flirted with me like this when I was alive. Maybe we were all just less encumbered by self-consciousness now. But seriously, didn't he know flattery would get him anything?

No, no, I mean nowhere! Focus, Audrey, focus. You've got a possible case of stranger danger standing right in front of you. "So . . . where are we exactly? Is this an extraction point?"

"Not exactly. More like a safe house."

Turning to the left and right, fields of wheat stretched out in every direction. I cocked my eyebrows.

"Less emphasis on the 'house' part, and more on 'safe,'" he said.

I eyed the red beast and curbed my need to pace. "Can that thing take us back? We're miles, maybe states, away from my family's house."

"Which is why we're here. You're not supposed to be there anyway, am I right?"

My back went rigid. "And what would make you think that?"

"I know the rules. We're never allowed to fight in battles surrounding our loved ones still on Earth."

"Well, I'm different," I bluffed—or maybe I was trying to convince myself. "I have this." I pulled my sword from my back and it blazed to life, causing the dragon to lift on its hind legs and hiss at me. "What's his problem?"

Morgan spoke some soothing words to the creature before it lifted off and flew into the distance.

"Hey, that was our ride back!"

"Don't worry. Your sword just makes him uneasy. He'll be back after we've had a chance to talk."

I frowned at the sky where the dragon had disappeared. "Why would it make him uneasy? It can only do real damage to demons."

"Is that so?"

"Of course." I gave him a quizzical look. "Why don't you know more about this? I thought my story had made its way around to everyone in the realm by now."

Morgan brought a hand to his face and pinched his bottom lip between his knuckle and thumb before releasing it. "Those of us on the fringes don't get information quite as easily."

I watched him suspiciously. His answers were plausible, I supposed, but something seemed off. "How did you get a dragon?" I asked. "Why don't more of us fight with them? I'll bet if we had dragons, we could wipe out a ton of demons all at the same time."

"I don't doubt that," Morgan agreed, "but they are very rare. They were almost completely wiped out by the great flood. The ones that have survived are reclusive, and they don't trust easily."

What? *Dragons* had escaped the flood? First unicorns, now dragons. I rubbed my tired eyes. This was messing with my understanding of history. "How did you came across yours, then?"

"I wouldn't consider him mine. He's more of a temporary partner," was all he revealed. He sat down in the middle of the golden field. The breeze blew the stalks around and over his head. "Would you like to sit and talk for a little while? I'd love to hear more about that amazing sword of yours. I've never seen anything like it."

I shifted from foot to foot. Now that my thoughts had cleared, my anxiety about getting back to help the other hunters and my family started to intensify again.

"Do you think you could call the dragon back? I appreciate the rescue and all, but I'd really rather get back to the fight and try to help out. I'm worried about my family and the other hunters. There were a lot of demons around when we left. My sword can be really handy in a fight. I just need to be more strategic this time so I don't get tagged down."

"How exactly does it work?" Morgan asked.

I looked down at him. One arm was thrown around his propped-up knee, and the other lazily supported the rest of his weight behind him. He didn't look eager to take me back. Rescuer or not, I started to get a bad feeling about this situation. Was he trying to pump me for information? The details of my sword were the least important thing in my life right now.

"Maybe I could explain on the way back?" I tried.

Morgan heaved a sign. "I'm sorry, but after all the flying, the dragon's most likely left to hunt and won't be back for a while. Until then, I'm afraid you're stuck with me. I promise to take you back when he returns. Does that put you more at ease?"

This was just perfect. I was stuck with a strange hunter in the middle of nowhere, and despite his gentlemanly behavior, he'd orchestrated this trip—and our seclusion. I decided then and there that I didn't trust him. I wasn't giving him any more information until I got some answers of my own, or at least until we landed in more recognizable territory.

I took what I hoped was a discreet check of his weapons. Blades were strapped all over his body. Two on his thighs, another pair at his ankle. A blade—much longer than my own—looked to be strapped to his back in a similar fashion to mine. And his armor was different. It wasn't the iridescent, metallic black my friends and I wore but instead was solid black. It was also stiff, not conforming to his body as our body armor did. I had no idea what was happening, but alarms were going off in my head left and right. I took a tentative step back, but it didn't matter—there was nowhere to run, no cover to be found.

"What kind of hunter are you anyway?" I asked.

Morgan frowned, marring his beautiful face. "Audrey, what's wrong? I only want to talk."

My hand itched to reach for my blade. I bent my elbow in reflex, then fisted the hand at my chest. One of the biggest downsides to wearing a baldric rather than a belt scabbard was there was no subtle way to reach for my sword.

Morgan didn't miss the move. His eyes flashed . . . with anger?

"Is your plan to use that on me? All I've done so far is pull you from danger."

I narrowed my eyes. Information seemed to be the name of the game right now. I bet this next bit would help me discern his true intentions.

"This blade can't be used against those who fight evil," I said.

"Is that so?"

"Yes. So, you wouldn't mind if I tried it on you?"

Morgan's eyes narrowed in response. "Why would you think I was evil? I am human like you, after all."

And there was the crux of the problem. I'd always assumed humans, any human, would be on our side. Was I about to be proved fatally wrong?

A PIECE OF LOGAN'S PAST

"*A*udrey, get behind me."

The familiar voice, laced with ice, caused my spine to straighten as I looked wildly around.

It couldn't be. But it was.

Logan stood to my left, having appeared from thin air. His posture was rigid, muscles bunched as if anticipating a fight—or holding himself back from one. His sword was drawn and ready, his gorgeous eyes fixed not on me, but on Morgan. Without his helmet, his light hair—longer than I remembered—ruffled slightly in the wind.

My eyes shifted between him and Morgan. "What's going on?" I unsheathed my blade, its heat warming my gloved hand.

"Audrey, don't get any closer to him."

"Wasn't planning on it," I admitted.

Logan's tone was so menacing I scanned the area for another threat. I didn't sense a demon, but who was to say my internal demon-radar was flawless? It hadn't worked on Satan, after all. There was a blur of motion and I found myself behind Logan. His broad shoulders and muscled back offered a shield of protection. I found that comforting. I wished I didn't.

"What are you doing?"

"Protecting you."

"Touchy, touchy. Relax, Logan. We were just having a chat." Morgan spoke with an English accent that wasn't there a moment before.

They knew each other?

"I doubt it was just that," Logan said, his voice even icier.

I peeked around Logan's shoulder. Morgan was still seated, looking as unconcerned as ever.

"So, there's no demon?" I asked.

"No, luv, he's trying to protect you from me. Although I didn't anticipate he'd get this worked up." Morgan's smile was pleased.

"Don't call her that." Logan's voice lowered even more.

"What . . . luv? I didn't realize that endearment was already spoken for, mate."

Waves of fury came off Logan. I sheathed my blade and lay a reassuring hand on his arm, confident that Logan with a blade was formidable enough to protect us from one seated hunter—even a strange one. Maybe if he calmed down, I'd figure out what was going on.

"Logan, what's happened?" I whispered into his ear.

My human shield remained mute. Frozen except for the tightening of his fist.

"He's just overreacting luv, like usual."

"You. Are. Not. Allowed. To speak to her."

Morgan cocked an eyebrow, a small smirk playing on his lips. "Are you worried history will repeat itself, or is it more than that?" He laughed softly. "I don't remember bringing out this much of a protective streak in you when I was your trainee. I suppose we're both your former trainees at the moment. Isn't that right?"

Logan's voice dripped with an emotion I couldn't identify. "She's nothing like you, Morgan. She's stronger. She'd never be seduced by evil."

What? This was getting interesting. Confusing and intense, but definitely interesting. I looked around Logan at the young man sitting in the field with new eyes.

"Well, I did have help with that, if you recall. Part of the blame for what I've become will always lie on your shoulders."

Logan tensed impossibly more. "I'm well aware. I'll always carry the shame. But you still chose your path. It didn't have to be like this. Now you have an eternity of suffering to look forward to. But he won't have her. Never her."

"She'll make her own decisions, Logan. Your job isn't to protect her. Not as her mentor, and not as her bonded. One of those positions has already been filled. My guess is there's someone else willing and waiting to fill the other."

Morgan tilted his head so he could see me around Logan. His eyes filled with lasciviousness. "She is rather lovely. I understand the appeal."

Logan moved so fast he blurred, but his sword only struck air. Morgan had ducked and rolled away, drawing his own weapons. His movements put him between Logan and myself.

As I stared at Morgan's back, his armor changed just enough to look like scales knitted together. Dark shadows clung to his weapons like smoke. A black-bladed sword was clenched in his right hand and a mace with a spiked ball appeared in his left.

I jerked my sword from its sheath.

Logan's eyes widened a fraction before narrowing with determination. He'd recovered his stance and readied for another attack.

"I wouldn't do that if I were you, mate," Morgan said with deadly calm.

"There are lots of things you wouldn't have done if you were me," Logan retorted.

I stepped closer to Morgan, allowing the heat of my sword to emanate off the blade. The blaze was so hot it burned blue. Even from a few feet back, some of the scales on Morgan's armor begin to scorch. It was then I realized what his armor was made of.

Demon skin.

"Unless you want to see how easily my weapon cuts through demon flesh, I suggest you put down your weapons," I said.

I only caught a flash of Logan's surprised expression as I focused on the threat in front of me. Morgan was not the hunter I'd assumed him to be. Still keeping his eyes trained on Logan, Morgan replied to him rather than me.

"You see, Logan, she doesn't need you to baby her. She has a backbone of her own."

I touched the tip of my sword to Morgan's back as a warning. He hissed and arched as the scales sizzled before ashing into shadows, leaving part of his back exposed. Yet he didn't drop the weapons pointed at Logan. I gritted my teeth. My sword hand quaked with restrained anger.

"I wasn't taught to cut down humans, Morgan, but with your back unprotected like this I don't think it would be too hard to hit something important."

"Oh, luv, you have no idea what type of man you are protecting. But I never intended to fight you, so here is my act of goodwill." Morgan lowered his weapons as he spoke and they, along with his armor, dematerialized. I blinked once, then twice. How was that possible on Earth?

He stood between us in plain street clothes, a black T-shirt and dark-washed jeans. Logan and I kept our weapons up and at the ready. Regardless of my bravado, I don't think I could have actually struck him, but he didn't need to know that. I looked to Logan for direction. His focus was solely on the young man standing between us.

"It seems the two of you have a little talking to do. I'm going to let you have at it, then." Morgan shoved his hands into the pockets of his low-rise jeans. "Besides," he continued, "I believe my ride is here."

My gut tightened when I spotted the red dragon overhead, moving toward us at an impossible speed. As it swooped down from the sky, Morgan lifted his arms, grabbed hold of its claws, and was lifted from the ground. He used the momentum and flipped forward to ride astride the creature's back.

"See you soon, luv!" he yelled and winked at me before skyrocketing off.

My eyes were still glued to Morgan's retreating form when Logan jerked me back against him. His protective arm wrapped around my stomach. Suddenly heavy, my head tipped back to rest on Logan's chest. As adrenaline seeped from me, my sword became too cumbersome to hold. I let it fall to the ground and extinguish.

It happened again. Just like in the alley after my encounter with Satan, electricity zinged between Logan and me. I jerked in his arms. But this time he didn't let go. He held tighter and the energized current faded.

"I feel . . . tired," I admitted. I was owed an explanation for what had just happened, all of it, because the game had just changed.

Changed in a big way.

But bone-deep exhaustion overrode my desire to know. I wasn't sure I could even handle an explanation right now.

"Exposure to evil will zap your strength quickly. Like coming off an adrenaline high." Logan's words vibrated in his chest, and so I felt as well as heard them. "Between the dragon and *him*," he all but spat, "you've had an overdose on evil. Come on, we've got to get you rested, and then we can talk."

I took a deep breath and then a shaky and reluctant step out of Logan's embrace. I chided myself. I shouldn't have found comfort there.

I reached down and returned my sword to its sheath on my back, then turned and watched Logan return his weapon to his scabbard. His eyes were haunted.

"Any idea how to get out of Kansas?" I asked.

He chuckled a humorless laugh. "This is Ohio, not Kansas. Come on. We've got a hike ahead of us."

We walked for almost a half-hour before coming upon a church. It was the first church I'd been to since I had died. It was a simple structure—nothing fancy about it. The white paint on the siding looked like it had seen better days, but the landscaping was well kept and the stairs leading to the sanctuary had recently been power washed. Someone cared enough for this small congregation to take care of upkeep.

We entered the open doors, and a refreshing charge of energy flowed into me. I stood soaking it in . . . whatever *it* was.

"This way," Logan beckoned.

As quaint as this little place was, I had no idea what Logan was up to. "What are we doing here?" I asked as I followed his lead.

"Getting back to where we should be. What do you know about churches on Earth?" He moved toward the front where the pulpit stood.

I planted my hands on my hips. "Are you serious?"

He rolled his eyes. "Just humor me."

"They're places of worship?" I had no idea where he was going with this.

"So, you don't know about the portals then?"

Portals? Like the one in my closet for my faux birthday party? No one had ever mentioned anything like that existing on Earth before. "Portals?"

He nodded and then crouched to examine the floor of the raised dais. Only half his attention was directed toward me.

"The Cliff's Notes version is that churches across the globe are interconnected with each other by portals." His hand swept lightly over the polished wood as he spoke. "Once you find the trigger point in each of them, you can activate a portal and use it to travel to any other church."

"Any church? Or does—"

"Found it."

Without further explanation, he settled his hand on the ground and murmured something I couldn't hear, then stood. As if he'd hit a power button, a shimmering oval the size of a person appeared on the back wall. It was strange enough to cut off my train of thought.

Hesitant, I took Logan's outstretched hand. He didn't give me a chance to think as he yanked me through.

We emerged in an all-too-familiar location.

The breath in my lungs caught as my eyes scanned the surroundings. This was a bigger church than the one we'd first entered, but there was still nothing fancy about the large room we now stood in.

Padded seats that went back at least thirty rows had replaced the ten pews of the former sanctuary. The ceiling height had expanded as well, vaulting a few stories into the air. The walls were painted a soft blue-gray color, and the floor was mostly gray on gray geometric industrial-grade carpet, the kind you see most often in heavily-trafficked public places like schools and hospitals.

There was nothing particularly spectacular about this place, except this was *my* church. A stone's throw from *my* home. I'd grown up in this building.

"Audrey?"

I had difficulty tearing my eyes from the comforting sights. "Did you know this was my church?"

"Sorry, I didn't think to warn you this might happen." He reached a hand up to rub his neck. I recognized it as one of the gestures he commonly used when he was uncomfortable. "I just picked the closest location I knew of. I hope this isn't too upsetting for you."

I shook my own head to clear the cobwebs of memories. "No, it's really fine. I just wasn't prepared, that's all. A bit of a shock. I'm fine. Let's get back to my house. I know the way from here. We can walk." I started toward the rear exit.

"No." Logan's voice echoed off the empty sanctuary walls.

"Excuse me?" My fist found its way to my hip once again.

"Remember, first you rest, then we talk."

"No, first we make sure my family is okay, then we talk," I shrugged. "I can rest when I'm dead."

He shot me a droll look. "The battle is over . . . for now. Your family is safe. We have a lot to discuss, and I'm not doing it until you've had some rest."

Stubborn as always. Still, learning my family wasn't in any immediate danger did make me more pliable—and I was awfully tired. What was the harm in humoring him? I gave a quick nod and staggered a little with residual exhaustion. I hoped he hadn't seen that.

His body relaxed and I frowned. He'd expected every interaction with me to lead to a verbal sparring session. I hated that I still caused him so much grief. Another reason we were better off apart.

"This way." He turned and walked from the room, not even bothering with a side glance to see if I followed.

I rolled my eyes. I was once again reduced to a duckling.

Logan led me to the bowels of the church, the forgotten places with dark hallways and dust bunnies large enough to be real.

I only had one memory of this part of the building. Playing hide-and-seek as a child. I hid a little too well, and it took church leaders and my parents close to two hours to find me. After I'd crawled under a bunch of stacked chairs to hide, I'd gotten too scared to leave when it was obvious the other kids weren't going to find me. It was an emotion-laden memory for a seven-year-old, so I'd avoided this part of the church ever since. I'd always found it kind of creepy.

He stopped to face me. "This is going to be a little weird," he warned.

"O-kay." I wasn't sure I was ready for anything weirder than what I'd already encountered today. Human traitors, dragons, and portals linking religious places of worship were strange enough.

"Follow my lead."

"Don't I always?" I lifted my eyebrows.

He quirked one of his own in response before turning to the wall. He put his hand on the drywall, and it glowed right before a hidden door popped open. It reminded me of my room fridge. Definitely freaky.

Logan held the door open and angled his head to indicate I should go first.

I did, hesitantly. The door softly clicked behind us. I looked around. This was weird in a way I wasn't expecting. We were encased in a cement block. A single light hung from the ceiling with a pull chain to operate it. The walls were craggy and gray. A wrought-iron twin bed sat in one corner of the room. Two metal folding chairs were stacked against the far wall. A crude doorway led to another room I couldn't quite make out. This place would never be mistaken for homey. Efficient perhaps. Not homey.

But if I'd hidden in *here* as a kid, I would never have been found.

"What is this place?"

"A safe haven for hunters. When we're on Earth for a while, we need to rest and recharge. You already know what exposure to evil feels like." He motioned with his chin. "You take the bed. We can talk after you've gotten a little sleep."

I would have argued if I weren't already fantasizing about sinking into the mattress and falling asleep. I unbuckled and unlatched my baldric and set it, along with my weapon, down on the stone floor.

"Is it safe to take off my body armor?" I asked.

"Sure. I'm staying up to stand guard anyway."

"Logan, don't you need to rest too?"

I knew the answer without asking. His shoulders sagged with exhaustion and the lines around his eyes were telling.

"I can rest without sleeping. Don't worry about me. I've been doing this for a while. I'm used to going without."

"That's what I'm worried about," I replied without thinking.

His head snapped up, his eyes sharp. I turned to escape his gaze.

I peeled off my armor while he looked the other way, leaving me in tight-fitting spandex shorts and a sports tank. I crawled into bed, already half-asleep. I was settling under the covers when Logan sat on the side of the bed. Unsure of his intentions, I froze.

He let out a breath of air. "Get comfortable, Audrey," he ordered. I apprehensively obeyed. His nearness made me nervous, but also somewhat excited.

I internalized my frustrated sigh.

When I was fully laid out, I turned toward him. He pulled the blankets further up so they were almost to my chin, then reached out an ungloved hand and caressed my forehead. I held my breath. The empathy link didn't work on Earth—so this was the only place Logan ever touched my skin. I didn't know if I was relieved or disappointed that I couldn't sense his emotions.

When he seemed satisfied about whatever he was checking, he removed his hand and simply looked down on me. I should have rolled over and ignored him, but I couldn't. He seemed so sad.

"Is this where you've been all this time?" I asked.

He nodded, not quite meeting my eyes.

Against my will, my heart melted a little. I felt a fracture wanting to close. All this time while I'd been feeling abandoned, Logan had been watching out for my family. I quickly shut those feelings down and turned over to face the wall. The pain that tore me apart was also what kept me together.

THE TRUTH BURNS

J awoke with a start and sat up. Logan sat in one of the folding chairs only a few feet from the bed, fast asleep. Even in slumber, it was evident he wasn't taking care of himself. Dark smudges ringed his eyes. His body slumped as if in defeat. This wasn't Logan. This was a worn-out shell.

As if he felt my eyes on him, his popped open. He straightened so fast he almost fell off the chair—another indicator of his physical condition. Logan's movements were never short of graceful. Like a jungle cat, his moves were usually not only precise, but fluid. They were neither at the moment.

We stared at each other for a few more heartbeats.

"You're awake," he stated, most likely to fill the silence.

"Yeah." I crossed my legs and leaned against the uncomfortable twisted metal headboard. "Why do you look so bad?" *Oops . . . too blunt maybe?*

He snorted a self-deprecating laugh, then ran a hand over his face. "That bad, huh?"

I shrugged. It kind of was, but I didn't want to say it again.

"Remember when I told you being on Earth too long is hard on a hunter?"

I pulled my knees to my chest and nodded.

"Well, physical exhaustion is one of the consequences. I'd just arrived back in the realm to recharge when I received word that you'd slipped down here. I came back to find you."

It was my fault he was this tired. I frowned. "Why didn't you sleep instead of me then?"

He looked away. "You needed it."

"You needed it more."

He just shrugged. It wasn't worth fighting over. I would insist he nap the moment the opportunity arose.

"Is exhaustion the only consequence of being on Earth too long?"

He looked into my eyes. Despite the red tingeing his, they were still beautiful. "No."

"What else?"

Another weary shrug—a strange response from him.

I huffed. "Then you need to get back."

"Will you come with me?" he asked.

"No."

He nodded as if expecting that answer. "Then I can't go back yet."

I waved a hand in his direction. "You look like you're going to keel over."

"Being in this place will help me recharge a little. Not fully, but it helps."

That made some sense. My body was certainly stronger and more rested than before. Knowing Logan, this wasn't a discussion I would win.

So maybe we should have a different one.

"Tell me about Morgan."

It was several heartbeats before Logan released a heavy breath and nodded. "Yeah, I suppose it's time you knew about him."

I sat quietly as I waited for him to continue.

"Morgan was my last trainee. He was more than that, though—he was my friend. I failed him, and now he's here, working for the enemy."

I sucked in a quick breath of air. I'd gathered as much from their strange conversation, but I still didn't understand how that was even possible. "I don't get it. How did something like that even happen?"

"Yeah." He hastily ran a hand through his disheveled hair. "I know. It's rare, so it's not talked about much. I'll start from the beginning so you understand." He looked me straight in the eyes. "You'll think of me differently soon."

His tone told me *different* wasn't going to be a good thing.

I returned his stare with a steady one of my own. "It can't be that bad."

Rather than arguing, he started his tale. "Like I said, Morgan was my last trainee. I think we were paired because they knew we'd get along so well. That's what usually happens."

An unrestrained half-laugh, half-snort escaped me. "Sorry, but are you sure that's taken into consideration with mentor-mentee assignments? If it is, why did they pair *us* together?"

The corners of his mouth lifted. "I think we were the exception, not the rule. Doesn't mean there wasn't a reason for our pairing, though. Probably an important one." He looked at me pointedly, silently shaming me for requesting a new mentor.

"Perhaps we were supposed to fit together in a different way." The words popped out of my mouth without forethought. I mentally slapped my hand over my mouth. Heck, I almost did it physically.

Logan considered me for a few tense moments. "Perhaps," he finally said, "but now we may never know."

I chewed on a lip in discomfort.

"Anyway," he continued, deflating the moment, "mentoring Morgan was relatively easy. He was an athlete in life. A soccer player, actually. About to go professional before he was murdered."

I sucked in a quick breath. "Murdered?"

"Yeah. That kind of plays into what happened to him eventually. I don't think I ever told you, but I used to be a professional surfer, so we had the athlete thing in common."

I couldn't be sure, but I think his cheeks reddened slightly. He coughed into his hand, obviously uncomfortable discussing his life on Earth. I restrained an eye roll. Of course, he was amazing enough to be a professional athlete. Was I supposed to be surprised?

"I'd been training Morgan for months. He progressed as a hunter so quickly I wouldn't have been surprised if they'd promoted him to mentor himself within a short period of time. But that was before we were captured by demons."

My stomach sank. I wanted so badly to fire off more questions, but I held my tongue. A rarity for me, but I didn't want to do anything to stanch the unusual flow of information coming from Logan.

"We were scouting an area of reported heightened demon activity. An abandoned house some kids had been using to conduct a fake séance, not realizing they'd actually attracted a lot of real demonic attention. We were supposed to observe only, but when we got there it looked like there was just a lone demon lurking about. We were confident we could handle a single demon together, so we ignored our orders and engaged the creature. We were right—we took the demon down fairly easily. What we didn't notice was the trap we'd fallen into. By the time we'd vanquished the demon, we were surrounded by others. We tried to fight, but the demons didn't attack us like they normally would. Instead we were herded into the house."

He took a deep breath before continuing. "A group of hunters was eventually dispatched to find us. Generally speaking, we know where a hunter is while he's on Earth. That's how I found you in the middle of nowhere. But if a hunter is in the midst of overwhelming darkness, they can't be located. The house we were herded into was one such place, so once we were inside, we dropped off the map. Other hunters didn't know where we were to rescue us."

"But they knew the last place you were. Shouldn't they have figured it out?"

He nodded, "Yeah, it certainly gave them an idea. But we'd been fed on a number of times and were weak. We were thrown into a hidden cellar under the basement level. Even after the hunters who came for us cleared out the demons on the surface, there were enough of them with us below to hide our location. We were too out of it to even know a rescue party had been so close. After the initial attack, we were held there for days. Weeks actually."

Logan stopped talking. There was a blankness to his stare. A chilling quiet settled on the room as he mentally relived those days. There were horrors in the details he wasn't giving me. He refused to meet my gaze.

"I don't see why Morgan blames you," I said quietly.

Logan shook his head. To shake off the memories or bring him into the present, I wasn't sure. He turned to me then. Listless eyes connected with my own.

"It was my call to go after the demon. He went with it, and sure, he might even have encouraged it, but it was my job to enforce the rules. If I had done what we were supposed to do, we never would have been captured. After a while we lost track of days and kept time by how often they fed from us. When we were weaker than I'd ever thought possible, Satan finally came to us."

I shivered and rubbed my hands up and down my arms to rid myself of the bumps.

"He came to us once a day, or at least as well as we could tell. Saving us from another feeding, 'protecting' us with his presence. Satan couldn't have gotten a stronghold to corrupt Morgan if we hadn't been captured. He used Morgan's own murder against him. He claimed a loving God wouldn't have allowed it to happen. He said Morgan's life was unduly cut short and he should have been a star on Earth. He claimed it wouldn't have happened if only God had sent an angel or hunter to protect him. Bitterness eventually took root in Morgan. Even though we'd been tortured by the darkness, Satan tried to convince us it was ultimately for our own good, so we would finally see God clearly—not as a loving father but as a selfish deity."

Logan sucked in a lungful of air. "Morgan eventually believed him. Once Satan's manipulation took hold, Morgan began to change. Rather than growing weaker, he steadily grew stronger. Then his other powers started to develop."

I couldn't help the "Huh?" that slipped out.

Logan nodded and continued. "When a hunter changes sides, he gains new abilities. In Morgan's case, he lost his skill with a bow, but he gained the ability to manipulate shadows. He can pull and stretch darkness to make fighting more difficult for us."

That thought was as frightening as it was fascinating.

Logan's head hung in defeat. "I knew things were hard on him, but I hadn't realized he'd fallen so far until that happened. Even after we were captured, if I had been stronger for Morgan, maybe all this wouldn't have happened. But it was so hard not to fall into despair. It was possible we'd never be rescued. Morgan not only gave up on himself, but on God as well. If I had been the mentor I was supposed to be, the outcome might have been different."

I was shaking my head before I was conscious of the movement. "No."

Logan's gaze lifted, a questioning look in his eyes. "No?"

"Yeah, that's what I said. You can't take responsibility for someone else's weakness."

His eyes didn't even flare—they just stayed dull and listless. I'd never seen him so defeated. "If I'd been stronger, better, we would never have been in that position. I know it's my fault."

"Are you serious?" I scoffed. "You really need to get over yourself."

Logan jerked back as if slapped. "What?"

Something about his shock angered me. "I get it, you screwed up. Heck, you both screwed up. But you're not responsible for Morgan's decisions any more than you are responsible for mine." Perhaps I shouldn't have gotten so worked up, but it frustrated me to hear him take all the blame. I felt for Logan, I really did. But how long had he been beating himself up about this? "You're being egocentric by taking responsibility for the whole thing."

Logan's eyes were impossibly wide. "Egocentric?"

I was on a roll. And angry. Not angry because of Logan's mistake, but angry that he'd carried the blame around for someone else for so long. Morgan's choices were Morgan's. I'd seen him in action. He wasn't some pansy, haplessly following a mentor's lead.

I sat up straighter and moved forward so I could get in Logan's face and drive my point home. Anger built up behind his eyes. He could blow at any minute, but I didn't care. I welcomed it.

"Morgan's the one who gave up, not you."

"Yeah, but—"

"There is no 'but' about it. You should not be carrying around guilt over this. And I think deep down you know it. You're holding on to it like a toddler cuddling his blanket."

Logan pushed out of his metal seat so fast it fell to the ground with a loud bang. He breathed hard and fast. My guess was people had been handling Logan with kid gloves ever since this happened. Perhaps no one had wanted to tell him the truth—that holding on to this guilt was wrong. No wonder he still carried the physical scars.

And, I realized suddenly, he'd been relating to me all along through this stupid, stupid perception of his. Any type of normal relationship between the two of us had been doomed from the start, and not because of *me*, but because of Morgan.

I sucked in a quick breath. "That's it, isn't it?" I asked.

"That's what?" Logan asked through clenched teeth.

"That's what this is all about. You're trying to protect me to prove something. To right some previous wrong."

I swung my legs over the side and stood, leaving the softness of the bed behind. "That's why you are so overbearing. Do you even really care about me, or is this just some sick form of redemption you've cooked up in your head?" Now I was really steamed.

Logan's own fury was palpable. "No!" he roared. "You are not Morgan."

I flinched at his intensity, but I refused to back down. "Dang straight I'm not," I snapped back. My words carried the venom that simmered in my heart.

A stupid means to an end. That's what I was. That's what I'd always been to Logan.

Oh, it burned.

I turned to walk away, not able to take him at the moment. How many times could one person hurt me? Inside, I hated that I'd taken Logan's pain and turned it into something about me, but this was just too much.

I glanced over my shoulder to see Logan advance on me. The look in his eyes was nothing short of feral.

A spike of fear surged through my body. Perhaps I'd pushed him too far.

Not trusting my back to him anymore, I spun around. His advance forced my retreat until I bumped into the wall. Without speaking, he lifted both arms and placed his fists on the flat surface on either side of my head, effectively caging me in.

A shock of alarm zinged through my body.

He was over the edge of tired, and who knew what else was at work in him from his exposed time on Earth? I trusted Logan, sort of, but I wasn't sure what to expect from him right now.

His expression was unexpectedly carnal. My throat constricted, but no words emerged. His eyes skated across my face, looking at nothing and everything at once.

What was he searching for?

Deliberately, and ever so slowly, he used one hand to gently grasp my chin and tilt my head to the side. My eyes widened, and my body locked.

Satisfied, he returned his hand to the wall and lowered his head. Breathing in and out, warm air caressed my neck, his nearness paired with his scent— uniquely his—made me lightheaded.

What's happening?

"You. Are. Not. Morgan," he repeated gutturally.

And then it happened. His soft lips pressed a gentle kiss, so at odds with the rest of him, against my neck, then another behind my ear as he nuzzled in closer.

I tipped my head back, my eyes sliding shut as he placed a third lingering kiss. I made a noise in the back of my throat and Logan froze. My lids were too heavy to open.

His breath bathed my neck again. "Audrey, you need to tell me to stop."

What was he saying? Stop?

Things had changed so quickly I wasn't thinking straight. I was floating on a cloud. Why would I want to come down?

"I . . ." My dry throat made it hard to speak. I opened my lids a fraction to stare down at Logan's head, still bent only a breath away from my neck. "I . . . I don't want you to stop," I whispered.

Logan sucked in a quick breath of air. The arms on either side of me tensed suddenly, bulging, then contracting only to bulge again.

And then without warning, he moved my head to sample the other side of my neck. With his body held away from my own, he buried his face in the thick mass of my hair. He drew in a long breath and let it out excruciatingly slowly. The hot air fanning across my neck caused a full-body shiver. His lips just barely made contact with the sensitive skin below my ear. It was not a true kiss, but more of a tasting.

My knees weakened.

Using the wall behind me to stay upright wasn't going to be enough, so I reached up to grab his biceps.

When his lips closed on the bottom of my earlobe, I couldn't help the gasp that escaped.

Just as suddenly as he'd begun, he tore himself away, ripping my hands from his arms as well as his lips from my skin.

I stumbled. Off balance and with unstable legs, I landed in a heap on the hardened ground, too stunned to form a coherent thought.

What just happened?

Logan's shoulders heaved up and down with the force of his breath. He stared at the opposite wall. I stared at his back. With three violent inhalations, he fisted a hand and ran the other roughly over his face. My butt remained firmly planted on the ground.

Logan half-turned his body and watched me out of the corner of his eye. "That shouldn't have happened." His accusatory tone said it was my fault.

"Huh?"

His eyes reached my face and softened a bit before turning away again. He took another steadying lungful of air. "Has anyone explained to you why *exactly* it isn't good for us to be on Earth for too long?"

I shook my head "No," still staring. All I knew were the bits and pieces Logan had told me, which I realized now was precious little.

"We are spiritual beings now. We're meant to stay close to the Creator. The longer we're on Earth, the more susceptible we are to sin."

Logan spoke as if giving a lecture he'd given a thousand times before. "Our inhibitions are slowly stripped away. Our ability to sort right from wrong becomes clouded. If we are here for too long, our base desires become almost impossible to resist." He turned slightly, far enough to catch my eye out of the corner of his. "Do you understand what I'm saying here?"

Another shake of my head. Apparently the only thing I was capable of doing at the moment was that small physical gesture.

"Audrey, I was not a great guy when I was here, not even a good guy . . . except maybe a little at the end." He pinched his nose and lightly shook his head. "Man, you taste sweet, like strawberries."

He said it quietly to himself. Heat accompanied an involuntary full-body flush. I tasted like strawberries? *What does he taste like?* The last thought skidded through my mind, causing a second blush. I squashed it before it took root.

"You shouldn't have let me do that," he said.

And all at once I was angry again. "This was somehow *my* fault?" I asked incredulously. "Like I even knew what you were going to do when you stomped toward me like He-Man on a mission to conquer Castle Grayskull."

He blinked at me. "You know who He-Man is? He doesn't conquer Castle Grayskull. He defends it."

"Is that really the point here?"

"No, not the point." He ran a hand roughly through his hair, fisting a chunk of it before letting go. "It obviously wasn't your fault, but you shouldn't let me do it next time."

"Next time?" I practically squeaked. "There's going to be a next time?"

He gave me a long, soulful stare. I knew there was no way my hair wasn't completely pink with all the blushing I was doing. There was a hunger in his eyes he either couldn't or wasn't trying to hide. "If we don't get back to our realm soon, there will most definitely be a next time."

My knees went weak again. *Oh my.*

"I can't promise I won't take it to the next level and get both of us stuck in a serious bind. I know that's something neither of us wants to happen."

Dumping a bucket of ice water all over me couldn't have done more to change my demeanor. I finally got what he was saying. He was attracted to me only because he'd been on Earth too long and I was the only girl around. He was scared he would kiss me and bind us together, and that had *always* been the last thing he'd wanted.

I stood as gracefully as I could, straightening and pulling my shoulders back before coolly assessing Logan. The wild and reckless incident that had left me breathless a moment before, now made me feel tainted and used.

"Don't worry," I said with a glare. "That's not something I'll ever let happen again. If you need help with self-control, you can remind yourself I've been training with Kaitlin too, and she's taught me some very interesting self-defense techniques that would be particularly painful for a male attacker."

Logan grimaced. A look of sadness quickly shrouded his face.

For me it was all bravado, but the lie was eerily easy to tell. I turned my back on him and walked out of the room and into the adjoining one. I needed some space. I thought I was over Logan, but hearing him reject me again pierced a spot in my heart I hadn't eradicated, only buried.

And those kisses. I forced myself not to shiver. No, I couldn't think about that. Just the thought caused my neck to burn with remembrance.

Out of the corner of my eye I spotted a strand of pink hair darken to red, and I welcomed the change.

COMING HOME

*N*ight had begun to fall when we started the short trek to my family's home, less than a mile from the church. The evening air was chilly. Goose bumps appeared despite the protection of my body armor.

Logan hadn't said more than a few words to me since I'd left him alone in the room, only enough to indicate what the plan was before leaving the church.

Tension was thick between us, palpable in an itchy and uncomfortable way. My anger toward Logan for his misguided sense of guilt about Morgan had long since burned itself out, and I wondered why I'd been so hard on him. There had been no compassion in my words, only self-righteous anger.

The other *incident*—as I had come to call it in my head—between us wasn't something I had the extra brain or willpower to tackle further than to admit it had happened. I was eventually going to have to dissect all that had gone down between the two of us in the basement of the church, but the time wasn't now.

I balled up all the passion and hurt from Logan's actions and shoved them to the far corners of my mind. I focused on what I could, our fight over Morgan.

I worried a fingernail as we continued on in silence. A nervous habit I still hadn't broken. Logan had been incredibly vulnerable with me, and I'd been cruel. There was a way to speak the truth in love, but that wasn't what I'd done. My pride struggled with my desire to apologize and make things right. I actually felt the ball of self-righteousness lodged beneath my sternum that kept my lips closed.

And then there was a whisper in my mind. A memory of one of the many conversations I'd had with Hugo.

"Pride goes before destruction, a haughty spirit before a fall."

"Huh?" I lay on my back, catching my breath from my latest literal fall.

Hugo smiled a knowing smile at me and tilted his head. "It's that pride of yours that most often gets in the way. You need to watch out for that."

"That doesn't make sense," I complained. "I know I'm struggling here. Getting beat down on a regular basis is actually pretty humiliating."

"Yet your prideful attitude stands in the way of you truly learning. You're motivated by your pride. You want to do better because you won't humble yourself. You'd pick up these lessons even faster if you yielded to humility."

I sat up quickly. How did he know this stuff? Did I push myself because I didn't like not being good at something rather than because it was important for me to learn? "How do I learn to do that then?"

His smile grew. "Being open to surrendering your pride is the first step, my dear. Congratulations. He guides the humble in what is right and teaches them His ways."

Logan's hand on my shoulder snapped me from my thoughts. I hadn't even realized we reached our destination. His eyes were riveted on my house.

I was about to tell him not to touch me when his tense voice stopped me.

"It's too quiet."

A scan of the surroundings proved his words to be true. Had it really been earlier in this same day and spot that I'd fought a horde of demons? But now there wasn't a single one in sight. My internal demon-radar wasn't being tripped either. Where had they all gone? And stranger still, where were the good guys?

"I thought you said there were hunters protecting my family."

"There were."

"Where are they, then?"

"I don't know."

A chill brushed up my spine. The evening wasn't fully dark yet, but the lights from the house in front of me—as familiar as anything could be but no longer truly my home—chased away many of the shadows that stalked the area. Movement across one of the front windows caught my eye.

I gasped.

"What's wrong?"

"I think that was my mother." I moved forward without thought. Logan caught me around the waist and turned me from the house, his eyes broadcasting his thoughts.

"Audrey, there's a reason we aren't meant to return to our former lives. You'll be able to observe but not interact with your family members. It's painful. Have you truly thought this through?"

"Yes." *No.* All I wanted was to see my mother. I'd ached with the loss of my family. Until now, I hadn't realized how much.

His arms were slow to leave my sides. He was letting me make this decision on my own, even though he didn't agree with me. That was a big step for Logan.

I was at the window in moments. My face practically pressed against it like a child in front of a toy store at Christmas. My heart leaped. There she was! I only caught a glimpse of her before she stepped into another room. I couldn't read much from the profile of her face before she turned her back on me.

Mom padded into the kitchen without shoes or socks, wearing some of her favorite comfort clothes—worn jeans and a snug green T-shirt I recognized as one of my old ones. The dark hair twisted into a knot high on her head with a pencil sticking out of it told me she was working. She always did that to her hair when she was busy with paperwork. The familiarity of the simple quirk was soothing. Logan stood behind me, giving me silent support.

"Is there a way in?"

"We can look for one."

Only after climbing a tree did we find an unlatched window on the second floor. I gave an unladylike snort. No wonder my older sister, Jessica, had always managed to slip out of the house undetected.

We stealthily entered the house without incident. Logan soundlessly swung through the open window after me. Both of my parents were talking, but we were too far away to make out their words.

After gently closing the window, leaving it unlatched as before, Logan nodded in the direction of the stairs. We crept down as silently as possible. He followed in my footsteps exactly to avoid the creaky steps. Easy to understand how ghost stories sprang up when there were hunters constantly running around the globe. At least no one had caught the window opening and closing on its own.

My parents were seated at the kitchen table, papers spread out in front of them. Their shoulders sagged as if in defeat. My dad's hair had a little more gray in it than I remembered. The fine lines around my beautiful mother's eyes seemed more pronounced.

They had aged more than the short period of time I'd been gone. My chest ached. What had they gone through to age them like this? Oh, right—I had died. But something else was going on here too.

Mom opened an envelope and black smoke puffed out of it and ringed her head.

I gasped. "What is that?" I frantically swatted at the blackness around her. Most of it dissipated.

Logan's eyes were sad when they met mine. "It's demonic," he stated. "Your family's home is protected, so the demons can't actually breach it, but there are still ways Satan can get in to oppress your family. That substance doesn't last long, and it isn't as strong as if a demon were here trying to influence them, but it does its job casting doubt and depression just the same."

I was horrified. How could we protect them from attacks on so many levels?

"They just keep coming," Mom said, holding one of the papers in front of her face as she read the contents silently.

Dad laid a comforting hand on hers and forced her to lower what I could now see was a bill of some sort. "We have options."

"I know," she sighed. "I just don't like going into all this debt. I figured by now the bills would stop rolling in. Isn't that what insurance is for?"

"It would be so much worse without it."

"You're right." She bowed her head and closed her eyes, and a glowing halo appeared around her. Soft, silver-tinted brightness chased away the remaining blackness.

My gaze snapped to Logan for answers. "What's happening? Is she all right?"

"She's praying," Logan simply stated. After a moment, Dad once again laid a hand on hers and mimicked her pose. The soft glow emanated from him as well. I'd never seen anything like it. It encased their heads as if creating a protective barrier around their minds. Within the light, specks of silver twinkled like fairy dust. It was mesmerizing.

"The light would keep any demon off them, if it could even get in here. It burns demon flesh. The power of their prayers clears the air of any demonic influence as well."

I looked on with eyes of wonder. After only a few more moments, they both lifted their gaze and looked on each other with love.

"We'll be taken care of," Dad said.

My mother nodded in agreement. I slid closer, and one of the bills caught my eye. It had my name on it. This was about me. They must be still paying off the bills from the accident. *I* was what put my family in debt. How was it fair that the loss of their daughter caused them to be plagued with debt?

A hand flew to my mouth and I shook my head in a feeble attempt at denial. I took a quick but shaky step back from the table. If it wasn't for Logan's wall of muscle behind me, I would most likely have crashed into something. He held me around the waist with one arm, supporting most of my weight as my knees lost their stability.

"No. Please, God, no. This is all my fault," I whimpered.

A now recognizable jolt of electricity passed between Logan and me. It caused my muscles to cramp before relaxing.

"I'm sorry," he whispered. "I lose control over it sometimes. Did I hurt you?"

I craned my neck to look at him. It was the first time he'd admitted the energy flow had actually occurred. He couldn't avoid the question in my eyes, and with a heavy sigh he acknowledged its existence. "I'll explain it too. Later."

I nodded, my vision started to cloud with tears. "Logan, they're in debt because of me. They're still hurting because of me."

"This is not because of you, Audrey." Logan's words brokered no room for argument. "These things are a part of life. And you saw Satan's army for your-self. They are under attack. You're not doing that. The enemy is."

Doubts and fears flooded my mind. Didn't you have to open a door for Satan to attack you in some sense? What if it was *me* doing that—opening the door? Maybe I'd done something wrong in the afterlife that negatively impacted my family. They were obviously struggling with debt because of the accident. Was it possible that breaking so many rules in heaven or being a bad hunter was causing the spiritual attacks?

"But what if that *is* my fault? We don't actually know why they're being attacked. What if it's because of me?"

Logan was silent for a moment as he took the time to really consider the possibility. Then he turned me in his arms. I didn't know when I had become so comfortable there, but I wasn't about to move away, even if I had been ready to throat punch him just a little while ago. I needed all the consolation he was willing to give, and physical touch was soothing right now.

"Even if your family has been targeted because of you, none of this is your fault. You didn't do this to them. This may have something to do with you, although since you are already dead that doesn't make much sense, but even if that were the case, it doesn't make it your fault. And it's not your responsi-bility to fix it."

I must have looked pathetically desperate for answers, because he went on. "God uses trials to strengthen people. When in despair, both your parents just turned to God. They are in a place where they need to rely on Him to get them through this. If you could take all this away from them, you would be doing them a disservice. It may seem the best thing to lift someone's burden yourself, but it's not yours to bear. It's God's, and it's your family's chance to learn to put their burdens where they belong. You'd be robbing them of something far more precious than money if you got in the way of what God has planned here."

I didn't like that answer. I just wanted to fix everything for them. Hadn't they been through enough? They'd lost a child. How much could they truly bear on their own?

Nothing, something whispered inside me. *On their own they can bear nothing.* The soft voice continued. *I will carry their load.*

"What-the-what?" I spun out of Logan's arms and frantically searched the room for whoever had spoken.

"Audrey?" Logan asked tentatively.

"Who was that?"

Logan was back to giving me the look that said I'd grown an extra head. Oddly enough, I had a moment of nostalgia before shaking it off.

"There was someone else here. I heard his voice."

"Oh." Logan's eyes lit with recognition. "Did you hear it with these," he pointed to his ears, "or in here?" He gently laid a hand on the top of my head.

My silence spoke volumes.

"He never leaves us or forsakes us. His Spirit goes with us, Audrey, and if we are sensitive to His presence, we'll hear what we need to hear."

I caught my breath. "That's what that was?"

He smiled in response. His smiles always threw me. He was gorgeous.

A loud engine backfire made me jump. I ran to the front window with Logan on my heels. I recognized my brother's junker of a car immediately as it cruised toward the house. What wasn't familiar was the blackened creature attached to its roof.

I whirled toward Logan. "There's something we can do about that, right?"

"Definitely." He turned and sprinted back up the stairs, heedless of squeaky steps. I followed in his wake.

A SPIKY SITUATION

*W*e took far less care leaving the house than we had entering. The wheezing of my brother's car camouflaged the noises of our hasty retreat. The *squeak* then *bang!* of the front door opening and closing echoed throughout the house just as I slipped through the window. I barely bothered with the tree, only gripping a branch before dropping two stories to the ground.

I beat Logan around the side of the house just in time to watch the demon detach and land on the paved road, the moment before the car rolled into the driveway, seemingly on fumes alone. I flew by my parents on their way to meet my brother and charged the creature, sword already drawn, flames licking the blade.

The demon prowled haughtily at the property line. I was sure it couldn't see me coming or it would have already fled. My sword was no joke, and word had to have gotten around about the damage it inflicted. A horde of demons was one thing. There was something to be said about safety in numbers. A single demon hardly stood a chance.

As soon as I crossed the protective barrier I became visible to the creature. It shrieked, revealing row upon row of sharp, snake-like teeth. Too late to flee, it took an offensive position and swiped its spiked tail at me.

I squinted my eyes . . . I knew this demon. It was eerily similar to the one I'd faced in the gauntlet. Apparently, they hadn't used creative license after all. My lips twitched in the ghost of a smile. I so had this.

No more useless metal sword for me. Charbroiled spikes coming right up! Given the right position, I might even be able to dispatch this ugly guy in one swipe.

A second tail I hadn't seen at first whipped toward me. Okay, make that two swipes.

"Audrey, stand down!"

Logan's yell penetrated my battle focus. I choked down my frustrated scream. Why were people always holding me back? Despite my annoyance, I complied and launched myself to the side, rolling away and out of reach of the demon. It swung around and immediately picked up pursuit.

And that's how I ended up running from the demon I should have been cutting down.

"Logan!" I growl-yelled as I sprinted back toward the property line. I made the mistake of checking behind me and stumbled on the curb. Logan's arms were there in an instant, and he threw me through the air toward the house and beyond the demon's reach. I landed on my back and the air punched from my lungs. Rolling over, I lifted my eyes toward the demon, whose jaws were moments away from shredding Logan.

Logan stood with his feet braced and one arm stretched out in front of him, palm open and pointed at the demon. His sword hung uselessly at his side.

Fear for him froze me. I watched in horror as he was about to be impaled and bitten.

My mouth opened in a silent scream that would never reach his ears.

And then blinding white lightning shot from Logan's hand and slammed into the fallen angel's chest.

The thing cringed in on itself like a dying spider. Logan wasted no time bringing his sword into play and severed its head in one mighty blow. He stood above it, breathing heavily. I watched his shoulders heave from where I lay sprawled on the ground. My unblinking eyes were probably the size of saucers.

Logan didn't turn away from the corpse until it disintegrated into nothing. Only then did he face me, a haunted expression shadowed his features, before hurrying over. He dropped to his knees by my side.

"Are you hurt?" He scanned my body for injury. When I didn't answer, his eyes met mine, and he cocked his head. "You actually listened to me," he said. There was something akin to awe in his voice.

I found my own. "Are you serious right now?"

"You never listen to me."

"That is not true."

His eyebrows dropped as if to say, "Yeah, right."

"There have been other times I have listened to you," I argued. I couldn't think of any right now, but that was inconsequential. "But look where it got me! You threw me. Like *through the air* threw me! And this time I didn't land in water. I have a seriously sore backside right now."

He looked at me like he was trying to stay serious, but couldn't. His mouth twitched as he stood and offered me a hand up. I narrowed my eyes and took his hand, yelping as a spark of electricity or . . . something, leapt from his hand to my own. My wide-eyed look came back.

"What was that all about?" My voice was small, my bravado abandoned. Logan, I remembered, had just electrocuted a demon . . . with nothing but his outstretched hand. The revelation currently overshadowed the fact he'd called me off my own attack.

Logan's eyes dropped. "Yeah, that was part of the story I never got to because you got so . . ." he struggled to find the right word, ". . . salty before."

"Salty? I do not get salty."

He pointed a finger at me. "You're acting salty right now."

I locked my lips after huffing out a breath. All right, he might have had a point. I did kind of get that way sometimes. But he wasn't supposed to call me out on it.

"Come on," he said. "Let's get somewhere safe, and we can talk further."

I cast a worried glance at my house. It shone in the darkness, yet it was no longer able to chase away the shadows as the last vestiges of light disappeared over the horizon.

"It's getting late. They're probably in for the night." He pointed toward the backyard shed. "We can stay there." I cast him an unsure look. "You already know no demons are making it onto the property. Come on."

I wasn't actually thinking about demons. "You want us to hang out in the shed? That place is a stinky mess." My nose scrunched of its own accord.

"Hunters have been protecting your family for a while now. We've made some upgrades." He chuckled over his shoulder as he led the way. I reluctantly followed.

Logan stopped in front of the structure, which was about the size of a small bedroom. Dad used the shed mostly to store his tools, including the lawn mower, so my expectations of comfort were low. We'd probably be sitting on overturned utility buckets amidst the smells of gasoline and decomposing leaves. This would be a long night.

After taking meticulous care to make sure no one was watching, Logan gingerly opened the door and quickly ushered me inside.

O-kay. I was wrong. He was right. The shed no longer resembled the shed. The walls weren't the rough, unfinished barn boards I remembered. Dad's equipment was absent, and the dimensions of the one-room outbuilding weren't even what they should have been. I recognized the physics of the afterlife at work. This place was easily three times the size of the shed we'd just entered. Four white walls—I hated white walls—enclosed the space.

Logan bumped into my back and forced me inside a step further as he slid the door closed behind us, but I hardly noticed.

At the back of the room were twin beds with—you guessed it—white bedding. I grudgingly admitted they looked fluffy and soft.

The wall between the beds reminded me of a mini version of the training center's gyms. Various weapons had been strapped, hung, and placed there. A small shelf was secured to the wall above each bed. I assumed they were there to hold one's weapon of choice

A small two-person table was set to my left, with two chairs neatly in place. Thankfully they weren't white—both table and chairs were made from a honey-colored wood.

A vase of flowers even sat in the middle of the table pushed against the wall. To our right was a small kitchenette with a narrow fridge, two burners, and a few cobalt-blue cabinets the same shade as Logan's eyes, giving some much-needed color to the washed-out space.

Shiny globes filled with light and suspended in the air illuminated the whole space. They cast a glow just strong enough to lighten the interior without all the white hurting my eyes. I turned my head sideways. There was a thick, lumpy fur rug adorning the floor. Wait a sec, that wasn't a rug—it was snoring.

"Bear?"

My golden retriever's tail wagged once, and his oversized head lifted fractionally before he huffed and lay back down.

"I think he's mad you left him."

I wouldn't be surprised. "What is this place?"

Logan rubbed his neck before answering. "It's an alternate reality pocket. It was created inside this shed as a refuge for hunters so they can sleep or relax between shifts."

"What if my family comes inside here? What will they see?"

"Your shed. This is a pocket where two realities exist at the same time. They're actually very rare. We try to disturb Earth reality as little as possible. But when it's necessary . . ." he shrugged.

"Wow."

"Want something to eat?" he asked.

I nodded, and he led me to the table. "Here, sit. I'll cook for us, then we can talk."

"You cook?"

The smile he shot me was nothing short of cocky. "I have so many hidden talents, if you knew them all your head would spin."

As my face darkened, the tips of my hair turned pink.

"I didn't mean it like that, Audrey." He turned toward the fridge to pull out some food then cleared his throat. "I was just trying to lighten the mood." He continued after a few beats. "Although it's not like I wouldn't say the same about those other talents. I'm sure you'd find I'm more than—"

"Oh my gosh!" I practically shrieked. "Enough! Seriously, enough. I don't want to hear another word out of your mouth right now. What is wrong with you? Do you have some split personality disorder I'm not aware of?"

I was more than half-serious. His behavior since finding me with Morgan went way beyond mere mood swings.

Even with his back to me, his low chuckle reached my ears. The pink in my hair spread. I pinched the bridge of my nose. *This boy is going to be the death of me.* I winced at my internal word choice. But seriously, what was I going to do with him? I mean, what choices did I even have?

The corner of my mind where I'd shoved 'the incident' started to prickle. I batted it back in to its hidden place. I didn't want to sort through the complications of our relationship—or lack thereof—at the moment. Maybe . . . maybe when this mess with my family was sorted out, I'd get the courage to actually have a grown-up discussion with Logan. But for now, I would pretend it didn't happen. That was the only way I could focus on what was really important, which was my family.

Logan grabbed items from the fridge and pulled a pan from the cabinet to place on the stovetop. His back and the expanse of his broad shoulders blocked most of what went on so I gave up trying to see and turned my attention elsewhere.

Bear snored on the floor between the two beds. He was so darn cute. As if hearing my thoughts, he lifted his head and craned to see me before he huffed again and put it back down. Definitely mad at me.

I lifted myself from the chair and crossed the space between us. A belly rub would soften my old friend's heart. His eyes followed me until I sat cross-legged at his side. "Hey you," I whispered.

He shifted away when I leaned forward to pet him.

"Okay, I understand, you're upset I didn't take you with me."

He looked back at me, his eyes watchful. I moved in for the kill. I scratched his chest, softly at first, and then more vigorously. Eventually his back leg kicked in tune to the rubs.

"That's more like it. I don't like it when you're mad at me." His big head flopped onto my lap. "I also don't like the thought of you getting hurt." He lifted his gaze and growled softly at me—a warning sound. "Whoa, when did you start doing that?"

"When he learned to understand you, and started to disagree with you." Logan set the plates down at the now fully made table. Drinks, utensils, and napkins were laid out.

"Is that right?" I turned back to my furry friend. He actually bobbed his head up and down. I laughed. "Well, I suppose it's about time you had a say."

Bear opened his mouth and his tongue lolled out, making it appear as if he smiled in agreement. I rolled my eyes as I stood and faced Logan.

"Looks like you're ready."

Logan smiled and held a chair out for me. As I sat, he eased it forward. An omelet sat artfully on my plate with a side of cut-up fruit, accompanied by what appeared to be a glass of orange juice. It all smelled amazing.

Logan's chair lightly scraped against the floor as he nudged himself forward. The table was so small our knees bumped slightly. I tried rearranging my legs, but all I managed to do was play a quick game of footsies with him. We both pretended not to notice.

"So," I cleared my throat, "it's breakfast for dinner?"

Logan lifted a shoulder. "It's a favorite. And I make a mean omelet."

"You seem pretty confident."

"What's not to be confident about? Taste it."

Accepting his challenge, I cut into the cheese and what looked to be ham-and-spinach-filled dish and brought a forkful to my mouth. He observed me closely. Too closely. I couldn't resist the urge to mess with him a bit.

"You know not everyone knows how to make a good omelet," I said, pulling the fork slightly away from my mouth.

"Audrey, just eat the food."

"I don't know . . . I mean, we've had our differences in the past, so how am I to know you didn't put something in here?"

He looked baffled. "Like what?"

"Oh, I don't know. Maybe something to knock me out so you can just spirit me back to our realm without my permission." I brought the fork closer and sniffed it skeptically. Hiding my real reaction to the scent was a challenge because, yum, there wasn't much better than cheesy goodness. "Maybe I should learn how to smell poison."

"Audrey." Logan's hand wrapped around mine. The simple touch set warnings blaring in my mind. "Just eat the food." He gently led my hand, and thus the fork, to my mouth, his eyes holding mine the whole time.

"Open," he commanded softly. And like a puppet, I did just that. When the fork was in my mouth, he trailed his hand down my arm and to my elbow before nodding toward my mouth. "Close and chew."

Oh boy, was he condescending. But why all of a sudden didn't I care?

The omelet was so good it broke the spell Logan had cast over me. I closed my eyes to savor the bite. The eggs were perfectly fluffy and the tangy bite of cheesy mixed with the salty ham in just the right way. I already couldn't wait for my next taste. "Oh, Logan." I made an appreciative noise in the back of my throat. "You were not wrong. Your omelet-making skills are superior. And you know, coming from me that's pretty high . . . what?"

I used the napkin to wipe at my mouth self-consciously. Logan's hand was still on my side of the table, and it appeared as if he was in some sort of trance. His eyes were locked on my lips in a predatory way. My body temperature rose because I'd seen that look before. I was a moment away from waving a hand in front of his face to break the tension when he suddenly pulled himself together. He snapped back against his seat, going so far as to move his chair back. His eyes dove to his omelet and he started shoveling it down.

"See," he said after clearing his throat a minute later. "I told you it would be good."

"Yeah, ah." We ate in silence, eyes focused on our food. My mind focused on everything but my food.

"It happened the day I was rescued."

"What?" I looked up. Logan's gaze was still locked on the remaining egg he pushed around his plate.

"The shocks, the electricity, whatever it is. It happened for the first time while I was still captive. Morgan had been released because he'd chosen his side. His new skills at manipulating shadows were developing quickly. He'd come to visit me instead of the demons, talking about how amazing it was, how freeing it was to experience his new existence. How much more things made sense to him now. Whatever he could say to make it appear he'd made the right decision and I should give in, too."

My hands lay limply in my lap as I silently encouraged him to continue. Logan's eyes lifted and held my gaze hostage.

"It was so hard," he admitted. "It was so attractive. I was in so much pain, physically and mentally. Every shield had been stripped in the weeks we'd been held captive. And I watched as Morgan grew stronger while I grew weaker. My prayers had gone unanswered, and the thread I was hanging onto frayed a little more each day. I was angry."

"That's understandable. I'd be angry at the people who had been torturing me as well."

"No," Logan tensed. "I wasn't angry at them, I was angry at God. Angry at Him for leaving me there. Angry for letting so much happen to me. Angry He'd let Morgan turn sides. I honestly don't know how I resisted them. Through my anger, I should have caved as easily as Morgan did."

"But you didn't." A statement, not a question.

"No, not fully, but I must have cracked at least a little, because the last day of my captivity I gained a power I shouldn't have. One that still shows itself on Earth."

"So, you can electrocute things. Or something like that. Why couldn't that be from God?"

"Do you see any other hunters walking around with abilities like it?"

"Do you see any other hunters walking around with flaming swords?"

He smiled a little. "Touché."

"So, why couldn't your new ability be something God gave you? Why do you believe it's from Satan?"

"Because that's how it works. Once your heart changes, you get new skills. Other skills, things we don't get in our realm. Morgan started the same way. His skill with shadows started in that dank basement as well. The only difference was I escaped that very day."

"How?"

Logan's hands clenched and unclenched on the table in between us. I don't even think he was aware of the motion. "Morgan untied me. I was so weak and he was so strong he knew I wasn't a threat. I think he was trying to work the 'good cop' angle. Anyway, I was out of my chains and shackles and struggling to even sit upright on the dirty floor. Morgan was spouting some platitudes I wasn't even listening to, and I became so enraged about my situation —and then it just happened."

Logan stopped talking then. The sound of my own heartbeat drummed in my ears as I waited for him to continue. It was several beats more until he did, picking up the story exactly where he'd left off.

"He grabbed my arm because he didn't think I was listening to him, which I wasn't, and the power shot out of me before I even knew what was going on." Logan shoved a hand in his hair and fisted it. "It threw Morgan across the room, but he was still conscious. In fact, he was elated. He knew what it meant as surely as I did.

"When he ran from the room to report it, I saw my first real chance to escape." His hand slid from his hair and landed with a thud on the table. Vacant eyes stared at nothing. "I somehow found the strength to pull myself up the basement steps and out of the house. I had to use my power on two demons before I was ultimately rescued.

His eyes refocused on me. "Once I left the house I showed back up on the radar, and a team was immediately dispatched to retrieve me. I've never told anyone about the energy, though. I do my best not to use it in battle, but sometimes when I get too emotional it leaks out. I think that's why I keep shocking you."

"I make you emotional?"

"Frustration is an emotion."

"Har har." The corners of Logan's lips lifted while I turned the information over in my head.

"Do you feel . . . I don't know, evil, or darkness when you use it?"

"No. I feel powerful."

"That doesn't sound too bad."

"It's where the power's coming from that concerns me. For a long time I expected, or hoped, it would just go away on its own. But that's obviously not going to happen."

"Why haven't you talked to anyone else about this?"

Logan shifted his gaze somewhere over my left shoulder. His breaths were strong and steady, but despite appearances, he waged an internal fight. I'd become too accustomed to his tells to miss it. His eyes locked back on my own, and I braced for his answer.

"Fear."

My eyebrows bunched. "Of what?"

His casual shrug was anything but. After a while I realized he wasn't going to elaborate.

"Why are you telling me this then?"

"Because I want you to know."

"But why? There are lots of people you are closer to."

"Aren't there things you want me to know, Audrey?"

The use of my name was like a defibrillator to my heart. I wasn't sure why. "No," I answered too quickly.

He gave a sad, hollow smile and placed his forearms on the table in front of him. His body shifted slightly toward me. Not enough to make contact, but enough to remind me of how close he was.

"You don't have any secrets you want to share with me?"

There was actually a growing list of things I didn't want him to know. Things I had been lying to myself about, let alone being truthful with him. I had a strong suspicion my list was filled with some of the same secrets he referred to.

I swallowed.

"That's a hard 'No,' Logan," I managed in an even, if slightly breathy, tone.

He sat back in his chair and crossed his arms over his chest with a satisfied smile. "I'll take that as a soft 'Yes,' then."

"I have no idea what you're talking about."

His eyes narrowed shrewdly. "Oh, I believe you have at least an idea. But we'll leave this for another time." He pushed back his chair and stood up. The wood scraping against concrete woke Bear, whose paws scrambled for purchase on the smooth floor before he jumped to attention. "Sorry, buddy," Logan said in Bear's direction. "Done with your dinner?" he asked me.

I gaped at him. He winked and collected my plate without permission.

Is he flirting with me? Again?

"I think we should get some rest for the night. Wouldn't you agree?"

I stared at his back as he cleaned and rinsed off our plates. His hair was getting distractingly long. I would take scissors to it myself if he didn't trim it up soon. It was in danger of reaching man-bun length.

"I guess so?"

"You don't sound so sure."

I gave myself a mental shake to clear the cobwebs. "What I meant to say is, what about my family? Shouldn't one of us stay up and watch the house?"

"Your family is in for the night. This place is here for hunters to rest. So, rest."

After drying and putting the dishes away, he turned back to me and leaned up against the counter. One foot crossed over the other and his arms folded over his chest. Something about that pose made my pulse pound a little harder.

Feeling at a disadvantage, I stood and brought our drinking glasses to the sink. He blocked part of the way. I looked up at him and raised my eyebrows, shaking the glasses gently to indicate I needed him to move. He stood there like a frozen centurion.

I rolled my eyes and leaned around him to set the glasses in the sink. If he wouldn't move, then I wouldn't bother washing them. I was about to pull back when Logan leaned down and inhaled deeply.

I think he just smelled my hair.

It was a moment before I thought to step away, and in that time Logan shifted, placing his hands on the counter on either side of me, but no part of our bodies touched. My synapses flared.

It was my turn to freeze. Logan's head lowered further until his face was practically buried in my dark mane of hair. I prayed it was still brown and not some random rainbow color.

Why aren't I moving? I thought to myself. *I should definitely be moving. I know how to take him down eight different ways from this position.*

His lips grazed my earlobe and created an involuntary shiver. "You're supposed to be stopping me," he whispered, warm breath fanning the sensitive skin beneath my ear . . . but his words were a bucket of ice. The stupid hormone-charged man-child had taken up residence in Logan once again, and of course it was somehow my fault.

I jerked my elbow into his gut and stepped on his left foot with the heel of my own. He faltered a half-step, leaving just enough space for me to turn and use the heel of my hand to strike him in the throat, followed by a knee directly in the stomach.

Logan stumbled back and caught himself on the small table where we'd just shared a meal, doubled over and coughing. I walked by him and chose the small bed on the right. Bear looked back and forth between us before trotting to my side, a seeming smile on his face to mirror my own.

That had felt good.

I climbed into bed facing the wall. "Thanks for the reminder," I threw over my shoulder before settling and pulling up the covers. I didn't expect the wheezing laugh from him in return. It was followed by an indiscernible mumble.

What? Did he just call me adorable?

"I guess I had that coming." His voice strained with the effort it took to talk.

"You think?" I answered. I wiggled in the bed, unable to find a comfortable position.

The springs on the opposite bed groaned. *Too close.* My imagination conjured the heat of his body burning into my back. It was probably just the death stare he was surely giving me.

After a moment, the rustle of bedding told me he was settling in. When movement stopped, I forced myself not to sneak a peek behind me. I had a sudden sick need to know whether he faced the wall or me. My answer came a moment later when his words washed over me, too loud for him to be facing the opposite direction.

"Sweet dreams, Audrey. And just for the record, I think the hues of pink are lovely on you, but I'm not too manly to admit red and black are a little scary."

I groaned in silence.

"Lights off," he said, and the room blackened.

NO MORE FUN AND GAMES

"—*U*p now!"

I jerked awake with a scream in my throat and just enough time to see Logan book it out the shed . . . without me. Bear was hot on his heels.

"What the . . . " I flew out of bed and snatched my sword off the wall, its weight a comfort rather than a hindrance. Thank goodness I'd slept in my body armor. Gritty-eyed but fully awake, I pushed the door open and chased after the two of them.

A sheet of cold water slapped me the moment I exited the shed. The rain hissed and dissolved into steam when it hit the flames running up and down the blade of my sword. I pumped my arms to catch up. The downpour was so torrential I could barely make out Logan in the distance as he skirted my house. My unbound hair plastered to my face and neck as I slogged through wet grass and mud, both seemingly determined to slow my hurried steps.

A deafening roar shook the ground beneath my feet. I took a giant step off course to steady myself and then pushed ahead. I had a wild fear I knew exactly what I'd see when I rounded the corner.

I skidded to a halt when I cleared the house.

It was worse.

The dragon and rider I'd expected, but not the additional demons that paced and shifted in front of the property line. One of them dragged its claws over the slick pavement, sparks shooting off in its wake, as if sharpening them before the attack. We were two hunters against five demons. I didn't like that equation at all. But it wasn't the dark creatures that made the blood pumping through my veins turn to ice. It was the red beast and its rider, towering over everyone.

Morgan's features were obscured by the sheets of rain separating us, but I saw his head working on a slow swivel back and forth, most likely searching for what couldn't be seen . . . us.

Logan stood precariously close to the very barrier that made us invisible. One outstretched hand would be enough to give away his location. With only his back in sight, I recognized the tension in his body. His sword was drawn and ready for use. Similarly, Bear had readied himself for the battle in the only way he could. His body crouched low to the ground, hackles raised and teeth bared. These were vicious looks I'd never seen on my precious companion before.

I stood in the middle of the yard in front of the house, facing the threat. I was momentarily confused by the stalemate until the garage door groaned and slowly lifted. My eyes tracked the movement until my family came into view.

Another roar from the red dragon, and the ground shook once again.

The gasp that left my mother's lips couldn't be heard, but I saw it. I sprinted toward them, my mind's eye seeing clearly the horrifying scene to come but not knowing how to stop it.

Mom laid a hand on her chest and laughed off her discomfort. "Well, that was an angry clap of thunder."

Dad planted a kiss on her forehead before moving to the driver's side of their small SUV. "It can't be too bad, hon. We haven't even seen any lightning. This rain's bark is worse than its bite."

He was so very wrong.

"James!" my father called. "I've grown a few more gray hairs waiting for you. Let's get moving."

My brother jogged out the door connecting the house to the garage. "Don't worry," he quipped, "they'll just make you look more distinguished." With a cocky smile and fake salute he hopped in the back seat.

It was just a car—but with a dragon and a small squadron of demons waiting just outside, it was a potential death machine.

Dad shook his head at Mom over the roof of the car. "Just wait until he reaches my age. Is it bad I'm kind of hoping he has some premature hair loss? Not like the whole head or anything, but maybe some thinning up top to give him some healthy respect for my hair?"

"Dean! You don't mean that."

"Don't get me wrong, I want the boy to be good-looking enough to snag the right girl someday, but a little character building wouldn't hurt."

"And hair loss is the way you want him to build character?"

He shrugged, a giant grin on his face. "Character for him, amusement for me, win-win."

"You guys know I can hear you, right?"

Mom laughed as they both slid into their respective seats. They were going to pull out. God wasn't stopping them. No one was stopping them.

No, this was not happening. This was seriously not happening right now. They were laughing. And soon they might be crashing. I had little doubt as to the enemy's intent. Where were the other hunters? The ones I'd seen yesterday, who had been guarding my family for weeks? Where had they disappeared to?

The engine turned over as the car came to life. I threw a stricken look over my shoulder at Logan, whose body was angled toward me. Determination punched through his blurred features. I'm sure my own face broadcasted the horror churning inside like a belly full of soured milk.

As the silver car began to slowly roll backward, I did the only thing I could think to do to get it to stop. I kicked it. Hard. Hard enough that it came to a sudden stop, and my dad's door opened and his head popped out.

"Yeah, I felt it too. Did either of you leave anything behind the car last night? James, if I just hit your skateboard, you're using your own money to buy a new one and fix the damages."

The car was halfway out the garage, but still somewhat protected from the rain by the raised door. My father came around the car to inspect the damage. I'd kicked it hard enough to leave a small dent in the passenger's-side bumper.

"What in the world?" he said to himself.

"What was it?" Mom yelled over the deluge, her window rolled down and head poking out to see my dad.

He lifted his gaze and shrugged, his eyebrows drawn. "There's a small dent," he leaned over to brush the spot with his fingers, "but there's nothing here I could have hit."

I missed what my mom said next because a piercing shrill rent the air. I swung around. Logan had passed the barrier and attacked a demon.

It was noble. But with four others, an ex-hunter, and a freaking dragon looking to join the fight, he didn't stand a chance.

I sprinted to the other end of the line of demons. Perhaps I could draw some of their attention away? The one I headed toward made creepy chirping noises as if encouraging his companions. It was the smallest of the group and its body the most humanoid. Blackened like the rest, with a birdlike beak filled with rows of serrated shark teeth, it had four appendages protruding from the trunk of its body that somewhat resembled human arms and legs. That is, if fingers and toes were long sharp knives instead of flesh.

It didn't have time to be surprised when I burst past the property line and severed its top half from its bottom. Its newly separated halves hit the ground before dissolving into black smoke and ash.

The first kill was so silent I wounded the next demon before it became aware of my presence. I stabbed my sword deep into its shoulder. Having missed anything of true importance, the demon turned on me with a vengeance. The charred hole in its shoulder did nothing to stop it. I should have tried to sever one of its limbs instead. That might have at least slowed it down. Stupid move.

It advanced on me, slashing at the air with its deadly claws. I was too preoccupied dodging the sharp objects to notice much of what else was going on around me. That is, until I narrowly missed getting run over by my own family's vehicle as is took off down the drive. Rather than smashing into the car, as I expected it to do, the demon jumped out of harm's way as well, stumbling as if knocked over by something unseen.

The momentary reprieve gave me a glimpse of the larger fight. Logan had managed to kill the first demon he'd fought, but now he battled two at a time. And although he was holding his own, he was still outnumbered.

Bear exposed his teeth and growled from the front yard, unseen by the creatures we battled. I was glad he was somewhere safe. He had no place in a fight like this.

The dragon and its rider surveyed the fight from their lofty perch, content to let the demons do their dirty work for the moment.

My big mistake was turning to check on the car as it drove past me.

A punch to my gut sent me flying. My uncovered head snapped back and struck the rain-soaked asphalt. I hadn't had time to grab my helmet before running into the fray. The crushing weight on my chest, barring me from breathing, indicated I'd gone down with the demon that struck me. My vision was blurred grays and blacks. My hands were empty. Where was my sword?

Temporarily blind, I brought my palms up and pushed in vain against the weight on top of me. Remembering the wound I'd inflicted, I punched the area I thought might be injured. My right hand found purchase in something soft and squishy. The demon screamed its high-pitched wail, and putrid-smelling moist air blasted me in the face. Something sharp pierced my side and I cried out.

A growl as loud as a trumpet blast shook the very air around me. The sound was deeper than a demon's usual screech, but what it lacked in pitch it made up for in decibel. I vaguely wondered if my ears bled.

Dang.

Where were noise-dampening angels when you needed them?

The weight above me was jerked off and I took a full breath of rain-soaked air. With the return of oxygen, my vision began to clear. I scanned the asphalt for my discarded sword, the world still hazy from the rain, frantic to help Logan. He must have somehow pulled the huge demon off me.

I forced myself to all fours when a bundle of forms collided not three feet from where I crawled. The ground quaked with the force of their weight. I gaped.

A golden paw, tipped with what had to be at least six-inch claws, batted at hardened demon flesh. Black ichor dripped from several wounds on the demon's body—wounds my sword hadn't inflicted and which looked suspiciously like claw marks. The furred beast lumbered up on two feet and let out another hair-raising growl before opening its giant mouth and chomping down on the flesh under its opponent's jaw, ripping a large chunk of it away, then spitting the clump to the ground.

Ew—and mad respect at the same time.

The demon's mutilated and lifeless face reflected what might have been shock or horror before its body slammed to the ground and disappeared into smoke and ash.

Still on my hands and knees, I looked up at the grisly beast above. The demon's black fluids mixed with its matted pelt. I stared at an overgrown golden bear—at least, that's what I thought it was. Its bulk was easily equal to a full-size SUV. The dark claws protruding from its paws were elongated to an almost cartoonish length.

The creature sank to all fours, drawing my attention to its muzzle. Its jowls pulled back in what might have been a smile. A macabre one, considering it still had some demon flesh stuck between its teeth, but a smile nonetheless.

What the what?

"Audrey!"

The shout jerked my attention to the side in time to see Logan run toward me even as the dragon and Morgan took flight. The rest of the demons were gone.

When he reached me, Logan hauled me to my feet. "They're going after your family," he yelled over the rain.

Despite the hit I'd taken to my noggin, my brain clicked back into high gear. My eyes snapped to the dragon gaining elevation and distance. "How are we going to follow?" I turned in a frantic circle.

Logan handed me my missing sword, grabbed me by the shoulders, and pushed me forward. "Get on. He'll get us there."

The only thing in front of us was the giant, demon-blood-covered bear.

The beast suddenly made me remember my dog. "Bear! Is he okay? Where is he?" My heart dipped and plummeted to my stomach. I looked around wildly. Bear was just a little thing compared to the demons. If one got hold of him while we fought, they'd have broken him in two.

"Audrey, get on!" Logan commanded.

"But Bear—"

"That's bear."

"Yes, I know, some weird mutant bear, but where's *my* Bear?"

Logan grasped my shoulders and shook—hard. He pointed to the giant grizzly. The beast nodded. I stared, not putting together the pieces.

With a frustrated huff, Logan picked me up and threw me over his shoulder fireman-style before taking a leap and landing on the back of the bear. "Find them," was all he said, and the beast started running. Logan set me astride the grizzly in front of him while we barreled down the street. He took my hand and fisted it in the fur of the creature below us.

I recognized this texture—softer than it should have been.

Not *a* bear's fur, but *my* Bear's fur.

"You get it?" he yelled in my ear.

I nodded, then shook my head. I had always assumed Bear was a pacifist.

"I'll explain it later. Right now, we have to take care of your family."

How could I have forgotten about them, even if just for a moment? The rain pounded our bodies and the houses flew by, blurred by our speed rather than the rain.

I twisted my body and neck to look at Logan. Riding atop a giant galloping bear was not conducive to conversation, but I did my best. "Where are they?"

"We will find them," was all he said. His gaze held a promise.

I nodded back and then turned to face forward. The rain and speed obscured the world around us.

We were out of the neighborhood and Bear ran down the street, dodging cars that couldn't see us. It was a surprisingly smooth, if surreal, ride.

A sharp pain in my side reminded me I hadn't escaped our battle unscathed. I put a hand to the wound and it came up bloody before being quickly washed clean by the rain.

I couldn't be worried about my injury right now. Instead, I focused on searching for my parent's silver car, but the rain and speed made it hard.

The creature that was once my dog lifted his head slightly and cocked it to the left. That was our only warning before he took a sharp turn.

So, sharp, in fact, his claws scrambled for purchase on the wet pavement. We slid several feet before changing direction. Logan's chest slammed into my back as he leaned forward to wrap an arm around me and reached with the other to ground a hand in Bear's fur.

Good thing, or I might have flown off of Bear's back.

Logan remained where he was, keeping me safe within the cage of his arms. I didn't have the brainpower to overthink that one.

The smaller road we'd turned onto was free of traffic and surrounded by woods. Within a short period of time the pavement gave way to packed dirt. Or at least, that's what it would have been if torrents of water hadn't been eroding the ground, making it more river than road.

"No," I whispered.

"What is it?"

"I know where we are. There's a bridge not too far up ahead. With all this rain the river below must be raging by now. It's a shortcut Dad likes to take to town."

The dragon's thunderous roar was akin to hearing my worst nightmare edge closer. I could picture it in my mind: the narrowing of the road past the bend, the old one-lane bridge, and my family in their car careening off the side into the angry waters below.

"No!"

My horror-filled scream spurred Bear on, and we rounded the bend just in time to see my fears come true.

Morgan and the dragon stood apart from each other at the far end of the bridge. The dragon spit something dark into the middle of the road. With all the rain, it was impossible to identify the substance. The car—really just a metal casing protecting my loved ones—moved at a reasonable speed considering the storm, but once they hit the spot in the middle of the bridge where the dragon had spat, they started to spin out.

And we were too far away. We wouldn't make it to them in time.

Bear bellowed and before I even knew what happened, I flew through the air.

Logan took the brunt of the impact, but it still hurt. We'd landed in some wet and muddy foliage off to the side of the road right before the bridge and rolled for several feet before stopping.

I scrambled to my feet in time to see Bear ram into the car before it had a chance to smash the guardrail. His big body acted as a buffer. The car did a few more spins before coming to an anticlimactic stop.

The side where Bear had rammed it was dented, as was the guardrail. My big monster of a bear-dog lay between the two on the rain-soaked concrete, not moving.

My feet pounded the ground as I sprinted in the direction of the wreck. I reached Bear first. His breaths were labored, but he was still breathing. A gash in his side—almost a foot long—oozed blood where he'd hit the guardrail. His enormous head lifted for a moment, and I looked into his pain-filled but clear eyes.

And then a ginormous tongue came out and licked the whole right side of my face.

Oh, nasty.

The golden beast in front of me made noises as if he were snickering at me. Okay, he was hurt, but if he still retained his personality, it couldn't be as bad as I feared. I quickly hugged his scary muzzle and turned to check on my family.

The car sat cockeyed in the middle of the bridge, right beyond a patch of black goo. I dashed past the substance, giving it only a cursory glance on my way to the car. The windshield wipers were still going furiously. They allowed me an unfettered view of the family members inside.

For the first time that day I breathed a sigh of relief. Dad was on his phone, most likely with the police, while Mom was turned in her seat, talking to my brother. James had been sitting on the opposite side of the damaged part of the car. As I watched, he unbuckled his seat belt and slid to the center seat, setting a hand on top of my mom's in a gesture of comfort. I couldn't hear them, but they all appeared unharmed. At least physically. The warm trickle of blood down my side and the throbbing of my head reminded me I wasn't so fortunate.

Muffled shouting drew my attention away from the car and up the road. Adrenaline shot through my body.

I skirted the car to stand at the back bumper and reached behind me to pull my sword free. The rain was no match for the fire that blazed from it.

Thirty feet in front of me, Logan and Morgan squared off with their weapons drawn. If possible, the rain came down even harder, creating a veil of water between them and myself.

Their body language told me everything I couldn't hear above the rain and the river. It was only a matter of time before they exploded into action.

A chill skated down my spine when I realized something was missing. A very large something. A red and scaly something.

Ungluing my eyes from Logan and Morgan, I searched the sky for the dragon. Rainwater blinded me. It was like trying to see while someone steadily dumped a glass of water in my face.

I snuck a glance back at the guys to see Logan shake his head once and slash his arm through the air in a gesture that said he was done with their conversation. But instead of charging on Morgan, he turned his back and took swift and determined steps toward me, a hard look on his face.

Sirens wailed faintly in the distance. Could the battle possibly be over? Could we have won this round?

No sooner were the thoughts formed in my head, then I was running screaming toward Logan as Morgan's mace arced through the air from behind him, sure to land a blow. Logan spun around and pulled his blade, but I didn't see the outcome, for the moment Logan turned I was yanked into the sky.

This wasn't over. It was far from over.

A DEAL WITH THE DEVIL

$\mathcal{B}$ony fingers tipped with razor-sharp claws wrapped around my chest like a vise, cutting off my ability to scream. My hair whipped around my face, obstructing my view of the ground as my body shot straight up into the air. I gulped for breath. Fear, speed, and immobility made it hard to get in enough to keep from passing out. The air around me grew colder as we ascended. I tried to look up, but the angle made that impossible. My view was filled with hair and sky.

We banked sharply to the left, and the flesh and bones constraining me tightened further. Lights blinked in my vision. I was going to lose consciousness. The wind howled in my ears, and as suddenly as I had been plucked from the Earth's surface, I was hurling straight back toward it.

This time an overabundance of oxygen stole my scream as I flailed in a free fall. The terror was so overpowering I grappled with the air as if I could find purchase to stop my descent. My body spun on a topsy-turvy axis. The ground and sky blurred to smudges of color that flashed by like a kaleidoscope.

The claws surrounded my torso once again a moment before a violent jerk that cracked a few ribs and halted my plummet. My head whipped forward, followed by a painful pop at the base of my skull. My vision blurred in and out of focus as we neared the ground at a leisurely pace.

Ten feet up, the dragon dropped me unceremoniously to the ground. I crumpled and rolled after the initial impact, stabbed with pain. The earth shook a moment later.

When my brain caught up enough to take stock, it was the contrast of pain and coolness that first seeped through. I lay like a rag doll, face down on spongy grass. The rain had stopped, but my clothes and hair and skin were soaked bone-deep. With every breath, I sucked in mud along with air. I turned to the side and hacked up what I'd unwillingly ingested. Sharp pains came from multiple spots around my rib cage as well as the back of my neck.

I felt like a squeezed tube of toothpaste.

My legs were tangled up in each other, twisted in a weird pretzel position. Both arms were flipped behind me like limp, featherless wings. I whimpered as I forced myself to my back. The sky above spun. My stomach rolled and I turned on my side just in time to throw up on the ground instead of myself.

"I must sssay, I did expect a little more fortitude."

With a cry I sat up as much as I was able and crab-walked away from the voice. When I looked up I wished I hadn't, for the red beast itself stood over me, glaring down with unveiled disgust. At least what I perceived it to be, having never had the opportunity to study a dragon's facial expressions before.

"You can talk?"

"Obvioussssly."

Its forked tongue caused its words to hiss in a cartoonish manner. It'd be funny if I wasn't so terrified.

"Wh-what am I doing here?"

"I thought it wassss time we had another little chat, you and I."

I couldn't be sure, but I thought the beast was smirking at me.

"Another?"

"Ah yesss. Let me ssslip into sssomething more comfortable."

Shadows, like living beings, crawled out of the ground and slithered their way up the red scales. When the monster was completely shrouded in darkness, the popping and crunching of bones and muscles rearranging themselves assaulted my ears.

The dragon bent its neck and covered its body with its massive wings as it began to shrink. The wings hid most of the transformation from my eyes until they, too, became shadows, darkening the form they concealed within.

And then the shadow wings spread and folded, revealing a being I'd hoped never to lay eyes on again.

A fathomless abyss stared back at me from where its eyes should have been.

"Ah, I see you finally recognize me."

The fear that should have rushed my system when I'd first met Satan hit with a vengeance this time around. At our first introduction, I'd confused him with an angel of light, rather than seeing the abomination he truly was. He was back to looking all too angelic now, for through the fear, I was still struck by his unmistakable beauty, even despite his blackened pits for eyes.

He reminded me of the marble busts in museums—perfectly formed, symmetrical and polished, but utterly cold and lacking humanity.

He took a step back and leaned casually against the trunk of a tree. He wasn't absently playing with a knife this time. Instead, I was the plaything he toyed with.

I took stock of my surroundings. He'd flown me to a clearing, perhaps in the same forest, but since I didn't recognize it, I had no way of telling. I was half-sitting, half-lying in muddy grass and dead leaves. So early in the season the trees around us were still bare of leaves, gnarled and dead rather than teaming with vibrant life. A strange part of my brain accepted this as a perfect spot to have a chat with the devil.

"Why am I here?"

Without a change in facial expression, he cocked his head in an almost birdlike manner.

Creepy.

"I don't intend to hurt you, if that is what you are thinking."

"You don't intend to hurt me? You almost squeezed my guts out and then dropped me from the sky!"

This time he did smirk. "Well, yes, that was just for a little fun. So few things amuse me these days."

"You dropped me simply because it *amused* you?"

Any levity immediately dissolved. I half-expected him to hiss again.

"Yes, my little huntress. I care not what you've heard of me, but know that I am the ruler of the air and sky. I am what rules this realm, and you are but a trespasser in it. Should it amuse me to drop you from the sky again, don't doubt I will do it."

My heartbeat picked up. I didn't doubt him.

"But," his posture changed to one of bored indifference as he leaned back against the trunk of a nearby tree, "my current plans are not to cause you harm, but rather to offer you a deal."

"A deal?"

"A deal, a bargain, an exchange . . . whatever you feel most comfortable calling it. You see, you have something I'm curious about, and I hold the future of something you care deeply about. For me it's simply an opportunity to scratch an itch, so to speak, but for you it's a matter of life and death. Or more correctly, lives and deaths."

My family. He wanted to barter with their lives. But for what I couldn't fathom. I shoved my growing hysterics down into a hidden corner of myself and pushed myself up.

Whatever evil manipulation was about to spew from his mouth, I wanted to be standing to hear it. Considering the circumstances, it was as dignified a stance as I could take.

He may have me in the middle of who knows where and at the mercy of his might, but I refused to remain cowering on the ground in front of him.

As I straightened up, it suddenly became clear what I'd forgotten until now. This evil being might call himself the ruler of this world, but he wasn't the ruler of all.

There was a limit to his power—a leash on his reign.

And he would someday be held accountable for his deeds.

"What do you want?" I was over the power play. Time to get to the point.

"You should be less concerned with what I want and more concerned with what I have that you want." He flicked his wrist and a small knife appeared in his hand, similar to the one he'd messed around with during our first encounter.

Was his weapon supposed to intimidate me? I had a sword that caught fire when I touched it. I wasn't impressed.

"You don't have anything I want."

"Are you so sure about that?"

"Yes." And I was. This being had nothing I *truly* wanted. Whatever he might offer would have strings attached so long they were sure to tie me in knots. The power he claimed was nothing but smoke and mirrors in comparison to the Creator's will.

"I would have thought your family would be of some concern to you."

Even though I'd known they would make an appearance in this conversation, my stomach still dropped. I schooled my features. Deep inside existed a wellspring of power beyond my understanding. I was experiencing something Hugo had often talked about: a peace that surpassed understanding. Or at least a little of *something* beyond understanding, for on my own strength I would have broken apart at the first hint of a threat to my loved ones.

He still played around with his knife, but his attention was still on me. My lips remained sealed. It wouldn't do any good to deny or confirm his claim. I'd read enough of this drawn-out stuff in books or watched it in movies to know the drill. I'd refuse whatever it was he wanted. He'd threaten my family. I was injured, exhausted, and angry.

"Is that not the case?" he went on. "It appears you don't understand—"

"No, I understand plenty. Like how you are about to seriously exaggerate your power right now. I witnessed that demon bounce off my family's car when it rolled out of the driveway. I'm thinking this whole ordeal was an elaborate bit of theatrics to scare me into agreeing with whatever you want to save my family. But that's the thing," my eyes narrowed, "I don't *need* to go to you to save my family. You're not really in control of their lives."

"Don't be so naïve." The narrowing of his empty eye sockets were the only real indication anything I'd said bothered him.

"Oh, I think that's exactly what you want me to be," I spat back.

"I actually prefer stupid to naïve. Looks like with you I've got both. But let's look at the facts. You've seen what I've already done to them. That's only a fraction of what can be done."

"I've seen what you've been *allowed* to do to them. There's a difference. There may be plenty more you could do, but I'm starting to see there's a limit. They're protected. Perhaps not as much as I would like them to be, but they are still protected. You can't really harm them. You can't even enter their property."

He laughed. And it made me uneasy.

"As if that paltry security line really means anything to *me*. But considering the lengths you've gone to in order to protect them, I'll admit I'm a bit surprised at how cavalier you're being with their lives." He made a *tsk* sound with his tongue. "Disobeying a direct order to come to Earth? That would normally be something I'd admire, but in your case . . . well, let's just say I find your belief you could do anything to stop my forces humorous at best."

His insult rolled right off me. I didn't expect him to be threatened by me. What didn't roll off easily was he knew about my disobeying an order. I didn't care *that* he knew, but the question of *how* he knew alarmed me.

Tendrils of doubt started to sneak their way inside my mind. Some of the peace holding me together leaked from my heart like water through cupped hands.

"Ah, now you may be beginning to see you've underestimated my reach. That it may stretch a little," he used his index finger to point up, "higher than you thought. Considering that, we both know the bravado you're holding onto is paper-thin. Tell me, little huntress, where are the angels to protect your family? Where is the legion of hunters? Hmmm? I've not seen them. Without them your family is, oh, what is the phrase you humans like to use? Oh yes, sitting ducks. Your knowledge of how things work here, in *my* realm, is riddled with holes. Perhaps I need to educate you further?"

His countenance didn't change, but the implied threat moved like an ice cube slowly being dragged down my spine. I tried not to show it, but his words unnerved me.

He noticed.

"Yes, I think that's it after all. This conversation is premature. We've not had enough fun together, you and I, to strike our accord." His fathomless gaze fastened on my face. The smile tugging at his lips struck more fear into me than any of his words so far. "I'm so looking forward to your education."

I took an involuntary step back. Thoughts of what Logan had endured at this maniac's command forced their way to the surface. I crammed the fear down to the same place I'd put my earlier hysterics and slammed the lid on tight. "I already know what you've done to other hunters. It won't work on me. I won't betray my God."

He waved a hand in the air. "Oh, I have no interest in freeing you from your deity's shackles. In fact, I'd much prefer you keep them on while bending to my will. It will make victory that much more sweet for me."

What did he mean? I still didn't even know what he wanted. Perhaps I'd played this wrong? The convictions I'd stood on began to shake.

"This is between you and me," I said.

"Indeed, it is. And there are so many ways to mess with that minuscule brain of yours."

"What do you want?"

He looked at me as if considering again. "I'm no longer interested in bargaining today. I feel a little demonstration is in order. You doubt my power. I plan to exert it."

I braced myself. He chuckled and cocked his head to one side, a Cheshire smile in place. "Oh, but insignificant one, I don't think I'll start with you. The game I've already set in motion hasn't come to fruition yet."

Somewhere along the way his insane prattle had wormed its way into that place inside where I'd sealed away my fears and sprung the lock. The peace which had held me resolute only moments before shattered, and the remnants blew away with the wind. And with it, so did my confidence.

"No. You have something you want from me? Then deal with me. Leave my family alone!"

"Ah, there's the concern you've been hiding. I have no intention of leaving anyone you may care about alone."

"But that's not fair. You're not playing by any rules."

"Rules?" His face scrunched in as much of a reaction as I'd seen so far. As if I'd said something extremely distasteful to him. "Haven't you figured it out by now? I don't follow anyone's rules. I make my own."

14

THE RETURN

I widened my stance and braced myself for an attack. My legs shook with fatigue as my hand reached over my shoulder for my sword. The flames lighting the blade when it was pulled free from its sheath were such a bright blue they were tinted silver. The fallen angel's lips curled into a snarl.

"As if you are, or will ever be, a true match for me."

With that sentiment, shadow wings spread out in a fan behind him. His body curved forward and then shot into the air with a single powerful downward stroke.

The displaced air hit hard enough to push me a few steps back, and my shaky legs did the rest of the work, landing me on my butt as I watched his inky form disappear from view. Like residue in the wake of a jet plane, a strange, shadowed line followed him into the sky before it too faded from sight.

I wasn't sure how much time had passed, but I was still staring up when my name was shouted. Only then did I notice the shivers racking my body. They hit like waves, ramping up until my teeth chattered and then subsiding after a few moments to quivers before gaining strength again.

"Audrey?"

My head turned in the direction I thought the voice came from.

Logan.

The world outside my interaction with Satan slammed into me with the force of a train. Logan, my family, the failed bargain.

What had I done?

Or what hadn't I done?

For the moment I was lost in the confusion of shifting convictions. My mind warred with itself. The knowledge that the Creator was in control of all no longer encased my heart in a peaceful bubble.

Instead, it battled with my desire to take control of the situation myself. My mind screamed at me that I'd just made things worse, even as it tried to reassure me this wasn't my war to win.

My soul felt fractured.

Full-blown shakes held my body captive, strong enough to keep me from shouting a response. I waited helplessly to either be found or passed by.

For a moment, I wasn't sure I wanted to be found. What if I'd doomed my family? Satan certainly wanted to make me believe that was the case. I had only one thing to hold onto now—God was big enough to take care of a situation I obviously was not capable of doing anything about.

Except perhaps making it worse.

I wanted to put my face in my hands, but the violent storm racking my body made even that simple gesture impossible. Why had I disobeyed and come down to Earth? I had played right into Satan's hands, and now my loved ones would suffer even more because of it.

What. Had. I. Done?

Brittle tree branches snapped and crunched to my right, and within moments, Bear crashed through the remaining trees and entered my clearing, still in his hybrid bear-beast form.

Logan leapt from his back and closed the remaining distance separating us before Bear's giant form even stopped running.

Every muscle in my body—including those in my fingers and toes—flexed and tightened painfully as Logan's bare hands gently cradled my face. Not even the steadiness of his touch could stop my head from bobbing and weaving.

"You're not okay." It wasn't even a question.

His eyes swept my face before meticulously, yet gently, checking my body for injuries. He started from the top down, forcing my limbs to bend as he checked for breaks. Despite my locked muscles and forceful tremors, he managed to shimmy me out of the top half of my body armor. The tight athletic tank I wore underneath allowed him to inspect my bruised flesh.

His fingers probed my side and I cried out. He stilled.

"I'm going to lift this up to take a look." His eyes held mine for a moment in case I protested.

Latent tears swam in my eyes. From the mental or physical trauma, I wasn't sure. Probably both.

His eyes dropped to my waist as he gingerly lifted the stretchy black material up my rib cage. He didn't have to move it far to see the start of the damage. Dark bruising around my ribs started almost as far down as my waist. He sucked in an almost indiscernible breath of air. He continued his examination without checking my facial responses.

"I know this hurts. The ribs are at least bruised, most likely cracked as well, but I need to check to see if any are worse off than that."

Even Logan's light touches were painful enough to make me grind my teeth. I wouldn't be surprised if all my ribs were cracked. But sometime during his careful ministrations I'd stopped shaking. If he noticed, he didn't comment.

"The right side is worse than the left," he said almost to himself. "I think you have some broken on this side, but they are clean breaks. None are puncturing the skin or caved into your abdomen. You do have a sizable gash here, but the blood flow has already stopped."

He looked up into my eyes, his blue ones stormy.

"Is there anywhere else you might be hurt?"

"No." My voice came out hoarse, even though it didn't have any reason to be.

"What happened?"

"The dragon . . ." I croaked.

His whole body tightened. "Yeah, I watched it fly away with you after I knocked Morgan out."

The last moment I'd seen him before being snatched into the air came rushing back at him.

"Are you hurt?" My eyes now frantically searched his body. He looked more disheveled than usual, but fine. Even during battles Logan had a way of looking put together. Artfully unkempt was usually as messy as he got.

I was sure I looked like a horror-movie victim. Only half my hair was still pulled back, and the rest hung in stringy jet-black strands to the left and right of my vision. I caught a glimpse of a white streak to one side—that was a new color—but I couldn't spare it more than a fleeting thought. It must have seemed ridiculous, asking Logan if he was hurt when I was in such bad shape.

"No. I'm fine. I'm more concerned with you right now."

I let out a humorless laugh. I guessed it was good I could laugh at all, with or without the humor.

"Yeah, I guess I can understand why. Finding someone shell-shocked in the middle of the forest, shaking and unable to string even a few syllables together, would be concerning. I'm okay, Logan, really."

He didn't comment, but the look in his eyes said how worried he still was. The more I came back to myself, the more I remembered I had my own reasons for concern.

"Oh my gosh, how's my family?" I swatted Logan away as I tried to stand. He ignored my attempts and held me in place. "Logan, stop. We need to get back. They're in trouble."

"No, Audrey, stop, you're not ready to be moved yet. The police had shown up when I took off, and the rain stopped. Your family is fine."

Tears filled my eyes. "No, you don't understand. They're really not okay.

Like really, *really* not okay. Or not going to be okay. You don't know what I did." I dropped my head into my hands.

"Audrey, talk to me. What's happened? I can't help if I don't know what's going on."

"The dragon . . . it wasn't just a dragon at all." I lifted my face a tiny bit, only enough to capture Logan's gaze. "It was Satan."

Logan froze. "What?" Static electricity brushed across my skin, a sign I now knew meant Logan was becoming overwhelmed by emotions.

"He wanted something from me," I continued. "Wanted to make a deal, or a trade or something. But I threw it back in his face. Mocked him even."

"What did he want?" There was a hollowness in Logan's expression that frightened me.

"That's the thing. I don't even know. I refused before he even said what he was after. The only thing I do know is he was trying to use my family as leverage. My family!"

I lifted a shaky hand to cover my mouth. Where was my wellspring of peace? I needed it, like pronto. I couldn't stop the words from vomiting out my mouth. "He threatened them in exchange for my cooperation, and when I threw it back in his face, he seemed . . ."

How exactly had he seemed? I spit out words faster than I was making sense of them.

"Almost excited. Like I was making this a bigger game for him. Then he went on about how he was going to prove to me how powerful he was, and I just know he's planning to do something to my family to make his point. At first I wasn't scared for them . . . but now I am."

"Audrey, Audrey, wait. Slow down. I don't understand everything that's going on right now. But we'll figure it out. And whatever you did, it was right. Refusing Satan is always the right choice."

"Oh my gosh, no, Logan. I think I made everything worse. I think all of this is really about me, somehow. I should never have been so careless with their lives."

A sob escaped, and the floodgates of tears finally opened. I rocked myself back and forth, ignoring the pain from my sides. I was one puddle of drool away from needing a straightjacket.

After who knows how long I realized I wasn't rocking myself anymore. I'd somehow found my way into Logan's arms and he gently stroked my back and whispered words to me so softly I couldn't make them out.

My sobs gave way to silent tears as I accepted his comfort. I admitted to myself I didn't want to move from his embrace. I closed my eyes and snuggled in closer. Logan's breath hitched a moment before he laid a tender hand on my cheek and tilted my head upward.

"Audrey," he whispered as he peered into my eyes. His thumb stroked my cheek. My eyes had cleared enough and I could make out his face clearly. His eyes looked pained, as if my agony were his own.

I didn't reply, just returned the pain-filled gaze he reflected back to me. His breath fanned my face and dried the tracks tears had created.

It was then, looking into his beautiful face, that I let the wall down and admitted what had been true the whole time.

He was it for me.

This man who held me as if I was his most precious possession. My feelings for Logan ran deep and were strong.

It didn't surprise me.

Rather, I breathed a sigh of relief at the internal acknowledgment. Regardless of how he might feel toward me, my emotions were my own and no longer denied.

The energy it took to bottle everything up was more than I'd realized, and stripped bare as I was, I simply didn't have the reserves to do it anymore.

Perhaps it shone through on my face, or perhaps something simply changed in Logan as well, but his pupils dilated slightly and he sucked in a sharp breath of air. The thumb caressing my cheek stopped its movements, and I held my breath as if the world around us were doing the same.

His eyes left my own and traveled my face before stopping at my lips, and as his face traveled slowly closer to my own, my eyes closed.

"This time I definitely know I'm interrupting something." Alrik's booming voice held no trace of apology, rather its usual, humor-filled cadence.

My eyes snapped open, and I jerked my head toward our intruder.

"You guys look . . . cozy."

I glanced back at Logan for help, only to notice his eyes hadn't left my face.

"Why are you here, Alrik?" Logan asked.

"Funny you should ask." Alrik was leaning up against a tree, similar enough to Satan's stance that a latent shiver racked my body. "I'm here to relieve your post so you can go back for a recharge. You've overextended your stay here . . . by a lot. But you already know that."

"Not going to happen."

Alrik's laughter boomed. "Yeah, I can see that. The thing is, friend, whatever is going on here right now," he used his hand to gesture between the two of us, still embracing, "could very well be because of your overextended Earth stay. You really want to do something you might regret later? Truth is, they want you both back, but I think I'll have a better chance talking sense into you, than Miss Stubborn Pants over there."

His statement hung in the air between us growing stale before he continued. "You know I'll take good care of her. Aud's like the little annoying sister I never wanted . . . I mean never had."

I narrowed my eyes at his last comment. But what if he was right? What if Logan was about to kiss me simply because his emotions were raw and twisted from being on Earth too long? *My* feelings went deeper, but I couldn't speak for him.

I moved my hands to Logan's chest to push away from him. His embrace only tightened. I looked up at him and spoke softly. "Logan, maybe he's right. You shouldn't be down here anymore."

Hurt flashed in Logan's eyes before resolve replaced it. He gave a curt shake of his head. "No."

"No?"

"I'm not leaving you here."

"You know there's an obvious solution to this little dilemma, boys and girls." I waited for Alrik to enlighten us. "Aud, you just need to return like you should have done in the first place, and Logan, like a lovesick puppy, will follow you right on home."

Logan actually growled at Alrik, who shoved off the trunk and put his hands up in front of him in a don't-shoot-the-messenger way. "Look, Logan, you know you're not thinking a hundred percent clearly right now. How many days has it been? We all know you want to protect her. That's not what's up for debate here. But how do you even know what you're feeling right now is real and not just some messed-up hormone lust boost you're getting from Earth's exposure?"

I gasped and shoved hard at Logan. I tumbled from his arms, freed by his surprise, and scurried backward until halted by a tree, lightly banging my head in the process. My ribs also protested the movement. Logan looked helplessly on.

"Audrey, I—"

"No," I held a shaky hand up to stop his progress. Alrik hadn't said anything I didn't already fear. "You don't know for sure what he said isn't true. Back when we were at the church, you said yourself you were struggling because of Earth's influence. And then again at the shed—"

"Audrey," Logan practically pleaded with me, "that doesn't change anything. It doesn't matter if it's true. It doesn't change—"

I didn't want to hear it. If he was just a victim of hormones right now, I wasn't going to let him into the deepest parts of my heart. "Oh, you betcha it matters, mister."

"Betcha? Mister?" Suppressed mirth shone in Logan's eyes and the barely visible upturn of his lips.

Oh yeah, I know. I'm just adorable when I'm angry.

I didn't bother to stop my eye roll. "Yes, that's what I said." I crossed my arms, earning me another angry body pain, and sent him a look, daring him to make fun of me.

Oh, shoot. I had an itch on my nose. I gave it a little twitch, but the itch remained. The corners of Logan's mouth lifted minutely before flattening again.

"Okay, all I'm trying to say is I'm not leaving you here. I've been crystal clear about that since the beginning when I saved you from Morgan."

I grunted. 'Saved' was a liberal term. Morgan hadn't actually been attacking me at the time.

"All right, you two." I'd forgotten about Alrik. "Here's the deal. They want you both back, so I'm going to lay your choices out real clearly. Door number one, Logan leaves, Audrey stays, and I take Logan's place. Door number two, Logan stays, Audrey stays, and Logan continues to pant after Audrey like she's a dog in heat."

My jaw dropped. He did not just say that.

"Alrik." Logan's deep timber showed his displeasure.

Alrik simply shrugged and continued, "Or door number three, the best option for everyone, you both return to heaven, and a whole group of hunters will be dispatched to protect Audrey's family." He looked straight at me. "Because the only way your family is going to get the backup they need is if you get yourself tucked away back in our realm. You don't leave, they won't send anyone else. So, which door are you walking through?"

"Are you kidding me? They won't send protection unless I leave? That's blackmail."

"That's just the facts, sweetheart." He pointed a finger at me, then Logan. "You were never supposed to be down here. He was never supposed to be down here for this long. If you think you can protect your family better than a seasoned bunch of hunters, then be my guest and continue to stay down here and cry on whoever's shoulder you'd like. But even ignoring the fact you look pretty banged up right now, the truth is we both know they'll be in more capable hands if you two leave."

"That's not very nice." I scratched the itch I had been trying to ignore and glared at Alrik, as if this was all somehow his fault.

He glared back. "That look there you're giving me? You need to find a mirror and give it back to yourself. If you choose to stay here, you're not only putting yourself in danger, but also your family and this guy here, who for some reason keeps putting up with the crap you shovel his way. And I get the honor of being your new babysitter."

I gasped and jerked back. Alrik had never been this harsh with me. Sure, he made fun of me all the time and never let a mistake go unnoticed, but it was always laced with humor and camaraderie. His attitude now was glacial.

"That's enough." Logan's words rang. "She gets the point."

The point being I'd been selfish to come down here, and it would be selfish to stay, and everyone knew it. Yeah, I got it. Shame smothered me. I couldn't meet either of their gazes.

"Fine," I finally said. "Logan, Bear, let's go. Alrik, where's our ride?"

"Perfect," Alrik's once-again jovial voice boomed. The quick change in his attitude was alarming. "I knew you'd pick the right door. Your winged chariot awaits."

I still didn't look him in the eye. Not only had his words cut me deeply, but their harsh delivery had eroded some of my trust in him. I surveyed the area outside our clearing. "Where are the other hunters?" I asked.

"They'll be sent down directly to your family's house as soon as you're sent back up."

"Are you coming back up with us?"

"Nope, I'm staying here to keep an eye on things in the meantime."

"Good." I meant it for more than just one reason. I was as glad he wouldn't be around me as I was that he was staying on Earth to watch my family.

I spotted the angel's glow in the trees, growing shadows as he silently waited for us. I headed his way. Bear, having magically returned to his normal dog size without my notice, trotting happily at my side. Whatever injuries he had sustained from the battle appeared to have already healed. Neat trick. The pain in my ribs reminded me I didn't heal the same way.

Logan stopped to talk to Alrik. I couldn't make out their conversation— wouldn't have been interested in it even if I could—but there was heat in Logan's voice. How could I have gone from feeling so secure in Logan's arms to once again teetering on the fence of uncertainty?

I couldn't and wouldn't hide my feelings from myself anymore, but that didn't mean I had to broadcast them as clearly as I had just done in his arms.

I imagined my family members' shadows crossing over the windows of my old house while I waited for Logan. The strings of my heart pulled once again. I knew, once back, I'd feel just as impotent as I had before I'd snuck myself down here.

I took a deep breath. A whisper in my head and heart told me to trust that my family would be cared for.

Closing my eyes, I willed myself to believe. In some ways, having my memories back was more of a challenge to my faith than not having them at all. I cared about so much more, and I had to trust it all to the Creator's care. I'd already proven my faith was small by coming down here. It would take a miracle to boost it to the level I should be at.

A gentle hand touched my lower back, giving me a start.

"Are you ready?" Logan tried to capture my gaze, but I refused.

"Yeah, let's go home."

15

HEARTBREAK

"*W*e're at the healing center? What are we doing here?"

I scowled at the building in front of us. The healing center was as eye-catching as any of the other white marble buildings in the heavenly realm. The intricate mason work would rival even the most beautiful cathedrals on Earth, but I wasn't a fan.

Even though it didn't resemble the boxy hospitals on Earth, it was essentially our version of one, and who actually enjoyed staying in a hospital? At least this time, Logan didn't have to carry me through the doors. I walked forward on my own two feet.

"You're joking, right?" Logan's stare was incredulous. "It looks like you let someone use your torso as a piñata."

"Well, yeah, there's that I suppose." I pressed the heels of my hands into my eyes and rubbed before letting them fall back to my sides.

Logan simply took my hand and led me into the building, Bear trotting along happily beside us. Even though I still had my gloves on, my heart fluttered at the gesture. I was used to Logan doing stuff like that on Earth, but in our realm he steered clear of any physical contact—all except the kind involving training. He was all about being up in my business during sparring, but he still never risked a touch that could possibly betray emotion.

We entered through a giant revolving door, which dumped us into the main lobby of the center. Oddly enough, I'd never been in the lobby before. The only other time I'd been to the healing center, we'd skipped the formality of checking in and gone straight to the surgical wing. I didn't remember much of the operating room before I'd passed out, and when I woke up, I was already in a private recovery room.

I took in my surroundings this time. The three-story lobby of the healing center was quite picturesque.

A circular information desk was situated in front of us, made of pink- and blue-hued quartz. Prisms of light reflected within the material, changing colors as we moved closer to it. The top of the desk was metallic, allowing the workers to use it without being distracted by bright lights. A story above the information desk hung a giant crystal chandelier. Not the traditional type, but rather a crystal chandelier in a very literal sense. Suspended in the air was a large chunk of natural rock emitting light. It looked to be strung up by only a thin silver chain.

Varied shades of tan-colored stone and crystal coffee tables were scattered throughout the spacious room, circled by sleek sofa chairs. Behind the quartz desk a set of curved stairs led to the second and third stories of the building. In contrast with the stone materials in the lobby, the stairs were made out of wood: sliced trees, natural and unfinished except for the lacquered tops you stepped on.

The coffee bar in the back of the lobby looked to be made completely of ice. I was completely transfixed by the hot liquid flowing from an ice luge perched on top of the translucent counter. Logan squeezed my hand to get my attention. We'd reached the front desk.

Despite our disheveled appearance—okay, mostly *my* disheveled appearance—the attendant looked up at us unalarmed. Bear was already sprawled at our feet and out of view. I'd put my body armor back on before leaving Earth, so I supposed the attendant wasn't seeing the extent of the damage, but my multicolored hair and tearstained face had to look a fright. I couldn't imagine what the workers here must see regularly for us not to faze him.

"How may I help you?"

"We need to check her in immediately," Logan answered for the both of us. "She has extensive damage to her ribs and torso that needs to be attended to."

"Of course. I'll get her checked in right away. I just need some basic information."

I turned to Logan.

"You're getting looked at too, aren't you?"

"I will eventually." His eyes stayed on the courteous attendant. "Her name is Audrey Lyons. Her injuries were sustained during a mission on Earth."

The man nodded, and his fingers flew over the desk in front of him, which lit up like a computer screen as he input information.

I studied Logan's profile, then tugged on our connected hands. "You promise?"

Logan looked down at me. His face was hard, but his eyes softened a bit. "Yeah, I promise. I just want to make sure you get taken care of first."

I may have melted a little where I stood. I allowed myself to drown a bit in his cobalt eyes.

"Audrey?"

The surprised shout jarred me, and I instinctually released Logan's hand. I caught a flicker of emotion in his eyes before I turned to find Jonathon jogging down the wooden steps. His eyes bounced over my face and body as if he could detect my injuries from a single glance.

He reached us faster than I would have liked.

"Where have you been?" he asked and pulled me into his arms.

I cried out at the painful embrace. Jonathon immediately released me. The concern in his eyes ratcheted up. A shuffle and low growl from the floor said Bear was issuing a warning.

"Be careful." Logan's low angry voice sounded at my back. "She's injured."

Jonathon's eyes only skated toward Logan for a moment before settling back on me. "Of course. I'm so sorry I hurt you. I've just been so worried about you I didn't think."

My cheeks flushed with embarrassment and guilt. It hadn't crossed my mind he would be worried about me. I hadn't thought about him even once since this whole ordeal began. What did that say about me? Perhaps more importantly, what did that say about us?

"I was on Earth." I mumbled the words and found my feet extremely interesting.

"Yes, we all knew that much. But none of us had any idea how you were doing. The last report that came in was from Alrik, who said you flew off with a stranger on a dragon."

"But Logan was sent down right after that."

Jonathon spared Logan another look. This one wasn't friendly. "Is that what you told her?"

"Do you really think this is the best time?"

"Best time for what?"

"Logan hijacked a ride down to Earth, and from the rumors going around, the two of you disappeared shortly thereafter."

My gaze snapped to Logan in disbelief. "You came down against orders?" Perhaps I shouldn't have been surprised, but I was. My straight-laced former mentor was breaking all the rules these days.

Logan let out an exasperated breath. "Audrey, we can talk about this later." He looked over my head. "Jonathon, she's actually in pretty bad shape. You just can't tell with her body armor on. She went into shock on Earth not long ago. Can I suggest we get her helped before diving into a Q and A session?"

Jonathon's eyes snapped back to me, and as if Logan no longer existed, he placed a hand on my back and ushered me toward the stairs, sparing only a cursory nod at the information attendant to let him know he'd get me taken care of. Jonathon led me up the stairs to the third floor and then to an elevator bank. Logan and Bear trailed along behind us.

Jonathon glanced over his shoulder at Logan as we waited for the elevator. "I've got her now. You can go."

Whoa, man. Possessive much?

Before I could say anything, Logan said, "You're crazy if you think I'm just dropping her off and leaving. I risked everything to make sure she was safe. I've been taking care of her all on my own for the last few days."

"Yeah, you've done a bang-up job of that so far. I mean that literally, by the way."

My mouth dropped open. Jonathon never acted hostile. Ever.

The hard set of Logan's jaw broadcasted his irritation. The two of them faced off, both visibly angry with the other, but neither of them said another word. A corner of my brain said there was a really simple explanation for all this animosity, but the rest of my mind was a pile of mush, only capable of staring back and forth between the two in confusion.

The sharp ding of the elevator broke their testosterone-filled standoff.

"Come on, Audrey, let me get you into a room so you can get looked at."

I obediently followed Jonathon into the elevator, Bear close to my side, and turned to see Logan remained where he was standing.

I pushed the button to keep the doors open when he didn't move. "You're coming, right?"

His face was a blank. "Let Jonathon get you situated."

"Excuse me?" It was my turn at incredulity.

"I have to go fill out our report." Keeping his eye on me, he flicked his chin at Jonathon. "He knows how to take care of you now."

"Are you kidding me?" They still looked mad at each other. "Did you have some telepathic conversation a moment ago I wasn't privy to? What happened to," I dropped my voice, "'you're crazy if you think I'm just dropping her off and leaving'?"

Great, now we were all angry. Okay, maybe not Bear, whose head just lobbied back and forth as if he followed our conversation perfectly.

Logan took a step back. He was really leaving me.

I jammed my finger on the close-door button three or four times. "Fine, just fine. Just great. See you around then. Have a nice afterlife. I'll see you when the next life-or-death situation crops up. Or not. Whatever."

"Audrey, don't be irrational."

"Irrational?" Just as the doors were about to close, I jammed my arm in the space and forced them open. I sputtered, caught on his words as much as how quickly and unexpectedly he'd changed his mind. But what else was new with Logan?

He wiped a hand down his face. "I've got some stuff to figure out. This is where you need to be right now. I'll—" his pause was an awkward one. He flicked his gaze to Jonathon before it settled back on me. "—come for you when it's right."

Was that some coded way of telling me our timing was off? Or was he just saying he'd see me later? Even after all the time we'd spent together, I still didn't understand Logan-speak. I was so tired of feeling like I was being kept on the back burner.

"Great then. Go ahead and shove me into someone else's arms. Just don't be upset when I don't fall back into yours," I shot back at him.

Jonathon took in a sharp breath. His hand resting on my lower back fell away. Clarity as to what I'd just revealed seeped in immediately. I was going to have the inevitable conversation with Jonathon, and I already dreaded it.

But the conversation with Logan wasn't over yet.

"That is not what I'm doing," he said.

Yeah, it totally was. I looked back at him sadly. There was no way my heartbreak wasn't being broadcast through the depths of my eyes.

"Let's go, Jonathon," I said weakly. "I'm in a lot of pain right now." Truth. Just not all of the pain was coming from my ribs.

Without a word, Jonathon pushed the close-door button. He left his finger on it. I held Logan's conflicted gaze until it disappeared behind the closing doors.

Uncomfortable. That pretty much summed up the next two hours of my life.

Jonathon ushered me to a vacant room on the eighth floor of the healing center. His words weren't unkind, but they weren't overly warm either as he instructed me to change into a tank and scrub pants while he located a healer to attend to me. He said and asked all the right things. Checking with me before he left if I needed someone to help me undress—I said no, but probably should have said yes—telling me I'd be taken care of shortly, and sending someone to bring me food and water.

But he never once looked me in the eyes after we stepped out of the elevator, and he didn't return. It didn't take a genius to figure out why.

Susie, a young female healer with brown hair and pretty green eyes, came in while I struggled to wiggle out of my body armor. Every move caused some ache or pain to flare up. She graciously helped me remove my clothes and put on the ones issued to me.

Last time I was here I was unconscious during most of my treatment, so I wasn't awake to be embarrassed. This time was different. Thank goodness Jonathon wasn't my primary care provider this go-around.

With freshly-wrapped ribs, I settled into bed. Pillows were situated at my back to prop me up. Bear snored on the floor. I didn't have a window, so I stared at the ceiling and tried to ignore the way I ached all over. My whole body had taken a beating, either directly or from overexertion.

The ceiling wasn't very exciting. My mind skipped from topic to topic like a Mexican jumping bean, never settling on just one thought to examine it too closely. Logan, Satan, Jonathon, and my family cycled through my head over and over again, but I couldn't come up with closure for any of them.

The knock at my door was a welcome interruption. That is, until I was hit with the look on Romona's face. Where Jonathon had radiated concern for my well-being, anger rolled off Romona in waves.

Oh boy, was I in trouble.

"I feel like we've been in this situation before," I joked to lighten the mood. It backfired.

"Yes, we have." She stepped into the room and crossed her arms. "And I believe that instance was from poor decision-making as well."

"Ouch. Okay, maybe I deserve that—"

"Maybe?"

"But I'm injured, here. You have to be nice to injured people. I'm pretty sure there's a rule about that." I gave her my impression of puppy-dog eyes.

Concern flickered in her own before she extinguished it. "What were you thinking?"

The lectures would come, but I wasn't prepared for all the hostility. First Alrik, now Romona. I shivered to think of my unavoidable conversation with Hugo. He was going to be so disappointed in me, and that was going to hurt.

I blew out a breath of air before going with the truth. "I was thinking I was bigger than God. I was thinking out of fear, and I regret my decision." I hoped my honesty would disarm her, but her response was still just as acerbic.

"Well, I'm not going to lie, I'm surprised you figured that out on your own."

"Okay, double ouch. Hey, did you know I have some broken ribs over here?" I gestured to the right side of my bandaged body. "Would you like me to lift my arm so you have a clear shot? I'm thinking that might hurt less than whatever might come out of your mouth next."

Romona finally deflated and the concern I expected to see filtered fully into her gaze. Her body sagged, and she took a seat on the bed near my feet. "Audrey, we didn't know where you were." Her eyes took on a sheen. "Do you know what that could have meant?"

My brows knitted together. "What do you mean you didn't know where I was? I was at, or at least around, the house."

"You and Logan were shielded. No one knew exactly where you guys were. We thought . . ." Her voice caught. "I thought the worst."

Her face said it all. Remembering back to my conversation with Logan, I realized what she'd imagined and gasped.

"You believed we'd been captured?"

"Only a high density of demons can shield hunters from our instruments while on Earth. When you guys didn't show up, we *all* believed the worst."

Well, that might explain Alrik's hostility too. And yet, it didn't add up.

"But that doesn't even make any sense. We were just staking out the house. The greatest number of demons we were ever around was six." I didn't think it was the time to explain about Morgan or Satan quite yet. "And there were long periods of time we weren't around demons at all. In fact, we spent a lot of time in some really secure demon-free locations. You should have been able to find us. In fact, if anyone had bothered to provide some support for our family, they would have found us right away."

Her expression darkened. "When you dropped off the map, hunters were sent to your last known location to search for you. That's why there wasn't anyone at your house. The demon activity broke up when you left with that man and the dragon, which we will be getting back to." She gave me a pointed stare. "And so our efforts were spent locating and recovering you and Logan. Do you have any idea how many miles of Ohio I've covered in the last two days?"

I blinked. Twice. "Do you mean to tell me our family was left unprotected because everyone was searching around the Midwest for *me*?"

"Yes."

I dropped my head back and used my hands to cover my face. I'd made an even bigger mess of things than I'd thought. Romona jolted when I screamed into my hands. Tilting my head, I looked at my grandmother. I didn't even try to hide my tears, or my fear. "It's so much worse than just that."

CONFESSIONS

*R*omona stared at me, her face expressionless. I'd told her everything. And I mean *everything*. From the way I got down to Earth, to my conversations with and confusion over Logan, to my interactions with Satan. She listened without interrupting. When I was done she just . . . stared. I waited several minutes before prompting a response.

"You still with me?" I asked.

She blinked. Had I broken her?

I reached a hand as far as I could from my semi-seated position and brushed my fingers over hers. The suspension of the empathy link in the healing center didn't allow me to get a read on her emotions.

"I don't know where to start," she finally said.

A short laugh burst from me. "Tell me about it."

"Bear turns into a bear?" She looked at the sleeping lump of fur still happily snoring away at our feet. She was so serious I couldn't help but laugh. Of all the things for her to start with.

"Yeah, surprise. Right? Poor Logan. I was really slow putting the pieces together." Mentioning Logan sobered my mood again.

"Maybe we should start there," Romona said. "What are you going to do about Logan?"

I shrugged. "What is there to do? One second he was all 'I'm not letting her out of my sight,' and the next he was practically tossing me at Jonathon. He all but ran away from me."

"That last part sounds familiar."

My eyes narrowed at my grandmother-slash-best-friend. "That was different."

It was her turn to shrug. "If you say so."

"It's not even remotely the same situation."

"Okay then."

"It's not."

She heaved a sigh. "Audrey, why did you ask for a new mentor?"

I couldn't look her in the eye. "You know why."

"Yes, I do, but I don't think you do."

"I had reasons." I crossed my arms over my chest. "Lots of really good reasons."

"Yes, I know you did. And some of them were valid, but at the heart of it, you were scared. Your decision was fueled by fear. Fear of rejection, sure, but I think also fear of moving forward."

If I were having this conversation with anyone else, I would have been incredibly embarrassed. As it was, I was simply uncomfortable with the topic. "What does it matter anymore anyway? What's done is done."

"I'm merely trying to help you understand the parallel between your and Logan's decisions. You two may be more alike than you realize. Perhaps he's struggling with fear as well."

I looked away from her probing eyes. "Well then, he should get over it and man up."

"Just like you did, right?"

"Hey. Whose side are you on, anyway?" I grumbled.

Romona started to laugh.

"What part of any of this is funny to you?"

"Quite a bit of it, as a matter of fact."

"Part of this mess is your fault, you know." I pointed a finger at her face.

"Me?" Romona stopped laughing. "What did I do?"

"Your whole 'Logan's not really available right now' statement gave me a huge complex. Do you know how long I thought something was going on between him and Kaitlin because of that comment?"

"You thought Kaitlin and Logan were together?" Her face mirrored the note of surprise in her voice.

"Well, yeah. They are super close and look perfect together. It wasn't a stretch. They never made it obvious they weren't."

Romona stared at me like I was crazy. "They never did anything that made it obvious they *were*."

I threw my hands in the air. "Well, what else was I supposed to think? I still don't know what you meant by that whole comment. Cryptic much?"

"Well gosh, I didn't mean for you to think *that*." She was thoughtful for a moment and then cringed. "Yeah, it was poorly phrased."

"How about you break it down for me?"

Romona's gaze was guarded. "I still don't know if I should."

"Are you serious? I'm tired of jumping to the wrong conclusions. I think it would be in Logan's and my best interests if you took a little time to set the record straight. I'll take whatever you say as opinion rather than fact."

She chewed her lower lip. "I suppose I should clean up my own mess. What I meant was what happened with Morgan."

I wasn't expecting that.

"Morgan?"

"Yes. You obviously know about him now."

"Unfortunately."

Romona looked sad. "Morgan was a good guy once."

"You're defending him? He's literally attacking our family. Maybe as we speak." A spike of fear shot through my body. I shoved it aside. "That guy is high on my hit list, so don't even try to defend him."

She put her hands up in surrender. "Fair enough. But Logan wasn't the same after he returned from that ordeal. Believe it or not, Logan used to be pretty carefree. When he returned to our realm, after all that had happened to him and without his trainee, it changed him."

"I don't know how a person could go through what he did and not be changed."

She nodded. "So, I meant he was *emotionally* unavailable. Not literally unavailable."

I groaned and ran a hand over my face. "Romona," I whined, "saying someone is unavailable is always code for 'he is in a relationship.'"

She had the decency to look regretful and laid a comforting hand on my shoulder. "I'm truly sorry to have caused so much confusion, Audrey." Sadness still lingered in her eyes. "But it wasn't my place to tell you about Morgan. Logan has been filled with shame over him. No one blames him but himself. I didn't think he was emotionally capable of having strong feelings for anyone at the time. But maybe I was wrong. All I've ever wanted to do was protect you. And protecting your heart was part of that."

She heaved a heavy sigh. "But it's not my place. I realize that now. Maybe the best thing for you and Logan is to lay it all out there for each other. So many of your interactions are tainted with assumptions."

I took a fortifying breath. "Truth?"

She nodded.

"I trust Logan . . . with everything but my heart. I don't know if I'll ever be willing to hand that over to him. The truth is, his fickle behavior scares me."

She pressed her lips into a straight line. "I can understand that. But we're not created to let fear dictate our actions. I'm less concerned with you trusting Logan and more concerned with you trusting your Creator."

Something inside me reared back. We were talking about Logan. Why did she have to drag my relationship with God into it? A knot formed deep in my gut.

"What? Who says I'm not trusting God?"

"If you were," she continued, "you wouldn't fear for your heart. You'd know He'd take care of it for you. Whether that be to protect it for, or from, Logan."

"You sound like Hugo."

"I'd take that as a compliment if I'd ever met him."

I cocked my head. "You didn't see him at all while I was gone?" The guy was something of a recluse, but I still assumed he'd be working with the team trying to locate me.

"No. He wasn't part of the recovery mission."

My brows pinched in confusion as I tried to reason that one out. Perhaps it had something to do with Hugo's claim that he wasn't *officially* a hunter.

"He hasn't stopped by here either. I thought for sure the moment I stepped back in the realm he'd be waiting to berate me for disobeying his orders. That's strange, right?" I grimaced. "What if he doesn't want to see me because he's too mad?"

"I honestly don't know."

"Yeah, me either." I threw my head back to stare at the ceiling. You'd think with the amount of time I spent looking up, there'd be something up there worth looking at. There wasn't. "Romona," I asked in a small voice, "do you think they're going to be all right?"

"Believe it or not, I don't like this anymore than you do. But they're in the Creator's hands. That's where they've always been."

Images of the bridge, the dragon, and Satan's empty eyes plagued me. "Yeah, but when I was there it was pretty bad. And I made things so much worse. I feel even more responsible now. It's taking everything in me to stay in this bed rather than run back down to Earth to be with them."

"They're not your responsibility. They never were. Satan's manipulation was to make you believe they are. You did the right thing by refusing him."

"I hope so." The anxiousness I'd been warding off settled in the pit of my stomach. Its fingers reached out and anchored itself in my heart as well.

Two days passed. Thanks to the magical healing properties of our realm, I was back in tiptop shape—except for the heart hammering in my chest.

The doors in front of me looked innocent enough. I'd shoved through them a hundred times before without pause . . . but the uncertainty waiting on the other side kept me rooted in place.

Besides Romona, I'd received visits from Kevin and Kaitlin. There were a few noticeable absences. Alrik, I assumed, was still on Earth. Logan had pulled the same disappearing act he did the first time I'd landed myself in the healing center. And Jonathon never came back to check on me, which left me both concerned and relieved.

Now, I stood in front of the doors of my training gym, working myself up to face Hugo, who had also not made an appearance while I'd healed from my injuries. I could only assume it was because of how angry he was.

I tilted my head side to side and then shook out my shoulders while bouncing up and down on the balls of my feet, hoping my trainer would be there, and dreading it, too. To an outsider, I probably looked like I was getting ready to step into a boxing ring rather than my training space. I took one more deep breath and placed my hand on the cool metal, then pushed it forward.

Hugo sat with his back to me in the middle of the gym. The top of his white head was bowed, and his hands were clasped in front of him. He was as still as a lifeless statue frozen in time. Was he meditating? Was there a chance he didn't realize I was there?

I quietly moved forward and skirted his body until I stood in front and to the side of him. His eyes were closed and his mouth moved in soft whispers too quiet for me to interpret. He prayed.

Oh shoot. What was I supposed to do now?

Taking his lead, I slowly lowered myself to the padded mats and tucked my legs under me. I watched Hugo with silent reverence. It was obvious he was communicating with the Creator. What wasn't obvious was whether or not he was aware of my presence.

On my knees, I bowed my head. How long had it been since I'd taken even a moment to do this? The forefront of Hugo's training had been the importance of my relationship with the Creator. To him, that took precedence over even the physical aspects of the work we did together. But I'd never taken the spiritual side of his lessons as seriously as I should have.

Why hadn't I?

I didn't really know. Even after meeting God face-to-face, He had just seemed so . . . so big. I was easily overwhelmed by thoughts of Him. Time and time again, Hugo had urged me to learn more about Him, probably sensing my struggle, but I'd been so focused on being independent I'd gotten in my own way.

Now was as good a time as any to start working on what should have been my focus on all along—the amazing Being who claimed to want an intimate place in my heart.

As I sat with my head bowed, I reflected on how I'd done a pretty good job of keeping my heart locked up since I'd been given my memories back. I'd thought that was the only way to keep it safe.

I was beginning to realize how wrong I was.

I'd slowly been turning my heart into a heart of stone believing that was the way to keep it whole. But stone isn't impervious to damage. It cracks and chips and can be broken to pieces. The only thing I'd really done was make myself hard. Flesh was soft and pliable and could endure wounds and be healed again, but stone could never mend like that. What might bruise flesh could take a chunk out of stone that would never regrow. Yes, flesh was more vulnerable, but also more resilient.

I moved my lips in an apology to my Creator. As I was lost in my confession of hardheartedness, a gentle hand cupped my cheek. It startled me. I looked up and Hugo's face filled my vision. His eyes brimmed with kindness rather than the condemnation I expected.

"Welcome back, child."

Tears filled my eyes, and I flung my body at his deceivingly strong one. "I'm so sorry," I whispered as silent tears tracked down my face. "I should have obeyed you. What I did was wrong, and I'm afraid I just made a bad situation worse."

I waited for the chastisement to come, but it never did. Hugo simply held me tight as I struggled with my emotions. After a while, I composed myself and sat back.

"I thought you'd be mad."

My mentor gave my shoulders a squeeze before laboring to a stand. "Do you think I should be mad?" he asked with his back to me as he moved toward the weapons wall.

"Well . . . yeah."

He turned his head so I had a view of his profile. "I have a complex range of emotions and feelings toward you right now that I don't think you have the capacity to process."

My mouth dropped. "Did you just call me dumb?"

"By whose standards?"

"You *are* calling me dumb!"

His laugh boomed. "No, I'm just messing with you."

I pressed on my temples, convinced a headache was starting to form. "What's happening right now?"

"Oh, nothing. Just an old man trying to lighten the mood. Let's train a little before we get too deep today. I think your body could stand to burn off some energy first."

If I was going to get off without a lecture, who was I to complain?

Two hours later, sweat rolled into my eyes and down my back. Hugo held his sword to my throat. I had yet to see anyone wield a sword with such excellence. He was more precise than Logan and deceptively strong and fast. He also possessed the energy of a sugar-hyped two-year-old.

I stood with my sword in one sweat-slicked hand and the other resting on my knee, bent over to catch my breath.

"How," *pant,* "do you," *pant,* "do that?"

A secretive smile danced on Hugo's face. It was a one-sided conversation we'd had numerous times.

My breathing evened out. "Okay, so if you won't answer, at least tell me why you aren't a hunter. You fight better than anyone I know."

"I have many talents, Audrey."

"But with your fighting skills and strategic knowledge, it doesn't make sense that you aren't one."

"My talents are extensive. For now, I'm pleased to come alongside you and help you grow."

My eyes narrowed suspiciously and I pointed a finger at him. "You are a strange little man, do you know that?"

Hugo's laugh bellowed throughout the gym. "Oh, Audrey, so blunt. So perfectly you."

I'd heard that before.

"You have improved immensely. I hope that's something you recognize."

I nodded. "Although I'd feel a little more self-confident if you'd let me win every now and then."

"Where would be the fun in that?" He hobbled to the wall to put his sword up. He then took up his cane and shuffled back to me. I shook my head as my eyes followed him across the room. A strange little man indeed.

"You had the chance to test your skills on Earth," he said suddenly.

Not a question. I nodded anyway. Oh boy, here was the conversation I'd been dreading.

"And?"

"And . . ."

"And how did it go? What is your assessment of your skills?"

"Oh." No one had ever asked me how *I* thought I was doing before. What was a truthful answer? I tried to remember how the confrontations had gone. "Well, I can see some definite improvement. Especially with the technical part of my fighting," I let out a short laugh, "and even with following orders. If only marginally with the latter. Logan was pretty surprised when I listened to him. Which is rather sad, when you think of it."

I frowned when thoughts of Logan entered my mind.

"My backside would have been handed to me in a big way if it wasn't for him and Bear. I struggled a lot with being distracted, but I'm not sure if it was because it was my family at stake, or if I just sidetrack easily. Probably a little of both. Fighting the demons was more . . ." I struggled for the right word, "instinctive than before. If that even makes sense. It's not that I wasn't thinking as much during the battles, but more like I was finally thinking the right way."

My eyes had fixated on a random point on the weapons wall while I gave my report. When I finished talking, I looked back to find Hugo watching me with a small smile on his face.

"Well," I shrugged out of a silly sense of embarrassment, "and my sword is kind of amazing, so it makes my tasks easier than the regular hunters'."

He chuckled. "It is a rather powerful weapon, but it sounds like things are clicking into place appropriately." The way he said it implied he had a plan mapped out for me I wasn't aware of. "I'd like to hear about everything from the beginning," he went on before I could question him.

"Everything?" My voice was a pitch higher than normal.

"I'm sure I already know more than you think I do," he said with a twinkle in his eye, "but for now, I'd love to hear you recount your battles. We can talk about them and break down what went right and where you could improve."

"Oh, battles." *Phew, fighting. I could talk about that. Let's stick to the safe topics.* "Yeah, sure, no problem. I got dropped into the middle of the first one, like literally. I poofed down to Earth and *wham!* fighting all around me. Alrik was so mad when he found me, even before I hitched a ride outta there with an evil ex-hunter and rode atop Satan's back while he was in dragon form. Of course, I had no idea at the time that it was Satan."

Hugo sat down at one of the benches along the side of the gym and motioned me over. "I can already tell this is going to be an interesting tale."

TRIALS UPON TRIALS

I spent several hours recounting my stories to Hugo. He stopped me throughout my retelling to ask questions or point out specific things I'd done well or could have done differently to defeat my opponent.

It was a happy surprise how helpful he was despite not having seen the fights himself. But what was truly unexpected was what never happened—the lecture I had been bracing myself for since the moment I made up my mind to go down to Earth without permission. Hugo listened carefully to my adventures and smiled broadly when I retold my victories, but sadness crept into his eyes when I recounted my time with Satan.

My own eyes filled with unshed tears. I had been injured and alone when I'd faced off against, not only the physical manifestation of evil, but the fears gripping my soul. He seemed to understand how hard it had been.

There was never any condemnation in his words or actions. He admonished me over some of my mistakes, but it was for the purpose of teaching, not to shame me. And for the ease with which he forgave me—I loved him all the more. His gentle teaching encouraged me to do better, to be better, for him. Not simply because I wanted accolades from him for my good deeds, but because he cared so much about me, I wanted to make him proud.

We ended our long discussion with my confession of how perplexed and disturbed I was over Satan's cryptic obsession with me and concerns about whether I'd made the right decision about my family.

Hugo picked up my chilly hand and pressed it tenderly between his two withered ones. The heat from his hands immediately soaked into mine.

"Audrey, Satan is the father of lies. His currencies are deceit and manipulation, and he liberally gives both to all he comes into contact with. Even those foolish enough to consider him an ally." His hands tightened around my own. "Standing against him and holding on to faith in the Creator will never be the wrong choice, regardless of what you may predict the outcome to be. The forces working around you, and through you, are far greater than Satan's."

A strange thing happened then. It was as if the warmth from Hugo's hands spread from my hand up my arm and throughout the rest of my body, then wrapped itself around my heart, pressed tight, and sealed itself there. I gasped at the sensation, but rather than pull away from his hands, I turned mine so I was able to grasp him back—holding on tight not only to his hands, but to his words as well.

"Is that true?"

When I expected gentleness, fierceness radiated from his body. "Yes. And heed my words, Audrey, for the next time the temptation to surrender to his demands will undoubtedly be stronger."

"Next time?" I squeaked.

"Fear not, little one." Hugo released my hand and stood with a broad grin that didn't match the tone of our conversation. "Today is not that day. Today is a day to rejoice in your safe return and in your resistance to the enemy."

"Rejoice?" I'd just poured my heart out and shared my concerns for my loved ones, and he thought this was a time to celebrate?

A boisterous laugh to rival Alrik's rumbled from his gut. "You think me dismissive?"

"Am I that easy to read?"

The smile on his face let me know he wasn't offended. "To me, as easy as a book."

Several days passed, and I fell back into a routine—a familiar, Logan-free routine. There hadn't been any coincidental sightings and I was too stubborn to seek him out. The sting of his most recent rejection was still fresh, and besides, if he truly wanted to see me, I could be easily found. I, unlike him, hadn't sequestered myself away from the rest of the realm.

Yes, he'd been keeping a low profile. I'd done some impressive Double-O-Seven work—meaning I'd pumped my friends for information on the sly. Just because I wasn't planning on hunting him down didn't mean I wasn't curious. It would have been nice if my covert inquires had gone unnoticed, but in all likelihood my friends were probably one step away from having "obsessive stalker" tattooed on my forehead. I was almost past the point of humiliation, but not quite. Though futile, my new motto was 'deny, deny, deny.'

Romona was the only one to whom I'd confessed my hurt and confusion. The more time passed, the more it seemed as if Logan's romantic interest in me really had only been a result of his prolonged exposure to Earth and boy hormones.

And that stung.

Yet . . . his indiscretions aside, there had been moments of gentleness and comfort that spoke of a genuine regard for me. It was those moments that made his avoidance truly confusing. Where was the friend I had grown closer to those few days?

Jumping to my own conclusions would have been easy for me, but I was trying to heed Romona's advice not to. My only alternative seemed to be perpetual confusion, so confusion was a constant friend.

Then there was the guilt.

It sat low and heavy in my belly, souring more every day that passed. I hadn't seen Jonathon in days, and as much as I wanted to stick my head in the proverbial sand and pretend the issue would work itself out, we needed to talk. No, we'd never established the exclusivity of our relationship, and on a technical level I hadn't done anything wrong—but deep inside I knew it was wrong to have let things go on with Jonathon as long as they had.

The harsh truth was I'd used Jonathon as a Band-Aid for my heart, and he hadn't deserved that. Logan or not, my feelings for him were never going to deepen, a certainty I was now aware of. He was a wonderful human being and deserved to be with someone whose feelings for him ran hotter than lukewarm.

"You know, Hugo," I started, "these nunchakus are starting to look mighty interesting to me."

He chuckled. "Oh, are they now?"

"Yep. I'm not going to lie, I can't really picture myself killing a demon by hitting it repeatedly with a couple of wooden sticks. I mean that's a lot of work, right? There are much easier ways to dispatch them. But handing out a good bruising could be cathartic."

"Becoming a little bloodthirsty are we?"

I shrugged. "I'm just saying."

"How about if we leave some of the advanced weapons training until after you finish the gauntlet? Then I can show you how those . . . wooden sticks can be useful for more than anger management in a fight."

I groaned and flopped to the floor. "Stupid gauntlet. I'm still on the hook there?"

"You sure are. In fact, you're on the schedule to run it again today."

I twisted in his direction. "What?"

"Yep, we have about . . ." he checked his wrist where a watch would be, if he had one, "ten minutes, give or take, before we need to get going."

I jumped up and started to pace, my heart suddenly pounding hard. I wasn't ready to run the gauntlet. "Oh my gosh. You're just telling me this now? Oh my gosh. I'm freaking out. Can you tell I'm freaking out right now? It's super obvious, isn't it?"

He laughed.

Laughed. At. Me.

"Oh yes. I can very much tell you're freaking out. Come on." He took my arm and hauled me out of the training gym. "I have a surprise I think will help bring the freak-out factor down a notch or two."

I followed along like a zombie. Full on foot-shuffling the entire way. When we arrived, Hugo squared my shoulders and looked me in the eyes. He patiently waited for me to focus on him. When he was satisfied, a smile broke his face that lit his eyes. "There she is."

"There who is?"

"My little warrior. I knew she would break through." He squeezed my shoulders and his smile dropped as he held my gaze. "Audrey, listen to me. You have got this."

I nodded woodenly.

"You stay focused. You listen to your instincts and rely on your training. It's going to be a cinch this time."

"You think so?"

"I know so."

"Can Bear come with me?"

My dog was now coming to training with me daily. He'd followed me around almost everywhere since returning to our realm. He even made it a habit to sleep on the bathroom floor when I showered. We both looked down at the fluffy mop already half-asleep at our feet.

"No, I'm afraid not. Besides, he wouldn't be much help to you in there. He'll only change when you're in real danger. The gauntlet is only smoke and mirrors."

"Oh."

Hugo removed his hands from my shoulders and grasped mine. A jolt of energy shot up my arms, this time traveling the length of my body and dispelling stress in its wake.

Oh my. That's better.

"Audrey, I am proud of you," Hugo said. "Not only of what you've accomplished, but of what I know you still have to accomplish."

I warmed under his regard, and a genuine smile broke free. "Thanks, Hugo. You're the best."

"That is what they tell me." Only Hugo could get away with saying that without sounding proud. "Now get in there and do your thing."

"You're not coming in with me?"

"Of course, I'll be with you. But you have some people who want to talk to you first. This one can stay out here and keep me company." He patted Bear, who leaned into his touch.

With an encouraging nod from my mentor, I turned and entered the monitoring room.

Who was here to talk to me? No one had ever come to watch my gauntlet trials before. A few familiar technicians waved before turning back to their tasks. I knew they were loading the computers with the information for the simulations. After facing a plethora of real monsters on Earth, this shouldn't be so intimidating to me, but it was. I'd failed it so many times already I was psyching myself out.

Romona's comforting voice interrupted me. "We wanted to be here to support you this time. We should have done it sooner."

I turned to the left, and there stood Romona, Kevin, and Kaitlin.

I smiled lightly at Romona. "You guys have always supported me."

"Yeah, but as your closest friends, sometimes you have to go above. Words aren't always enough."

As I looked at the three of them, I couldn't help notice the few friends who were still missing. I shook it off. The three standing in front of me were waiting for me to respond. I was more than lucky to have them—I was blessed. A shaky smile filled with equal parts nerves and love for these people broke free on my face.

"It's kind of awesome you guys are here."

Three sets of arms swallowed me. I yelped along with Romona and Kaitlin when Kevin tried to lift us all off the ground.

"Okay, enough, you nut." Kaitlin swatted at Kevin until he released his hold.

"Just trying to show my love for Audrey in my own manly way."

"Oh, is that what that was?" she asked with an amused smile on her face.

"Well, that and these things can't be contained." He flexed one of his lean biceps and then struck a few bodybuilder poses.

I burst out laughing.

"Now that there," he pointed at my face. "That's what I was actually trying to do. This girl was in serious need of a good laugh."

"You weren't wrong. I feel much better now." It was true. I couldn't wipe the grin from my face. "You guys are the best."

Romona stepped forward and took my hand. "Remember? I said you had family here, too."

"You did."

Kevin clapped his hands together. "Time to set some new records."

"I'd settle for completion."

One of the technicians tactfully interrupted. "All right, Ms. Lyons, we're ready for you now."

I took a deep, solidifying breath and materialized my body armor.

"You're getting so much better at materializing," Romona said.

I warmed at her praise. "Thanks. Okay, guys, wish me luck."

"You won't need it."

Nerves threatened to break through again. I bounced up and down to shake them off. I waved to my friends, who would be observing my trials from above, and followed the technician to the belly of the testing arena. After giving the same old safety speech for the fourteenth time, he left me alone.

I stood in the open area and waited for the gauntlet to start. I held my sword at the ready. I never knew if something was going to jump out at me right away.

"Okay," I whispered to myself, "let's do this thing."

"There she is!"

My friends rushed me at almost the same moment the final simulation disappeared, returning the room to its warehouse-like appearance. I barely had time to turn toward them before my exhausted body was picked up into a constricting hug.

"Kevin," I squeaked. "Air, please."

"Oh, right." My lanky friend set me on my feet, but it was only half a heartbeat before I was swallowed in another hug. This time I was the meat in a Romona-and-Kaitlin sandwich.

"You did it," Romona squealed loudly. Her normally composed exterior took a back seat to her excitement.

"We're so happy for you," Kaitlin added. She pulled back and looked me in the eye, her expression morphing from excited to serious. "That was some impressive butt-kicking."

"Thanks."

I used the back of my hand to wipe the sweat from my forehead. The gauntlet had been intense, but . . . good. It hadn't been easy, but it had been different from any of the other times I'd run it. I'd been focused beyond the reach of distraction. My movements had been fluid and my instincts spot-on.

And then a new voice chimed in.

"I wholeheartedly agree."

A zing of awareness shot up my spine. When had he arrived? I turned slowly, allowing myself a few extra moments to brace for impact.

The purple smudges under his eyes were gone. Normal color had returned to his complexion. The gauntness of his features was transformed as well. He stood with his arms crossed over his chest, and his blue eyes practically sparked with energy. Unlike the last time, we stood face-to-face, Logan was the picture of male health . . . and then some.

I couldn't help it. *Man, he is hot! Yum! Did I just think that?* My stomach bottomed out. *Oh dear. Hair stay brown, stay brown, stay brown.*

As if mind reading were part of his skill set, Logan gave a cocky grin. I pulled my ponytail forward under the guise of twirling it and snuck a peek at its color.

Brown. Thank goodness.

"What are you doing here?" I asked. I couldn't decide which emotion I was supposed to bring into play. Anger. Happiness. Irritation. Sadness. Relief. Frustration. Confusion. Yeah, I was going to go with the last one—confusion.

Any of the others would likely lead to my least favorite of them all . . . embarrassment.

"Same as the others, I suppose." He put his hands in the pockets of his jeans and kicked at nothing on the floor. The movement made him appear unsure. Everyone was uncharacteristically quiet. The others looked anywhere but at the two of us.

"O-kay. So, yeah?" That wasn't supposed to come out a question. Too late. This was headed toward awkward.

A soft hand squeezed my upper arm. "Hey, maybe we should go and let you two have some time." Romona's voice was low, but no one missed her words.

"No, that's—"

"That'd be great," Logan cut me off.

"Hey, wait a minute." Apparently, irritation, frustration, and anger were ready to come out of hiding. "You," I pointed a finger at Logan's chest but stopped short of actually touching him, "left me alone in the healing center . . . again. I'm not so sure I want to be alone with you right now. I still have some strong emotions moving around inside. You know, reoccurring abandonment issues I'm probably going to need a lot of therapy to overcome."

Romona, Kaitlin, and Kevin slowly tried to shuffle around me to get to the exit.

Not a chance! "You three, don't move!"

Logan released a heavy breath of air and ran a hand through his hair. It looked like someone else was about to jump onto the frustration train to nowhere.

"Yeah, that's kind of one of the things I wanted to talk to you about."

"You don't say?" I jutted a hip and planted a fist firmly on it.

"Audrey, if you're dead set on not hearing me out, how are you ever going to be able to forgive me?"

"This is not about forgiveness." *Not mostly, at least.* "This is about the Jekyll-and-Hyde personality thing you have going on around me."

"Okay, you have a point. But do you really want to get into it with an audience?" Logan gestured to our friends, who despite my command, managed to slip several feet closer to the exit.

"I definitely want an audience. They've been privy to most of our shenanigans so far. Why stop now?"

Logan's lips twitched. He lifted his hand to his face and coughed to cover his laugh.

"Oh, and are you finding me just *adorable* right now?" I snapped at him.

His smile formed unfettered this time. "Yeah, a little. Shenanigans?"

I growled. "It's an awesome word. I'm going to start using it all the time now."

"So now we're discussing your word choices?"

"You're the one who brought it up, mister."

"I guess I did. So let's."

Huh? "Let's what?"

"Talk about our shenanigans. In front of an audience comprised of our closest friends. Let's start with the time we were hiding in the church, and you can go into detail about how you felt when I had you in my arms and we almost—"

With a gasp, I lunged at Logan and slapped two hands over his mouth, surprising us both. If the widening of his eyes didn't give away his shock, his feelings through the empathy link would have. But the moment the shock wore off, a bigger emotion rushed me. The very one I'd been waiting desperately for, yet somehow still was not quite ready to receive.

Logan loved me? Logan was *in love* with me?

But that couldn't be true. Without doubt, what I picked up from him was simply the aftereffects of Earth's exposure.

In a surprise move, Logan didn't wrench away. We were both frozen for the moment.

Amusement flooded the empathy link a split second before he licked my hand.

"Ah, yuck!" I squealed and jumped back.

Logan belly laughed.

"This is the weirdest thing I've ever seen," Kevin said from the peanut gallery.

"Agreed," Kaitlin answered. "Do you think they've finally cracked? I feel like we should be making bets or something."

"Your hair is pink," Logan said.

Ahhhhh! "You're so helpful."

"That's me," he said with a smile. "And by the way," he leaned toward me, his voice lowering an octave, "I know exactly what the colors mean."

I inhaled his yummy scent on a gasp. *Oh gosh, please have that not be true.* A tendril of hair that had fallen in my face darkened to magenta.

"Okay, you don't want to talk about the church basement. How about—"

"Logan!"

He lifted a shoulder, a wicked smile in place. "You're the one who wants to publicly discuss our shenanigans."

"You know that's not—"

The resounding boom of the door being thrown open and slamming into the wall cut me off.

"Alrik!" Romona gasped and rushed toward him.

Our warrior friend took two steps into the room before stumbling to his knees. A gash in his body armor ran along his left arm, and a steady stream of blood leaked from it and onto the concrete floor. One eye was swollen shut, while the other searched our faces until he found mine . . . and stopped. A foreboding chill wracked my body.

Alrik was supposed to be with my family.

A COHORT

We coaxed Alrik into a seated position before starting the inquisition. Refusing to let the fear show on my face, a fine tremor still ran through my hands. I balled them into fists. Logan crouched down at Alrik's good side while Romona and Kaitlin attempted to stanch the blood flow from his arm with a towel they'd found somewhere. Kevin and I hovered above the four of them, uncertain about what to do next.

"What happened, man?" Logan asked the question I was too scared to.

"I was overrun."

Logan shot a concerned look at me before giving his attention back to Alrik. "What do you mean *I*? Where were the other hunters?"

"It was just me. After you and Audrey returned, a group of hunters were dispatched to watch over her family like I said they would be. Everything was fairly quiet, so after a few days some of them got called back." Alrik's features pinched and he let out a low groan. "It didn't give me any red flags at the time, but now I see what was happening."

"What was happening?" I couldn't hold my tongue any longer. Kevin reached over and pulled me to his side for comfort, but it hardly registered.

"A few hunters were sent back at a time until there was only one of us left on rotation." He hadn't truly answered the question.

"Only one? That's crazy!" *Who was the dummy that made that call?*

"That's not routine," Logan spoke up, thinking aloud for us all. "We always work in a minimum of two. With only one hunter, there wouldn't even be anyone to send back to alert the rest of us of trouble. Why would you even allow that?" His tone was just short of accusatory.

"I didn't . . . I was working with another hunter, and then he just . . . disappeared. I was about to send a message to base when it happened."

"What happened?" I asked sharply. My fists were clenched so tight my fingers started to ache. We needed to get to the point, and fast. And Alrik needed medical attention. It was obvious he'd sought us out before seeking any kind of help.

His apologetic eyes lifted to me. "There were so many, Audrey, it was all I could do to escape. I had to let you know what was happening."

Which was? I only just held myself back from screaming.

"They've been swarmed."

Romona gasped. "How many?"

"I'm not sure. At first it was only two. I stepped out to fight them. While I was distracted the rest descended."

"Ballpark it for me," I ordered. The strength in my voice hid the turmoil churning in my gut.

"A cohort at least. Maybe more."

It was Kaitlin's turn to gasp. Her hands flew to her mouth, and the blood on them distracted me for a moment.

"How many is a cohort?" I asked.

"Several hundred." Logan's voice was hollow.

I closed my eyes. *Do. Not. Panic.*

"How many hunters have been sent down?" Logan's switch flipped to full hunter mode.

"I don't know. I came straight here."

"You didn't check in before finding us?" Logan sounded furious.

Alrik speared me with his eyes. "I figured Audrey should know first."

Perhaps I should have been grateful, but that was bizarre. Telling me before briefing the higher-ups would do nothing but slow down the response time to this attack. What was he thinking? Maybe he'd taken a hit to the noggin we couldn't see?

I looked sharply at Logan. His face said his thoughts were similar to my own.

"We need to let command know so they can counter the attack," Logan said. "Kevin, get Alrik to the healing center and then come back here right away. Kaitlin and Romona, come with me. We'll be able to get down there the quickest."

Everyone began to move.

"Wait." Alrik's voice was stronger than I thought it could be considering his injuries. "Audrey, aren't you going down, too?"

Four pairs of eyes snapped to me.

"I . . ." *Oh, this hurt.* I swallowed my pride and my pain simultaneously. "I can't. I'm not allowed to go."

"But it's your family," Alrik practically pleaded. "They need *you.*"

I reared back a step and blinked at him. "But . . . but you know I can't go. Last time we spoke, you lectured me on what a horrible decision it was to try to fight for my family to begin with." What parallel universe had we just entered?

"I was wrong. You should go down with them."

He was telling me exactly what my heart wanted to do. But I knew I couldn't. I'd defied orders before and lived to regret it. I couldn't go down, wouldn't go down, without orders to do so. Squeezing my eyes shut, I shook my head. My ponytail slapped me in the face from the force of my movements.

"No, I can't. I won't do that again."

"We have to go now." Logan's voice was sharp. "Audrey's right. She's already been explicitly told not to interfere with her family anymore. But the rest of us can do something. Let's go."

Kevin switched places with Logan and helped Alrik to his feet.

What was up with him lately? First, he'd chastised me for going down to Earth, now he was practically begging me to do it again. Was he drinking some of Logan's Jekyll-and-Hyde crazy Kool-Aid? As he was led away, Alrik's eyes bored into me. The accusation in them was clear. My heart jack-hammered.

I didn't understand!

Logan followed them to the door, but right before pushing through he turned and pierced me with a stare. There was a lot he was trying to convey with one look, but I wasn't in the right frame of mind to pick it all up. There may have been a promise there.

I hoped so.

With a short nod he disappeared, Kaitlin close on his heels.

"Have faith," was all Romona said before jetting, leaving me completely alone.

I stood stock-still, staring at the exit. I needed Hugo.

Stat.

As if conjured by my desire alone, Hugo's hand, frail in appearance, settled on my arm. His powerful energy surged through the point of contact.

"Where have you been?" It wasn't an accusation, just a question. My voice was full of the same impotence that filled my circumstances.

"I've been here the whole time."

I turned a quizzical eye toward him. "I haven't seen you."

"That doesn't mean I wasn't here."

"You heard what's happened?"

"Yes." His eyes were gentle. "I know what's going on. How are you holding up?"

"Truthfully?"

"Always."

"Not well." I took my eyes off him to stare at the door my friends had disappeared through.

It was oddly quiet in the gauntlet arena. None of the usual activity of resetting the system was going on. Strange. I was used to the flurry of activity from the technicians after I'd failed a gauntlet. Instead, Hugo and I stood alone in the massive space. Perhaps they'd seen what had happened and were giving me space? Perhaps they still watched. I couldn't muster the emotion to care.

"That's understandable. A very human reaction."

"Human reaction? What's that supposed to mean?" I would have worried about being offensive, but there wasn't enough oomph in my voice to warrant a strong response from him.

"This is a heavy situation you're in, and I wouldn't expect you to be unaffected. The real question is what are you going to do about it?" Hugo's voice was full of patience, but his line of questioning began to irk me.

"What's there to do? I learned the brutal way the consequences of disobeying orders. I don't have much of a choice but to do nothing. Nothing but wait." A dull throbbing pain pounded behind my eyes.

"You see no other options?"

"You're saying there are some?"

"I simply asked if you saw any other way."

I took a moment before responding. For the life of me I couldn't see any but the two extremes. Do what I'd done before or sit around and wait. The former was what I wanted to do; the latter was what I should do. I possessed enough sense to stop myself from making another foolish decision, no matter how badly I ached to be part of the action.

"No," I finally answered. "I honestly don't see any other options."

"I feared that might be the case." There was disappointment in his eyes.

What had I done this time?

I threw my hands in the air and rolled my eyes. "I'd love to be enlightened."

"Audrey, what do you know of God?"

The question threw me off. Weariness tugged at me as I shifted my weight from one foot to the other. The sweat from the gauntlet had long since dried on my skin, but the muscle fatigue still remained. "God? Like in general, or in a specific situation? That's a pretty broad question."

"You're right, it is. But He's a pretty broad guy, wouldn't you say?"

"I suppose."

"You've met the Creator of all. Spent time in His presence in fact. Yet you still operate as if He exists separate from your existence. As if He's an observer rather than an active participant in your day-to-day activities."

Ouch. He wasn't wrong. I thought perhaps I knew where he was going with this.

"Despite everything, inside, you still believe He doesn't care."

"I'm showing some restraint right now," I said. "It has to count for something."

"Yes, you are. But is it because you learned the consequences of your actions, which don't get me wrong is an important lesson to learn, or because you trust in a Higher Authority?"

I let out a heavy breath. "Can't it be both?"

"Absolutely—but is it? For you?"

He waited patiently for my answer. A heavy breath escaped my lungs. "Hugo, this is hard."

"It doesn't have to be."

I scoffed. He ignored me.

"Audrey, tell me what's in your heart." There was a slight note of pleading in his tone. Inspecting the contents of my heart seemed like a really bad idea right now. There was ugliness churning there I didn't want anyone to see.

I crossed my arms and refused to meet his gaze. "I don't know what you want from me right now. I'm doing what I'm supposed to. Absolutely nothing."

"You are never called to do nothing."

"Could have fooled me."

"I'm not the one who's fooled you."

"It's a figure of speech." I uncrossed my arms and shifted my weight back and forth.

"One that is accurate at the moment, for you have been deceived."

"By who?" I took a step toward him.

"Yourself mostly, but that's beside the point. Why won't you tell me what's on your heart?"

"Because they were forgotten." I wailed, finally snapping. "I'm supposed to keep my trust in God, and He's abandoned my family!" My eyes filled with tears of frustration, at all of this, at myself.

Gosh, I was angry.

Whether at Logan or God or circumstances, I always seemed so angry. It was exhausting. Why couldn't I be better than that? But I wasn't. "How am I supposed to have faith in a God who's so unpredictable? I feel totally adrift."

"Ah, finally, there it is." There was a strange gleam in Hugo's eye. Part amusement, part annoyance. "You can't work through your personal demons, Audrey, until you're willing to be truthful with yourself. If you're struggling with your faith, name it. Face it. Don't bury it."

"But . . . I'm ashamed. Underneath all this anger, I'm ashamed that I don't trust God. What does it say about me that my faith is so small?" I answered in a weak voice.

"My dear child, it simply says it's an area that needs to be worked on. But perhaps more importantly, you need to know what it doesn't say. It doesn't say the Creator loves you any less. It doesn't say He thinks of you any less. It doesn't say He cares for your situation, circumstances, loved ones, hopes, dreams, or future any less."

The words struck my heart with peculiar pain. Wasn't that what I had feared all along? That He didn't really care.

"How is it you know my heart better than I know it myself?"

"I do have some practice in that particular area." His secretive smile made another appearance. "When your faith is small, God is always present and reaching out a hand to help. Faith is both a choice and a surrender. You have to choose to believe the God of all works all things for good, and you have to surrender to His will above your own."

"I'm scared He won't do things the way I want them to be done." I hunched and wrapped my arms around myself.

"I can pretty much guarantee that will be the case. But what if your way isn't the best way?"

"But this is what I'm supposed to be doing. I'm supposed to be helping people by going down to Earth, by fighting demons. Yet I feel like my wings have been clipped. Why make me a hunter if I can't even fight for the ones I love? I'm supposed to just sit back and never do anything?" I threw my hands in the air.

"Quite the contrary. You will be called to do a great number of things. In fact, God's power is made perfect in your weakness. But apart from Him, your deeds are quite worthless. Surrender your will and reach your hand back to His. Accept His help. You have been like a hamster running in a wheel, using up your energy yet never actually getting anywhere."

I huffed. "If this is some new tough love campaign of yours, I don't like it. Why are my mentors always comparing me to animals? With Logan it was a dog. Now you're calling me a hamster. It's degrading."

His gaze had never left my face. "This isn't about what you like. It's about what you need." His already impassioned words were amplified by the other-worldly fire that radiated in his eyes.

"But I'll never be perfect. I'll never do everything right." The movement of my hands punctuated my words.

"Exactly my point. Your deeds will never make you perfect. No matter how many good decisions you make, no matter how good your scorecard of right versus wrong, it will never be good enough."

The crushing weight of despair settled on my chest. What good was any of this, then, if I was never going to get it right?

Hugo's voice was gentle, yet he was unrelenting. "I'm not trying to shame you, Audrey, but to speak truth into your heart. How effective was your trip to Earth?"

"Counterproductive at best." I stared at a spot on the wall over his left shoulder. It was as close to meeting his gaze as I could get.

"See, apart from God our deeds are dead. But with Him it's another story. God can do amazing things, even with faith the size of a mustard seed."

He'd momentarily lost me. "What does a mustard seed look like?"

A belly laugh followed my question. "Let's just say it's really small." He held up his index finger and thumb, and there was barely a sliver of space between the two. "I believe it's time you see what God can do with your mustard seed of faith."

"What do you mean?"

"Audrey, the Creator is incapable of abandoning His own. With that in mind, do you think your family's predicament is by accident or by design?"

"I know for a fact Satan is gunning for them."

"Yes, but time and time again God uses Satan's evil intentions for good."

Huh. "Well, what can I do about it? I'm not allowed on Earth."

"Correction. You *weren't* allowed. I believe it's time you showed that bully down there what he's up against."

He'd caught me completely, one hundred percent off guard. I stammered for a moment before I managed to get out, "Me?"

"You, with the power of heaven behind you."

There was a spark of excitement and anticipation in Hugo's eyes. He reminded me of a parent the moment before his child opens a birthday gift. It struck me as an odd reaction, and I was shocked into silence.

"Go now. Gather your friends and go to your family. I'll make sure you have the clearance you need."

WHEN DARKNESS DESCENDS

I materialized to the right of the small line of hunters who stood their ground within the boundary line of my parents' property. Covered from head to toe in body armor, swords drawn against the overwhelming force that blackened the already darkening day, they waited.

Dusk was upon us.

I drew my own weapon, the sudden brightness drawing the attention of my fellow warriors. With all eyes on me, one hunter broke away from the rest. Even in the low light I would recognize his form and movements anywhere. His hurried steps brought him to me in mere moments. His blue eyes sparked with emotion.

"You shouldn't be here." Logan scanned the sea of demons surrounding the property. "For a number of obvious reasons."

"Hugo sent me," I said. I held his gaze and waited. "I have orders."

Alrik had not been exaggerating. The black bodies of the demons stretched down the street and along the sides of the property. They were not only littered across the street, but on the neighbors' properties as well. In their yards, on their houses, some even perched in trees.

The demons' numbers had grown. Several hundred wasn't even a conservative estimate. I wouldn't have been surprised to hear it was closer to a thousand. Up against only . . . I looked to my left and counted—eight hunters, including me. Why so few? What was heaven thinking, sending so few fighters down? If it came to it, this wouldn't be a fight. It would be a slaughter.

"Audrey, please." Logan's eyes begged me to leave.

"You need every hand you can get."

"No. We're not planning to engage in a fight. The odds are too overwhelming. We're just holding the line. This isn't meant to be your fight. You shouldn't be here," he repeated.

My face softened as I took in his concern. "Logan, this isn't any of our fight. We both know there's no way we could subdue this much evil. This is out of all of our hands. We have to trust it's in Someone else's much more capable ones." My eyes skimmed the area around us. "Shoot," I said softly to myself. "I shouldn't have left him behind. We need Battle Bear."

Logan's brows pinched. "Battle Bear?"

"Yeah, you know. Grrrrrr!" I pulled my lips back from my teeth and bent my fingers, slashing them through the air as if they were claws.

Logan blinked, and then the left corner of his mouth quirked ever so slightly.

"Stop it." My fist landed on my hips.

"What?"

"This is not cute."

He pressed his lips together tightly.

"I'm serious."

"Yeah, I know."

"I'm not being cute." I stomped my foot. I had a feeling I might not be helping my case.

"You're right." He was losing the battle with his lips. "Definitely not adorable at all. Not a bit. Really quite unattractive, actually. I think you need to show me that claw imitation again, though, so I know what you're talking about."

I threw my hands in the air. "If you knew they were claws, I don't need to show to you again. Geez, I cannot believe you're joking at a time like this. Hell is quite literally breaking loose around us!"

His blue eyes locked with my brown ones, and I watched the humor leak from his face. After several heartbeats he nodded, reached forward to grab my hand, and led me to the others in our small defense. He released his hold on me when we reached the line.

I checked the faces of the other hunters. There were no welcoming smiles, only a palpable level of anxiety. I expected and recognized Kevin, Kaitlin, and Romona. The three other hunters were only vaguely familiar to me. They displayed the usual muscular build of a typical hunter. Rather than exchange names, we only nodded a brisk greeting to each other.

"Why are the demons so silent?" I asked.

It was Romona who answered. "We're not sure. I've never seen them behave this way. Almost sedate. It seems like they are waiting for something, but demons aren't known for their patience."

I knew what she meant. Even during the battle at the school several months back, the demons circling the air were so loud before they attacked that a battalion of angels was tasked to block out their noise.

Somehow, the silence was more frightening.

"Since they can't get through the barrier, do we have any idea why so many are congregated here?" I asked.

"Theories only," Logan answered. "And not any good ones. We can only assume they're waiting for someone to leave, but from what we can tell, your parents and brother seem to be in for the evening." He jutted his chin toward the house. "They're eating dinner now, and we heard James say he was staying in tonight to finish a paper. Your parents are working on taxes."

I chewed a lip. Maybe the horde of demons was Satan's way of posturing? I said as much. Logan looked thoughtful.

"He said he wanted to teach me a lesson about his power. Maybe this is his way of doing that. At the very least we know he wants to scare me."

"But if that's the case, where is he?"

I wasn't sure what he meant. "How do you figure?"

"If this was about intimidation alone, I'd think he'd be here to try to force your hand again. Something is off. We're missing something."

The sun kissed the horizon as he spoke. Shadows lengthened around the neighborhood. I vaguely wondered if any of the living could feel the overwhelming presence of evil in the atmosphere. Thanks to my internal demon-radar, it was as if a suffocating blanket was thrown over my head. I forced myself to ignore the sensation.

"Should we just—" Romona started, but she was cut off by a shrill scream from the direction of my parents' house. My insides froze. I turned quickly enough to see my mother drop her phone and crumple like a sheet of paper.

I sprinted to the bay window, heart pounding. When I reached it, I put both hands on the glass. Dad talked loud enough I just made out his words. He asked her what was wrong, but Mom was sobbing too hard to get anything out. James had abandoned his place at the table and paced behind the two of them.

With infinite tenderness, my dad took my mom's face between his hands and kissed her forehead. "What's happened?" he asked again.

"It's Dad," she wailed between sobs. "He had a stroke . . . while driving." Tears streamed down her face. James stood frozen as he listened. His face was as white as a ghost. "He ran into another car."

I wanted to stop the words from coming out of her mouth, but I couldn't.

"It was a young family. They're not sure who is going to make it."

A loud gasp wrenched my attention away from my parents. Romona was behind me, eyes impossibly large and standing unnaturally still except for her chest, which moved rapidly up and down. She would hyperventilate if she didn't calm down.

"No," she whispered, bringing a shaking hand to her lips. "Not Garrett."

My grandfather on my mother's side had been Romona's husband in life. Although I was sure she was anxious for him to join her in the afterlife some-day, we were still hardwired to want our loved ones to live out a long and happy life on Earth. The possibility of lives lost at his hand, even accidentally, was horrific to consider.

"Romona," I began, but paused when the start of piercing noises from the horde surrounding us attacked my eardrums.

As if the demons woke from a dream, the night shadows undulated with the movement of their bodies. Their excited shrieks built in frequency, punching holes in the silence. Five hunters still remained on the property line, facing adversaries blind to their presence.

Logan stood in the middle of the yard, looking between the drama playing out in the house and the awakening mass of demons. His expression didn't divulge the obvious tension in his body.

"I just can't take any more tragedy!" My mother's voice rose above the swelling noise. Her plea was desperate: "Where is our God?"

Over Logan's shoulder, the final sliver of sun dip behind the horizon. As if a gunshot signaled the start of a race, demons tore toward the property line and beat their twisted forms against the invisible shield that held them at bay.

One of the hunters on the front line stepped back and stumbled over his feet. I think it was Kevin. Romona and Logan whipped their attention to the demons. At once we all rushed to the invisible barrier. Loud screeches drew our attention overhead as demons dive-bombed the top of the protective dome around my parents' house.

"What's going on?" I screamed to be heard over the noise.

"They're trying to break through the barrier!" Logan answered, eyes still fixed on the dark shapes above.

"Is that even possible?" I asked.

Logan's eyes finally met my own. "The prayers and faith of your family are what put this barrier up."

Romona finished what he left unsaid. "Their lack of faith could theoretically take it down." Her eyes weren't fixed on the demons, but rather on the remnants of my family still visible through the bay window. "The demons must have been waiting for that call."

Her words sent ice to my heart. Satan orchestrated all of this. Hugo's words about faith in the Creator were all I had to hold on to, because if the demons did manage to break through the shield, it would take an unimaginable amount of power for eight hunters to protect the people within that house. I wasn't sure we had access to power like that.

Father, I called out silently. *Where are You? We need You now.*

A sound like shattered glass rent the night air. I spun toward the house expecting to see a smashed window, but everything was intact.

Then came the shout from a hunter I didn't know. "They're through! Arm yourselves!"

No!

Turning back to the small group of hunters, there was an obvious breach in the protective barrier. Rather than being uniformly transparent, the barrier flickered as if light was bouncing off glass. A demon tumbled into the opening and battled with Kevin and one other hunter. The rest of the demons were either trying to break holes at other points, or clamoring to get past the existing jagged opening.

The sharp edges cut into their flesh when they pushed through, but they paid it no mind. So far, only three small demons managed to fit. The others were either too big to squeeze through the space or fought each other to advance, bottlenecking themselves in the process.

There were so many of them. We could only hold them off for so long before the rest of the barrier broke or we became overwhelmed by the demons who managed to make it through the opening. The reality that the protective dome had failed because of my family's hopelessness cut through me like the blade of a knife.

Hugo sent me down here with the promise of being backed by a God big enough to handle any situation. It was time I started to fight like I believed that.

I reached behind me and grasped the hilt of my sword, pulling it free from its sheath. Fire engulfed the blade as I ran toward the breach, determined to do what I could to stop demons from slipping through.

The demons on the other side could see through the gap. Once I came into view, they momentarily shrank back. The brightness of my sword reflected off the barrier, creating a bubble of light around me. The sight only gave me a moment's reprieve before one of the braver—or dumber—creatures rushed the opening.

I slashed up with a speed that surprised me and cleaved his head clean off his body, which dissolved to smoke and ash before even hitting the ground.

There was hardly any resistance when my weapon bit through the demon's flesh. Nor had I ever seen a demon disintegrate that quickly. I glanced down at my sword in amazement.

Had it downloaded an upgrade without me knowing?

Well, whatever that was, I wasn't complaining.

I glared at the demons swarming the opening before me.

Bring it.

As if one entity rather than hundreds of individuals, the demons let out an earsplitting shriek. A sliver of trepidation slid down my spine.

"Shoot. If that's not the definition of creepy, I don't know what is." The voice came from my right.

Truth.

I caught a glimpse of Kaitlin's blonde ponytail out of the corner of my eye. I wasn't willing to risk a full look. My eyes were diligently trained on the increasingly organized creatures in front of me. Abandoning their self-warring, they formed what appeared to be a rudimentary line.

"They're going to rush us."

"Yep." Kaitlin popped the last letter.

"I'll take out or injure as many as I can. You handle the ones that get past me?" I glanced in her direction and caught her nod. Her eyes were laser-focused on the demon horde on the other side of the barrier. We ignored the attacks on other parts of the shield and the other hunters. We had our own battle to focus on.

Without warning, the next demon rushed forward. The difference this time was that the creature behind it, the one behind that one, and so on down the chain they'd created, moved as well, one after another.

A freight train of demon flesh bore down on us.

I steeled my resolve and ran forward to meet the attack. An unplanned battle cry left my throat as I slashed through the first demon, ashing it immediately before the next struck. The next two were so close together I took them down with one well-placed plunge of my blade. The fourth dodged at the last moment, and I only managed to hack a limb from its body as it tumbled past. I trusted Kaitlin would take care of it as I faced the next monster.

On and on it went. Hugo had ingrained movements so deeply into my subconscious and muscle memory that I fought almost without thought. The smallness of the breach was a blessing, because no more than one demon at a time was able to enter. Most fell quickly to my blade, but the ones that made it past were all wounded in one way or another. I had to depend on my fellow hunters to take care of them. The onslaught was relentless.

I was covered in a layer of ash in no time. The black smoke of fallen demons swirled around my ankles even as I took out another. I heard nothing, saw nothing but my next opponent.

I'd never been so focused.

It was as if someone else had inhabited my body and I was just along for the ride. My muscles remained strong, I didn't feel any injuries, and the breath in my lungs was steady and even.

Whatever power I used to fight off these demons was not my own. I'd turn that over in my head later, but for now I had a job to do.

However I was doing it, I was doing it well.

Despite the circumstances, a small smile touched my lips. This felt good. This felt *right*.

Suddenly the mass of demons rushing toward me stopped. Perhaps a sense of self-preservation finally sank in. I'd long lost count of how many demons had spilled through the breach. A deafening silence alerted me that the attack on the dome around my family's home had also abruptly ceased.

I stepped a foot back and angled my body to check on the hunters behind me while still keeping an eye on the threat. I was surprised that not a single one of my companions was involved in a struggle of any kind. Breathing hard and covered almost completely in black blood and demon ash, they all stood ready behind me. Against the odds, we were succeeding in keeping the horde at bay.

The last light from the set sun tinted the horizon with color. The once elongated shadows were now masses of darkness. I squinted. It was hard to see the demons. They blended well with the murky evening. I was sure we took out a good number of them, but looking at the throng through the shadows it was impossible to see the dent. The darkness played tricks on my eyes, making their numbers appear infinite.

"Everyone all right?" I called back to my friends.

"We're hanging in there," came Kevin's out-of-breath reply. "Your head's doing its thing again."

"What?" What thing did my head normally *do?* Shoot! Somewhere along the way I'd lost my helmet.

"You know, the crazy color stuff."

I shot Kevin a look. Like that was on my list of concerns right now.

"No, seriously, it's kind of gold and shiny now."

Well, that was new, but I wasn't going to take the time to worry about it. There were more pressing concerns than my hypercolored hair. I turned in the other direction.

"Logan?"

"Yeah." He stepped forward to stand by my side. His eyes were trained on the demons in front of us. He was actually . . . pretty nasty looking. Black ichor was splashed over his face in a gruesome splattered paint pattern. Clumps of I don't even want to know what were mashed in his disheveled mop of hair.

And he smelled.

Not sweaty guy smell, but more like putrid sulfur. My disgust must have been written all over my face, because when Logan shifted his gaze to me, he started laughing.

A full-blown laugh straight from the gut.

Completely surprising coming from him, and totally inappropriate for the situation. When had I become the serious one?

"That bad, huh?"

I scrunched my noise. "Worse."

He started to lift an arm to wipe his face and then realized he was so covered in general grossness he'd only make it worse. He shrugged. "I can't be pretty all the time."

My mouth fell open a little. Then I shook my head. "I'm not even touching that one. What do you think is going on? And I don't just mean with the reprieve we're enjoying right now. How did they know to attack the barrier? And more importantly, how did they bust a hole in it?"

Logan sobered. His eyes returned to the uncharacteristically quiet creatures in front of us. They narrowed as he thought. He glanced behind us before returning his attention to me.

"I've never seen a barrier fail like this. We all knew it could happen—hypothetically—but I always assumed it would be an all-or-nothing thing. I've never heard of only a portion of one failing."

"Can't we do something to put it back together again? Or at least plug the opening?"

He paused before answering. I knew what it looked like when someone didn't want to deliver bad news. "We can't do anything about the state of the dome. Your family's faith is being shaken. We have to hope they hold on to what they have left so the breach is the only problem we have to deal with. Your grandfather's accident has hit them hard."

Grandpa. My heart squeezed. I jerked my gaze to the house to find Romona practically pressed up against the bay window.

"I need to check this out."

Logan gave a quick nod to indicate he understood. I sheathed my blade and sprinted to her side.

I'd never seen Romona so . . . unhinged before. Her palms were pressed flat against the window, while her eyes darted frantically between family members on the other side of the glass. Her bloody post-battle appearance only added to the air of desperation clinging to her. I didn't think she even noticed I was there until she spoke.

"They haven't received any additional information on the accident since the attack began."

"How do you know?"

"Your father's been making calls, but he can't find anything out. They aren't even sure which hospital Garrett is at yet, so they can't go to be with him." She turned haunted eyes to me. "They're falling apart."

Romona's behavior, more than even my immediate family's, scared me.

"And that's why they were able to mess with the barrier?"

She nodded. "I think this is the straw that broke the camel's back. We don't know how Satan's been messing with them this past week, but considering what's going on right now," she took a moment to sweep the area around the house, her gaze taking in the demons restlessly shifting in the shadows, "it's obvious he expected something like this to happen."

Satan's words in the clearing came back to me. His threat to my loved ones. Guilt tried to climb up my throat and choke me, but I pushed it down with Hugo's words of truth and encouragement. *Have faith.* Blaming myself for Satan's psychotic nature wouldn't help the situation.

Almost to my surprise, I remained levelheaded. Very not me. Maybe I was maturing? Maybe it was something else? I placed my hand over Romona's right one still pressed to the window. The contact caused her to start.

"It's going to be okay." I snuck another peek at the scene surrounding us and wished I hadn't. "I'm not sure how, but I know it's going to be."

She nodded but replied, "We can't hold them all off."

"I know, but we—"

A low hissing noise started from the demons surrounding us. It sounded like a multitude of voices whispering all at once. Each word slithered over the other, obscuring their meanings.

"What the . . . ?" Kevin exclaimed, followed by a half-scream from Kaitlin as she frantically stomped the ground.

It was almost fully dark now, so I couldn't see much past the glow emanating from the house. Romona and I exchanged a glance before jogging over to the unit of hunters. When we neared the group, I bit back my own gasp.

Heavy gray smoke-like fog slid along the ground, headed our way. I followed the trail with my eyes from the ground in front of us through the hole in the barrier and into the night.

Dark mist poured from the demons' mutilated jaws as they chattered. Combining, it formed a denser substance. The noise slowly grew louder, and with it the movement of the fog increased.

Other than the chill it carried, the mist passed harmlessly over and around our feet. I watched helplessly as it progressed toward the house, undulating like a ravenous swarm of snakes gliding over each other in a race to reach their prey.

Desperate to do something, I pulled my sword from my baldric. The flames that enveloped the blade were more blue than red. I swiped down in a movement that resembled a golf swing. The fog in close vicinity to my blade scattered, dissipated, or simply displaced—I couldn't tell. Even if my sword had eliminated some of the substance, there was too much of it for me to stop its forward progression.

I looked up and caught Logan's eye before swinging my sword at the fog at my feet again.

"That's not doing much."

"You don't say?" I gritted my teeth. "What happens when it reaches the house?"

"Nothing good." He turned his head toward our group. "You guys stay here and guard the opening. If the demons start trying to battle their way in again, you know what to do."

He jerked his chin toward Romona and me. "Come on, let's see what's going on with your family. They're fighting this battle right now every bit as much as we are, even if they don't realize it. We can't do anything to repair the barrier, only hold off as many of the demons as possible until . . ."

"Until what?" My muscles stiffened. I forced them to loosen as we turned toward the house.

"Until something changes."

Well, that sounded ominous.

"Can we expect more backup?" We cut our way through the putrid matter clinging and swirling around our feet. Even without corporeal form, something about it was very serpentine. The hissing demons probably contributed to the image.

When Logan didn't answer, I cut my gaze toward him. His stoic expression wasn't comforting.

"We should have already received backup," Romona's soft voice answered instead. "There's something . . . not right going on right now."

A chill went up my spine, as much from her words as from the hollowness with which she delivered them. She appeared almost hopeless. Even as my grandmother on Earth, I'd never seen her like this.

"We'll have to worry about that later," Logan said. "One thing at a time. That's all we can really do at this point." He veered to the left of the house.

"Where are you going?"

He glanced back over his shoulder toward us.

"We're going in."

THE SHATTERING

*W*e entered the house the same way we had before. Up the tree in the back and through my sister's window.

"I don't even want to know how many times Jessica used this tree to sneak out of the house," Romona mumbled behind me as we gingerly descended the stairs.

"I totally should have moved into her room when she left for college."

Romona snorted but sobered quickly when sobbing reached us from the living room. We filed into the room one at a time and surveyed the scene.

Dad held Mom on the couch, rocking her back and forth as she cried. James sat in the sofa chair across from them, arms bent and resting on his knees as they bounced nervously up and down.

Wide-eyed and pale, his gaze jumped between my parents. Seeing my usually infallible parents this worked up unnerved me. I could only imagine how much more it affected my little brother.

"Love," Dad said softly, "we don't know for sure your father won't be all right. I know it hurts, especially . . ." his voice caught, and he had to swallow a few times before going on, "considering Audrey, but we need to stay strong right now."

Mom lifted her eyes and the despair in them ripped me to shreds. "Sometimes I don't know how to keep going on. Sometimes I wonder if He still cares."

Had I not been standing almost directly above them, I wouldn't have caught her hushed confession. I glanced at James. Nothing in his posture indicated he'd heard her. For that, I was glad.

"The windows," Romona gasped, jerking my focus away from my family.

Over my brother's shoulders, inky tendrils of demon-induced fog crawled its way up the panes of glass. Layer upon layer of the mysterious substance soon blanketed the entire bay window. I dashed into the kitchen, and sure enough, the windows in there were covered as well. In my mind's eye I imagined the whole house encased in a blanket of darkness. I ran back into the living room, and the look of horror on Romona's face brought me up short.

"What?"

Without looking at me, she lifted a shaky finger toward the front door.

I didn't notice anything at first . . . and then I looked down. It was such a small amount it was almost indiscernible. Wisps of black fog slid under the door and into the house. The fragments moved independently, yet with the same trajectory, like centipedes with a hive mentality.

"It's coming in through the glass too," said Logan.

With my mouth hanging open, I watched long slivers of fog snake straight through the glass.

I vaguely processed Mom's sobs subsiding to small hiccups. Dad whispered in her ear while continuing to rub her back gently.

With terror clawing at my heart, I watched the first bit of darkness come near my parents. Like insects attracted to the light, it traveled straight for them.

"I don't think so," I said to myself and pulled out my sword. I might not be able to stop the mass of fog outside, but I could certainly handle the little bit in here. I swiped at the ground and warded off the small amount that had condensed in front of the couch. For some reason, it stayed clear of my brother, and for that I sent up a quick word of thanks.

Another small wave of darkness moved toward my parents in an uncharacteristic jerky manner. This time when I swiped at it, it skirted my movements. Some of it managed to slide up the side of the couch.

The substance that wove its way under the front door and through the windowpanes collected on the floor faster than I could swing my sword back and forth.

It wasn't long before I couldn't keep track of what was on the ground and also catch the stuff sneaking up the couch. Without a weapon of their own against the fog, Romona and Logan could only look on with matching expressions.

"I don't," there was an obvious quiver in my voice, "I don't think this is going to work."

It was then I spotted the first tendril of smoke slide smoothly over my mom's forearm. It wrapped itself around her limb like a python about to squeeze its prey, then curled along her arm in an upward motion spiraling around her neck.

"No!"

Without thought, I lifted my sword high, ready to hack off the evil now attached to my mother. Before I could complete my downswing, I was knocked clean off my feet. The air was punched out of me when I hit the rug-covered floor face-first. My body groaned in pain. The heaviness pressing me down quickly lifted. I flipped over to see Logan crouched above me.

"What the—"

"You don't know what your sword would have done to her."

"What are you talking about? The sword only affects evil."

"You really want to test that theory on your mom?"

One heartbeat, then two. "Oh my gosh. I could have hacked her arm off?"

He frowned. "I don't think so, but we don't know exactly what that sword of yours would do to a living person. All we really have is theories."

He grabbed my hand and hauled me to my feet. I looked toward my mother. More smoke slid fluidly over her, occasionally slipping to my father as well. She was once again sobbing.

"I don't think this is a battle we can fight for them." Romona's soft words were laced with sorrow. Her eyes lifted to meet my own. "Some things in life even we can't protect them from. They're losing hope. This," she gestured to the darkness filling up the remaining spaces on the floor, "is a test of their faith, not ours. They're currently not even trying to fight it."

I didn't want to believe it. "But my parents . . . they're so strong."

"Even the strongest of us can stumble sometimes." Her eyes were haunted. "We do what we can, but their choices, their free will, their *faith* dictates the outcome of some battles. The condition of the barrier out there has already given us a clue to their current state of mind. When despair hits, sometimes we forget we're not alone."

"But that's what we're here to do. To help."

I could see from Romona's expression that this was as hard for her as it was for me. "They need to reach out for help, or at the very least hold on. The struggle isn't against flesh and blood, but against the forces of darkness. Forces they can't see for themselves. For us to be able to fight for them, they have to stand firm and resist. When they give up, Satan's forces are given an entry into their lives. Without their resistance, we're impotent against this type of attack."

I realized I still clutched Logan's hand. "You think this is all their fault?" I asked, my voice quivering.

"I'm saying they're beat down and not thinking straight. We'll do what we can, but we can't do—"

A sonic boom cut off the rest of Romona's sentence. I ducked and covered my ears with my hands, half-worried they'd come back bloody from perforated eardrums. My eyes swung to the windows.

The noise had come from outside. I could just barely make out the hunters on the front lawn through the thick layer of demon fog. They were all in various positions of cover, some with their arms thrown over their heads, others crouched low to the ground. Kevin's whole body engulfed Kaitlin, who huddled in a ball on the ground.

It was then I noticed reflective pieces of something littering the ground at their feet. It glittered like pixie dust.

A demon to the right of the house let out a scream. The hunters jumped to their ready positions and pulled their weapons. The demon rushed forward, unfettered, into the yard.

And I knew.

The barrier had fallen.

We didn't bother with stealth mode anymore. This time we left right through the front door. I didn't know if my family noticed us open and close the door.

I didn't have time to care.

With the barrier down and hundreds of demons surrounding the property, our team was literally being swarmed. We slowed our steps and took a quick moment to assess the situation from behind the large bushes that flanked the front entrance.

Not all the demons were attacking. At least half of them stood still, doing that weird hissing whisper chant that caused the foggy substance to pour from their mouths. If that was the only thing we had going for us, our situation was truly dire.

"I'm going to help Kevin," Romona yelled. Before either of us had a chance to reply, she took off, running to where the lanky hunter battled three demons.

"I honestly don't know if I wish Bear were here or not."

Logan cleared his throat and sliced a glance across the yard. "Okay, no Battle Bear . . ." his serious look slipped for half a blink, "so we're fighting this tandem style."

"Huh?"

"Turn around. We keep our backs to each other so nothing can sneak up on us."

That sounded as good a plan as any. I was only half-turned when Logan yelled, "Duck!"

He pushed my head down with his left hand and swung his sword around with his right. Liquid splashed my back at the same time the creature let out its angered cry.

Ew.

That was my cue.

I spun around and finished the creature off with one stroke of my blade.

I didn't know how long we'd been fighting. I only knew my muscles shook with fatigue and the attacks were relentless. No amount of training could ever have prepared me for an onslaught like this. I didn't know how my fellow hunters were faring.

What I knew for sure was Logan still fought at my back, and I only knew that because I hadn't been attacked from that side yet.

No sooner had the thought flitted through my brain than I was knocked over from behind. With a grunt, I landed on my side, but quickly rolled out of the way of a spiked appendage that embedded into the soft ground rather than my body.

Ouch, that would have seriously hurt.

I bounced to my feet and sliced through the limb that had tried to impale me. Its owner let out a piercing sound of pain before stumbling back and disappearing into the madness surrounding us.

Logan!

Another demon rushed me before I was able to check for him, but I quickly reduced it to smoke and ash. I turned in a circle and finally spotted Logan's limp body to my left.

I started toward him immediately, exhaling the breath of air I hadn't realized I'd been holding only when he got to his knees. He shook his head once as if to clear it, and then with fear-filled eyes, swiveled his head quickly until our gaze locked. He released his own breath of relief.

With eyes on me, he didn't see the creature rear up behind him, but I did. A warning scream broke through my throat, but before the air could even be expelled through my lungs it was already too late.

I watched as Logan grabbed for a sword that was no longer there. As he turned to face his opponent, he was backhanded in the face and sent flying through the air at least ten feet. He landed face-up on a hardened walkway, his head snapped back and connected with stone.

This time he didn't stir.

The demon advanced on Logan with single-minded intent, its jaws already open wide in anticipation of ripping into his flesh. I sprinted after the monster, which was easily two or three times my size. Focused on its prey, it didn't notice me coming.

At the last moment, I jumped, landed on its back, and stabbed my sword straight through to its chest. With all my strength, I pulled my weapon down and sliced through its body in a move that would have disemboweled it had it not charred to ash first.

The fight took place close enough to Logan's prone form that some of the demon's remains settled on his chalky skin. With fighting all around us, I didn't have the luxury of checking his wounds. I needed to get him somewhere safe so he wouldn't become demon fodder.

With every bit of my strength, I dragged Logan toward the house. With its walls at our back, that left only one side to defend. I had to drop his weight and battle standing over top of him twice before I reached the siding next to the garage. With Logan relatively safe, I fixed my attention to the conflict raging in front of me.

Like water running over a dam, darkness and whispered hisses still dripped from the jowls of the immobile demons. The fog continued to move steadily, weaving in, out, and around the limbs and bodies littering the ground in its undeterred trudge to reach my family.

The rest of the demons maintained their relentless attack. I'd gained a momentary reprieve hidden in the shadows of the house, but I couldn't just stand there and watch while my friends and fellow hunters struggled.

Scanning the grounds, I considered my next move. The demons' flesh was black on a night backdrop, making them nearly invisible. I was so going to have a conversation about night-vision goggles with Hugo when we got back.

Through flashes of darkness the hunters fought on. Our body armor captured whatever light it found and reflected it. Most hunters fought in pairs like Logan and I had been . . . but then a flash of blonde caught my eye off to the right.

Kaitlin battled a demon on her own. Her movements were so fast they blurred, but the demon she faced matched her blow for blow.

I blinked and she was down, blindsided by another demon who came in from her right. She tried to get to her feet but was tackled by both demons at the same time and buried beneath blackened flesh.

Her scream rang out a moment later. My feet desperately wanted to take off, but I cast a quick look behind me. Logan was still unconscious. How I could leave him completely unprotected?

A heartbeat lapsed as I made my decision. He wouldn't want me to abandon Kaitlin. Her terror-filled scream filled the air again.

I only got one step before one of the creatures was thrown off her and into the street. I came up short to absorb what my eyes were seeing.

Morgan's sword cleaved the head of the other demon clean off its body. His gaze swept the war zone and came to a sudden stop on me.

Kaitlin lay unmoving on the ground at his feet. He quickly hefted her into his arms and ran straight for me. Conflicted and confused, I positioned myself on guard.

Morgan tried to move past me, but I held my blade up to thwart him. With the help of the flames I could easily see his expressionless face. There was no mockery in his eyes, no hatred written across his features. He stared back at me with a face cut from stone.

"Let me put her with Logan so you can protect them both."

"What are you doing?" I demanded.

"Audrey, move!" he yelled, finally showing emotion. "I'm trying to keep her safe!"

"Why?"

"Does it really matter right now?"

I supposed he was right. I stepped cautiously to the side, keeping one eye on him and the other on the chaos in front of us. Whether from confusion or curiosity, it wasn't long before the movement in my peripheral vision snagged my full attention—Morgan gently set Kaitlin's motionless body down next to Logan. Once she was out of his grasp he scrambled away from her in haste.

"Will she be okay?" I asked.

"She's been fed on. She blacked out." His shoulders lifted and fell with angry breaths. His eyes remained fastened to Kaitlin's immobile form. "You need to get your people out of here."

"We can't. In case you didn't notice, we're the only ones here to fend them ...*you*, off."

"Which is exactly why you need to leave." His deadened tone chilled me.

"We can't," I repeated.

He stared at me then, his face once again a stone mask.

"Then you are all bloody fools." He uttered something under his breath and shadows leap from the ground and cocooned his body. I didn't even try to hold back my gasp. Through the darkness he was almost invisible. He ran a rough hand through his hair before racing back into the mass.

What the heck *was that?*

I stared in the general direction in which he'd disappeared, in stunned silence until a demon rushed me. My weapon whipped up so fast even I couldn't track the movement. The demon was toast. Burnt toast, to be exact.

A familiar mechanical sound caused my heart to jump to my throat.

Oh please, no!

To my left, the panels of the garage door ascended as it opened. The chugging sound of the motor lifting the door might as well have been the sound of impending doom.

With the barrier down, I had no idea how the demons would be able to affect my family or their vehicle. The last time they'd taken the car out while under attack, they'd almost gotten into a wreck—even with their protection in place.

This time there wasn't even a way for me to follow to help ensure their safety.

An ear-piercing roar forced my attention away from the garage and into the darkened night. Black on black made it near impossible to make out, but unless my imagination was filling in the blanks, whatever was up there looked like a dragon. It was far larger than any demon I'd laid eyes on, and it cut through the sky like a missile.

Satan was here.

At the last moment, the red beast spread its wings, dipped low, and landed on the roof of a house half a block away. Its shape contorted and shrank, and although it was impossible to clearly discern what it had morphed into in the low light, I could make an educated guess. The figure leaned against the chimneystack that jutted from the roof, lounging as if unaffected by the surrounding violence.

So, he'd come to watch his handiwork after all.

With determination, I shifted my attention back to my family. The garage door was fully open now, and Mom fumbled with the keys in the box next to the door. She was having trouble locating the right set with her shaky hands.

Suddenly, the house door swung open and Dad appeared. His arrival surprised her, and she dropped the set of keys she held. She bent over to retrieve them, but dad went down on a knee and placed a hand over her own to stop her movements.

I watched in dismay as the enemy's fog poured into the garage from both the interior door and the backlog pooled around the house itself. It slithered straight for my parents, my mom specifically.

"Love, what are you doing?"

Her shoulders sagged even further. "I was going to drive to the county hospital and wait. I think there's a good chance that's where he'll end up."

"I don't think—"

"I have to do something!" Mom wailed and placed her hands over her face. Her body shook from the force of her sobs.

Dad immediately engulfed her in his arms. Worry was etched on every inch of his face.

I snuck a quick glance behind me to where Logan and Kaitlin still lay unmoving. The foggy substance covered parts of their bodies, but since it didn't seem to affect us the way it did my family, I tried not to add that to my list of concerns.

I sucked in a large breath of air and instantly wished I hadn't. Man, that stuff stank like bad demon breath. Like demon breath after they'd eaten a truckload of rotten eggs. I choked a little on the stench, and for their sake, was glad Logan and Kaitlin weren't conscious.

Dad rubbed a soothing hand over Mom's back. "Okay. If you think it will make you feel better, we can go. Just let me drive, all right? I don't want you handling a vehicle right now." He lifted her face and waited for her to nod. She did.

He pressed his lips together, then gave her his own fortifying nod. He helped her stand, then took the keys in her hands. "Just let me grab my wallet. I'll be back in a second." Dad slipped back into the house. Mom moved toward the car. Her back was to me, head bent and shoulders hunched.

Watching the drama unfold in the garage was a stupid idea. I realized that a moment too late, when I was knocked over and a stabbing pain raked down my back. I bowed my spine to escape the agony.

A demon was on me, pressing my face into the soft earth. Its talons squeezed my sides, unable to puncture my body armor. It screeched, and its steamy, maggot-filled breath blasted the back of my neck.

I was about to become demon chow.

My right eye had a view of the opening of the garage. I couldn't even take comfort in my family being safe inside. The distraction of hunter blood in the yard was probably the only thing that had kept them off the demons' radar so far. It wouldn't be long until they were discovered. It was a miracle they hadn't already been noticed.

Nasty spittle dripped on my cheek and in front of my face as the creature on my back salivated in anticipation of his snack. Bones popped as it extended its mouth. I imagined it probably looked a lot like a snake dislocating its jaw before swallowing its prey whole.

Adrenaline punched through my system, and I thrashed beneath the monster's weight.

I spotted my sword several feet in front of me—too far to reach—and cried out in frustration. I was seconds away from being sucked into a vortex of blackness from the demon's bite. Once those teeth pierced my skin, I'd be less than useless.

I was *not* going down this way! "Get off!" I screamed.

"Audrey!" Someone yelled my name and dropped my sword within reach. Shortly thereafter the beast on my back grunted in pain.

I didn't waste a moment.

I wrapped my hand around the sword hilt and awkwardly shoved the blaze in a general upward direction. It wasn't the most technical of moves, but it did the job of dislodging the demon holding me down.

Gritting my teeth through the pain, I jumped to my feet.

The demon had turned and was battling another hunter. Only the wild arc of his blade was visible. With waning strength, I plunged my weapon into the creature's back. I pulled it out and then cleaved off one of its lower appendages, causing it to fall to the ground.

A sword came down and hacked off its head. Black substance sprayed into my face. It was easy to forget how gory a demon kill could be when my own sword quickly reduced them to a pile of burnt nothingness.

Kevin stood over his kill, his chest heaving. "You okay?" he asked. I wouldn't say he looked good, but considering the situation, he didn't look too battered.

"Yeah, I think so. Do I have any flesh left on my back?" I turned to him so he could inspect it for me.

"Your armor protected you. There isn't even a tear."

A shiver wracked my body. Thank the Lord for this magical covering.

"Audrey, I've got them." Kevin motioned to Kaitlin and Logan behind him. "You protect the garage."

I nodded and took off.

"Mom, wait!"

My mother's delicate figure appeared just outside the garage, but my brother's voice stopped her. She faced him, her eyes red-rimmed, face lined with worry.

My heart stopped beating.

"Get back in the garage," I yelled, even though I knew she couldn't hear me.

I wanted to wake up from my personal nightmare, but it just got worse as my brother stepped out of the relative safety of the house to meet her. The fog skirted him in a five-foot radius, but I was too concerned with the whole situation to find much comfort in one small victory.

The garage couldn't really protect them from the demons, but they'd at least remained out of view. There was no hiding them from the enemy now. I stood in front of them with my eyes on the battle they were unable to see.

"What?" Mom asked in a shaky voice. I cast a furtive glance in her direction. The fog ran over her body like dark veins of poison. It was repulsive to watch, yet I couldn't look away.

"We haven't prayed, Mom." James's voice trembled, as if he sensed the evil surrounding them that he couldn't possibly see.

A glimmer of hope blossomed in my chest.

"I don't know that I can right now," Mom said.

My gaze bounced from the danger in the yard to the drama unfolding behind me. Back and forth, back and forth.

"Then I will." Looking like a soldier going to battle, James stepped forward to take my mother's hands in his own. The darkness clinging to her hands fled on contact. He gave her an assured nod before reverently tipping his head down. I only caught the words "Dear Lord" before my mom's sobs drowned the rest of his prayer out.

I looked on in awe as my little brother started to glow. As he spoke, his arms came around my mother in comfort, and the sickening darkness that had clung to her like a parasite ran from the light he was projecting and dripped from her body like blood.

Within a few short minutes she was free of the evil influence, and a ring of at least five feet around them had been cleared.

But the hope blossoming in my chest was swept away when my gaze drifted to the battle. Demons suddenly jerked their bodies in my direction, and as one, the horde charged.

I gripped my sword and crouched into a defensive stance. We'd finally run out of time. They were coming for them.

They were coming for us all.

LEGIONS

*B*OOM!

The explosion swept the yard with a deafening roar. When I looked back at that moment, I would always remember the grotesque face of the demon who managed to scrape me with its claws from chin to temple before the lot of them were blasted away from us. The image of its face, void of eyes with two off-center slashes acting as what I assumed were nostrils, burned into my memory forever.

From behind me, light detonated like a land mine, tossing demons in every direction. It blew the hair escaping my tight braid forward, but otherwise left me unscathed. The demons shook themselves off and ran at us again. I didn't dare sneak a glance over my shoulder. I wasn't sure what the explosion had been exactly, but it didn't keep them from coming at us again.

I braced myself for the attack when the first demon exploded to ash in front of me. I flinched and took a step back when the same thing happened to the second and third. I watched with morbid fascination as demons, one after the other, connected with something invisible and ashed much like they did when I delivered a deathblow with my sword.

Several dozen had heedlessly run to their own demise before the swarm finally retreated, leaving a diameter of at least fifteen feet clear of my family and myself in every direction. Their anger-filled shrieks left no doubt as to their feelings about their forced withdrawal. I watched a few more minutes to be certain they weren't getting any closer before I focused on my family again.

Sometime during the commotion my father had joined his wife and son. But the three of them weren't alone.

Hugo?

My mentor stood with his arms extended around my family, his head bowed and mouth moved with silent words even as James spoke out loud. My brain could not process what he was doing here.

As if I watched a tennis match—rather than being immersed in a battle with evil—for the umpteenth time that evening my attention was wrenched in another direction when a shock wave nearly knocked me over.

Lights dropped from the sky like shooting stars. Their impact didn't physically shake the ground, but each collision sent a tremor of life-giving electricity through the earth and up into my body.

From all around, demons let out agony-filled shrieks as their limbs seized and convulsed. Scurrying away from the lights their twitchy movements were grotesquely similar to dying spiders.

Blinking through the tears created by the blinding lights, I began to distinguish forms.

"Angels," I whispered.

Within moments, the angels created a hedge with their bodies around my parents' home, standing side by side along the property line where the barrier had once been. Any demon dumb enough to try to break through was dispatched immediately, their broken bodies flung out into the street. It didn't take the creatures long to figure out that wasn't a good option.

More angels dropped into the battle zone where the enemy still fought the exhausted hunters. They formed rings around the hunters, finally giving them a cessation from fighting. Angels fell from the sky in a steady stream and fought the demons littered throughout the neighborhood and down the street.

"A legion."

"Huh?" I needed to stop using that word so much. I twisted around and found Kevin—battered, bruised, and covered in both his own and demon blood, but still standing. One of his arms hung at an unnatural angle. His eyes were fixed on the miracle unfolding in front of us.

"It's a full legion of angels," he said. Later I would find out what a legion was, but for now I assumed it was a lot. Like a lot a lot. Their brightness dimmed after they descended to Earth, but their sheer numbers bathed the area in much-needed light.

My attention snapped to the rooftop Satan had descended upon. There was no sign of him anymore, in dragon form or otherwise.

At some point he had fled with his followers. I was glad he was gone, yet a knot of trepidation for the future still remained.

I turned back to my parents and James. Hugo was still with them. The slight glow that had started when James began to pray had turned into a brilliant white light, bright enough I shouldn't have been able to even look at it.

But for some reason I could.

My family was pressed together in a football huddle, each member touching the other in some way. Hugo's arms embraced both my mother and brother, and his hand extended to my father's shoulder as well. I startled when looking at my brother. He was covered in ghostlike armor, reflecting the light around him but still transparent enough to reveal his plain clothes underneath. The arms touching him went right through it, settling on his person rather than the bulky encasement. Straps of what might have been leather crisscrossed over his favorite pair of worn converse sneakers, which looked to have grown spikes out of the bottom. The effect was a cross between a sandal and a soccer cleat, if soccer cleats had razor-sharp spikes.

I took stock of the rest of him. The translucent armor also included a fitted plate across his chest, a belt around his waist with a sword hanging from it, and a helmet that not only covered his head but his cheeks as well. And finally, a large rectangular shield rested on the ground, propped up against his back, reaching almost his full height.

I stared dumbfounded at the vision in front of me. Perhaps someday the unexpected wouldn't throw me so much.

Today was obviously not that day.

My brother's voice finally broke through my shock. He thanked the Lord for being with our family, for protecting them, for loving them despite their weaknesses.

When did my little brother get so wise?

My eyes shifted to my mother. Her posture had transformed. Her head remained bowed as she quietly soaked in James's words, but her shoulders were no longer sagged or rolled forward. The arms encircling her husband and son no longer shook in fear, but were solid and resolute. Tear tracks still ran down her face, but her eyes were dry. And most importantly, the grotesque wisps of demon fog had completely left her. My mother was no longer defeated.

She stood victorious.

Without realizing it, I moved closer to them, deeper into the light. When I was close enough to reach out and touch them, I stopped.

Without looking up, Hugo grasped my wrist and placed it on my brother's back.

My hand landed on James's ghostlike armor rather than passing through like the others. It was warm to the touch. I took in a sharp breath of air. I was used to the strange power Hugo's touch brought, but being connected to my brother, was a hundred times more intense—as if currents of it flowed between each family member.

This was truly supernatural. The evidence shown on each of my loved ones' faces.

Gone were the terror and panic I'd witnessed earlier. In their place was a deep-seated well of peace.

My brother finished his prayer with a soft-spoken *amen*. My parents looked at him with matching smiles on their faces.

"We needed that, son," my father said.

Mom nodded her agreement. She opened her mouth to say something—and right then her phone rang. She answered it immediately, watching Dad's face as she listened to whoever was on the line. I let my arm drop to my side as I turned my attention to Hugo, whose arm stayed wrapped around my mother.

"When did you get here?" I asked.

"I've always been here."

I lifted my brows. "Where?"

He smiled at me, and his eyes trained on something over my shoulder. I turned to see the yard—heck the neighborhood—cleared of demons and their manufactured fog.

Glowing angels were everywhere, all bent on one knee with heads bowed and right arms crossed over their chests. The hunters who were conscious took up a similar posture. Kevin knelt off to my side, but his eyes were large as he glanced back and forth between Hugo and me, silently trying to tell me something.

"What am I missing this time?" I asked.

"Something rather big, I'm afraid," Hugo answered with a chuckle. "But we'll talk soon so you understand."

"He's at Memorial General. They've stabilized him." Mom's voice cut off our short conversation. "They said we could come and be with him."

"Any news on the family in the other car?"

Mom shook her head. Sad, but not panicked like before. "We're not family, so they won't release any personal information to us. We'll just have to wait to find out." She reached out and took my brother's hand. "And pray for them, too." The tears glistening in her eyes this time were full of pride.

"Let's go now," Dad said as he rounded the front of their car. Mom and James followed suit and opened the car doors to settle themselves inside. The semitransparent armor my brother wore never faded.

"Are they going to be all right?" I asked Hugo. With all the angels in the vicinity, my family's home was now a veritable fortress, but they were about to leave it.

"They'll be fine now, Audrey. This battle has been won. I'm leaving this legion of angels to watch over them until Satan moves on."

At the reminder, I jerked my gaze in the direction of where I'd last seen the angel of darkness overseeing his forces from a neighbor's roof. It remained cleared of his presence. I hadn't realized I'd been holding my breath, but I could suddenly breathe again. "Really?"

"Yes. Watch." He tilted his chin toward the car slowly backing out of the garage. A group of eight angels formed rank around the vehicle and took flight as it turned and traveled down the street. Occasionally their wings brushed because they flew so close to each other. The car was almost indiscernible in the middle of the warrior cluster.

Someone whimpered to my left. Romona knelt on one knee like the others, but her attention was focused on the receding car and she had a fist pressed against her mouth to stop sounds from coming out. Silent tears streamed down her face.

"Go," Hugo said beside me. At first I didn't know who he was talking to, but when Romona turned her hope-filled face toward him and answered, it was clear.

"Truly?"

"Yes. Go be with him now."

She bowed her head in reverence. "Thank you, Your Majesty." She stood, and an angel swooped down and picked her up. They flew in the direction the car had disappeared.

"Your Majesty?" I looked wide-eyed at Hugo.

"Did I not once tell you I went by many names?"

"Well, yeah, but I thought you just meant nicknames like Hugh, or H-man or something. 'Your Majesty' is a little . . . ah . . . loftier than I imagined." The last sentence came out sounding like a question.

Hugo chuckled. "Time to get you and your friends home. Then we'll talk."

I gasped. Way too many things had happened to keep track of them all. I ran to Logan and Kaitlin, still unconscious from their wounds. Logan's face was bruised, but the blow to the head when he'd been knocked backward probably kept him out cold.

Kaitlin's wounds were more visible. I hadn't had the chance to inspect them before, but for her benefit, I was glad she was still unconscious.

I fortified my stomach as I peeled back the tear in her body armor to survey the damage. It wasn't pretty. The flesh around her shoulder had been almost completely ripped away. Bone and muscles were easily seen. She'd lost so much blood it practically soaked the ground around us.

Her face was devoid of color except for her lips, which had a bluish hue rather than their usual red. Only the knowledge we couldn't die kept me together, but even then, panic clawed at my insides at the extent of the damage to her shoulder and neck.

These wounds were serious.

"Is she going to be all right?" a softly accented voice whispered at my right.

Morgan was down on a knee beside me, doing his own visual survey of Kaitlin's wounds. The mystery of his appearance and assistance was still that —a mystery.

I stared at him in confusion. "I think so. They should know how to help her in the healing center, right?" He probably knew more about this than I did.

"Yeah, yeah, of course." His stony features couldn't hide the concern written on his face. There had to be a story here somewhere.

"It's not too late, my son."

At the sound of Hugo's voice, Morgan leapt to his feet, spun, and pulled his weapons—both of them—a sword in his right hand and a spiked mace at the end of a chain in the other.

"I want nothing to do with you," he spat at Hugo.

Hugo's face reflected deep sadness but not surprise at Morgan's reaction. "Perhaps that won't always be the case. Forsake your unrighteous thoughts and turn to me, and you will have mercy."

Morgan's face reddened. He took in and expelled breath like a provoked bull. "Look at what you allowed today," he practically growled at Hugo. "Why would I want anything to do with a God who stands idle while such evil attacks?"

"Like a petulant child, you look to blame others for your poor choices." Hugo's voice boomed with authority.

Oh snap! Morgan was a half second away from a verbal beat down.

"Who are you to question my actions? My thoughts are not your thoughts, neither are your ways my ways. As the heavens are higher than the earth, so are my ways higher than your ways and my thoughts than your thoughts. It's only when you choose to surrender that you'll be set free."

Why did his words sound familiar?

After such wise counsel, I expected a look of disgust from Hugo, but his expression was filled with disappointment peppered with sadness, before he shook it off and turned his back on Morgan.

"Be gone from this place, and do not return."

As if against his will, Morgan's spine straightened and he sprinted from the property. The line of angels separated to let him through before closing ranks and obscuring him from view. In the back of my mind, I wondered why they let him go.

"That's Hugo?" Kevin's frantic whisper was a few octaves higher than his usual baritone voice.

I turned to look at him. "Yeah?" Hugo was obviously more than just a part-time trainer.

A nervous half-laugh burst out from him. "That's no ordinary hunter you have for a mentor. You've been training with—"

"I'd like to explain myself, if you don't mind, Kevin."

Hugo had turned back around and approached us. Kevin's eyes snapped up. "Yes, of course. Totally understand." His head bobbed up and down like a bobble toy.

Hugo smiled his thanks. "It's time you all returned to the realm now." He turned his gaze to the angels around us, and without a spoken command, the ones nearest the fallen hunters scooped them up. It was then I realized Kevin and I were the last ones standing—we were the only hunters still *capable* of standing.

Brilliant wings snapped out before one mighty downward motion shot the angels into the air and out of view. When my eyes returned to the ground, they landed on a familiar imposing form.

Gabriel's eight-foot frame towered over the other angelic beings. He was dressed in white linen, with a thick belt of polished gold. From it hung his new sword. New, because the one I now carried had once been his. When I used it in an attack and it blazed to life for me and me alone, he had refused to take it back—something I didn't appreciate at the time but was immensely glad for now.

Gabriel's bronze skin glowed as he made his way toward me. "My lady." A smile spread on his face as he bowed.

"Gabriel, you know that kind of talk makes me uncomfortable." My grin was just as big.

"Which is only part of the reason why I keep using it."

I rolled my eyes. When I'd first met him I'd been so intimidated by his stature I'd assumed he was incapable of humor. I'd been wrong.

"May we?" Gabriel gestured toward the two unconscious bodies I was still unknowingly guarding.

"Yeah, of course." I scurried to get out of the way as Gabriel directed two formidable angels to collect Kaitlin and Logan.

"Thanks." I looked around. "Which one is my ride?"

"That honor would go to me, little one." Another, less formal, term of endearment Gabriel liked to use for me. He extended his wing almost as if he were extending his arm to escort me. I turned to Hugo before grasping the downy feathers.

"Go be with your friends," he said. "When the dust has settled we'll have our talk."

I nodded and then reached forward without hesitation. It was time to compartmentalize. The mystery of Hugo had held for months now. A few more hours wasn't going to make a difference.

FACE THE MUSIC

*T*he pristine whiteness of the healing center's rooms and hallways was maddening.

For once, my presence here wasn't as a patient. There was a time I might have said that sounded refreshing, but considering the circumstances, it was pretty miserable.

I was acutely aware of what it had been like for my loved ones when I'd been in here. It was nerve-racking, and scary, and I didn't like one thing about it.

What I used to consider tranquil was simply irritating now. The calmness of the healing specialists was annoying. The soft music floating around the air was grating. The forced serenity of the building seemed just that, forced, and rather than capitulate to its effects, my agitated mind screamed to punch through its façade.

Oh yes, I had issues.

I paced the waiting area, still clothed fully in blood-and-ash-covered body armor. I barely registered the occasional gasp at my appearance, but a twisted part of me enjoyed messing with the tranquility of this place. A few brave souls approached me from time to time to ask if I needed any care and offered to help me get cleaned up, but I refused them without so much as breaking my march back and forth across the small space.

The only reason I was still in the waiting room was because I didn't know where to go first. All the people I cared about in this realm were strewn throughout various parts of the building, and I couldn't go to them all at once —so I'd opted not to go to any of them. I stayed were I was and uselessly paced out my concern for them all.

The last update I'd received, Kaitlin was still in surgery. Logan remained unconscious but solidly on the mend. Kevin's arm and wounds were being checked out by a specialist. Alrik was most likely still here somewhere, recovering from his injuries, but I hadn't taken the time to figure out where.

My heart was already pulled in too many different directions. The other hunters who'd fought with us were also being treated, but I didn't know them well enough to feel comfortable popping in on them.

Even though everyone would assuredly heal, I struggled with something akin to survivor's guilt for escaping relatively unscathed.

I wished Hugo were here with me.

He would know the right thing to say or do. My only peace of mind came from knowing Romona was safe and with my family on Earth.

The updates had stopped coming a while ago. Maybe the healers who had been keeping me informed assumed I'd taken some kind of action by now.

After what may have been hours of pacing, I finally succumbed to fatigue and plopped down in a chair. I pressed the heels of my hands to my eyes and rubbed hard enough for white blotches to mar the black behind my lids.

Rather than continue to wish Hugo were here, I took a deep breath and tried to figure out what he would say if he was.

My hands dropped to the armrests of the chairs. My vision took a moment to clear, and my mind did the same. Hugo would say guilt was never the answer—that it was a trick of the enemy.

Feeling that way because I was unharmed when the rest of my friends suffered in one capacity or another was not only unproductive, but also a giant waste of time. There was a difference between guilt and conviction.

Conviction prompts positive change. Guilt paralyzes us from taking steps in faith.

So, with a heavy heart, and with strength I knew I didn't possess on my own, I swallowed the guilt eating me up inside and pushed it from my mind.

As the ugly emotion subsided, conviction moved forward to take its place. It was what gave me the strength to shove myself to my feet.

Thank You, Father, I sent up in a silent prayer.

I left the waiting area in a hurry and roughly grabbed the first person in a white coat who passed me. She made a sound of surprise as she stumbled.

Whoops.

"Sheesh, I'm so sorry." I smoothed out the sleeve I'd grabbed. "That was rude. I'm a little jumpy today." I offered her a crooked smile and hoped all was forgiven.

She took a few moments to assess me before speaking. "That's okay. This place can make people a little nervous. I can't say I've ever been accosted on my way to do lab work before, but I suppose it keeps the job interesting." She offered me a tentative smile.

"Yeah, I . . . guess, I . . ." I floundered with my words. "Ah . . ."

This time she laid a comforting hand on my arm. "It's all right, truly. What can I help you with? You seem," she gave me a quick once-over, "a bit frantic. We're all here to help."

"I came in with a group of hunters a few hours ago. I was wondering if you knew where I could find out some information on their status. It's been a while since I've heard anything, and I'm not sure who to ask."

"Of course," she said with a friendly smile. She surprised me by turning and going straight to the wall. The shiny whiteness of the corridor reminded me of my room in the Redwoods before Romona helped me redecorate. She pushed a few undetected spots, and a touchscreen appeared. Her fingers flew across the screen, and images and words flashed by so quickly I didn't have time to make sense of them.

"Here we go."

The screen showed a two-dimensional layout of what I assumed was the healing center. It reminded me of the maps you see in a mall. There was even a red blinking circle saying "You are here."

"So, who is it you're looking for?"

I gave her the names of my friends, and with a few more movements there were five blinking circles on the map. Each circle held a name. Logan, Kevin, and Alrik's names were in the green circles, and Kaitlin's was in the yellow.

Turning to the woman for an explanation, I was surprised to realize she only looked about college age. Truthfully, I hadn't noticed much beyond her white coat at first. Her jet-black hair hung in a straight curtain down her back almost to her waist. We were about the same height and had similar petite builds.

"These colors indicate their level of trauma and recovery. These three," she gestured to the green circles, "are all through with their treatment and just resting and recovering. They'll be good as new in no time. This one here, Kaitlin," she said and pointed to the yellow circle, "is just recently out of surgery, but she looks to be doing fine. She'll most likely be here for at least another day. They are all cleared for visitors, though."

She turned her heart-shaped face toward me. "Would you like me to take you to one of them?"

"Yes, I'd appreciate that. Could we go see . . ." I paused. Who did I want to see first? Okay, so that was a no-brainer . . . but should I go straight to Logan's bedside? I just didn't know. Indecision weighed me down. The healer patiently waited for me to choose.

"Kaitlin. Could you take me to see her? I should check on her first."

Coward, my mind whispered.

I told it to shut it.

"Knock, knock."

Kaitlin's room was yellow. Perhaps I shouldn't have been surprised. It was a color I'd come to associate with her anyway, but all the patient rooms I've been in had whitewashed walls. I wondered how she'd swung the upgraded digs.

Perhaps she'd flipped her perfect blonde hair and batted her ridiculously long eyelashes at the right gentleman. Kaitlin was hard to say no to when she put on the charm.

For once, the thought brought a small smile to my face rather than a bolt of green-eyed jealousy. It was refreshing.

Look at me being all mature and stuff.

Kaitlin's signature smile only slipped a little as she struggled to sit up.

"Oh no, you don't." I rushed to her bedside. "I've been where you are before. Just take it easy."

I propped a few pillows behind her back so she could be more comfortable. She smiled gratefully. "Thanks. I'm still pretty sore actually."

I blew out a short breath of air. "Yeah, no kidding. That'll happen when you spend time as a demon chew toy."

She grimaced. I mirrored her expression.

"Sorry, that was insensitive."

She released a burst of laughter. "But true. I'm just glad I blacked out for most of it. What I do remember . . ." She shivered, rather than going on.

I'd been fed on by a demon before, so she didn't have to go into detail about what it was like. It was the worst experience of my life.

Dying included.

Nothing could compare to having pure evil forced into your system while simultaneously having your soul ripped apart—and that was just the mental anguish. Physically, your flesh was also being torn to shreds.

The remnants of Kaitlin's attack were visible through the bandages along the left side of her body. They were clean and free from any blood, but her neck, chest, and shoulder were wrapped like a mummy. The healers had most likely repaired as much of the muscle damage as possible, but she'd need time for parts of the tissue and skin that had been violently ripped away to regrow.

I released my own shaky breath and nodded. "Yeah, I know."

"How is your family? What happened? No one has told me anything yet. Did we kick butt or what? And Audrey . . ." her nose scrunched, "I hate to tell you this, but you're kind of nasty-looking right now. A shower, fresh clothes, and a little foundation wouldn't hurt."

Lifting a hand to my head, I winced at the crunchiness of my hair. Most likely dried demon blood. "That's gross."

Kaitlin nodded. "Truth."

I waved it off. "I've been too worried about all of you to pay much attention to my appearance. I'll get cleaned up once I've checked in on everyone."

"You sure? You could take a shower here." She pointed toward the closed door to her left. I seriously considered the offer but decided against it. I'd rather shower at home in the Redwoods when I was all done visiting.

"Nah, I'm good. I think I'll take the armor off, though. No need for it now."

I turned my back to Kaitlin and peeled the crusty fabric off my body. Dried flakes of black demon blood drifted to the floor. Kaitlin gasped behind me.

"Sorry, I know I'm making a mess. Maybe I should have just left it on." I turned with the offending fabric in my hands, trying to find a place to put it.

"Oh for goodness' sakes, just throw it away. Then get over here and let me look at your back. You're all bruised."

My thoughts had been so outwardly projected I hadn't even considered my own battle wounds. I found a waste bin in the corner and placed the soiled material in it before returning to Kaitlin.

She indicated with her finger that I should turn around. When I did, she gingerly picked up the length of my braid and placed it over my shoulder as she softly prodded my sensitive back and shoulders.

"You have three long bruises running from your shoulder down," she lifted the bottom of my shirt, "to your waist. Looks like you've been whipped."

"Claws."

"Yep, that looks about right. You should get it checked out."

I shrugged and turned to face her, settling on the bed to her right.

"Bruises will heal."

She huffed. "All right, spill then." She reached out and took my hand. Her eyes filled with renewed concern. "Is your family okay?"

I'd never been so glad to give a good report. "Yes, it looks like they're going to be fine."

I took a few minutes to fill her in on how everything had gone down, from my brother's see-through armor to the light explosion that vaporized the demons to the angels' appearance and finally to Satan's disappearing act. She was uncharacteristically quiet as I relayed the story.

"Wow. That's just . . . wow." A frown marred her pretty face. "I am so annoyed I missed it all. Boo. I had to go and get myself bit and miss all the—"

"So this is where the party is!" Kevin's friendly voice came from the doorway.

I almost said, "I was going to come visit you next," but the truth was I hadn't decided.

Kevin walked into the room with a bandaged arm in a sling. He was clean, and only a few of the cuts from the battle still remained visible. The others had already faded. All things considered, he didn't look much worse for the wear. Which hadn't been the case a few hours ago, though. I frowned at the remembrance.

"I was really worried about you guys," I said in a small voice.

"Nah." Kevin flopped his lanky body into a chair on the other side of Kaitlin's bed. "It wasn't all that bad. I've been in worse situations."

I shot him a droll look. "Really? You've fought against a few cohorts of demons with only a small handful of hunters before?" Kevin opened his mouth to reply, but I pushed on. "Without any protective barrier, not to mention unstoppable creepy evil mist-fog everywhere?"

Kevin's smile was huge. "It was kind of epic, wasn't it?"

I rolled my eyes. "Such a boy."

"I should hope so!" He choked a laugh. "Besides, it's all part of the job."

Hoping for backup, I glanced at Kaitlin. With a smile of her own, she just shrugged her uninjured shoulder.

"Well, I just spent the last few hours pacing the halls of this place like a skittish animal. So, I don't think it was all awesomesauce like you two do."

"Now you know what it's like for the rest of us when you land yourself in here. A little taste of your own medicine was about due," Kaitlin said cheerily.

"Now, Kaitlin," Kevin chastised his friend, "is that any way to speak to your own personal hero? When I found Audrey, she was guarding you and Logan like a pit-bull protecting the last bone on Earth."

"Oh yeah?" Kaitlin asked with interest. "Hey, thanks. Last thing I remember is getting chomped on by a demon."

How she was talking about her attack so casually, I didn't know. It had been violent and brutal, and the repercussions went beyond the physical. But she was her usual spritely self. She was most likely going to walk out of here without any scars.

Absently, I rubbed the spot where my own fading scar still remained. It was practically invisible now, but I could still feel phantom pain every now and then which reminded me I hadn't completely worked through the mental aspects of the attack.

"Yeah, well, I can't take all, or even much, of the credit for saving you."

Her eyebrows pinched.

"You don't know, do you?" I checked with Kevin, but he appeared just as lost as she was. Did I have a story for them! "Oh boy, you're going to really love this. I didn't actually get you away from the demons, Kaitlin, I just kind of protected you and Logan after you were brought to me."

"Oh." She paused. "Well then, who did?"

I chewed on my lower lip. "Morgan."

"What?" Kevin straightened quickly and almost fell out of his chair.

Kaitlin's eyebrows shot so high it was a wonder they didn't reach her hairline. "Yeah, what he said."

I settled back in the chair, preparing myself for an onslaught of questions I wasn't sure I could answer.

"After Logan was knocked unconscious, I managed to drag him to the side of the house. I figured I had a better chance of keeping him safe if the demons could only attack from one side. I had just made it to the house when you were overtaken, and then your screams followed."

I brought a finger to my lips and started to chew on a nail. I quickly pulled it away when I realized what I was doing. Disgusting nervous habit I wished

I'd broken already, all the more disgusting at the moment since I had dirt and demon blood under my fingernails.

"I was going to come for you, I swear. But before I had a chance, the demon was flung away. You had passed out, and Morgan had you in his arms and was running toward me. He left you with me and then disappeared back into the fighting. I didn't see him again until after the battle was won."

"But that doesn't make any sense," she said.

"You're telling me. At first I thought I was going to have to fight him to get you back. To say, I was shocked when he practically pleaded with me to take care of you would be an understatement."

"Morgan, pleading?"

"Yep." I popped the "p," mimicking her.

She stared straight ahead, her mind working to make sense of it all. I wasn't sure she would be able to. I knew I couldn't.

"I didn't know you were well acquainted with Morgan," I said.

"I'm not," Kaitlin answered quickly. "I wasn't even in the same part of the realm when he was training with Logan. I met him a few times on visits, and he's obviously, I mean, you know he's like, um, well you *know*." I thought her face darkened a shade. Oh, what I wouldn't give for her to have emotion-revealing hair like mine right now.

I forced my lips to stay neutral. "I know what?"

"Never mind."

"No, really, what exactly is he? Do you mean British?"

She shot me an irritated look. "He's not exactly the ugliest guy I've ever seen."

"Oh, now I see what you're trying to say. You think he's a hot piece of man candy." How I delivered that line with a straight face is a mystery even to myself.

"Audrey," Kaitlin all but shrieked. "That is *not* what I said." Yep, there was definite redness staining her cheeks. It shouldn't have given me as much pleasure as it did. "He's like completely messed up, and evil. Yeah, he's totally evil now. Evil is *not* hot."

Kevin's eyes ping-ponged between the two of us.

"Hey." I held up my hands in defense. "I never said it was. I was just trying to interpret your girl-coded speak."

It was her turn to huff, and she folded her arms across her chest. "Well, you interpreted incorrectly."

"If you say so," I replied in a singsong voice.

A look of discomfort and disapproval had settled on his face. "Well, maybe that's why the H . . . Hugo just let him go," Kevin wondered out loud.

"Because Kaitlin thinks he's hot?"

"No, of course not. Because he rescued her." Kevin was clearly annoyed at me now too.

"Hugo? Your hermit mentor?" Kaitlin's face twisted even further. "What was he doing there? Okay, now I'm beyond confused."

Kevin's face morphed from annoyed to smug. "Oh, I haven't even gotten to the best part yet, Kaitlin. I'm not allowed to say in front of Audrey, but when she leaves I'll tell you all about it."

"Hey now. No fair. No talking behind my back."

"It's not talking behind your back when we tell you we're going to be doing it," Kevin argued. "Besides, once you have a talk with your—" he used his fingers as quotation marks, "—'mentor,' I'm looking forward to hearing more about it from you."

"Cryptic much?"

He laughed at my obvious irritation. "Trust me, this is a good one."

I didn't know whether to laugh or be annoyed. "On a scale of clueless to extremely stupid, how dumb am I going to feel when I find out this big mystery?"

His smile couldn't have gotten bigger. "What are a few steps above extremely stupid?"

"Oh, great." I tried to run a hand through my hair but met crusty resistance. Yuck.

"Now, I have to know what's going on. Audrey, skedaddle." Kaitlin made a shooing motion with her hands.

"Are you kidding me? I just spent hours out of my mind with worry about you guys, and you're kicking me out of your room so you can talk about me behind my back."

"Audrey," Kaitlin went on, "we've already established it's not behind your back, because you not only know we are going to be talking about you, but you know what we are going to be talking about."

"You both stink." I stuck my tongue out at them as I rose from my chair. "I'm sure there are other people in this place just dying for me to visit. I'm going to go grace them with my presence instead."

"Oh yes, you do that. I can think of one, how did you put it? Hot piece of man candy who is probably just dying for a visit."

Too embarrassed to ask her for specifics, I scurried toward the door.

"Oh, Audrey," she called before I slipped out.

I turned.

"You've got a little something-something going on here." She indicated the hair on the right side of her head.

I pulled a chunk of my matted hair forward to find it fuchsia. "Shoot," I muttered under my breath as I left the room. Kaitlin and Kevin's laughter echoed all the way down the hall.

The room was empty. The rumpled bedding made it obvious it had been recently occupied, but Logan was no longer there.

I stared at the wrinkled sheets. It had taken me several silent pep talks to make it this far, and finding the room empty left me with a hollow feeling inside.

Logically I knew Logan wasn't one to sit around with nothing to do. Heck, half the time he didn't even make it to the healing center to get his wounds taken care of in the first place. But I couldn't help but feel like he'd purposefully left without waiting to see me.

The comfort zone we created while fighting together always seemed to dissolve when we returned to our realm. Perhaps it was because things were just simpler on Earth. We were there for a job. We protected people, we fought the bad guys, there wasn't much room to explore emotions, and accidental contact couldn't result in exposed feelings. Our interactions, even as imperfect as they were on Earth, became downright dysfunctional in our realm.

I'd hoped it would be different this time. Apparently not.

I let out a disappointed sigh.

"He checked himself out about thirty minutes ago." I jumped at the sound of Jonathon's voice. He stood in the doorway wearing a white lab coat, arms crossed over his chest and a frown marring his handsome face. "Seemed to me like he was in quite a rush to get out of here."

"Oh, well . . ." How exactly did he expect me to respond to that? "Logan has never really liked staying in the healing center longer than absolutely needed."

"Funny you should mention it. I wondered about that myself. Thought it was kind of weird how antsy he was around here. The center usually has a calming effect on people." Jonathon took a deep breath and then ran a hand though his brown hair, leaving a few strands out of place. "I ignored it for a while, but something about this whole situation wouldn't settle with me. So, I checked his records."

"You did what?" The tone of my voice was borderline shrill. I stepped back. What whole situation? What was he talking about?

"See the thing is, he used to have a typical pattern for a hunter. He came in regularly after missions to get checkups and always stayed the recommended amount of time before leaving, but then something changed."

"Should you be telling me this? Isn't there some patient-doctor confidentiality thing you should be adhering to?" Without realizing it, I'd taken a defensive posture with my arms crossed over my chest and my chin notched up. Jonathon plodded on, heedless of my body language.

"He rarely comes in after assignments anymore, and only if he's severely injured. And rather than waiting the full time to recuperate, he jets almost as soon as he's assigned a room. Do you happen to know what changed?"

I didn't actually. Jonathon's behavior was accusatory, but I didn't know why. Rather than answer I just shook my head.

"I have an idea it has something to do with you."

"Me?"

He nodded. "There was an obvious turning point in his patterns. It all started after you ended up in here for the first time. I think his aversion to this place is because of you."

I stared at him slack-jawed for a full ten seconds before responding. "What you're saying doesn't even make sense. I don't work here."

"No, you don't. But I do."

"So?"

"So maybe there's a reason Logan isn't too keen to run into me."

Oh. Suddenly I knew what this was about.

"And what do you believe that reason to be exactly?" I asked wearily.

"That's actually what I'd like you to tell me."

Silence stretched between us. Part of me wished we could keep avoiding this conversation. The other part knew it was already way overdue.

"You told me nothing was going on between the two of you."

I sighed. "There wasn't. I mean there isn't. I mean nothing serious or anything."

"Nothing serious?"

"I didn't mean it like that." I brought my hands up to scrub my face.

"Then how did you mean it?" When I just stood there staring at him, he went on. "Why did you request a new mentor, Audrey?"

"That is none of your business," I snapped. I was not about to go into those details with him when I hadn't been willing to talk about it with anyone else, not even my closest friends. When hurt filled his eye, I instantly regretted my harsh tone.

"I think maybe it is," he stated softly. "Have you just been leading me on this whole time?"

The words made me want to scream. "What? Of course, not."

"I didn't want to believe that at first either, but the more I look back, the more little things add up. I feel like a complete idiot. Here I thought we were working toward something really meaningful, but all I ever was to you was a nice placeholder until what you really wanted came to his senses."

Did we have to talk about this here—like this? My brain was muddled at best, and he deserved so much more than a casual brush-off.

"Jonathon, it wasn't like that." I reached a hand out to do . . . well . . . I wasn't sure exactly. He flinched away from my touch.

"Just don't." His words came out gruff and harsh as he held up a hand to ward me off. He'd never spoken to me in that tone before. "Just tell me how long it's been going on. How long have you been with him behind my back?"

I sucked in a sharp breath of air. His words were hurtful and full of spite, and whatever kernel of truth might have existed in his version of events was completely overshadowed by the falsehoods he'd convinced himself of.

"We're not together," I argued almost desperately, but my own words from before were incriminating enough. *Go ahead and shove me into someone else's arms. Just don't be upset when I don't fall back into yours,* I'd yelled at Logan in front of Jonathon. It was no wonder he felt betrayed.

He let out a harsh laugh. "Oh yeah, you expect me to believe that? You expect me to believe you don't have feelings for him?"

I reminded myself Jonathon spoke from a place of deep hurt, but he was getting dangerously close to making me lose my cool. Taking a deep breath and holding it for a count of three helped me simmer down.

"This," I gestured between the two of us, "is about us."

"Let me guess, you're about to tell me 'it's not you, it's me'?"

"No, that wasn't what I was going to say. That's a stupid saying anyway." There was no coming back from what I was about to say. "We're just not right together."

"How can you even know? There was never a real chance for us to figure it out. There was always someone standing in the way."

I opened my mouth, but then stopped for a moment. Was he right? Even if Logan hadn't been physically present, had the idea of him ruined what could have been with Jonathon? Had I ever truly given the two of us a chance? Maybe I *had* strung Jonathon along. If Logan had never been, would I have learned to be happy with Jonathon?

They were impossible questions to answer. The reality was there was a Logan, and even though I wasn't with him, might never be with him, my feelings for him were as real as he was.

"Jonathon, I don't know what you want me to say right now."

"Yeah." He looked away so I was staring at his profile. "I guess a small part of me hoped . . ." The unfinished sentence turned stale. "I never really meant anything to you."

"No, Jonathon, that's not true. You're amazing." I recaptured his gaze and wouldn't let go. "You're thoughtful and caring. You cherish the people you're closest to. You work so hard to let others know they are important and have worth. You make me smile and laugh, and you've lifted my spirit during some of my darkest times."

With each declaration, something in his gaze deadened, and I couldn't understand why.

"You're one of the most important people to me," I finished. It was true. It was all true. Even though I had finally acknowledged to myself that what I felt for him wasn't what it should be for us to be a couple, all those things were still so true.

"And yet you're willing to throw it all away?"

I could have argued that he was the one forcing my hand, but the truth was if he hadn't, I would have eventually worked up the courage to end things between us. My heart ached. What had I gotten us both into? "I don't want to throw you away." I took a step toward him. He countered with a step back.

"But you don't want to be with me anymore?"

"Not in the way you want us to be together."

"Meaning, you're with Logan."

He was so fixated on that. I let out a bitter laugh. "No, I already told you, Logan and I aren't together." I gestured to the empty room around us. "He didn't even want to wait around for me to visit him." My heart pinched.

"But you want to be with him?"

Why was he putting me through this? Did it make him feel better to see me miserable?

"Honestly, I don't know. If you really want to know, I won't lie. Yes, I feel something for him. But in our case I don't know that it's ever going to be enough."

His eyes carried a strange mix of sadness and bitterness as he held my gaze for a moment longer. "It would have been enough for me."

And with that he turned and left me standing in the empty room, wondering how I'd messed up so badly and if I'd just seen someone I cared about walk, not only out of the room, but out of my life.

THE EFFECTS OF THE WIND

*N*umb.
That's what I was.

My feet carried me out of the healing center and through the city, but the active part of my brain had disengaged. I didn't remember entering the training center, or walking down the hallways and into the locker room, but that's where I found myself.

Of all the places I could have gone, I found myself in the almost deserted building at one of the few times I didn't have to be there.

I stood staring at the lockers and shook my head as if I hoped to dislodge something. I'd long ago lost track of time, but it must have been just shy of the early morning hours. The smart thing to do would be go back to my room and get some much-needed rest, but instead I stood under the shower spray, letting the hot water massage some of the pent-up tension from my body.

For the first few minutes, I stood there watching the red-and-black stained water circle the drain as the battle filth was finally washed clean from my skin and hair. When the water ran clear, I robotically finished my shower. Occasionally my thoughts attempted to stick on a subject for deeper introspection, but when that happened I focused on the mundane task at hand.

Numb.

I wanted to remain numb for a little while longer.

When I was finished and dressed, I stared at my reflection and wasn't able to hold onto the numbness anymore. The image staring back at me spoke of hidden pain. Lack of sleep and overexertion made my face pale and gaunt in the harsh lighting. I wasn't standing tall, but rather hunched in upon myself as if protecting my vital organs from attack. My numbness cracked and splintered like a dropped mirror. Pieces of it fell away to expose the unattractive backing hidden beneath the shiny façade.

The reflection in the mirror confused me. We'd been victorious over the enemy the night before. Through a miracle of the Creator we defeated Satan and his demon army. At the brink of certain defeat, I'd personally borne witness to the mighty hand of God through His supernatural power and a legion of conquering warrior angels. And it wasn't as if that was only the battle won. I had assurance of my family's ongoing protection against evil.

So why wasn't I standing tall in the triumph I'd witnessed with my own eyes? Why instead did I look—and feel—so beat down? A celebration was in order, yet instead, I fought the desire to cower in a darkened corner.

Am I broken?

In disgust or weakness—I wasn't sure which—I turned away from the damaged image and woodenly trekked down the halls to the far recesses of the training center. In a short time the building would fill with hunters, and I wasn't in the mood to be disturbed. I headed to one of the gyms tucked in the corners of the center. No one would stumble across me there. Musty air greeted me when I pushed open the doors to an abandoned gym.

"Solitude isn't a bad thing as long as it's being used for the right reasons."

I yelled and tripped over my feet. I laid a hand on my beating heart as if the pressure alone could slow down its speed.

"Hugo, where did you come from? This gym was empty."

His fluffy hair waved back and forth with the movement of his shaking head. "No, I was always here. You're still learning to recognize my presence." He gestured to the middle of the padded floor. "Come, let's talk. We've much to discuss."

I nodded in agreement and settled myself across from him. He sat with his legs crossed and waited patiently for me.

"I don't even know where to start," I confessed.

"How about if we talk about what you are doing here? You want to be alone right now. Why?"

I had a strong sense Hugo understood why even better than I did myself, but I searched for the reasons behind my actions.

"When things get overwhelming, I tend to pull away from people."

He nodded his agreement. "Why do you think that is?"

Pulling on a strand of my hair, I looked at the floor. "I just don't feel like putting on a front for people, I suppose."

"Why would you feel you need to do that?"

I shrugged again. He slowly forced me to verbalize what I had never really wanted to think too deeply about before. "I don't know. I guess it feels like people expect me to act a certain way, and sometimes I just don't want to feel like I'm trying to be someone I'm not."

"Who do you think people expect you to be?"

"Someone . . . more."

"More?" It was an invitation to continue rather than an inquiry.

"Someone more put together. Someone stronger. Sometimes I feel so fragile, and I guess I don't want anyone to see that part of me. I certainly don't like feeling breakable."

Hugo nodded as if he understood perfectly the imperfect explanation I'd just given him. "Audrey, I don't want you to feel that way."

"Neither do I," I admitted, my voice small. I watched my finger draw patterns on the dark blue padding beneath me.

"You weren't created to be alone. Seeking solitude isn't always a bad thing. In the stillness you can find intimacy with your Creator. But it is downright destructive when you pull away simply to hide yourself."

Shame slammed into me hard, because that was exactly what I'd repeatedly done.

Hugo's unexpectedly sharp tone cut into my thoughts. "Stop it." He slapped a hand on the floor between us. "What you are doing to yourself right now, I want you to stop."

"What?" My gaze snapped up and connected with Hugo's. A fire burned behind his denim-washed irises.

"You're letting yourself fall into a shame spiral when my words are meant to correct and teach, not disparage. I'm giving you hope, Audrey. Whether mighty or small, the size of your strength matters not, because you have my wellspring to pull from, and it is unending."

"H-how did you know what I was feeling?" Perhaps it had been written across my face.

But a part of me knew that wasn't the case.

The lines on Hugo's weathered face softened as he reached out to lay a hand atop my own. Power poured into me from the point of contact and rushed up my arm and throughout the rest of my body, filling me with supernatural warmth that made my blood buzz.

It validated the reality of what Hugo was trying to tell me.

"Audrey, I always know how you are feeling. Up here," he pointed his finger at my head, and then lowered it to my chest, "and in there. I've acted as your trainer these last several months, but I've always been so much more than that. I am your comforter, your helper, the still small voice inside. I am the Spirit within and without. I am the one who knows you best and loves you most. I make intercession for you to the Father when your words fail you."

He looked at me with meaning. Willing me to catch on. And I did.

"You're the Holy Spirit." I knew my eyes were full of wonder.

His smile confirmed what I didn't need confirmation of.

"Kevin was right. I am completely dense. I mean, I think I might have known, but not really. You know?"

His laughter caught me off guard. "No, this was the moment orchestrated for you to become aware. If it would have benefited you to know earlier, you would have. And if it would have benefited you to remain unaware for a while longer, you would have remained so. Nothing in my kingdom is ever too late or too early."

"But why now?" I was still struck a little dumb by the revelation that my mentor had been one of the Godhead this whole time.

"You've seen my power work in many ways. You've been physically, mentally, and spiritually trained by me. You've even seen my power on Earth, although you haven't recognized it as such. And there are times I am like the wind." He lifted his hand and moved it rhythmically back and forth, as if dancing with the air. "You can't see the wind, but you can see its effects. It's time you fully grasp what my power is so you can take hold of it and use it for yourself. So you can be assured of what can be accomplished through my power. So you know whatever battle you enter, you aren't entering it on your own strength, but mine. You are fully equipped to fight the enemy, because I will never leave or forsake you." A fire burned in his eyes.

"Wow. Okay, I'll admit. This is all a little much to take in." I pressed the heels of my hands into my eyes and rubbed. I'd always known something was different about Hugo, but it had never even crossed my mind it could be this big. For all intents and purposes, I'd been training and spending my days with God without even realizing it. "Can we start small and work our way up?" I asked.

He chuckled, already knowing how I processed information.

"You said I've seen your power on Earth but didn't recognize it. Are you talking about something other than the battle with my family? The way you poofed those demons out of existence was pretty awesome, by the way."

He nodded. "Audrey, go over to the wall and pick up a sword for me, will you?"

"Ah, sure." I rose and walked over to the weapons, looking back at him before selecting one. "Anything in particular you want me to grab?"

"No, your choice."

"O-kay." I reached a hand out toward a long katana, a curved, slender, single-edged blade with a squared guard and a long grip to accommodate two hands. I lifted it from the wall with my right hand. The instant my left joined my right on the grip, the blade was set ablaze. Dropping the sword immediately, I jumped back as it clattered to the floor.

"What the . . ." I turned frantic eyes to Hugo.

"The sword was always only the vessel of power, not the source."

My mind spun. "You mean *I'm* the reason my sword burns like dry kindling?"

"Yes and no. More accurately, it's my power working through you that makes your weapon unique." He indicated the katana lying harmlessly on the floor at my feet. "That was my holy fire burning along the blade. Without me it's just like any other weapon. In one way or another, I've been with you on every step of your journey. That is just one of the ways I've come alongside you."

Questions swirled in my head. They ran so quickly through my mind I had difficulty settling on just one. I grasped the first one I could hold on to.

"Why are you telling me this now?"

"Because now you need to know. There are hardships in your future unlike any you have faced before, and you will need to be reminded of where your strength comes from when you feel you have nothing more to give."

A shiver ran down my spine. Those were not comforting words. "I don't like the sound of that."

"No, I don't suppose anyone would. Come sit back down with me. We have more to discuss."

I looked down at the sword at my feet, hesitant to return it to its place.

"Don't worry, you can pick it up. I've only imbued your angelic sword with my holy fire in any sort of ongoing way. That was just for the sake of demonstration." With a soft smile Hugo returned to his spot on the mat.

I returned the katana to the wall without incident and took a seat across from Hugo once again.

"Why doesn't everyone's sword, you know, do the lite bright thing? Why just mine?"

"Each one of my children has their own set of special gifts. This is just one of yours. There is a plan and a purpose for it, just as there is a reason you've been chosen to be a hunter. The road you've been set on is not an easy one, my dear Audrey, but it is a good one. And I don't intend to let you move forward without everything you need to succeed."

"Do we all have hard roads to travel, or am I just extra lucky?"

He chuckled, even though I hadn't meant it to be funny. "Wide is the gate and broad is the road that leads to destruction, but small is the gate and narrow the road that leads to life."

"Say what?"

"In other words, though your path may seem hard at times, it brings the greatest reward. Some may choose to take what appears to be the easy way, but in the end they've only hurt themselves. The Father cares for you deeply, and although you will face challenges, it is in the furnace that your character will be refined."

"Character? Your talk of challenges and difficulties and furnaces is making character sound a little overrated right now." Uncrossing my legs, I hugged my knees to my chest.

"Ah, but your noble character has brought you this far. I am so proud of the woman you are and the woman you will become. Now is not the time to lose heart, dear one."

I chewed my lower lip. My hands were clammy. "You're freaking me out a little right now."

"That's not my intention, but I do want you to be prepared. None of my children are promised an existence without trials, but with me, there will never be a trial you cannot overcome. And Audrey, there is beauty and happiness in your future as well. But if you aren't prepared for there to be hardships, you'll easily fall into a pit of bitterness when they come." His eyebrows pinched in concern.

"Is my family really safe now?"

"They are doing well." I didn't miss that he hadn't answered my question. "I would tell you not to worry about them, but before you can do that, you have to understand and believe they each have their own demons to battle." He lifted a hand to stop the words desperately clawing to burst from my mouth.

I wanted to help them fight those demons.

"Their paths are different from your own, and yes, there are times you will be able to come alongside them to help, but you will never be able to shield them from every hurt the world may throw at them. Even if it were possible, doing so would be a disservice to them. You can care deeply about someone but still trust the Father will ultimately take care of them. Until you surrender their lives over to me, you will be trapped in a cycle of worry and anxiety over them."

"I don't want to be caught in that cycle." I lowered my eyes.

"Then don't be."

"I'm not sure I know how not to."

His gentle finger tilted my chin and expressive eyes met my gaze. The smile he offered was neither happy nor sad, but it was fleeting. His other hand hovered over my shoulder before dropping back to his lap. "You fight against what you can't change with what you know to be true. When anxieties surrounding your family members crop up, give them over to me. They are not your burden to bear. When you don't let go, you are really saying you don't believe I can work in their lives. Those chains of unbelief will keep you captive. You'll remain stagnant in your journey, unable to move forward as you were intended. You'll miss out on the riches waiting for you."

My thoughts turned introspective. It wasn't as if I didn't want to do exactly what he said, but it seemed so difficult. Part of me was hardwired to worry about my loved ones, but I knew concern and care for them shouldn't turn me into a ball of anxiety.

I nodded. "I'll try to remember that."

"I'll remind you," he promised. This time his hand did land on my shoulder, giving it a squeeze before letting go. The squeeze packed a punch of power behind it!

"Why didn't anyone tell me who you were?" I asked next. Kevin knew who he was right away. Others must have recognized him as well.

"Before you saw me with your family on Earth, I never revealed myself to anyone when we were together. If you think back, you'll remember times where you thought I was overlooked. It was because others literally couldn't see me."

"Well, that explains the gauntlet technicians. I always thought they were really rude to you." Looking back, I almost laughed. "Wow, I wonder if they thought I was talking to myself all the time? And then none of my friends knew who you were either. But why keep your true identity a secret?"

"I wanted you to get to know me without being intimidated by who I was. Your heart needed time to know me, to trust me, in order to fully accept who I am. You may be slightly overwhelmed right now, but you're handling all of this with a great amount of maturity. Your heart and head were finally ready for this mystery to be revealed."

"I wouldn't have been—" One look at Hugo reminded me that he knew me better than I knew myself. "Okay, yeah, I probably would have been weirded out." I took in a big breath of air and held it a moment before blowing it out. "Where do we go from here?"

"Why, forward of course. Always forward."

"And that means . . . ?"

"You've completed your formal training."

"I have?" My heart picked up its cadence and I resisted the urge to pump my fist up and down in the air. *Score one for the tiny female!*

"Yes, you have. I'm very happy with your progress. You did exceedingly well yesterday evening."

"Does this mean we won't be training together anymore?" I deflated a little.

"Not in the same way we have been the last several months. You've moved on to a different type of training. More like a buddy system than a mentor-mentee relationship."

"Oh, good. So, we'll be—"

"You'll be working mostly with your grandmother."

That could be fun. And challenging. But mostly fun. Romona was, after all, my best friend. Deep inside, I'd sometimes wondered if I would ever move on to the next step. "Oh, that will be good. I—"

"And also with Logan, of course."

"What?" My heart started to chug like a freight train. This had 'bad idea' written all over it. "You can't be serious."

"As a heart attack, my dear."

I blinked. Twice. "Did you just make a joke?"

"That I did."

"You can't honestly believe training with Logan again is a good idea." I scoffed . . . at the Holy Spirit.

Whoops!

Having known him as only Hugo for so long, it was easy to forget whom I really spoke to. My eyes did a quick check of the ceiling.

Phew.

No thunderclouds to strike me down with lightning.

Hugo chuckled. "No, I don't think it, I know it. You push each other to be better. And the level of care you have for one another means you will always look out for each other."

"But . . . we . . . it's terribly complicated." I bit my lower lip.

A small smile appeared on Hugo's face. "Do you honestly think I don't know every facet of your feelings for one another?"

I didn't have to look at my hair to know it had changed colors. "Do I have to answer that?"

His response was a full smile.

"In the past, Logan and I have been nothing but a disaster together." I abandoned my lips and started chewing on a fingernail. I didn't even care. This news was worthy of a good fingernail chew.

"You've both matured since then. At least, somewhat." That was a back-handed compliment if I'd ever heard one.

I fell back on the mat and let out a pain-filled groan. "Why are you doing this to me?"

"I'm sure there will come a day when you will thank me for this. You two have some things to work through, but once you do, I have no doubt you will be a force to be reckoned with."

I sat up so quickly I had to throw a hand out to steady myself. "Like as in a force together?" I interlinked my fingers. "Like you know," I lowered my voice to a whisper, "together, together? Or just like a good fighting team together?"

The volume of his laugh startled me. "Oh, wouldn't you like to know?"

"Well, yeah." I threw my hands in the air. "Why do you think I asked?"

"Always trying to read ahead in the story. I'm sorry to say you're going to have to take this one a page at a time."

"You laugh at me a lot, you know," I grumbled.

"It's because you amuse me so." His gentle hand rested on my shoulder. "It endears you to me even more, Audrey. You are so uniquely you. But now I must go."

He rose smoothly to his feet and started toward the door.

"What? You're leaving me? Now?" I scrambled to my feet much less gracefully.

Don't leave me!

He stopped and turned back to me. "My lovely daughter, I have never left you, nor will I ever. I'm simply making myself less obvious for the time being." He opened his arms, and I rushed forward in an instant.

The arms I had once considered so frail wrapped around me with strength. The Holy Spirit's power buzzed from my toes to my head. I closed my eyes and burrowed my face in his chest, determined never to let go, but after a moment the weight of his arms disappeared.

Looking up, I found myself standing in the gym alone. Yet Hugo's energy still hummed in every cell and fiber of my being.

I was alone, but not really. I stared at nothing, absorbing the wonder until the sound of a new voice broke my trance.

"I had a feeling I'd find you hiding out in one of these deserted gyms."

SOMETHING STOLEN

"*L*ogan."

Logan strode into the room, only stopping with a few feet of separation between us. He looked every bit the part of male perfection.

My breath caught.

His hair was *finally* trimmed up a bit—thank goodness there was no danger of me having to take a scissors to a potential man-bun anymore—but still on the long side the way I liked it. There was a healthy glow to his sunkissed skin, and a spark shone in his electric blue eyes.

My eyes swept over his body before I could stop myself. He wore those dark-washed jeans and faded graphic tees better than anyone I knew.

Yum. No, shoot, stop it.

I forced my eyes to remain on his face.

"I've been looking for you," he said.

A delicious shiver shook my body at the deep timbre of his voice.

Stop it. I ordered myself again. *We are not happy with him.*

Why was I referring to myself in the plural? I needed to pull it together.

"Funny, because that's what I was doing when I stopped by your room at the healing center. You'd checked yourself out early, though. I was told I'd just missed you." I didn't temper my accusatory tone.

Rather than looking properly chastised, Logan smiled. A real smile. A rarity for him, so of course it made me uneasy.

"Really? Well, that's very interesting." He took a predatory step closer.

I stepped back. "Hardly." I rolled my eyes, avoiding his—they were starting to do funny things to my stomach. "You'd been knocked unconscious during the battle. The least I could do was pop my head in to make sure yours was still working correctly."

"Is that so?"

"Yes. But you weren't even there." I wasn't sure why I felt the need to remind him again.

"I'm sorry to have missed you."

"Are you?" I challenged.

His eyes softened. "Always."

His candidness took me aback. Was he riding high from his little Earth-induced infatuation with me? I narrowed my eyes.

As much as I hated to hear the words, I had to know. "So, I, ah, just wanted to check and make sure you're okay now with the, um," I waved my arm awkwardly between the two of us, "you know, the ah, issue you were having back on Earth."

Logan cocked his head and the side of his mouth. "Exactly what issue are you referring to?"

"You know, the *thing* you were struggling with down there." I flushed as I remembered *The Incident*. Then gritted my teeth. "The thing I was supposed to be helping you out with because you were having some self-control issues."

Logan drew his eyebrows together as if he were trying hard to figure out what I was saying. I didn't know if it was sincere or simply a ploy to make me uncomfortable. If the latter, I was going to make sure he paid dearly for my discomfort.

I huffed. "Okay, fine. I can't believe I even have to ask this. Your self-control problem specifically pertaining to your attraction to me. Remember how you could hardly keep your hands off me? I just wanted to make sure that was all squared away now that we're back. Because you're still acting a little strange. Is that specific enough for you?"

My hands fisted.

"Oh, that. Yes, I believe that's something I have worked out now. I appreciate your concern." He was mocking me with that smooth smile of his.

"Logan, seriously, this is not funny. I don't *appreciate* being laughed at."

"Do you know how adorable you are when you get annoyed?"

Argh, not this again! Aggravation wrestled with confusion over his words. Why was he saying this?

He wasn't done. "You get this cute little scrunched line between your eyebrows that makes you impossible to take seriously. And you put your hand on your hip like you really mean business. It makes you almost irresistible."

"I do not do that!" I took a quick look down and found I did in fact have a hand planted firmly on one hip. I quickly straightened my arm. "Um, I guess this means you *are* still having problems in the area of, um," I used my hand to gesture again because words failed me. Adorable? Irresistible? Was he on something?

"I wouldn't call it a problem. Well, to be honest, I did at first. In the beginning I thought it was a huge problem."

I looked away. *Geez, don't be scared to tell me what you really think.* But I wasn't really expecting where he took the conversation next.

"I was your mentor and constantly struggling to stay professional during training because I didn't know whether I wanted to yell at you or kiss you silent sometimes."

"Kiss me?" I squeaked out. "Mentor? Wait, I was just talking about the most recent issue. Are you really going there right now? Wait, where exactly are you going?"

Do. Not. Hyperventilate.

Logan plowed ahead as if he hadn't heard a thing I said. "And then you took matters into your own hands the first time we went to Earth and the problem, as you call it, only got worse, making me think we were bonded and you'd be stuck with a broken person when you deserved so much more. But now that I've acknowledged the *problem*, I don't see it that way anymore."

I wished my voice wasn't such a squeak. "You don't?"

"No, I don't."

"Then what do you consider it now?" Was it getting hot in here?

"A challenge."

"A challenge?"

Logan nodded. He took a few leisurely steps forward, invading my personal space in a way that should have caused me to move back. But my brain was cycling the words *kiss, irresistible,* and *challenge,* and it wasn't functioning beyond that.

"Yes, Audrey, a challenge. Something worth waiting for. Something worth fighting for."

"Waiting? Fighting?"

"Yes," he nodded slowly, "waiting and fighting."

I stared back. My mind was blown. He was saying everything I wanted him to say but had never expected to hear.

Warm hands reached forward to cup my cheeks. Tingles of his emotions mixed with my own, and as always, it was difficult to discern which were his and which were my own.

"You're worth waiting for, Audrey. You're worth fighting for. I should have been clearer about that a long time ago. I'm sorry I waited so long."

With a half-step forward and a guided tilt of my chin, his lips descended on mine without first garnering permission. He tasted of peppermint as he gently coaxed my response. A hand left my cheek to wrap around my waist and pull me closer. The onslaught of heightened emotions, both Logan's and my own, was a leap beyond overwhelming—something I'd never experienced before. I'd been kissed, but this—this was something more than a simple kiss.

As my lips responded to his invitation, my arms, which had been hanging limply at my sides, found their way to him without thought.

One hand boldly inched up his neck to find its home in his hair, while the other bunched the material of his T-shirt at his waist. He made a pleased noise deep in his chest as he deepened the kiss. As connected as we were, I was pleased he was pleased and returned his fervor without further thought and as if nothing else existed.

Each brush and pressure of Logan's lips quickened my heart a fraction more than the one before. I moved forward and slanted my head back in a silent plea for more. Logan's hand tenderly cradled the back of my head as I forced mine not to fist in his amazingly soft hair.

I was impossibly out of control, but I got the sense Logan had never been more in control. Each stroke of his hand along my back and each guided move of my neck perfectly complemented the others to invade my senses without pushing us too far.

When he finally tried to pull back from our kiss, I greedily refused to relinquish my hold, my lips unsatisfied with the length of their taste. He only got out the first syllable of my name before my treacherous hand fisted in his hair and brought him back to me.

I sighed into his lips when he gave up his fight and obliged me for a few more precious moments. The hand on my lower back pulled me impossibly closer. I tilted my head to stay connected to him.

Logan's emotions flowed through me freely like blood through veins, and the first indication that he was losing control seeped through the bond. I both welcomed and feared his release of control. But before that moment occurred, he ripped himself from my grasp.

"Don't."

He held a hand up as if to bar me from coming any closer.

We stood, staring at each other. Our breaths quickened. As his arm lowered and Logan's mouth quirked in a small smile, it hit me. I gasped and it echoed throughout the empty gym.

"You bonded us," I yelled the accusation at him. My arm moved of its own volition. I slapped him hard across the side of the face, and then I stumbled a few shaky steps back.

He didn't move as the reddening spot appeared across his face. His smile only grew, as if the mark appearing on his cheek were a badge of honor rather than shame.

"Why yes, I'm fairly certain we are bonded now. It probably would have happened with even less . . . shall we say 'energy'? But I appreciate your vigor. Rules out any chances of it not taking."

My eyes grew large. My nose flared as I sucked in a breath of outrage. *Vigor?* He had some nerve.

"Logan, this isn't like kidnapping a date for prom. This is *forever* we're talking about. This is serious."

My mind raced with what I knew about being bonded in this realm—the heavenly equivalent to engagement could be made with just one simple kiss. It was hard enough when we only *thought* we'd bonded, but this time it was for real. We'd feel more connected to each other now than ever. There might be side effects my currently muddled mind couldn't remember.

One thing I knew for sure, it was going to be extremely hard to unstick myself from Logan.

Was that what I really wanted? I didn't know. Since ditching him as my trainer I'd not allowed myself to get this far down the rabbit hole of thought in our relationship. I wasn't sure if we were suited even to date, let alone spend the rest of eternity together.

I think I'm going to be sick.

"Kidnapping a prom date? Is that a thing? Wait, are you saying you want me to take you on a date first?" Brows drawn, he appeared genuinely confused. Granted, it wasn't a strong analogy, but it was the only one I could come up with on the spot.

"Ha," I let out a bitter laugh. "Yes, dates do usually come before you commit yourself to someone for eternity . . . but that is not the point here. Do you even fully grasp what you've just done? And without my consent?"

"I'm well aware of the implications and ramifications of my actions." The smile, which had slipped a fraction, amped back up.

Logan leaned a shoulder against a practice dummy and crossed his arms smugly. "And I don't know if you can claim there was no consent. You could have pushed me away immediately if you wanted, but that's not what happened, did it?" His raised brows dared me to deny it.

"But that . . . it was . . ." I sputtered and stuttered until finding my true voice. "It doesn't matter how I reacted. I wasn't given a choice." I stomped my foot for emphasis. A move which surprised me, and only seemed to ramp up Logan's amusement.

"Oh, I believe your reaction matters a great deal when it comes to bonding."

I took two steps forward with the intent to acquaint his cheek with the palm of my hand again, but he caught it mid swing and used my momentum against me, spinning me so my back was pressed tightly against his chest. I found myself trapped in his arms.

I struggled in his hold, but he dodged all my moves. Not surprising, since I'd learned most of them from him.

"Agh!" I shouted. "Will you just let me go already?"

But he kept me immobile, grasping my forearms and pulling them tight against my chest. His bare hands against my arms caused his emotions to leak into me, and they caused me to squirm even more. As my frustration built, so did my confusion over whether I wanted to escape his hold or burrow into it.

"What is wrong with you?" I managed to get out. "You're aloof, then sweet, then angry, and now professing your undying love for me. You switch from hot to cold like you're changing a pair of shoes. How do you expect me to take anything you say seriously?"

"No more flipping between hot and cold. Only hot now."

"You drive me insane."

"But only in the best way possible."

"You're delusional."

"I don't think so."

"What delusional person ever does?" I pulled against his hold.

"Audrey," Logan whispered into my ear, his soft breath tickling its fine hairs. "Don't you think it's time we stopped fighting and just faced what is right in front of us?"

"What are you talking about?" I stilled. I knew exactly what he was talking about. I just didn't want to concede.

"Our kiss proved our mutual attraction toward one another. I may have surprised you with it, but it wasn't forced. You reacted as passionately to me as I did to you."

"So? You can be attracted to someone and not want to be bonded to him forever. You can be attracted to someone and not be in love with him."

If I had been facing him, I would have been screaming into his face. His surprise and sudden sadness crashed into me through the link. It was quiet after I spoke. Only my ragged breaths were echoed throughout the gym.

"You're right," Logan said softly into my ear. "Attraction isn't everything. But I needed to prove there was at least that. For now I'll wait."

"Wait for what?"

"Wait to see if you have a change of heart. Whatever you've been told about bonding, there is always a choice. Even if it's only on the subconscious level. If you don't choose me, the bond will cease to exist, and you have nothing to worry about. You can go on your way dating as many princes and dukes and whoever else you don't truly have feelings for as you want in order to hide from what's real." I heard rather than saw the smile return to his face. "But if you do have true feelings for me, things are about to get interesting."

My world spun, and then Logan stole another kiss, to which I responded far too eagerly and which ended far too quickly.

His hands gently cradled my cheeks. "The damage has already been done," he said. "That last kiss was because I'm not sure when you'll let me within close proximity again."

He stepped back and released me. He crossed his arms over his chest and looked down at me. "Think about what I've said. I'm not going away this time, Audrey. You can't dismiss me as easily as before. I'm prepared to wait or to fight, whichever the season calls for, but I promise you one thing: my waiting period has an expiration date. When that time comes, I plan to fight for you like my very existence depends on it."

He stared into my eyes, allowing his words to really sink in.

I gulped.

He nodded as if satisfied and relaxed against the practice dummy again. There was a teasing note in his next words. "And now that we'll be spending more organized time together, I'm sure we'll have lots of opportunities to get this straightened out one way or another."

"What are you talking about?" I asked cautiously.

"Your new training setup. We'll be spending a lot more time together again." Nothing short of a wicked smile broke across his lips, and he leaned in close. I didn't have the good sense to step back. "That means you're mine again," he whispered.

"That," I floundered in my response for a few moments, "is not exactly true. We're only buddy training. You're not my mentor anymore."

"Exactly."

While I stood in a state of semi-shock, he cocked a smile and turned for the door. He waved a hand without looking back. "I'll see you around."

I stared at the door behind him, unable to pull my unruly thoughts and emotions into coherence.

Did that really just happen?

ONLY TIME WILL TELL

*H*ours later, I stopped to take a breath.

Destruction. Carnage. Everywhere. Scattered limbs. Splintered wood. Weapons embedded in the walls, floor, and even the high ceiling.

Practice dummies shredded.

I stood in the middle of the wreckage, panting, with sweat not just dripping but drenching me. Had I been in my right mind, I surely would have been disgusted by my own appearance. Even after all this time as a hunter, I still wasn't a fan of excessive sweat.

I looked down to find myself holding a mace—a club-like weapon of war with a bulbous spiked metal head.

What in the world was I doing with a mace?

My mind was so distracted I hadn't even been aware of what I'd been doing for the last . . . well, however long it had been since Logan left me standing struck dumb in the remote training gym.

But seriously, a mace? That was a brute-force kind of weapon, and not at all my style.

I snuck a glance at the practice dummies littered across the floor like fallen foes. Most were not only missing appendages, but had their lifelike innards splattered all over as well.

Gross.

Dropping the handle I'd been clutching, I flexed my fingers to loosen the stiffened joints.

"Oh my," came a soft gasp from behind me.

I turned to see Romona surveying my handiwork.

"Temporary insanity." I laid a hand on my forehead to massage the start of a headache.

"I should hope so."

I chewed on my lower lip, not knowing where to start the cleanup, but then I remembered where she'd been. I snapped to attention.

"How are they? Did they make it to the hospital all right? How's Grandpa? Did you find anything out about the other family? Have you been to the healing center yet?"

This time I gave Romona more than a cursory glance. She'd cleaned herself up, and except for a cut running from her left brow to her hairline, she looked unharmed.

"Whoa. That's a lot of questions. I haven't been to the healing center yet, but I don't have much that needs to be attended to. The short answer about our family is it looks like it's going to be all right, but we have some things to talk about."

"You don't know the half of it." I let a self-deprecating laugh slip. Ever since Logan had stepped out those doors, there'd been a tugging sensation deep in my gut, pulling me to follow him. I'd pulverized everything I could get my hands on in an attempt to ignore it. I had an uneasy feeling that following the tugging would lead me to exactly where he was.

Stupid bond.

I couldn't believe I was going to have to explain to my grandmother how it had been formed once again. Well, technically for the first time—but it was the second time I'd have to confess to her about it.

If I had to put words to the emotions I was feeling, I'd label them as panicked embarrassment. There were other, less aggressive sentiments churning inside, but I didn't want to deal with them yet.

Romona's eyebrow quirked. "Is that so?"

I blew out a hot breath and twisted my limp ponytail into a tight bun. "I'm afraid so."

"Why do I have a strange feeling we're about to repeat a conversation we've already had?"

"I think that's called intuition."

"So, it's more than just Logan being assigned as one of your companion trainers?"

"How do you guys find out this information so quickly?" I cracked my neck to hide my irritation.

"Some of us actually check in with our superiors from time to time."

I grimaced. "I do tend to overlook the chain of command sometimes, don't I?"

"I'm assuming that question was rhetorical."

My response was a stare.

"But in this case," Romona said, "I actually ran into Logan on my way over here."

"You did?" The interest in my voice was unmistakable.

"Yes," she answered slowly.

"Oh." I attempted to fake nonchalance. Most likely failed. "And what did he say?"

"That you've moved on from mentoring to companion training. And he and I had been assigned your training partners."

"That's it?"

Her eyes narrowed.

"Pretty much. He was on his way to check on Alrik."

I experienced a quick stab of regret for not checking on Alrik when I was in the healing center, but the rest of the conversation drove it from my head. "He omitted something of import." I shook my head and muttered under my breath, "Coward." He was probably scared to admit what he'd done to my own grandmother. As well he should be.

"What was that last part?"

"Nothing. I'll explain the rest to you. Maybe not here."

"Right then," she continued. "Let's get you some fresh air. You obviously need it."

I cast a look around the chaos I'd created. She waved a dismissive hand in the air. "It's not going anywhere. We can deal with this mess after you've had a proper break."

This mess I could clean up on my own. Time to find out if she had any advice for the quagmire I didn't know how to navigate.

"That water is deceptively cold." I glared at the large pond in front of us. Romona's laugh was like the chiming of bells.

"You would know."

We were seated on a bench overlooking the very body of water Logan had pitched me into so many months ago. The memory of that event usually both irritated and amused me, but as I sat with my best friend and grandmother, the tug of the bond telling me exactly which direction Logan was relative to my position, I felt only vexed. I shook off the feeling and concentrated on what was important.

"How's Grandpa?"

"Doing well, considering the circumstances. He was pretty beat up in the accident, but when I left they'd removed him from the intensive care unit. They think he had a mild stroke. Healing will be slow for him because of his age, and there's a good chance he may get his driver's license revoked, but he'll live. Your parents were talking about having him move in with them. For his sake, I hope he agrees, if for nothing else than companionship. He's been alone for too long. I think living with family will be good for him." The sigh she heaved gave me a clue as to the true state of her heart.

"Grandpa can be pretty stubborn."

"Ha, don't I know it." Her eyes took on a faraway quality. "Only time will tell how things are going to play out."

"And the family in the vehicle he struck?"

"Broken bones, bumps and bruises mostly. The mother is still in intensive care. She sustained a head injury, and they are keeping her in a medically induced coma." She breathed deeply. "That one's rough. The whole lot of them are at the same hospital."

"Oh gosh. How's Mom doing? Is Grandpa with it enough to understand what happened?"

"Yes, he is. He's pretty devastated about the whole thing. He doesn't remember much. Your parents are holding it together. It could have been much worse. Right now, I think everyone is focusing on the fact there wasn't any loss of life. Your brother has been talking with the other family. Praying with them."

"What? Really?"

She nodded. We sat in silence for a few minutes. Both of us lost in our own thoughts. The mention of my brother had me reliving moments from the battle.

"Did you see what happened to James at the house? After he started to pray with Mom?"

"Only some of it. I was trying to fight my way to them. That was some powerful stuff. I'm proud of him."

"Me too. Who knew my little bro had it in him?" I laughed.

"Strength in the face of adversity is a family trait." She gave me a cheeky grin. "You all got that from me, you know."

"I don't doubt it. But that whole glowing transparent armor thing was crazy! I've never seen anything like that before."

"He truly did step up to the challenge. He bore the full armor of God. Once he did that, the demons didn't stand a chance. Speaking of God," she turned her body toward me, "it seems like you've been holding out on me."

"Hey." I held up my hands in front of me. "I had no idea who he really was. To me he was just Hugo. I didn't have a clue I'd been training with a deity —*the* deity—for the last several months. I just thought he was a little . . . quirky."

Romona busted up laughing. "Only *you* would come up with that, Audrey."

I flushed. "Please don't make me feel any dumber than I already do. It seems so obvious to me now."

"Hey, don't be too hard on yourself. If Hugo didn't want to reveal to you who he truly was, you weren't going to stumble across it on your own. It's all in His timing, you know?"

"I think I'm finally starting to grasp that. Even if I don't like it."

"I'm sure, given the opportunity, many of us would be tempted to choose our own timetables, but they wouldn't be what is best for us. Considering my finite knowledge versus God's omniscient and omnipotent power, I'm glad I'm not the one in charge."

She had a valid point. It was my impatient nature that repeatedly reared its ugly head. "Yeah."

We lapsed into a comfortable silence once again.

"So, Logan and I are bonded again . . . or rather, for real this time."

"What?" Romona's body jerked so violently she almost fell off the bench. If we'd been about to dive into a different subject matter, I might have laughed.

"Yep. He smacked a good one on me earlier today. And I . . . well," heat rose to my face, "didn't exactly do a good job of stopping him."

Romona's giggles brought my gaze to her. My eyes narrowed.

"Déjà vu much?" I asked.

"Oh, my. Audrey, you look so grumpy. You two just couldn't stay away from each other, could you?"

"How can you seriously find this funny?"

"How can you seriously not?" she countered. "You are probably the only one who didn't see this coming from a mile away."

"Apparently so," I grumbled. "Come on, I'm your granddaughter. Shouldn't you be more protective of me or something?"

Romona did her best to iron out her expression. She failed. A sly smile still lit her face. "I don't fully understand why you are so upset. It does, as they say, take two to tango."

At that moment, I hated the saying. I wasn't ready to admit my own guilt. I crossed my arms over my chest and slumped into the bench. "See, that right there is why I'm so mad. It was a total sneak attack. Like a kiss and run."

Her eyebrows shot up. "Oh, this is getting interesting indeed. A kiss and run. It sounds rather . . . quick."

"Never mind about the length. We're not talking about that right now."

"Oh, my." Romona's eyes flitted around my head, looking everywhere but my face. "I don't think we need to actually have that conversation for me to make an educated guess."

Why was I always the last to realize my hair was doing its thing? "Argh, this stupid hair!"

She shrugged as if to say 'you said it, not me'.

Closing my eyes, I smiled at Romona's soft gasp. I had turned my hair green on purpose. For some reason the thought of me ruining my brown hair was always a little disturbing to her.

"There, that feels better."

The grimace on her face told me exactly what she thought of the new shade. "It reminds me of a booger," she said.

"Well that's perfect. I love boogers." Oops, that was a little loud. I snuck a glance around, and sure enough there were more than a set or two of eyes on my neon hair. Just on principle, I wasn't going to change it back right away.

Romona patted my hand. "Whatever you say, dear." Her disgust had morphed into amusement once again. "But back to the point. I'll tell you what I told you before. You let him go in your heart, and you won't need to worry about this pesky bond. Poof, problem solved." She waved her hands in the air like she was batting a mosquito away. Her sly smile was back in place.

"Like I'm capable of that anymore," I grumbled under my breath.

"What was that?"

I let out a frustrated breath of air. Time to get real. We both knew this bond wasn't going to disappear. "I have feelings for him. Big feelings. The bond's not going anywhere this time."

"Well, of course I know that."

"I know you know."

She frowned. "Then what I can't understand is why you are so upset."

Did *I* even understand why? "I'm upset because I didn't get a say in the matter."

Her eyebrows lifted as if she didn't believe me.

"Seriously, it was like a smash and grab."

"You're likening it to a robbery now?"

I sat up a little straighter and pointed a finger at her. "Yes, exactly. It was like a bonding heist. And I was the bank. What's a girl got to do around here to get a little wooing before committing her eternity to someone?"

"Oh, Audrey." Romona's light laughter filled the air, "I have a feeling Logan has quite a bit of wooing in his future before you fully come on board with his plans. Some groveling probably as well."

I flopped back against the bench and folded my arms. "Dang straight. Like right now, I know he is . . ." I reached out to that newly awakened part of me that zeroed into Logan like a stinkin' GPS signal, "Right in there." I pointed back toward the training center. "When we first came out here he was over there." I pointed off to the right. "I'm not interested in knowing where he is at all times, let alone being all in tune and aware of it. How am I ever going to not think about him?"

"You can tell where he is right now?" She sounded surprised.

"Yeah. Is that not normal?"

She shrugged. "Maybe it is. I wouldn't know. I'm not bonded to anyone."

"Aren't you supposed to know all about this stuff?"

She gave me a stern look. "Audrey, I'm your grandmother, not your bonding guru."

"So much for older and wiser." I cracked a smile.

"Hey. I'm still plenty wiser."

"If you say so." I used my most patronizing voice. She rolled her eyes at me.

"But you do have a point," she conceded.

"I do?"

"Yes." She finally, *finally* sobered. "Bonding is a huge commitment. You are rather young. And I am your closest Earth relative here." She crossed her arms and studied me closely. "I should be more adult about this with you."

I nodded. Yes, yes, she should. This was some serious—

"What were you thinking kissing Logan, young lady?"

"Wh-what?"

She leveled me with a look. "Audrey, you are a very intelligent young woman. What did you think would happen if you allowed Logan to kiss you?"

If Romona was only pretending to be authoritative, she was a really good actress. This wasn't exactly what I was going for.

"What part of 'hit and run' or 'smash and grab' didn't you get?"

"The part where your hair went bubble-gum pink when the length of the kiss came up."

She was serious, too. This was *so* much worse than her playful ribbing.

"Ah, there it is again," she said with a self-satisfied smile. "I knew I could get rid of that putrid shade of green."

"Are you messing with me right now?"

She looked at me with a straight face and blinked. Twice. Then a smile broke through. "Of course, I am. I think the world of Logan. He's really come a long way in the months you two were apart. And just because you're bonded doesn't mean you can't still take things slow."

"It doesn't?" A sharp slap of relief jolted my heart.

"No. In fact, I am going to get parental for a moment and insist you take your time. It's not like you're going to be going ahead with the ceremony and moving in with each other tomorrow."

I choked on nothing.

"Right?" she demanded sternly.

"Oh my gosh. Of course, not. There's a ceremony?"

"This situation is a little like an engagement, so of course there's a cere-mony. But there's no limit on how long the 'engagement,'" she used air quotes, "period has to last."

"Oh, thank goodness." I sagged back in my seat. "Everything has just seemed so out of control lately. It's nice to know it's possible to slow this train down. A century or two ought to teach him a lesson."

Romona actually snorted at me. "Like that's going to happen."

"I don't like what you are implying." I stuck my nose in the air. "I have amazing self-control."

"Sure you do, dear." She patted my hand. "But do you think that's maybe what's truly bothering you? The afterlife moving a little too quickly for you?"

I thought about it for a minute. It had only been how long since I'd died? Not even a full year. And in that short time, everything had changed.

"Perhaps. Most likely. Maybe?"

Romona slung an arm around my neck and pulled me forward into a hug. "If it's one thing you have now in spades, my darling granddaughter, it's time."

"You really did a number on this place," Romona said, looking around the gym after we returned. "How do you suppose you managed to get that sword stuck all the way up there?"

With arms loaded down with bits of a practice dummy, I tracked her gaze up to where a rapier was impaled in the ceiling twenty feet above our heads.

"I'm going to be perfectly honest with you, I have no idea. I don't even have an educated guess."

"Huh."

"Exactly."

I returned to the task of putting the gym back together, but a seed of something unpleasant had taken root in my gut, where it had been blooming for the past half-hour. It was an uncomfortable sensation of unease I just couldn't shake. Shortly after it started I noticed I couldn't detect Logan's presence anymore. I almost said something to Romona a handful of times, but I didn't know how to explain it to her.

"You know, I think we may need to track down a ladder to—"

The gym doors slammed open with a bang, cutting off whatever Romona was going to say next. Kevin stood panting hard in the doorway. I glanced at Romona, and I'm sure I mirrored her look of surprise. I wanted to ask Kevin what was wrong, but the unpleasant bloom in the pit of my stomach said I wasn't going to like whatever he was here to tell us.

A part of me I almost didn't want to acknowledge already knew what was wrong. If I could stop him from uttering the words, would the realm keep moving forward as it should? For surely once the truth passed through his lips, whatever peace I'd made with my afterlife would be ripped away.

He looked straight at me. The whites of his eyes stood out in stark contrast to his dark irises and mocha-colored skin. "You have to come right away. He's gone."

"Who's gone?" Romona asked in confusion.

Kevin answered, but it was for Romona's benefit alone. I didn't even hear his words, for I already knew. My intuition had been screaming at me for thirty minutes.

Something terrible had happened to Logan.

26

A TRUTH REVEALED

"Oof. Sorry," I mumbled at the hunter I'd just bumped off of like I was the metal ball in a pinball machine.

Romona snuck a worried glance over her shoulder for about the millionth time as she and Kevin gracefully moved through the mass of bodies like shifting mist. I was taking the bull-in-a-china-shop approach to navigating the foot traffic. Bouncing, rebounding, and plowing right into people.

Logan was gone, and my mind felt as if it was missing right along with him.

Logan.

I didn't know exactly what was going on, Kevin hadn't been forthcoming with information, but still my heart twisted painfully. Each hurried step forward brought me closer to finding out what in the world was happening.

"Whoa. Whoops, we just passed it." Kevin skidded to a stop, then brushed past me back to the nondescript door we'd all flown right by.

They seriously needed to label these doors. How anyone knew where they were going was still a mystery to me. I still got lost more often than not.

Kevin twisted the handle, and the three of us pushed through the doorway all at once. There was a momentary jam before we popped through the bottleneck we'd created.

The glowing figure in front of us turned upon our entry.

"Shannon?"

It was Shannon who had first introduced me to Logan, and although I didn't know it at the time, she was an angel. Back when I was training with Logan it was somewhat common to see her, but not so much since I'd been working with Hugo.

Shannon appeared just as put together as I remembered. Her severe, yet beautiful, features didn't convey any of her underlining emotions. That is, if she had any. Her raven hair was pulled tightly back into her signature bun. Her fitted navy dress and suit jacket were all business, just like her. Only the ethereal glow of her skin gave her away as a being other than human.

"Good, you're finally here. We can start the official debrief. In this situation, we really don't have a moment to lose."

A sniffle from somewhere behind Shannon caught my attention. I stepped up to the rectangular table along with everyone else and noticed Kaitlin was already there. Tears ran down her cheeks, and her normally flawless skin was red and blotchy. My anxiety ratcheted up.

"Hey, guys," she said in a small voice as she lifted her hand in a weak hello.

My lid had officially been flipped.

"Someone better tell me what's going on in the next three seconds or I'm going to start . . . start throwing some chairs or something!"

Yeah, that was good. Throwing chairs was surely a scary enough threat to loosen their tongues. Sometimes I was a complete moron. The look Shannon shot me said she agreed.

"Audrey. Sit."

My butt hit the seat without hesitation. She had that authoritative thing down like no one I knew.

"What's going on? Where's Logan?" I demanded. Kaitlin let out a wet crying-choking sound I completely ignored.

"Before I start, I don't want any of you panicking," Shannon said. "You've all been called here because you're close to Logan. I want you to know a plan is being created as we speak to ensure his safe extraction, but we didn't think it was wise to keep you in the dark."

"Extraction!" I panicked whether Shannon liked it or not. "Where does he need to be extracted from?" He was just here. Foreign anxiety mixed with my own, but since it wasn't as severe as my own, it actually calmed me a bit. I looked down to see Romona had taken hold of my hand.

Shannon blew out a breath of frustration. "Audrey, I understand the delicate nature of your concern right now, but will you please let me finish?"

"Delicate nature?" Kaitlin asked in a small voice.

Shannon plowed forward. "To cut to the chase, Logan has been lured out of the realm, and we believe he's being held by the enemy." Shannon held up her hand to cut off anything I might say. Wise woman. "As of this point, we don't know exactly where he is, which brings up some serious concerns. There are only a few reasons we wouldn't be able to locate him."

The blood drained from my face. He'd never come to terms with the last time he'd been held by the enemy. He had both the physical and emotional scars to prove it. I raised a shaky hand to cover my mouth. My heart didn't just twist painfully this time, it bled.

"Before I continue, Audrey," Shannon fixed her crystalline blue eye on me, "do you feel anything that might give us an indication of where he may be?"

"Um, I don't think so."

"Are you sure? The link between the two of you could be very useful to us right now."

"What are you talking about?" Kevin broke in. "Why would Audrey be able to tell where he is?"

"Because they're bonded," Shannon answered.

"You and Logan are bonded?" Kaitlin's face was a strange mix of confusion and excitement.

"Yes, it's kind of a recent thing. Recent and unexpected," I threw in for good measure before turning my attention back to Shannon. "How do you people know about these things so quickly?"

"Hey, way to go Aud." Kevin held his hand up for a high-five. The look I gave him withered the smile on his face. "Ah yeah, not the right time, huh?" He dropped his hand to the table with a thud.

Shannon ignored my question. "Sometimes bonded pairs have a sense of where the other is, geographically and emotionally. It doesn't happen all the time. But I needed to ask. That must not be the case with you two. Perhaps the bond is too new. Or maybe it's not meant to stick." That was inserted a little too casually for my taste. Not meant to stick? Something churned inside me. "Moving on—"

"Wait." I cut her off. "It did happen. At least the geographic location part. Up until about an hour ago I did know where Logan was. It was like I developed an internal compass that pointed toward him at all time. But it disappeared. I've had this really uneasy feeling I couldn't shake ever since."

She looked sharply at me. "That makes sense. That would have been about the time they left the realm. Not being on the same plane of existence must be blocking your connection."

"*They* left?"

Shannon's frown deepened, and she cast a glance at Kaitlin, who'd started crying again. Did Kaitlin know more than we did, or was this just her reaction to the news?

"Yes, they. We're not sure, but we believe we have discovered our mole."

I held my breath without meaning to. Shannon was taking far too long of a time to get this out.

Finally, she said it. "We believe Alrik tricked Logan into leaving the realm under the guise of your family being in jeopardy again."

Forget holding my breath, my heart stopped beating for several seconds then sped up to recover from the lapse.

Alrik?

Alrik was the traitor? Our fun-loving resident Viking had deceived and betrayed us all? I shook my head without even realizing it.

"I know it's hard to believe, but the evidence we've uncovered can't be ignored. He got sloppy covering his tracks at the end. We recently found a hunter in the bunker at your family's home who says Alrik knocked him out and chained him to the metal bed frame before he could ask for more backup, as he planned to do. Further, Alrik sent messages to us that your family was overprotected. Those reports were what caused us to pull hunters back when they should have been left there. We believe he did it so your family would be in a precarious enough situation that you'd cave to Satan's demands. We also suspect he may have found a way to conceal your location on Earth, which is why we were looking for you all over northern Ohio. We're not sure when he turned sides, but the more we uncover, the more incriminating the evidence appears."

Shannon's succinct explanation made a sick sort of sense, but it also didn't. This was Alrik we were talking about, for goodness' sake. The man had a pet polar bear. Or at least he claimed to have one. When I thought of him, the first thing that came to mind was his larger-than-life smile and booming laugh.

A heavy silence hung in the air. It wasn't just me who'd been struck mute by the news. Kaitlin's teary-eyed state made sense now.

"How certain are we of the validity of this information?" Romona, always practical, asked.

"Of Alrik's actions? We're positive."

"And you're saying you think this is all about me? That Alrik is trying to use Logan against me somehow?"

"With your family heavily protected, we think he may have gone after someone else you care about. You're now bonded to Logan. Who better to use as a bargaining chip?"

"But that's so new, how would he even know about the bond? Satan isn't omnipresent."

"No, he's not. But who do you think Logan would have told about it?"

The answer was as plain as day. Of course, Logan would have told Alrik. They were best friends.

"Having failed on Earth, it's possible Alrik acted on his own to devise a plan to capture Logan. Delivering your intended to Satan himself might have granted him a boon he was hoping for." Shannon spoke exactly what my mind came up with.

"If that's true, he truly is an idiot," I said. "Anyone who thinks they are going to get something of value from Satan is a fool."

"I don't disagree with you. I'm only relaying what we think might have happened."

"I'm assuming this means you can't track Alrik either."

She shook her head.

"No, this doesn't make any sense." I put my hands on my temples. "Why would Alrik do something like this? Why would he work for Satan? There has to be a motive. What is it?"

"We're not sure."

"You're not sure?" I scoffed at her.

Her lips pressed together in a fine line. "All of this is happening very fast. Information is still coming in. We're going off our best assumptions at the moment. Alrik's motives are still unclear, but we do know he sabotaged your family's security, and we do know he left the realm with Logan. Right now there's no evidence to say Logan had any knowledge of Alrik's motives, and for that reason we're treating this like a hostage situation. Should anything come up to indicate Logan did—"

"Wait!" I jumped up from my seat. "Are you telling me you think Logan may be a traitor?"

Shannon remained unaffected by my passionate response. "Logan's always behaved completely above board, so besides the slightly suspicious timing of your bonding, we have no foundation for misgivings of that nature at this time."

At this time?

I was struck speechless. How could they think Logan would betray any of us? Alrik was hard enough to believe, but Logan too? No way. Besides, we were bonded now, and . . .

And then it fell together. That was it. Shannon had just hinted at it herself. They thought there was a chance Logan had bonded with me to lure me back to Earth.

"Our bonding," I whispered to myself.

Old fears and insecurities rushed to the surface. Could that actually be what happened? I'd always doubted Logan's feelings for me. What if I was right the whole time? Everything had happened so suddenly today. Could it have all been staged?

Push beyond your fears.

It was a small voice inside that spoke to me. A whisper to my heart rather than my mind.

And I listened.

I pushed aside the insecurities that rode me hard. The lies that said there was no way Logan would be interested in me because I simply wasn't enough. Pretty enough. Smart enough. Strong enough. Brave enough. Good enough.

I turned Logan over in my brain with as unbiased a view as I could manage. He wasn't perfect by any stretch of the imagination. He was stubborn, pushy, and bossy, and he had a serious issue with forgiving himself.

But he was also loyal and reliable and brave and kind. He didn't hold grudges against people. He was selfless to a fault, and under his stoic mask, he was caring beyond belief. It was a combination of the things he wasn't as much as the things he was that made up my mind.

He wasn't untruthful, wasn't selfish, wasn't self-serving, wasn't unfaithful. He wasn't any of the things that would make me doubt him now.

I knew Logan. He wasn't a betrayer.

I don't know what look was in my eyes when I finally met Shannon's gaze, but it must have been powerful. Her features pinched for only a moment, and then she gave me a curt nod before plowing forward with her agenda.

"We'll let you know once our plan has been put into action. Audrey, we may need you on the ground at some point because of your link with Logan, but we'll let you know if it comes to that." She stepped toward the door.

"You mean we won't be helping with the rescue attempt?" For once it wasn't me complaining about being left behind. Kaitlin beat me to it.

The angel let out a quiet sigh before turning back around. "Look, due to the emotional nature of this mission, we don't think it's wise—"

The door behind Shannon abruptly opened, cutting off her words.

"Sir?" Shannon's voice was full of reverence.

The familiar man laid a hand on her shoulder. "Plans have changed. I'll take it from here. These ones are coming with me."

"Yes. Of course, sir."

I blinked at Shannon's quick obedience. I mean, this guy had a habit of showing up in weird places, but I wouldn't have dreamed he outranked her.

"You're seeing to this yourself?" It sounded as if she expected him to correct her.

"That's right. He's no longer on Earth, so I'll be heading this mission."

"Oh, I see." Shannon turned to us briefly. If I were better at reading the facial expressions of a cyborg, I might have been able to interpret the look on her face before she slipped silently out the door.

I was confused. Again.

"Joe?"

"Hello, Audrey." The slight smile on his face was both kind and sad. "I'm glad to see you again, but not under these circumstances."

My friends remained mute, so I continued to ignore their presence. "Logan's not on Earth? Does that mean he's back in our realm?"

"I'm afraid that isn't the case. He's somewhere far worse. Somewhere hunters can't venture alone. That's why I'm going with you."

"No!" Romona's sharp exclamation was jarring. "It can't be! Alrik wouldn't have taken him there."

Joe's eyes broadcasted regret.

"Where exactly is he?" I asked, looking between my grandmother and Joe.

"Hell," Romona answered for him. Her voice was eerily hollow. "The one place we can't venture alone is Hell."

27

IT BEGINS AT THE END

"Hell! Logan's in Hell?"

"Yes, Audrey. I'm sorry this has happened." The sincerity in Joe's eyes was unmistakable.

"But . . . but how do you even know how to find him?"

"Because I'm the only one who's been there before . . . and made it back. You'll need my protection to travel there."

"This is insane." I placed my hands on either side of my head and squeezed. Maybe it was me who was finally going insane?

Joe reached forward and removed my hands. He looked deep into my eyes with a hand on my shoulder. "We will bring him back."

It was a promise I would hold him to.

He turned to the rest of the group. "All right, you all know who I am." Nods all around. Great, I was missing something . . . again. This was getting old. Was I going to have to play twenty questions this time to figure it out? Jump through some burning hoops. It was so seriously awesome to always be the one who—

"Audrey?" I glanced up. Joe watched me expectedly. Apparently, he'd been talking while I was fuming.

Whoops.

"Yeah, sorry, what?"

"I know you know me as Joe, and you're welcome to call me that, but you need to know who I really am."

Thirty minutes later we were gearing up in the locker room, and I was still going over and over the unexpected introduction.

The Son of God.

Joe was the literal Son of God, and he was going to help us get Logan back. I was still digesting Hugo being the Holy Spirit, so finding out Joe was really Jesus just added another log to the burning fire of news I had to process.

I gave myself a mental shake. It didn't matter. I mean yes, it did matter, because it meant we were about to kick some serious demon butt with the Son of God with us, but more importantly we were going to bring Logan home safely. My focus needed to stay on that one goal. Eventually I'd digest the information about Joe properly, but right now I had a job to do.

Joe gave us a rough layout of his plan and then sent us off to gear up. We were only a small group, because a large contingent of hunters entering Hell would be more likely to be noticed. This was a covert infiltration mission, not a siege. The hope was we could slip in, locate Logan, and leave before being detected.

I was the first to arrive in the transportation room. I leaned against the wall and distracted myself by watching the engineers scurry around to get things ready. There were at least twice the number as usual manning the different desks and equipment. Lights flashed rapidly on the panels as the engineers' fingers flew over them. The mechanical whirl of the machines was routine, but the hard—and somewhat frantic—looks on the faces of the people around me were not.

An eerie sort of quiet permeated the air. Some of the engineers' brows were dotted with sweat. Apparently being transported to Hell was a heck of a lot harder than going down to Earth. They had started prepping for our trip before we even knew we were making it.

I looked over my shoulder when the door squeaked open.

"What are you doing here?" It was rude, but it was equally shocking to see Jonathon stride into the transportation room decked out in hunter armor. Shocking. Bizarre. Confusing. Take your pick.

"Ever heard of triage?" he said without sparing me a glance. "I'm your med unit on this mission."

"But you're not a hunter." I stood up straight and faced him.

"I can take care of myself." With jerky movements he strapped a leather scabbard to his waist and roughly thrust the thin blade of a rapier into it. He looked up and caught my look of incredulousness.

"I used to be a prince, remember? Fencing was part of the job description. I was a champion swordsman." When my face didn't change, he sighed. "Just because I don't know how to glide down a sheet of ice while balancing on planks of wood doesn't mean I'm not good for other things."

"If you were so good at this stuff, why weren't you assigned to be a hunter instead of a healer?" I didn't say it to be impolite. I genuinely didn't understand.

He seemed offended anyway. "Despite my obvious set of skills, I was better suited as a healer than a hunter. I'd think you, of all people, would understand that looks can be deceiving."

I didn't miss the jab. Jonathon was obviously still upset about how things had gone down between the two of us.

"Why are you doing this?"

"Because they asked me to." His gaze wouldn't quite meet my eyes.

"But you don't even like Logan."

"Don't have to like the guy to help find him." He crossed his arms.

"I think it would certainly help. Not to mention where we're headed. Can you honestly tell me Logan is someone you're willing to go to Hell and back for?"

"Funny."

"It wasn't meant to be."

He finally looked me in the eyes. "If we're talking about literal interpretation, then yes, it looks like he is."

I wasn't used to this new, snippy Jonathon. It both annoyed and saddened me. My hands fisted and ended up on my hips. "Jonathon, I appreciate your willingness to do this, I truly do, but it doesn't have to be *you*."

"Doesn't it?" he asked. Before I could respond, he turned on a heel and strode to the opposite side of the room.

I worried my lip. Part of me thought having him along was a colossal mistake, but I couldn't argue the fact that having a warrior medic with us would be a huge help. There were no guarantees where we were going, and like it or not, there was a solid chance we'd need his skills at some point in this mission. I was once again left in complete confusion as to what God was thinking, but . . . God either knew what He was doing or He didn't. It was time for me to choose to believe that He did.

Jonathon positioned himself as far away from me as possible and stared at the busy engineers. His face was hard as granite. Regret filled me.

A gentle hand brought me out of my reverie. "Interesting development, isn't it?" Romona lifted her chin in Jonathon's direction.

"Yeah." I pressed two fingers to my temple and rubbed. "I wish I'd done things differently. He's so bitter now. I was stupid."

She squeezed my free hand before letting go, not agreeing nor disagreeing with my words. The situation just was what it was.

There was no going back, only moving forward.

A commotion drew my attention to the door where the rest of our rescue crew had appeared. Kaitlin and Kevin were decked out in just as much armor and gear as the rest of us. Joe—I was having trouble thinking of him by any other name—followed. For once he wasn't in his signature T-shirt and jeans. He looked regal in his own armor.

Movement around the room stopped upon his entry. Joe made a motion with his hand that they should continue what they were doing and then beckoned the hunters to him. Jonathon crossed the room to join us, and we arranged ourselves in a semicircle around our leader.

"You are all acquainted with the plan?" Joe asked.

We nodded. The faces around me were focused and serious.

"I know I've already said this, but you must prepare yourselves for the horrors you are going to see. This place was not built for human souls. It was intended as a prison for the evil ones, but the fall of mankind brought with it a steep price. There is nothing you will be able to do for the souls who chose darkness instead of light. Our objective is to locate Logan as quickly as possible. I will then be able to bring all of us home. Stay together as a unit." He took a moment to make sure we all paid attention. "This mission will challenge you physically and mentally like nothing has before, but I will be there with you."

Joe then looked straight into my eyes. "No matter what happens, remember the Father works all things to good. Never forget that." His words were for all of us, but with his eyes on me, I claimed them for myself.

"We're ready for you, sir."

"Thank you." Joe nodded his acknowledgment.

We all shuffled onto the glowing pads. I took a deep, fortifying breath. How were you truly supposed to prepare yourself for a trip to Hell?

Romona nodded at me encouragingly. "Let's go get your man."

"He's not . . ." I started to say Logan wasn't mine, but I stopped. It was time to stop pretending things weren't exactly what they were. Logan was as much mine as anyone would ever be. Perhaps losing him was what had finally firmed that up in my mind. Just this morning he'd staked his claim on me.

It was time I returned the favor.

"Yeah, let's do this thing."

EPILOGUE

LOGAN

I pulled in vain at the shackles on my wrists, ignoring the pain caused by the raw skin beneath them. I spit out another mouthful of blood. A good portion of it dribbled down my chin before hitting the rough floor. The heat in this realm was like nothing I'd ever experienced. It was so dry every inhalation burned my parched throat. I struggled not to sag against my restraints—not to show weakness.

There was only one good thing about my situation. She wasn't here.

"Enjoying your stay with us, I presume?"

I ignored the evil being trying to provoke me. With his façade in place he resembled his noble brothers of the angelic realm, but he could never again completely replicate his former glory. The evidence of that was written on his face, as if to prove the saying "the eyes are the windows to the soul" to be true —for the soulless creature before me had none.

"Perhaps you're a little lonely. I wouldn't concern myself with that if I were you. I'm expecting company to join you anytime now."

I wheezed out a humorless laugh that ended in a dry cough. She'd called me delusional, but the deranged beast in front of me truly earned that title.

"You doubt she'd come for you then?"

My eyes lifted in defiance. A low growl escaped my throat. It sounded more beastly than human. When it came to her, staying rational was a struggle.

I never should have bonded with her. It was a burden she didn't need right now. I didn't regret being honest with my feelings for her. She deserved that. In fact, she deserved to be told a lot sooner. But if our separation caused her to feel even a fraction of the pain I was enduring, then our bond was something I deeply regretted. Not to mention it was something Satan could easily exploit . . . if he knew about it. No matter the torture, I'd never reveal that truth.

"She resisted you when you tried to use her family as leverage. Why would this pathetic attempt be any different?" My voice was filled with gravel and grit.

"Perhaps you're right. But you see, there's one major difference here." He took several steps toward me, invading my personal space. Not that I really had a right to it anymore. "The pain I inflicted on her family wasn't quite as . . . literal as what I can do to you."

As if to prove his point, the nails on his left hand elongated to sharpened points that he sunk into my chest and then slowly raked downwards, leaving a bloody and shredded trail of flesh in their wake. I shut my eyes and clenched my teeth to keep from shouting out in agony.

"And who could resist the pull of the bond?" he asked in a singsong taunt.

I tried not to react, I did, but my eyes betrayed me.

"Oh yes, I know about your bond. Very well-timed, in fact. I should be thanking you. I'm sure it's going to add a layer of desperation she might not have felt before."

"She's stronger than you're giving her credit for."

He backhanded me. Hard.

My face slammed into the jagged stone wall, and my vision flickered black and white before clearing. I wasn't given the luxury of passing out. The look on his face said he'd done it out of boredom more than anything else.

He turned his back and strode from the room, speaking to himself instead of me. "I know these vapid beings far better than they know themselves. They are all so utterly . . . stupid. So ridiculously predictable. I've been at this game for millennia. What lamb has ever outsmarted a hungry wolf?" The shake of his head indicated his disgust.

He turned back to me right before leaving the chamber. I was losing the battle to remain upright. Streams of blood trickled down my forearms from my wrists where they rubbed the restraints. The blood was almost cooling to my skin.

"I hope she is as you say, for an overabundance of weakness could prove to be irritating for the both of us. It pleases me to hear she may not be as feeble as I perceive her to be, for to be the key, she has to possess a measure of strength."

"The key to what?" I croaked out.

"True freedom."

As he exited, chains scrapped across stone. The grinding vibration lessened as the distance between us spread. The skin of my chapped lips cracked as I smiled. Satan was bound tighter than even I was at the moment—he just hid his discomfort better.

I was both fearful and hopeful she would come to my rescue. But either way, only one thing mattered.

My girl was sure to give him hell.

Thank you for reading *Warfare*!
If you loved it, please write a review at
http://review.WarfareBook.com

Up Next: Have you ever wondered what's going through Logan's head? You're not alone! In ***Logan (A Life After Companion Story)*** you'll get Logan's perspective and dramatic backstory; a view into his trials, his demons, his powers, and his weakness, including his first introduction to Audrey.

... or skip ahead for the epic conclusion of Audrey and Logan's story, in *Dominion (Life After Book 3)* →

LOGAN

A LIFE AFTER COMPANION STORY

JULIE HALL

USA TODAY BESTSELLING AUTHOR

To my devoted readers.

I heard you. Your love for the seemingly grumpy mentor with a mysterious past and a bruised heart is what made this book a reality.

This story gives you Logan's perspective and backstory; a view into his trials, his demons, his powers, and his weakness.

INSTRUCTIONS

FOR THE AUTHOR COMMENTARY AND BONUS MATERIAL

You're in for a special treat! This book includes chapter-by-chapter "author commentary" videos, to help you read between the lines and go deeper into the story!

At the end of each chapter, you'll see a web address (URL), and a square bar code, also known as a "QR" code. Simply go to the URLs, or scan the codes, and you'll unlock the bonus commentary and material.

Thank you for reading in LOGAN, and investing in me!

STEP-BY-STEP INSTRUCTIONS

How to scan QR codes with an iPhone or iPad:

1. Open the camera app on your iPhone or iPad *(requires iOS 11+)*
2. Hold the device's camera up to the QR code.
3. Your device will automatically recognize the QR code and provide you with an on-screen notification.
4. Tap the notification to be taken to the video.

How to scan QR codes with an Android device:

1. Open the Google Chrome browser.
2. Click on the search/URL box.
3. Click the little square icon that resembles a QR code.
4. Hold the device's camera up to the QR code.
5. Your device will automatically recognize the QR code and provide you with an URL to visit.

6. Press "Go" to be taken to the video.

AUTHOR COMMENTARY

INTRODUCTION

I'm so excited to give you this extra commentary, to help you read between the lines and go deeper into the story! Get started by watching the first video: JulieHallAuthor.com/logan-intro

LOGAN'S SOUNDTRACK

LISTEN WHILE YOU READ

These handpicked songs perfectly describe Logan. I often listened to these songs while writing this book. I hope they inspire you while you read!
JulieHallAuthor.com/logan-playlist

Click "play" or scan the QR code below. You must have a Spotify account to listen (it's free).

CHAPTER 1

$\mathcal{I}$ gritted my teeth as my opponent's blade connected with mine. I was glad the sparring mask I wore hid the effort I had to make. My muscles bunched as I gathered strength to separate our blades, hoping to throw him off balance, but he remained steady on his feet. Still, I had managed to free my weapon and evade his next strike.

Sweat—from both exertion and the stifling nature of the mask—dripped down my face as I traded blows with the warrior in front of me.

Hinges squeaked somewhere behind me, and for a few seconds the sound of rancorous voices and loud jeers from the rec room drowned out the clashing of our blades. Then the room fell quiet again.

Someone had entered the gym.

Curious, I tried to check over my shoulder and lost my footing instead. I shoved the intrusion out of my mind and focused on the task at hand.

Winning this match.

I spotted the swing aimed at my shins from a mile away and swiftly jumped out of the way, landing a couple of body lengths from where I'd been standing. The sharp gasp that burst from the unwanted spectator almost threw me off my game. Again.

This time I gritted my teeth out of annoyance.

The warrior ran straight at me and we exchanged a series of quick blows. Despite being a friendly sharpening of skills, neither of us was willing to let up. After several years of training, deflecting an attack had become instinctive for me.

I was an experienced hunter, capable of defending Earth's inhabitants against all sorts of evil—evil they neither saw nor accepted. When I fought, whatever weapon I wielded became another extremity, a simple extension of myself. So today my sword was part of my arm—arching, slashing and deflecting with barely a thought.

Where my opponent's advantage lay in his massive size, mine was my speed. As the blade intended for my neck cut through the air, I ducked and rolled out of the way, watching it sail overhead.

I sprang to my feet in one liquid motion.

The challenging-warrior was frustrated so his attacks became sloppy.

I took full advantage of his irritation, so it wasn't long before I had an opening to snap my leg out and hook his right ankle, bringing him to his knees.

If the giant could have seen my face at that moment, the grin I wore would have annoyed him to no end. I was just about to deliver the final blow—which wouldn't actually injure him, but rather signal the end of the match—when someone cleared their throat loud enough that the sound echoed throughout the gym.

A sign that we were not only being watched, but that our playtime had come to an end.

We froze in our positions. No doubt my opponent was just as disappointed by the interruption as I was. He fisted a dagger in his left hand. I almost chuckled. Someone had just foiled his plan for a surprise attack.

Nice try, but I was already two steps ahead of you, my friend.

"Logan, may I have a word with you?"

Ah, Shannon—the kill-joy of the hunter community—and strict mother to all of us lost boys. But what would we do without her?

I took a step back and lowered my sword. "Sure, Shannon. Just give me a sec." I reached down to offer Alrik a hand up, giving it a shake once he was standing, followed by a pat on the back for a job well done.

"Nice try with that dagger there, but I would never have let you get close to me."

Alrik chuckled, the sound muffled beneath his face guard. "That trick would have definitely worked on you half a year ago."

"Yeah, well, half a year ago I was a different person." And wasn't that the truth?

Recognizing he'd hit a sore spot, he changed the subject. "What do you think the Head Mistress over there wants?" He jerked his head in Shannon's direction.

I shrugged. Alrik was always finding new ways of referring to Shannon, knowing full well she could hear him, but not caring in the least.

"Who knows? But if you don't want to get roped into something along with me, you might want to start a speedy retreat."

"Good point."

Heading for the far door, Alrik didn't even bother dematerializing his armor before fleeing. He just gave Shannon a curt nod and was gone.

I started my trek toward her, ridding myself of my armor along the way. It was then that I realized she wasn't alone.

A small female stood with her, positioned almost behind the stoic angel as if using her for a shield. The girl's eyes zig-zagging across my body in an almost frantic way.

Ah, I thought, *newbie. Must not be used to seeing people materialize and dematerialize things from thin air.*

"Hey, Shannon, what's up?"

I snuck another glance at the girl next to her, keeping my features neutral. She didn't glow, so she was definitely human. Maybe Shannon was taking on an apprentice or something? Getting help with clerical work?

This wisp of a girl couldn't have looked more out of place or uncomfortable in the training gym—my home away from home—if she tried.

I mentally dismissed her as I focused back on the formidable angel in front of me. Girls were the last thing on my mind these days.

"Actually, I've brought you a new trainee."

Hope filled me. A sliver of trepidation slithered through my chest as well, but if they were allowing me to be a mentor again after what happened with Morgan, I must be doing something right.

I'd waited six long months for this day.

I scanned the area behind Shannon but there was only a closed door to the rec room. Maybe she was just giving me a heads up on what was coming down the pipeline soon.

"Oh, yeah? That's great! Where is he?" I asked.

Shannon gave the wisp a gentle shove forward, causing the girl to stumble a bit before righting herself.

"Here *she* is," Shannon answered with a knowing smile.

My usually controlled expression broke. *Oh. Heck. No.*

The widening of my eyes was completely involuntary as I really took stock of this supposed new hunter. Starting at her feet and moving my eyes up her body, I took in every inch of non-hunter in front of me. I'm sure the appraisal had to be uncomfortable, but it couldn't be helped.

She was clearly assigned the wrong job. The top of her head didn't even reach my shoulders. And it wasn't just that she was shorter than any hunter I'd ever met, or even that she was a girl, but she was also incredibly petite in stature as well. Her softly-curved figure also lacked the muscle definition needed for our job. From her tiny feet to her delicate heart shaped face this chick screamed 'damsel in distress,' not 'big bad fighting machine.'

What in the world were they thinking?

I had the crazy urge to bundle her up and whisk her off somewhere safe. There was no way I was going to be able to train this girl.

Her long mane of brown hair matched her large doe eyes, which were glassy at the moment. Oh no, was she going to start crying?

I did not do tears.

I meant to look away, but her eyes wouldn't let me go. I forced words from my mouth. "You have got to be kidding me." I couldn't help the icy bite to my words.

The young girl, who was probably around the age I had been when I'd died, flinched. I instantly regretted my words, but refused to take them back. They were calloused and insulting, but our job—protecting the living from the evil that stalked the Earth—was no joke.

Barely a second passed before Half Pint turned and headed back toward the rec room door, muttering something under her breath the whole way.

Shannon moved faster than either of our eyes could track and the wisp walked right into her, bouncing off the angel, before landing heavily on her butt.

I pressed my lips together tightly to keep the corners from lifting. Maybe there was a little bit of fight in this wee leprechaun after all?

I was focused solely on the girl until I felt Shannon's gaze on me. When I lifted my eyes, the angel was glowing brightly—a clear sign she was agitated.

Well, if *I* could glow, I'd be a flippin' Lite Brite right now, so she wasn't intimidating in the least.

"You know we don't make mistakes about these things. There's a reason for this."

I ran a hand through my hair and indicated the wanna-be huntress with the other. "She'll be eaten alive out there. Just look at her, Shannon."

A moment of doubt crossed Shannon's face. I saw it and Half Pint probably noticed it as well.

Couldn't they find some nice, safe, more appropriate job for her? Or at least a trainer with a little more patience than I had these days. Even *I* could admit I was a bit of a loose cannon after what went down with Morgan on Earth.

There had to be someone better suited than me.

"Logan, it is what it is," Shannon's voice drew my attention—which had subconsciously drifted to the damsel still sitting on the ground between us— once again, "You've been chosen as her mentor. You need to train her as you would anyone else."

Did that last comment come with a pointed look, or was I just reading too much into it? And then a thought occurred to me.

"Is this because of what happened?" My tone darkened.

"No, Logan, this isn't some sort of punishment. You know things don't work like that here." Shannon paused for a moment. Her features softened and that was almost worse.

I didn't want her pity.

"What do you think they said about Romona when she first joined?"

I looked down at the girl, who in truth wasn't that much smaller than Romona—one of our best fighters—and let out a heavy sigh.

What else could I say?

Shannon knew me well enough to recognize my defeated sigh.

"Thank you, Logan. I'll leave her with you now. You know what to do."

I almost laughed at her words. I had no idea what to do with her.

"Wh-what?" The little sprite had been listening to our conversation with rapt attention, and it appeared that she had just now realized her fate had been sealed—and she wasn't going down without a fight.

I watched silently and with raised eyebrows as she clumsily tried to regain her footing to chase after Shannon. When the door banged shut behind the angel, she stopped and stared. Most likely frozen in disbelief.

I could relate.

Hmm, what's the wisp going to do now?

I was surprised by my own mild interest in this tiny creature. She remained turned toward the door, which gave me a nice view of her—

With a huff, she spun on her heel.

I schooled my features. I had a master poker face. No need for her to know the path my thoughts had taken a moment before.

"Okay," she plopped her hands on her hips and let out a breath. *That absolutely wasn't cute,* I chanted over and over in my head. Maybe if I said it enough it would become true. "So, will you at least tell me what exactly it is that we do?"

I stared straight into her eyes. How could they not have explained her job to her, at least in part? Man, talk about throwing someone right in the deep end. Time to rip off the Band-Aid and see if Half Pint knew how to swim. This chick was in for the shock of her afterlife.

"We kill demons."

She blinked twice. I thought she was going to say something, but instead her eyes rolled back and she dropped to the ground like an anchor hitting the ocean floor.

She was out cold.

Author Commentary: Chapter 1
JulieHallAuthor.com/logan-1

CHAPTER 2

TWO AND A HALF YEARS EARLIER

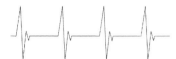

*T*he drink in my hand was tepid and soured in my stomach. To an onlooker, I probably looked wasted. But the glazed expression emanating from my eyes was less from the warm beer I was drinking and more from the thoughts rolling around in my head.

Despite the noise from the beach party around me, the splashing and receding of the surf washing up on shore wouldn't be silenced. Salty waves beat against the beach again and again only to be sucked back into the vast ocean. The sand would either be covered in water during high tide, or dried out by the sun's rays at low tide.

Underwater or dried out. That's exactly how I felt these days.

This party was like any other I'd gone to during high school. Booze, drugs, music, and filled with over-exaggerated everything. Loud laughing, sloppy dancing, and poor decisions we all blamed on the booze, drugs or music the next day and just moved on.

Everything was the same, except this time the only difference was me.

But no one seemed to care and I couldn't drum up the emotion to care that they didn't care.

An ocean breeze blew my shaggy hair around my head and with it the smell of brine and warm beer. I hadn't drunk that much, but there was a chance I was still going to be sick.

What am I still doing here?

Just as I was about to get out of the lounge chair I'd taken possession of for the last half hour—the one I'd pointed at the water rather than the festivities —a body plopped into my lap, sloshing the warm drink on both of us.

I let out an annoyed growl as I dumped the remainder of my cheap beer into the sand before it could do anymore damage. My mind more on thoughts of how it was going to stink up my car than the drunken girl trying to straddle my lap.

In her quest, she elbowed me in the gut and my annoyance turned to her.

"Oops, sorry Logan," she said before dissolving into a fit of giggles that brought her stale breath and unfocused gaze closer to my chest. I restrained myself from standing up and dumping her on her butt into the sand. I knew Rachel. We went to the same school and under normal circumstances she wasn't nearly this . . . annoying. I told myself she was just having a good time and I shouldn't bring her down. But I was done with this party tonight. Maybe done for a while.

"Hey, what's up with you? Whatcha doin' sitting over here all by yourself?" she asked after she regained some semblance of composure.

She wasn't wrong. This wasn't my usual M.O. for these parties. I was often one of the loudest and most annoying of them all. But something just wasn't sitting right with me these days and it couldn't be ignored anymore.

"Just feeling more like chilling tonight, I guess," I answered, trying hard not to stare at the ample amount of cleavage on display, exactly at eye-level.

"I could be up for chillin'." Rachel's attempt at casual seduction was anything but. There was nothing subtle about her literally throwing her body at me. Her eyes weren't half closed with desire, but rather due to whatever drinks or pills she'd consumed that night.

That was not hot.

I fought against another wave of irritation that called for me to shove her body harshly off of mine.

What was wrong with me?

In the past, this would have been the type of scenario I would have been down for. Rachel was cute; I'd never cared how much someone else was under the influence before going for it. Heck, I was usually just as plastered as they were and sometimes didn't remember much the next day, but right now, I was just disgusted. Not at Rachel, but at myself.

Is this really how I want to go through my life?

I gently, but firmly, removed her hands from my shoulders and then lifted her off my lap as I stood up. She teetered on her feet and giggled some more as she used my body to keep her own upright. I gritted my teeth and waited for her to regain at least some of her balance before removing her hands from me once again.

"I'm gonna head out." I jerked my chin towards the parking area up the way to indicate that I meant I was going to leave the party, not just leave her. I was never one to needlessly hurt people's feelings, but if this chick didn't get the hint soon, it might come to that.

Something was roiling inside my gut, screaming at me to run from this place. Itching to get out of there, I was little more than a ticking time-bomb, unsure of when the countdown would reach zero. When I exploded I wanted to be far away from this place.

"Aw, come on, Logan. Don't be like that. It's not even late. You can't leave yet." She jutted her lip out into an exaggerated pout. Did girls think that was attractive?

Rachel made a move to latch on to me again but I quickly side-stepped and took off. I think she landed on the lounge chair because of the racket behind me, but I refused to turn around to check. I was *so* done.

Long strides took me closer to my car. And each step away from the party lifted some of the pressure in my chest, making me feel lighter somehow.

"Hey, handsome, where are you headed off to?" The clear and crisp nature of her words and familiarity of her voice tempered my need to flee. Kaitlin was just getting out of her lime-green VW Bug Convertible when I reached the rows of parked cars. My black Mustang was a few cars down from hers, but the itch to reach it lessened for a moment.

"Just not feeling it tonight, I guess," I answered. Kaitlin's quintessential California girl look with her blonde hair pulled up into a high ponytail, tanned skin, and athletic build was probably an exact match for my laid-back surfer persona. I'm sure lots of people assumed we were a *thing* at one time or another. But it had never been that way between the two of us.

I'd known Kaitlin for practically my whole life. In a weird way, she was the closest thing I had to a sibling. We'd bonded over who-knows-what sometime along the way and now we watched out for each other.

Her eyes narrowed and her brow pinched. I braced myself for a round of twenty questions, silently cursing the wind as I shoved the hair from my face, and waited for her to come up with the first one. Clearly, we knew each other a little too well.

Kaitlin was probably the only girl here I wouldn't blow off if pushed too far. Maybe that was wrong, but it was the truth.

Her slow nod spoke of understanding and I almost dropped my jaw at her next comment.

"Yeah, I get where you're coming from." She looked out over the beach where the bonfire blazed. From up here under the lights, you couldn't see much down past the circumference of the fire's light. "These things don't seem as exciting as they used to, do they?"

I opened my mouth to respond but no sound came out.

Kaitlin didn't wait for me to speak. "I'm just gonna pop in myself and say hi to a few people before heading out too," her gaze jerked back to me, "You haven't been drinking have you? You're okay to drive?"

I ignored her first question and answered the second. "Yeah, I'm good to drive. You have fun. I'll see you later."

She nodded her approval—probably assuming I was confirming the not-drinking-anything question—and I waved a quick goodbye.

I was fine to drive, so she didn't need to know I'd had a few drinks of beer in me. Really only one because the second barely counted. I wore more of it than I had actually drank. *Thank you very much, Rachel.*

I reached my car a moment later and breathed a sigh of relief. Something was seriously wrong with me.

I started the muscle car and enjoyed the rumble of the engine before carefully reversing and pulling out onto PCH—Pacific Coast Highway ran north and south along most of the pacific coast of California—leaving the festivities behind.

Both literally and figuratively.

I carefully maneuvered my car around the bends and turns in the road because although I felt like I was one hundred percent okay to drive, I still didn't want to be caught by a cop. Being underage at eighteen, any number that popped up on a breathalyzer would be too high. So, regardless of how fast I might push it during the day, my hands remained firmly at the ten-and-two position as I carefully made my way home.

But that restless mind of mine just wouldn't shut up and I found myself pulling off at one of the scenic overlooks along the road. It was a favorite late-night spot of mine because it was far enough away from the city to see the stars, and hidden enough that it was hard to find. The singular deterrent was the occasional car that did stumble across my hidden oasis to use it for a different sort of privacy. Tonight it was blessedly empty when I pulled off the road. I got out of the car and hopped up on the hood so I could lean back and gaze upon the heavens.

It was a cloudless night, so the cosmos was out, its full glory on display. I could even see the edge of the Milky Way, like a dusting of freckles set upon the darkened sky.

I inhaled a deep breath of salty air and was warmed by the metal beneath me as a cool breeze washed over my body. Even though most of my clothes had dried since their earlier beer bath, the faint smell still infused the air around me when the wind died down. It was washed away with every new gust of air off the Pacific, only to return between breaks.

I was going to have to be extra careful to get these clothes in the wash before my parents woke up in the morning. I'm sure they already suspected what I was doing when I went out with my friends, but no point in giving them any reason to get on my case when I hadn't even done anything this time.

Thoughts of the party slowly leaked from my brain as I continued to stare at the expanse above. For the last few years, my life had consisted of three main things: surfing, parties, and girls. But lately, deep life questions had begun to haunt me, making me feel much older than I truly was.

What was I doing with my life? Where was I going? Was I making a difference in the world? Did I even care if I did?

My mind was a cluttered mess. I beat down the uncertainty and let all thoughts fly from my head on a loud exhale. A perfect moment of silence followed as I watched a star streak across the sky. I gulped in the ocean breeze and a question bigger than myself trickled into my subconscious.

Could all of this beauty in the world really have been put here by accident? What if there was something bigger at work?

"My will, not yours."

Those words echoed in my brain in an unnatural way.

I jack-knifed into a sitting position and turned my head from side to side making sure I was truly alone.

Had I actually heard those words . . . or was I hallucinating now? Had someone slipped something into the one drink I'd had?

My gaze was prowling the surrounding area for the person who had spoken when I was momentarily blinded by a set of headlights.

Great, my reprieve was over. Might as well head home, I guess.

I slid off the hood of my car and was about to open the driver's side door when the short *whoop* of a police siren froze me in my tracks.

I yanked my guilty hand from the door handle as if it had been burned. I couldn't get in trouble if they hadn't actually caught me driving, could I?

As I turned, the police cruiser came to a stop in the spot next to my own.

I groaned silently as a door opened, then slammed shut.

This was just great. I should have just stayed home tonight.

I turned my body and leaned up against the side of the car, crossing my arms over my chest. Might as well find out what the cop wanted. I'd been here too long for him to have followed me under suspicion of drinking and driving, but the second I got behind that wheel he could slap me with a DUI *and* underage drinking charge.

No thank you.

An older man with salt-and-pepper streaked hair came around the front of his standard issued police cruiser. He reminded me of my dad for some reason. Maybe it was the man's athletic build—despite being past his prime— or perhaps it was just the air of authority cops gave off in general.

Whatever the reason, I shook it off and forced a neutral expression on my face.

"Everything okay out here, son?" the officer asked.

My knee jerk reaction was to tell him I wasn't his son, but that wasn't going to land me anywhere I wanted to be.

"Yeah, I'm good." Short and to the point. Why offer any more information than was necessary?

His eyes, although not hostile, remained locked on my face. I returned his stare hoping it sent him the I've-got-nothing-to-hide vibe.

"Well, that's good to hear. I happened to see a car parked here on my way back to the station and just wanted to check to make sure everything was okay. Glad to see no one has any car trouble."

I almost snorted. Yeah, he was probably checking to make sure no one was getting it on, was more like it.

"Nope. The car is fine, sir, just doing some star gazing to clear my head."

This guy wasn't a fool, but it didn't appear like he was looking for trouble either.

He nodded at me and cracked a small smile. The gesture seemed friendly, but what did I know? I didn't have much experience with cops.

He could check my car if he wanted. He wasn't going to find anything incriminating in there.

"Well, then," he began, "seeing that everything is alright here, I'll just be on my way."

At that moment, the wind shifted and blew my beer-drenched scent directly at the cop.

The officer stopped in his tracks and turned back toward me. His gaze wasn't as friendly as it had been a moment before.

Not moving a muscle, I remained casually leaning against my driver's side door with my arms folded across my chest. My face held the same look that I was sure gave nothing away. But I did hold my breath and sent up a silent prayer to whomever was out there that this guy would just turn back around and drive off.

My prayer went unanswered.

"Did you drive this car out here tonight, son?"

I was not this guy's son. And what could I say to that? There wasn't anyone else around, so a lie wouldn't have been convincing.

"Yes, sir."

"And have you been drinking tonight?" He didn't beat around the bush.

Lie or truth? Which one would get me in less trouble? Because right now this cop was like a dog with a bone.

"Someone spilled their drink on me. That's what you smell, officer. That's why it's so strong." Half-truth and evasion, it was.

This guy wasn't an idiot, so I knew he would be able to tell right away that I wasn't drunk. But I also didn't look twenty-one, and I smelled like a brewery.

My only hope was that he'd take my word for it or let me off with a slap on my wrist. I got underage drinking was illegal, but come on, didn't everyone do it? And he had to actually catch me driving to slap me with a DUI, right? But I'd just admitted to having driven the car here myself.

Shoot.

Author Commentary: Chapter 2
JulieHallAuthor.com/logan-2

CHAPTER 3

"*Y*ou know getting off with only community service for the rest of the year is actually pretty lucky."

I cracked my neck and shot Kaitlin an irritated look. She wasn't wrong, but the whole ordeal was a mess and I would never hear the end of it from my parents. They'd had to pick me up at the police station. The lectures hadn't stopped since, and they'd revoked my 'car privileges' for the next month.

I slammed my locker shut and walked down the hall without responding to Kaitlin. I was being a jerk; it certainly wasn't her fault I was arrested for underage drinking. I was lucky they hadn't stuck me with a DUI charge as well. They certainly could have because it was obvious that I had driven the car to the overlook.

I was eighteen and about to graduate from high school, and hated being treated like a child. It rubbed me the wrong way.

Bumming rides off friends was a real pain.

But not only that, the feeling of 'off-ness' still hadn't gone away. It nagged and picked at me daily.

"Hey, wait up!" Kaitlin called after me. I slowed my gait. "Come on, Logan. I know you. There's something else bothering you."

I arched a brow. She wasn't wrong. She knew me well enough to pick up on that fact, but she also should have known I wasn't big on talking about my feelings and such. I liked to work stuff out on my own. Even though Kaitlin and I were close, the number of times I had actually confided in her about deeper issues was minimal.

"Are you being serious, right now?" I asked.

She gave me a playful shove. "Don't give me that look. I know I'm right, and it isn't something that just came up. You've been acting . . . different, for a while now. Something is bothering you. I can tell." She narrowed her eyes and went up on her toes, and forcefully grabbed my head, tilting it side to side as if she was searching for something buried in my hair.

"Hey, cut it out," I swatted her away, "What the heck are you doing?"

"Yep, it's just as I feared." *What was this chick talking about?* "The gears in there are definitely turning, but they're a little rusty and covered in cobwebs, so it's taking you extra long to work it out. You are in obvious need of a good friend, right now."

I barked out an involuntary laugh before rolling my eyes at her. "You're a weirdo, you know that?"

She shrugged, her smile still in place. "Takes one to know one."

"Whatever." Sometimes there was nothing to do but shake your head at Kaitlin. "I'm headed to class." A few more weeks until I was out of here, then I could concentrate on my surfing career full time.

That was another point of contention with my parents. I wanted to go pro, and they wanted me to go to college instead. I'd been accepted to several schools. Between my decent grades and my surfing skills I had even snagged a few privately-funded scholarships for student athletes.

I'd been competing in the juniors for years . . . and yeah, I may be jumping the gun a little early by trying to go pro right out of high school, but I at least wanted to give it a shot.

My parents' argument was to go to college and spend the time getting a degree and perfecting my sport, but I didn't want to waste four years when I could be doing what I loved every day.

Before I could leave, Kaitlin grabbed my arm, her expression morphing into one that rarely graced her face . . . seriousness sprinkled with a dose of uncertainty.

"Hey, do you think we could talk sometime? Even if you don't want to open up—I get that, by the way—but there has been some stuff I've been thinking about lately and I wanted someone to . . ." she lifted and dropped a single shoulder, "I don't know, I guess just someone I trusted I could talk to it about."

My body drained of all levity as my concern for Kaitlin rose. I grasped her shoulders and turned her to face me fully. She wouldn't look me in the eyes as she played with the end of her ponytail.

"Kaitlin, what's wrong?" My voice had dropped an octave. If someone was messing with her, they were in for a world of hurt. A shiver of fear ran through me at the thought that she might be in some sort of trouble. I ignored it as I waited for her to answer.

She heaved a sigh before finally meeting my gaze. "It's nothing like what you're thinking, Logan. I'm fine, really. In fact . . ." she paused and her brows pinched as she chose her next words, "for the first time everything might actually be . . . right."

Confused I tilted my head like a puppy trying to interpret its owner's words. And then she laughed.

Laughed. In. My. Face.

Was she messing with me right now? If so, I was never going to take anything she said seriously again.

"I'm sorry, Logan. Your expression right now . . . it's just priceless." She hiccuped, and then slapped a hand to her mouth to stop any more noise from escaping.

"Hey, you two, get a room already!" someone down the hall yelled. The comment was followed by a couple of hoots and inappropriate remarks.

I rolled my eyes. We got random junk like that all the time. Just because we looked like we'd make a cute couple or whatever, didn't mean it was ever going to happen. She was like a sister to me.

Kaitlin scrunched her nose in disgust, mirroring my thought. If I hadn't felt the same I might have been offended.

"That's gross."

I grabbed my chest as if I'd been shot. "Ouch. You mean you *don't* want to get a room with me? That hurts. Haven't you heard? I'm irresistible," I said with a wink.

"I repeat, gross. Maybe if I hadn't seen you eat your boogers in middle school you might be marginally attractive to me, but yeah, no. That's never happening."

A roar of laughter rose in my chest and escaped my lips.

"I'm a guy, Kaitlin. We all do gross stuff at one time or another. It's a given."

"Yeah, well, that pretty much sealed the deal for me. You," she finished her statement with a pointed finger in my face, "are forever planted in the friend zone."

I chuckled at our banter since it put me in a better mood, all of our heavy talk forgotten for the moment. Messing with Kaitlin was a fun sport of mine. I tossed an arm around her neck and led her in the direction of both of our first-period classes.

"Don't let my adolescent behaviors get around. I got a rep with all the ladies to uphold."

"Yes," Kaitlin deadpanned, "I'm very aware of your rep."

Nothing like a good friend to keep your ego in check.

"Say something," Kaitlin pleaded with both her eyes and words.

"You . . . found God?" I shifted awkwardly in the too small plastic chair. Being after school, we had the library basically to ourselves. I cast a quick glance around just to make sure no one had overheard Kaitlin's confession. I didn't want to make her feel weird, but her admission had been a little out there, even for me. I'd prepared myself to sit through an emotional monologue about her failed attempts at snagging some guy . . . boy, was I wrong.

"Don't say it like that. You make it sound like I've joined a cult or something."

"Well . . . *have* you?" I widened my eyes unnaturally large, "Wait, did you drink any funny-smelling Kool-Aid while you were at one of those meetings?"

"Gosh, Logan. No! Geez, dramatic much?"

I lifted my hands up in defense. Truth was I didn't know what to say, so I resorted to jokes. What Kaitlin had just described to me poked at that spot inside I'd been trying to ignore. The itchy feeling was back and something about this conversation made me really uncomfortable, and I was using humor to hide it.

"Look, it's not like I'm trying to convince you of anything. I just wanted to tell you what's been going on with me."

Kaitlin's shoulders hunched and she played with the end of her ponytail, something she often did when nervous. Her eyes were downcast. Everything in her posture spoke of vulnerability and here I was cracking jokes to cover my own conflicted heart.

I took in a huge breath of air and let it out slowly, then ran a hand through my hair, not caring in the least the crazy directions I sent it.

"Hey," I laid a gentle hand on her shoulder, "I'm sorry for making light of this. I just don't . . ." It was my turn to look for the right words, but they were missing. "I just don't know what to say."

A weak smile touched Kaitlin's lips. "You don't need to say anything, okay? I just wanted an ear to listen."

I could do that for her. "Okay. Whenever you want to talk about this stuff, I promise I'll listen. I may not get what's going on with you right now, but I can be that friend."

"Thanks, Logan," she leaned forward and gave me a quick squeeze, "I'd better head to practice now. I'll see you later, okay?"

I forced a wide smile. "Yep, definitely."

An hour after Kaitlin left I was still sitting in the same chair, running over everything she'd said.

"Give me a break, Logan," Kaitlin's eyes, as well as her words, held a world of skepticism, "Like you never thought all of this could be part of a bigger design." Her hand swept wide to indicate the world around us.

We were hanging out in my favorite spot. Or rather ex-favorite spot. Getting arrested for the first time in a location kind of steals the luster away. We watched the ocean's waves tumble and roll toward shore. Salty mist would irritate my nose a few moments after each large wave crashed against the cliff beneath us.

"I don't buy it," Kaitlin continued, "I've seen you deep in thought enough—especially these last few months—to know that something else besides 'girls' is rolling around that dusty shell you call a brain."

I scoffed. "We both know my brain is very high functioning—" I was cut off by Kaitlin's own scoff, "What? Would you like to compare SAT scores?"

She sealed her lips and narrowed her eyes in mock anger.

"And I think you're severely underestimating the amount of time guys spend thinking about girls."

"You're probably right about that second one."

"And the first?"

"Oh, shut it!" she said and smacked my mid-section. Laughter rumbled from my gut.

"Don't be a hater."

She rolled her eyes and I knew we were on safer ground. She was right. Some of the things she had been talking about these last few months had started to make a little too much sense to me. We'd graduated a few weeks back and after many arguments with my parents, I was about to start my run to become a pro-surfer. So, I don't even know why I was giving Kaitlin's talks a second thought.

I had agreed to be a sounding board—it was the least I could do as her friend—but that was it. Somewhere along the way a God of the universe didn't sound quite as crazy as it had when she had first brought it up to me. And now that didn't just make me uncomfortable, it scared me on a level even *I* didn't understand.

All it would take would be to let go of my old beliefs, and embrace what was starting to resonate as truth . . . but I wasn't ready to pry my fingers loose quite yet. I didn't want anything to derail the plans I had for the future. Even if that meant ignoring the changes stirring inside my heart.

Three months into the pro-surfing circuit and it was exactly how I had expected it to be. Which left me feeling exactly how I *hadn't* expected to feel.

Hollow.

I lay on my board, staring into the cloudless blue Hawaiian skies as I bobbed in the water past the break. My body moved up and down to the lazy rhythm of the ocean as the coolness of the water on my backside warred with the Pacific sun's rays beating down on me from above.

It was still too early in the fall to worry about sharks migrating up from the south, not that sharks were ever a big concern of mine. For the most part you left them alone, and they left you alone. With arms stretched out on either side, I probably appeared to be a juicy snack to any great white. But my mind wasn't really focused on any of that. Instead, it was rolling around making friends with that hollow feeling inside.

It made no sense. The surfing was amazing. Yeah, the competition was intense, but I lived for that kind of stuff. I enjoyed the challenge and constant drive to excel, adrenaline pumping in my veins, my focus crystal clear. Almost nothing else could compare to being out in the free, wild waters where I was one with the ocean.

Most of the other surfers were cool guys, so no complaints there. The parties . . . well they were as unbelievable as I'd expected. So again, no surprises. And the girls . . . ah . . . yeah, the girls were also something I expected would come with going pro. I'd never had trouble in that department before, but I didn't like the feeling that I was a commodity to them now. Even though I was new to the major leagues of this sport, the girls looked at me like their meal ticket now . . . or at the very least a bragging right.

I watched other surfers use what was freely offered to them and consider it a perk of the sport, but something about it didn't sit well with me anymore. No one around me seemed to care the way I did. Part of me longed for the oblivion I had lived in before, even if I now saw it for what it was . . . simply chasing after the wind. A poor imitation of something that was supposed to hold more meaning.

For the millionth time, I wondered what exactly was going on with me. There was only one thing for certain; something needed to change.

I was straddling a fence refusing to pick a side, and it made my life grayer by the day.

I was currently in off-season training. Technically speaking, surfing was a year-around sport. The athletes simply chased the warm weather and the waves. After getting my feet wet in the pros so soon after graduation, I had decided to take a short break from competition to get ready for the official winter season to start. There were lots of surfers who did the same, so I was still surrounded by the community and lifestyle. Currently in a lull between tournaments, I used this time to train where the next big tournaments would start to pick up again.

I kept loose track of some of my friends from high school via one form of social media or another, but for the most part, I knew those friendships probably wouldn't last much longer. Except for Kaitlin, who reached out over calls or texts on a weekly basis, mostly with updates on her life at UCLA where she'd joined the volleyball team as a walk-on. But, sometimes she'd ask me deeper questions about how I was doing. I considered ignoring some of her messages, though years of friendship and loyalty refused to let me.

Some vital part of me had begun to change so many months ago, and I tried my hardest to ignore the constant scratch that pestered me. I kept telling myself to move on, that it would go away with time. But more and more my conversations with Kaitlin crept back into my consciousness. No amount of shoving them to the recesses of my mind would keep them buried any longer. And that annoyed me to no end.

I was due for a trip home in a few weeks and I knew there was a reunion party brewing already. *Ha!* Reunion party for people who had been apart for less than six months seemed silly to me, but I promised Kaitlin I'd be there, so I would.

If only this restlessness would leave me. I just wanted . . . peace.

"Be still, and know that I am God."

I sat up so fast I dumped myself right off my board. Some pro-surfer I was. I surfaced quickly and coughed to free my lungs of the briny water I'd inhaled, and then grabbed my board with one arm as I looked around the ocean to see who had spoken.

What was that?

It was just like the night I'd been stargazing, before I'd gotten arrested. A voice that sounded clear as day, but echoed in my head instead of the air around me. This time I couldn't blame it on the possibility of a hallucinogenic dropped in my beer. Despite the ease of availability these days, I actually hadn't had a sip of alcohol in months.

I was stone cold sober.

So, there were two explanations here. Either my mind was playing tricks on me, or there really was someone—or something—out there trying to talk to me. The grip on my old life just tightened a little more. I was getting off of this fence, today, and I knew exactly how to do it.

Six hours later, I was exactly where I told myself I wanted to be. Sitting poolside, with my vision just the right amount of hazy, a bikini-clad brunette at my side. I had always had a thing for brunettes, who really knew why.

I was young and attractive . . . heck, I was a pro-athlete. This was exactly how I was supposed to be living my life.

Correction, this is exactly how I was supposed to be enjoying my life.

Then why aren't you enjoying yourself right now? My mind whispered defiantly. I told myself to shut it.

"What was that, baby?" asked the almost-naked girl at my side.

Dang. Had I said that out loud? I must be drunker than I'd thought.

"Nothing." I waved her off and she shrugged in response.

After a few minutes, her arm skated across my naked chest. I told myself that it felt nice, not that it made my skin crawl.

"So, Jace said that there were some guest bedrooms upstairs. Want to go check one of them out with me?"

Shocker, another girl who lacked a subtle bone in her body. But I was doing this. I was shaking off the doubts that had plagued me for months and robbed me of the fun I should be having. This was exactly the type of night I had been expecting when I had shown up to this party.

I shot the girl a cocky grin and simply lifted my chin to let her know I was down. What was her name again? I honestly couldn't remember. Maybe she didn't remember mine either, and that's why she'd called me 'baby' before. I told myself it didn't matter.

We both got up, me a little less graceful than was normal—I'd lost count of the shots I'd taken that evening—and walked into the house, the girl leading the way because I didn't have any idea where Jace's guest bedrooms were. I barely even knew Jace.

She stopped in front of a door and turned to send me a sly smile over her shoulder. It looked more creepy than seductive to me, but what did I know? I was wasted, and committed to the course of action.

She opened the door and beckoned me in. I watched with glassy eyes as she moved her hands up to untie the top of her swimsuit. I had a vague thought that I should be more excited about this, but shoved it away.

Just as she was about to untie the strings that would cause her top to drop away, something in my stomach turned. And I didn't mean that in a metaphorical sense. I meant that in an, 'I'm-gonna-blow' sense.

My stomach's revolt must have shown on my face because she stopped short and sent me a confused look, brows scrunched and upper lip pulled north.

"Um, are you feeling alright there, babe?" Yep, she definitely didn't remember my name.

I made an attempt to laugh it off. Like I was going to let an upset stomach ruin my night. "Yeah, I'm totally—" I couldn't even make it through the sentence before vomit spewed from my mouth, as if someone had forcefully squeezed my stomach, causing the alcohol mixed with bits of food to project right onto the brunette and her pristine white, barely-there bikini. It slid down all her ample curves. Suddenly, they weren't as attractive as they'd been a minute before.

We both stood motionless for a beat before the girl began to scream in disgust. She fled the room, and I ran for the door that I prayed would lead me to the bathroom.

It *was* the bathroom. Finally, something was going right. Or as right as it could, because I continued to vomit and heave into the porcelain toilet for at least another fifteen minutes until nothing else came up.

Perhaps I should have been embarrassed by what had just happened, but after the alcohol was ejected from my body—*nothing like a good puke to sober a guy up*—I realized more than anything, I was relieved. And that was all sorts of backwards.

I knew I was too messed up to drive, so after I stopped dry heaving I drank as much water from the tap as I could keep down, and stumbled out of Jace's house and onto the beach. The one place I always felt at home. I walked a short distance before dropping to the damp sand, hanging my head between my arms.

I'd changed. I was still changing. And I was finally ready to let go.

Author Commentary: Chapter 3
JulieHallAuthor.com/logan-3

CHAPTER 4

"*Y*ou're actually here!" Kaitlin's scream slapped me in the face the moment I opened the car door. I'd barely unfolded my long legs from the bucket seat of Reeve's sports car to stand to my full height before a blonde bundle of energy slammed into me.

My back hit the side of the car as I absorbed the impact. Thank goodness, I'd positioned myself a little to the side or we both would have fallen back inside the car. She hadn't even given me the chance to close my door.

"Hey, Kaitlin," I chuckled as I squeezed her and then returned her to her feet, "It's good to see you too."

The smile on her face couldn't have been brighter. It was so wide I was pretty sure she was showing off a few molars at the moment.

"Let me check." She tilted her head to the side and twisted it back and forth as she ran her over-exaggerated gaze from head to toe and back again, bobbing up and down as she went. One of her eyes was closed and the other was squinted as if she was examining me. Something about the way she moved reminded me of a baboon.

"Cut that out." I forced her to stop and shot her an annoyed look.

"Yep, there's definitely something different about you." Her mega-watt smile was back.

"Give me a break." I rolled my eyes at Kaitlin. That night on the beach, several weeks ago, after I'd vomited on the chick I was looking to score with —whose name I still didn't recall—something had happened. I'd finally let go of my old life and put my trust in someone greater than myself. I'd called— perhaps mistakenly—Kaitlin the next day to tell her what had happened. There was lots of squealing involved on her side of the phone.

It's not as if everything had changed overnight, but some things had. That itchy restlessness I'd been struggling with for months had finally quieted. And I had something I didn't before—hope.

"Welcome to the club, little brother."

"Little?" I arched a brow and tilted my head to look down. It wasn't as if Kaitlin was short, she was actually quite tall . . . for a girl. But my six-three height gave me at least four or five inches on her.

"Yep, my birthday is two months before yours. That makes you the little sibling."

"If you say so."

"What club?" Reeve asked. He was a buddy from high school who'd given me a lift that evening. His parents had just bought him a new Camaro Z28 for having made it through his first few months of college without being kicked out, and he was looking to show it off tonight.

"Nothing," I answered, "Ignore the annoying blonde in front of me. She just likes to hear herself talk."

"Hey! That's not true," She turned her attention to Reeve with a gleam in her eye that caused an involuntary groan to crawl up my chest. She was about to say something to embarrass me. I could feel it. "I'll have you know Logan has some pretty big news. A few weeks ago—"

I slapped my hand over her mouth, stopping whatever words were trying to make their way out of that devious head of hers. I did a quick check of her clothes to make sure I wouldn't be causing any indecent exposure, bent Kaitlin under my arm and picked her up, removing the hand from her mouth to keep a strong grip on her while I strode towards the group of our high school friends.

"Logan Barron London, you put me down right now."

Uh-oh, she'd just used my full name. Was that supposed to be intimidating?

I chuckled.

"Listen up, you. I know some defensive skills that could take away your ability to have kids someday. You drop me right now!"

Ouch.

An involuntary wince overtook my body, wiping the cocky grin from my face. You don't joke about things like that. If that was how she wanted to play it, fine.

"You want to be dropped? No problem."

I released my hold on a squirming Kaitlin, making sure I crouched so that her fall to the sand wasn't far, and listened as she sputtered when the surf rode up the shore and knocked into her.

"Logan!"

I turned and continued walking backwards. A full-on belly-laugh burst free. It started in my gut then moved up to my chest. She scurried out of the water's path on her hands and knees. The glare she shot me promised retribution. I didn't doubt for a second that one day I'd be paying for that sin.

When she finally got to her feet, the left half of her body was covered in wet sand and her once perfectly straightened hair was a tangled mess. She assessed her condition as if she couldn't believe what had just happened.

Another bark of laughter from me drew her attention.

The smile she shot me was nothing short of chilling. It said she already had a plan of retaliation brewing in her head. That look alone should have given me cause for pause, but I just laughed louder and waved her over.

"Come on, Kaitlin. You're missing all the fun."

She stuck her tongue out at me in the perfect sibling gesture before jogging to catch up, and then punching me in the arm when she had.

"That was sneaky. You know I'm gonna get you back for that."

"Oh yes, I'm aware. Now let's go say hi to all of our old classmates."

"You're lucky there's no one here I'm looking to impress." She brought a hand up to the soggy side of her head and tried to finger comb through her now-matted hair.

"Hey, I just did you a favor."

"Oh, yeah? How do you figure?"

"The lucky guy who ends up with you should think you're beautiful even at your worst."

She returned the eye roll I gave her earlier.

"Okay, Mom. Thanks." Sarcasm dripped from her voice.

"Mom? I can honestly say that's the first time anyone has called me that." I curled my upper lip, "Yuck. Hopefully the last as well."

"Oh, new nickname for you. I like!" Kaitlin clapped with glee.

"Hey look, Logan's here!" someone yelled, cutting off our conversation, "The party has finally arrived." A round of cheers went up from the rather large group around us.

Apparently, quite a few of my old classmates were trying to relive their high school glory days. And even though I'd been more subdued in my attendance and participation of parties those last few months of school, my reputation as a partier was still locked down.

Well, I thought to myself, *this ought to be an interesting experience.*

I kept a bottle of water in my hand the entire night to keep people from shoving red solo cups at me. It helped a little, but it still seemed like every third person was trying to get me to drink that evening. Especially the girls. Something about me not partaking in recreational drinking seemed to make people nervous.

I'd gotten more than one strange look each time I'd declined an invitation, whether it was for a drink or something more. At one point in the night I'd happened to accidentally catch Rachel's eye, the girl I'd turned down all those months ago. *Whoops!* She quickly looked the other way and disappeared into a group of her friends. What might have been a twinge of regret pinched my chest. Not regret for having turned her down, but for having caused her embarrassment in the process.

I'd done my fair share of embarrassing things in a drunken haze—something I hoped was in my past—but I knew it was different for girls. Personally, I'd just groaned about it the next morning and then pretty much forgot it ever happened. Girls seemed to take these types of things harder. It was somewhat of a mystery to me, but I guess there were some areas in which we truly were different.

I'd never cared before what a girl might have felt like after making a fool of herself, but now I did. That alone was proof of the change happening within me. I steered clear of her for the rest of the night. Talking with me would not lessen her embarrassment, and I also wasn't looking for a repeat of that evening.

I used to call most of the people around me friends, but in reality, they were more like acquaintances. When all you had in common with someone was that you liked to party together, you weren't truly friends. I hadn't seen the difference before, but I did now.

Everyone wanted to know what it was like to be a pro-surfer. I'd been an excellent surfer in high school, but skipping college to go straight pro was something of a novelty. The guys wanted to know about all the perks, and they didn't mean the endorsements. They wanted the nitty-gritty details on the girls and parties. Something I was uncomfortable talking about.

As the night went on, the girls got bolder and sloppier in their pursuit of me, some latching themselves on to my arms as they tried to hold a conversation with me even as they slurred their words. So not attractive.

"Hey, Mr. Popular." Kaitlin slid up next to me body-checking one of the girls away. I pretended not to notice.

"Hey, yourself. Where've you been the whole night?" I'd noticed Kaitlin had taken up my approach and clutched a half-full water bottle with the cap secured.

She waved her hand around indicating a couple of different groups. "Oh, you know, just catching up with people." There was a beat of silence between the both of us as we looked upon the group. Part of it all, yet somehow not. "It's different now, isn't it?" she finally asked.

"Yeah, it is. Being the life of the party doesn't seem as interesting, or as important, as it once was."

She nodded, her eyes still fixed on everything and nothing in front of us. She mumbled something under her breath.

"What was that?"

She shook her head, clearing her thoughts. "Oh, nothing. I just said 'in the world, but not of it.' Something I've been thinking about lately."

I'd heard that before. Read it for myself. I knew what she was talking about, and it perfectly described our situation at that moment.

"I know what you mean."

She turned her head to me and smiled. A genuine smile of friendship. And so I did what any good friend-brother would do . . . snaked my arm around her neck, pulled her into my side, fisted my hand and ran it back and forth on her head messing her hair up even further.

"Argh, you are so annoying sometimes." She said it with a laugh in her voice—so I knew she wasn't really mad at me—and wriggled from my grasp. "Do you realize that?"

"I am very aware," I answered solemnly, "I'm lucky to have a friend like you."

"Yes, you are." She crossed her arms over her chest in what was supposed to be a disgruntled pose, but she had a horrible poker face.

The party had been going on long enough that people were finally beginning to ignore me. I breathed a sigh of relief. This just wasn't my scene anymore.

"So, Mr. Deep Thinker," Kaitlin started.

I pointed a finger at my chest. "Me? Deep? Never."

One side of her lips curled up in a smirk, "You can't fool me, Logan. I know there's more to you than your pretty face."

"Do not let anyone hear you say that," I said swiftly glancing around in mock frustration to see if anyone had heard, "I have a rep to uphold."

Her laugh was loud, but so were the festivities around us, so no one turned to look. "Oh yeah, I can tell that you're really concerned with upholding your old rep." She nodded down at the water in my hand.

"What can I say? I've turned over a new leaf."

"Which is exactly what I want to talk about. So, tell me what's really been going on these last few months?"

I turned weary eyes to her. There had been a lot of ups and downs during that time. Definitely decisions I wasn't proud of, but also some stuff I needed to talk to someone about.

Kaitlin's face was filled with anticipation. As if she'd been waiting to have this conversation for a while now. And in hindsight, I could see that she had.

"There was a man," I began, "and his sacrifice for all of us is what made all the difference."

Time flew by, and by some miracle, Kaitlin and I weren't interrupted. We'd talked about everything. I told her all about what my time as a pro-surfer had really been like.

All the details, leaving very little out.

I had expected her to look at me, eyes full of condemnation, but that never happened. Kaitlin had too big of a heart for that.

She shared about the changes happening in her life too, and when they had really started, which was far before she'd ever mentioned anything to me.

We were so engrossed in our own conversation that we didn't realize the party had died down and we were some of the only people left. By the time we had noticed, Kaitlin thought to check her phone.

"You've got to be kidding me."

"What?" I asked.

"Ugh, Jessie. She left me here to go 'hang out' with Ryan." Kaitlin used her fingers to mark the quotes around 'hang out'. I didn't need an explanation of what that meant. "She said she's had too much to drink and let him take her home. How annoying. If she'd just left her keys with me I could have driven her car home."

Stuff like that happened all the time, but I could still understand Kaitlin's frustration. In fact, who knows if *my* ride was even still here? Time to go look around I guess.

"Come on, let's go see if Reeve ditched us, too."

We walked around for a few minutes before we found him quite literally tangled up with Rachel. I tilted my head to the side as I watched the show, feeling a little bit like a creeper for staring, but his tongue had to be halfway down her throat and it was like a train-wreck—I couldn't look away. That was some serious skill right there, just not the type you wanted to actually have.

"Logan," Kaitlin swatted my arm, "break them up or something."

I gestured towards the sand-covered couple. "I'm not breaking that up. I'm even sorry we went looking for him. That right there, is something I can never un-see."

Kaitlin huffed her irritation and then walked up to the couple and kicked Reeve's shoe. It didn't deter him from his current course of action, which I'm pretty sure was a hybrid between CPR and making-out. Kaitlin kicked the bottom of his sandal one last time with similar non-results.

Apparently fed up with the spectacle, she reached down and grabbed a handful of sand and chucked it at them and then yelled, "Hey, dork, gimme your keys so we can get home."

I laughed out loud at Reeve's shocked face when he came up for air. It bellowed out of me in waves. What tempered my amusement was Rachel's look of mortification when she realized both Kaitlin and I had been privy to her. . . ah . . . moment with him. For her sake, I forced myself back under control.

"Did you just throw sand on us?" Reeve brushed some of the granules off his shirt, but whether it was from Kaitlin tossing it on them, or them rolling around in it, who really knew.

"Yep, sure did. Now hand over your keys, lover boy. Logan and I want to head home. And we all know with his ugly face he needs all the beauty sleep he can get." She threw a smile over her shoulder at me, as if to say, 'Did you hear what I just said about you?' Guess she didn't get the memo that guys aren't as sensitive about their looks as girls.

"Yeah, that's right," I chimed in and took the wind out of Kaitlin's sails, "I need a lot of beauty rest. So, let me have them. You can come pick your car up at my place tomorrow."

"No way, man. That's my baby. No one drives her but me."

This was getting annoying. "Come on, dude. We live down the street from each other. You can walk over to pick it up in the morning."

He got to his feet. His hands and jaw clenched. It was obvious he was annoyed, but I wasn't sure if it was from us insisting we drive his new *baby*, or having interrupted his time with Rachel. I was too tired to care.

"I said no one drives her but me." Well, I guess that answered that question. He was definitely more concerned about his car than the girl he was with. I just hoped Rachel saw his behavior for what it was and used it as an excuse to leave his sorry butt behind.

"Hey, why don't you drop them off and then you and I can head somewhere together?" she suggested.

I ran a hand down my face. Nope. Lesson not learned.

He finally glanced at Rachel. "Well, yeah, I guess I can do that," he pointed a finger back at me, "but I'm just driving to your house and then you can drop her off yourself." I assumed he was talking about Kaitlin.

"Yeah, man, whatever. Let's go." At this point I just wanted to be off this beach. Kaitlin and I led the way to Reeve's car.

"Do you think he's been drinking?" she whispered in my ear.

I glanced over my shoulder. His steps were straight. Now and then he veered off the path, but it seemed to be from Rachel tugging on his arm. She was the only one of us who appeared to be tipsy, but it wasn't worth the risk. If I had to, I could call someone else to come and get us.

"Hey, man, you been drinking at all tonight?" I asked when we reached his car.

Reeve scoffed at me and opened his door. "You guys get the back."

I eyed the small backseat. Could I even fit in there? "Are you being serious, right now? There's no way my legs are gonna fit back there."

"Get in or don't, I don't care. But my girl gets the front seat." Rachel smiled widely at his words. Too bad she didn't know they were less for her benefit and more to express his irritation with me.

I grabbed the handle and jerked open the door, then moved the seat so Kaitlin and I could crawl in the back.

"I'll go in first," Kaitlin said, "Rachel can at least pull her seat up a bit to give you some more leg room," she added with a pointed glance at Rachel, who was looking everywhere but at us.

I nodded my thanks. Kaitlin crawled across the first seat and then wiggled her way into the tiny back seat, just barely squeezing her legs in between the driver's chair and her own. She winced once with the effort. It was obvious her shins and calves were being pinched.

"Reeve, come on, at least give her a few extra inches."

Without looking my way, he grunted and moved his seat up a fraction. Well, at least that was something. Kaitlin's legs were trapped for sure, but at least her circulation wasn't going to be cut off. I climbed in next and settled into the remaining tight spot. My shoulder was smashed against Kaitlin and I had to tilt my body at a weird angle to make my lower body fit. Maybe I should have called for a ride instead.

At least it was a short drive.

After adjusting the seat back and giving me a few extra inches—thank you, Rachel—she jumped into the passenger seat and bounced with excitement.

"I love your new car. I can't wait to see what it can really do," she purred suggestively in Reeve's ear. I pressed my fingers to my eyes and pushed down until I saw spots.

Real classy, Rachel.

I gritted my teeth as I waited for Reeve to start his stupid car.

That turned out to only be the start of the 'Reeve and Rachel' show. For the next ten minutes Kaitlin and I sat in uncomfortable silence as Rachel did everything except unbuckle and climb into Reeve's lap to get his attention.

Rubbing the heels of my hands down my face, I tried my best to ignore the noises from upfront. At one point, I looked over at Kaitlin, who was red in the face, but not from embarrassment. She was trying really hard not to laugh. With every added mile we drove, Rachel's antics kicked up a notch.

Seeing Kaitlin's tightly-pressed lips and bugged eyes almost made me lose it. Especially when I caught Rachel lick the side of Reeve's face. He made a move to jerk his head away, but remembering he had an audience in the back-seat he caught himself and stayed still, making some bogus comment about how sexy that was.

Big mistake, bro.

She did it again and the car veered into the oncoming lane for a moment before he forced it back.

"Okay guys, why don't you cool it while we're driving," I spoke up. "We get the point."

Wrong thing to say.

Reeve white-knuckled the steering wheel. "You got a problem with my driving, man?"

I heaved an annoyed sigh. "At the moment, yeah, I do. So, if you could just keep your focus on the road for a couple more miles, you can drive this thing however you want once you drop Kaitlin and me off."

What was his problem tonight?

It dawned on me slowly. When I would look back at this moment, I would ask myself time and time again how I couldn't have seen it sooner. Reeve only ever turned into a real jerk like this when he'd had too much to drink. I should have done more than just check his steps and take his word for it.

"I can drive this car however I want. Who are you to tell me how to drive anyway? You spend more time in the water than you do on the roads." Reeve yelled at me, and even Rachel—in her impaired state—looked a bit shocked.

Kaitlin's nails bit into the flesh on my forearm as Reeve sped the car up, swerving around corners at unsafe speeds. This portion of the road wasn't lit, so only his headlights guided him around each new bend.

Time for a new tactic.

"Yeah man, you're right. This is a pretty sweet ride. I'm sure you can really open her up on the straightaways. Why don't you slow it down, though?"

Once we got to my house I would somehow get the keys to make sure he couldn't endanger himself or Rachel further.

"You want to see her really open up?"

"No!" Kaitlin yelled.

But it was too late.

Reeve had turned his head slightly to glance at me in the backseat just as the hairpin turn appeared. Even Kaitlin's warning cry didn't give him enough time to make the proper steering corrections to keep us on the road.

Rachel screamed.

We hit the guardrail at an angle on the passenger's side of the car. My head whiplashed and smashed into the side window.

The next few moments—the last of my life— blurred into a maelstrom of noise and sensation. My life didn't flash before my eyes, but bits of glass and steel did as the vehicle tumbled on its descent.

There was a small part of my brain that knew this was very bad; people didn't just walk away from an accident like this.

Between the head injury, the chaos of the accident, and the constant tornado of bodies and debris, I could only discern the crunching of the metal around us, the screams of the people in the car, and the pain that wracked my body.

This shouldn't be the end. I didn't have enough time.

The thoughts whispered through my mind just as the motion of the car came to a jarring stop. My head once again slammed into something hard, my vision winked in and out until it was no more.

Author Commentary: Chapter 4

JulieHallAuthor.com/logan-4

CHAPTER 5

I was dead.

What other reason could there be for waking up in a field of multicolored flowers? I lay on my back with my arms stretched out on either side of me, blinking against the brightness of the sky and the rainbow sprinkled greenery around me. I closed my eyes, squeezing them tight to push through the memory block I seemed to be having, and snippets of a car accident filtered through.

"Well sh—"

"Hi, there."

I jackknifed to a sitting position and turned to my left. A man—probably somewhere in his thirties with tanned skin and facial hair—sat beside me.

"Whoa, where did you come from?"

He smiled and faint laugh lines appeared around his eyes. "You wouldn't believe me right now if I told you."

"Try me," I challenged.

He shrugged. "Okay, I've always been here."

"You're right, I don't believe you."

"Told ya."

"So, I'm dead, huh?"

He just shrugged again. Not a full answer, but I guess my question had been rhetorical anyway.

"All right then, what's next?" Why prolong the inevitable?

The man beside me chuckled. "You're going to fit in here just fine, Logan."

Logan, right, that was my name. How the heck did I forget my own name? In fact, there was lots of other stuff I couldn't remember.

"Why are my memories all jumbled, right now?"

"To better adjust, everyone's memories come back at their own pace, but don't worry, you'll get them back pretty quickly."

My gut told me to trust this dude, and at the moment, I was inclined to listen to it. Not that I had much choice.

I scrubbed a hand over my face. A gesture that felt familiar to me.

"Come on, Logan," the man stood and offered me a hand up, "let's get you to orientation."

I grasped his hand and was yanked to my feet. "You have to go to orientation after you die?" That was weird.

"You're in for a lot of surprises."

"I don't care how long I have to stand here, I'm not moving until you tell me what happened to my friend. Do you need me to spell her name out for you again?"

The blonde angel behind the intricately-carved mahogany desk looked around nervously, obviously flustered by my behavior. I'd just been assigned the job of something called a 'hunter' and was supposed to head to their training facility to meet my mentor.

But I couldn't have cared less about that right now. I wanted to know what had happened to my friend and would wait as long as it took to get answers.

That's right, I remembered Kaitlin. In fact, I'm pretty sure I remembered everything about my life on Earth. But there was no way for me to really be sure because the irony was you never would know if there was something you'd forgotten.

"Sir—"

"Logan."

"Right, Logan. You attended orientation, so you understand how things work here," she drawled out in a sweet, southern accent. Sure, put a southern belle at the front desk so we can't get frustrated without feeling bad.

I'd been hooked up to their Matrix-like machine—the information-download minus the large insertion of needles—and received the biggest brain dump ever. Apparently, I now knew all there was to know about this realm.

I had knowledge about materializing and dematerializing objects, knew where all the main buildings were in this city, learned there were different parts of the realm, that we could feel each other's emotions through a simple brushing of skin—creepy—and even that I needed to keep my lips to myself unless I wanted a soul mate for the rest of eternity.

No, thank you.

I can do without that for a few hundred years or so, because now I had all the time in the world. I was going to live . . . er . . . um, well, be like this for the rest of eternity. No need to worry about settling down anytime soon.

So yes, I got where this lady was coming from, and even knew from the faint glow she let off that she was some type of angel, but Kaitlin had been in that car with me and I needed to know if she'd made it or not. And by 'made-it' I meant made it out alive, not made it to where I was now.

There was a soft click that came from behind the blonde angel, and then a panel opened up from what I previously had assumed to be a flat wall.

Out walked another faintly glowing angel. This one had her jet-black hair pulled into a bun and wore a severe expression to match her businesslike attire.

I'll bet she was a barrel of laughs.

I refused to be intimidated.

"I've got this, Celeste," she said as she laid a hand on the blonde's shoulder.

"Oh, phew, thanks Shannon. I'll just pop out for a minute so you guys can get this sorted."

Shannon, the new angel, nodded and waited for Celeste to leave before turning her attention to me.

"What can I help you with?" she asked calmly.

I gritted my teeth. As if she didn't already know.

"I want to know what happened to my friend, Kaitlin, who was in the same car accident as me."

"She's in this realm as well."

My heart both sank and lifted with the news. It meant that she had died, but it also meant I wasn't here alone. "I want to see her."

"You cannot."

"What?" I stiffened, stepping back sharply. Blood rushed to my head and I ground my teeth together harder than before. My jaw started to ache. "Why not?"

"For several reasons actually, but the two most pertinent to your situation being that she's been assigned to a different part of the realm—"

"Why would you do that?" My hands clenched with the desire to punch my fists through the plain white wall.

"And because she doesn't have her memories back like you do."

Well, that made a little more sense. Shannon and I stared each other down. Slowly a softer emotion leaked into her gaze.

"Logan, when she regains her memories, you'll be able to visit her. But she needs a little more time than you did. Can you give that to her?"

I sighed heavily. When it was put that way, how could I say no? The fight leaked from my body and soul. I pinched the bridge of my nose.

"How will I know when she remembers everything again?"

"I'm sure she'll reach out to you when she does."

That would have to be okay for now.

"Alright. How about Rachel and Reeve? Are they floating around up here somewhere as well?"

Shannon's lips pressed together, forming a harsh line before she spoke. "No."

"You mean they're still down on Earth walking around, living out the rest of their lives while Kaitlin and I paid for their stupidity?"

There were a few beats of silence before Shannon answered. She squinted and her upper lip curled before her features smoothed out. "I wouldn't exactly say that was the case. Reeve is currently a quadriplegic. That means that there are lots of things he will most likely never again do independently. Some of those things include getting dressed, feeding himself, using the bathroom, getting into bed, driving a—"

"Stop!" I lifted a hand to halt her flow of words, "I get what you're saying." Shannon had rattled off that list in a monotone voice that might have seemed uncaring, but I got her point. Reeve was paying dearly for his mistake.

I shoved a hand in my hair and fisted it. Bile churned and boiled in my gut.

Yeah, I was mad at him for the accident, but I didn't want him to suffer like that for the rest of his life.

I stared at the blank wall to the right of Shannon before asking my next question. "What about Rachel?"

"Rachel is physically fine. She escaped the crash with some broken bones and cuts, but nothing life threatening or permanent," I almost breathed a sigh of relief, but it would have been too soon. Shannon continued, "Except mentally she has to live the rest of her life as the only one who walked away from that accident. Many people in her situation struggle with survivor's guilt, which can manifest itself as severe anxiety, depression, social withdrawal, insomnia, night terrors, mood swings and posttraumatic stress disorder."

I couldn't see myself, but I knew the blood had drained from my face. No longer satisfied with residing in my stomach, the acidic taste of bile crawled its way up my throat.

Shannon continued, "Only time will tell how this event shapes her future. I think it's safe to say that no one escaped that crash unscathed." The last sentence was a censure to me.

I looked the angel in the eye and nodded, "Yeah, I believe you're right."

"Any more questions, or can we move on now?"

Swallowing once, I shook my head and stared at nothing. My thoughts were on the two people suffering on Earth and the one here that I wasn't allowed to contact.

I startled when she laid a hand on my shoulder. Shannon waited until I met her gaze to speak. Her eyes weren't harsh, but they spoke of a core of steel.

"Are you ready to start the first day of the rest of your existence?"

I arched a brow at her and a small barely-there smile touched her lips. Was anyone ever really ready for that?

I was a natural. I wasn't being prideful, it was just the simple truth. I picked up fighting skills quickly and efficiently. I'm sure being an athlete on Earth hadn't hurt either as my body quickly adjusted to the new routine of the afterlife. I knew I was a good surfer, but this was really what I was built for. I couldn't wait to go up against my first demon. The thought of protecting the living against evil didn't leave me cowering in fear, but rather got my adrenaline flowing and heart pumping.

Through hard work and practice, every weapon I touched eventually became an extension of myself. I wielded them all fluidly, gracefully, and with deadly precision.

I spent extra time in the gym simply because I wanted to, not because I had to. When I was there everything else melted into the background. And it stopped me from thinking about what I'd left behind on Earth.

And there was a hefty list of things I sometimes found myself obsessing over. My surfing career was one of the things I'd had to come to terms with losing, but it wasn't the most difficult by far. The hardest part was letting go of my parents and friends. I'd built surfing up as a big part of my identity while alive, but I now realized I should have spent more of my energy on the people that mattered instead.

It was a mistake I wouldn't get the opportunity to atone for. And that was hard. Finding meaning in my new job—what I was literally created to do— made it better. Yet even now, I had to hold myself in check. If I weren't careful I would put being a hunter at the center of my universe, exactly as I had done with surfing on Earth.

I wouldn't let this job consume me. I'd gone down that road already and knew my identity was rooted in something much more powerful than that.

After only a matter of weeks, my mentor Stephen, a former knight during the Crusades, was already talking about sending me to the gauntlet—the trials every trainee had to pass before becoming an active hunter. After passing the gauntlet, I would not only become an active hunter, but eventually a mentor myself. I truly looked forward to the challenge.

Kaitlin had visited me for a few days the previous week before returning to her part of the realm. It had been a bittersweet reunion between the two of us. There was sadness about everything she'd left behind, but training to be a hunter—her assigned occupation as well—came almost as natural to her as it did to me. Having a true purpose revived part of her soul.

She was also something of a novelty being one of the few female hunters. There were all types of hunters, but the vast majority of them looked like professional body builders.

Looks could be deceiving though. I'd learned that the hard way by underestimating a fellow hunter, a girl named Romona, during a sparring session Stephen had arranged. The dark-haired beauty might have appeared fragile, but she moved like the wind and packed a mean punch.

I'd learned about more than just fighting techniques the last several weeks.

I'd made some interesting discoveries about my new home as well. I lived on the outskirts of a sparkling city nestled against a magnificent mountain range and giant forests. But the area I now considered home wasn't the only part of this realm.

The topography where Kaitlin resided differed from my slice of heaven. She was in a part of the realm more suited to the California girl I believed she would always be at heart. Her training center was steps from a beach, with warm light-filled days, ocean breezes, and laid-back evenings. Everything she said about it reminded me of where we'd grown up.

She tried to convince me to transfer to her part of the realm—something I'd learned was possible—but this was where I needed to be. Maybe I didn't want to be there because it was too much like my old life. Maybe it was for some other reason. I couldn't quite nail down my own hesitation.

Perhaps someday I'd go back to what I'd always known, but for now I listened to my gut and stayed put. There was a reason I'd been assigned to this part of the realm and I was curious to see what it was.

"Yo, Logan, stop showing the rest of us up," a voice boomed from the entrance of my training gym. My mentor had long since left, and I recognized the deep timbre of Alrik's voice, the mountain of a man who never seemed to take anything seriously.

"Is it *my* fault you can't keep up with this awesomeness?" I taunted back still striking the punching bag in front of me.

"Oh, young Skywalker, you have much to learn."

I grabbed the bag to stop it from swinging and shot Alrik a look. "How in the world do you know lines from *Star Wars*, old man?"

"Old man? *Old man?* That, my young friend, is a wounding blow. We both know I don't look a day over 600."

In reality, Alrik appeared to be in his late twenties. But here, where people rarely aged, it was impossible to guess anyone's true age. He claimed to be a Viking, but something about the chuckle he couldn't contain every time he mentioned it had me wondering if it was true—either way, he did play the part to perfection. With his large stature, blond hair and beard, he also happened to resemble Thor a bit too much.

"Come on, call it quits for the day. We're hitting the town tonight. Go get your smelly self cleaned up. I don't want you scaring off any of the ladies with your foul stench."

I gave myself a sniff. He wasn't wrong about my needing a shower.

"Hitting the town, huh?"

"Yes. You know. Go out with a group of your friends and do normal people things together. You did used to have a life, right?"

"Funny."

His grin widened. "Why yes, that I am."

"Humble, too," I added with mirth.

"Whoa, there. Let's not get ahead of ourselves. That's something I've never claimed to be."

I pointed a wrapped hand in his direction. "And I'll bet it's something you've never been accused of before, either."

"That is also true." He puffed out his chest as if extremely proud of that fact. I laughed off his antics.

"Where are we meeting?"

"Well, I'd say your place, but you live like a hermit out there in that cottage."

"Hey, now. It's a manly cabin and we both know it," I answered him.

He lifted his brows and hands. "If you say so. But in light of your hermit-like abode, we're gonna meet up at Kevin's place."

"The big glass building that looks like an open book, right?"

"Yep, that's the one," he backed out of the room, "We're leaving in an hour with or without you. So, you'd better get moving if you want to have time to perfectly style that head of yours."

He let the door bang shut behind him before I could defend my grooming habits. Alrik was always giving me a hard time about my hair. He was convinced I spent hours in front of a mirror styling it, when in reality I just showered, towel-dried it, and let it fall where it wanted.

Unwrapping my hands, I threw everything in my gym bag and spent a few minutes tidying up the gym before leaving the training center.

I skipped the locker rooms in favor of showering in my cabin instead. Maybe Alrik was right. I did kind of live like a hermit out by the edge of the forest. There wasn't a path that led to my house, so I'd made a crude one with a borrowed sword from the training center. I had to hike through part of the giant redwood forest to get home. Most people lived in the populated, bustling city, but this place fit me better.

I cleared the tree line and made my way to the front of my rustic and incredibly manly cabin. It sat just within the shadows of the giant trees over-looking fields of flowers. The same one, in fact, I'd first woken up in when I'd arrived in this realm.

From the outside, it didn't appear to be anything other than a small hunting cabin, but the inside . . . well that was a different story altogether. I guess every detail hadn't simply been downloaded during orientation . . . just the highlights. Because what we could do with our living spaces was almost beyond my imagination.

I opened the front door and stepped into my beach bungalow. What one could do with a simple thought in this realm was also beyond belief. When I'd first arrived and was assigned this home to live in, I'd been less than impressed with its Spartan appearance. It had been a couple of days before I'd remembered I could change my living space into anything I desired.

Decorating wasn't really my thing, but at one point I had wanted to go to school to be an architect, and at the end of all my experimenting the inside of the cabin looked a lot like a two-story beach-themed bungalow. Smaller than the house I'd grown up in or those of my friends, but more fit to my personality.

No extra frills, mostly just the necessities, except for the sweet master bathroom I'd thought up. The shower alone was worth waiting the extra fifteen-minute walk to clean up.

If Alrik wanted to tease me about something, it should have been the exorbitant amount of time I spent in there.

My body relaxed as the spray from multiple showerheads pounded out the knots in my sore muscles.

Ah, now this is heaven.

Author Commentary: Chapter 5
JulieHallAuthor.com/logan-5

CHAPTER 6

----

*S*weat dripped down my brow, and it wasn't because of the heat. My first trip back to Earth was also my first assignment. I was more nervous than I was willing to admit, but my body's response to the unknown was giving me away.

I accompanied a small group of hunters tasked with clearing an intersection of a few demons. They were messing with the streetlights and had caused a few head-on collisions, but no deaths.

We'd been sent down to take care of the problem. Which meant killing the creatures responsible. They were lower-level demons, so it wasn't a high-risk mission, but it was still my first.

Romona was team lead on this one, and that surprised me. Not because she was a girl, but because Alrik was with us as well and I'd thought for sure he would pull seniority over her. From what I'd gathered, she'd been a hunter for a relatively short amount of time—meaning less than a decade—compared to some of the others with us.

But the team leads for each mission were chosen for more than just the number of years they'd been a hunter. They were chosen based on their individual skills and talents, and the amount of focus they put into their missions.

I respected and appreciated that.

I glanced at my giant friend, Alrik. He'd never complained about it, but I did wonder what he thought of that way of doing things. If he truly was as old as he claimed to be, he'd be the senior ranking officer on this mission. From what I could see of his helmet-covered head, he was the picture of concentration. Exactly what I should be doing at the moment.

Snap out of it idiot!

The six of us moved forward together as a unit. I'd practiced enough times in the form-fitting body armor to be used to the weight and feel of it. Formless until we put it on, the tactical wear for hunters had hardened plates protecting our vital parts and was almost impossible to penetrate. An absolute must when fighting demons because their appendages were often sharp or serrated, not to mention their teeth which had evolved to bite into a hunter's flesh.

I'd been warned against ever letting my guard down against a demon. Demons gained their strength by feeding on negative human emotions. It was vital to their existence and part of what drove them to do the things they did. Hunters were somewhat of an addictive drug to them. We weren't necessary for their survival, but from what I'd been told we were a favorite tasty treat of theirs. If feeding off of human's negative emotions was their sustenance, then hunters were the dessert they would forgo their main course to consume.

Of course, generally speaking, they hated humans regardless. Thinking themselves the more superior beings, every demon had once been an angel who'd fought against the Creator, and had ultimately been cast out of His perfect realm. They'd been condemned to live out their existence on Earth, or worse, the realm beneath. So, their manipulations against the human race went deeper than mere survival; they enjoyed the pain, chaos and destruction they caused.

I shook my head to get it back in the game. The helmet I wore weighed my head down and restricted some of my view. It was the one part of the armor that took a little getting used to. I wished we didn't need them, but since we could still be knocked out, it was a necessary evil.

It felt very strange to be creeping around at night in the suburban areas knowing that no one except other hunters or demons could actually see us. After being in another realm for the last several months, being back on Earth was odd. Like discovering I'd spent a lifetime colorblind, but never realized until I was healed. Earth now seemed dull in comparison to the brilliance of my new home.

The streets we walked down looked nothing like where I'd grown up, which I appreciated. We were in the middle of America, far away from the ocean. That helped me concentrate so memories of my home, family, and friends wouldn't cloud my judgment.

Romona held up a fist signaling we should all stop. Being toward the rear of the line of hunters, I wasn't sure what lay ahead. She motioned for us to draw our weapons, which meant that she'd spotted the demons we'd come to slaughter.

I drew in a steadying breath. This was it; this was the moment I'd been incessantly training and waiting for.

I stayed light on the balls of my feet. Romona turned to the group and held up two fingers, indicating there were two demons. With a few more hand gestures she let us know we were splitting into two groups and attacking all at once. Romona, Alrik and I in a group, and Jason, Kevin and my mentor, Stephen in the other.

Stephen was being reassigned to another part of the realm on request, so this would be our first and last mission together. He gave me a wide grin before slipping away with the other hunters to attack from a different angle.

"You sure you're ready for this?" ribbed Alrik. I pressed my lips together and nodded once. Now wasn't the time for a chat.

"Okay then, you just yell if you need some saving. Damsels in distress are my specialty."

Romona glanced back and rolled her eyes at us before shaking her head.

"They're in position," she whispered. She was peering around the side of a building, so she alone knew what was going on. "We're going in three . . . two . . . one." And she took off sprinting into the street.

Dang, the girl could run fast!

Alrik and I caught up to her just as she reached the intersection and jumped straight into the air. I wasn't expecting that move. And where were the demons?

The shriek that rent the air could only be described as ungodly.

I gritted my teeth and almost dropped my sword to cover my ears.

It wasn't just the volume of the noise that was awful, but the pitch was high enough to make you drop to your knees. Stephen had warned me about it, but even his explanations didn't come close to the real thing.

Something fell from the sky with a thud that shook the ground.

Romona stood on the creature's chest, breathing hard with her sword positioned at its unprotected . . . ah, stomach . . . I think.

So that's where she'd been.

I checked my surroundings and sure enough another demon was up on a pole across the intersection and the second group of hunters was fighting to bring it down.

Man, demons were ugly.

Blackened scale-like skin stretched unnaturally over its flesh. Formerly angels, the demons' bodies had transformed to mirror the evil that lurked in their hearts. Since all their goodness had been twisted and warped into something evil, their bodies were twisted and warped as well.

This fella must have been extra evil because it looked like he'd fallen out of the ugly tree and hit every branch on the way down . . . and then some.

One of his limbs stuck out of his midsection and he used it to swat at Romona, who was trying to hack it off with her sword.

Most of their skin was extremely hard, like armor, which was unfortunate when trying to figure out where to stab to pack the most punch. Demons had a few vulnerable parts, usually around the joints, but they were difficult to locate and even harder to reach.

The thing didn't have a neck, but rather a head that attached directly to its upper body. We were trained to go for the neck first—if it had one—because that's one of their most vulnerable places.

Decapitation was a very successful way to vanquish a creature of any kind.

This monster reeked of sulfur, and the scent burned my nostrils.

This demon-fighting business was going to take some getting used to.

"Anytime now, guys!" Romona roared.

Right.

I'd been gawking at my first view of a demon rather than helping her fight.

Rookie mistake.

I don't know what Alrik's excuse was.

I jumped into action. Plunging my blade forward, I expected the tip to sink into the being's side.

I'd put a lot of force behind my attack, but was thrown off balance when it skidded across the side of the demon's armor-like hide, giving off a piercing metal-on-metal sound.

My training finally kicked in and I scanned the demon for weak points. Spots on its body where the flesh was slightly different meant we could pierce it with our weapons.

There, just under the appendage protruding from its midsection the blackened scales were missing and there was a section of penetrable flesh.

The creature threw Romona from its body and struggled to its . . . er . . . feet? Less like feet, more like stumps with jagged looking claws.

Alrik took the opportunity to attack from behind, swiping with his massive sword. The demon let out another ear-splitting cry, and swung around to its new threat. Alrik had cleaved a nice chunk of flesh from its back, but it wasn't enough to slay the creature.

Time to get back in the fight.

I aimed for the spot Alrik had already opened and my blade sunk a few inches into the unprotected flesh. One second, I was getting ready to push my weapon fully into the demon, and the next I was flying through the air.

My face throbbed and the sky above spun. I blinked until my vision cleared and was forced to sit up as my mouth filled with blood.

I spat on the ground and along with the unsavory bloody mix was a chunk of something familiar.

I ran my tongue along the top row of my teeth and sure enough, I was missing one of the front ones. I looked down to see it lying on the asphalt beside me.

Just great. I'm never going to live this one down.

"Logan! Break time is over, man. Time to help us finish Big Ugly off."

I sprang to my feet. I'd worry about the tooth later.

"Keep it distracted," I yelled to Romona and Alrik, "I see one of its weak points and I'm going to try to reach it."

Without questioning me, my fellow hunters obeyed my command and both moved in to attack together, purposefully keeping its attention on them, even though none of their blows would leave more than a scratch on the creature.

They trusted I had a plan. And I did.

While Romona and Alrik played a game of swing-and-duck with the demon, I moved around its side, and just as it lifted that weird arm-like thing coming out of its stomach, I used all my strength to thrust my sword into the base of where the limb met its body, and forced the blade into its innards.

The guttural cries of the dying demon were loud enough to make me wish I'd figured out a way to lop its head off instead.

It flailed and tried in vain to pull out the sword that I'd left in its gut. But the thrashing proved futile. My weapon was lodged at just the right spot that it couldn't be reached.

Without my sword, I backpedaled a safe distance from the raging creature. Romona and Alrik used that as an opportunity to hack off its middle appendage and sink their own weapons into its guts.

Black blood shot out of the wound and sprayed Alrik, who wiped his face with the back of his arm. Since that was also covered in the demon's goo he only managed to smear it around more.

I may have lost a tooth, but at least I wasn't covered in that foul-smelling liquid.

Romona delivered the killing blow to the demon by sinking a dagger into one of its slitted eye-sockets.

The creature crashed to the ground, and after a few moments dissolved into ash and shadow.

Our weapons, although still covered in black ichor, lay unharmed. I bent over and retrieved my sword, wiped it on a nearby bush and slid it back into the scabbard.

Whoops and howls came from the other group, who had dispatched their demon first and apparently—rather than helping us—had stood back to enjoy the show. Stephen stepped forward and slapped me on the back . . . hard. I forced myself not to stumble.

"Well done, Logan. It looks like my work here is complete," he said with his thick French accent.

I smiled back at him. I was going to miss my friendly crusader.

He grimaced. "Sorry about your face, though. You're going to have a hard time getting a girl to take you someday looking like that." He shook his head. "It's too bad too, because you used to be so good-looking."

Surely they could replace my tooth. Right?

Stephen bent over and started laughing.

"Don't worry, Logan, we'll get you to the healing center and get you fixed up right away."

"Thanks," I said, hearing a lisp in my voice and rolling my eyes at the howl of laughter it brought from not only Stephen, but Alrik as well. I hoped I'd live this down one day.

Author Commentary: Chapter 6
JulieHallAuthor.com/logan-6

CHAPTER 7

"Don't look behind you, the Harbinger of Death is headed this way," Alrik whisper-yelled in the cafeteria.

"Alrik," Kevin reprimanded, "she can probably hear you."

"I think he's counting on it," I piped in.

"Which is why I always choose not to entertain his antics," Shannon said as she stepped up to our table.

I tilted my head back so I could see her. Her hair was up in a tight bun, like always, not a single wrinkle on her business-like attire, while a very faint glow emanated from her.

Shannon often interacted with the hunters. Kind of like one of the overseers of the business-end of our operation. Many of our missions and orders came through her, although I'd put money down that she'd never been in an actual battle before. Yet, despite her somewhat-stuffy demeanor and her dislike of smiles in general, in a weird way she was growing on me.

Sure, she wasn't the cuddliest of angels, but she took her job seriously and worked hard, and I respected that.

"What can we help you with today, Shannon?" I asked with my head still tilted backwards. She frowned down on me in disapproval. My smile broadened.

"Logan, if you're finished eating I have a new trainee to introduce you to."

"Fresh meat? Oh yeah, I'm definitely in!" I jumped out of my chair, ready to meet my next mentee. I'd already trained two other hunters, so I held a certain amount of confidence now about my assignments. "See you guys later," I waved to the table as I turned to follow Shannon.

"Don't forget to bring him around later so we can place our bets," Alrik bellowed when I was on the other side of the busy room.

I winced when Shannon came to a sudden stop.

Thanks, Alrik.

I glanced over my shoulder and he was doubled over, laughing at the predicament he'd purposefully put me in.

Shannon did a slow turn to face me.

"Tell me you all aren't still mistreating our new hunters."

I held my hands up in front of me; a look of pure innocence sculpted my face, "Mistreating? Noooooo. No one is doing that."

"Hazing is not allowed."

"I can promise you, Shannon, we are not hazing the new hunters." Nope. We were just taking bets on how long they'd last on their first day before puking their guts out. In fact, it was kind of a bonding experience since it had happened to all of us. I grinned broadly at Shannon when she lifted one brow at me.

"You'd better not be. I expect more from you, Logan."

I cleared my throat and nodded once. I couldn't help but feel like a scolded child. Alrik was probably dying of laughter right now.

"So, the new guy?" I prompted to keep us on track.

"Right. His name is Morgan. Let's go so I can introduce you two and you can get started." Back to business. At least she was predictable.

When we walked into the training gym a few minutes later, someone was wailing on the punching bag. His dark mop of black hair was slicked to his forehead with sweat. I immediately went into mentor mode and began to assess his stance and movements.

I was somewhat impressed.

"Morgan," Shannon raised her voice to be heard over his fists smashing into the bag.

The guy stopped his jabs and turned his head to look at us. He lifted his chin in greeting as he started unwrapping his hands. Once done he tossed them into a gym bag and made his way to us.

"Hello there, lovely Shannon. It's good to see you again so soon. Hey there, mate," his British-accented voice rang strong as he addressed me and held out his hand, "My name is Morgan. So, you're to be my task master, eh?"

I waited a beat before grasping his hand. Not because of anything he said or did, but simply because the empathy link still made me a little uneasy.

This guy was an open book. All I got from him was a laid-back vibe laced with mild curiosity.

"Hey, man. Yeah, I'm Logan," I pumped his hand in return. I glanced toward the punching bag and then back at him, "Looks like you have a little head-start over most of the new hunters."

Morgan lifted an arm and scratched the back of his head, "Yeah, I know my way around a gym."

"Morgan was on the cusp of being a professional soccer player," Shannon informed me.

"That would be football where I'm from, luv."

Shannon tipped her head in acknowledgement.

"Really?" My interest was piqued. "I was a pro-surfer for about two minutes before I died." I chuckled at the career that never was.

"Hey mate, that's terrific," he held out a fist for a bump and I knocked knuckles with him.

We were going to get along just fine.

I stretched a gloved hand down to help Morgan up off the ground. It had taken me a full five minutes longer than usual to best him today. Training him was almost effortless.

He picked up techniques quickly, worked hard, learned how to materialize and dematerialize objects faster than anyone I'd ever seen—myself included—and on top of that was easy going and quick to laugh.

We'd hit it off immediately and he was quickly becoming not *just* my trainee, but my friend as well.

"Good job, you," Morgan said as I helped haul him to his feet. He dematerialized his sparring helmet, which had covered his face, and I did the same. Because he was so proficient in materializing, I'd moved him to only working with weapons and armor he could create himself. His breathing was slightly elevated from exertion, but still far more controlled than either of my other trainees at this point.

"I should be saying the same to you. You made me work a little for that one."

"Oh, get off it," he shoved my shoulder good-naturedly.

My laugh was cut off by a metallic blur and then I was lying flat on the mat with the wind punched out of my lungs, staring at the ceiling rafters.

What just happened?

A weight on top of me was making it hard to breathe. A hunter, covered from head to toe in armor, except for a white-blonde pony-tail shooting out of the top of her helmet—well she'd obviously made an adjustment to the standard issue gear—was sitting on my chest. Not straddling me or even trying to hold me down. But sitting on my chest . . . with her legs crossed in front of her . . . and laughing.

I shook my head and then gave Kaitlin a good shove. She tumbled off me to the mat, but continued to laugh as I caught my breath.

"I told you I'd best you eventually, Logan."

I lumbered to my feet and pointed a finger at her, "That was cheating."

She rolled on the ground like a puppy, giggling like a maniac. "Yeah, like demons fight fair," she sat up suddenly and threw her arms in the air and yelled, "I win."

"Brat," I rolled my eyes at her antics even as I cracked a smile. Kaitlin had an infectious personality that was hard to not go along with.

Finally gaining control of herself, she rolled to a sitting position and dematerialized her armor, leaving her in typical workout clothes—tight-fitting black leggings and a yellow sports tank. She resembled a bumblebee.

"You have to admit, that was pretty good."

Before I could answer her, Morgan's deep British voice cut in, "I'm not sure if he's capable of admitting defeat, luv. It's not hardwired into him. But anytime you want to spar with me, I'd be a willing participant. I might even concede defeat."

Watching Kaitlin's eyes widen, I coughed to cover my laugh. Morgan was a shameless flirt, but he'd just laid it on thick. My California girl was speechless. Not something that happened often.

I glanced back and forth between the two of them.

Morgan stood in full armor—except for his helmet—his arms crossed over his chest, feet spread wide, and a cocky smile on his face while he boldly ogled Kaitlin.

Kaitlin sat cross-legged on the padded mat. Leaning back on her arms she stared up at him with rounded eyes and parted lips.

The longer the silence stretched on, the greater my urge grew to slowly back out of the gym and leave the two of them alone.

This was an interesting development.

"Do you need a hand up, luv?" Morgan stretched his arm out so that his hand was within Kaitlin's reach. She did her best impression of a deer in headlights. A deep rumble of laughter finally burst from my chest. It snapped Kaitlin out of whatever trance Morgan had put her in.

Maybe it was the accent that had gotten her? Maybe it was more?

She cleared her throat and avoided eye contact with Morgan as she got to her feet—without his assistance—and immediately started playing with the end of her ponytail.

"Don't be a jerk," Kaitlin growled under her breath as my laughter subsided. Her eyes narrowed as she said it, which recharged my amusement.

"Logan, are you going to introduce me to this lovely bird of yours?"

Kaitlin turned on me, "Did he basically just call me a 'chick' and insinuate I was your possession?"

"Yes. He totally just did that," I said. Then, seeing shock on Kaitlin's face, quickly followed with, "But, I think it's just a British thing. He didn't mean any harm by it."

"Yes," Morgan jumped in, clearly not bothered at all by Kaitlin's ire, "please excuse my coarse language, lovely friend of Logan's whose name I still don't know. I've spent entirely too much time with a bunch of rough-around-the-edges male hunters and it has obviously affected me in a most negative way. A thousand apologies." Morgan hammed it up by bowing at the waist to Kaitlin. Her brow furrowed in return.

"Is he for real?" Kaitlin asked me, jerking a thumb, but not her gaze, in his direction, "Does he talk like that all the time?"

"No, not usually. I think you're getting special treatment."

"Oh, lucky me."

"Hey, mate, what kind of wingman are you? Bad form," Morgan complained.

"Sorry man, I didn't realize my duties as a mentor also encompassed wingman."

"When a beautiful lady who isn't already spoken for is involved, it's implied."

Kaitlin cut her hand through the air, "Okay, enough with the fake charm. Logan, introduce us already so I can go back to ignoring him and spend some time with you. I have an afternoon off today and I'd planned on gracing you with my presence."

I couldn't hide the amused smile on my face as I made the introduction. "Kaitlin, this is Morgan, my new trainee. Morgan, this is Kaitlin, an old friend of mine not just from here, but Earth as well."

"Well, that hardly did me justice," Morgan grumbled.

"Nice to meet you . . . ah . . . kinda, Morgan. Now I'm planning on stealing your mentor for the rest of the day. Have a nice afterlife." Kaitlin grabbed my arm and tried to haul me from the gym, which she found was a fruitless endeavor, but was entertaining to both Morgan and myself.

Kaitlin was becoming a great huntress, but I had almost a hundred pounds on her. Unless she did another sneak attack, she wasn't going to be able to make me budge unless I wanted to be moved. And messing with her was way more amusing than going along with her plan.

"Come on, you over-grown toddler," Kaitlin grunted and jerked on my arm. I took half a step in her direction.

"You know, Kaitlin, I can't leave Morgan all alone."

"What?" she dropped both my arm and her jaw.

"Yeah, he's my trainee. I have to look out for him now. He's going to have to come with us if you want to hang out." Morgan's smile broadened and Kaitlin scowled at me.

"You're joking, right?"

"'Fraid not, my dear friend. It's just the right thing to do. I can't leave poor Morgan to fend for himself when he's so new here." My straight-faced delivery testified to my ability to cloak my emotions, as inside I howled with laughter. Morgan certainly didn't need help making friends, but she didn't know that.

Kaitlin played with her ponytail as she looked back and forth between us. Morgan dropped his head forward a bit as if rejected, and gazed at Kaitlin with puppy-dog eyes.

I remained stone-faced because I knew if I moved a muscle, I would break down with laughter. I'm pretty sure Morgan was going for the see-how-pathetic-and-humble-I-am expression, but he just reminded me of a cartoon character.

"But, Logan," Kaitlin whined, "I only have an afternoon and evening to hang out. Do we really have to bring him with us?"

"Standing right here, listening to every word you say, luv."

Kaitlin shot him a withering look. "I don't know," she said to me, her voice lowering slightly, "you know I don't trust guys with beards and accents."

"Since when?"

"Since now."

"Hey, this isn't a beard. Just a bit of scruff. I can shave it off if that's what you'd prefer." Morgan chimed in.

Kaitlin rolled her eyes. "Fine. He can tag along," she pointed a finger at Morgan, "But just so you know, I'm going to pretend you aren't here."

"Oh," Morgan perked up, "a challenge. I like it," he rubbed his hands together, "Let the games begin."

"See!" Kaitlin turned on me, "That's exactly what I was worried about. Have a talk with your boy here about proper American manners. I'll meet you at the pond outside the gym when you guys have cleaned up."

"Luv, I'm British. We invented manners. Or didn't you know?" Morgan said and winked at her.

"You got it," I cheerfully answered and held my fist out for Morgan to bump without looking in his direction.

"Men," she grumbled and then stomped from the training gym, letting the door bang unnecessarily loud on her way out.

Kaitlin rarely got this flustered around guys, but somehow Morgan had quickly gotten under her skin. I'd let Morgan work out whether that was going to turn into a good or bad thing.

"Oh, I like her," Morgan said, his eyes still fixed on the gym door, "That one has spunk and spirit." There was a gleam in his eye that gave me a slight pause in my decision to force the two of them to spend time together. I liked Morgan, and wanted Kaitlin to like him, too. I wanted my friends to get along. Still, she was like a sister and I didn't want Morgan playing with her emotions.

"Man, she's basically my oldest friend and like a sister to me. You act inappropriately towards her and I'll have to break something important. We clear?"

Morgan's eyes drifted to mine, and a smile lit his face. "Crystal, mate."

Author Commentary: Chapter 7
JulieHallAuthor.com/logan-7

CHAPTER 8

————————

I crept along the deserted driveway, each step calculated to avoid making noise. It was late in the afternoon and the sun hung at the horizon's edge. Our rendezvous point was a mile behind us and we had about another hour to scope out the old house.

"So, you're saying she hasn't mentioned me at all?"

I shot Morgan a look that clearly said *shut up*, but he ignored me. We'd been training together for several months and Morgan was flying through the program. He'd passed the gauntlet several weeks ago and had already experienced his first few missions on Earth. He wore a sword secured at his waist, but archery was what he really excelled at. His bow was slung across his chest and a quiver full of arrows strapped to his back.

I'd never seen anyone's arrow slice the air with such accuracy. The more he trained, the faster he became at notching and aiming. When we were at the archery range, his movements blurred from his frenzied pace and then I'd look up to see he'd hit the bull's-eye on not just his own target, but the others lined up to the right and left as well. A few times a week he trained with one of our archery specialists because he'd far surpassed my skill level with that weapon.

I'd started calling him 'Katniss' every now and then just to mess with him. It was one of the few things that actually got under his skin.

We moved slowly, scouting an area of reported increased demon activity. An abandoned house some kids had used to conduct fake séances not realizing they'd attract the attention of a horde of demons instead of Casper the friendly ghost.

Morgan, however, seemed more interested in pumping me for details about Kaitlin than the mission. At first, I was amused at Kaitlin's response to

Morgan—interest covered with wary suspicion. It had been entertaining to watch Morgan turn into somewhat of a performing monkey the few times Kaitlin had come to visit. Now, it was just plain annoying.

Morgan continued peppering me with questions as we crept up to the property.

"Dude," I glared at him, "Not the time, alright?"

He winced, "Yeah, sorry mate. You're right, I should be taking this more seriously. Okay boss, following your lead."

I nodded and started forward, but jerked to a stop when a shadowy figure crossed in front of the ransacked house. Morgan and I crouched low to the ground to avoid being seen. Our mission was supposed to be strictly recon. We were not there to engage any demons.

We watched the creature pass by the front of the house two more times, but didn't see any other activity.

It appeared the reports had some merit to them, but rather than a horde of demons, there was only a single one preying off the unsuspecting high-schoolers who thought they were having a night of silly fun.

"There's only one," Morgan said in a low voice a touch above a whisper, "It's not even that big. We can take it, between the two of us."

I couldn't say the thought hadn't crossed my mind as well, but dispatching the demon would be against our orders.

"That's not what we're here for."

"Yeah, I know. But it's just one. And I'm kinda itching for some real action."

I glanced back at Morgan. His face was serious and his eyes blazed. "Better to ask forgiveness than permission?"

"Easy for you to say when it's *my* neck on the line with Shannon when we come back covered in demon blood."

"Might be worth it just to see the look on her face."

I shook my head, wanting to be responsible and follow-through with our orders.

"Oh, come on Logan. Look, it's just a little one. I only see two spiked tails. You know we can easily take it out. Then, ta-da, demon issue gone. We return conquering champions, knights-in-shining-armor, blah, blah, blah. We'll be heroes, mate!"

I shook my head again. Why he and Alrik didn't get along was a mystery to me. Maybe it was because they were too similar; although, while Morgan had Alrik's humor and charm, he took hunting very seriously and trained hard. Maybe Alrik had been in the game too long and it was getting to him. Or maybe it just wasn't his personality to take anything too seriously. Either way it didn't matter. I'd accepted Alrik for who he was.

As if I couldn't tell exactly what he was doing, Morgan slowly crept forward. I could've stopped him, and probably should have. But I hadn't spilled any demonic blood in a while, and this creature appeared to be easy pickings.

I pushed down the nagging feeling in my gut and moved forward with Morgan.

"Okay, fine. But if we're doing this, we're going to do it the smart way," I whispered my plan of attack to Morgan and he nodded in understanding.

I was going to engage the creature first, and while it was distracted, Morgan would swing around and attack from behind. Strategically speaking, it was a sound and simple plan, and I had zero doubts we'd take care of the problem quickly.

Had we stumbled across one of the greater demons—who used to be warrior angels before their fall from grace—I never would have entertained the idea of a fight without at least a full unit of hunters and even perhaps a few angels, but this creature appeared to be some sort of underling. A bottom feeder in the demon hierarchy.

It even appeared to be sickly. Its dark, scaly skin was stretched tight over its distorted features. This one was somewhat humanoid in appearance and its appendages that mimicked arms and legs appeared devoid of muscle of any kind. Like flesh wrapped around bone.

How did a demon even become that emaciated?

My subconscious issued a warning, but at this point, I'd already stepped into the clearing in front of the dilapidated house and drawn attention to myself.

The shriek the demon let out upon spotting me was one of the loudest I'd ever heard. What this thing lacked in girth it made up for in noise.

Something warm trickled down the side of my neck and I wondered if the sound had ruptured one of my eardrums. No time to check, I lifted my weapon and rushed the blackened form.

I slashed my sword up at the creature a moment before its claws reached me. I aimed for its midsection, but my blow was deflected by one of its boney upper limbs. Hitting it was like striking my sword against a piece of hardened steel, making my weapon shake and the vibrations travel up my arms.

The demon swung at me again with its sharp claws and I rolled out of the way. I kept the creature busy, making sure its attention stayed on me while I waited for Morgan to sneak up behind it.

I managed to get in some superficial hits, which did minimal damage and only seemed to make it angrier. The longer we fought, the more the creature's energy flagged. It was obvious in the decreased speed of its movements and its clumsy attacks. Something else was going on here; this wasn't how demons usually behaved, but I couldn't focus on the mystery at the moment.

I'd spotted Morgan as he sprinted straight for the demon from behind. I kept it engaged and then with one powerful thrust, Morgan's blade punched through the demon's midsection. It howled again and pawed at the sword protruding from its gut, cutting itself as it tried to push the blade back out the way it had come through.

With as much strength as I possessed, I brought my own sword up and across its neck, cleaving its head right from its body. The pieces of broken demon—head and body—fell to the ground and crumbled to ash.

Morgan looked up at me with a broad smile and then retrieved his sword from the mess at our feet.

"You see mate, that's what I'm talking—"

"Down!" I shouted at Morgan, who despite being mid-sentence heeded my command. A barbed demon tail sailed through the air where Morgan's head had been a moment before.

Having trained together, we worked like a well-oiled machine. Morgan rolling and shot to his feet, quickly taking position behind my back..

"Where did they all come from?" he asked. Whether the question was meant for me or just for himself, I wasn't sure.

"This was a trap. We're surrounded," I answered him anyway. "That first demon was the bait."

"What do we do then?"

"We fight."

I lost track of time as Morgan and I slashed, hacked, and fought against the onslaught of demons. They landed a few blows on us, but our armor had taken most of the beating. Morgan now fought with his left arm because the right one was most likely broken.

This was no ordinary demon ambush. I'd been a hunter for almost a year and a half and had never seen or heard of demons behaving this way. Demons were a little like sharks around hunters. It was something we often used to our advantage. They were easy to work into a frenzy in their desire to chomp down on us, and that made them sloppy and marginally easier to fight.

But this group of demons was different.

I'd witnessed demons fight and injure each other to get to a hunter first, but these ones fought as a unit, and seemed uninterested in taking us down.

They were trying to wear us out—which was working—but for what reason I didn't know. Since the fighting never ceased I didn't have a chance to think through the logic of it.

"The house!" Morgan yelled to me.

We'd found ourselves herded at the front of the abandoned house we'd been scouting earlier. It was now fully dark, and with no electricity inside it was hard to see, but with demons around us on three sides, and an empty building at our back, there was one obvious choice of retreat.

We'd already missed our rendezvous for our transport back to the realm, but if we could somehow manage to free ourselves of this mess, we could still get home.

"Go! I'll cover you until you get the door open. I'll follow after."

Morgan didn't need any more encouragement. He lifted a foot and shoved the demon he'd been fighting off him, then sprinted for the warped door at my back.

The snap and groan of wood splintering reached my ears.

"I'm in!" he yelled a moment later.

I swung my blade in a wide arc to give myself as much room as possible to make a run for the door. Once inside, I wasn't sure what we were going to do. I just prayed there was a back entrance we could escape from that wasn't surrounded, or that a group of hunters had already been dispatched to find us since we'd missed our rendezvous window.

I dashed up the rickety steps, expecting to either feel the slash of a claw at my back or for my foot punch through the decaying wood beneath me, but by some miracle, I actually made it into the house safely.

Slamming the door shut behind me and pressing my weight against it to stop the demons from entering, I scanned the room for Morgan.

There was a thud at my back and my whole body jarred as demons struck the door from the outside.

My eyes darted around the room, but Morgan wasn't there.

Morgan was as loyal of a person as I'd ever met, so the idea that he'd left without me only flitted through my mind. He had to be around here somewhere.

"Morgan!" I yelled as the door behind me shook violently with the force of demons' bodies being thrown against it.

"Logan, run!"

Morgan's muffled shout came from somewhere below, to the right. I jerked my head in that direction and barely made out an open doorway in the dim light. It was pitch black beyond the threshold.

Why in the world would Morgan have run into the basement when we should have been leaving the house?

The door behind me shook again, reminding me I was running out of time.

If there were living humans in the area, the demons wouldn't have been allowed to slam into the door like they were now, but seeing as we were alone in the middle of nowhere, without any witnesses, they could bring this house to the ground without repercussions.

I couldn't leave Morgan, so there really wasn't a decision to be made.

I pushed back on the door, only then noticing the deadbolt—the lock on the handle having been busted by Morgan upon entry.

Stupid, why didn't I check for another lock sooner?

I was bending under the very pressure I'd been trained to endure. I twisted the deadbolt. That wouldn't keep the demons out for long, but it might buy me a few extra moments.

I gritted my teeth and suppressed the urge to punch my hand through the wall.

How could I have been so reckless? I let this happen. This was all on me.

Shoving off the front door I sprinted for the black hole in front of me and was swallowed by the darkness.

Author Commentary: Chapter 8
JulieHallAuthor.com/logan-8

CHAPTER 9

———————

I awoke to yelling. Loud agony and despair-filled shouts.
They were my own.

Blackness filled my vision and pushed its way into my being. Hatred and fury rolled in my gut in merciless never-ending waves. I was emotionally undone, physically restrained and out of my mind at the same time.

And then the agony stopped.

Had I just imagined it?

My eyes slowly adjusted to the dimly-lit room at the same rate as my mental haze dissipated. It was only when clarity returned, that I fully appreciated the horror that had befallen us.

My arms were spread wide overhead. My wrists locked in chains that were attached to some old, rusty pipes in the basement of what I assumed was the house we had entered. My shoulders ached from having my full weight on them for who knew how long. My toes brushed the floorboards, bare feet scrambling for purchase on the floor below me, only to slip in something warm and slick.

I shuddered when I realized it was my own blood, which had poured out of the gash on my shoulder.

Stripped of my body armor to the waist, the shirt underneath was shredded to rags. I tilted my head far enough to recognize the shoulder wound for what it was. Not made from the slashing of claws or weapons, but distinct bite-marks gouged deep into my flesh.

I'd been fed on. And I probably would be again soon.

A moan from the other side of the room drew my attention. I squinted, barely able to make out the figure across from me. He mirrored my position.

Morgan, from what I could tell, wasn't fairing much better than myself—

worse in fact. A rope looped around my gut, like a lasso, and tightened. Dread locked in my chest and spread its icy tendrils throughout my whole body.

"Morgan," I tried to call out to him, but was hindered by the rasp in my voice. It was as if my vocal cords had been stripped from me. I moved my tongue around to build up moisture in my mouth, but it was in vain. There wasn't enough wetness to swallow and help sooth my damaged throat.

Putting ever reserve of energy I had into the one action, I called out again. This time creating more volume to wield, but my words were unintelligible.

"Logan?" Morgan's voice sounded as shredded as my own.

I gulped down what little liquid had accumulated in my throat. "Yeah. Are you alright?"

Morgan made a noise that I interpreted as a humorless laugh.

"Just peachy," was his sarcastic response, "So, mate, what do the training books say about getting out of a situation like this?" It took him several tries through fits of coughing, to get the words fully out.

There was a rattling sound in his voice that concerned me. I had to remind myself that our bodies couldn't be destroyed. But right on the tail of that thought was a stark reminder of how badly we could be hurt because of it.

What had happened? How we had ended up in this pit?

"They'll send a team to locate us," I assured him, as well as myself.

Yes, this was bad. But the other hunters knew our last known location, and could find us anywhere on Earth through their tracking system. It was only a matter of time before we were rescued.

A fit of wet coughs racked Morgan's body before he spat something to the ground. Probably a wad of blood, we were both drenched in it—demons' as well as our own.

The slow creak of a door opening above us gave me a burst of hope. Thank goodness, they'd come for us quickly. But my heart plummeted and adrenaline spiked when the chirping and gurgling sounds of demon communication snaked its way to my ears.

After that the door closed and something came stomping down the steps.

A darkened mass blocked my view of Morgan.

A fire hose of flames shot out from the black mass and momentarily blinded me, forcing my lids closed. When I opened them again, an angel stood between us.

But there was no comfort in that. For this was the one angel every hunter hoped never to meet.

"I have a proposition for you." His silky voice was a clever disguise. As clever as the false skin that he now wore. For standing before Morgan and me, was the King of Hell himself. And apparently, he'd come to make a deal. But everyone knew you didn't make a deal with the devil without trading in your soul.

I'd lost track of time and existed in cycles of pain, broken by short reprieves. It had to have been days, yet we still hadn't been rescued.

They were searching for us though. A group of hunters had passed outside the single window that opened to the basement where we were being held. The glass was small and covered in grime—impossible to see through—but the quiet steps of my fellow hunters still penetrated my fogged mind.

I had strained to yell out to them in my broken voice, but barely a sound escaped.

At least a dozen demons scurried into the basement with us, leaving a few of their companions above to be slaughtered by the contingent of hunters sent to retrieve us.

This was it, this torture would finally end! I'd thought.

We waited and waited through the sounds of battle above us. But they never came.

Despair strangled any joy I had felt, and tears streamed down my face when I realized they were retreating—leaving Morgan and me behind in this never-ending nightmare.

Morgan remained unconscious the entire time, and there was a small mercy in that. It would have been another form of torture having come that close to freedom, only to watch it slip away.

As far as I could tell, Morgan and I were demon chow twice a day. After weeks, our bodies were riddled with scars and torn flesh. Our minds were just as broken—maybe even more so.

Demons were beings filled with everything dark and ugly in the world— they absorbed and churned in all the hate, wrath, lust, greed, jealousy, and just plain blackness out there. Whenever one of the creatures visited us, the empathy link we experienced in our realm sprang to life.

Day after day we were forced to absorb what they felt, and it was incapacitating in a way that went beyond physical pain. The demons got some sort of drug-like high in return.

The bite was necessary during battle so they remained latched to our body, but trussed up like this, they could also sink their claws into our flesh to open the link. I didn't know which method was worse.

The cycle of agony went on and on for days that never ended.

The only thing keeping us from fading into oblivion was the impossibility of doing so after death. Our immortality in the afterlife had become a curse; there was something truly worse than death, and we were experiencing it.

And then one day, the Prince of Darkness came to us again.

He sauntered down the stairs, his pace unhurried. I noticed the difference in his stomping from the claws that normally scraped against the wooden planks leading to our basement prison. A faint rustling of something brushing down the steps reached my ears. Like the sound of heavy fabric being dragged, although I doubted that was it.

When he finally came into view I recognized the noise for what it really was, large black wings—similar in size to those of the archangels—jutted up from his back. But where angel's wings had feathered layers, his looked to be made of black, membranous leather cloaked in smoke and shadow.

Devoid of any strength, Morgan and I hung listlessly from the chains wrapped around our wrists that bound us to this prison. My body was clothed in remnants alone. Rags hung from a body that had not only lost muscle mass but had stopped healing as well. Old wounds oozed what little liquid still pumped through my veins. In some ways, I had become a creature of darkness.

I hissed at the monster that was a picture of vitality where Morgan's and my ravished bodies were little more than mostly-drained meat suits.

There was something so unbelievably grating about watching him walk around in his angel disguise, the ultimate wolf in sheep's clothing. I supposed he took on the likeness of what he once was, an angel of light.

I wanted to yell and lash out at him, but I barely had enough energy to lift my head.

He ignored us for a while, moving around the small space, adjusting various objects I could not see. Then he began to sing softly to himself. The song was simultaneously beautiful and terrifying, causing images to swim through my vision of existing in perfect light with countless other beings, then ripping away, falling, falling, falling into flame and darkness.

The song was filled with regret and above all a terrible malice that chilled my soul and my ragged flesh. The very temperature in the room dropped as he sang and our breath became visible as we exhaled.

I don't think he sang for us, or even knew he was doing it. After a long time, he stopped and finally faced Morgan.

"Do you know what you could have been if He'd protected you before?"

Morgan flinched at the mention of his death. It was the one subject we never talked about.

"That's right, Morgan." Satan's velvety voice gave me chills. "I know all about the mugging in the alley. Such a shame to have lost your life for the paper in your pocket."

His back was to me as he faced Morgan, but his head tilted to the side in a jerky movement, almost as if he wasn't used to making the simplest of gestures and was imitating another being instead.

"Do you know what you would have accomplished had He sent his angels to protect you instead?" Satan continued spewing his lies, "You would have been one of the greatest athletes your country had ever seen. You would have had it all. Wealth, fame, power. You were stripped of all those glories along with your life that night. Where's the fairness in that? Where's the justice? You think your God is good and merciful? What is good or merciful about striking down someone on the cusp of greatness? Perhaps He worried that if He didn't allow your death, He'd eventually lose your love? Why serve a God like that?"

Satan stood in front of Morgan as he spoke, softly and confidentially as a friend, someone who understood the man's sorrow. Then, he laid a hand gently on Morgan's shoulder.

"And now look at you. Worse off than you ever were before, and where is He? Do you think he doesn't know exactly where you are? That paltry attempt at a rescue was simply for show to keep the other slaves in line. What I'm offering you now is a chance to truly be free. Be free of your bondage to a careless God—one who has only brought misery to your door. Instead you have a chance to be your own master, and join my ranks."

"I will never leave you nor forsake you," a gentle voice whispered in my ear.

I wanted to yell at Morgan to resist the lies even as my body begged me to give in. With what little strength I possessed, I pulled at the chains binding my wrists, hoping that the noise would draw Morgan's attention.

Part of the plan worked. Morgan's eyes slowly left the face of evil incarnate and drifted to mine. But what I saw in them grieved my soul. And a shadow rose between us, cutting off my view of my friend, and I knew at that very moment, he was lost.

I watched day after day as Morgan's body grew stronger from the hate against our Creator that he let consume him. It was a slow transition. Satan continued his daily visits to pump Morgan full of lies. And the more Morgan swallowed, the healthier he looked. But his renewed vitality was only on the surface, for inside my friend's soul had surely begun to rot and twist into something as grotesque as the rest of Satan's minions.

My resistance was rewarded with further torture. With each new demon feeding, my body weakened past the point I'd thought possible. And rather than having a companion in Morgan, I now had another manipulator urging me to give in to the darkness as he had done.

He'd tell me how much stronger he felt. He'd even hinted at something inside of him transforming. Until the day came when the change he'd spoken of manifested into something tangible.

Still chained to the pipes as I was, I watched his eyes move back and forth over the dank basement floor as the shadows followed his unspoken commands. It was like observing a macabre dance as he learned to master his new skill. It was horrifying, but I found myself fascinated even as my chest ached with the proof of the depths my friend had sunk into darkness.

I had completely lost track of time. The feedings were no longer helping me gauge the days that passed. In my misery, there were times I'd believed I'd always existed in this hell. The day came when I woke and Morgan was no longer strung up across from me, but standing tall, wearing in a new type of armor—coverings that blended with the very shadows around us.

"I'm finally free," he said. They were the first clear words he'd spoken to me since our capture. "Logan, don't you understand, we've been fighting the war from the wrong side all along."

I could do nothing but weakly shake my head at him. There was a fever in his voice that hadn't been present before. Where there used to be joy, I only heard anger.

"If you let go, the pain will stop. You'll be a new man. A better man than you ever were before. A more powerful one as well. Look," he stretched out his arm and called the darkness to himself. It covered his hand and then slid up his bicep until it looked like his arm from shoulder to fingertips had simply disappeared.

I looked into Morgan's eyes with disbelief. He'd not only fully given up on himself, but on our beloved Creator. And for what? A cool party trick?

I woke to a blinding pain in my shoulders, but for once it wasn't from a demon bite. One arm hung limp and useless by my side. There was a good chance both shoulders were dislocated from being stretched apart and taking the brunt of my full body weight for so long. Sensation in my hands was almost non-existent, only a slight tingling feeling remained. That was a small mercy.

I turned my head and watched with half-lidded eyes as Morgan moved to my other arm and started to unfasten the chains that held me in place. My shoulder was screaming now as it bore all my weight. I'd long since lost the ability to stand on my own.

Morgan wrapped a steady arm around my waist as he freed my hand and then staggered under the dead weight of my body. My raw and torn flesh shot jolts of pain throughout my being with every jostling movement as he lowered me to the floor—but it was nothing compared to the agony in my shoulder joints.

What was happening right now? Was he setting me free? Was his surrender to Satan all a ploy to free the both of us?

My logical mind strained to snap the pieces together, but it was sluggish after weeks of torture and lack of sustenance. I struggled to shake the cobwebs from my brain, but they'd been there so long I feared they'd now taken up permanent residence.

"I'm gonna put those shoulders back in their right place, mate," he sounded more like the Morgan I knew, but what if this was a trick? "I'm not going to lie to you, it's going to hurt like the dickens, but it needs to be done. You ready?"

I managed a wobbly head-bob, which resembled a nod.

"Alright, I'm gonna lay you on your back to do this."

He lowered my torso to the floor with zero help from me. Once I was splayed out on the grimy basement floor, Morgan grabbed my right wrist and slowly pulled on my arm. I gritted my teeth through the intense, searing pain.

Morgan's face pinched with concentration and exertion as he continued to pull my arm away from my body, standing to get better leverage. An eternity later, there was a clunk as the bone slid back into place and although still incredibly sore, there was a lessening of pain from that shoulder.

"One down, one to go. You still with me, mate?" Morgan asked.

"Yes," I managed to rasp through my dry throat and parched lips.

He nodded and took hold of my left wrist, repeating the agonizingly slow process again until I heard the familiar clunk of the bone being reset followed immediately by the same relief I'd felt from the previous side.

I wiggled my fingers as sensation flooded back into my arms. Morgan helped me up to a sitting position.

My throat worked to swallow, but nothing happened because of the absence of moisture. I fastened my eyes on Morgan and croaked out a single word, hoping he knew what I was trying to say.

"Escaping?"

Morgan's eyes blazed and his mouth set in a hard line.

"No. That's not why I unchained you. We both know you're too weak to go anywhere right now. I wanted to talk to you about why you should join forces with us."

My stomach turned. Had there been any food in it, I would have thrown it up.

Morgan wasn't here to orchestrate our escape, even though he was now in a position to do so. He was here to try and talk me into turning my back on our Creator.

"Satan was right," Morgan was saying, "Where was God and His army when we needed Him? Satan did this to us to show us the truth. To set us free."

I shook my head. Incapable of having a real conversation with him, it was the only way I could communicate. Satan wasn't trying to set us free, he was using us to grow his own army.

I wouldn't lie to myself and say my faith hadn't been shaken by this experience, but I wasn't willing to sell my soul for freedom.

"I am here," a voice whispered in my head.

Morgan droned on and on and at some point I just blankly stared back, not hearing anything that was coming out of his mouth. Eventually he realized I wasn't paying attention to him. He grabbed my sore shoulders and shook me roughly.

"Wake up!" he yelled in my face. His own features had turned red and were now filled with rage. Nothing about that was from our Father. Was it too late for Morgan? "The Creator doesn't care about you. He doesn't care about any of us. We're all a big joke to Him. Pawns to move around His chess board while He's bored."

A rage filled me like I'd never experienced. It bubbled up from my chest and shot down my arms.

That wasn't the Truth.

No matter the amount of abuse Morgan or Satan or his demons dished out, it was on *their* heads, not our Creator's.

The maddening anger that filled my soul at Morgan's words burst from me all at once, and with a shout I threw my arms up to dislodge his hold on me, shoving him back with both hands.

Morgan flew across the room as twin bolts of blue and white light shot from my palms and hit him in the chest. A crackling sensation weaved over my fingers as I looked down at the remnants of whatever power I had wielded.

Hunters didn't have abilities like this.

When the sensation and light disappeared from my hands, I jerked my head to gape at Morgan. There was a charred hole in his armor—right in the middle of his chest. He shook his head once and returned my stare with wide eyes.

Then a slow grin appeared on his lips.

Author Commentary: Chapter 9
JulieHallAuthor.com/logan-9

CHAPTER 10

*M*organ's hurried steps echoed as he ran up the basement stairs, no doubt rushing to report that I'd finally snapped.

I stared down at my hands in horror.

What had I just done?

My rage against Morgan's words had fueled some power inside me and now the floodgates were open.

Hunters don't have powers like this, I repeated to myself.

Would I even be allowed back in the heavenly realm now? This power had to have sprung from evil, didn't it? A result of my long weeks being linked with demon-kind? It had burst forth in a fit of blinding fury.

"Run."

That whispered voice in my head snapped me back to attention. The adrenaline pumping through my veins afforded me a moment of mental clarity.

Now was my chance. Morgan had freed me from my chains and had run from the basement, leaving me completely alone. Whether it was an oversight on his part, or simply an assumption that I didn't have enough strength to move, I didn't know.

And I didn't care.

I gathered every bit of strength I had and pushed myself to my feet. I wobbled before being able to take a step toward freedom. Grinding my teeth together, I set my mind on a single endeavor: leaving this wretched basement of horrors behind.

One step turned into two and eventually I'd made it to the stairs. I used the handrails, despite the objection of my recently relocated shoulders, to push and pull myself to freedom.

I stopped at the top of the landing and listened for any noises. For all I knew there could be a horde of demons camped out in and around the house. But time was a luxury I didn't have.

After waiting thirty seconds without hearing the scrape of a claw on the floor, or the shrieking chirp they used to communicate, I slowly opened the door.

My eyes darted around the empty room, expecting a creature, or even Satan himself, to materialize at any moment. I paused momentarily, then— with a spurt of energy—I stumbled to the front door and pushed out into the open air.

My eyes watered at brightness they were no longer accustomed to, but I couldn't wait for the temporary blindness to cease. I lurched forward, tripping and rolling down the few steps to the ground.

I hit the packed dirt with one of my injured shoulders and a bolt of pain lanced through my body. An anguished cry burst free.

Forcing myself to my feet once again, I ran into the forest surrounding the prison I'd just escaped, stumbling repeatedly as I fled.

Weaving around foliage and trees, I almost ran right into a demon before skidding to a stop.

It turned on me with an otherworldly snarl.

I had nothing to defend myself with. They'd deprived us of our weapons before I'd even awakened to find myself chained to those awful pipes.

Oh, Father, please help me.

The creature charged and I held up my hands in defense, sure they were going to be sliced from my arms at any moment. But the strange power I'd exercised against Morgan sprang to life once again, hitting the demon square in its middle and immediately stopping its forward momentum.

I kept my hands outstretched and watched in morbid, detached fascination as the demon let out a final shriek and its body shook as if electrocuted. Is that what I was doing? Electrocuting it?

Finally, the demon's appendages folded in as if every muscle was contracting at once. And then it stopped moving. Several heartbeats passed, and the creature's corpse turned into a pile of ash.

Bile churned in my stomach as I stared at my defeated foe. I should be running. I knew that, but I was frozen.

Something sliced into my back from shoulder to waist, splitting the flesh and muscle and allowing blood to flow freely down my spine.

This wasn't over.

I barely had time to turn before the demon was on me. Its teeth snapped, inches from my face. I pushed back with my hands, but my strength had left me. It was just about to bite into my neck when the lightning shot from my palms once more, and sent the creature flying off me, crashing into a nearby tree.

It screamed its outrage and came rushing at me again. I lifted my hands and found the power inside to blast the demon just as I had done with the last one. After the beast dissolved into smoke and ash, I didn't linger.

I turned and fled.

I ran, stumbled, and even crawled as far as I could until my body finally gave out on me somewhere in the middle of the wooded area. Only then did I sink into darkness once again.

"I said back up!" boomed a voice.

I winced at both the volume and the brightness behind my closed lids.

"I think he's waking up." This voice was softer.

"Do you think he's going to be weirded out that we're all just staring at him?" That sounded an awful lot like Kevin, but how could that be when I was trapped in the basement dungeon of that old house? That didn't make sense either because there was no light in the hovel I'd been surviving in for weeks.

I tried to open my eyes, but they were weighted down by lead.

"Seriously, he's waking up. We should listen to Alrik and back up."

Kaitlin.

How were my friends here? Where was I?

I wasn't going to find out until I pried my lids open.

It took a bit of effort and time stretched. My friends must have held their breaths, because when I finally managed to wrench my eyes open, a collective whoosh of air sounded. I viewed the room around me through the screen of my lashes.

"Oh, thank goodness you're awake." Kaitlin threw herself at me and began to cry. The force of her sobs shook the bed. I winced at her weight on top of my sore body, but held back the groan.

"Woman, get off of him," Alrik barked. "Can't you tell the poor guy is in pain?"

"Oh, my gosh," Kaitlin scrambled off of me and jumped from the bed as if it were on fire. "Logan, I'm so sorry. I'm just so happy that you're back. And okay-ish," her features pinched, "*Are* you okay?"

"Yeah, of course." That probably wasn't an honest answer, but what else was I supposed to say?

"What happened to you, man?" Kevin asked timidly. His brows pulled together, "We've been looking for you and Morgan for weeks. It's like you just . . . disappeared."

I took a deep breath. Overwhelmed, but trying to hide it.

"I think I should talk to one of the superiors about what went down first."

"Oh, yeah, right. Of course." Kevin nodded his agreement, but it was simply a tactic to prolong the inevitable.

If I could go the rest of my existence without having to relive the last few weeks in any way, shape or form, I would. But people were going to want to know what had happened. It wasn't something I wanted to talk to my friends about right now. Or ever for that matter, but especially not right now.

Everything was too raw. My mind—along with my body—was damaged beyond my friends' comprehension. And then there was the problem of my new power. I didn't know what it meant. And as hard as it was to admit—even to myself—I wasn't sure I wanted the truth.

Things were different now. I had changed in that dark basement. And I wasn't sure if I'd ever be the same person again.

Author Commentary: Chapter 10
JulieHallAuthor.com/logan-10

CHAPTER 11

"*Y*ou're joking, right?" The look I shot Shannon was ice cold. Because of the extensive damage that was done to my body, a week later I was still in a room at the healing center, our realm's version of a hospital.

All I wanted to do was go home and sleep in my own bed—just one night —and then get back to training. But I'd been temporarily benched.

Didn't they realize I needed to get back to a normal routine?

"I'm afraid not, Logan. Considering what you went through, it's absolutely mandatory for you to talk with someone before we reactivate your status as a hunter." She delivered her short speech with the same tone she did every-thing, but there was a glimmer in her eye I didn't like. It looked an awful lot like pity.

"This is ridiculous." I crossed my arms over my chest and refused to make eye contact. Instead, I stared at the white wall in front of me. Whoever thought white was soothing was an idiot. The urge to punch my fist through the wall hit me hard and fast. I wiped a hand down my face instead.

"Logan." The softening of her voice startled me into looking at her. Her face remained stoic, but I had never heard compassion like this in Shannon's voice before. "You've been through an ordeal that very few people have ever experienced. Thank the Lord for that. You'd need therapy even if only half of the things you listed in your report happened. But I would still insist you seek counseling for the wounds we can't see."

I pressed my lips together tightly, knowing exactly what she was referring to. They were basically expecting me to go crazy at any moment. And they didn't even know about my new ability. I'd left that out of all my reports, written and verbal.

"With everything you've gone through, it's a miracle you're healing as well as you are." She gestured to my body, which at this point was devoid of all the visible scars that had been inflicted on me during my captivity.

My friends knew nothing about the three long, angry wounds running across my back that hadn't healed. I'd spotted them in the mirror the night before. So, no matter how *well* I looked on the outside, until those disfigurements healed, it meant that I still carried the mental scars of my torture as well.

That's just the way things worked around here. Our physical scars were a manifestation of emotions or experiences we hadn't fully recovered from.

There was no way for me to hide those marks from the healers who came into treat me. Shannon, being part of the hierarchy of hunters, most likely had been informed of them as well. Thus, I was being sent to the realm's equivalent of a shrink to talk about my . . . *feelings.*

My lip curled at the thought of sitting down and openly talking about the conflicting emotions churning around inside me. I'd much rather work my issues out on a punching bag, practice dummy, or sparring partner.

"Physically speaking, you could be ready to go back to training with a few days' more rest."

Correction, I was ready to go back two days ago.

"But your mental state is just as important to us."

I refused to engage her in conversation anymore.

"Logan," there was that softened voice again. I hated it, "you were held captive and tortured for six weeks straight."

Keep your expression neutral. Don't show any emotion.

"You haven't spoken a word about Morgan since we retrieved you from Earth. We only know what happened to him from your written reports. What happened was awful. The reality of the situation is that you need to heal more than just your body. I'm sorry you don't like the idea, but if you want to remain a hunter, this is the only way to do it. Otherwise we'll be forced to find a different position for you."

At that last comment, I jerked my gaze to her.

They were considering reassigning me to a different job? She read the question and fury in my eyes.

"Don't let that happen. Keep fighting."

Without any fanfare, she turned on her heel and walked from the room.

Squeezing my eyes shut, I pinched the bridge of my nose. Would this nightmare ever end? I guess this meant that I was going to get my head shrunk.

I felt like a voyeur as I watched through the doorway as the couple embraced. The man and woman looked to be somewhere in their forties, but honestly, I wasn't that good at judging age. He leaned down and whispered something in her ear, and she giggled.

It was strange to watch a grown woman giggle. She nodded at whatever he'd said to her and then went on her toes to place a chaste kiss on his lips. They finally broke apart and I stepped back from the doorway, pretending to find something on the opposite wall really interesting.

"I'll see you for dinner, sweetheart," the man called back over his shoulder before leaving the room and continuing down the hallway. He passed in front of me and offered a smile and small nod of his head.

"You can come in now, Mr. London."

Totally busted.

I schooled my features into the hardened mask I'd been perfecting ever since being captured by Satan and his demons, and strode into the room. The woman was now seated behind her desk, so I picked a chair and sat—waiting for her to speak.

I didn't have anything to say.

Those scars on your back tell a different story, my mind whispered to me.

"Hello, I'm Deborah. May I call you Logan?"

I nodded.

"Wonderful," she smiled, and it lit up her whole face. It was still hard to make out her age. Her silver hair was pulled back in a twisty thing, but rather than looking grey from age, it shone with vitality. Her face had some fine lines, but it added interest to her appearance.

Why was I bothering to even try to nail down her age in a realm where appearances meant very little? Oh right, because it distracted me from why I was here to begin with.

When I didn't respond, she pushed on undeterred.

"So, Logan, tell me about yourself."

On her desk, I spied a folder with my name written clearly across it. I looked at it pointedly and then up at her.

"Don't you already know everything about me?"

"Do you really think you can get to know someone by reading a small list of facts about their life and afterlife?"

Touché.

I sighed. If this is what I had to do to get back to being an active hunter, I guess I was going to have to grin and bear it.

Leaning back in the chair, I folded my arms across my chest. "Fine. Where would you like me to start?"

"How about your earliest memory? And we'll go from there."

An abrupt laugh burst out of me, "Are you serious? You want to hear my whole life story?"

She leaned forward in her chair with a gleam in her eye, "Oh no, Logan, I want to know so much more than that."

"You're messing with me right now, aren't you? She actually drove a tent peg through his head?"

Lapidoth laughed at the look of shock on my face, "I promise, I'm telling the truth. And as you can imagine, it was a big deal back then to be taken out by a woman. Barak had won the day, but the glory went to another. And to think it was all because he wouldn't go into battle without her. Ha! Served him right. My Deborah is always right."

"What are you two talking about out there?" Deborah called from within her office.

Lapidoth poked his head around the corner, "Just some of the highlights from the glory days, dear. All good things."

"Well, don't scare the poor boy, LD. Times were different then."

"Should I be more offended that she referred to me as a boy, or that she suggested your story would scare me?"

Lapidoth chuckled and moved out of the way so I could enter Deborah's office. "My advice is to ignore her comment altogether."

"I heard that," Deborah yelled back to her other half from behind her desk. I took my usual chair just as he shouted, "I know," from what was probably the end of the hall.

Deborah smiled showing the playfulness of their relationship, "What am I going to do with that man?"

"For as many years as you've had together, I'm pretty sure you have it figured out. You're putting on a show for my sake. And speaking of, I think we should reserve these little meetings to talk about your life instead of mine. You've obviously led a more interesting existence than I have, so I don't understand why we're wasting our time discussing me."

She rolled her eyes.

Deborah rarely talked about herself during our sessions. But Lapidoth— LD for short—was usually here before my appointment and we'd fallen into a somewhat friendly acquaintance. He was always ready to brag about his wife and I'd learned quickly he had every right to do so. At one time, the woman had actually been the leader of Israel. Way back in ancient times before they even had official rulers. We're talking many millennia ago.

When I'd joked about her having been a queen she corrected me and said that she was a Judge during that time. And then, with a soft smile on her face, she'd rolled her eyes at me.

They were a hard pair not to like.

After three months, I was finally not dreading these sessions. Although my scars still hadn't disappeared. The one time I brought it up, Deborah waved it off, telling me some things just took time, and other things were all about the right timing.

"So, today will be our last session."

My eyebrows shot up so far they hid behind hair I'd let grow too long.

I'd gone back to training a couple of months ago, but it was under the strict understanding that I still wasn't cleared for active missions.

"Does this mean . . . ?" It was almost too much to hope for. If I was done with my counseling, that meant they'd made a decision about my status as a hunter.

I'd leaned forward in my chair without realizing it—my hands white-knuckling her desk.

Her smile widened and she nodded. "Yes, Logan. You've been cleared to get back into active duty as a hunter," she reached across the desk to pat the fingers that were probably leaving indents in her wooden desk, "I know the scars are still there, but—"

Deborah's words cut off abruptly the moment her hand touched mine. Her eyes widened and she sucked in a sharp breath of air.

"Deborah?" Her eyes stared right through me and a pained look pinched her features before smoothing out again. "Deborah?" I asked again, forcefully removing my hand from beneath hers.

Her strange spaced-out look was as disturbing as her touch. Skin-to-skin contact meant the empathy link sprang to life. Sharing emotions when we touched is a part of this new existence that I have always been uncomfortable with. Now I hated it because it instantly brought back memories of my captivity, and thoughts of the time spent in that dank basement were coupled with dark emotions I didn't want to share with anyone else.

When Deborah's hand had landed on mine, her happiness had pushed into me, but that emotion was quickly swept away by a strong feeling of shock.

"What just happened?" I demanded.

"You'll figure it out." Her voice had taken on a monotone quality that frankly, was just plain freaky.

"Figure *what* out?" I demanded.

She continued as if I hadn't spoken. No longer staring through me, her eyes seared into my own, "This existence isn't going to be what you expected. Your time here is only *part* of the journey. It may take a while to get there, and there are times ahead that are going to be harder than you've ever experienced, but in the end, you'll make the right decisions and figure it out. Don't run from your purpose. Embrace everything you'll learn, and use it to continue your journey. It will be worth it. *She* will be worth it."

"What the heck are you talking about?" I slammed back into the chair so fast it rocked on two legs before settling to the ground with a thud.

The noise made her jump, and then she blinked a few times. The intensity left her gaze, but a frown still marred her face.

"What's going on right now?" I demanded. Nothing like this had ever happened in our sessions before.

"Calm down, Logan." Deborah held both hands up in front of her in an attempt to pacify me. At least she seemed to be back to herself at this point.

"Are you done speaking to me in Chinese proverbs?"

Deborah's lips pressed together and her nostrils flared. She took a deep breath.

"I'm sorry about that. Let's wrap up this last session. What I said a moment ago . . ." she paused and I leaned even further away from her, "Well, we can discuss that another time. Right now, you just need to figure out who it is you want to be, and what it's going to take to get there."

"Is that what you meant when you told me I'd figure it out?"

She stared at me in silence for an uncomfortably long time before answering, "In part. But for now, let's see you get back into your normal routine, and go from there. I'm always here if you want to talk."

That wasn't likely to happen. Especially after what had just gone down.

She went on as if knowing my thoughts, "You don't think that day will come, but it may." She lifted her hand and gestured to the door.

I sat in stunned silence until it dawned on me that I was being dismissed. Deborah had never acted this way before. And to do so during our last session was even more bizarre.

"Okay. I guess I'll just get going now."

She nodded and a small smile appeared on her face, "This won't be the last I see of you, Logan."

I simply waved as I walked out the door. What else was I supposed to say to someone I respected, but who I hoped I never had a reason to meet again? Especially after the wacky sendoff she'd just given me.

Not paying attention to where I was going, I almost ran into LD a few doors down from Deborah's office.

"Oh, sorry man," I said and started to step around him. He mirrored my movements. I looked up at him with a question in my eyes.

"She wasn't only a Judge," LD's face was as serious as I'd ever seen it, "She's a prophetess too."

At my blank look, he continued. It's obvious he'd caught the last few minutes of our conversation, although why he was creeping in the hallway was a mystery to me.

"She sometimes still has visions, and is never wrong. What she said to you might not make sense now, but I believe someday it will. And know that her words were meant to encourage and strengthen you for your journey."

This was, by far, the strangest day I'd experienced in the afterlife. And that was saying something.

LD clapped me on the shoulder, gave it a gentle squeeze followed by an encouraging smile, and slipped into his wife's office.

"Hi sweetheart! I forgot to leave this with you. I know you wanted . . ." His voice faded as I walked down the hall, each step taking me further from them.

If Deborah was right, and what lay ahead was worse than what I'd already gone through, I'm not sure this was a journey I wanted to take.

Author Commentary: Chapter 11
JulieHallAuthor.com/logan-11

CHAPTER 12

Three months had passed since I walked out of Deborah's office. I'd gotten back into the routine of being a hunter. I'd had several dozen successful missions to Earth. The afterlife was just beginning to settle back into place. And now this.

I had tried my best over the months to push Deborah's words—her prophecy—from my mind. But after doing some digging and finding out that the prophetess stuff was legit . . . well . . . that will mess with any guy's head.

Staring down at the sleeping beauty at my feet, I couldn't stop the last part of her cryptic message from floating to me. *She will be worth it.*

I shoved a hand in my hair and fisted the strands. What could the Creator be thinking? I didn't need this added complication.

I released my hair and with a frustrated growl stomped closer to the figure lying crumpled on the dirty mat. I crouched down to get a closer look at her.

Her mass of hair was everywhere, blocking my view of her face. Gingerly reaching out, I pulled some of it back to get a better look at her.

She'd fallen on her side, her head tilted toward the ceiling. With her hair out of the way, I had a perfect view of her face.

Man, I was starting to feel like a creeper. I should probably wake her up or something.

As if it had a mind of its own, my hand moved towards her cheek. The moment my fingers brushed her soft flesh, sparks of electricity—the same power I'd used on Earth to escape from captivity—encased my hand and I jerked it away.

Amazingly, she appeared unharmed. Still passed out, but no charred holes in her—which was good.

I stared down at my hand as if it wasn't my own. The last vestiges of light were blinking out.

What just happened?

My heart pounded in my chest. It had been six months since I'd escaped Satan. When the new power to shoot lightning or electricity from my hands hadn't reappeared, I'd thought it was gone for good.

Maybe heightened emotions brought it on?

It's the one thing about my captivity I'd never told anyone. I'd let people believe I had escaped when Morgan's guard had been down. I hadn't brought it up to Deborah, or even any of my friends. I was ashamed that I'd somehow given in to the darkness and I just hoped that it hadn't damned my soul.

I had no idea what this meant, but it couldn't be good. I didn't want anything to do with this girl, but I didn't really have a choice in the matter. We were stuck together, whether we wanted to be or not. The sparks had to be a fluke.

I was truly a different person than the one who'd foolishly rushed into battle with Morgan that day. I had more control than this. I'd make sure I never used that power again.

No one had to know, especially not my new trainee. It was widely known I didn't like the empathy link, so it would be easy to keep from touching her.

A plan started to form in my head. One in which I would be able to train this newbie, and then we could both move on with our own afterlife . . . separately.

It was a while before I came back to myself and realized I needed to deal with her. I couldn't just leave her on the ground like that. I should like, flip her over or try to wake her up.

Taking a deep, calming breath, I tentatively reached out again, taking way too much time to try and figure out where to put my hands.

Waist was a safe zone, right?

I finally grasped her around her tiny middle, ignoring how fragile she felt in my arms as I began to lift and turn her over. Halfway through my maneuver the door behind me banged open.

I straight up dropped her. She landed sunny side down in a tangle of limbs. I spared her a quick wince before spinning around.

Yeah, way to go Logan. That didn't seem guilty or anything.

Shannon had walked back into the room, but had stopped just inside the entrance.

"What in the world did you do to her?" she asked, wide eyed.

"Nothing. I didn't do anything to her. If anything, this is your fault."

"Me?"

"Yeah, you didn't give her any prep for what we do. When I told her what the job was, she passed out cold."

"You didn't think to ease her into it, either?"

"Shannon, get real. I'm a dude. I wasn't about to hold her hand and give a watered-down version of her new reality," I glanced down at her, "I had no idea she would pass out, though. Do you think she does that a lot? Is that a girl thing?"

Shannon scoffed at me, then rolled her eyes.

What? That's a legit question.

"What are you doing back here, anyway?"

"I forgot to tell you where she will be living until she regains her memories."

Since she was my charge now, I should have thought of that already.

"Right. Big glass building?" That's where a lot of the temporary housing people lived.

"No. She'll be moving into the Redwoods."

I furrowed my brows, "Why did they stick her way out there?"

Shannon took a deep breath, "I don't know, Logan. Contrary to popular belief, I don't know everything. I'm just relaying what was told to me."

"But that's so secluded. Don't chicks need to be around other people or something . . . for socializing?"

She pinched the bridge of her nose, "First off, I'm pretty sure young ladies these days don't like to be referred to as *chicks.*"

I shrugged.

Shannon continued, "And I'm confident she'll figure out a way to socialize despite her living quarters. *You* do, after all, and you live out in that area as well," she cocked a perfectly-groomed black eyebrow at me, "Or is it that you don't like her that close to your cottage?"

"It's a cabin," I said through gritted teeth.

Shannon's lips pressed together and for a second I thought she might actually crack a smile. Then the moment passed. "Yes, of course. You're right. Well, now that you know where to take her, I'll leave you to it. I'm sure she'll wake up soon. Those who pass out from shock never stay down for long," she turned to leave.

"Wait!" I shouted before she escaped, "You never told me her name."

Shannon's brow creased as if she couldn't believe her own oversight, "Oh, her name is Audrey. And I can already tell you're going to have your hands full with that one."

As she strode from the room I stared down at the enchantress sprawled on the ground. The whispered words that escaped my lips were too quiet for even an angel to hear.

"You have no idea how right you are about that."

I had a feeling this Audrey girl was likely to be the end of me.

But maybe it wouldn't be a bad way to go.

Author Commentary: Chapter 12

JulieHallAuthor.com/logan-12

. . . and don't forget the blooper reel:
JulieHallAuthor.com/logan-bloopers

Thank you for reading *Logan*!
If you loved it, please write a review at
http://review.LoganBook.com

NOTHING COMES WITHOUT A COST

DOMINION

LIFE AFTER
BOOK THREE

JULIE HALL

USA TODAY BESTSELLING AUTHOR

HELL

I coughed for the hundredth time. Hell was . . . well, hot as Hell. As clichés went, this one was turning out to be extremely accurate. We'd only been here for an hour, tops, and I was already dying to leave.

Oh look, I made a funny!

My quiet laugh turned into another round of nasty coughs. Once they subsided, I half expected to find a lung lying on the ground.

If the incessant hacking didn't get me, the stench was going to kill me.

I'm on a roll.

The atmosphere was filled with a nasty cocktail of rotten eggs, rotten meat, and rotten souls. That last one was just a guess—but if souls could rot, I'm pretty sure the mystery scent in the air was what they would smell like.

Our small group—my fellow friends and hunters—baked in the funk as we trudged through the barren and rocky terrain on our top-secret mission. We'd been transported from our realm to this barren one only an hour before. The conditions were just shy of unbearable, despite the protection provided by Joe. I mean Jesus. I mean the Creator's Son. Oh geez, I was still struggling to wrap my brain around Joe's identity.

He'd been the first person I met when I woke up in the afterlife. He'd introduced himself as Joe, so that was how I thought of him—even after he'd recently revealed himself to be the Son of God. I could swallow the news that he was the Savior of mankind, but actually processing the implications of that information was a little too much for me right now. My finite brain could only handle so much at a time.

In the last twenty-four hours alone, I had discovered my beloved quirky mentor, Hugo, was actually the Holy Spirit; defended my family on Earth against a horde of demons, including Satan; and contracted the heavenly equivalent of a fiancé. And yes, I say contracted as if the engagement were a virus, not the romantic proposal every girl dreams of. It happened much like one would get mono. One kiss and bam I was stuck with him forever. Technically we'd shared a couple of kisses, but who was counting?

As I trekked along behind my friends, my face reddened at my thoughts.

Oh gosh, I really hope no one was counting.

The slight tug on my brand-new internal Logan-GPS—the sense I had of his whereabouts and well-being, activated upon the fateful kiss—was physical proof of the bond between us, as certain and permanent as the Epstein-Barr virus. So here I was, sneaking around a realm I had no business entering and sucking down sulfuric fumes on a quest to rescue my viral love.

Another round of rib-cracking coughs racked my frame. I pressed a hand to my burning throat. Every breath seared my windpipe.

Gosh, he's lucky he's so good looking because rescue missions in Hell are totally overrated.

Something slimy rolled in my gut. I tried hard to ignore the sensation.

Jokes and grumbling could only cover up so much of my concern for Logan's welfare. A throbbing awareness in both my wrists accompanied the pull of my Logan-GPS. I suspected the pain was an echo of what he was experiencing. Phantom twinges had sliced my body since we entered Hell.

I tripped on what looked to be a black lava rock, and Jonathon shot his arm out to steady me. I started to offer thanks, but he was already walking past. The rapier hanging from his waist slapped his thigh with every step. Covered from head to toe in hunter's armor, Jonathon blended well with our trained band of warriors. He looked the part, even if he was a skilled healer rather than a proven fighter.

"Watch where you're going." His words carried a frosty bite that contrasted with the suffocating heat bearing down on us.

Sigh. There was another unneeded complication to this mission. My ex-boyfriend was along for the ride as our group's medical support—the "ex" was for sure . . . the "boyfriend" part debatable.

Why he'd even bothered to stop me from face planting into the craggy red ground was a mystery. He'd made it clear he wanted nothing more to do with me when I told him there could never be anything more than friendship between us. He threw that suggestion back in my face like I'd offered him a bite of a moldy sandwich.

A peace offering he wasn't interested in—and actually offended by.

My chest tightened as sadness blanketed my heart. I lost his friendship, but whatever attraction had existed between us was never going to be strong enough to go the distance. Maybe when he realized that, he'd forgive me.

Of course, he thought I'd cheated on him, so maybe that day would never come.

Another round of coughs compressed my chest and burned my throat. I sucked in the putrid air like it was laced with honey rather than whatever dark pollution caused the stench, but I couldn't catch my breath.

"Hey, you all right?" Romona's chocolate eyes were round as she patted me on the back until my coughing fit subsided.

"Yeah," I croaked.

Great. Apparently a frog had crawled down in my throat and taken up residence.

I did a quick sweep of my traveling companions. All five of them: Kaitlin, Kevin, Jonathon, Romona, and Joe. They all struggled to varying degrees in our new environment. Kaitlin covered her nose with her hand. Romona's eyes watered, whether from the smell or emotions, I wasn't sure.

My throat screamed for some moisture-filled air.

Whoever said dry heat wasn't as bad as humidity didn't know what they were talking about.

Kevin wasn't doing anything to ward off the stench, but sweat dripped down his face. He lifted an arm to wipe the moisture away every few minutes. Guilt washed over me when I realized I was mollified that someone else was suffering from the heat.

Jonathon strode forward as if completely unaffected by our environment, but I suspected his bravado was out of pride and sheer determination to appear strong.

As for Joe, the only sign of distress he revealed was the expression on his face. A sadness had invaded his eyes the moment we reached this realm. The emotion showed itself in the creases around his eyes and the tightness of his features as he surveyed the landscape.

Stumbling and hacking, I was having the worst time of it.

Romona grasped my elbow to help me stand upright, and she kept her hand loosely on my arm to steady me as we continued. We'd fallen a little behind the rest of the group and hurried to catch up.

A stabbing pain in my gut caused me to lose my footing again and cry out. If not for Romona, I would have been on my hands and knees on the scorched ground. The agony was enough to double me over and stop my forward progression.

I took deep breaths with my arms around my middle, protecting myself from the phantom pain.

My Lamaze-like breathing probably made me sound like I was about to give birth. I'd laugh about that if the truth weren't so horrific. I half expected to look down and see blood leaking from my gut. But this wasn't my pain. This was a whisper of whatever Logan was enduring. Panic churned in my stomach, but I stuffed the dread down.

Horrible as that was, the knowledge kept me going. If I didn't know to the very fiber of my being that he was here somewhere and in a tremendous amount of danger, I wouldn't subject myself to this misery any longer.

First train back to the heavenly realm? Yes please. Sign me up.

But I wasn't physically capable of leaving him here, thanks to our bond. And even if I were, I'd never abandon Logan in this horrid place.

"Guys, hold up," Romona shouted.

One breath in. One breath out. One breath in. One breath out.

A cool hand touched my forehead, and the pain subsided. I looked up into Joe's sad, kind eyes.

"Better?" he asked.

"Yeah, thanks." The frog had vacated my throat, and I could speak again. I straightened my frame.

He nodded once. "I know. I can feel it too."

"You can?" Could have fooled me. Besides the hidden sadness in his gaze, he appeared fresh as a daisy.

He rolled his eyes. "Appearances can be deceiving."

Right. He probably knew every thought flitting through my mind. Awkward.

Turning his head, he addressed the small group, "Let's stop for a bit."

No one talked as we all pulled out our canteens to gulp down some water. I took a seat on a spiky rock. That had to be a better alternative than the ground. Wrong. My backside had become a pincushion.

I chugged my drink too quickly, and some of it dribbled down my neck and fell to the dusty soil where the liquid sizzled before evaporating. The desire to drink it all rode me hard, but I'd need it later.

I capped my water and secured it to my belt. Waiting for the go-ahead, I looked around.

Red ground littered with small mounds of black stones stretched as far as the eye could see. When I looked up, there was no blue sky but rather a rocky surface that could have been a mile above our heads.

We were truly entombed in the Earth.

I had no idea what dim luminescence lit this place, but whatever the artificial light was, rather than enhance color, it drained it. The faces of my companions were chalky. Even the dirt beneath our feet seemed leached of color. Devoid of vegetation, the barren wasteland laid out in all directions.

Hell was bleak.

Looking at the grey faces and dull eyes of my friends was a bit like looking at reanimated corpses. Waves of trepidation rolled down my spine, wracking my frame with full body shudders as my thoughts, steeped in the macabre, worked their way through me.

"Is it all like this?" Kaitlin swept her arm in an arc as her eyes scanned the vicinity.

"No." Joe was the only one of us still standing. His gaze remained outward even as he addressed Kaitlin's question. "This part hasn't been filled yet."

Filled? What did that mean?

The look of disgust marring his face was unmistakable. "I wanted to make sure we weren't detected, but entering an empty part of this realm calls for a lengthy walk. You all are holding up well." His eyes found mine. "Considering the circumstances."

He turned to face the whole group. "Listen. There are a few things you all need to know before we go any farther. This realm was created for the Betrayer and his followers, but there are others here as well. It isn't Our desire that a single soul should end up in this vile place, but . . ."

He paused and scrubbed a hand down his face before going on. His expression was tormented, his mouth was pressed into a hard line, and veins pulsed at his temples. "You're not going to like what you see. You need to prepare yourself. We're here for one reason alone, and that is to bring Logan home. You are going to have to come to terms with the fact that you can't do anything for anyone else here. They are not your responsibility."

Then whose responsibility were they?

I snuck a glance at my companions. Mouths pressed in hard lines and scrunched brows were a common theme.

"What else can you tell us?" Romona asked.

Joe motioned for us all to come forward. With his sword, he drew a circle in the red volcanic cinder at his feet.

"This realm is composed of rings." He drew several more circles within the first, each one inside another until there were nine circles. The center one was no bigger than a quarter.

"We're currently in the outermost ring." He indicated the space between the largest circle and the next one with the tip of his sword. "As we travel farther, each ring is more inhabited, and the discomfort you're all feeling will intensify."

I blinked back at him. *Intensify?* I wasn't going to make it.

Squirming, sharp pains of discomfort stabbed my backside. This rock made a horrible seat.

"Audrey."

My attention snapped back to Joe.

"A lot of what you are feeling is leaked to you from Logan, so you're already experiencing what it's like to be in a deeper ring. I'm not saying it won't get worse for you, but not by much."

Dread sunk my heart to my belly. *Logan.*

Multiple pairs of concerned-filled eyes swung my way. Jonathon didn't look at me. He was staring at the circles Joe had drawn in the ground as if they held the meaning of life. Jonathon's features were hard. I couldn't help the tendril of compassion that spun around inside when I looked at him. Knowingly or not, I'd played a part in the stone-like façade he now wore.

"Do you know where he is?" I asked, turning my attention back to our leader.

Joe nodded and made an X in the space between the fourth and fifth circles, four rings away from where we currently resided. "Logan's there, and we're here. This is an oversimplification of the realm, but it's basic information you should have."

"Why didn't we just drop into his exact location, grab him, and get out of here?" Cocking my head toward Kevin, I silently admitted he had a point.

"Your bodies need some time to adjust to the atmosphere down here. The demons are extremely active where Logan is. If we'd gone straight there, you'd be forced to defend yourselves against upper-level demons while you struggled to breathe."

We nodded, our faces broadcasting a range of emotions.

"Your bodies weren't meant for this realm, but by going through the circles slowly, you'll be able to handle its intensity better. We're going to skirt around as much of the demonic activity as possible, but at some point, you will all have to fight to defend yourselves. The creatures residing in this realm have been here many millennia and have adapted to its climate. This is their home turf, and it's important you remember that. Our primary objective is to get Logan and get home. You need to readjust your thinking." He took a moment to look each of us in the eye. "You are no longer the hunters, but rather the hunted."

ZOMBIES

*D*espite the heat, chills raced up and down my spine.

Joe sheathed his sword and turned to continue our journey. We wordlessly followed, each one of us likely processing the information he'd just given.

We walked and walked, and the scenery never changed. This journey felt like an exercise in futility—like a nightmare where we were running from something without actually getting anywhere.

I struggled against the feeling of despair as much as I fought to remain upright. Romona stayed suspiciously close, with her gaze on me as often as our surroundings. As my best-friend-slash-grandmother turned kick-butt huntress in the afterlife, her concern for me was expected—if not slightly overbearing at times.

Kevin was up ahead with Joe and peppering him with questions like an inquisitive child trying to make sense of the world around him. For his part, Joe was playing the patient parent well. Kevin wanted to know how big the realm was—*Big.* How many different demons resided here—*A lot.* Why was the ground red—*It was, in fact, made up of volcanic cinder.* When would we run into another being—*Hopefully not for a while.*

"So where is the light coming from in this place? It looks like we're in a giant cave." Kevin tilted his head up to survey the stone-like sky above.

"It comes from the lake of fire that makes up the innermost ring. The flames shoot up from the lake like a pillar."

Kevin jerked his head toward Joe, mouth hanging open.

"But we won't be going anywhere near there." Joe's steps halted. "Okay, everyone, we're here."

Here?

I looked around. We stood in the same barren wasteland we'd been trudging through for hours.

"Wow. Yep. This is . . . something?" Kaitlin's confusion was mirrored on the faces of my other companions.

The corner of Joe's mouth twitched as if he were struggling to hold back a smile. "This is the beginning of the next ring."

"But how can you tell?" I asked. Scanning our surroundings, the landscape was still a flat plane of red sprinkled with black rocks.

"I can feel it," Joe answered with a frown. The strain around his eyes told me there was more he wasn't saying. "Join hands."

I bit my lip and grasped Romona's left hand with my right. I was at the end of the chain. Joe held Kevin's hand and walked forward. On the second step, our leader disappeared.

I gasped as Kevin said, "What the—" before he disappeared too.

I started to pull back on Romona's hand, trying to slow my steps as Jonathon was swallowed by the nothing, but the momentum of the group propelled me forward.

"This is trippy," Kaitlin said a moment before she vanished.

"Romona, are we sure—" Romona turned her head toward me, and I watched her fade out of sight. I squeezed my eyes shut. I was next.

A flash of heat washed over me—like when passing a finger through the flame of a candle without lingering long enough to actually get burned.

My eyes popped open when the feeling passed.

The world had transformed. The ground was still red, but that was where the similarities ended. The terrain was dotted with the skeletal remains of trees. Gnarled and bone-white branches protruded from twisted trunks at awkward angles, a distorted mass of intertwined appendages that appeared to have grown with the intent of hiding from the life-giving light rather than reaching for it.

Beyond the blanched dead forest was a blackened mountain range that cut a jagged line across the horizon.

Not comparing the frightening sight with the peaceful landscape of our own realm was impossible. They were opposites in every way. But just as the mountain range had been the first site to captivate me in the heavenly realm, the hellacious mountains were what drew my attention now. Rather than standing in awe of its majesty, my attention was captured by its grotesqueness. Lined up like rows of shark teeth, multiple peaks were completely black except for occasional pustules that oozed red magma down the sharpened slopes like never-ending streams of tears.

"This is seriously disturbing," Kevin said, and I couldn't have agreed with him more.

Bile churned in my stomach with the wrongness of this place.

"Why do the trees grow like that?" Jonathon asked.

Several heartbeats passed before he received an answer. "They are the pathetic attempt of a creature trying to create life in its own image. But even in this desolate place, there is only one Creator." There was a hollowness to Joe's voice, and his face was stoically masked, hiding whatever emotions might lie beneath. "Let's go, everyone. We have several more rings to go through until we reach Logan."

That I could have forgotten about Logan even for a moment caused guilt to settle into my gut.

"Yeah, let's get going." I started forward without waiting for direction.

"Yo! Audrey!"

I stopped walking and turned in the direction of Kevin's bellow. He—along with the rest of the group—was about thirty feet behind me.

"It's this way." He hitched his thumb in the opposite direction.

"Oh." I grimaced. "Sorry." I scurried to join back up and this time waited for Joe to lead.

After five minutes of traveling in the eighth ring, the sensation of being watched washed over me like a surge of static electricity.

The fine hairs on the back of my neck prickled. I swiveled my head, searching for the source of my discomfort.

Was that movement in my peripheral vision? I snapped my attention to the left. The only thing there was one of those creepy dead trees.

My gaze stayed glued to the tree as we passed. Nothing there. Just as I turned my attention forward, a cracking noise like brittle twigs being snapped in half echoed in the gloom. I cast a glance over my shoulder to see one of the bleached branches of the tree I'd just passed stretching in my direction—reaching out to me.

I yelped and tripped over some rocks—okay, my own feet—in my haste to get away. Landing with a thud on my right hip, I threw my arm out to catch my upper body.

Without bothering to stand, I scurried on my hands and knees to put distance between the tree and me. Thank goodness for the body armor. I would have been a scraped-up mess without it. Nothing about this realm was soft.

"What are you doing?" Jonathon's voice held only disgust.

Jarred out of my fright, I assessed him. Where was the compassionate guy I knew? Had he never been that person to begin with, or had I somehow broken him?

A gentle hand tugged on my arm and helped me to my feet. If I didn't know any better, I'd say Joe was trying hard not to laugh at me.

My companions stared at me, waiting for an explanation. "Dude, I think those things are alive. And I don't mean like they're sucking-nutrients-in-from-the-ground alive, but rather they're-moving-their-branches-at-will alive."

"They're not alive," Joe assured me. "They're reanimated."

"What? Reanimated? Like . . . like zombies?"

Joe just blinked once but didn't expound.

"You're telling me we're walking through a forest of zombie trees?" I let out a yap when I accidentally brushed up against one of the boney branches, almost flattening Kaitlin in my haste to get away. "Oh my gosh! Are they going to try to eat us?"

Finally my point was getting through. The others shifted on their feet and started looking around with wary eyes. Jonathon even pulled out his sword, although what he expected to be able to do with the thin blade he carried against a hardened tree limb, I had no idea. We needed a machete . . . STAT!

Oh wait, I had a sword that caught fire. That was, if it worked down here. If so, I could char these things in no time. As dry as they were, they'd probably ash as quickly as kindling.

I followed Jonathon's lead and pulled my sword from its sheath on my back. With a sigh of relief, I watched the blade catch fire like usual. It looked like the holy fire was ready to torch some petrified zombie bark.

A deep belly laugh had us all looking in Joe's direction. *Seriously?*

"Are you messing with me right now?" I asked. I wasn't willing to put my sword down until I knew we were safe. A quick look around the group said that despite Joe's blasé attitude, they all agreed with me.

A long few minutes passed before Joe composed himself enough to speak.

"I'm serious. These things aren't alive. Reanimated is the best way to describe them, but they aren't going to try to eat your brains." The last few words were spoken with a chuckle.

"Well, what do they want then? Because they are definitely interested in something." Over the time we'd been standing still, a few more branches had slowly stretched my way.

"They're attracted to what you have that they don't."

"Which is?" I prompted.

"Life."

I wasn't willing to lower my sword just yet. "But I'm dead."

Joe shrugged a shoulder.

I swung my sword at a branch that was a little too close for comfort. My blade cut through it as easily as warm butter. In response, the tree let out an ear-piercing shriek—from where exactly I wasn't sure, because it's not as if it had a mouth—and I stumbled back a step. The remainder of the limb retracted, burying itself within the tangle of branches closest to the trunk.

Hands down the creepiest thing I'd ever seen. No lie. And I'd seen a lot of creepy things since becoming a hunter.

"What. Just. Happened? That was a very lifelike reaction for something that's not supposed to be alive!" I held my weapon out in front of me like a flamethrower rather than a sword and turned in a circle to make sure no other limbs entered my personal space.

"This place is seriously messed up," Kevin muttered, and I nodded my agreement. We were so in sync at the moment.

"Okay, my vote is we get through this forest of horrors as fast as—" My words were cut short as my body convulsed violently and I dropped my sword.

I fell to my knees hard, and my back bowed in pain. A scream caught in my throat. One I desperately wished I could expel.

My vision flickered to another scene.

A smirk appeared on the sadistic face in front of me. "I told you the fun had only just begun."

The pain at my side was beyond what I thought I had the capacity to feel. My instinct was to fold over and protect myself from the worst of it, but with my arms restrained, I could do nothing but bear it.

I blinked. Romona's face blocked out part of the rock-like sky overhead.

"Audrey!" someone screamed and reached for me.

I sucked in a lungful of air, and with my next blink, I was gone.

LOGAN

"*That's enough playtime for now, Adramelech.*" *The dark being cocked his head to the side. "He looks properly tenderized for the moment."*

If I weren't in so much pain, I might have laughed. Through my non-swollen eye, I could see bits of my flesh. Whatever wasn't torn was covered in layer upon layer of blood. These short reprieves from the torture would give the blood just enough time to dry before the next round began and the sticky wetness started flowing again. I was like a bloodsicle now—nothing more than a battered hunk of flesh.

My human body would have failed long ago, and at this moment I wasn't sure whether to be glad for or curse the new one the afterlife provided me.

The creature who had just been dismissed bowed and scampered out the room on all fours.

The creature left standing in front of me was less vile in form but infinitely more so beneath his façade. His attractive illusion was only that: an illusion. "Ah, Logan, this all feels so familiar to me."

I lifted my chin and stared him straight in the face—right where his eyes should have been. He was right. We'd been in this position before. And just like the last time, I would endure.

"I believe I recognize that look in your eyes. Excuse me, I mean your eye. One is out of commission at the moment. The look I'm seeing is"—the sockets narrowed around where his eyes should be—"ah yes, I'm right. It's defiance."

He leaned in closer and put a hand on my bruised shoulder. I flinched involuntarily but refused to look away from the face of pure evil.

Satan.

The sharpened tips of his fingers grew into claws that slowly cut into my skin, sending trickles of hot blood weeping down my shoulder and onto my exposed chest. The liquid was almost cooling in the oppressive heat of this place.

He ripped his hand from my shoulder, increasing the blood flow from the wounds he'd inflicted, and took two leisurely steps back.

"That look is fine by me." The cruel twist of his lips said that the shredding of my flesh pleased him.

"Whada you wa?" Like honey clinging to a jar, my words stuck in my throat.

Blood started to ooze from a crack on my lip.

I didn't bother trying to spit the coppery substance from my mouth. It would have only dribbled down the front of me anyway.

He heaved a breath as if this was all a giant bore. "Haven't we already been over this? From you? I want nothing more than exactly what you are already doing. And might I say you are doing it beautifully. Even the weakest bond would be pulsating in agony right now. You're acting as a beacon, drawing in exactly what I want."

Audrey.

Fear sliced through my heart. Not for myself but for her. Oh God, I sent up a desperate prayer, Please don't let her anywhere near this horrific place.

A pull deep inside me said it might already be too late. I'd been trying hard to ignore the feeling. The torture drowned it out, but during my few short respites, I'd sensed she was close.

I hoped I was simply delusional, that the sense of her being near was a fabrication of my psyche that wanted her close even as my rational mind wished her as far away from this place as possible.

"Hmm. I wonder if He'll answer whatever pathetic plea you just lifted up to His name."

The sound of footsteps echoing off the walls outside my cell halted our conversation.

"Ah, a visitor." Satan clapped his hands together as a figure entered the chamber.

The air punched out of my gut even as my brain scrambled to put together the pieces.

Alrik. My friend. My closer-than-a-brother friend.

Yes, a deeply buried part of me had considered this as a possibility ever since I'd woken up in this God-forsaken place, but seeing reality was more painful than any of the wounds that had been inflicted in this realm. I had been betrayed.

Again.

Something inside me began to boil.

"You were right." Alrik's voice was steady. "They've been spotted in the eighth ring. They'll cross over to the seventh shortly."

A flicker of annoyance crossed Satan's face before the emotion was wiped clean. "Perfect. It's like they heard the dinner bell and have come running, not realizing they're on the menu. Let me know when—"

"You!" a shredded voice bellowed. A moment passed before I recognized the shout as my own. What I lacked in clarity, I made up for in volume. "How could you?"

Pure rage punctured my skin like rusty nails. With energy I shouldn't have possessed, like a rabid animal I struggled against the manacles that kept me tethered to the stone wall.

Alrik had led me to Earth and directly into an ambush. We'd been attacked the moment we'd materialized. I'd lost track of him when I was taken down and feared he'd been captured as well. To think, this whole time I'd been hanging here I'd also been concerned for his safety. The snake.

"History does seem to be repeating itself, doesn't it?" Satan mocked.

"Betrayer!" I spat at Alrik. My gaze fixated on my ex-friend even as staring at him made me sick.

Deadened eyes stared back at me. I'd seen that look from him on the battlefield, but I'd never been the recipient of that expression before.

I breathed like a raging bull. Before I even realized what I was doing, electricity crackled to life inside me, building in my heart and then exploding outward. White-and-blue zigzags of energy shot from my hands, harmlessly scorching the walls of my cell rather than the two beings at whom my fury was directed.

I'd revealed my hidden power.

Big mistake.

Yet the dread that should have settled in my chest was snuffed out by my righteous anger.

I strained against my chains with an otherworldly power. They groaned, and for a moment I thought I might be able to free myself. That was until Satan flicked his wrist and a second set of binds clamped down on my forearms, further securing me to the jagged rocks at my back.

"Interesting. You might be worth more than I thought." Satan tilted his head in a birdlike manner, examining me like an alien specimen. "That little trick of yours betrays your alliance. Interesting that you've been able to hide it from me for so long." A grin spread across his face. "My arms are always open to welcome another solider as fodder for the battlefield."

He turned from me and addressed an uncharacteristically stoic Alrik. "I think it's time we thin the herd a bit, don't you agree?"

Alrik merely shifted his weight and gave a quick nod of agreement.

They both turned to leave, but before stepping out of sight, Satan turned his head my way.

"It appears that prayer of yours has gone unanswered after all."

Logan!

I jerked upright with a silent scream lodged in my throat and my face wet with tears. Turning to the side, I retched not once but twice onto the ground. The measly amount of food and water in my stomach was expelled the first round, and yellow bile came up the second.

A face filled my watery view, and hands came down on my shoulders, straightening my hunched form.

"It's okay." Joe's voice soothed me. "It's going to be all right."

I whipped my head back and forth, still unable to find my voice.

Joe pulled me forward and squished my face against his chest as sobs wracked my frame. Rubbing soothing circles on my back, he let me cry.

I didn't have the luxury to fall apart. Every moment we wasted was extra torture for Logan. And that vision confirmed my deepest fear—Satan was using Logan to lure me closer, but I still had no idea what the evil being wanted with me.

Terror pressed on my bladder. I beat the fear back as best I could; my welfare wasn't my primary concern right now.

"N-no," I stuttered. "You don't understand." Still seated, I pushed away from Joe's chest so I could look him in the eye.

"I do." His eyes bore into mine, a fire burning deep within them. He nodded, his gaze never wavering from mine. "I promise, I do."

My pulse started to calm.

"And when the time comes, you'll do what you think you need to do. Just know that you've already been forgiven."

My heartbeat kicked right back into high gear with Joe's bizarre statement.

"Huh?"

He placed his hand over mine, and sadness overtook the righteous fire burning in his eyes.

"You'll know soon enough." He squeezed my hand before standing. "We should keep moving now that you're back with us."

I hadn't considered the rest of the group or even my surroundings for that matter, until Romona stepped into view.

We appeared to be in a cave. A fire burned several feet away, giving light to the cramped space as well as adding to the already unbearable heat.

I turned my head and located Kevin, Kaitlin, and Jonathon standing close by.

They all stared in silence. Seeing me jolt awake and then proceed to have a complete meltdown must have been unnerving. Did they have any idea what had happened while I was out?

They watched me with wide eyes and faces leeched of color despite the orange glow of the fire's flames. They were spooked. Even Jonathon's expression matched the rest.

"Audrey"—Romona drew my attention—"your hair . . . it's white."

I swallowed a gasp and brought a chunk forward to inspect. Color usually streaked my hair, but this time the white completely swallowed any trace of pigmentation. I shivered despite the heat then took a moment to change it back. It had never turned that shade before, but considering what I'd just witnessed, the color change shouldn't have been a surprise.

I set my hand on the ground, intending to push myself to my feet, but snatched it back when I connected with something warm and sticky. My gaze tracked down, and with a yelp, I rolled-crawled off the makeshift bed I'd been sitting on.

Oh no they didn't!

"Please tell me you didn't drag me through Hell on a bunch of dismembered zombie tree limbs?"

Romona's eyes twinkled. "Okay, I won't tell you that."

I spared a glance at my hand, smeared with—something warm and sticky.

"Is that blood?" My voice was shrill even to my own ears.

I glared at the pallet I'd been resting on. A dozen or so skinny branches had been secured together to make a semi-flat surface just wide and long enough to fit my frame. With caution, I leaned forward. The dim lighting made it difficult to see, but sure enough, something red was leaking from the broken tree limbs.

"Oh my gosh! Did they suck my blood while I was unconscious?" I frantically searched my body armor for rips or tears. "How could you put me at risk like that?"

"Vampires suck blood. Zombies eat brains," Kevin piped up.

"Well then, why the heck are those things leaking blood?"

"It's not blood," Jonathon snapped, clearly over any concern he had for me. "It's sap."

"Sap?"

"Yeah sap. You know, like maple syrup." Jonathon's tone and eye roll made it clear he thought I was an idiot.

My stomach churned at the thought of pouring the blood-like substance on my pancakes. I slapped a hand over my mouth as if the action would somehow ward off my macabre thoughts, unintentionally spreading the substance over my lips and chin.

"That's nasty." I furiously scrubbed my face with the back of my clean hand, the bile in my stomach churning once again. "I can't believe you guys dragged me around on that thing."

"Well, technically we didn't drag you; we carried you." Kaitlin shrugged at the glare I shot her. "What? It helped disperse your weight and allowed us to move faster. You were all floppy and stuff."

"This is by far the most bizarre thing that's happened to me since I woke up dead." A day jammed with firsts.

"That's saying something," Kaitlin noted.

"Truth." I bobbed my head in agreement.

"So what happened?" Romona laid a gentle hand on my arm. Leave it to her to recognize my very real need for comfort.

"Yeah." I swallowed in a vain attempt to wet my suddenly parched throat. "I saw Logan." Correcting myself, I shook my head. "No, that's not entirely true. I didn't see Logan. I *was* Logan."

Kaitlin gasped.

"Trippy," Kevin whispered.

"He's . . ." I closed my eyes and rubbed them with my clean fist before going on. "He's in real bad shape right now. They're doing . . . things to him that are beyond horrible." Letting my hands drop to my sides, I speared each of them with my gaze. "If we don't get to him soon, I'm not sure how much of him there will be left to save."

"What's that supposed to mean?" Jonathon demanded.

How could I explain the horror Logan was experiencing right now? "It means he's on the verge of breaking."

"Was Alrik there?" Kaitlin asked in a small voice. Her eyes were wide and glassy.

Just the mention of his name spiked my anger. With gritted teeth, I nodded curtly. When I got my hands on that traitor, he was going to suffer.

"Audrey." Joe's soft but assertive voice broke through my haze of fury. "Alrik's ultimate fate is one you wouldn't wish on anyone."

"Do you . . . feel *sorry* for him?" Every word came out with a bite. I wanted to expose my teeth like an angry dog and snap at him.

The skin was literally being peeled from Logan's body while Alrik stood and watched. After witnessing his betrayal firsthand, I'd never have anything but hatred in my heart for him. He'd led Logan to a fate worse than death.

Willingly. Knowingly. For personal gain.

My muscles tensed, fingers curled inward, and knees bent as I readied myself for a fight. I was acting like a provoked animal—ready to fight dirty to protect what was mine.

"It is not Our desire that We would lose even one. If you truly understood what awaited him, you'd have a measure of compassion as well."

I growled. Literally growled at Joe. He only shook his head and turned from me.

A moment of shame settled on my heart before I shoved the disgrace aside. I didn't have anything to be ashamed of. I got that Joe's ability to forgive was larger than mine, but no one responsible for the atrocities being done to Logan should be forgiven. There was no room for that kind of forgiveness. Their actions were unforgivable.

Alrik deserved the punishment coming to him, and nothing Joe said could make me feel otherwise.

I turned my back on him and walked away from the fire. "You're right," I threw over my shoulder, "we should get going."

RINGS

"You carried me through the rest of the eighth ring?" I asked in a whisper as we trudged along behind Joe. Sometime while I'd been unconscious, we'd left the zombie forest behind and entered a completely new terrain.

"Yep." Kaitlin nodded.

"I don't know whether to be impressed or embarrassed."

"Definitely embarrassed."

I half-heartedly shoved Kaitlin, lacking the energy to do much more. She took a step to the side and righted herself, not even bothering to try and hide her smile.

Brat.

If Romona was my best friend, then Kaitlin was the annoying—and somewhat immature—older sister I hadn't asked for. Rolling my eyes at my friend, my mind wandered elsewhere.

The ground crunched beneath my feet with every step. I'd been told the volcanic stones and cinder had disappeared when we crossed through the last ring. If I tried hard enough, I could pretend we were walking on bleached seashells, but the shape and general appearance didn't quite line up with that theory.

But, whatever, I preferred it to the zombie trees. Shivers wracked my body when my mind even brushed against the thought.

The seventh ring had similarities to the eighth. The same jagged mountain range cut a crooked path along the horizon. When we'd emerged from the cave, I learned we'd actually been taking shelter within the black monstrosities to hide from any roaming demons. Joe explained that the creatures inhabited the rings closer to the center, but occasionally one would appear in this section. The height of our hidden shelter had also given us the advantage of being able to scout great distances.

How they hauled me up the sharp terrain to find the cavern was a mystery. Dragging my unconscious body straight up that hunk of rock must have been near impossible, but I was thankful.

Even without carrying my dead weight, it took the better part of a half hour to descend. From our perch, I had assumed the area was covered in desert sand.

I was so wrong.

The particles were larger than granules of sand, ranging from the size of a dime to a quarter in a variety of distorted shapes. A sickening snap and crack sounded with each heavy footfall.

No, this wasn't sand at all. I knew these were bleached bone fragments.

I shoved all thoughts of the ground we traversed into a tightly sealed box and stored it in the far recesses of my mind. We were one ring closer to Logan, that's all that should matter—even if I had to fight the urge to wince with every crunchy step.

As we'd been warned, the heat increased, but after experiencing what Logan was going through, I hardly registered the uptick in temperature. If anything, I was actually doing better than I was before. Perhaps I was just that much more motivated. Seeing the person I lo—

I caught my thoughts. *Whoa, wait a minute. I almost just let the "L" bomb drop.* Did I actually lo—lov . . . Oh. My. Gosh. I couldn't even spit the word out mentally. There was a time I had thought my feelings ran that deep for Logan, but was it even possible I felt that way when I couldn't even force my conscious mind to say it?

Our relationship had gone through so many ups and downs. Just when I thought I knew where we stood, he kissed me, and we were bonded. Then he was kidnapped and gone. My head and my heart ran into each other like colliding freight trains. I'd been acting mostly on instinct, but when I stopped to really think about us, my head throbbed.

I took a casual look around to make sure no one was paying attention to me and my existential crisis. Kaitlin morbidly kicked bone fragments as she strolled forward—blessedly ignoring me. Kevin and Jonathon trudged on in front of us, their attention firmly forward.

Up ahead of them, Joe and Romona led the way. I squinted and tilted my head just a bit as I stared at Joe's back. His shoulders were hunched in a way that had my suspicion meter spiking. Was he . . . laughing?

He put a hand up to his face and shook his head. A moment later, he glanced over his shoulder and shot me a quick look before turning back again. The smile on his face said it all.

That booger *was* laughing. At me.

"Yeah, live it up!" I yelled.

His shoulders just shook harder, and he brought a hand up to wipe something from his eyes. Were no thoughts sacred?

Kevin and Jonathon looked my way, both set of brows furrowed.

"What's going on?" Kevin asked.

"Nothing," I grumbled and pushed forward, leaving our footprints as well as my thoughts about love behind.

"Sooo. This is it, huh?" I stared ahead at nothing. And by nothing, I mean the exact same thing we'd looked at for the last few hours: a sea of white with the angry dark mountain range to our right.

We'd followed the mountains until Joe called a halt and let us know we were about to enter the next ring. I cocked my eyebrow and pursed my lips, ready for another optical illusion of some kind that hid the entrance of the next ring.

"Do we need to hold hands again?" Kailtin asked. "Because if so, I think this time we should sing Kumbaya."

"Did you have to do that when you passed between the eighth and seventh ring?" I asked.

"Sing songs?"

I rolled my eyes. Smart-mouthed blonde.

"Hold hands."

She grinned back. "Yep." She popped her p as usual. "It was tricky, since we were lugging around your dead weight. We all had to keep one hand on your zombie stretcher and another on you so we could all get through together."

"Do not call it a zombie stretcher." I cringed even saying the words.

Her smile grew.

"Join hands. No singing. I'm expecting company this time," was all Joe said before he clasped Jonathon's hand and walked through the invisible veil.

Company?

Wait, maybe we should discuss this "company" before going through an invisible wall.

Before I could voice my concerns, Jonathon grabbed Kevin's hand and disappeared. Kevin grasped Romona's, Romona snatched Kaitlin's, and then Kaitlin grabbed mine and everyone was steadily moving forward.

"Seriously, peeps, I'm thinking that maybe we should . . . Oh shoot."

Kaitlin vanished. This was happening whether I wanted it to or not.

Rotten eggs. I choked on the stench. Great, we were back to the stinky part of Hell. When I crossed over to the sixth ring, my eyes started to water from the intensity of the smell. The nasty odor had been absent from the last two rings but was back with a vengeance.

I waved my hand in front of my face to clear the air of not only the stench of rot but of some sort of smoke or mist as well. This ring was a little like stepping into a smelly, dense cloud. Foul-smelling and horrible visibility.

Someone to my right retched. Jonathon bent at the waist, dry heaving into the skeletal remains of a bush. The leafless twigs did little to hide the sight. A gag worked its way up my throat, but I managed to choke the bile down.

Everyone else's complexions were tinged green, but the others fared far better than Jonathon. Most covered their mouths with their hands.

Pfft—like that's going to do much. Not even a gas mask could clean this air.

Despite the distracting assault on my senses, something familiar rolled in my gut and punched awareness to the surface. And it wasn't my Logan-GPS . . . this sensation was something altogether different.

Turning in a quick circle, I scanned our murky surroundings. We were no longer alone.

They're everywhere.

"Huh?" Kevin asked.

I must have spoken that last part out loud.

"Demons," I answered without allowing my eyes to rest on any of my friends. I was too busy searching for unseen enemies. In this crazy fog, they could be upon us before we spotted them.

"You know, my built-in demon-detector thing. It's going berserk right now." That indescribable feeling that wasn't a feeling. The smell that wasn't a smell. I'd never been able to properly articulate the freak power that had sprung to life on Earth that no one but me seemed to have. Right now my gut churned, and awareness poked at my senses.

I grabbed the sword from my back, and when the blade blazed to life, a fresh wave of heat flared along my arms.

"Where are they?" asked a straightening Jonathon. "I don't see anything."

I spared him a glance. He wiped his mouth with the back of his glove and scanned the hidden terrain with a squint.

Had Jonathon ever actually seen a demon before? It's not like he would have had the opportunity to do so from the safety of our realm. This might very well be the first time he would come face-to-face with the reality of our enemy.

I hope he's up to the task.

Something shimmered around us, and I recognized Joe's dampening effect on the environment. The smell became somewhat bearable again, and the heat lessened.

"The Fallen do inhabit this and the remaining rings of Hell. We'll have to be more vigilant than before."

"Is that the *company* you mentioned before pulling us into this ring?" I was still wary, ready for an attack at any moment. Why hadn't they already charged?

Joe nodded. He was the only one of us whose focus was on the group rather than our surroundings. "You're feeling their presence because there are so many of them here. It's overwhelming your senses. It doesn't mean any are as close as you think. You're feeling them like I do."

My gaze snapped to Joe. His stare remained locked on mine . . . steady and unflinching.

"Yes, Audrey. That part of you comes from me." He answered my unspoken question.

My muscles locked. So. Many. Questions.

"Whoa." Kevin's murmur reached my ears.

I didn't disagree.

Joe shook his head. "Not now. We'll have to discuss this later. Just know that you can't trust your instincts down here. Not like you do on the surface. You're going to feel suffocated by their presence sometimes, but that doesn't mean you have one breathing down your back."

"Are you seriously going to drop that bomb on me and just leave it hanging there? I mean . . . what? I'm not supposed to ask any more questions? All I've ever had regarding this . . . this ability of mine . . . has been questions."

"We'll talk later." His eyes told me that was a promise. "Let's find shelter and a place to rest first."

I wanted to argue, but it would be fruitless. Joe's answers would come when he was ready and not a moment sooner. I released an unintelligible grumble and let it go. Maybe this meant I was maturing?

Pfft. Yeah right. It simply meant I was starting to recognize battles I wasn't going to win.

"You guys." Something about the tone of Romona's voice caught me off guard. "Maybe we should start looking for that shelter sooner rather than later."

The mountain range that had been our steadfast landmark was still with us, but in this ring, it wasn't simply ugly . . . it was angry. The pustules that had leaked molten lava in the previous rings were spewing it freely here. They were also spontaneously erupting on the mountainside like exploding zits.

One of which had just appeared several hundred feet above our heads. Its contents were headed straight for us.

"Move!" Joe commanded.

As a unit, we ran forward into the hazy mess. We weren't going to luck out and find shelter in the mountain this time.

SHELTER

*H*ours later, we were still traveling on high alert. We grouped close together because if one of us strayed too far, there was danger of being swallowed by the dense fog. The shrieks that occasionally emanated from it were far from comforting. Kaitlin jumped more than once at the sounds.

My blade was out and on a near-constant swivel. The whoosh of the fire as I swung the weapon back and forth to ward off the inevitable attack grated on my already frayed nerves.

The sense of demons—everywhere—never dissipated.

Sweat dripped down my back and between my shoulder blades. My arms shook with fatigue. The strain I'd felt ever since the ninth ring was now evident on all my companions' faces, save Joe's. I didn't take any satisfaction from the fact that my friends were finally experiencing my level of discomfort.

To my left, Romona stumbled. She took several shaky steps before losing the battle against gravity and landing on her hands and knees.

I sheathed my blade and helped her to her feet. She teetered a bit before finding her footing then sent me a weary smile and nod of thanks. Sweat dotted her brow and upper lip, and her breathing was labored despite our slow pace. Lines of exhaustion ringed her eyes, and she weaved as if drunk.

"Joe," I whisper-yelled to our leader. When he turned toward me, I jerked my chin in Romona's direction.

His lips thinned to a grim line.

"Almost there," he called back.

I cringed at the volume. Despite Joe's assurance that no demons were close enough to attack us, the creepy feeling in my gut said otherwise.

A few long minutes later, Joe held up his hand, signaling us to stop.

Romona sank to her knees. I watched her with concern. The others in the group were bent over, hands on knees and sucking in air as if they'd just run a marathon.

Phantom pain still zinged throughout my body, causing me to jerk from time to time with the intensity. Fatigue weighted my limbs, but at least I could remain upright. Perhaps my earlier exposure to this discomfort had conditioned my body for the hardships of the sixth ring? Or maybe the little "nap" I'd taken allowed me to rest when the others hadn't gotten that luxury? Referring to the experience of Logan's torture as a luxury seemed beyond wrong, but I couldn't ignore the fact my body had the chance to refresh while my friends had hauled my unconscious form through an entire ring.

Joe was hunched over a spot on the ground, doing who knew what. His lips and hands were moving, reminding me of the first time we'd met—back in a time outside of time—when he'd literally created the heavenly realm in front of my eyes. There was a strain to his face that hadn't been there before.

A moment later, the ground shook beneath our feet. The other hunters jumped and pulled out their weapons, searching with wild eyes for the perceived threat. I was too busy watching the hole growing at Joe's feet to join them.

What the what? Are those stairs?

When the shaking stopped, Joe stood and called us forward.

Kevin's eyes grew when he spotted the hole that had appeared while he was scanning for threats. The rest of my friends simply shifted their weight back and forth with unsmiling faces. I'd wager a guess none of us were wild about going down there. We stood in a circle, looking into the darkness.

"Abandon all hope, ye who enter here."

Had Jonathon not been standing right next to me, I might not have heard his whispered words.

"Huh?"

Jonathon didn't spare me a look; he only rolled his eyes.

"Is that from Dante's *Inferno?*" I pressed. "Weren't you already dead by the time that was written?"

"No. I'm not that old," he sneered. "Did you remember that from a 'quote-a-day' calendar?"

Ouch . . . and he wasn't wrong.

I held up my hands in defense. "Geez, sorry. I didn't mean anything by it."

Okay, new strategy when dealing with Jonathon: Ignore his presence entirely. He seemed to prefer it that way.

A set of stairs led into a black abyss. Joe took the first step into the dark hole.

"Come on," he said. "We'll rest here for a while. You all need it."

"You want us to follow you into a black hole in the ground. Deeper into

Hell?" There was a wild glint in Kevin's eyes when he spoke. He took a step away from the rest of us.

I got it. This was unnerving but hardly the scariest thing we'd encountered so far. I mean, come on, zombie trees for the win. At least Joe was offering us a break. My weary body screamed for rest even as my mind rioted against anything that would slow our mission, but if we were going to be in any shape to rescue Logan, we all needed a breather.

Joe motioned the rest of us down before him as he went to Kevin, laying a hand on his shoulder and quietly speaking to him.

I strained my ears to hear their conversation even as I took my first step into the hole, but I couldn't catch a single word. Disappointed, I focused on following Kaitlin into the darkness. On the tenth stair, I lost sight of her completely. Only the sound of her feet crunching on the steps assured me she was still there. I settled my gloved hand on the grooved wall to steady myself and continued my descent.

"I'm at the bottom," Romona called up. "Careful walking. The ground is uneven down here."

Figures.

"Ouch!" Kaitlin yelped. "A little heads-up about the ceiling height would have been nice, Romona. Anyone have something to light this place up?"

"Oops, sorry. Anyone taller than Audrey and me needs to watch their head." Romona yelled up.

The belated warning echoed off the walls of the darkened chamber.

I reached the bottom without realizing and took a stumble-step forward, knocking into what I assumed was Kaitlin's back. We both staggered several uneven steps before righting ourselves.

"Yikes! Sorry."

"That's okay. It's impossible to see down here."

"What in the world are you girls doing?" Jonathon's perturbed voice was close enough that I knew he was about to walk right into me.

I spun around and put my hands up. They connected with overheated body armor a milli-second later. "Whoa there."

"Don't touch me," Jonathon spat, and he swatted my hands away.

I heaved a frustrated sigh. *Geez, it's not like I was trying to cop a feel.* Would he rather have run into my back? I wanted to march farther ahead of him, but in the total black that engulfed us, I wasn't sure what I'd run into. Scooting as close to Kaitlin as possible, I kept my mouth shut.

"We're coming," Joe called down to us. "I'll start a fire in a moment so you all can see."

I heard, rather than saw, Joe and Kevin shuffle into the space with us. After several long moments, a spark ignited off to my right. By the time I'd fully turned my head in that direction, a small flame danced on Joe's palm. I cocked my head and blinked.

Joe transferred the light to a fire pit in the far corner of a small enclosure.

The flame grew in size until a full-fledged fire, large enough to light the entire space, blazed. I had no idea what material was actually burning. The already oppressive heat ratcheted up, the space becoming almost too hot to breathe in, but I preferred the heat to the darkness.

"Holy fire," Kaitlin whispered in my ear. "It burns clean so we don't need a vent."

Right. Had I been thinking clearly, I could have pulled my sword out a minute ago to act as a torch.

Joe put his hands flat on the soil beneath our feet, and the ground shook again. Loose dirt fell around us in dusty waves. Coughing, I glanced toward the stairs and found they were gone. I shivered.

We were literally encased in earth and stone. Kaitlin, Romona, and Jonathon looked around our surroundings with eyes filled with unease, but at least they were holding it together. Kevin was hunched over; his unblinking gaze darted from the floor to ceiling, and his breaths came out in snorts. He was one second away from hyperventilating.

Joe motioned for us to sit as he went back over to Kevin, murmuring something in soothing tones. Kevin squeezed his eyes shut and nodded. A violent tremor shook his body before he sank to the ground with the rest of us.

Someone was not comfortable in enclosed spaces. But who could blame him? I felt both oppressed and oddly safe in our mini-sanctuary.

Just don't think about it, I chanted to myself.

There was enough space for all of us to lie down if we wanted, but that was about it. Sleeping on the uneven, rocky ground was going to be challenging. I looked around at my companions, some of whom were practically sleeping sitting up. Exhaustion would make up for the lack of comfort in this refuge.

"We'll stay here for a few hours," Joe announced. "You all need the rest. I expect to reach Logan tomorrow, so use this time to recharge."

The statement was met with nodded heads and softly spoken thanks as my friends all shuffled into as much of a comfortable position as possible. Joe waved his hand in the direction of the fire, and the light dimmed.

I tried to settle, but as much as I squirmed, I couldn't find a position where something sharp wasn't poking me. It was distracting. And annoying.

I flipped over again . . . and swallowed a scream. Joe was hunched down in front of me, with his knees bent and his weight resting on the balls of his feet. I pressed a hand to my chest and felt my heart pumping furiously.

"I thought we could talk now." Joe spoke softly, probably so he wouldn't disturb the group.

"Okay, yeah." I nodded and pushed myself up on my elbows. Quiet snores rose from behind me. My money was on Kevin.

Joe sank down into a seated position while I carefully wiggled up into one as well, careful not to disturb Kaitlin to my left. I bumped her once and turned to apologize, only to find her out cold, her even breaths in tune with the rest of the sleeping forms in the dirt bunker.

No worries about being overheard, I suppose.

"You have questions," Joe started.

"When don't I?"

He chuckled. "An inquisitive heart was stitched into the very fibers of your being. It's part of what makes you, you." He held his hands out as if that explained everything.

"O-kay. So, my demon radar?" I left the question open ended.

Joe's lips pressed together, but the corners of his mouth tipped up. I waited for several moments before he spoke. As if he needed that time to compose himself. "Audrey, as I'm sure you've noticed, you have certain . . . abilities and skills, that most hunters or others who have passed on to our realm do not possess."

"Yep. Flaming sword was the first thing that tipped me off."

Again with the pressed-together lips. I got the impression he was finding something I was saying amusing. He reminded me of Hugo.

"Right, well, the flaming sword isn't the only thing that has set you apart. Being able to sense the presence of demons is another."

I nodded at him to continue.

"Just as the power from your sword comes from Hugo, sensing demons comes from me."

He leaned back a bit, as if that was explanation enough. My mouth dropped.

Ah, no. "Let's back up," I whispered. "The flames from my sword are actually Hugo's power. Check. I got that one. But sensing demons? That's not an external thing; that's an internal one. I don't get it. And more importantly, why am I the only one who has that ability?"

"Audrey, I am part of you. I am part of your very soul. You were made in Our image."

"But wasn't everyone else as well?" I gestured to the sleeping forms around us.

"Yes, of course."

"But I'm the only one with demon-dar."

"Demon-dar, huh?"

"It seems like a fitting description."

He laughed under his breath.

"You're not wrong about that. There is no short answer for your question. Nor should every question be answered. But to *attempt* a short answer anyway—you've been equipped with everything you need. And so your . . . demon-dar . . . is just another talent you've been given to fulfill your purpose. If you didn't need it, you wouldn't have it." He smiled at me, knowing full well I wouldn't be satisfied with that response.

"But—"

"Get some sleep, Audrey. And learn to trust that the Creator not only has a plan but your best interests in mind as well."

I scrunched my nose and bit my tongue to keep from peppering him with questions. When Joe was done talking, that was that. Didn't mean I had to like it though.

I awoke to the ground trembling beneath me, coughing and choking on dry dirt that swirled in the air. The rest of our group was in various states of waking up as well. All except Joe, who stood with his eyes fixed on the low ceiling above.

"What's going on?" Jonathon asked after a coughing fit subsided.

I already knew what Joe's answer would be, thanks to the familiar rolling in my gut.

"It's a horde of demons passing right above us," he answered.

"Dude, that's not cool." Kevin's knees were pressed against his chest with his arms squeezing them tight. An impressive feat for such a tall guy. The whites of his eyes practically glowed in the low lighting. He rocked back and forth gently with his head immobile, staring at nothing but the wall of rock across from him.

If we stayed down here much longer, he was going to either lose it or turn so introspective who knew when we'd be able to snap him out of it?

"Once they pass, we're going to head out. We're almost to the end of this ring; then we'll be able to cross into the fifth. The one where Logan is being held."

Joe lowered his gaze. His eyes passed over each of us briefly. "I won't lie to you. We will come into contact with opposition before we reach him. The most important thing from here on out is to make sure we get Audrey to Logan."

"Me?" I squeaked.

Five sets of eyes blinked back at me. I mean, yeah, I wanted to be there when we set Logan free, but why was it so important that I be the one to make it there? Was it something to do with our bond?

"This is your mission, Audrey," Joe said, answering my unasked question. Knowing he could get into my head that easily was freaky. "I can send the rest of them back at any time if I need to, but you're the one who's going to have to free Logan. It's the way it was meant to be."

The way it was meant to be? Cryptic much?

Wouldn't that play exactly into Satan's plans? In my vision, he'd been clear that Logan was the bait to lure me to him. I still didn't know why.

Terror punched my gut like I'd been run through with a rusty blade. I rammed my reaction down, hiding my fear.

Joe's gaze lingered on me a moment longer before he scanned the faces of my friends. "So that means it's all of your jobs to ensure she makes it there. Got it?"

There were nods all around. While he'd been speaking, the rumbling from above stopped, and it left an eerie sort of quiet in its wake.

Joe placed his hand on the wall. Another mini-earthquake revealed the set of stairs we'd used to descend into this pit.

We scrambled to our feet. A world of horrors might be waiting above, but I was ready to leave this tight enclosure. The feeling of being buried alive was a little too strong within its walls.

Joe motioned for us to follow him. We shuffled in his wake; somehow I found myself at the rear of our little train. The moment I placed my foot on the bottom step, the fire that had lit the cave extinguished, pitching me in almost complete blackness.

A chill skated up my spine despite the oppressive heat. I used the wall as my guide as I ascended until some of the unnatural light from above filtered down.

When I reached the surface, my companions had already formed a semi-circle around me, all facing out with weapons drawn. Whatever might or might not be out there was shrouded in a thick layer of fog.

How had I forgotten about the fog? Or the smell?

Barf.

The assault on my nose was worse than I remembered.

"Let's move," Joe said.

We fell in step together and progressed as if we were a single being—yet this time I found myself surrounded on all sides.

I rolled my eyes.

Was this really necessary? I was the one with the sword loaded with holy fire. Shouldn't I be given a prime defensive position?

I elbowed my way to the front between Kevin and Joe. Kevin tried to push me back into place, but I pulled out my sword, looked pointedly at the flames, and then back at him with lifted brows. He shook his head but didn't try to reposition me again.

No attack came. The farther we marched, the less I remembered to be on my guard and the more my mind wandered. Between my Logan-GPS and my overactive demon-dar, my insides were a mess.

Everything was going fine . . . until Romona's pain-filled scream pierced the silence.

DEMONS

I swung around. Kaitlin and Jonathon were spinning in circles, looking for Romona, who up until a moment before had been right between them.

"Where is she?" I yelled, no longer caring about detection.

Kaitlin's frightened gaze snapped up. "I don't know. Sh-she was just here."

Joe barreled through the lot of us and took off in the direction we'd just come from. No one questioned his decision; we all just ran after him. He moved so quickly the thick fog swallowed him, making it challenging to keep up.

We heard nothing more from Romona after that first scream.

My heart beat fast and erratically. Exertion wasn't the only culprit. I didn't allow my mind go down the rabbit hole of what could have happened to her. I completely focused my attention on staying with Joe.

I looked down to search for footprints. Big mistake.

Was that blood?

Dark, narrow lines appeared and disappeared on the dry ground as we flew over it. They might have been left by her fingers as she was dragged away from us.

Joe disappeared and reappeared in the fog time and time again. Were we running in circles? There was no way to tell. The only consistent was the bloody trail we followed and the glimpses of Joe.

I yelled Romona's name time and time again, careless of the repercussions. But she never answered. And then Joe appeared, crouched over Romona's motionless body.

In my haste to reach her, I almost tripped over him but managed to stop myself just in time. Kaitlin, Jonathon, and Kevin skidded to a stop as well. I leaned over Joe to get a better look and immediately clamped both hands over my mouth, holding in a scream.

Romona lay on the ground in front of him. Pieces of her armor had been shredded at her thigh and abdomen. Thick, gooey blood spread in a circle around her, and the ground slurped up the scarlet liquid almost as fast as it left her body.

A low groan left her lips. With horror, I realized she was still conscious.

"Fan out," Joe barked. "Protect us. We've been discovered."

We obeyed without argument.

I felt them. Demons.

Now that I was paying attention, their presence practically slithered under my skin. But I couldn't pinpoint exactly where the threat was coming from, leaving us blind to their location.

"Jonathon, switch places with me. Try to stanch the flow."

Joe didn't wait for Jonathon to comply before joining the circle around Romona. I heard clothes ripping and Jonathon's murmured words behind me, and I knew he was tending to Romona the best he could.

"They're here!" Joe shouted, and then the rest of the world fell away as I found myself in a battle with abominations that were hidden and half-invisible in the fog.

Sharp, blackened appendages came at me from multiple directions. I couldn't see the creatures attached to them to anticipate their moves. They were using the dense fog to their advantage. Their strikes were precise and powerful; the fog clearly wasn't affecting them negatively.

My sword cut through every attack aimed my way, and soon I was cringing under the onslaught of demon shrieks. My eardrums throbbed, but I did what I could to ignore the pain in my head and continued to hack away at anything that appeared out of the mist.

Abruptly, the attacks on me stopped.

I scanned the area, but it seemed I no longer interested the demons. In contrast, my friends' struggles echoed around me. The sound of metal meeting hardened flesh rebounded off the blanket of vapor. Without the ability to slice off limbs, they were only able to defend themselves against the demons. A demon's vulnerable points were concealed in the trunk of its body, but no creature came out of the fog far enough to be seen. I made a split second decision I hoped I wouldn't regret.

"Kaitlin," I yelled in her direction, somewhere to my right. "Close the gap between us. I'm going in."

"Wait, what?" she yelled back. "Are you crazy?"

"Probably."

I ran head-on into the fog, blind to the creatures I stalked. My hope was the demons would be so distracted trying to injure everyone else that I could ambush them from behind. That is, if I could even find them.

My eyes failing me, I strained my hearing to its limits. To the right were sounds of battle and the distinctive piercing chirp of a demon. It must be the one fighting Kaitlin. Oh gosh, I really hoped I was right.

Here goes nothing.

I ran toward where I *thought* the demon was with my sword held out in front of me, the blade blazing like an inferno. I'm sure I looked like a complete idiot, but if I was going to accidentally run into something demonic, I wanted the pointy end of my sword to hit first.

I skidded to a stop when the mist cleared enough to reveal the backside of the Goliath battling Kaitlin. My gamble paid off—the giant creature was too distracted fighting my friend to notice me—but its sheer size gave me pause.

Thank goodness Kaitlin couldn't see this thing, or she'd probably pee herself. Heck, I was close to losing bodily control, and that beast wasn't even facing off with me.

One cut was not going to do it, holy fire or not. The thing was easily the size of a small house. Even if I plunged my blade right into the creature, it would most likely swat me away like a fly before I got the chance for a second blow.

An idea formed in my head. Not one I liked, but the only one I could come up with. If I could take care of the tentacle-like appendages attacking Kaitlin first, there was a chance I could then climb up its back and sink my sword into something that would put the creature down.

This was insane.

Once I started cutting off appendages, this massive demon was going to start attacking me right away.

Shoot, I'd better be fast. This was going to get messy.

I bounced on the balls of my feet for a quick second before jumping into the fight.

I managed to cut through two of the barbed tentacles in one swing. They flopped to the ground and wiggled as if still attached. *Nasty.* The stumps that remained squirted black blood. That was new. Usually my sword left only charred flesh in its wake. And the things I cut off weren't turning to ash either. It had to have something to do with the realm we were in.

Lost in thought, I ducked a moment too late, and one of the creature's wiggly arm-like things clipped me on the shoulder. I slammed into the ground, hard. With a shake of my head I bounced back to my feet and charged.

Now that I could see clearly, I zeroed in on the demon's remaining limbs. They flailed through the air like knives aimed at my head.

Time disappeared as I fought. Any blow I landed cut through its shell-like flesh without difficulty. Shrieks of pain and outrage rent the air.

One more wiggly limb to go, and I would be on to phase two of my plan. The crazy part where I somehow managed to get high enough on the demon's body to take off its head, or at least plunge my sword into its skull . . . repeatedly.

With a satisfying swipe, I lopped off the last limb. I was covered in the demon's slimy black ichor. I preferred it when the creatures charred and ashed. So this was what the other hunters went through when they fought with the enemy.

Didn't like it one bit.

In a surprise move, the demon suddenly threw its body in my direction. I dove to the side to get out of its way. My sword flew from my hand and landed somewhere unseen.

Did that fat demon just try to squish me?

Dazed, I shook my head and looked up in time to see the creature lumber to its feet and come at me again.

Scrambling for purchase on the parched ground, I only just managed to evade getting flattened a second time. The demon's razor sharp jaws were only feet from where I lay, and it twisted and snapped at my feet.

Holy cow, it's trying to eat me!

It would almost be funny if this weren't so dangerous.

The demon twisted to its feet once again. Shoot! My sword. It had landed somewhere to the left. I dashed into the mist with my eyes down, searching the ground for a glint of metal and praying I didn't get crushed before I found my weapon.

Tripping over something, I fell to my knees. Looking back, my sword lay at my feet. My own weapon had thwarted me. So stupid.

I grabbed it, and it blazed to life. The ground shook around me as the demon took another kamikaze dive at my body.

Thank goodness this thing's aim was so off. But it had also unknowingly done me a favor. With its body sprawled on the ground, scaling its side was a breeze.

As the creature rose, I jumped and threw myself as high up on its body as I could get.

Needle-like spikes penetrated my armor, and I screamed out in pain. The demon's flesh was covered with thin barbs, some as long as four inches. No wonder the fatty had been trying to get me under itself. The spikes alone would have shredded me. They had already pierced several spots in my left hand and thigh.

I was close enough to its head that I could do some damage—no need to chance climbing higher. Not exactly where I wanted to be, but it would have to do.

With a loud cry, I brought my arm down and sliced through the demon, roughly where the neck would be. When it tried to let out its own scream, black blood spurted out of the hole I'd created instead.

I choked down the bile rising in my throat and took another swing.

The creature began to tip. I gritted my teeth and held on tight to the spikes that had impaled my hand, readying myself for the fall. The impact almost dislodged me, but I managed to keep from being flung through the air.

The blood that had been gushing out of the demon slowed to a gurgling river. I wasn't taking any chances and took another swipe at its flesh. Its head was halfway off its body, and the demon finally stilled.

Pushing the savage battle out of my mind, I jumped off my perch and landed in a roll before popping to my feet. My shoulder throbbed, as did the hand and thigh that had been on the receiving end of the nasty demon's barbs.

Hardly giving my body a thought, I turned in a circle to locate my group.

The land was unnervingly quiet.

I cupped my hands and shouted for Kaitlin. Her answering cry came from my left. I took off running, heart pounding with relief. I stumbled onto the group in no time. We were a mess, but we'd been victorious. Or as victorious as we could be in Hell.

No more demons attacking meant we'd won, right?

As I stepped closer, I got a better view of the scene. Kaitlin stood with her sword still out. Her wild gaze locked behind me, like she expected the creature to come back through the fog at any moment.

"What happened?" she asked.

"I took out the demon you were fighting. Big ugly thing. Lots of tentacle-like appendages and spikes all over its body." I shuddered. "And it bled a lot."

"I can tell."

"Yeah."

Behind her, the rest of the group was on the ground. Jonathon held his post over Romona. A tourniquet had been tied around her upper thigh to slow the bleeding. He was applying pressure to her stomach area with a white piece of cloth that was quickly turning red. He'd stripped the top part of his body armor off, revealing a torso drenched in sweat, and used his shirt to slow down the flow of blood. To her side, there were two other clumps of cloth that were already soaked through.

"I can't stanch the flow," Jonathon called to Joe, who was bent over an obviously injured Kevin.

Ignoring Jonathon, Joe looked into Kevin's eyes and said, "On the count of three, okay?" Joe held Kevin's arm at an awkward angle—his shoulder was out of joint. At his nod, Joe yanked up on his arm without giving the count. Kevin screamed out in pain.

"Sorry. I thought surprising you would be kinder than the anticipation of the pain."

Kevin panted and nodded. Sweat streamed down his face. I was sure he'd sustained more injuries than were evident.

"I said I can't stop her bleeding!" Jonathon shouted this time. Joe leaned over and put a hand on the medic's shoulder.

"I heard you." Joe's voice was clear and calm and free of censure.

Jonathon's shoulders sagged, and a vein in his forehead stopped pulsing as some of the tension left his body.

"What do we do now?" he asked.

"You're going back with Romona and Kevin," Joe told him.

Jonathon started to argue, but Joe silenced him with a look. "Romona and Kevin are in no shape to continue on. I need you to take care of them. Make sure they arrive safely and are cared for." His eyes shifted to Romona's prone form. "Especially her. If only Kevin was injured, I'd send him up alone, but she needs your attention."

Jonathon's shoulders sagged, but he nodded his agreement.

Joe shifted his gaze to Kaitlin and me. "The three of us will continue on."

"Yeah, okay, can I just . . ." I gestured to my grandmother's still form. Joe nodded, stood, and walked a few paces back.

I rushed to Romona's side. The shirt Jonathon held against her was almost completely drenched now. The ground around her body was oddly dry, although stained red. My earlier impression had been right—the ground was actually drinking up her blood.

My stomach turned.

I pulled off a glove and pressed my hand to Romona's face. Her skin was clammy, and she didn't stir. Bending over, I pressed a kiss to her forehead before looking up at Jonathon.

"Please take care of her." My eyes welled with tears.

He returned my look with compassion. "I will. She'll be fine."

I nodded and stood.

"Thank you for being here," I told him sincerely.

He nodded back.

I turned toward Kevin, who was watching me with hooded eyes. He was barely conscious. "You heal up fast."

"You get him back," Kevin croaked.

"I will," I promised.

"Kaitlin and Audrey, step back," Joe instructed. He urged Kevin to scoot closer to Jonathon then laid hands on them both and closed his eyes. Within moments, the four of them were encased in a light so bright I was forced to turn away. It faded quickly, and only Joe remained.

Where we had been six, now we were only three.

Joe stood and brushed his hands against his legs. "Let's go."

HIDDEN

*T*he rest of our trek through the mist-filled ring was somber and tense. No one spoke until Joe signaled for us to stop and explained we were about to cross into the fifth ring. I was anxious to leave the sixth, regardless of what new horrors we'd face.

The first thing I noticed when we crossed into the next ring was that I could breathe again. Yes, the ever-present smell of rot and sulfur still lingered in the air, but I was able to suck in a lungful without wanting to retch.

The second was the light. Where we had just traveled through a land of fog-induced blindness, this new ring was overexposed and washed in brightness.

My eyes watered, and I blinked several times before adjusting to the change. I swiped at a tear that leaked out the corner of an eye and ran down my cheek. Finally acclimated enough to take a good look around, I choked on a gasp that escaped my lungs.

My legs gave out, and my knees hit the packed ground. Hard.

There were people. Everywhere.

They wore manacles around their wrists, feet, and even sometimes necks, connected to glowing lava-red chains that were anchored into the earth.

Each one of the poor souls was tethered to the ground by at least one point of contact, sometimes several. Their bodies were fully corporeal. Their flesh torn and scarred, though no blood leaked from their wounds as if they'd already been drained and there was nothing left. Their anguished faces cried out in pain, yet barely a whisper of sound could be heard.

These were the ones Joe had warned us about. The ones who couldn't be helped.

I turned my head to beseech Joe to give us some kind of instruction.

Surely there was *something* we could do. But the Savior of Man was on his knees as well. His hands were fisted in his hair, and water rolled from his eyes, raining tears to the ground.

The souls closest to us stretched as far as they could in their chains, even tearing at the flesh that kept them captive in a desperate attempt to get to Joe —to reach the water flowing from his eyes.

His face crumpled. I had never seen a look of such anguish on a person before. It was as if he himself was one of the bodies surrounding us, yet their despair and torment was piled upon him a hundredfold.

With wide eyes, I looked to Kaitlin, who watched Joe with a worry-filled gaze as well.

"Who are they?" she asked him in a whisper.

"They are the lost ones." His hands slid from his hair to clench at his sides, his gaze falling on the person closest to him—a woman, or what had once been a woman. He squeezed his eyes closed as if he could shut out the world around him. When they opened again, renewed suffering washed over his features. Sweat trickled down his temples and mixed with the tears still dripping from his cheeks.

The . . . thing—for she barely resembled a human anymore, with only patches of hair and flesh sagging off her bones—reached out as far as her tethers would allow. A single word was desperately trying to escape her cracked and split lips, but the only sound that emerged was a scratchy whisper too quiet to hear.

Pleading arms stretched forward—even her bent and broken fingers strained to their limit. I stared at her mouth as she repeated the same thing over and over again.

Water.

The rest of the bodies around us appeared to be asking for the same thing. Some of them drew out their soundless plea in one long word, while others hysterically repeated it in a rapid loop.

If water was all they needed to find a moment of peace, that was something I could offer—at least to some of them. I reached for the canteen attached to my belt, my hands shaking, but Joe placed his hand on mine and stilled my movements.

He stood tall beside me, with dried tear tracks on his cheeks. "That's not what they need."

"What do you mean?" I swept my hand across the macabre crowd. "They're obviously asking for water. I still have some in my canteen. I can help some of them."

"No. That water will never quench their thirst."

I yanked my hands away from Joe. There must be something we could do. Something *he* could do. He was the Creator's Son after all. With a word, he could probably flood this place if he wanted.

I glared at him. Accusing him with my eyes if not with my words. Yet Joe heard my unspoken words as clearly as those that passed my lips.

"I cannot ease their suffering." His voice was hollow.

"But if you would just—"

"I can't!" he yelled back. "They have already rejected me, so there is nothing I can do for them. I did not pick this fate for them. My gift was freely given, yet they didn't claim it. Whether from pride, fear, or disbelief, they didn't take it. We did not want this fate for even one of them. Not one." He punctuated his words with a slash of his arm.

"But if they had understood . . . "

Something in Joe's eyes made my words falter.

"Yes," he said, "if they had only understood."

He turned his back to me and swiftly set off through the sea of bodies, not once looking back.

Kaitlin and I silently followed Joe through the sea of bodies for what must have been hours. Occasionally one of the poor souls would get ahold of our legs or ankles and we'd have to tug ourselves free. The sensation of their stiff fingers grasping at my body stayed with me long after I untangled myself from their hold.

Joe moved forward at a relentless pace, seemingly unaware—or uncaring —if Kaitlin and I still followed. If I hadn't seen his initial reaction when entering this ring, I'd consider him cold and compassionless. But the remembrance of the agony etched on his face, his hands pulling at his hair as he fell to his knees, was forever burned into my memory.

Out of all the horrors we'd witnessed in this realm, this was by far the worst. Forward progression was like walking through a mass grave of desiccated corpses that were not yet dead but were dying forever.

I tried to numb myself, but hopelessness for these people, or souls, or whatever they were, hung heavy in the air and saturated everything it touched. It seeped into my pores and settled unnervingly in my gut. Much more of this torture and I wasn't sure I'd be able to keep my sanity. I was already half mad. My brain wasn't built to process these monstrosities.

Yet to reach Logan, I was forced to press on. There was no going back. Joe had warned us this realm would challenge us physically and mentally, but I still hadn't been prepared.

Joe's raised hand was the only warning we received before he halted.

Kaitlin and I skidded to a stop, almost barreling right into him. Kaitlin's weary glance skated to me before landing back on Joe. Neither of us knew what was going on. Joe remained silent.

I forced my gaze to remain on our leader, not wanting to get another look at the scene around us.

"There's an illusion in front of us."

I jumped at Joe's unexpected voice. Even though I couldn't see his face, emotion clogged his words, making them slightly hard to understand. He cleared his throat before continuing. "Once I dispel it, we are going to be at the base of a mountain. Logan is hidden away in a cell deep within these caves."

Logan!

My heartbeat sped at the mere mention of his name. When was the last time I felt one of his phantom pains? It had been hours.

The absence of the discomfort should have been reassuring, but it alarmed me instead.

Why couldn't I feel anything from him? What did that mean? Had our connection somehow been severed?

"I can't feel him anymore! Why can't I feel him?" My frantic thoughts fed my hysterics. "Is he still all right? That was stupid, of course he's not all right. But what I mean is—"

"Audrey"—Joe turned and took my face between his hands and pinned me with his gaze—"he's passed out. That's the reason you aren't feeling his pain anymore."

I inhaled a breath of relief.

"It's a small mercy Satan hadn't intended to grant him, but it will help you keep your head for the moment."

I nodded and opened my mouth to ask what was ahead. I had no idea what we were going to see beyond this illusion he spoke of, but to have a fighting chance, we needed as much information as he was willing to give us.

Kaitlin stole the words right from my mouth. "So what should we be prepared for? I doubt we're going to be able to walk right in, find Logan, and then strut back out the front door with him. What's the plan?"

"Finding Logan might be easier than you expect. After all, he's only the bait." His gaze flicked to me and lingered. "It's getting him and ourselves out unscathed that's going to be the tricky part. Follow my lead, but stay on guard."

"What aren't you telling us? What is it Satan wants with me?" I crossed my arms over my chest. I was pretty sure Joe was being purposefully vague. Satan had attacked my family and then, when that failed, stolen Logan practically straight from my arms. Whatever the game was, there was a part scripted specifically for me. I just needed to figure out what it was. What could I possibly have that Satan wanted badly enough to go through all of this trouble?

Joe stared at me a moment longer before turning forward, effectively evading my questions. "Let's get going."

Before I could press him further, he swiped his hand at the air in front of him, and the illusion dissolved.

There was no longer a never-ending sea of bodies in front of us. The face of a blackened mountain range jutted up high into the sky. Stealing a look behind me, the bodies had disappeared there as well. A cracked and barren desert landscape replaced that horrid nightmare.

"Did we just cross through another ring?"

"No. They're still there, just covered by the same illusion that blocked these mountains from sight. The land itself is poisoned with lies and deceit. You can't take everything you see at face value." Joe pointed toward the base of the mountains. "We'll enter there. The caves under this range form a labyrinth you'd never be able to navigate alone. Don't stray from me once we enter."

A chill skated up my spine even as sweat trickled down it.

This didn't feel right.

"Why aren't there demons at least guarding the entrance? They obviously know we're here. We fought them in the last ring."

"Like I said before, finding Logan is going to be the easy part. Satan wants us to find him. Logan was brought here for a reason. There's something he wants."

Yeah, me. "Then why even bother attacking us in the last ring? Why not just let us stroll right up to where he's been leading us this whole time?"

"Thinning the herd." Kaitlin's words were as hollow as her gaze.

Joe's stare shifted to her blank face, and he nodded. She was right. We'd lost half our group in that one attack.

"What's he truly after?" I asked Joe . . . again.

I thought Joe's gaze flicked over to me, but it happened so fast I couldn't be sure. When I blinked, he was staring back at the opening to the cave. "I'm sure it will be revealed soon enough."

There was something Joe knew that he wasn't sharing with me. I just didn't know what or why. Why wasn't he keeping me informed? Making wise snap judgments wasn't really my thing. I had an embarrassing history of rash decision making that if put to the test could very well bite us all in the butt.

I bit my tongue to keep from voicing my annoyance.

For probably the millionth time, I wished I just knew how everything was going to play out in advance.

Waiting stank worse than Hell.

I trudged along beside Joe and Kaitlin, just short of dragging my feet. Half of me wanted to break out in a run—we were closer to Logan than ever—but the other half was filled with trepidation. Joe's cryptic comments and pointed looks, losing half our team, and knowing that at some point in the near future there was more than a good chance I'd be facing off against Satan again had my anxiety—and adrenaline—levels spiked higher than ever before.

Best-case scenario, we find Logan quickly and are magically able to slip out of this demonic realm with him right under Satan's nose.

Worst-case scenario . . . well, I didn't even know what that could be. Was it possible to end up like those living corpses we'd just picked our way through? I wasn't sure. Maybe there was an even worse fate?

Heck, I already knew there was. I'd been privy to some of what Satan had inflicted on Logan. Even the echoes of his pain were debilitating at times. Kaitlin and I could end up in adjoining torture cells for all I knew. And Joe . . . I didn't know the rules of the game when it came to him. Was there anything Satan could do to harm him? If so, this would be the realm where Joe would be at his weakest. But as the Son of God, wasn't he untouchable?

We were completely off script now. There were things I didn't even know I didn't know.

My internal demon-radar was blaring as well, but not one of the disgusting creatures was in sight as we reached the cave's entrance and descended into darkness.

DESCENT

*T*he moment we stepped foot into the cave, we were pitched into complete darkness. Considering the blinding desert terrain at our backs, there was no logic in the sudden change of light. Some of that brightness should have bled into the cave—eventually being swallowed by the darkness—but instead it was as if we walked into a windowless room with the lights off.

Did anything make sense here?

I pulled my sword from the sheath strapped to my back, and we used the blade's light to illuminate our path. Joe's strides were even, and he seemed to know exactly where he was going without the assistance of the blaze to direct him. Kaitlin and I, however, stumbled along the uneven and rocky ground like toddlers. Our shared struggle was my only consolation. There was something satisfying in not being the only bumbling one in our shrunken group.

I pressed a hand to my temple as we trekked forward and forced my eyes to remain open even as I ordered myself to ignore the crushing sense of being surrounded by demons. I trusted Joe to let us know if we were in any immediate danger, but there were definite lurkers nearby.

Besides the sickening sensations on a constant roll in my stomach, the heat was even more intense in the caves, furthering my discomfort. The hot breath puffing from my lungs was actually cooling to my skin. I imagined that with every step we descended closer to the Earth's molten lava core. Sweat didn't simply dot my skin but poured down it. At some point, I was going to run out of moisture to sacrifice to this forsaken realm. I itched to strip out of my body armor, but doing so would be the height of stupidity—and I was working on lowering my stupidity batting average.

A ghostly wail echoed from the tunnel in front of us, and Kaitlin and I lurched to a stop.

"Wh-what was that?" I managed to stammer through my dry lips.

"You don't want to know," Joe answered.

He was right. I didn't.

"So . . . are we there yet?"

Joe shot me a droll look over his shoulder. "Did you seriously just ask that?"

"What? It's a legit question. It's hot as you-know-what down here. We've got ghost noises added to the mix, demons are practically breathing down our necks—and quite frankly, I'm hangry and would like to get my . . . my Logan back."

Apparently a bad case of cranky pants, sweating worse than a sumo wrestler, and going a couple rounds in Hell made me extra salty.

I glanced at Kaitlin for some back-up, but she just gaped at me.

"What?"

She cupped her hand to the side of her face and whisper-yelled at me, "Did you really just talk to him like that?"

Crap. That was a teensy bit disrespectful . . . I mean, he was the Son of God. Wincing, I offered Joe an apologetic grimace. He swiped a hand down his face before rolling his eyes and gesturing for us to keep moving.

"Well, I'm still hangry," I whisper-yelled back to Kaitlin.

"I can hear you," Joe called back.

Whoops!

"I'll just pretend to get over that then."

"Good luck with that," Kaitlin piped in.

"Alrighty."

"In the meantime, give this a try." Joe pitched a small drawstring bag over his shoulder at me. I snatched the sack out of the air one handed without dropping my sword-turned-temporary-torch.

Score one for improved reflexes!

The bag was no larger than my fist. Tugging open the sides, I couldn't see anything, so I reached in and pulled out a loaf of bread.

What the what? How did that fit in there?

There was still some weight in the small pouch, so I awkwardly shoved my hand in and drew out some sort of dried piece of meat. Bringing it to my nose, I sniffed then used the very tip of my tongue to lick the supposed food. Its briny tang assaulted my taste buds.

Is this a dried piece of fish?

"Hey, what's in there?" Kaitlin asked.

"See for yourself." I handed her the bag.

A few minutes later, she chuckled before starting to munch on her own loaf and fish.

"Classic," she murmured.

"If it's not broke . . ." Joe mumbled in response.

As Kaitlin and I filled our empty stomachs, we continued through the winding tunnels. Whenever we'd hit a section where the tunnel branched, Joe always continued forward without breaking stride, as if he was as familiar with these underground pathways as the back of his hand.

Just as I finished my fifth piece of fish jerky—it sounded grosser than it actually was—Joe held up his hand, signaling us to stop.

Kaitlin lifted her eyebrows and shoulders to confirm she didn't know what the holdup was either.

"Quickly, this way." Joe tore off down the tunnel then banked to the left, disappearing from view.

Kaitlin and I scurried to keep up. I didn't even realize there was a small opening off to the side until we had almost passed it.

We ducked through and followed the sound of Joe's feet smacking against the stone.

He was suddenly standing in front of us, facing what appeared to be a wall. He'd stopped so fast I almost stabbed him with my sword.

"Whoa!" My feet slid forward on the gravelly floor as I came to a stop. My hand shaking at the close call, I sheathed my weapon. Joe had created another blue-and-red fireball that lit the area around us.

"In here," he ordered.

What? In where? He wants us to walk into the cave wall? Last time I checked, this wasn't Harry Potter.

Joe stepped forward, and the stone that had been there a moment before dissolved and revealed a crude doorway.

Didn't see that one coming.

An agony-filled groan struck my ears and my heart in the same moment. In the next instant, I was pushing my way past Joe and Kaitlin without even realizing it.

Logan!

A lone figure sagged against the far wall. But something was wrong with the hair. Logan's wasn't black. He had a gorgeous blend of blond and honey browns.

Even matted and dirty, that hair was not attached to the person I was expecting. This wasn't Logan.

The prisoner's head slumped forward, effectively obscuring his face. He was trussed to the stone wall in exactly the same manner Logan had been in my visions. Logan or not, we couldn't just leave this poor soul here. He was obviously being tortured.

Rivets of dried blood ran from his shackled wrists down the arm suspended above his head. His chest was covered in so much blood that whatever color his shirt might have been before, it was now dyed completely red. There were gashes along his left rib cage, deep enough to see muscle and bone.

I swallowed back a gag.

He was wearing pants, which obscured any damage to his legs, but his bare feet looked like they'd been dipped in blood before they'd been rolled in black volcanic cinders.

Like a soft-serve ice cream cone dipped in chocolate and rolled in sprinkles.

Why did I have to think that?

Vomit rose in my throat, but I choked the chunks down before they made an uninvited entry into my mouth.

As if the world ran in slow motion, I took stock of the man and our surroundings in a matter of heartbeats. Even so, these were moments we didn't have.

"What do—"

Before I could finish asking what to do, Joe pushed past me. He tenderly took the man's head in his hands and tilted his battered face.

The gasp that echoed throughout the chamber was not mine, although it might as well have been.

The young man's face was covered in bruises and lacerations, and only one eye was partially opened, but there was no mistaking who he was: Morgan.

Kaitlin's eyes were wide and glassy. Her hands covered her mouth. I didn't know the history between the two of them—if there even was one—except that Morgan had fought off demons to make sure she was safe when we were outnumbered on Earth.

Perhaps just seeing a person so broken affected her?

Perhaps it was something more.

My insides swirled with confusion. Morgan was the enemy. A traitor. He'd threatened my family and betrayed not only Logan but the Creator as well. Yet the traitor in front of me also risked much to save Kaitlin and was obviously being horribly abused in this place.

I just . . . I just didn't know.

In the back of my mind, there was a clock tick-tick-ticking down every moment we didn't reach Logan. I both wanted to leave Morgan to the fate he'd chosen and stay to help. If I hadn't been staring at Morgan's beaten body with my own two eyes, the choice to bolt would have been easy. But seeing the devastation in front of me, I froze.

As I watched with one foot in the room and the other in the hall, ready to run in either direction at a moment's notice, Joe spoke quietly to Morgan. His one good eye opened to a slit, and he groaned. A trail of blood leaked out of his mouth when he tried to talk.

Joe laid a hand on Morgan's neck and supported his head. I was unable to see the look on Joe's face as he continued to speak quietly. Despite Morgan's ravished face, his expression crumpled at Joe's words as he weakly shook his head back and forth.

Not in defiance but as a broken person would.

"It's true." I heard a note of steel in Joe's voice as he forced Morgan's attention. "Not too late."

Tears leaked from Morgan's functioning eye.

Joe pressed a kiss to the crown of Morgan's head, not unlike a father would his son. He then placed a hand over each shackle holding Morgan upright, and they broke one at a time. His body slumped into Joe, and he took a step back to support the weight. Although conscious, Morgan couldn't stand unassisted.

Shoot, what are we going to do? We can't drag around his dead weight and search for Logan.

"Kaitlin"—Joe's voice was quiet yet strong—"come here."

Kaitlin rushed to Morgan's other side. He mustered enough strength to tilt his head in her direction.

"Extreme measures to get me in your arms, luv," he mumbled.

Oh my.

Was I more shocked by what he'd said or that he'd managed to speak at all? Joe rolled his eyes and shook his head with a soft smile on his face.

As for Kaitlin . . . whoa. Her face puckered as if she tasted something particularly disgusting. For a moment, I thought she might take a swing at him. That was certainly a one-eighty mood flip.

"Kaitlin."

Her attention snapped back to Joe, ending the murderous stare directed at a partially conscious Morgan. "You're going to take him back, and Audrey and I are going to go ahead."

"What?" Kaitlin was already shaking her head. "No! I can't leave you guys down here alone. We already lost the rest of the group."

"Yes, you can, and you will. Audrey."

I jumped at my name.

"I want you to go ahead and continue checking these cells room by room. Logan is here somewhere. Go find him."

"Alone? But I can't even see the rooms."

"Don't use your sword to light your way. You won't need to, and it might attract attention. I'll catch up to you."

My feet might as well have been superglued to the floor.

"You can do this. Keep one hand on the right side of the wall. When your fingers touch an opening, the illusion will shatter. This was something you were always going to have to do. I'll be there soon. You can't get back without me, remember."

I nodded, half-numb. The fire in his eyes was telling me something I wasn't picking up.

"Audrey, I'm so sorry." Kaitlin was practically in tears now. "Please, find him. If he's anything like this . . ." Her voice caught. She didn't need to spell it out for me. Seeing Morgan in this shape she could now imagine what Logan was like.

Why was I still here?

"Right." I nodded. Resolute. "I'll see you soon."

"Soon," she repeated.

With a final glance at Kaitlin and Joe, I bolted into the darkness.

BROKEN

*H*e was close. I suspected he was still unconscious because the phantom pain was missing, but every step I took brought me closer to Logan.

His nearness wasn't just something I hoped for. It was something I knew to be true.

His soul cried out to mine, latched on, and dragged me forward. I didn't even bother putting my hand against the wall as I blindly ran forward. His presence was like a lighthouse beckoning me home.

I was so close . . .

And then I was there.

I pitched my body against the stone, expecting resistance where there was none, and fell to the ground, sliding forward on my hip and shoulder. A single torch lit the room I'd busted in on. The light was secured to the stone wall to the left of the shackled man.

Logan's head hung forward much in the same way Morgan's had. His body was . . . I could hardly finish the thought. As if a wild beast had attacked, Logan's flesh was shredded in spots.

His once silky hair was no longer blond, now red-stained, matted clumps. His whole body sagged forward, suspended by the shackles on his wrists. One of his shoulders hung at an odd angle. It was dislocated.

My heart shattered.

His body jerked as if in reaction to my broken heart. Broken for his pain. Broken because I hadn't been there for him when he needed me. Broken because even now that I was present, I didn't know what to do.

His eyelids fluttered before his gaze locked onto mine. A garbled sound came out of his mouth.

With a cry, I scrambled to my feet and ran to where Logan hung from the wall. My hands fluttered around the air in front of him before I fisted them and brought them back to my sides. I couldn't chance touching him anywhere for fear I'd cause more pain.

A muffled noise came from his mouth again. His words were so faint and distorted I couldn't make them out.

"What can I do? How can I help?" I asked as I stared into Logan's pain-laced eyes while my body throbbed with the aftershocks of his agony.

His throat worked as if he were trying to swallow, but lack of moisture made it impossible. Chains scraped against the uneven stone wall as he tried to move one of his hands closer to me but failed.

"Don't cry." His weak words finally made sense.

I reached a hand and wiped at the tears I hadn't even realized were free flowing down my face.

Don't cry? I didn't know if I would ever stop.

This picture of him hanging here, beaten beyond what a normal person could endure, would forever remain burned into my psyche.

"I'm going to get you out of here. *We're* going to get you out. Joe is with me. Oh, or rather Jesus, but I know him as Joe too. Never mind, not important." Apparently I still rambled when I was nervous.

I brushed a clump of red-stained hair off his face, so I could see his eyes and know that he understood what I was saying. His beautiful blue eyes, so filled with pain yet also with longing and tenderness for me.

This man was truly amazing. He was the injured one, yet he was desperate to offer me comfort in any way he could.

Forget my insecurities and hang-ups. I loved him. We were getting out of here, and I was going to shout that word at him as soon as we were safe.

I threw a glance over my shoulder. Where was Joe? We needed to leave this awful place, like five minutes ago.

No sounds of pounding feet on the stone floor of the hallway reached my ears, which made me both relieved and nervous.

Focus, girl. One thing at a time. Get Logan out of those shackles. Then worry about the next step in this super messed up rescue attempt.

Focusing on the chains that held Logan suspended, and the manacles secured around his wrists and ankles, I quickly realized I wasn't going to be able to use strength to pull him free. If that were possible, he would have already freed himself. His dislocated shoulder said as much. The echoes of his injury shot down my arm.

Reaching behind me, I pulled my sword from its sheath. The warmth from its flames was different than the oppressive heat of Hell. This fire wasn't stifling; this blaze was filled with life.

"Time to see what damage some holy flames can do to these chains," I muttered to myself.

Logan had slumped forward once again. He'd either passed out or was close to it. I didn't want him to fall on me while his feet were still bound, so I started on the restraints down there first. "Here goes nothing."

I swung my blade like a golf club, aiming so the sharp edge would break the chain from his ankle. We could worry about getting the actual manacles off later. Right now I just needed to get him off the wall.

At the point of contact, the chain shattered, freeing his left leg. I really wanted to do a victory dance, but there wasn't time for that.

This was going to work.

I took a swing at the chain attached to his other leg, and that fell away with ease too.

Almost there. Almost free.

Chewing my lip in indecision, I took a precious moment to consider my next step. When I broke the chains holding him up, he was going to fall forward, so I needed to be careful. Whatever way I sliced, it wasn't going to be a pleasant experience for Logan. But if I could somehow keep him from crashing to the ground, that would have to help a little.

Just as I brought my sword up to hack at the first chain attached to his wrists, a sharp sound caused me to whirl around toward the entrance of the cell.

Alrik stood in the entrance, leaning against the wall. He clapped—slowly, mockingly.

I clenched my sword hilt, itching to lash out.

"You," I spat at him.

His eyebrow arched, and his hands finally stopped moving.

"This is touching." A cocky smile rode his lips. "I see you finally came to your senses and noticed what was right before you the whole time. He makes a pretty damsel in distress, doesn't he? Well, at least he did before Satan turned him into a bloody pulp."

The bones in my hand cracked as I gripped my sword even tighter.

"I gotta be honest, little Aud, I didn't think you'd make it this far. I may even be a bit impressed."

"Do not call me that," I growled. "You are the worst kind of scum this universe ever spit up."

He tsked. "Sticks and stones, little Aud, sticks and stones."

If it didn't mean leaving Logan exposed, I would have attacked Alrik. Human or not, I was confident my sword would inflict damage on his blackened soul.

"He was your friend," I said.

"Was he?"

"It couldn't have all been a lie."

He lifted a shoulder. "Some of us are just more convincing than others. You, my dear, have a horrible poker face." He tilted his head, his smile widening. "Oh, I am getting you worked up, aren't I? A whole head full of black-and-red hair doesn't lie."

I couldn't care less what color my hair was right now let alone what it broadcasted to him. I had a super good reason to be angry and wasn't trying in the least to hide it.

"When I get Logan to safety, I'm going to make sure you suffer in every way he did . . . tenfold."

Alrik laughed at me—laughed until tears streamed down his face. He ran a hand across his eyes to clear them before responding. "Hon, when this is all over, you're going to be rocking in a corner, a drooling puddle of nothing."

His attitude and words stoked the coals of anger in my soul. How long had he been spying on all of us, reporting back to his real master? How long had he been our true betrayer?

I asked. "How long?"

He didn't pretend to misunderstand me. "From the very beginning, of course. I have a few neat tricks up my sleeves that none of you knew about."

He lifted a hand in front of his face, and before my eyes, it transformed into a familiar ominous mist before solidifying back into a hand.

I only just kept myself from gasping. That was the same mist that had chased me through the forest when I'd tried to follow Logan. Even then, I'd known something about that fog was off, but I'd been the only one to see it. Alrik had been spying on us for ages.

"That's right. I see the hamster finally turning the wheels in your head. This handy skill let me slip in and out of lots of interesting places."

I understood where he'd come by the ability. When souls chose darkness, they developed a new power—one given to them not by the Creator but by Satan. Morgan had been able to manipulate shadows. Logan thought his electricity came from the same place, but I had my doubts. Alrik's ability reminded me of the grotesque substance that had poured out of the demons' mouths during the battle at my family's home. That fight was only days ago but felt like years for all that had happened since.

"Why?" My cool had long ago been lost, but the volume of my voice finally matched the boiling magma churning in my gut. That one word echoed off the chamber walls. "Why would you do this? Why would you turn yourself into this . . . this monster?"

And for what?

What could possibly be worth not only betraying the people who cared about Alrik but also risking the fate of his soul? What could be so important that he'd knowingly ban himself from our realm, let alone the Creator's love?

Alrik had to know that once he'd crossed that line and lured Logan into a position to be captured and taken to Hell, he'd be exposed for the traitor he was.

The betrayer's face hardened, and his joking demeanor disappeared. "That," he said, "is none of your business."

He shoved off the side of the wall and straightened to his full impressive height. I had to tilt my chin up to keep holding his gaze, and that annoyed me.

The sense of another presence nearby slid over my skin like the scales of a snake, forcing an involuntary shudder.

"Time's up, little Aud, the boss is here. A bit of advice: Play nice and just agree to his terms. It will be easier on everyone that way." He looked pointedly at Logan before stepping to the side.

I swallowed hard as Satan himself walked right into the cell, wearing his fraudulent angelic skin. A pretty covering to conceal the twisted form of the evil being inside.

At his arrival, I wanted to both scream in frustration and cower in fear. I should have just stabbed Alrik and figured out a way to haul Logan out of here when I had the chance.

Where is Joe?

I was in no way prepared to face Satan with an unconscious hunter pinned to the wall behind me. An unconscious hunter I loved. Joe was the powerhouse. I was simply the semi-hysterical human trying to get her man back, and more than a little scared to admit the lengths to which I would go to protect Logan. Breaking some of the Hugo-approved rules was a definite possibility.

I needed backup, STAT.

"Sorry I missed the reunion." A smirk curved Satan's lips. "It would have been entertaining to watch." He examined one of his hands, turning it this way and that at an unhurried pace. Where a human's nails should have been, sharpened claws gleamed and dripped red fluid to the ground. "But as you can see, I was busy elsewhere. I'm looking forward to picking up where I left off."

No doubt he was trying to intimidate me. I'm not too proud to admit that it was working. My only hope was that my face didn't betray my fears.

I lifted my sword higher so the flames danced blue between us, the blade's holy fire my only comfort.

The last time we'd had a physical showdown, I ended up feeling like a squeezed tube of toothpaste, but I was ready this time. If I had to hack through him and every other forsaken creature in this grotesque realm to get Logan to safety, then that's what I would do. I braced myself for the hardest fight of my life.

"Don't point that at me like you intend to use it." Satan flicked his wrist, and an unseen force tried to bat my weapon away.

I held firm. His eye sockets narrowed, and his jaw worked back and forth.

"Well, it must be time to have some fun with your boy-toy. Wakey-wakey, sleeping beauty."

Satan lifted a clawed hand and raked it through the air in front of him. Logan's pain-filled yell threw me off. I cast a glance over my shoulder to see a very conscious Logan with a fresh set of tears on his chest, blood running freely from the injury. How?

I almost dropped my weapon as I swung around to face him. With tears running down my face, I tried to use the remaining rags hanging off his body to stanch the flow of blood, but I only managed to coat my glove-covered hands in it instead.

Logan grunted, and I looked up to see a fresh slice appear on his cheek. He sealed his jaw and gritted his teeth as he fought to keep from shouting in pain.

I snapped like a rubber band. With a banshee cry, I used my sword to break the remaining chains holding him captive. A moan slipped past Logan's lips as his battered body slammed into mine, forcing me to take a step back. I lowered him to the floor then tensed to deal with the threat behind me. Satan and Alrik first. Then I'd drag Logan out of this place, fighting off demons with one arm if I had to.

Bring it.

The righteous anger building inside me was a breath away from shooting forth like steam from a teapot. But before I could spin around to face my foes, a warm, wet hand landed softly on my cheek. I halted.

"Shouldn't . . . have . . . come." Logan's voice was weak but clear. His eyelids were heavy and he blinked slowly, battling to remain conscious.

"I will always fight for you." I stared intently into his eyes, willing him to absorb my words. "Always. Just like you would for me."

A strange wheezing sound started in his chest. With a gasp I leaned forward. Was he having trouble breathing?

No.

He was laughing.

"Took you . . . long enough," he got out between breaths.

"Are you kidding me right now? You're going to give me crap at a time like this?"

"Always." His eyes slipped shut as he succumbed to his body's demands.

Our audience had been suspiciously quiet.

"I hear that was a long time coming," Satan said conversationally to Alrik.

I jerked my gaze over my shoulder.

Alrik dipped his head. "Indeed."

With one look at the smirk on Satan's face, my frustration and anger increased and my fear diminished. I was sick of this twisted being messing with my life . . . or rather my afterlife . . . and the people I cared about.

I lifted my chin as well as my sword. The blaze turned entirely blue. The openings where Satan's eyes should have been narrowed slightly.

"You're not hurting him anymore," I said.

His head cocked in that creepy bird-like manner of his and sent a slimy shiver down my spine. Alrik stayed a silent statue behind him, acting as a sentry for the door.

"It's so . . . interesting, that you think you have control over that."

I lifted my sword higher to act as an unspoken reminder. This sword held the power of the Holy Spirit. This sword he was afraid of, even if his pride would never allow him to admit it. This sword—wait, what?

He stepped closer to it without a lick of apprehension in his movements. This shouldn't happen.

His odd behavior threw me off my game. He came within inches of the flames and stopped to inspect the blade. His head tilted one way and then another as though appraising the weapon rather than fearing it.

I watched, transfixed, as he reached a claw-tipped finger out and ran it through the blue blaze. The flesh on his finger bubbled, but he simply considered it with a tilt of his head and a slight narrowing of his eye sockets.

"Hey." I pulled the sword back and took a fighting stance, my voice shrill. "Don't touch that."

"That sword, my ugly sheep"—he pointed the same clawed finger at my weapon—"is the whole reason you and your bonded are even in my realm. The whole reason I sent my demons to attack your family. The whole reason for all your pain"—he ticked his chin toward Logan—"and a good deal of his pain as well. Had you been willing to listen the last time we stood face to face, you could have prevented your boyfriend from being turned into a bloody hunk of flesh."

Guilt nipped at my gut, but I pushed the shame away. This was the Father of Lies; I couldn't take anything he said as truth.

"You want my sword?"

"In a way."

"But it won't work for you," I blurted. "Didn't Knuckle-Head behind you report on that?"

A bubble of near hysterics threatened to burst free from my chest. If all of this pain and suffering was due to a misconception, I was seriously going to lose it.

"I won't be using the sword . . . You will." Satan's lip curled.

I blinked. Twice.

"You *want* me to stab you?"

Satan blew out a breath of air and turned slightly to Alrik. "She is exceedingly stupid, isn't she?"

Alrik simply tipped his head in agreement. He'd never been so quiet before. It gave me the creeps.

"That insult might have bothered me if it came from anyone other than you."

Satan lifted an eyebrow above those creepy empty eye sockets.

"And *you're* stupid." I couldn't believe the word vomit coming out of my mouth.

Gosh, what was I, five?

If Satan had eyes, I think he might have rolled them at me. Can't say I blamed him for that last comment. "You won't be stabbing me, you idiot sheep. You'll be using that blade to cut through this." He reached behind him and roughly jerked something forward. He pulled it with such violence that sparks shot from the rough ground where it grated.

It took a moment for my eyes to adjust to what I was seeing. Clenched in his fist was a semi-transparent chain. Each link at least the size of my fist. Rather than metal, it appeared to be made of black smoke encased in a transparent glass-like material—though clearly much stronger than glass. How long had he been dragging that thing behind him?

My eyes widened. What exactly was I looking at?

"What is that?" I stammered.

"That, Daughter of Eve, is the chain that binds me to this and the earthly realm. And you are going to be the one to break it. Then I will be free, and you will be one of mine."

CURSED

The tip of my sword shook, but not from fatigue. "Yours?"

"Yes, my little lamb. The one who frees me, willingly or not, from these chains will be cursed to become one of my children, bound to me for eternity. The rules were established by the Creator Himself. But your beloved Logan will be free."

He tilted his head toward the still form behind me. "Well, what's left of him at least. I'll even grant you some time with him before I come to collect what is rightfully mine."

The dam keeping my hysterics on lock-down burst. I didn't scream or cry —I laughed. It sounded maniacal even to my own ears, wild and uncontrollable.

The creature in front of me was beyond insane. He was delusional. I wasn't going to help him. I would never help him.

An unearthly growl burst from Satan and vibrated throughout the small chamber where we stood, causing dirt and small stones to rain down on us. His outburst snapped me out of my hysteria and reminded me exactly where I was. Standing in a cell, deep within the earth, with Satan, a traitor, and the man I loved.

Satan grabbed the smoke-wrapped, transparent chain and chucked it toward me. It landed dangerously close to my feet. I had no idea where it attached to him, and I wasn't going to ask. I flicked my gaze down to what, according to him, was the only thing keeping him out of the heavenly realm, and then back to his face.

"Break it!" he roared.

For all Satan had done to me, this was the first time he raised his voice in my presence. Something inside begged me to search for cover. Evil-soaked power permeated the very air we breathed in the aftermath of his furious bellow.

I held my ground, standing firm and tall in front of Logan as if my fragile flesh and bone could protect his broken body.

"No." My voice was quiet but firm.

"My patience has run its course. You will do this, or I will end him." Satan brought a taloned hand up in front of his face and slowly closed each digit into a fist.

At first I was confused . . . until I heard Logan in agony behind me. His cries of pain echoed off the walls like the sounds of a dying animal, and fresh second-hand pain sliced across my chest.

I dropped my sword, the flame instantly extinguishing, and fell to my knees at Logan's side. He thrashed on the blood-soaked ground. I moved my hands frantically over his body, trying to find an uninjured spot to touch to lessen his convulsions.

Suddenly Logan's back arched, and all the muscles in his body contracted. His fingers contorted and bent like claws. The arch in his back was so severe that only his shoulders and part of his legs touched the ground. His eyes were squeezed shut and his mouth open in a silent scream—as if the horrors being done to his body were so atrocious that they couldn't be verbalized.

And then a gurgling noise started deep in his chest. The cough that worked its way up his throat was wet and splattered blood on my face when it finally escaped.

My entire being vibrated with the watered-down version of his agony. With black-dotted vision, I battled my body's defense mechanism to shut down in the face of the painful onslaught. Gritting my teeth, I forced myself through the invasion and willed my body to obey my commands.

"Stop it!" I screamed over my shoulder. "What are you doing?"

"Ending him." Satan's cold demeanor was once again in place.

"You can't do that!" I yelled, but Satan's depthless gaze was trained on Logan and not on me. A steady flow of blood bubbled out of Logan's mouth and dribbled down his cheek.

I spotted Alrik behind the evil being. There was a horror in his eyes that was surely reflected in my own.

"Do something!" I yelled to him, but when the words left my mouth, a mask of fake detachment slid over Alrik's features. I'd find no help there.

"You can't do this," I reiterated. "He is a Child of God! He's not yours to end!" The shriek in my voice shredded my vocal cords. I was coming undone in a way I never had before.

But as quickly as it started, it ended. Satan opened his fist, and Logan's body unclenched and fell unconscious in a pool of his own blood. Relief flooded my limbs as well, and I was able to unclench my muscles.

My tears fell unfettered onto Logan's prone form. I didn't even try to stop them. The shock of seeing him so destroyed caused my hands to tremble.

I didn't know what to do.

I didn't know how to comfort him.

I didn't know how to fix him.

Why hadn't I tried to stop this? Instead I just threw insults at Satan and made it worse.

"Oh God, what have I done?" The whispered words of desperation slipped unknowingly out my mouth.

The deep chuckle behind me was chilling. "You think He hears you? You think He actually cares?"

I must have verbalized my plea.

"Yes," I whispered, not bothering to turn to the monster behind me.

"He doesn't. If He did, He would have stopped me. But look what I've done to your beloved."

"You can't take him. He's not yours." My whispered words were barely a breath leaving my mouth.

"I know this game better than you do. I can, and I will." Satan's voice was so close his hot breath washed over my neck. He brought his clawed hand in front of my face, taunting me. My vision blurred through a veil of tears.

Ever so slowly, he closed his hand again.

I watched in horror as Logan's battered body responded as if the evil being was squeezing his heart of flesh. A spasm and crushing pain pierced me deep inside.

With a crazed scream I spun, whipping my sword off the ground. My hands gripped the pommel tight enough to hurt as I brought the holy weapon behind my head and used all my strength to arch it downward.

The flames flashed blue before my face as the fiery blur headed toward its target—Satan's head.

But with a clang that echoed throughout the chamber, the blade connected with the chain that bound Satan instead.

The force of the impact threw me back into the stone wall. My head smacked against the hardness, and my vision winked in and out before clearing.

I shook my head to clear the fuzziness. Big mistake. My brain felt like a giant bruise rolling around in my skull. Every movement hurt.

Logan? My sword?

I pushed through the pain and realized my legs were sprawled over Logan's injured body. I let out a noise of distress and as gently and quickly as possible pulled myself off him.

Next I noticed my sword lying in the dirt to my left, the blade broken in two.

I grabbed the handle and gasped when nothing happened. No fire sprang to life.

Had the sword itself rejected me?

What had I done?

The edge of my sword had been intended for Satan's skull, not his chains. Striking his bonds had been an accident.

"No!" His angry roar shook the chamber.

I put a hand against the wall to keep my balance. What was happening?

Satan stood in the middle of the room, his back to me, the leathery shadow of his wings blocking my view of whatever he was holding in front of him.

I blinked, and he was in my face. His contorted in rage as his angelic mask melted away. Bits of charred flesh peeked out from holes in the porcelain skin he hid behind.

"Strike it again," he ordered with a growl. Red dots lit the middle of his eye sockets—the beast inside peeking out.

Several heartbeats passed before I even understood what he was trying to command me do.

He held the chain that I had struck.

Held it *intact.*

The blow hadn't worked. But my sword no longer wielded holy fire. Was my soul condemned, or had I somehow been saved?

Logan lay on the ground between us. Satan's hate-consumed face filled my vision. Without breaking eye contact, I brought my sword up between us.

"I can't. The flame is gone."

Satan didn't utter a word, but the very ground beneath us began to shake.

And it didn't stop.

A fissure appeared in the ground by Logan's head. I gasped and took a step back as the crack climbed up the wall to my right. Large rocks began to fall from the ceiling. I released my broken sword and threw my body over Logan's, grunting when chunks of debris pounded my back.

"Stop!" I screamed.

And suddenly, it did.

I looked up. Through the debris still floating in the air, Satan stood in the middle of the room, looking at the chain in his hands and muttering to himself. I heard only snatches of his nonsensical ramblings—"Must be," "blood," and "key."

Where was Joe? We needed our ride out of here, like yesterday. I didn't know what the ramifications of my rash act would be, but I was supremely glad Satan's trick hadn't worked. Even if it had cost me my weapon. The real question was what else had it cost me?

That was a concern for another time. Now was my opportunity to get Logan out of the room while Satan was lost in his own insanity. I inched my fingers under Logan's arms—ignoring his dislocated shoulder—prepared to drag him out.

"Blood." The melodically vile voice broke the silence.

"What?" I crouched in a protective stance over Logan's head.

"You need to coat the blade with The Lamb's blood."

I didn't even try to pretend I misunderstood what he was saying. The thought was so horrific, words thoughtlessly tumbled from my mouth. "Are you insane?"

"That question is idiotic . . . even coming from you." Satan's calm demeanor was back, but the melted patches on his face revealed his true nature.

"It was rhetorical," I spat back. "Of course you're insane. Only an insane being would expect me to stab the Son of God."

"The fire didn't work. So the key must be in the blood instead."

I didn't answer. I shook my head so violently that my hair slapped my face.

"It's the only way. And when you do this, you will be one of mine. Your soul will forever be covered in blackness. You will become the betrayer."

"I'm not doing anything you want me to do."

"Oh, yes you are." The calm confidence in the smile that split his grotesque face made my stomach churn as if snakes were wiggling inside and wanted out.

"I already said . . ."

He brought his hand up, fingers spread wide and itching to curve inward.

Threat received, I cut off my words.

"You find him and run him through with that blade of yours. You come back here and cut the chain, and I'll send you and what's left of him"—he indicated Logan with a jerk of the chin—"back. You will have time to say your goodbyes before I claim you. It's more than fair."

My mouth opened and closed. I didn't even know how to answer. Of course I wasn't going to stab Joe. That wasn't an option. Apparently I took too long to respond because Satan's fingers started bending inward.

"No!" I held a hand out in a pathetic attempt to stop him. "No. Take me instead. Let Logan go, and keep me down here."

"Our bargaining period is long over. You passed that up when we conversed on Earth. You either do what I want, or you both—"

I let out another banshee scream and rushed Satan with what was left of my weapon. He easily sidestepped, and I crashed into another rough wall.

I spun. "I. Will. Gut. You." *Was that my voice?*

"Oh, I highly doubt that."

I saw red as I ran at him again, focusing on the exposed parts of his face. The real beast behind the façade. With a soul-shredding scream, I was just about to impale the monster when I was jolted to a stop. My arms were forced to my sides and caught in a bone-crushing grip.

I struggled like a wild beast against the hold. Kicking, grunting, and even trying to bite whoever, or whatever, was holding me back.

A voice at my ear stopped me. "I'd do what he says, Little Aud. It's the best deal you're going to get today."

Alrik. Liar. Coward. Betrayer.

I'd forgotten about him. A fresh ball of rage consumed me, and I thrust my elbows back into his gut, forcing the air from his lungs. A hot whoosh of breath coated my exposed neck and accompanied a surprised grunt of pain.

He was the one I would end.

I spun and blindly lunged forward with the jagged end of my sword, right into the space where Alrik's blackened heart should have been. Before I could enjoy the satisfying feeling of shoving my weapon into his body, he dissolved into a poof of mist.

My forward momentum continued, and my sword struck something else. I came to an abrupt stop. I pulled my weapon back through the dissipating cloud of mist—to the sickening sound of suction.

My hand shook when I saw the red liquid that coated the entirety of the jagged blade.

I snapped my head up and stared into the eyes of my friend.

BETRAYER

*N*O! *No, no, no!* This couldn't be happening.

Joe squinted in pain, and he brought his hand to the wound in his chest. His blood flowed over his fingers and down his front to drip onto the dry dirt. The ground sizzled wherever his blood touched, slurping up the life-giving substance and bubbling its thanks.

The sword slipped from my fingers. My pounding heart was so loud it drowned out the rest of the world.

Tha-thump, tha-thump, tha-thump.

Joe's mouth moved. The words didn't register. They were buried under layers of shock and the crazy erratic beating of my heart.

What have I done?

I fell to my knees, overcome with emotion as I watched Joe struggle for breath in front of me. Because of what I had done to him.

Satan hadn't driven that blade into his chest. Alrik hadn't done it. I had.

I stabbed the one being who loved me unconditionally. Who had traveled through a realm filled with fire and brimstone and horrors—things I was never going to forget—all to save the other half of my heart.

He'd been with me every step of the way, and in repayment, I made him bleed.

I had become the betrayer.

My eyes were glued to his bloody wound.

And then, by some miracle, his words penetrated the fog that weighed down my senses.

"Audrey, look at me." His words carried such love my heart broke all over again.

I blinked and shook my head. My vision blurred and filled with crimson. I didn't need to touch my cheek to know my face was coated with tears.

"You have already been—"

A blast of power from behind thrust me forward onto the unforgiving ground. My mouth filled with dirt and grit. Stones pelted my body as a shockwave of energy washed over me. I covered my head with my arms. The pressure was unrelenting and seemingly unending. Despite my efforts, I remained flattened against the earth.

I spotted Joe through the maelstrom of debris whirling around the cell. His eyes were focused on something beyond me. They held a mixture of sadness and disgust. He was propped against the craggy wall; the only part of him affected by the blast was the hair whipping around his head.

And then the chaos stopped.

Pushing to my feet in one fluid motion, I whirled around, steeling myself to face the source of the pandemonium. Bending an arm behind me, I reached for a blade that was no longer there.

I didn't immediately recognize the beast as Satan. He stood tall, his body in some half-transformed state. Flesh-like skin only splattered his body now. Spikes jutted out from the joints in his arms and hands, some as long as six inches.

He rolled his shoulders, and his leather-and-smoke wings stretched as far as possible in the confined space.

In his right hand, he held what was left of my weapon and its blood-drenched blade; at his feet, lay the shattered pieces of the glass-like chain.

He was free.

I pressed a hand to my stomach to stop its revolt and only just managed to keep myself from falling to my knees.

Satan's head swiveled in my direction in a very inhuman manner. Fluid and fast. Not a single part of his body had moved except his head. It reminded me of an owl, and in my overwhelmed state, I vaguely wondered if he could perform a 360-degree turn. Would he vomit green bile next?

"Perfect, my child," he said, and his voice bounced painfully in my head. "You did well holding up your end of our bargain."

No, there had been no bargain. I hadn't agreed to any of this.

I shook my head. "No—"

"Oh yes. This"—a claw-like hand gestured to the broken binding on the ground—"couldn't have happened without you. No need to be modest, my dear."

He distorted the truth. It was an accident. Not a premeditated action.

But in the end, Joe had bled and Satan was free, so did it even matter? Willingly or unwillingly, I had been the instrument used to release Evil Incarnate—and according to what he said before, I now belonged to him.

The snakes in my gut writhed and snapped their jaws. I was going to be sick.

Then Satan swept his wing out of the way, revealing Logan's motionless body.

A fresh wave of panic washed over me. Logan's features, at least what wasn't covered in blood and gore, were pasty white. The rise and fall of his chest was imperceptible.

Since we were already dead, I didn't know what his death-like vitals meant, but they frightened me nonetheless.

"I believe per the conditions of our deal this now belongs to you; at least, what's left of it."

Without thought, I rushed to Logan's side. Practically sliding into his body, I fell to my knees to be closer to him.

Was he breathing? His skin was that of a chalky vampire. Dirt and grime from the floor was mixed into every wound. Some seeped blood, and others were crusted over.

He was bleeding. That meant his heart was still pumping . . . right? I held tight to that unverified hope. He couldn't truly be gone.

"And you," Satan spat.

I jerked my head up, but he wasn't speaking to me. He was angled toward Joe, who was still bleeding freely from the wound I'd inflicted. "In your supreme arrogance, you never thought I'd figure out how to free myself from your chains?"

Joe took a weary step forward. His gaze was locked on Logan and me, and Satan's taunts went unanswered. The enemy did nothing to stop Joe's advance. His eyes lightened when he reached us, and he lifted a hand to wipe the wetness from my face, but the warmth of Joe's freshly spilled blood coated my cheeks in his hand's wake.

Satan continued to mock Joe, throwing words at him like stones. But whatever was said garbled and bounced off me as I looked into the eyes of my truest friend.

Blood leaked from the corner of his mouth. Accidental or not, I'd done a horrible thing. But Joe had to be all right. There wasn't a force in any realm that could take him out. He was literally the Creator of all, right?

Satan's verbal jabs continued . . . until Joe roared, "Enough!"

I jolted. Joe spared a glance over his shoulder at the dark being. "Go do what you have been waiting to do."

Satan's eye sockets narrowed, and his eyebrows pinched. His gloating had been interrupted and ignored. Served him right.

His attention snapped to me.

"I'll be seeing you soon," he promised. His body coiled before he sprang straight up, punching through the layers of stone that trapped us. Rocks rained down on our bodies in the wake of his departure. I once again threw myself over Logan's defenseless form. We'd be buried in no time.

Where was Joe? I searched for him—and breathed a sigh of relief. He was right beside me.

"Fear not. You'll both be returned to your realm shortly."

"Joe," I coughed, knowing our time here was short. "I didn't mean—or rather I didn't know—"

He laid a gentle hand on my cheek. "I know. Let's go home."

Home.

I couldn't help thinking that the heavenly realm might not be my home for much longer if Satan made good on his threat. How much time did I have before I was dragged back to this pit of death and decay?

I nodded, but mid-bob, something struck my head, and my vision swam. I blinked, and my vision was filled with Joe's light-brown eyes before I was swallowed by black nothingness.

I sat up with a gasp and a sob. I was blind, drowning in blackness.

Wait, no, I was just in an unlit room. The muted outline of objects started to appear as my eyes adjusted to the darkness.

Breathing was like trying to take in air through a straw. There wasn't enough.

My heart pounded so hard I could feel it without laying a hand on my chest.

Where am I? Where are the lights?

As soon as the thought flitted through my mind, brightness flooded the room. My eyelids fluttered at the sudden change.

The Healing Center.

That's where I had to be. I recognized the chairs against the white walls as well as the small bed I was lying in. I brought a hand to my face and pushed my grimy hair behind my ear.

Everything came back with crashing clarity.

Logan's and Alrik's disappearance.

Our journey through Hell.

Romona, Kevin . . . fighting with me and injured.

Discovering Morgan.

Then Logan. Finding his broken and bleeding body chained to the wall.

My sword shattering when I tried to attack Satan.

And then the unthinkable. The blood I'd spilled that freed Satan from his chains and cursed my soul in the process. I didn't want to believe Satan, but how could I spill holy blood and not be cursed?

I put my face in my hands, but my tears had all been spent.

How long did I have with my friends before I'd be dragged to Hell for my sins? I'd sold my soul to Satan the moment I'd unknowingly plunged that sword into Joe's chest.

A wail lodged itself in my throat. If only I'd kept my head and hadn't gone after Alrik.

Regret was a bitter pill. Regret for the things I wish I'd done differently, and regret for the things I'd never get to experience.

Logan.

I'd done what I set out to do. I'd returned him to our realm. He would be safe here. That was a small consolation considering what I'd done to bring him back.

I'd been the tool that broke Satan free from the leash that had held him captive for eons. And to do so, I'd drawn holy blood.

My soul was now surely a shriveled black pit.

Would I end up like those poor souls tethered to the ground, begging for a drop of moisture? Or worse, would I somehow be forced to work against my loved ones?

No. I'd never do that.

There was nothing Satan could do to make me fight against the living, or against heavenly powers. I'd rather end up a wasted shell of a person in Hell for eternity.

Which was a real possibility at the moment.

I sucked in a deep breath. At least my lungs finally worked properly.

How much did people know? Did they realize Satan was free? Had Joe returned? Was it possible that he'd sent Logan and me back and not had enough strength to return as well?

Questions swam and looped in my head like darting fish. Every time my mind reached out to catch one, it zipped out of reach while I was distracted by another.

I drew my knees up and rocked back and forth in an unconscious effort to soothe myself. Too much had happened in the last few days—heck the last few hours—for me to process.

But one thing I knew with absolute certainty: What I'd done was too horrific to ever ask for forgiveness, let alone receive it.

If Satan didn't haul me back to the pit, the Creator would eventually cast me there Himself. I couldn't even turn to Him for help—which was what my soul was crying to do—because He was the one I'd betrayed.

Captivity to Satan was what I deserved for my actions. Actions that had ramifications not only for myself but for all mankind—both dead and alive.

Now freed from his tethers, it would only be a matter of time before Satan stormed this realm. Why else would he have fought and schemed to be free from his bondage? This had to be the one place his chains had forbidden him from entering.

He was right: I didn't know, didn't understand the rules. Was he now an unleashed beast with the freedom to roam where he pleased?

And should I out myself as a betrayer or hide what I'd done?

"Oh thank goodness you're back. We've all been so worried."

I snapped my head up and stopped my crazed rocking. Kaitlin rushed to my bed and pulled me into a fierce hug. All things considered, I was in pretty good physical health.

It was almost annoying. The Healing Center and I had a tumultuous relationship at best.

"How is—" I choked on my words, my face muffled against Kaitlin's shoulder. So many of my friends had been hurt, and I couldn't even find the inner strength to ask about them.

Kaitlin pulled away and looked into my watery eyes. "Everyone is fine. They're all going to be all right, Audrey. They are all safe. And it's because of you."

No, I thought, *no one will be safe. And that is all because of me.*

KINDRED

*K*aitlin left to find a change of clothes and grab me some water, but I slipped out of the room before she returned.

Once again, I stared at the wrong mop of hair. Black hair that should have been sun-streaked blond. Why my feet had taken me to this particular room, I wasn't quite sure. But here I was, standing at the foot of Morgan's bed, watching his sleeping form like a creeper, and I couldn't puzzle out why.

Or maybe I just didn't want to.

"Should I be flattered?" Guess he wasn't asleep. His usually smooth accented voice was full of gravel and grit. Raw as if his vocal cords had been stripped bare. Maybe they had been.

Old me would have startled at his voice, but new me felt dead inside. New me no longer felt whole.

When I didn't immediately rise to the bait, Morgan cracked an eye open. The other was still swollen shut but looked considerably better than the last time we met. The swelling had gone down, and the blood, both dried and fresh, had been washed from his skin. With all the stitches patching his face back together, he looked like Frankenstein's monster—but given time, the evidence of what had been done to him would fade to nothing. That was if he could work through the emotional damage that had been inflicted. If not, he might carry those scars for the entire realm to see.

Through my numbness, I wasn't sure if I even cared. Maybe this was what it felt like to be soulless?

With effort, Morgan shifted on his bed, and the smirk that was flirting with the corners of his mouth dropped suddenly as his good eye took me in. Did I have a scarlet letter pinned to my chest only other betrayers could see?

The change in his demeanor told me he'd picked up on something Kaitlin hadn't. I didn't have to wait long to find out what.

"I know that look." His voice might have been soft if his throat wasn't so damaged. I resented that.

"What look?" I went for neutral but heard the accent of defense in my tone.

"What did you do?"

"I got my friends back."

"How?"

"By doing what was necessary."

Morgan let out a sharp burst of air. "Yeah, that's what it looked like to me."

"What's that supposed to mean?"

"That you have the look of a girl who just made a deal with the devil and is going to live to regret it."

The hiss of air I sucked in was the only confirmation Morgan needed. I suspected he knew something, but not that he'd cut to the truth so quickly.

"What's worse, luv, is that I know enough about the monster to know he wouldn't have been satisfied to just bring you down. The taste of your soul was likely only his appetizer. What's to be his dinner and dessert?"

Probably the destruction of the world and this realm as we know it.

"What do you mean?" Why was I asking questions I already knew the answers to? I was perfectly and painfully aware of what Morgan was asking. And he wasn't wrong. If all I'd done was damn my soul . . . well that would have been bad, but what I'd done was so much worse than that. I couldn't even fully wrap my brain around the repercussions.

Not now. I didn't want to understand. Not now or ever.

"What I mean is—"

"Stop!" I held a shaky hand up in front of me. "Stop. I can't. I won't. I just . . . Everyone is back. That's all I can focus on for the moment."

Morgan was silent. For once.

His lips pressed into a grim line. We stared at each other for several moments before he gave me a sharp nod. A silent acquiescence to my request.

The air slowly leaked from my lungs. Whatever conscious or subconscious reason I'd sought Morgan out had been a mistake. There were some hard truths I was going to have to deal with in the upcoming days, but my heart of flesh was bleeding freely. My deeds were too fresh to face today.

I turned to leave but missed my window of escape when Kaitlin popped her head in the room.

"There you are! You were gone when I got back to your room with some water"—she waved a bottle in the air—"been looking for you everywhere. Logan's awake." Kaitlin's eyes were expectant and her smile radiant.

"Oh."

Her smile dropped.

My wooden demeanor was going to get the wrong person asking the right questions sooner or later.

"Oh? Ah, don't you want to see him?" Even the trickle of confused doubt in her voice wasn't enough to snap me out of the tortured haze that blanketed my mind.

Morgan saved me the trouble of a response by addressing Kaitlin himself. "It's nice to see you too, beautiful. I was just about to call for someone to give me a sponge bath, but now that you're here, it seems you'll be able to save me the trouble."

Kaitlin's eyes narrowed, buying me a few extra moments to pull myself together.

"You wish," she shot back.

"Oh, I do. I do very much."

She scoffed at him.

"Is that any way to treat someone who endured unspeakable torture on your behalf?" Morgan infused just the right amount of pout into his damaged voice. The man was skilled. I'd be worried for Kaitlin if I thought for a moment she might fall for his antics.

"Whatever you had to endure rests solely on your own pathetic shoulders."

"Well, I suppose that's true. It was my decision to rescue you from those demons." A flicker of something akin to sympathy rested on Kaitlin's face, but the emotion was erased by Morgan's next words. "I can't blame you for falling prey to them. You are only a girl after all."

"Ah, whatever." Kaitlin rolled her eyes and fixed her attention back on me.

I dug deep to find the shadow of an appropriate emotion. It was go time.

"Yeah, Kaitlin, you're totally right. Let's go see Logan. I'm so . . . happy he's awake."

Face palm. That was some seriously bad acting. And the look on Kaitlin's face confirmed it. But I was terrified of seeing Logan. Fear rode me hard, warring with relief that he was safe. I was worried he would take one look at me and see all my secrets, all the ugly deeds I'd done.

And that when he saw them, he'd reject me.

"Audrey? Are you okay? Do you maybe want to—"

"No, I'm good! Promise!" Internal cringe. That was way too loud.

"Smooth move." Morgan coughed.

Without sparing him a glance, I spun Kaitlin toward the exit.

"Yikes." The turn was so sudden she lost her footing before righting herself.

"Let's get going." I continued with false cheeriness in my voice, nudging her toward the doorway.

Kaitlin peeked over her shoulder at me as she moved forward. "Yeah, all right I guess."

I followed her while willing myself to hold it together.

"Some things can't be undone, luv. But others can." Morgan's final words were softly spoken, and they threatened to undo me.

The straightening of my spine was the only indication I gave that I'd heard him before striding from the room.

13

REUNION

*L*ogan was awake . . . just as Kaitlin said, but even so, part of me wasn't expecting him to be conscious considering the severity of his injuries. After ushering her out of Morgan's room, I sent her on some other meaningless errand I'd already forgotten. I wasn't ready to face Logan with an audience, but he apparently already had a visitor.

One of the voices that floated down the hall as I approached was most definitely Logan's deep timbre. It was scratchier than normal—making it sound as if he was recovering from a cold or had just woken up—but I still recognized it. The other voice was . . .

Jonathon?

I slowed my steps as I neared the open doorway, padding forward carefully. Was I planning on eavesdropping on their conversation?

Absolutely.

These two didn't have a cozy relationship. And considering my history with each of them, I wasn't about to pass up this juicy opportunity. Perhaps Jonathon's visit was only medical . . . but then again, perhaps not. Thank goodness I'd sent Kaitlin off on another errand, or she never would have let me do this.

Stopping a few feet from the doorway, I strained to catch their words.

"Thanks, man," Logan said.

There was a pause before Jonathon heaved a sigh. "I didn't do it for you."

"Yeah," Logan chuckled. "I'm well aware of that. It doesn't mean you don't deserve my gratitude."

"Maybe that's exactly what it means."

"Naw, your heart was still in a good place. That's all that really matters.

Just because you were doing it for her instead of me doesn't matter. In fact, that makes me even more grateful."

I bit back a groan. Did they really have to talk about me? I really shouldn't be listening to this.

"You know what she means to me." Logan's words were quieter, forcing me to take a step closer even as I chastised myself for listening to their private conversation. But if I was damned anyway, what was one more sin to add to the ever-growing pile? Besides, new Audrey's emotions were still somewhat on lock down.

The room was silent after that.

What I wouldn't give to be a fly on the wall in there. But not an actual fly, because, eww. Maybe have the power of invisibility? Yeah, that would be sweet.

I fidgeted as I waited for one of them to say something . . . anything.

Eavesdropping was overrated.

Why was no one talking?

Forever seemed to pass before Jonathon responded.

"Yeah, I do know. But I think more importantly, I finally know what you mean to her."

"Would it have made you choose differently if you'd known that before?"

Wait, was Logan Doctor Phil'ing Jonathon?

"No." Jonathon's answer came out gruff. He was agitated. "But maybe it should have."

"You're a good man, Jonathon. The right one is out there somewhere; it's just not her. You can't force these things." There was a bit of warning to Logan's words I wondered if Jonathon picked up.

A self-deprecating laugh shot from Jonathon. "Learned that lesson the hard way."

Another few beats of silence. What was happening in there? Were they staring into each other's eyes and having a bro moment or something?

"It's been . . ." Jonathon started and then stopped. Another deep sigh before he continued. "Lonely. I've been here for a long time."

Perhaps Logan nodded or something because I didn't hear a response. Since when did guys open up to each other like this? Were they having some sort of post-traumatic bonding moment, or did this happen all the time under our female radar?

"There's something special about her. If there wasn't, I wouldn't have held on so long."

Me? Special?

I slapped a hand to my face to cover my snort of disbelief—old Audrey stirring a little inside. A part of my heart that had hardened against Jonathon during our mission melted a bit.

He was lonely, and he had acted out of his hurt. I found it hard to stay upset at someone when they were in pain. Emotional or physical.

"Yeah, I know it, man. I've known it since the beginning."

Wait, what? He's known since the beginning? That didn't make sense with how he first treated me.

"Well, maybe if you'd done something about it right away, you would have saved us all a bit of trouble." Jonathon's words were just short of biting. The guys were civil to each other, but there was still more than a touch of animosity hanging in the air. Mind you, if I'd been in the room, I would have been nodding in agreement. *Took bonehead in there long enough to get with the program.*

Maybe that was a touch hypocritical. Whatever.

Logan ignored the not-so-veiled jab. "Thank you for keeping an eye on her for me."

The laugh that burst from Jonathon was humor-filled. "Yeah, right. No. It didn't go down that way. She's a true warrior, Logan. She singlehandedly took down a demon the size of a small building. It was pretty disgusting, but you would have been proud of her."

A sharp pain lanced my heart. Old Audrey was fully awake now and trying to shove new, cold, unfeeling Audrey out of the way. But if that happened, I'd fall apart.

No one should be proud of me after what I'd done. I existed in this realm on borrowed time. For all I knew, a portal to Hell could open any minute and suck me back down to that kingdom of despair.

I deserved nothing less.

I rubbed my eyes with my fists as an overbearing weariness permeated my body and soul.

"Except for perhaps if you'd seen her reaction to the hell-trees." Jonathon chuckled, and I cocked my head. What was he about now? "She squealed like a girl whenever one got too close to her."

Hey, I am a girl, you doofus!

My throat itched to spit the words at him. Too bad I was playing spy at the moment. I pulverized the warm fuzzies that had started to grow for Jonathon. Wonder if he thought a throat punch would be girlie?

Anger issues? Yeah, maybe. So what?

Wait, was Logan laughing too? Not cool.

Those blood-sap-leaking zombie trees were nasty.

Oh, shoot!

I'd missed the last few exchanges, but I heard the slapping of hands in some weird dude bonding handshake, and then Jonathon was saying his goodbyes.

And I was just standing outside the door . . . like a creeper.

Abort mission.

Where to go? Where to go?

I performed a ridiculous foot shuffle followed by a spin as I searched for a hidey-hole, but it was too late. There was nowhere to hide.

Jonathon strode out of Logan's room—and spotted me.

We both froze.

I grimaced, braced for a well-deserved tongue lashing, but after several moments Jonathon just rolled his eyes, shook his head, and then continued on his way down the hall without a single word.

Wait, what happened? Had I pulled that spy junk off without getting in trouble?

Old Audrey—the one untainted by Hell's nightmares—demanded a happy dance.

"You can come in now, Audrey."

Oh. So busted.

I reached up and patted my matted hair. I hadn't given it much of a thought until now. The mess was sure to be a kaleidoscope of colors. Looking down, I also took in my rather filthy body armor. The material was intact but caked with dirt and blood. Not even the dark color of the suit could hide the grime. My face was probably just as nasty.

Even though I'd woken up in The Healing Center, I obviously hadn't been tended to—probably because I hadn't sustained any serious injuries. I should have taken care of my disheveled appearance sooner. I had not thought this through.

Typical.

"After taking a trip to Hell to spring me free, you're gonna leave me waiting now?" There was a teasing note in Logan's voice I wasn't used to hearing.

I wiped a hand down my dirty face. How was I going to do this?

Pain-filled grunting noises reached my ears. "Okay, if you're not gonna come in, I'll come out there to you."

Wait, what? "No! Don't move!" I barreled through the doorway . . . to find Logan sitting in bed with an amused smile on his face. "Huh? I thought you'd gotten out of bed."

"I figured that's what it would take to get you in here." He laughed and pointed at my head. "Not amused I see."

"Let me guess. Red?"

"Yep." He didn't look the least bit remorseful.

I rolled my eyes and stepped farther into the room. He'd caught me lurking outside his door after all. I supposed that gave him license to mess with me.

I took a long moment to check him out. That is, check out his physical condition. Not check *him* out.

Yeah, keep telling yourself that.

I cleared my throat and chewed on my lower lip.

Logan appeared . . . fine . . . especially considering the condition I'd found him in outside this realm.

He was wearing a clean white t-shirt. There were some bandages on various parts of his exposed arms but no bruising. His face had a few small scratches, and a little discoloration, but no swelling at all.

He was certainly cleaner than I was. Another reminder that someone forgot my sponge bath. Did the guys get all the special attention in here now?

But the real question was how had he healed so quickly?

"Why don't you look worse?"

Logan choked on a laugh. "I'm going to take that as a compliment, even though I know you didn't intend it as one."

"I just meant . . ." How did I delicately explain that he'd looked like ground beef only a short while ago? Delicate didn't seem to be part of my skill set.

"You were in bad shape, Logan." A swell of emotion clogged my throat as I remembered what it felt like to find him in that underground cell. Old-weak-emotional Audrey was really fighting tooth and nail to take over new-cold-unfeeling Audrey. She took advantage of the cracks in my heart and slipped though. Before I could lock my feelings down, my eyes filled.

I turned and stared out his window before going on. I couldn't face him at the moment.

"You . . . I've never seen someone beaten so badly." A shudder wracked my body, and a tear slid down my cheek.

"Hey."

The gentleness in Logan's voice lulled my senses. I turned, and my gaze traveled up his body until my eyes connected with his. He wasn't smiling anymore.

"Can I hold you?"

His request was simple. And perfect. And exactly what I needed.

And rather than fight what we both wanted, I did what I should have done long ago—I surrendered.

14

REUNITED

I stayed in Logan's arms until I couldn't stand my funk anymore. There was only so long a girl could live in crusty clothes.

After slipping into the small bathroom in Logan's room, I peeled the bloody form-fitting armor from my body. The protective garb was extra crunchy from dried demon blood and stuck to my skin in places.

My gloves were coated in a different type of blood. Red flakes of it fell to the ground. My hands shook as I yanked the gloves off and stuffed them in the bottom of the garbage can. I stood for a moment, staring at nothing as I wrestled my thoughts into submission—but the questions slipped through anyway.

Joe, what had happened to him? Was he okay?

A fresh wave of guilt slammed into me over the result of my anger-filled actions. If only I'd not lost it, I wouldn't have lashed out at Alrik and accidentally struck Joe instead.

The feeling of my blade sinking into soft flesh was too close to the surface. Squeezing my eyes shut, I fisted my hands and wished those horror-filled moments away. But they were branded to the forefront of my consciousness.

"Audrey, you all right in there?"

Logan's voice and soft knock on the door jarred me back to the present.

"Yeah, sorry. It's just taking a bit to get this nasty armor off. I'll only be another minute." That sounded normal, right?

I set about ridding myself of the rest of my gear and chucked it all in the corner. That left me standing in days old workout clothes, but that was better than the alternative . . . still being in the blood-saturated armor.

My next step was to attempt to clean up. Although free from bloodied and dirty outerwear, I had sweated buckets in these clothes.

I seriously missed waking up in the Healing Center fresh and washed.

Surveying the small space, I found some washcloths. A sponge bath was the best I could do.

After soaking and lathering the soft terry cloth with soap, I pulled my tank with a built in bra over my head and set to work scrubbing off as much funk as possible.

Reaching my back was a challenge, and I twisted and contorted my upper body to scrub the hard to reach places. In the middle of a twist, I caught my reflection in the mirror over the sink.

I froze, limbs at awkward angles, and then half turned.

What was that on my back?

The soggy towel dropped from my hands and landed on the tile floor with a splat.

There, beneath my left shoulder blade, a black spot about the size of a quarter marred my otherwise flawless skin. I backpedaled closer to the sink for a better look. The mark wasn't perfectly round, nor was it all black. Thin black-and dark-green spider veins reached out in all directions from the central mark.

What is that? That's definitely new. Did I . . . catch something in Hell?

A more sinister explanation occurred and sent shockwaves of fear through my body. Was this part of the curse Satan spoke of?

A small part of me still believed Satan's words were a lie, that I wasn't actually cursed to spend an eternity in torment. But this . . . this hideous mark wasn't a lie. It wasn't made up. It was sketched on my skin like a tattoo. My own personal scarlet letter—a reminder of what I'd done and the consequences to come.

The door shook with the force of Logan's knocking, and I yelped. "Audrey, not to invade your privacy, but I'm a little worried about you out here. Are you sure everything's all right?"

I searched the floor and found my tank, quickly sliding it over my head and concealing my shame. No one could know of this.

"Gimme a sec." That was all I could push through my suddenly dry throat.

The last bit of hope that I could be redeemed slipped through my fingers.

This was real. This was happening. And there was nothing I could do to stop it.

Shortly after Logan banged on the bathroom door, I emerged from the small space to find him resting. I crawled onto the narrow bed next to him. I was still pretty nasty with my ratty hair and days old clothes, but I was too exhausted and soul crushed to care.

He stirred when I slipped in next to him and pulled me into his arms. Without the self-constructed barrier of self-doubt or suspicion I'd built for months to protect my heart, the feel of his strength encasing me was heaven.

My silent tears streamed down my face, but rather than snap into his usual fix-it mode, he just let me be. Softly stroking my back with one hand and holding me tight with the other.

If only he knew that my tears were not only shed for the horrors I'd seen in Hell, but also for the tomorrows we'd never have together. I wanted to tell him, but I couldn't. If he knew the full truth, the spell would be broken. And I was selfish enough to want whatever time I had left with him to be beautiful. We'd already wasted so much of it.

In that moment, I decided he wasn't to know. Not until the separation came. We'd enjoy the limited time we had together, and I would cherish the memory throughout the torturous days that I would endure for the rest of eternity.

We sat on his bed, tucked up against the headboard, Logan sitting with one knee bent and an outstretched leg, and me curled into a ball against his chest, practically cuddled on his lap.

When my tears were spent, I let out a shaky breath of air.

"Audrey, I can't—" Logan's voice caught on something. His head rested on top of mine. When he continued, his voice dropped an octave, thickened with emotion. "I can't imagine what you went through down there. I'm so very sorry. I should never have bonded with you."

I savored the warm thud of his heartbeat on my cheek for several seconds before what he'd said sunk in. The leakage from my eyes along with a bad case of the feels must have dulled my reactions.

I jerked to a sitting position to stare at him in disbelief—and anger. My face was crusted with the salt of dried tears. There was no doubt I was a hot mess and a half. But that was nothing compared to the mess he'd just spewed.

He reached for me again, but I put a hand up to ward off his movements and curled my upper lip.

Where to even start?

"What *I* went through? Are you insane?" His gaze jumped around my face as if he couldn't decide on a safe place to land. "Logan, I actually felt an echo of what you went through. I even experienced some of it in a dream or a weird out of body experience where I *was* you. What I went through was nothing."

He opened his mouth to speak, but I slashed a hand through the air to stop him. "*Nothing* compared to what had been done to you. You were torn to shreds. Literally, in some spots."

His face paled. I shouldn't have gone there and instantly regretted bringing it up—but I couldn't handle his concern for me when *he* had been tortured. We'd get to the "should never have bonded with you" comment next.

"You experienced some of . . . of what I went through?" he asked.

Shoot, I gave him another reason to beat himself up. Rookie mistake.

"Never mind about that. And what's this business about regretting bonding with me? Frankly, that's kind of—hey!"

He grabbed my upper arms and held me still as I tried to push away even farther. His blue eyes flashed, and his face was hard as stone. "If bonding with you caused you to feel even a second of what I endured in that place, then yes, it's something I deeply regret and would do anything to take back."

Buried under the caveman response was something sweet, but I wasn't feeling it.

"Argh. You . . ." I pointed a finger at his face. "You just . . ."

As I sputtered to find the right words, the corners of Logan's lips just barely tipped up. I stopped talking when I spotted his involuntary reaction. Of course I'd find a guy who thought I was cute when riled up. Actually, that was probably pretty lucky considering I did tend to have a short fuse.

I pressed my lips together and narrowed my eyelids before performing another visual sweep of his body.

Yep, he looked to be relatively healthy.

I launched myself at him and grabbed the sides of his face, and then I planted my lips right over his. Just like the first time I'd surprised him with a kiss, he was momentarily stunned.

I gently but firmly bit down on his full bottom lip in a silent demand for him to get with the program. Then I pulled back a fraction, just far enough that my lips grazed his when I spoke. "Less talking, more kissing."

I'd gone to Hell and back for this guy. I wanted to collect my reward . . . with interest.

A lazy smile spread over his mouth, and his lids dropped to half-mast. "Yes, ma'am."

I pulled back and lifted my eyebrows. "Ma'am? What am I, a zillion years ol—"

Oh.

A warm pair of lips cut off my rant, and I wasn't upset about it in the least. *Mmm, yes.*

My body flooded with warmth. Every nip of his lips and change of position spiked my heart rate until an electric current zipped under my skin, energizing my molecules and enhancing my senses.

I needed this. I needed to get lost in this moment and forget this world or any other realm existed.

I curled into Logan's embrace and slid a hand into his gloriously thick and soft hair. With my other hand, I grasped his bicep as if to hold him in place.

He growled low in the back of his throat, and with a grasp on my waist, he pressed me even closer. I liked that. His other hand made a slow trek from the hair beside my ear—probably the only non-crusty strand—down the side of my face, to rest in a light embrace at my neck. His thumb played lazy circles with my pulse point.

But I wanted more.

Despite the gentle touches, the soft press of his lips, and the light nips at mine, the fear that this—or any other time—could be our last time together stirred a frantic sort of panic in my gut.

If this was all I was going to get with Logan, I wanted as much as he would give me.

I made a sound of protest at one of Logan's toe-curling yet tender kisses. Moving even closer, I scooted to my knees and pressed my lips more firmly against his. A silent demand.

Logan tried to slow things down again, but I wasn't having it. Now both my hands were buried in his hair, and I was kissing him like there was no tomorrow . . . because I wasn't sure there would be.

There was only a slight hesitation before desire overcame Logan's sense of propriety, and he hauled me against his chest in a savage move.

Yes, the beast inside me whispered even as a soft voice cautioned me to slow things down.

I pushed the voice away. Desperation released the beast from its cage. There'd be no hesitation from me.

What had started out sweet and innocent was quickly moving toward unrestrained passion. I didn't care. Scratch that, I did care. I wanted it.

I dragged a hand from his hair down his neck to settle on his arm, unconsciously searching for warm skin. When my other hand reached the bottom of his shirt, I slipped it underneath. A shudder ran through his body, and the next thing I knew I was on my back. But not in the way I had anticipated.

Logan had broken our kiss and pushed me back onto the mattress. He held both my hands in his against the sheets but away from his body. With his arms straightened and his body to the side, he'd moved as far from me as possible while still holding my wrists immobile. His breathing was as hard and erratic as mine. A cobalt ocean churned in his eyes.

We just stared at each other. Me wondering why he had stopped. And him . . . Well, I had no idea what he was thinking. His gaze searched my face erratically, and his features were drawn and pinched, almost as if in pain.

"Wh-what?" I asked. "Why did you stop?" I didn't miss the breathy tone in my voice.

Logan squeezed his eyes shut and then pushed away from me, sitting back against the head of the bed. He shoved a hand in his hair and then fisted it for a moment before letting it go.

When he opened his eyes, they didn't meet mine right away. I propped myself up on my elbows to watch him. Cocking my head, I scooted back to a sitting position. The sharp pain of rejection pierced my chest. He was a guy. Why the heck had he just stopped us?

Logan finally looked back at me, and I licked my lips, tasting his familiar peppermint sweetness.

He slammed his eyelids shut again with a groan and shoved another hand roughly into his hair.

"Can you please not do that right now?" he asked. Just the deep sound of his post-kiss voice made my heartbeat spike again.

"Do what?"

His growl was followed by a reverse head-butt to the wall. "You're killing me. You know that, right?"

I grinned like the Cheshire cat. I found getting under his skin very satisfying. I made a move toward him again, but he put up a hand to ward me off. Did he really not know me by now? Like a hand gesture was going to deter me. *Ha!*

I grabbed his arm and used it to pull myself closer to him. His eyes and chin snapped down so he was facing me.

"I wasn't done with you yet," I said as I pulled him in closer, my eyes already shutting. Any second now, I'd get a second taste of heaven. But then the world tilted, and pain shot through my butt as it hit an unforgiving surface.

What the what?

My eyes snapped open, and I blinked several times.

I was on the ground.

With one very sore backside.

I looked up. Logan peered over the bed with an expression that was simultaneously angry and sheepish—an emotional mix that had to be hard to pull off.

"What was that?" I shouted at him. "And *ow*, by the way."

Getting to my feet, I rubbed the sting out of my tush. I think I bruised my tailbone.

I eyed one of the chairs, but sitting might hurt, so I jutted out a hip, crossed my arms over my chest, and glared at Logan instead.

The big jerk.

He rubbed his eyes with his fingers and then covered his face with his hand. I spotted a smile he couldn't quite cover.

"That was rude." I landed a fist on my hip as I pointed an accusatory finger at him.

He opened his fingers to peek at me and bit his lip to keep the smile from getting too far out of control.

"You better not be laughing at me right now." I crossed my arms back over my chest and attempted to stare him down.

A full belly laugh escaped his mouth and I widened my eyes in disbelief.

I. Am. Out.

I spun on a heel and marched to the door.

"Good luck saving yourself the next time you end up in a super stinky realm. I'm probably going to smell like rotten eggs for a week because of you," I grumbled on my way out—too quietly for him to hear the full sentence, but I was confident he'd picked up the gist.

A strong hand caught my arm and spun me back around, sending me tumbling into a warm chest.

This is more like it, the beast inside rumbled. I told it to shut up.

"Now, Audrey, come on, be reasonable." There was still a healthy dose of mirth in Logan's gaze and words.

I struggled against his hold, but the defiance was halfhearted at best.

He brought his other arm around and locked me in place. The urge to nestle into his warmth rode me hard. The man *had* just dumped me . . . literally.

"When have you ever known me to be reasonable?" I muttered. Wait a minute, I'd just insulted myself. Logan one. Audrey zero. "I mean, don't try to be cute with me now. It's not going to work."

His brows lifted. "It's not?"

"No." I shook my head and caught a glimpse of red-and-pink streaks. Argh, this hair.

"Are you sure?"

"Yes." But I refused to meet his gaze.

"Well, that's good. Because that means you won't be affected if I do this." He placed a gentle kiss on my temple.

"No, not at all."

"Or this." He brought his face down and nuzzled the spot behind my ear before placing another soft kiss on my skin.

Not responding to that one took a herculean effort. My throat dried up, and so I just shook my head while a quiet chuckle vibrated through Logan's chest.

"Perfect. That means I can do this as well." He slid a hand up and cupped the back of my neck.

I was caught in his spell without even knowing it had been cast. Obediently, I tilted my head back with only the slightest pressure from his hand. His lips grazed my neck before nibbling on the sensitive skin and finally placing a scorching kiss below my ear.

The shudder that wracked my body was completely involuntary. I'd closed my eyes without even realizing it.

Logan's breath touched the shell of my ear as he whispered, "You can't kiss a guy like you did before and not expect him to lose control. We don't have to rush. We have eternity together now."

His words doused all the warmth and passion coursing through my body. My eyes popped open, and without thought I wrenched from his hold.

We didn't have eternity anymore. I didn't even know if we had another full day.

Logan's brow pinched, but he let me go. The confusion on his face was clear, but he was a smart guy. He knew I was hiding something. His gaze roamed my face as he tried to pick apart the enigma. Like I was a puzzle that needed to be solved.

"Audrey, what's wrong?"

I opened my mouth to speak, but nothing came out.

"If you're worried I don't want you, that couldn't be further from the truth. But I don't think it's wise to get too . . . close until we've officially and therefore permanently bonded. We can have a short engagement period if you want; it doesn't really—"

"Engagement? Wait, what are you talking about?" I stumbled a step, and the back of my knees hit one of the chairs. I wobbled for a moment before regaining balance.

He reached out to me again, far more agilely than before, which made me think he'd been playing me in the beginning. I sidestepped his advances.

My head started to pound under the pressure of the secrets stuffed inside.

"You know our bond can only lead to one of two places"—Logan held his hands up in front of him as if to show me he was keeping his distance—or else he was treating me like a spooked animal—"and I think it's safe to agree we're on the same page with how we feel about each other." His gaze pierced me. "This bond is not going to dissolve, Audrey. We both know that. I just thought, considering"—he gestured to the crumpled bedding with his hand —"considering that, you wouldn't want to wait."

A hysterical laugh bubbled up my chest and burst from my mouth. A crazy sound I tried to shove back down my throat but failed. *Oh gosh, is it getting hot in here?*

"You expect us to get married because we made out?" My eyes were wide, and I started sucking in too much air. "That's nuts."

My emotions were bouncing around like a pinball, and I wasn't even sure if my reaction was because the idea of being bonded permanently freaked me out or because now it could never happen.

Hot mess . . . inside and out.

I glanced at the door. I'm not sure why. Maybe I was subconsciously looking to make a quick escape.

"Now, Audrey." My head jerked up. Logan had moved several feet closer to me, his voice annoyingly calm. "You know people don't get married here."

"Married, mated, soul-bound for eternity"—I waved a hand in the air —"who cares what you call it; it's all the same thing." Except marriage was 'till death do you part.' This was a way bigger commitment. Like I was going to let some overzealous hormones make that decision for me.

Oh gosh, did it even matter? I'd be gone soon anyway. Separated from Logan . . . permanently. I didn't even have a choice anymore. We'd never be whatever we were meant to be.

I started sucking in air like I was drowning. And in a way I was. Drowning in the folly of my foolish actions.

I held a hand out to ward off Logan's slow and steady advance. If the bond was doing the same thing to him as it was to me, he was probably itching to have me back in his arms. This bonding thing was seriously whack.

My breathing accelerated. I gulped air between phrases, panting like a dog in the desert. "I just need . . . a minute . . . to process."

Logan's face hardened, and he advanced on me anyway. I backed up until my rump bumped something. I glanced over my shoulder and spotted the bed. I yelped and jumped away from it, stumbling into the side table and smacking my shin in the process.

I bent over to rub the bruised limb while still sucking air as if I could inhale all the oxygen in the room. I started to see black spots around my vision and lost track of Logan.

Warm but firm hands took hold of my shoulders and forced me to sit in a padded chair. Right now what I needed was a padded room.

Logan's face appeared before mine as I tried to blink away the black spots. He'd crouched in front of me and filled my hazy vision.

"Audrey, love, I want you to take one deep breath and hold it for the count of two before releasing it."

Did he just call me 'love?' Something went a little melty and gooey inside. *Did he say something else? Oh shoot, black spots are blocking out his perfectly formed face. Man, he has perfect bone structure.*

I pitched forward. My stomach leaped to my throat, but with a grunt, Logan caught me before my face became acquainted with the floor. I held on to consciousness with both hands but felt it slipping through my fingers.

My back rested against something soft, and I was pretty sure I was horizontal. I blinked rapidly at my diminishing vision. Cobalt orbs were all I could see clearly.

"You know if you'd listened to me, you wouldn't be passing out." Logan's words, full of soft vibes, were missing his usual sarcastic bite. "But I appreciate the effort to make me feel like your rescuer again."

A gentle pair of lips kissed my forehead before my vision winked out completely.

15

AWKWARD

*N*aps were amazing. I loved naps. They were so magically awesome I wanted to marry them and have a nice long relationship with them.

My body buzzed with energy even as I snuggled into the soft bedding. Something warm and solid was at my back. Some sort of heated pillow?

Mmm, I like.

With eyes still closed, I shifted closer to it and nuzzled a second heated pillow beneath my head.

"Finally. She's alive," a campy male voice announced.

"Oh, don't wake her just yet. They look so cute together. I feel like I need to capture this with a camera."

Wait. What?

"You know how mad she's going to be when she wakes up and finds out you've all been staring at her sleeping. Especially with her hair all crazy-like."

That male voice rumbled along my back and shifted my warm pillow. I cracked an eyelid.

That's not a pillow; that's an arm! Which means . . .

I grabbed the top blanket and hauled it over my head. Jerking myself away from Logan's arm and the side of his body, I armadilloed into a ball beneath the covers.

"I hate you all."

"What was that?" Kaitlin asked. "You love us the most and think we are the best? Oh, so sweet! We love you too." She blew loud kisses at me from the other side of my makeshift blanket shield. She was the worst.

Tremors from Logan's direction started to shake the bed, reminding me that I was very much still lying next to him . . . in front of our friends.

Letting my legs lead, I slipped out of bed and then army-crawled beneath it. The room was silent for several heartbeats.

"Did I just see my granddaughter slide out of your bed and sneak under it?"

I slapped a hand over my mouth to hold back the groan. When did Romona arrive? I thought only Kevin and Kaitlin were in the room with us.

"Yes, yes you did," Kaitlin supplied helpfully.

"Um," Logan cleared his throat. "Romona, I'm so glad to see you're up and moving around already."

"Yeah, sure you are." Romona's voice dripped with sarcasm. "Care to explain to me what Audrey was doing in your bed . . . and now hiding underneath it?"

I covered my eyes with my hand as if that would transport me out of this situation.

Silence blanketed the room.

Logan cleared his throat. "It's not what you're thinking. Audrey was just—"

"Oh, it's exactly what you're thinking," Kaitlin cut in.

"Kaitlin." Logan's voice was a sharp censure.

Only their feet were visible to me, so I couldn't read their body language. But I knew Logan was both uncomfortable and annoyed.

I think I'll stay here for a while longer.

I snickered.

"I heard that, young lady."

I pressed my lips together and covered my head with my arms. *Stay very still and quiet, and they'll forget I'm here.*

"Logan, I'm waiting." Romona's foot tapped a quick staccato against the glossy floor.

"Well, Audrey got a little upset about something and started to hyperventilate. I couldn't calm her down, and she passed out, so I put her somewhere more comfortable."

Way to make yourself look like a hero, buddy. I rolled my eyes.

"Why was she hyperventilating?" Romona asked. There was a note of genuine confusion in her voice.

"I'm not sure. One second she was fine, and then she just freaked out."

"Are you kidding me?" I shouted from my hiding spot.

"You've got something to add down there?" Logan thumped on the bed, and a spring knocked my head.

I shot the offending mattress the evil eye and rubbed my head.

"You said we were going to get married."

Logan let out an exaggerated sigh. "Audrey, be reasonable. And I already told you people don't get married here."

I flipped on my back and punched the mattress as hard as I could in the limited space I had, hoping I'd managed to hit part of his body.

"You still don't spring a commitment of that magnitude on someone. You take your time and work up to it."

"Where's the popcorn? This is getting good."

"Shut it, Kaitlin," Logan and I said in unison.

"Oh cute, they're synchronizing now."

"Kaitlin," we both yelled.

"I think there's some popcorn in a vending machine down the hall," Kevin piped in, "but no way am I leaving now. This is like watching a movie in 4-D."

"Logan," Romona went on completely ignoring Tweedledee and Tweedledum. "You asked to spend eternity with my granddaughter without talking to me first, and in that brutish manner? Is she not worth more to you than that?"

I fist pumped in my confined space. *Way to go, Grams!*

"Audrey, will you please get out from under the bed now?" Romona's voice was authoritative.

"No thank you. I'm good."

"Audrey—"

"I'm too young to get married," I moaned, cutting off Romona's censure.

"That's right. You're obviously too immature to make a commitment like that."

"Yep, not even offended by that comment. You're totally right. One hundred percent too immature."

Logan huffed out a frustrated breath. "Romona, you're right, I should have handled the situation with a little more finesse. But in all honesty, Audrey was all over me, so it was kinda hard to think straight."

"What?" I squawked, nailing my head on a metal beam. I flipped over again and kicked the mattress where I thought his butt might be. "You did not just say that out loud."

The bed squeaked, and Logan's upside-down head appeared. The tips of his golden hair brushed the ground.

"I'm just keepin' it real, babe. You know that's how it went down." His eyes twinkled, and a grin lit his face.

"Ouch." I twisted an arm to rub my back, feigning pain. "Oh my gosh, can you see them?"

Logan's eyebrows pulled together, and the smile slid from his face.

"What happened? Are you hurt?" His hands landed on the floor by his head while I twisted my face to a mask of agony.

I blinked, and Logan was off the bed and on his belly on the floor, his head right-side-up and peeking under the bed at me.

"It really hurts," I whined.

"Did the mattress squish you?" He assessed the amount of space between the bed frame and me.

"No, no, it's just . . . the tire marks on my back from the bus you just chucked me under!" I screamed at him.

At my outburst, Logan's head jerked up and he nailed it on the bed frame. He gave me a side-eye while he rubbed the sore spot.

Kaitlin lost it. Her hysterical laugh was broken up by the occasional snort.

Logan army-crawled under the bed after me, which was quite a feat considering his size. The dude was a lot bigger than me.

"Wait, stop," I protested.

Ignoring me, he wrapped an arm around my waist and hauled me out from under the bed with him. We ended up grappling on the ground for a few minutes before a loud throat clearing reminded me of our audience.

Straddling Logan's hips with my hands planted on his chest, I froze. A quick check over my shoulder revealed Romona staring me down. Logan wore a smug smile, the back of his head rested on his crossed arms. He looked as if he enjoyed this spot on the floor immensely.

"You see what I mean?" he asked Romona without taking his eyes off me.

I was about to throat punch him when I noticed red blossoming on his white t-shirt.

"Oh my gosh, Logan, you're bleeding." Twisting, I scrambled off him and tried to tug his shirt over his head. I needed a better look at where that blood was coming from. How stupid was I? He was still injured, and I was wrestling with him.

A belly laugh rocked his body as he swatted my hands away. "Audrey, stop trying to undress me. This is exactly why I suggested a short engagement."

Did he not have one iota of self-preservation? He was so close to a throat punch right now. All it would take was one quick jab. But another look at the blood blooming on his stomach had me pushing aside my annoyance and renewing my search for the source.

"Stop fighting me. I'm trying to check out your wound."

"You're definitely trying to check something out," Kaitlin added.

Logan grabbed my hands and captured my gaze. "Audrey, I'm all right, I promise. How about you let me up and I'll go take a look?"

I chewed my lip in indecision but nodded, the concern for him threatening to overwhelm me.

We both stood. Logan let out a quiet grunt. "Hey"—he placed a hand on the side of my face—"I promise, I'm fine. There are just a few places still healing. You're here, you're safe. That means I'm all right too."

Oh. That was sweet.

He bent forward to kiss the corner of my mouth, and even that chaste contact sent my heart rate into overdrive. When Logan pulled back, his eyes broadcasted he'd been affected as well. Black pupils nearly swallowed the blue.

Someone cleared their throat, and he headed to the bathroom in the corner. I caught a glimpse of his smooth back as he tugged his shirt off and tossed it to the ground. Stepping into the bathroom, he turned and grasped the door. A bandage taped to the left side of his . . . I tilted my head—was that an eight pack?

One, two, three, four, five six, sev—

"Hey, Audrey. My face is up here."

Words tumbled from my mouth in a guilty rush. "I was checking out your bandage. Obviously. What else did you think I was doing?" The bandage was almost completely soaked through. His eyes danced with laughter as he closed the door, blocking his body from view.

Holy smokes. As in—Holy. Smoking. Hot!

I fought the urge to fan myself.

"Hey, Audrey," Kaitlin called to me, breaking my hormone-induced daze.

I spun to face her.

"Yeah? Huh? What?" My voice was fast and breathy.

"You have a little something-something right here." She indicated the corner of her mouth.

"What?" I scrubbed a hand over my mouth, but there was nothing there. "What are you talking about?"

"Don't worry. You got the drool wiped off."

"Funny."

"I thought so." She giggled.

I shot her a look that said you can shut up now, but she just laughed harder. *Brat.*

"How's Morgan, Kaitlin?" Her laughter turned into a choking sound.

Kevin started slapping her on the back.

"Pfft, I don't know." She shrugged and looked at the empty wall.

"Sure you don't," I said with a smirk.

She stuck her tongue out at me.

"What, Morgan's here?"

Shoot, how had I forgotten Romona hadn't been there? She'd been taken out of the fight before we'd found Morgan. Kevin, too, for that matter, but he must have been filled in because his face reflected a look of resignation rather than surprise. But she was my best friend, and here I was ignoring her.

"Romona." I rushed over and squeezed her.

"Ow."

I pulled back and scanned her from head to toe. She was in a tank and loose-fitting pants that reminded me of scrubs. "I'm so sorry. Are you still hurt?"

"Just a bit sore."

I cringed and looked at the floor, toeing a spot that didn't exist. I was the worst.

"Audrey." Romona's soft voice brought my gaze up. She gently placed both hands on my cheeks. "You did it, baby girl." Were those tears gathering in her eyes? "I'm so proud of you."

Guilt slammed into my gut like a Mack truck, knocking the wind from my lungs. I was incapable of speaking for several seconds. New unfeeling and blessedly numb Audrey wanted to take back the reins.

"You shouldn't be," I whispered back. Yeah, we'd brought Logan and Morgan back, but at what cost exactly? Besides my soul that is.

"Of course she should be," Kaitlin interjected from across the room. "She was amazing, Romona."

I craned my neck in Kaitlin's direction. "How do you even know? You were sent back with Morgan."

Kaitlin gaped like a fish. "You're joking, right? You single-handedly took down a demon the size of a yacht. You marched through that desert of—whatever those things were—with determination. You were fierce, girl. Tiger on steroids fierce."

"You weren't there at the end," I argued. "And if you had been connected to Logan and experiencing what he was, you'd have been laser focused on getting him out of there too. If you had seen what that . . . that abomination was doing to him, then . . ."

Logan wiped away the wetness on my cheeks with his thumb, and he rubbed my back. I hadn't even realized I was crying—or that he'd re-entered the room, where I could bring up all his horrific memories for him to relive.

Stupid old Audrey and her stupid emotions.

The fact that Logan wasn't rocking in the corner somewhere, but was comforting me instead, was a miracle. In fact, why didn't he have any scars? I saw his smooth back in my mind's eye. His old scars were completely gone.

I sucked in a sharp breath of air. He was standing in front of me now, gently cradling my face.

"Would you mind giving Audrey and me a few minutes?" He glanced over my shoulder, and the smallest of smiles ghosted across his face. "I promise, no more bed cuddling."

While Logan spoke, I caught the fast-paced clicking of heels in the hallway. As my friends started to get up, I cocked my head—the clipping grew louder and then abruptly stopped.

"Just a minute, everyone. I have some news." Shannon's voice made my blood run cold and struck fear in my heart, because deep inside, I knew what her announcement would be. And it wasn't going to be good.

16

HALF-TRUTHS

I twisted to stare at the formidable angel. Shannon stood in the doorway, barring retreat. I'm sure she wasn't actually trying to restrain anyone from leaving the room, but considering I had a fairly good idea what this announcement would be, unease twisted in my gut and crawled up my throat. Were the walls closing in on us?

Logan wrapped his arms around my waist. I itched to pull away—unworthy of his silent support.

Shannon glanced our way, the frown on her face deepening for a moment before her lips straightened. She surveyed the rest of my friends and then jumped right in. "I'm glad you're all back safe, but there's been a development. Satan's broken free of his chains."

There was a beat of silence, and then the room erupted in shouting.

I stayed quiet as everyone bombarded Shannon with questions. Eventually my transgressions would come to light . . . time was my enemy. My friends' voices turned into a steady buzz in my ears.

Shannon held up a hand, silencing everyone. Logan tightened his arms around me.

"You'll be briefed more thoroughly. But as you can imagine, this means all hands on deck until we neutralize the threat." Shannon's gaze landed on Logan and me. "That is except you two. You're both benched for the time being."

I shrank back into Logan's embrace. Shame filled my being.

Logan wasn't as compliant as I was. "Wait a minute. You need all able-bodied hunters. Forcing Audrey and me to sit this one out doesn't make sense."

"There will be no debate about this decision, Logan."

I didn't have to view Logan's face to know his eyes were narrowed in determination and that there was no way he'd let this go. But for the moment, he held his tongue.

"How do we know about this?" Romona asked.

Did Shannon's eyes linger on me a moment before turning to Romona to answer? "The Son himself confirmed the news."

I sagged in Logan's arms. The injury I'd inflicted on him hadn't prevented Joe's return.

"Shh, everything will be all right," Logan whispered in my ear, wrongly interpreting my body language as fear, when in reality relief pumped through my veins. Joe was back, which meant one less stain on my soul. Goodness knows it didn't clean my slate, but a weight lifted none-the-less.

"What does this even mean?" Kaitlin asked.

Shannon's gaze shifted to Kaitlin. "It means we need to prepare for the possibility of an attack."

Kaitlin's gasp filled the silence in the wake of Shannon's words.

"How is that even possible?" Logan asked. "Satan can't enter this realm."

"His chains kept him bound to Hell and Earth. He's now free of those restraints. We have to assume he's set his sights on us. We aren't sure of anything yet, so I ask you all to be very discreet about this information. We'll be disseminating emergency protocol methods throughout the realm, but without further information, we're not looking to insight panic."

"So, you're not telling everyone about this?" Romona asked.

"No." Shannon scanned the room once again. "You are all hunters. As such, it's your job to defend people against evil—and that extends to our home as well. Along with the warrior angels, you'll be our defense."

"But that means you need—"

"As I mentioned, there will be a full briefing." She didn't let Logan finish his sentence. "We're currently collecting data. Those of you who can, get cleaned up and meet at the training center in an hour. Strategy planning for all scenarios starts immediately." Without allowing further discussion, Shannon turned on her heel and left.

"How does she deliver news like that so calmly?" Kevin wondered out loud.

"I'm pretty sure she's stripped of regular emotions," Kaitlin answered. "My gosh, how did this happen?"

"I expect we'll find out soon enough. Come on."—Romona motioned to Kaitlin and Kevin—"let's get going."

They nodded, and chairs scraped the floor as they left. Before shutting the door behind her, Romona said she'd update us on as much as she could.

Logan nodded. "Thanks."

When the door clicked shut, he gently turned me in his arms. I knew he wanted to talk, probably to reassure me everything would be okay. But I didn't want to think about Satan any longer. In an hour's time, there was a solid chance my ugly secret would be exposed to everyone.

Joe was safe, but I wasn't.

I slipped my hands up the back of Logan's t-shirt.

"Whoa, Audrey—" He moved to extract my hands.

"No, wait. Just give me a second."

He froze, and we stared at each other. His blue depths connected to my brown gaze. I whispered my fingers over his back, starting at his waist and then moving both hands up toward his shoulder blades. When I reached his shoulders, I lightly brushed down the center of his back. I didn't miss the tremble that passed through his body. But he held my gaze and stayed still, allowing me my innocent exploration.

Okay, mostly innocent. I didn't have to linger quite so long on his skin to verify he wasn't scarred anymore—but he felt so good. The muscles and contours of his back were like warmed steel.

I dragged my hands off his flesh and brought them up to rest lightly on his shoulders. This time on top of his t-shirt.

"You're not scarred anymore." This was as good of a distraction as any.

He bit his bottom lip and then smoothed it with his tongue before shaking his head.

"Why not?"

He transferred his gaze to my lips. I unconsciously nibbled my bottom one. I freed the lip, and he ran the pad of his thumb over it. A small spark of his special brand of electricity pricked the tender flesh before he moved his hand away. Blue fire blazed in his eyes, but for the first time, I realized, he'd used his gift with no guilt.

"I let go."

"Huh?" What were we talking about again?

A smile touched his lips. One that said he knew exactly why I was discom-bobulated. "The scars aren't there anymore because I've forgiven myself. And I no longer believe that this"—he lifted his hand and formed a small blue globe of flickering lightning—"is because I'm cursed. I know I'm forgiven. I don't know what this is all about, but I don't believe it's from Satan."

"What changed your mind?" I asked.

"Love."

I scrunched my eyebrows.

"Love that I don't deserve but am given freely anyway. Truly accepting God's love and forgiveness gave me the strength to forgive myself and simply . . . let go."

"But how did you feel love and forgiveness when you were chained to a wall and tortured in Hell?"

He brushed a clump of hair behind my ear. I really needed to get cleaned up. "I was not forgotten, Audrey. I was not forsaken. Did I suffer? Yes. But it brought me you, and you are worth it. Worth facing whatever Satan tries to throw at me."

I was melting again . . . but the rush of emotion was quickly chased away by the sound of a clock tick, tick, ticking down to the moment I'd be forced to leave this realm—leave this amazing man I'd finally let into my heart.

I just . . . How was I to live with that?

I suppose the answer was that I wasn't. Life was more than just the time we spent living on Earth. The moment I became a slave to that fiery realm, that's the moment I'd truly lose my life.

Until that time came, I would live to the fullest. I didn't want to suffer through an eternity of regrets. The black mark on my back was proof I was here on borrowed time.

I knew exactly what needed to be done.

With a hand placed on his heart, I let my eyes sweep Logan's face. His strong jawline, the hint of stubble around his mouth, cheeks, and chin, his straight nose and masculine brow that led to his soft and beautiful sun-kissed hair—hair that was currently sticking up all over the place from our tussle.

I sucked in a deep breath, inhaling the woodsy and spicy scent that I would forever associate with Logan, and then finally I brought my gaze back to where they'd begun. Meeting Logan's. I saw a slight question in his eyes.

I smiled, at peace. Laying a hand on his softly prickled cheek, I inhaled in a quiet breath of air.

"Marry me?" I asked.

17

SOUL FUSING

"*H*old up a sec here." Kaitlin raised her hand to quiet us. "You mean he asked you to cement your bond and you freaked out so bad you passed out, and then you turned around and asked him to marry you like thirty minutes later?"

Kaitlin, Romona, and I were sitting in Romona's apartment on her plush antique couches with a full tea setting in front of us. I was chewing a cucumber finger sandwich . . . okay three sandwiches. I'd shoved one in my mouth right after the other. Those things were small, and I was hungry.

I lifted a shoulder and nodded, swallowing hard to clear my mouth. "Pretty much."

"And he said yes right away, right?" Kaitlin leaned forward, elbows propped on her knees.

Romona remained suspiciously quiet. That gave me an itchy nervous feeling. My grandmother-slash-best friend was too perceptive for her own good.

I'd opened with the news of Logan and my decision to be permanently bonded because I didn't want to hear about the briefing. I feared the truth. But by some miracle, they hadn't been told about the part I played in Satan's release. They would have brought it up if they knew anything. My knee bounced a nervous cadence as I wondered who knew besides Joe.

Since they hadn't already been told, I was assuming it wasn't going to be common knowledge anytime soon. And in that case, I'd already decided not to tell anyone my time here was limited. However, if anyone could put the pieces together, it would be my grandmother. Or Logan.

I would do whatever I needed to in order to keep that secret from them. I wanted to enjoy our time together while we had it.

"No," I absently answered Kaitlin.

I reached around to itch my back. I tried to ignore it, but when I finally got a shower, I couldn't help but notice the black mark on my skin had grown. The spot had doubled in size, and the veiny black-and-green fingers spreading from it had reached several inches long. I imagined the mark was an hourglass, its growth like dripping sand through a funnel and counting down my time in this realm. The spot remained hidden on my back, but I didn't know how far or to which parts of my body the blackness would spread. A time might come when it could no longer be concealed.

"What?" She huffed and slouched against the couch, arms crossed over her chest and brow pinched. "Are you kidding me? What's wrong with that boy? He's obviously insanely in love with you." Her words snapped me into the present.

Despite believing the same thing, I still blushed. "Well, you know Logan, first he had to explain to me—again—that we wouldn't be married"—I rolled my eyes—"that it would be a bonding ceremony or whatever." I waved a hand through the air. "Same difference, right?"

"Well kinda, except this is for eternity. No divorce and no till-death-do-you-part. But I guess if you don't count those things and the fusing of your souls then, yeah, it's pretty much the same."

I sprayed a mouthful of tea all over our delicious snacks.

"Excuse me? Fusing of souls? Whatever that is, it sounds painful. Can we do this thing without that part?"

Kaitlin and Romona shared a look. Kaitlin's eyebrows lifted, and Romona shrugged.

"What? What don't I know this time? Flipping orientation. Will someone please just hook me up to one of those machines that download all the important information about this realm already so I know what's going on?"

"Calm down, Audrey." Romona rested her fingers on my palm. Concern ripped through my body, and I snatched my hand back. Usually, Romona was all about transferring peaceful emotions my way.

"You can't expect me to calm down when you feel like that."

Romona sighed deeply and pursed her mouth. Her eyes scrutinized me for a moment before she decided to speak. "Audrey, what happened to being too young to go through with this right now? I thought the plan was to wait a few decades before any official ceremonies."

I shrugged and struggled to keep any physical sign of guilt from my body. "YOLO, right?"

"What in the world does that mean?" Romona tilted her head and studied me as if I was an alien species.

Kaitlin snorted a laugh. "As if that applies to this situation."

"I don't get it." Romona's questioning look bounced back and forth between Kaitlin and me.

Kaitlin waved her off. "It's just a saying that kinda means 'seize the day while you're young.' It obviously doesn't apply. Audrey's being weird."

"Hey."

"I call 'em like I seem 'em, girl."

"You're the worst. You know that, right?"

Kaitlin's smile broadened.

"That's cool, I only wanted one bridesmaid anyway." I slung an arm around Romona's shoulders.

"Hey, come on now." The pout Kaitlin put on would have had any guy on his knees in front of her, begging for forgiveness or asking her how they could fulfill her deepest wish.

I just scoffed. "That's what happens when you annoy the bride."

Romona shrugged off my arm. "Audrey, you're not a bride"—her gaze slid pointedly to Kaitlin—"and you know full well she doesn't get bridesmaids, so stop pouting."

"Hey, I don't? Well, that's no fair. What am I supposed to hold over Kaitlin's head to keep her in line for the next few days?"

Romona sputtered and choked on a mouthful of tea.

"Days?" she croaked.

I nodded.

"Days, Audrey?"

Didn't I just nod?

"Yeah, why wait, right? We're already bonded. It's obviously gonna stick. Let's just get this show on the road and all of that."

Romona looked at me as if I'd lost my mind. I turned to Kaitlin for help, but her expression wasn't much different.

"What? Logan was cool with it."

"Of course Logan was cool with it. He's a dude." Kaitlin snickered.

"Is this about sex?" Romona asked bluntly.

This time, the tea shot out of my mouth and nose. I coughed and hacked and blew my nose until my orifices cleared enough to speak.

"No. Oh my gosh. I can't believe you just asked that. This is not about sex."

Fuchsia. My hair was definitely hot pink right now. No doubt.

Kaitlin slapped her leg as she laughed. "If I were you, it would be. We all know you think Logan's a hot piece of—"

"Say it and I'll break something . . . on your face."

Kaitlin made a zipping motion across her mouth, but her shoulders still shook with unrestrained laughter. Oh man, I couldn't wait until she went through this. I was going to razz her so bad.

A blanket of heavy sadness settled on me when I realized I'd never see that day. I wouldn't be around when she fell in love. That wasn't the only thing I'd miss. I'd also never see my family again. After all the fighting I'd done, in the end, they would end up truly gone to me.

I mentally slapped myself. I couldn't fall apart in front of these two. They'd sniff out my secret like bloodhounds.

I plastered on a fake smile.

"If it's not sex that's rushing this, then what is it, Audrey?" Romona asked seriously. "Because, honestly, something seems off right now. Something's causing you to jump into this. What aren't you telling us?"

Too smart, that one. I needed to get some friends who weren't so sharp.

Oh, right, I wouldn't be making any more friends.

I shoved those thoughts to the back recesses of my mind where I was trying to bury all depressing feelings.

"You were right before. It's definitely the sex. What can I say? I can't keep my hands off Logan. Might as well make it official and do it the traditional way and all that. Listen, I really gotta go." I stood and inched my way across the room. "Lots of planning and stuff to do. Er, ah, or figuring out what needs to get done. I'm obviously way behind. Sorry I ruined your tea with my snot. Pretty sure I sprayed the whole table."

Romona and Kaitlin both stared at me as I backpedaled toward the exit. Romona's gaze was calculating and Kaitlin's was stunned. No doubt they'd be chatting about me the instant the door clicked shut behind me.

Who could blame them? I was acting supremely weird.

I was saved when my back hit a hard surface.

Thank goodness. I suppressed the urge to shout free-dom!

Turning the handle, I spilled into the hall and slammed the door shut.

Free—and alone—I turned and leaned back against the smooth surface then sank to the floor right on the welcome mat in front of Romona's apartment.

"What exactly does soul fusing entail?"

We were sitting on a white linen couch in Logan's cottage. I'd never been to his home before. In fact, before that morning, I didn't even know he lived in the same redwood forest that bracketed the mountain range as I did. I had assumed he had some small little studio apartment in the city with a bed, bathroom, and punching bag in the corner.

Sneaky boy.

Logan's cottage, which he insisted was a cabin—semantics—was lovely and charming and homey. Not at all the Spartan living abode I'd expected.

We'd been discussing Morgan when I opened my mouth about the soul fusing.

Logan ran a hand through his hair, looking slightly uncomfortable. "Right. Sometimes I forget you didn't go through orientation."

"You and everyone else," I grumbled.

"So, soul fusing, it's really just a fancy way of saying we'll be permanently bonded."

Permanently. There was that word again. My skittishness about the permanence of our bond had bounced back and forth—I was happy about it one moment and fearful the next. We were definitely linked in an irrevocable way, but there was still a choice. When I was sent to the abyss, what kind of existence would I be sentencing Logan to if we went through with the official ceremony? I didn't think it would be anything different until this 'soul fusing' concept came into play. Now I was back to agonizing over whether or not this was a good idea. I definitely needed more intel.

"Does it hurt?"

He chuckled and shook his head. "No. It doesn't hurt. I've heard it's quite enjoyable in fact."

He wiggled his eyebrows.

"Are you seriously trying to make this sound sexual right now?"

"Audrey, I'm a dude about to be officially joined with the woman I love for the rest of eternity. My brain functions in a very limited capacity. Speaking of, did you know we get a year off from hunting after the ceremony?"

"A year? For what?"

He wiggled his eyebrows again.

"You've got to be kidding me. No one can go at it all the time for a year."

"We can give it a go." He wrapped his arms around me, attempting to haul me into his lap.

I pushed him away, grazing his skin as I did. Joy like I'd never felt before shot through me during that brief moment of contact.

In response to his emotions, guilt flooded my system, and I pulled back even farther. I didn't want to taint his mood. I'd become as nervous about the empathy link—the transfer of emotions through skin-to-skin contact in this realm—as Logan had once been. Putting on a good face was one thing, but emotions were almost impossible to control.

"Be serious here."

"Okay, fine." He stopped to study me, and I wondered what he'd felt through our brief touch. Getting a reprieve from the link in the Healing Center had been nice. Since the transfer of emotions would be distracting to the healers, the Center was the one place in our realm the empathy link didn't work. "It's not just for that. It's so we have time to truly and properly connect. It's supposed to be a gift to us so we're not separated for that first year. It's a bonding time for us in all aspects. Emotional and spiritual as well as physical."

"Finally, a straight answer." I chewed on my lower lip.

"What's going on in that beautiful brain right now?" He tapped my head, and I swatted his hand away. This new lighthearted, touchy-feely Logan took some getting used to. I was finally seeing a Logan free of the demons that used to haunt him.

This was who Logan was created to be, and new Logan or old Logan, I loved him. To see him so happy both lifted my spirits and crushed my heart.

How would he be after I was gone? Would going along with this charade of a bonding ultimately break him? Was I pushing him when I should be pulling back?

I chewed on my bottom lip some more. "Logan, why are you okay going through our ceremony so quickly?"

He tilted his head a fraction. "What do you mean?"

"When I told Romona and Kaitlin we were going forward with the ceremony in a few days, they thought something was wrong with me. I'm just wondering why you're so cool with it."

"Audrey." He took my face in his hands. Something he'd gotten in the habit of doing.

I liked it but suspected he was using the move to force my attention when he thought I might try to avoid his gaze. Clever man.

Think happy thoughts.

Happy thoughts that let him feel happy emotions from me. Nothing that let him know my heart was shredded and my soul torn.

Waves of pure joy and love filtered through the empathy link from him to me. I closed my eyes to bask in it a moment. It helped lighten my mood, even if only temporarily. They were beautiful, these feelings he had. Beautiful and infectious.

It should be strange for him to be so comfortable touching me, but I guess after seeing his body broken and knowing I was running out of time—the growing black splotch on my back attesting to that—allowed me to soak up every moment to its fullest.

"Love, open your eyes." He brushed his thumbs over my closed lids before removing his hands.

Love. My insides melted when he called me that. I obeyed.

"I should have claimed you as mine the moment we met," he said. My breath caught, and he nodded. "I knew then there was no one in any realm like you. If I hadn't been so consumed with pushing you away, we'd already be together in every way imaginable. So in my mind, we've already lost time. I don't want to waste another moment not being with you."

"That was sorta the perfect thing to say."

His smile was gentle and free from pride. "Only because I'm perfectly made for you."

He kissed my forehead and released me.

Okay, that was cheesy, but still, I couldn't stop my eyes from filling again. This was becoming an incredibly vexing habit of mine. The unimaginable joy we might have had together clashed with my knowledge that it would not be our future, and as a result my eyes continually filled and spilled.

Thank goodness I'd held back the tide until he'd removed his hands. I was walking a tight rope with no safety net. One move that wasn't anticipated, and I ran the risk of my emotions freefalling right into Logan. I'd be completely exposed.

So far, I think Logan thought my tears were kind of cute. Like I was overwhelmed with happy emotions or some girlie junk.

He was clueless.

Maybe when he found out the truth he'd be mad enough that he would get over me quickly. As much as the thought crushed me, it was the best-case scenario.

For the hundredth time, I questioned whether keeping my shame hidden was the right thing to do. If I weren't such a coward, I'd try to find Hugo and ask him for advice. But I was both ashamed to face him and fearful of what he'd say.

Staying away from Hugo, Joe, and the Creator was imperative. I had little doubt that if they found me, they'd be more inclined to chuck me into the fiery pit than help me out.

"I don't like that look." Logan brushed a hand along my cheek, and I flinched.

I hadn't been ready for that touch, and my emotions were untamed. What had he picked up in that brief moment of contact? I tried so hard to keep my thoughts on him when we were together. To keep the darkness at bay . . . but I hadn't guarded myself at this particular moment.

Logan's brows furrowed, and his eyes darkened.

We stared at each other.

What was he thinking?

He was probably wondering what *I* was thinking.

He nodded to himself. "All right, you'll tell me when you're ready."

"Huh?"

"Whatever it is that has you feeling like that"—he nodded toward me—"I have faith that you'll tell me eventually."

"You're not going to harass me into talking about it?"

He was quiet for a moment. Thoughtful.

"Audrey, I'm always going to want to know what's going on with you, especially the things that bother and burden your heart, but I realize that I need to earn your trust. Yes, we're bonded and I believe with every fiber of my being that we were created for one another, but there are some things that need to develop over time. So yeah, if you've got some stuff you're going through that you're not ready to trust me with yet, I understand."

I released a breath.

"But, Audrey." He waited until he was sure my gaze was locked with his. "We're in this together now, which means that if you're ever in danger, I need to know."

I tried to swallow, but my throat was dry.

"I'll give you the time and space you need, but I need you to tell me if you're in trouble."

I nodded. What else was there to do? Lies were a slippery downward slope, but since I was already freefalling, I stuck with the program.

Logan clapped his hands once, making me start. "Now, I know just what to do to get you out of this funk. Let's get out of here."

18

ARCHIVES & THINGS

"*Y*ou're taking me to the training center?" I eyeballed the large building as we walked along the path I traversed most days. I was dressed casually in jeans and a tank, and Logan was definitely not cleared for a workout yet—but I wouldn't put it past him to try for it. "How . . . romantic."

"What?" He glanced at me, his arm slung over my shoulder. "It seemed to me like you needed to work off some extra energy."

I shoved him off. "Oh, shut it already."

He chuckled and rubbed his chest. Pfft, as if that actually hurt. Eye roll.

"Man, you seem extra strong. You taking some performance-enhancing drugs to up your game?" He smiled as he spoke, but ice chilled my veins.

Was I extra strong? Was I developing a new talent? I didn't have my flaming sword anymore. Had I traded my holy weapon for satanic super strength?

"Hey, what's wrong?"

We'd stopped walking, and I was too in my head to care. Logan faced me. The crease that settled between his eyebrows was the only indication he was worried. He looked very much like the familiar 'all business' Logan I'd known since my first arrival here.

"What just happened? You know I was joking, right? We're not going to the training center."

I shook my head and forced a wooden smile. "Sorry. Just got stuck in my head there for a bit."

He nodded. "I noticed. Are you sure you don't want to talk to me about it?"

That was the problem. Because I did.

I desperately wanted to talk to him about it and have him fix the unfixable and make it all go away.

But that was a fantasy. This wasn't going away. My fate had been sealed in blood.

I shook my head.

Logan heaved a sigh and continued down the path. This time, he didn't take my hand or put an arm around me.

I didn't blink as we walked through the entrance of a pearlescent, columned building. It appeared to be about five or six stories from the outside. We passed through the revolving doors and . . . were we outside again?

"What is this place?"

Logan's fingers grazed my hand. His happiness mixed with my wonderment. "It's beautiful, right?"

My eyes skated from one place to another. Taking in the dense tree cover, the beautiful flower-lined paths, and . . . wait, was that a purple bunny?

"Yeah, that's one word for it." I didn't realize I'd spoken out loud.

I closed my eyes and sucked in a lungful of sweet scented air. When I opened them again, rainbow light shimmered on the grassy path in front of us. I reached my arm out, and the multicolored light coated my hand and tickled my fingers with warmth.

"I don't understand. Did we just go through a portal?"

"No." With two fingers, Logan tenderly tipped my head and pointed up with his other hand. "We're in a solarium. Can you see the glass?"

I peered through the canopy of leaves above our heads. If I tilted my head just right, light reflected off a spot above us. I would have never known we were in a glass enclosure if Logan hadn't pointed it out.

"Wow . . . just wow." My eyes started to water from not blinking. I fluttered my lashes and glanced at Logan. "So, where are we?"

Logan looked back at me and blinked, unmoving—there was an intensity to the moment I didn't understand. Warmth filled my cheeks and then, like a wave, rolled through my body. There was a spark of blue that ignited from Logan's hand, even as his gaze remained locked on mine.

"What?" Did I have something on my face? Oh gosh, was I drooling or something? I wiped at my mouth. No drool. Phew. Something in my teeth? What was it? "Why are you staring at me like that?"

The blue in Logan's eyes flashed as if backlit, and the next moment the black pupils almost completely swallowed the color. He snaked his arm around my back and pulled me close, cupping my neck with his hand.

I struggled to stop a second full body blush. I had a pretty good idea of what was going through Logan's mind. His emotions overpowered mine.

"You are beautiful beyond words." His lips were a whisper away from mine.

He was the beautiful one.

He leaned even closer so that our lips were just touching. Neither of us moved.

"What color is my hair?"

He blinked once then buried his face in my neck, laughter shaking his body.

"Oops, was that a mood killer?" I asked.

Logan continued to laugh, the sound rich and deep. He placed a loud kiss to the side of my neck before pulling back. At least I still amused him.

"It's whatever color says 'I love Logan.'"

I pushed a hand into my hair and kept it from view. "You know, I don't even want to know."

"Probably not." Only his eyes were laughing at me now.

"Man, I need to find the receipt on this talent so I can return it."

Logan shook his head. "Never. How else would I know how you're feeling?"

"You're joking, right? Because I'm pretty sure I have the worst poker face in the world."

"That's true as well."

Rather than punching him in the gut, I pushed away with narrowed eyes.

"We're in the Archive Building." Logan's eyes still danced with mirth. I couldn't truly be upset with him. "Romona mentioned that you might have identified a new species a while back. I thought we could check to see if the little guys are recorded here."

"Oh. I'd forgotten about that." I slapped a hand to my face. "I really hope someone had already discovered them."

"Why?"

"Did Romona tell you what I named them?"

"No."

"Well, that's why."

With a smile I was still getting used to, Logan took my hand and guided me along the grass-covered path. "Let's go see if your genius is recorded for the rest of eternity."

"Oh, great."

After our quick jaunt through what was nothing short of an enchanted forest, we pushed through another revolving door. This time we emerged into a great library. Shelves upon shelves of books lined the perimeter of an open space reaching six stories into the air.

I'd suddenly stepped into a Disney version of heaven. Should I be looking for Belle?

People with wings strapped to their backs flitted around in front of the books, plucking them from their homes and bringing them down to be read.

No thank you, I was not going there again. Last time I'd tried flying with those contraptions I'd not only crashed into a floating chandelier but also an occupied table. I ended up wearing someone else's meal.

I was shaking my head before Logan could utter a word. "Nope. No way. Absolutely not."

"But you fly so gracefully," he teased.

"Yeah, you mean I crash so splendidly. I'm sure if I even tried that again, Alrik would be around to—"

Reality crashed down on my head. Alrik wouldn't be here to do anything anymore, ever again. He was in Hell, working with Satan.

Logan tactfully ignored my slip. "Aw, all you need is a little practice."

He just meant to tease, but his words pulled up a wash of emotion again. I wouldn't be here long enough to practice anything. All I had were the memories I could make before our time ran out.

Logan misread my face . . . or perhaps my hair color. "Don't worry. This isn't why we're here anyway. We're just passing through."

"It is quite a sight."

We walked down the middle aisle. To our left and right were long wooden tables with a smattering of people seated at them. Large books lay open in front of most of them.

"They're reading the history of their loved ones," Logan told me.

"What?"

I glanced at Logan, and he jerked his chin at the table in front of us where a middle-aged man sat reading a book several times thicker than an encyclopedia. He smiled softly smile even as I spotted the track marks of dried tears on his face. We brushed past his table, and I stole a peek over my shoulder. The man remained hunched over the book.

"These books hold the current stories of every living person on Earth. It's one of the ways people can catch up on their friends' and families' lives."

"This place is huge, but there can't possibly be enough books in this room for every single person in the world."

"The books are also stacked several rows back—as in, several thousand rows. You have to check in with a librarian first"—he pointed at a desk in the corner where a young woman stood in front of a monitor—"and then the book is brought to the forefront and you can go fetch it."

"But books? That seems like a rather impersonal way to find out about someone's life. Wouldn't a recording of some sort be better?"

He shrugged. "Have you ever read a book before? Some people would argue they're the best way to get sucked into a good story."

"Have you ever read someone's history here before?"

A muscle in Logan's jaw jumped—the only indication my question had affected him. I hadn't realized it would be a personal thing to ask.

"Never mind. You don't have to tell me."

He blew out a breath and tipped his head toward me. "No, that's a fair and simple question. Truth is I've been avoiding this place. I probably should have at least checked in on my parents, but I've been too . . . "

Despite not wanting to pry, I waited for Logan to continue. He ran a hand through his hair. "I suppose what I'm trying to say is that I dove into my new existence and did whatever I could to bury my past. With the exception of Kaitlin, this was my fresh start. I took hold of it and didn't look back. But I'm learning that burying my feelings isn't healthy. I need to make a trip here soon —if for no other reason than to honor my parents. They deserve that. Just not today, okay?"

"Yeah, of course."

"But if you have any questions about looking up someone's history, you should check with Kevin."

"Really?"

"Yeah, he visits at least once a week to check up on his family."

I didn't know why, but that surprised me. "Wow, that sounds . . . incredibly hard."

A strange look shadowed Logan's face, one I wasn't familiar with and gone as quickly as it came. "It's a little different for him. You'll have to ask him yourself, though. It's his story to tell."

My interest was piqued. "What does that mean?"

"Here we are." Logan pushed through a set of ancient-looking doors, cutting off my interrogation in the process.

This guy. Seriously?

I took my eyes off his face and scanned the new area. The room was small, with two unmarked doors and nothing else. I was underwhelmed.

"Ah, yep. Here we are all right." Logan smiled beside me. He pointed to the unmarked door on the right. "That door leads to the Artifacts Room. We're headed through this other door."

Before I could ask him more about the room we weren't entering, he'd opened the door on the left and let me walk in in front of him.

Ahhh . . . another white room.

"Is this a museum?"

Logan's low chuckle echoed off the bleached walls around us. Hallways stretched out forever in front of us and to the left and right. I took several steps to the left and encountered another hallway.

On the white walls of each hallway hung photographs of animals. Most I recognized. A few I didn't. Under each picture was a gold plaque with the name of the animal, dates listed—some with a date range like those seen on a tombstone—and then a person's name. Most of them had "Adam" listed, but a few here and there featured other people's names. It didn't take me long to figure out these were pictures of every species that ever existed, even the ones now extinct, and who first gave a name to them.

"Please tell me we don't have to search this whole place?" I did a slow turn. I couldn't even imagine how long it would take to check each picture.

"Naw, come here." He gestured to an empty spot on the wall with a tilt of his head. "We can look it up."

"Thank goodness. I don't want to waste any more time than I have to."

"You find spending time with me a waste?" The teasing note in his voice betrayed him.

I shot him a side glance. "That's not what I meant, and you know it."

"A couple months ago I might not have."

"Well, quite a bit has changed since then, hasn't it?" I lifted my eyebrows in a challenge to refute me.

"I certainly hope so." He turned to the wall and pressed his palm to it. A screen appeared in front of us, much like the ones at the Healing Center. At this point, things just appearing at a touch didn't surprise me in the least.

"All right, so, tell me what name you chose, and I'll see if it's in the system."

I grimaced and squeezed my eyes shut. "Maybe this wasn't a good idea."

Logan chuckled. "Come on, spit it out already."

"Ah, this is the worst." I covered my eyes with a hand before answering, "Star shooters." When I dropped my hand, I glared at him, daring him to laugh. He ran a hand over his mouth in an obvious attempt to wipe away any evidence of a smirk.

"I think it's cute."

I rolled my eyes.

He moved his fingers over the screen, and after a few moments, nothing came up. "Huh, that's strange. Maybe they'd already been discovered." Logan's eyes remained glued to the monitor, as though searching for something that wasn't actually there. "You sure that was the name you gave them? There wasn't any variation?"

"Yes, of course I remember. I just called them 'star shooter thingies,' and then Romona and I went and had lunch."

Logan shook beside me as he tried to bottle a laugh. His fingers moved over the screen again.

"What? It's not there. That means someone already named them, right?"

"Not exactly," he said. I'd been staring at him, but he directed my attention to the screen with a pointed finger.

"No." I rubbed my eyes and groaned. When I opened them, the picture on the screen hadn't changed. The same cute aquatic creature Romona and I had spotted was captured to perfection.

Its scales shimmered a pretty purple-blue. One tip of the star shape stuck out more than the rest. Two of the appendages opposite the long one were fish-like tales. The image came to life, and the other two points of the star flattened to the creature's body when it swam, allowing it to dart to and fro. It moved like an aquatic hummingbird.

Under the image in big bold letters for all to see was my name, AUDREY LYONS, along with the words STAR SHOOTER THINGIES.

"It's not that bad." Logan laughed behind me. I'd moved forward without realizing it, my nose only inches from the screen.

"Oh, those poor creatures. They sound like a bad frat party shot." I shook my head in shame.

Logan howled with laughter.

I wanted to complain, but I couldn't blame him his reaction. If the roles were reversed, I never would have let him live the embarrassment down. I deserved a good ribbing for this one.

"Can it be undone?"

Logan shook his head and wiped a tear from his eye. "'Fraid not. Those little guys will now and forevermore be known as"—he cleared his throat —"star shooter"—he cleared it again to get the last word out—"thingies."

I closed my eyes. "Promise me you'll never let me name another species."

He pulled me to his side and tucked me under his arm. My hand naturally came up to rest on his chest, and I looked up into his stormy gaze. He bent his head down and whispered, "Promise."

My heartbeat picked up. What were we talking about again? I nestled into Logan's embrace and sighed contentedly. Since when did a cotton t-shirt feel so good?

"It's nice to see this again." He brushed a hand through my hair and pulled some of it forward. The strands were a pretty lavender shade with only a few wisps of pink through it. "I'd like to believe this color means something good."

My stupid hair . . . but he was probably right. With his lips so close, I had to wonder why we were still talking. My eyes zeroed in on those kissable peppermint lips. With the limited time I had, I wanted as much of him as I could get.

That thought was like being doused with a pitcher of ice water. My body reacted in a visceral way—a chill shot straight up my spine, and my muscles locked. Logan's eyes widened. The hair he held in his hand turned to an icy blue before both our eyes. He dropped the strands and took hold of my face with both hands. My out of control emotions slammed into both of us, and I jerked out of his hold.

"What is it?" I hadn't heard the cold bite to Logan's words since before we bonded. "What just happened?"

"I . . . ah, um . . . I'm not sure what you mean." I stumbled over my words as if I were blindly walking through a field of rocks.

Logan's eyes narrowed. After several heartbeats, he swiped a hand down his face. When he looked at me again, his eyes were filled with sorrow.

He took a step closer to me; I forced myself not to retreat.

"Audrey"—the way he said my name caused my heart to ache—"you can lie to me with these"—he brought his fingers up and ghosted them over my lips —"but that doesn't lie to me"—he pointed at my hair—"and neither does this." He patted his chest. "Don't you feel it?"

I was honestly perplexed at what he meant.

His brow creased in frustration, and he thumped his chest. "In here, don't you feel me like I feel you?"

My eyes widened. He could feel my emotions even when we weren't touching? I still had the Logan-GPS, but I hadn't felt anything from him since we returned to this realm. The last time I'd felt anything of his without the aid of the empathy link was in Hell.

He read my answer on my face. "Well, I can feel you, and it seems an awful lot like you're not only shutting down on me, but you're hiding something. Something big. Something that scares you."

Right now *he* was scaring me. The level of intimacy he was describing felt . . . invasive. At least with the empathy link there was some sort of choice about whether to share emotions, but what he was talking about left me feeling vulnerable in a way I was far from comfortable with.

I took another step back. Logan's face twisted, a shadow of the agony I'd seen etched on his face when he was chained to that wall in Hell. Except this time, I was the cause of his pain.

"Audrey, please don't." He reached a hand toward me. He *did* know what I was feeling, because I was half a second away from bolting.

A sudden stabbing pain exploded in my chest. I cried out. Was he causing this sensation? Or was I? I pressed a hand to the ache and held the other up, warding him off. He'd almost closed the distance between us without me noticing. His jaw was clenched and his hands opened and closed to fists. The muscles in his forearms bunched up.

"I just." I choked on my words. "Right now I can't."

And then I fled.

MEMORIES

*T*he memories that blanketed this pond whispered through my subconscious. I'd passed the glassy waters right outside the Training Center almost every day since arriving in the afterlife. I had confessed my bond with Logan to Romona on the very bench where I was now seated. I stared at the blue-green depths. It looked so perfectly . . . normal. Its rim was speckled with people fishing or kids running in and out of the water along the edge and squealing in delight.

I knew the chilly bite of the water firsthand from when Logan had chucked me into the pond out of frustration. Frustration eventually led to mutual respect, which broke into an awkward limbo after we kissed. Awkwardness became doubt and, somehow in a crazy turn of events, translated into love in the end.

And that's what this was . . . the end. Logan thought this was the beginning, but I knew better. This was the beginning of the end.

Folding my body, I dropped my head into my hands, shielding my eyes from the view if not from the truth. Bear's paw landed on my knee. He'd joined me only minutes after I'd settled myself on the bench. His paw was his way of reminding me he was here to provide comfort. Comfort I wasn't sure I actually deserved.

Logan deserved more than this. He deserved more than me.

A weight dropped into the seat next to me and shook the bench.

I yelped and jolted upright, grabbing the seat to steady myself.

"Heard you've been visiting the archive building." Kevin's smile was so wide I'm pretty sure I could see his molars.

Bear jumped up on the bench on the other side of me and laid his giant head on my lap. I absently ran a hand over his soft, golden fur.

"Kevin. Geez. You know how to make an entrance, huh?" I squeezed my eyes shut and pinched the bridge of my nose. Kevin was an amazing friend. But I wasn't sure I was up to his level of chipper at the moment. Drained and emotional, I wasn't confident in my ability to fake normalcy.

He nodded with a blinding smile still in place. "I saw you over here and thought you looked a little down. Looks like you could use a friend right now."

I shrugged. "I have Bear."

Kevin leaned forward to survey my friend. "Yep. That's part of what tipped me off."

I looked at him. "What do you mean?"

His smiled dimmed and turned into a knowing up-tilt. "You haven't figured out this fluffy guy is pretty tuned in to your emotions yet? He was your Bear long before he was ever Battle Bear. His instincts are to comfort as well as protect. He's over here comforting. I figured that means you need it."

I looked down at Bear. The fur on his forehead scrunched as he looked up at me. A puddle of drool was already forming on my jeans. A small price to pay for good company.

Bear was my dog, but he was also his own. He came and went like a dog on Earth would never do. And when I took a moment to look back, I realized he was always around at exactly the right times. Just like how he'd found me today.

I looked into those big brown eyes and scratched the spot I knew he loved. *You little genius.* He guffawed out a noise that oddly resembled a laugh before closing his eyes and leaning into the scratch.

"So"—Kevin stretched his long body out; legs straight in front of him with ankles crossed and arms along the back of the bench—"wanna tell me what's up?"

Yes. My secrets were straining to be released.

"Not really," I answered.

"Hmm." Kevin looked at me from the corner of his eye, likely seeing through my façade but too polite to push the matter. "Why don't you tell me what you think of the Archives Building then? That a safe enough topic?"

He wasn't mad. He was simply looking for me to talk. I appreciated that and let out a deep breath. He wasn't going to give me the third degree.

"That place is definitely . . ." I struggled for the right way to explain it. "Otherworldly. But then again, look where we are." I swept a hand in the air to indicate the wonders of this realm.

Kevin nodded. His eyes fixed on the various groups of people in and surrounding the pond. A soft smile touched his lips. "Otherworldly. I suppose it is."

"Logan mentioned you spend time in the Archive Building pretty regularly."

For the first time, Kevin's smile faded. I studied his profile as his face tightened and relaxed again—almost as if I'd said something painful. Had I stuck my foot in my mouth without realizing it? Certainly wouldn't be the first time.

"Yeah." He nodded. "I spend a bit of time in there."

"I'm sorry," I began. I rested a hand on his shoulder. "It's really none of my business. I shouldn't have brought it up."

I hadn't even thought it through. For all I knew, Kevin could have a wife and kids still on Earth he was checking up on. I'd never even asked how old he was when he died. Considering Romona was in her seventies when she passed away, yet now looked to be in her late teens or early twenties, Kevin could have been any age when he passed.

"Naw." He turned his head and shot me a smile. "No worries, Audrey. I like to check up on my family. It's just . . ." He blew out a puff of air and squeezed the back of his neck before looking to the side and appraising me. I wasn't sure what was going on. "How much do you know about my past?"

I chewed on my lower lip, suddenly embarrassed I didn't know much. I was a lame friend. "I'm sorry, Kevin. I really only know that you're in Romona's building because you're waiting for some of your family members to arrive before settling into a permanent residence."

He nodded. "Yeah. Do you have any idea how long I've been here?"

I didn't detect any malice in his questioning, but I also wasn't following his train of thought. "Um, no. Was it rude that I didn't ask?"

Kevin started to laugh.

"What? I never know which questions are taboo here. I don't want to come across as offensive, but I also don't want to seem uninterested."

"Sorry, Audrey. I shouldn't laugh. I just wanted to know how much you knew of my past to know where to start. I've been here for eighteen years, four months, and three days."

"Well." I blinked twice. "That is very specific."

He ducked and bobbed his head at the same time—like that admission embarrassed him.

"So you haven't been aging since you arrived, because that looks about as old as you are now."

"No, I've been aging. In fact, I age every day. Since I arrived in this realm, I age as if it were a regular Earth day."

I widened my eyes as the truth penetrated my self-absorbed thoughts. "But that would mean that . . ."

That what? That Kevin had died as an infant? Died before birth? It meant that he'd died before he'd ever truly had a chance to live. "You grew up here?"

The questions ricocheted around my mind, and I studied his face, looking for answers. It wasn't my business, it truly wasn't. But there was a story here I never knew existed.

"My mother was sixteen when she became pregnant with me. Two years younger than you are right now. She was young and scared and didn't want anyone to know. And so after hiding her pregnancy for three months, she aborted me."

A gasp escaped my mouth at the same time my hands flew up to cover it. Kevin stared at me with sad eyes as I tried to tap down my emotions. I forced my hands to my lap, thumping Bear, and absently twisted my fingers. "Kevin, I—"

His warm hand landed on both of mine, stopping their restless movement. A wistful joy saturated my heart . . . straight from Kevin.

"She was so young, Audrey. And her heart still aches over what she did. I have brothers and sisters now. I have a whole family on Earth that I'm looking forward to meeting in person someday. But in the meantime, I like to check in on them from time to time."

"But aren't you . . . I don't know . . . upset at her? Angry at the life you never got to live?"

He nodded. "Yeah, I could look at it that way. But tell me, what would that really accomplish? Do I wish I'd had a chance to live a long life? Yeah, there are times I think about that. Maybe even a lot. But rather than dwell on what might be perceived as things I was robbed of, I choose to look forward to the day I'm reunited with my family. The day I see my mother, look her in the eyes, and tell her I love her . . . and that I forgive her. She needs to hear that."

Kevin sat back in his seat and turned his attention to the pond. "That's a day I'm really looking forward to. That will be a great day."

A single tear slipped down Kevin's cheek. He let the wetness fall to his chest as a soft smile overtook his face. "I choose love and forgiveness, Audrey, because the same has been given to me."

Kevin left hours ago, yet I was sitting on the same bench. Bear's head lay in my lap as I stroked him. His snore and the large wet spot on my legs said he'd long since fallen asleep.

I didn't want to leave here—this realm. I didn't want to give up all I had and spend eternity in misery. I wanted to be with friends and family, and I wanted to be here to welcome the ones still on Earth when their time came.

But there was nothing to be done. I'd committed an unforgivable offense by freeing Satan, and I couldn't even wrap my brain around the repercussions. Was there a way to count the lives that would be affected? If there was, did I even want to know?

My heartbeat picked up as my Logan-GPS told me he was near.

I couldn't do this alone anymore. He had to know what I'd done. Letting him fuse his soul to someone who was going to leave was just . . . selfish beyond comprehension. What had I been thinking? I had to tell him so we could break the bond. It would be hard, but not yet impossible.

No bonding ceremony for us. It would be cruel. He deserved nothing but the absolute truth.

Fingers wisped through my hair.

"You're sad."

Bear jumped off my lap and trotted off without a backward glance.

"What gave it away?"

Logan moved around the bench to sit next to me. He ran his hand through my hair again and brought it in front of my face. The strands were grey-blue. He let them slip through his fingers and pulled back, leaving what might as well have been a cavern of distance between us.

"I'm sorry for running away."

Logan angled toward me. One leg bent up on the bench so he could fully face me. I mirrored his posture. Our knees brushed against each other when one of us shifted, but besides that we were very . . . separate.

A crease formed between Logan's brows as he studied me.

Ducking my head to avoid his gaze, I chewed on my lip.

"We need to talk," I whispered.

He nodded. "Your place or mine?"

My mouth quirked. "That sounded really cheesy . . . and a little seedy."

With a twinkle in his eye, he did a one-shoulder shrug.

"All right, let's go back to your place," I said. *That way I can kick myself out after I've revealed the truth.*

20

COMING CLEAN

I was pacing. Most likely wearing a hole in Logan's rug. Whatever, he could materialize a new one. The real problem was I couldn't find words, which meant I couldn't stop pacing.

Logan sat on his couch in front of me. But from the look of things, he was just as wound up as I was. He leaned forward with his arms draped across his knees and hands hanging as he watched me walk back and forth. The crease between his eyebrows had returned, but he stayed silent. Whenever I glanced at him, a muscle in his face would jump.

Besides that he was a statue. "Would it help if you sat?"

I jumped at the sound of his voice. "Huh? What?"

The crease deepened. "Do you want to—"

"No, sorry. I heard you." I stopped pacing and pressed the palms of my hands into my eyes until I saw stars.

All my fault. All my fault. All my fault, my mind relentlessly chanted. My secret was a festering wound that wouldn't heal until I cut it out.

And to cut it out, I had to admit to someone it existed.

I had to admit to Logan it existed.

Removing my hands from my eyes, I found Logan's. "It's all my fault."

The words hung in the air between us. I waited for his reaction. And . . . nothing.

"Well?" I prompted.

"Care to give me a little more information than that?" he asked.

I gestured wildly with my hands. "Everything. All of it. Everything everyone's been talking about. Satan's imminent attack. His release. It's all my fault."

"How?" Besides the slight tilt in his head, not a muscle so much as twitched.

Really, that was all he had to say? "Does it matter?"

He straightened, shoulders back and hands gripping the couch cushions. "Yes, of course it does."

"Okay, first let me show you something."

"All right."

I turned away from Logan and lifted the back of my shirt high enough that he was sure to see a good deal of the growing darkness there. A physical representation of my mistake—and the consequence I would pay for it. I squeezed my eyes shut and waited for his outburst. He was going to blow for sure. But the room remained silent for several minutes.

"Love, why are you showing me your back?"

"What?" I turned my neck until I could see him. Logan's stare was blank. "It's right there. It's huge and black and ugly . . . and growing." I lifted my shirt higher so I could see the evidence of my cursed soul myself. Yep, still there.

"Audrey, I don't know what you're talking about. I don't see anything."

He couldn't see the mark? Was I the only one who could? There was actually a little bit of relief in that. Dropping my shirt, I turned to face him.

I rubbed my forehead. The threat of a headache beat behind my eyes. He couldn't see the darkness. So how was I to make him understand?

"Logan." I looked into those beautiful cobalt eyes. "We can't be together."

He shot to his feet and advanced. I took two hurried steps back.

"What? Why? You need to start explaining all this to me, quickly." His fists clenched at his sides.

I had no fear he'd use them against me, but his reserve of patience had apparently just run out.

"Well, it's . . . complicated." I twisted my hands, mimicking the churning in my gut.

"Uncomplicate it for me." The look in his eyes said *who do I need to destroy?*

My brain . . . blanked. Logan's hands crackled as he struggled to maintain his composure—his frustration leaked out in unseen waves.

I wasn't scared. I was . . . in awe.

"Audrey." One word. A command to start talking.

And so I did. I spilled it all without holding back one gory, ugly detail. The trek through the rings, how I'd somehow slipped into his mind at one point, our party getting sent back to our realm piece by piece until Joe and I were the only ones left. And finally what had happened in the cell he'd been strung up in. How my sword shattered, accidentally stabbing Joe when I went after Alrik, and Satan's release and promise to me.

By the end of my tale, my cheeks were drenched. Logan had taken his seat again on the couch, and I sat facing him on an armchair. The length of the coffee table was all that was between us, but it might as well have been an impenetrable wall for how isolated I felt.

Silence hung in the air.

Then the room exploded.

"No!" Logan roared. He shot to his feet and flung the glass coffee table against the wall. The furniture shattered into a million pieces. Lightning shot from his hand and connected to the window behind my head.

He pointed at something to my left, and a chair exploded. Burned stuffing littered the air around me, assaulting my sense of smell.

He was . . . unhinged.

"Logan." I jumped to my feet, intending to rush to him.

"No." A deadly calm overtook his features as he held his hands up to ward me off. Blue-and-silver lightning crackled around each finger, each knuckle, and halfway up his arm. His breath puffed out as if he'd just run a marathon. With each exhale, his hands sparked.

Throughout his rampage, I'd been more startled than afraid. But now the fear came. The fear that even though I was going to lose him eventually, I'd lost him sooner than I thought.

Was this anger at me? Rage at what I'd done—or at my selfishness in not telling him sooner?

But accusations didn't spit from his mouth. Instead he said, "No one is going to take you from me."

My eyes widened.

He went on. "I don't care what deals you may or may not have made. There isn't a being in existence who will take you from me. You. Are. Mine."

Steel rods pieced my heart.

"Logan." My voice softened, and I took a tentative step forward.

One hand raised higher even though he'd already warded me off. With the couch behind him, he'd have to hurdle over it or blow it up in order to retreat. There was a feral look in Logan's eyes I'd never seen before. My stoic-masked warrior had revealed a chink in his armor.

Me.

"Logan," I said his name again as my fingers grazed his jawline. The empathy link sprang to life between us. A sense of dread and desperation flooded me, like that of a dying man struggling to take just one more breath.

Logan was falling apart, right in front of me.

I pushed aside his feelings as best I could. Buried my own sorrow, guilt, and shame and focused on him. On us. That even though we'd only been given a speck of time together, at least we'd been blessed with that. I gathered all the love in my heart for him, and I poured it into our connection, determined to overwhelm him with positive emotions.

He crushed me to his chest. One of my hands remained gently placed on his face, and the other reached around to bury itself in his hair. Logan's face pressed against my neck. His arms were wrapped around my body in a vice-grip, as if he was determined to never let go. One wrapped completely around my waist, and the other crossed over my back with a hand, securing my shoulder.

Logan must have regained control over his powers because I wasn't getting electrocuted. The longer we stood, the more our emotions aligned. Comfort and love flowed in currents back and forth to each other.

I relaxed in his embrace, unsure of anything but this perfect moment we were experiencing in the middle of our mutual storm.

"Audrey." A whispered prayer into my hair. Logan shuddered.

I adjusted my grip on him, wrapping both my arms securely around his neck, as if I could hold him together by sheer force of will.

Then he was pulling back, and a sound of protest left my throat. My lips only began to form the word no—the actual word was smothered by Logan's kiss. The action was as desperate as he'd been a moment before, but I welcomed the wildness of it. That wildness was truth. There were no more hidden secrets or half-truths between us. And what this kiss might lack in finesse, it made up for in raw emotion.

I felt Logan compose himself through the kiss and empathy link. He was a star that had exploded but was now reversing time and tucking every burning ember and ray of light back into the places they belonged. Our kiss ended softly when he pulled his head back and used both hands to keep mine in place.

Smart man. He knew me well. Without restraint, I would have sought out those delicious lips for another taste.

I had to blink a few times to clear my kiss-fogged mind. Logan's smug smirk told me he knew exactly why I needed those few extra moments to compose myself. I rolled my eyes. Truth was he had a right to be smug, and I wasn't sure my voice wouldn't come out breathy if I tried to talk. An eye roll was the best I could do.

His smile faded, and his features ironed back out to warrior mode. His mouth and brow straight slashes. His eyes focused and intent.

I stared into the familiar face of my old mentor. The mask he had presented to me. The face I'd trained with for those first several months of our relationship.

Logan had slipped into his get-stuff-done mode. I struggled not to smile at his seriousness.

With hands on my shoulders, he guided me to a seated position on the couch. My gaze bounced around the room before focusing on him. Glass lay like splattered blood on the ground. Stuffing from exploded furniture littered the floor, and the skeletal remains of the unfortunate pieces of furniture bent at unnatural angles.

Logan had made a mess.

A giggle slipped out of me. I slapped a hand over my mouth and snapped my widened eyes back to him. *Shoot.* That wasn't supposed to happen.

Logan glanced over the carnage and shrugged. That simple gesture told me all I needed to know. He would destroy the world for me if he had to. What was one living room? Especially one that could be cleaned with a few concentrated minutes of materializing and dematerializing items.

"Audrey, I'll find a loophole."

I was shaking my head without even realizing it.

"I will," he said forcefully. "This isn't the end. There is no conceivable way that this is the end of us. This is the beginning."

My eyes filled with wetness at his words. At the fierceness with which he spoke them. I might have gone to Hell and back to rescue him, but this was a man who was telling me he would spend eternity searching for a way to destroy Hell itself for me.

But that wasn't the existence I wanted for him.

"No, Logan. What possible loopholes could there be? Satan was very specific about what would happen to me. The price of his freedom would be paid by the one who released him. The Creator himself set those terms. Nothing in any of our realms can change that. I stabbed Joe. I'm responsible for Satan's newfound freedom. I'm the reason our realm is in jeopardy. That's a stain too big to be removed from my soul. The time we have now is a gift I don't want to waste. But I won't shackle you to me. That would be the same as condemning you to an eternity of loneliness. Someday there will be someone else—"

"No." He nearly shouted the word, halting my speech. "No," he said again. "I will fight with every bit of my existence to keep you by my side. There will never be someone else. You are it for me. Forever."

I took a deep breath. My heart melted and broke at the same time. My next words would hurt both of us.

"For your sake, I hope you're wrong."

After Logan settled down, he riled himself right back up again when I told him I didn't want to go to Joe, Hugo, or the Creator. We'd had a fairly lengthy disagreement about that. Logan didn't let up until he saw the pure fear in my eyes. When that happened he agreed, for my sake, not to seek Their help. And so as a result, he was on a hunt to find a loophole to my damnation another way.

Logan was a man on a mission. I was pretty sure he wasn't even stopping to sleep. Rather than an idyllic last few days together, I hardly saw him.

I hardly saw anyone.

All my friends were running from one thing to another, or else they were missing in action on some secret defense plan for our realm. And me? I'd just been left adrift.

The original plan had been to train with Romona and Logan, but then he'd been kidnapped, and now everyone knew Satan was on the loose—no doubt with his gaze fixed on our realm—so all normal activity had been suspended. So that meant no training, and no active assignments for me since I was technically still in training. If anyone should be out there making sure the heavenly realm was protected, it was me. But even as the training center was a flurry of activity, I might as well have been invisible. Satan could literally come for me at any moment, and I was being robbed of my goodbyes. That made me . . . furious.

I didn't regret telling Logan the truth. He deserved to know. But his stubborn refusal to believe I'd doomed myself to an eternity in Hell took him away from me as he . . . Well, I actually wasn't even sure what he was doing every day. He was a mystery.

On the rare occasion I did get to spend some time with him, he'd kiss my forehead and tell me he was going to fix this. Like my unwilling bargain was a broken toy he could glue back together. I didn't know everything, but I knew enough to know that wasn't how these things worked. I'd crossed a line that couldn't be uncrossed.

I wanted this time with him, with my friends, and I was being denied it. Perhaps that's what I deserved. Really, this was just borrowed time anyway.

"Hey, wait up."

I glanced behind me to catch sight of Kaitlin jogging toward me, blonde ponytail bouncing. I slowed my stride so she could easily catch up. With nothing to do, I spent a great deal of time walking aimlessly around the perimeter of our city.

She reached me and wasn't even out of breath. "So, it's off then?"

"Huh?"

"The bonding ceremony . . . You called it off after all?"

Truth was, Logan and I hadn't spoken of the ceremony after I laid the 'my soul is going to spend eternity in Hell for my sins' bomb on him. Yeah, I'd say there would be no soul fusing in the future, but I hadn't told anyone anything one way or another.

"Um, why do you ask? Did someone say something to you?"

Kaitlin cocked her head. The blonde silk of her ponytail disappeared behind her right shoulder. "No. It's just that you said it was happening in a few days, and I haven't heard anything about it. It's been a few days . . . so I figured . . ."

She let the statement hang in the air between us.

"I suppose it's on hold for an indeterminate amount of time."

"What's wrong?" she asked point-blank.

What wasn't wrong? The 'groom' was MIA most of the time on what was most likely some random fool's errand, I expected to get sucked back to Hell at any moment, and the time I wanted to spend with my loved ones was slipping through my fingers like sand because of an impending siege on our realm that I'd unintentionally helped orchestrate when I let Satan free.

"Nothing."

"You know, you and Logan have been acting really strange ever since—"

"Oh, come now, luv—you have so much free time you can speculate over your friends' romantic entanglements? I was under the assumption that dear Audrey and I were the only two hunters in the realm not being run ragged right now."

Saved by the sarcastic bite of Morgan's British humor. I was grateful for that, especially since I knew Kaitlin wouldn't, perhaps couldn't, back down from his taunts.

"Seriously, Morgan, we were having a private conversation here. Is this really any of your concern?" She moved to flip her ponytail over her shoulder only to find the hair was already there. Morgan ruffled Kaitlin's feathers like no one I'd ever met. I'd be willing to bet they had a history of some sort that my fair-haired friend wanted concealed.

Morgan shrugged. "I'm bored out of my mind these days. So why not make this my concern? Not much else to do."

"Are you seriously going to stand here and annoy us simply because you're bored?"

"Annoying you? Who knew?" He grinned. "That gives me extra incentive. Cheers."

Kaitlin's face turned a shade of purple-red I hadn't seen before.

I took a concerned step back and checked her ears for steam.

"You . . ." was all she could get out.

"Are incredibly handsome? Why yes, I already knew that. Thank you for the compliment."

Kaitlin's nose scrunched up as if she smelled something extremely unpleasing.

Morgan pulled his lips back from his teeth as if he'd just witnessed a hideous accident. "Oh, luv, you should never do that thing you're doing right now." He twirled a finger in her face. "It might get stuck that way, and that would be a supreme disappointment to men everywhere."

The look dropped from Kaitlin's face, and she stared at him with a slack jaw. "Do you even think before words come spewing from your mouth?"

"I try very hard not to. Thank you for noticing."

"Ah, I can't. I just can not." Kaitlin turned toward me with pinched features. "I'm headed back to the training center. This whole 'Satan on the loose' thing has us all working double time. Let's talk soon though. I want to make sure you're all right."

"Sure." I nodded. "I'd like that." A half-truth wasn't truly a lie . . . right?

She waved goodbye and disappeared in the direction she'd come from.

"I accept gratitude in the form of verbal or physical affirmation. Whatever you're most comfortable with." Reclined against the back of the park bench, his arms and ankles crossed, he was the picture of male arrogance. I understood why Kaitlin was annoyed.

He opened his arms to me. "So it'll be a hug then?"

I rolled my eyes.

He inclined his head apologetically. "I'm saving these lips for someone else. Nasty business this, no kissing issue. But I suppose we both know there are ways to get around it."

He wiggled his eyebrows at me suggestively. *Ew.*

"Of course," he went on, "I also wouldn't fancy having my handsome mug marred by your beloved." Morgan indicated his face with his hand. He was undeniably handsome—yet he still bore many of the scars from his torture in Hell. He might no longer look like Frankenstein's monster, but several lines still crisscrossed his cheeks and forehead.

If I thought for a moment he was seriously trying to flirt with me, I would have walked away. But as strange as the development was, I was morbidly drawn to Morgan now. I felt a sense of kinship with him, which disturbed me.

I pinched the bridge of my nose. "What exactly am I supposed to be thanking you for?"

"Why, getting rid of Blondie of course, so that you didn't have to continue lying to her."

"I wasn't—"

"I have a knack for running that particular bird off. It's usually quite vexing, but it came in handy today. It's rather odd that she reacts so strongly to me, don't you think?"

"Probably because she hates your guts."

"Oh, Audrey, you above all should know there's a thin line between love and hate."

I ignored the jab and glanced in the direction where Kaitlin had disappeared. Even if there had been something between them before he sided with evil, he'd have a difficult time wooing that maiden now. She seemed determined to steer clear of him at all costs.

I was confident that, either way, Kaitlin could take care of herself.

"Well, good luck with that." I saluted Morgan and turned to continue my aimless walking.

"I figured someone who only had a few days of freedom left, at best, would be doing more than roaming around by herself."

I stopped so suddenly my feet crossed in front of each other, causing me to wobble. Finding my footing, I straightened and swung to face Morgan.

"What did you say?"

His mouth was in a straight line now, no hint of an amused smirk peeking through.

"Logan's spent the better part of the last two days grilling me for information. I'm sure he hasn't told me the full story, but I'm bright enough to fill in the blanks. Especially since I got a look at you shortly after your return."

The bottom of my stomach dropped out. "What do you know?"

"You see, the problem with deals with the Devil, luv," he said, ignoring my question completely. "You can never get out of them without paying a price. It seems to me that you may have bargained away all of your chips. Very unwise."

"I didn't bargain anything. I was tricked."

"Well, yes, they don't refer to him as 'the Great Deceiver' for no reason. Perhaps it makes you understand how Eve first fell prey to his schemes? And Adam followed right along. Tell me, have you ever given their story much thought?"

"Adam and Eve?"

"I've often wondered if it was the serpent who deceived Adam as well, or if Adam purposely damned himself to stay by Eve's side. Maybe he couldn't stand to be parted from her."

I blinked at Morgan. Was he saying what I thought he was? That Logan would willingly follow me into eternal damnation?

A sad smile touched his lips. Morgan pushed off from the bench and shoved his hands in his pockets, his shoulders hunched up near his ears for a moment. His pose screamed of hidden vulnerability.

Then his shoulders dropped, and his usual swagger returned.

"Well, it's been lovely talking with you, but I have a feisty blonde to nettle. Perhaps if I get good enough at it, they'll find something for me to do."

He set off but stopped after a few steps, turning his head to look back at me. "For what it's worth, Audrey, I hope you're able to take in as much beauty and enjoyment as you can. Take it from one who knows. However bad you're imagining your impending servitude might be, it will undoubtedly be worse. And I'm sorry for that."

His long strides ate up the distance quickly, and soon he, too, was out of sight. I stood there, staring at nothing. His words about Adam and Eve—and Logan—echoed in my ears. For the first time since returning from Hell, I was terrified for someone other than myself.

21

DESPERATE TIMES

*O*organ's cryptic talk about Adam and Eve didn't just disturb me, it terrified me. Only minutes after finishing the conversation with him, I abandoned my wandering and bolted for Logan's cottage. I was prepared to camp out on his couch if I had to, until he returned and gave me answers about what he'd been up to.

And what was I going to do next? The black mark on my back had grown to almost a foot in diameter. I couldn't shake the feeling that when it got to a certain size, or reached a particular part of my body, that would be the end. I just didn't know the size or its destination.

Was my only move to protect Logan going to the Creator? I wasn't willing to do that for myself, but to make sure Logan stayed safe—in *this* realm and not the one buried deep within the Earth—I would risk getting hurled to Hell. If Logan was looking to take my place in Hell, I had to talk some sense into him. If not, he'd force my hand and I'd have to go to the Creator. Hopefully it wouldn't come to that.

My feet itched to pace, but I forced myself to remain rooted to the cushion beneath me. A half-hour after I'd planted myself in his living room, I felt Logan's presence nearby. Finally the hinges on his cottage door announced his arrival.

Evening had come, and I hadn't turned on any of his lights. I was sitting in the shadows like a stalker, waiting to be acknowledged.

Logan slammed the front door after he entered then punched a fist into the wall, leaving a rounded hole. He pressed both hands to the flat wood, and his shoulders and head sagged.

Did he not know I was here? He could feel me through our bond just as well as I could him.

I held my breath as I waited for his next move. He stood like a statue, so stuck in his thoughts that my presence must not be registering. Was he even breathing?

The cottage remained quiet until I heard something dripping, the sound similar to a leaky faucet. But this was Heaven, and things here didn't leak. Which meant . . .

Logan's hand was dripping blood onto the marble tile.

I sprang into action.

Logan startled and spun when my hand connected with his shoulder. He really hadn't realized I was here. I took a step back when I saw the wild look in his eyes. His hair was a disheveled mess, and not in a stylish way. In the sticking-up-at-weird-spots-since-he'd-run-his-hands-through-it-and-grabbed-it-out-of-frustration-a-few-too-many-times way.

"What happened? What's going on?"

For a few beats, the only sound coming from him was the continued dripping of blood from the cuts on his hand.

"Can you seriously ask me that?" he snapped.

I took another step back.

"Are you mad at me?" My voice was small.

"At you? No." He ran his fingers through his hair again, leaving streaks of red in his hand's wake. Regret crossed his expression, and he said, "What am I doing?" His arms shot forward, and before I realized his intent, I was smooshed against his chest—face first into his t-shirt, squeezed so tight I could hardly breathe.

Definitely more uncomfortable than endearing. I pushed back a little to get a breath of air.

"I'm so sorry," Logan went on. "I'm just not going to lose you."

His grip tightened, and my heart sank . . . because he *was* going to lose me.

I cleared my throat. "Hey, why don't we take care of that hand of yours? Then maybe we can sit down and have a talk?" I pushed gently against his chest again, and this time he let me go and let me lead him over to the kitchen sink where I washed the blood off.

As I held his hand over the sink, the red swirling down the drain wasn't what sent my heart pounding—the fact that hardly anything filtered through from the empathy link was what freaked me out. Logan looked over my shoulder at nothing while I worked. The worst hadn't even happened yet, and the man I loved was already turning into a shell of himself.

I secured the bandage around Logan's hand. He could get it fixed easily at the Healing Center in the morning; tonight we had more pressing matters. I led him back to the couch, took his face in both hands, and forced his attention. Still, all that came through the empathy link was a numbing void. What was happening?

"Talk to me," I demanded. Finally a pinprick of emotion leaked though.

Fear. But he locked it up quickly and gently returned my hands to my lap, pulling his away. He clearly didn't want to be touched right now.

Okay, I could respect that. I didn't like it, but I could respect it. Sometimes emotions were so overwhelming that the thought of sharing them with someone else added to the burden. I wished he'd let me bear some of his pain, but that wasn't natural for Logan, and perhaps we just weren't there yet in our relationship.

Pain twinged in my chest as I realized we'd never have time to "get there."

"Really, Audrey, it's nothing. You know I'm just trying to find a way for us to stay together. I'm sure I'll figure something—"

"Don't lie to me, Logan." My voice was level, but his eyes widened. "And perhaps more importantly, don't lie to yourself."

"But, Audrey—"

I shook my head. "How much more time are you going to waste?"

He opened his mouth to answer, but I wouldn't let him proceed.

"I know you talked to Morgan about me. You can talk to whomever you want, you can search through the ancient texts, try to bribe angels, or whatever it is you do every day, but the facts aren't going to change. A price has to be paid for what's been done."

Logan shot to his feet. "Then I'll pay it instead."

I stood as well and craned my neck to look into his eyes. That was exactly what I was afraid of. "No. You stop whatever you're doing right now. I'm begging you. Begging you to stop and just be with me, here, now, while we can. This is my mistake. This is my price to pay."

"You wouldn't have even been in Hell if not for me. If I hadn't kissed you, you could have stayed safely in this realm. That would have been better."

I sucked in a lungful of air, suddenly angry. "There are so many things wrong with that, I don't even know where to start." A tendril of hair turned red. I batted it out of my way. "First, do you believe if we weren't bonded I would have left you in Hell to rot? Second, Satan was using *you* to get to *me* the whole time, so I was the reason you were down there to begin with. Third, you're not the one who literally stabbed the Son of God. I get that lucky title all to myself, and fourth . . . fourth . . . if you're saying you regret kissing me in the first place, I will hate you forever."

I poked his chest on the last weak point of my argument. I'd backed Logan up to the wall without even realizing it. He was breathing hard, jaw grinding. But I was breathing harder. For me, anger was probably a little too quick to mingle with fear.

But I wasn't the only one who was angry. "First," he bit out and took a step forward, forcing me to take one back, "if you think there is anything short of eternal damnation that would make me regret bonding us, then I obviously haven't done a good enough job of expressing my feelings for you—something I will fix the minute we're done with this ridiculous argument."

My thoughts ran away from me before I could beat them into submission, and my entire body flushed. But Logan wasn't done.

"Second, bonded or not, I would rather you left me in that den of horrors for a lifetime than watch you not only get taken from me but also spend an eternity with a similar fate.

"Third, I will find a way out of this. Even if you've already given up, I will *never* give up on you. And fourth"—He backed me up until I bumped into the couch, lost my balance, and sat down. Leaning in he put his hands on either side of my head—"we both know there is no scenario in which you would hate me forever."

A cocky grin appeared on his mouth that I both wanted to slap off and smother with a kiss. Vexing. He narrowed his eyes at me, practically daring me to do either.

"Well—"

I wasn't sure what my rebuttal was going to be, but it didn't matter because Logan crushed his lips to mine before I could get another word out. Whatever was going to escape my mouth was swallowed by his, and like every other time we'd come together like this, rational thought flitted right out of my brain.

He had skills. Mad-crazy, mind-boggling kissing skills. So good, in fact, I had no idea whose emotions belonged to whom as his mouth pressed against mine time and time again. Anger, fear, love, devotion, and desire all swirled into a tornado of feelings that were impossible to segregate. But who had time for sorting out feelings when they were kissing the love of their life? Certainly not me.

Logan pulled back, and like always, I mindlessly protested and leaned forward. He chuckled at my response. This was getting embarrassing.

When the fog cleared from my brain, we were both staring into each other's clear eyes. He uttered one word before diving in for a second helping.

"Mine."

It branded my heart and my soul. I knew that whatever lay ahead, we were going to face it together.

I opened my eyes and then slammed them closed again against the brightness streaming through Logan's large front window. I went to rub my face, but my arms were trapped.

Huh?

I looked down. A tanned, toned forearm was not only draped across my waist, but pinning my left arm in place. My other arm was somewhere above eye level. Whatever pillowed my head radiated heat and was oddly lumpy. My right hand was also really warm. I craned my neck to see the traitorous hand clasping Logan's.

Shoot!

How did I end up curled into him on his couch? I remembered a kiss, and that was about it. Did I pass out from lack of oxygen? It would have been worth it.

Whatever the reason, this was still an embarrassing situation. What if I drooled in my sleep? What if the weight of my head had caused his arm to go numb and he was too polite to shove me off? Why hadn't he woke me up and sent me home?

I mentally slapped myself. *Focus!* I needed to figure out how was I going to discreetly get off this couch. I shimmied my way toward the edge, ready to slide off the make-shift bed, when Logan made a sleepy sound and used the arm around my waist to haul me more firmly against him.

Ahh. Double shoot!

I tried to shimmy away again only to be hauled back a second time. But this time, a bolt of amusement shot through the empathy link.

I gritted my teeth and swatted at his hands. His arm was definitely higher now than the first time he'd pulled me back. Boys. My body shook with the rumble of Logan's laughter. I pried his heavy arm away and rolled off the couch . . . straight onto the ground with a resounding thump. Logan's chuckles turned into full-blown laughs.

I rubbed my hip.

"You're awful. You know that, right?" I called up to him.

His head appeared right above mine, and I yelped.

"We both know you don't believe that."

"You know nothing," I snipped back.

"I know enough." He wiggled his eyebrows.

I put my hand on his face and pushed.

"Pig," I said under my breath as I got to my feet and headed to the bathroom. I needed a toothbrush, STAT.

His laughs followed me down the hall, and although I was mildly annoyed, hearing him happy brought a secret smile to my face.

The grin stayed in place until I closed the bathroom door and turned to look at myself in the mirror . . . then screamed.

There was a thud down the hall, and then seconds later the bathroom door burst open. Logan was fully alert, all traces of humor washed away.

"What are you doing?" I yelled. "I could have been peeing in here."

His brow furrowed. "You screamed."

"Yeah, 'cause of this." I pointed a finger at my head.

Logan's features relaxed, and his eyes twinkled. He swept a hand down his face until he reached his mouth and covered it.

"Are you laughing at me?"

He shook his head, hand still over his mouth.

I pointed at the door. "Out."

He nodded once and left. As soon as the door clicked shut, I heard his bellows of laughter.

"I can hear you," I shouted.

"I know," he yelled back.

Shaking my head, I turned to the mirror. My hair looked like a birdie had made a nest in it, left, and then a rat had decided he wanted to give it a go. And the colors closely resembled Rainbow Brite's magical horse's mane.

I rubbed my eyes then pinched my nose.

"I think you're adorable," Logan yelled from somewhere in the house. Less to make me feel better and more to annoy me.

Jerk. This mess I called hair was at least eighty percent his fault. If he hadn't run his hands through it so many times yesterday evening, it wouldn't be this crazy.

My cheeks warmed at the thought, and I watched all the red lighten to magenta.

Maybe I wasn't as mad about that part as I was telling myself.

I shut my eyes and materialized a brush. Time to get to work. This nest wasn't going to fix itself. Over an hour later, I emerged from Logan's bathroom. I'd taken the opportunity to shower and change into fresh clothes as well as brush my teeth and fix my hair. The look on Logan's face when I sat down at the kitchen counter was worth the extra effort. I may have applied a little makeup as well. But he didn't need to know that.

He paused from making us breakfast. "Wow, you look amazing."

I cocked my head. "You mean I didn't look amazing when I woke up this morning?"

"Oh, you looked amazing all right. Just a different type of amazing."

I stuck my tongue out at him.

He winked. "You do realize that is in no way a turn-off to me."

When he turned back to the stove, I turned my hair brown again.

"Should we talk about last night?"

His shoulders tensed for a moment before he forced them to relax. "Talk, or reenact?"

Stupid hair, stay brown.

"Logan, you know what I mean. Talk about the big stuff we brought up before all the, you know, other stuff happened."

Brown, brown, brown.

Logan scooped something out of the pan in front of him and set the fluffy concoctions on two plates. He turned and put them down on the island then walked around it to take a seat next to me.

I looked down and smiled. He'd made me an omelet.

"Is this the only thing you know how to cook?" I asked.

He smiled back. "No, but I was feeling a little nostalgic today."

"Nostalgic about hiding out in a bunker in my dad's tool shed?"

"Something like that." His smile widened. "Eat up."

I dug my fork into the fluffy eggs already remembering how delicious they'd been last time.

"Audrey."

I stopped with my utensil mid-air, my mouth already half open. Logan reached over and steered the food home. He continued when I started to chew.

"I've considered what you said last night, and I see your point. I've been running myself like crazy these past few days. I've been a man obsessed, but I haven't considered what you need from me right now. So as long as you can accept that, I'm not giving up hope; I want to spend more time together. With or without this blood price hanging over our heads."

I went to interrupt him, but he silenced me with a tilted head and raised eyebrows, then continued. "It is *our* heads, not yours. We're in this together. But regardless of anything else going on, we should be together now."

I nodded my agreement.

"Great." He smiled broadly and then shoveled his omelet into his mouth, finishing his meal before I'd even gotten through half of mine. "Okay, so I gotta head out for a bit."

I started choking on my bite of egg. Logan slapped my back until the chunk was dislodged.

"What?" I croaked. "You just said we were going to spend time together until . . . well until we can't anymore."

"Yep. You're absolutely right." He stood and walked around the island to set his plate in the sink.

I watched him with wide eyes. He came back around and quickly kissed my forehead, the touch too brief to pick up much from the empathy link. I had a feeling that was the point.

"I'll be back soon. I promise. I need to handle a couple of things, and then the day is ours."

With that, he walked around the corner and out of view. He was really leaving me. What was happening?

The front door opened. I heard some muted shuffling, and then Logan yelled back to me, "Audrey, you have a guest to keep you company until I get back," and then the front door closed.

This was surreal.

A soft pitter-patter of footsteps echoed off Logan's wood floor before Bear appeared. I shoved a huge bite of omelet in my mouth and jumped off the stool.

"Hey, buddy. It's good to see you."

He sat on his haunches, and I knelt on the floor in front of him while he raised one of his overgrown paws and put it on my shoulder. I hugged my old friend. His chin came down on my opposite shoulder, and his furry arm kept me anchored to his warm body. I smiled into his fur, soaking in the comfort only Bear could give. He was a good boy. I was going to miss him.

It wasn't long before wetness coated my cheeks. As if he knew the reason for my sadness, he adjusted his chin so that I was more securely pressed against his warmth.

I'm not sure how long we sat like that, but when I finally pulled away, Bear rewarded me with a giant lick up the side of my face.

Gross. I could have done without that.

As if sensing my thoughts, he licked the other side before I could stop him.

"Thanks for cleaning off those tears, buddy."

His tongue lolled out in a doggy smile. Grabbing my unfinished plate off the counter, I set the food on the ground for him to enjoy. While he was happily munching away, I went and washed my face off. So much for the makeup I'd put on this morning. Logan had hardly even stayed around to appreciate the effort.

I stared at my reflection in the mirror.

"What's going on?" I asked myself.

Giving my head one good shake, I exited the bathroom in search of Bear. He was on the living room floor, wiggling around on his back, mouth open and tongue hanging out the side.

With a grin, I dropped to my knees to wrestle with the beast. He weighed as much as I did, so we were evenly matched. I laid my arms on the ground and put my tush in the air, moving it back and forth to mimic Bear's wagging tail.

"Whatcha got, old friend?" I playfully taunted.

He jumped from side to side before assuming the same position as me. Each of us waiting for the other to make the first move.

The front door opened and then slammed shut. I craned my neck to see Logan leaning casually against the entrance, a wicked smile on his face and his head tilted to the side. And he wasn't looking at my face.

"Hey there." I plopped down and turned so I was facing him. "Stop staring at—"

"Your lovely smile?"

"Haha."

"Please don't stop on my account. I was enjoying the show."

"When did you become such a guy?"

His eyebrows shot up, and faster than I was able to track, he was on me, pressing me back into the plush rug. I was shocked, but I can't say I minded. Bear jumped around us, barking in intervals, happy to be playing a new game.

"Audrey, my love." Logan's voice was quiet, but its timbre had deepened. "What could I have possibly done to lull you into the false belief that I am anything other than one hundred percent red-blooded male?"

"Not this for starters." Were my words a little breathy? If so, I'm sure the temporary lung hiccup was just because I wasn't able to get in enough oxygen. Not because anything he said was affecting me.

Liar.

Logan chuckled and pulled me to my feet, his amusement obvious through the empathy link.

Tease, I mentally shot at him.

Logan's eyes widened, and he took a step back. "Did you just call me a tease?"

I slapped a hand over my mouth. "Did I say that out loud?"

"No. No you didn't."

We both blinked at each other.

"Then how did you know that?"

"I heard it. Here." He tapped his head.

"Is that normal?"

"I don't think so."

"You try it," I said.

"Well, what did you do?"

"I don't know. I literally just thought the word at you."

He shrugged. "Worth a try I guess."

A moment later, his voice echoed in my head. I was prepared to hear something, but I still stumbled back and landed on my backside.

"Did you just say I was hot stuff?" My face mirrored Logan's, wide eyed and open mouthed.

"You really heard that?"

I nodded.

"Well that's . . . pretty cool. Let me try it again." He closed his eyes, and several loud thumps of my heart sounded before I heard him again.

"Logan, stop sending me secret messages about my body parts."

He bent at the waist and started to belly laugh. "Sorry, you're just too easy to fluster sometimes."

"You're awful, and I hate you."

"You said that last night too."

"Yeah, well maybe today I mean it."

He leaned back against the wall and shot me a smug look. "Not likely."

Why does he have to be so smokin' hot when he's being conceited?

Logan's smile widened. "I heard that too."

"Would you get out of my brain? This"—I frantically moved my hands around my head like a hyped-up rave dancer—"is off limits."

Logan pushed off the wall and extended a hand to help me up. His smug exterior hid a layer of worry and concern I didn't think he wanted me to pick up because he released me as soon as I was on my feet.

"I will do my best," he promised. "But it would probably help if you tried not to focus on how gorgeous I am. You know I'm more than just a pretty face. You're going to give me a complex that you only want me for my body."

I almost swallowed my tongue, but instead, a wad of spit went down the wrong pipe. I doubled over in a coughing fit.

Logan rubbed my back until the hacking subsided and then bent to look at me. A few latent coughs were still coming out every few seconds.

"I'm sorry, Audrey. I just really like knowing I can get under that shell of yours. That was immature. Do you forgive me?"

I might have believed he was sincere if he hadn't been grinning wildly.

I glared at him.

"Come on." He extended his hand. Now that everything was out in the open, I was no longer as apprehensive about the empathy link. "Let's go make some new memories together."

I grasped the hand he offered and straightened. "I'd like that very much."

22

MAKE BELIEVE

*T*he next days were some of the happiest and darkest of my existence. There was no more talk of a bonding ceremony, for which I was glad. I couldn't stomach the thought of Logan not moving on with his existence after I was gone, just as much as I couldn't stand to think of him with anyone else. But I loved him enough to want the best for him and chose to think not of some possible future love but instead of his having a future. Something I'd lost the moment I released Satan from his chains.

Logan made good on his word to spend time with me, but he would mysteriously leave for short periods of time and not tell me what he was up to. He never left longer than an hour, but his disappearances made me suspicious just the same. Whenever I started to grow morose, he did whatever he could to lighten my mood. And for my part, I tried to make these last few days happy for him as well. I put on a good face, but I knew there was truly no fooling him. We weren't just contending with emotions now. Worried or fearful thoughts would filter to him unknowingly, and he was always quick to reassure me that things would be all right.

But our bond went both ways. When he thought I wasn't paying attention, I'd catch glimpses of his worried thoughts as well. He wondered what an existence without me would be like and was always plotting ways to change my fate but managed to keep the details concealed from me.

I asked him to abandon his search, for I felt deep in my heart the efforts were hopeless. The darkness marring my back had finally reached its tendrils around my body. The grotesque veins that slithered around my waist and over my shoulder pointed toward the same place . . . my heart. I now felt as if that was the end game. Once the dark thread reached my heart, my time would be up.

But I deserved whatever dark punishment awaited me. Isn't that what the black mark was telling me? I begged him just to enjoy the time we had left. He said all the right things, but those fragments of thoughts still leaked to me.

Other than his odd disappearances, we spent all our time together. Our friends were extremely busy with the mess I'd made with Satan, yet they still didn't know the hand I'd played in those events. For whatever reason, Joe must have held back those details, and for that I was extremely grateful.

Logan and I managed one meal with our hunter buddies at Celestial Heights. The dinner was bittersweet. Logan held my hand almost the whole time, and we shared both joyful and sorrow-filled emotions.

Always in the back of my mind was the thought I should approach the Creator, Hugo, or Joe. The idea floated around my consciousness night and day. Distracting myself during the day was easier, but at night I had horrible nightmares of Hell. I'd wake up in a panic, desperate for comfort, but stopped myself from seeking it from the true source of peace, knowing I wasn't deserving. How could I go to the Creator? I'd betrayed Him.

Each nightmare was a penance I bore. A penance Logan bore when my screaming woke him up. He'd moved me into a spare bedroom at his house and would come running moments after I'd sit up, often drenched in sweat. But I refused to be consoled. I knew that whatever hurt me, hurt him as well. But I reasoned that each tortuous moment I endured would gain me a little more time in this paradise. There wasn't much logic to those thoughts, but without seeking guidance from the Creator of all, logic was elusive to me at best.

The last few nights, Logan had ended up sleeping on the hardwood floor beside me with only a blanket and pillow for comfort. Perhaps I was being cruel, but we were already too connected. Ceremony or not, our bond slid into place more firmly every day—even every hour—we were together. I was determined to keep some of him intact for the moment I was ripped from his life. Sharing a bed, even if all we did was sleep, was an intimacy I couldn't engage in.

Two weeks had passed since we returned to our realm. Fourteen days of a different kind of living hell. And then Logan announced at breakfast that he'd arranged some girl time for me.

"I just think it's important you spend some time with your friends and not just me right now."

I tried not to read into that too much. I chose to take him at face value rather than believe he didn't want me around.

"Yeah, okay." I speared a sausage link and brought it to my mouth.

"Audrey?" Logan waited until I met his gaze. "If you think I can't tell you're getting worse by the day, you're wrong."

I blinked at him before speaking. "What do you expect me to say to that? I'm trying."

His smile was gentle. "Yes, love, I know you are. And so am I. But it's selfish for me to keep you all to myself. You have so many other people here who love and care for you."

"If that's what you want, then all right." I shrugged. I didn't have much fight left in me.

Logan's concerned gaze bored into me. I felt it through our bond. He sensed I was emotionally slipping away from him.

"You'll have a good time today," he said in an upbeat tone. "You'll see."

I snapped my head up and looked at him. "A whole day?"

A day was practically an eternity for us now.

"Trust me . . . please?"

A knock sounded at the front door. He jumped out of his seat and jogged out of the kitchen.

"So, this is where you've been hiding her away," came the slightly peeved voice of my best friend and grandmother. Romona entered the room on high alert, as if looking for a defect in Logan's home. Her reaction struck me as rather funny. "How many rooms did you say this place has again?"

Way to not so subtly ask where I sleep at night.

"There are three, *Grandma*. Logan set me up in the guest room on the second floor." I didn't tell her he'd been sleeping in there too.

She smiled sweetly at me then turned back around the way she came. Kaitlin dodged her on the way into the kitchen.

"What's she doing?" I asked.

Kaitlin's smile was large. "I have an idea."

Logan entered the kitchen, shaking his head. "She just ran upstairs."

"Why?" This was weird.

"Logan!" Romona yelled from somewhere above. "Why is there bedding on my granddaughter's floor?"

I covered my face with one hand.

"Romona's trying to make sure your virtue is still intact. Like I couldn't have taken that whenever—"

"Not another word." I pointed at him.

Footsteps pounded the stairs as Romona came jogging down.

"Logan—" she began.

"Audrey's been having nightmares. I've slept on the floor a night or two so I'm there to wake her up if they get bad."

"Oh." Her brow furrowed for a moment as if trying to come up with something to condemn him for.

I was both mortified and amused. Especially when Romona seemed bent on giving Logan a tongue lashing regardless.

"So"—I clapped my hands once to break the awkward tension—"what are we up to today ladies?"

Kaitlin rubbed her palms together. "Oh, we have big plans for you today, Audrey."

I pointed a finger at her. "No. Whatever it is you have planned, cancel it right now. I want nothing to do with whatever plans are attached to that look. None whatsoever."

"Too late. Everything has already been set in motion, and your jailer over there"—she jerked her thumb over her shoulder at Logan—"has already given his stamp of approval. You have zero choice in the matter."

"Jailer?"

"Yep, total hostage keeper."

"That's hardly fair," I argued. "You all have been extremely busy, w-with"— I stumbled over my words—"with all the bad stuff going on."

"Today is different," Romona inserted. "We have it blocked off especially for you. Doctor's orders."

"What doctor?"

"It's just a phrase. Come on." She tugged my sleeve. "Let's go do some girl stuff."

I reluctantly slipped off my stool and followed the girls to the front door.

"I'll see you later?" I asked Logan.

He laid a palm on my cheek. Love poured into me through the empathy link.

You couldn't keep me away, he said directly to my mind.

With a soft kiss, he gave me a gentle nudge out the door with the command to 'just relax' right as Romona and Kaitlin linked arms with me and dragged me away from him and what had become my haven over the last few days.

I craned my neck to see him standing in the doorway, watching us walk from view. Something turned in my chest, and I had an ominous thought that I might never see him again.

Believing I existed on borrowed time, every moment felt as if it could be my last. If I had the courage, I would have prayed for more time. But when I dug deep to try, I found that well empty.

23

GIRL'S DAY

"What exactly is happening right now?" I lifted my eyebrows at Kaitlin—she was less than trustworthy—before turning to Romona for answers.

She was misty eyed with a soft smile on her face. The look did absolutely nothing to put my mind at ease.

The tent in front of me was a deep burgundy made of thick material. Velvet maybe? Kaitlin lifted the flap and pulled me through, Romona right on my heels. When the drape closed, we were in our own personal bubble. Just us and the eight—wait, no, ten—strangers standing around at different stations within the tent. What was this, a salon?

"Why are we at a spa . . . in a tent?" I looked around at the reclined seating area, complete with greenery and a bubbling water feature, and the pedicure chair with little fish swimming around in the footbath.

Ahh, no thank you.

Several seats were positioned in front of a mirror with large exposed light bulbs, and a massage chair waited in one of the corners. Curtains concealed two partitioned areas.

An ornate purple chandelier hung from the middle of the tent, and white twinkle lights ringed the sides, giving everything a soft glow. Next to each station stood several women with broad smiles on their faces.

I didn't get it. The space was quite magical and beautiful, but . . . huh?

"Not exactly a spa day," Romona started, "but it's probably best if you think of it that way."

Kaitlin clapped her hands. "You ready for some pampering? Because I know I am."

"Are you really going to keep me in the dark about all this?"

"Yes," they said in unison and then exchanged a look.

I considered being mad at them, but I couldn't do it. Honestly, getting pampered was my favorite guilty pleasure, and I *had* wanted to spend some more time with Kaitlin and Romona before . . . the stabbing sensation was back in my chest. I shoved the pain aside and reminded myself to live for the moment. I didn't have any other guarantees.

I needed to find a way to say goodbye to these two women. Kaitlin would be difficult . . . but Romona, she wasn't just my best friend; she was family. Leaving Romona was going to break me almost as much as parting from Logan.

I closed my eyes and shook my head, willing the tears to recede. A gentle hand grasped my shoulder.

"Audrey," Romona asked, "are you all right?"

I shook my head. They deserved more than I was giving. Maybe I should have come clean to all my friends like I did with Logan.

I just didn't know how.

Whenever I tried to pray and ask for guidance, I simply couldn't. I felt too . . . unclean to present myself to the Creator and ask for help. I was on my own.

"No," I answered honestly, "but this looks like a lot of fun. Where do we start?" I gave Romona a watery smile to reassure her. She pulled me into a hug and patted my back.

"We're all here for you, you know that, right?" she whispered in my ear. That was a strange thing to say.

I pulled back.

"Of course." I searched her eyes for answers to questions I didn't know to ask.

"All right, peeps," Kaitlin interrupted, "let the beautification begin."

"No! Five hundred percent absolutely not! This is not happening." I dug in my heels. I had just learned what was behind curtain number one and wanted nothing to do with it. "Kaitlin, stop pushing me forward, or so help me, I will throat punch you so hard you won't be able to talk for a month."

She shoved me forward, her shoulder against my back. My feet slipped over the plush carpet without my having to lift them. Darn this beautiful rug and its strangely slippery qualities.

"Stop being a baby, Audrey, and put your big girl panties on. Or rather, take them off so the aesthetician can wax down there as well." She snickered.

"Kaitlin, don't be crude," Romona snapped from somewhere behind her. "Audrey, it's just your legs and underarms."

I tried to turn, but Kaitlin did some weird mixed martial arts movement on me, and the next thing I knew, I was lying flat on my back across the semi-reclined table with the wind knocked out of me.

"I . . . will . . . kill . . . you," I huffed out.

"Oh silly Audrey." Kaitlin just laughed at me. "I'm already dead."

I tilted my head and caught Romona watching wide-eyed from behind Kaitlin.

"Traitor." I croaked out.

She held up her hands. "This was all Kaitlin's idea. I had nothing to do with this part."

"Guilty by association," I shot at her.

"Oh chill out, Audrey. I promise, you'll thank us later. Body grooming is very important." With that, Kaitlin spun on a heel and hightailed it out, pulling Romona with her.

I would kill them both.

"So." A woman with a kind smile and arms as thick as some of the bulky male hunters appeared above my head, holding a tongue depressor covered in what I could only guess was scalding hot wax. "Where should we begin?"

Double dead . . . both of them.

What must have been a million hours later, I limped out from behind the curtain, looking for my 'friends' with the intent to inflict some serious pain. Hair had been pulled, plucked, and ripped from various areas of my body. That was the first and last time I'd ever go through that. Friends don't force other friends into painful hair removal.

When I finally spotted Kaitlin and Romona, I stopped in my tracks. They were wrapped in silk robes, looking positively radiant. We'd all had relaxing facials, which gave our skin a lovely dewy look, but while I'd been tortured, they must have gone through a couple more of the stations because they both wore expertly applied makeup and sported Hollywood hairstyles. Romona's latte-tinted skin glowed even brighter, and her makeup accentuated all her best features without overwhelming her face. Her dark hair was pulled back into a low bun of loose braids that gleamed beneath the chandelier and twinkle lights.

Kaitlin's makeup was on the heavier side, with its smoky colors making her blue eyes pop like crazy. Her face was flawless and sun-kissed like the beach girl she'd always be. Her hair was swept into a side-do, and it looked like the stylist actually made flower designs out of her blonde locks. She did a little spin for me. The braid of interlocked blonde flowers wrapped around her head and flowed over her shoulder. I'd never seen anything quite as exquisite.

"You both look . . . amazing." I blinked a few times. This couldn't just be a girl's day. "Are we going to a pop-up-prom or something?"

The corners of Romona's lips curled in a secretive smile.

Kaitlin gave me a toothy Cheshire cat grin. "Getting warmer," she said. "Now it's your turn."

I practically jumped into the seat offered me. Yes please! I'd spent way too much of my afterlife in workout clothes or body armor. I was more than ready to pretty it up.

The makeup artist, a petite redhead, gave me a sweet smile and then turned me away from the mirror so I couldn't see her work. I found myself facing my friends again.

"Hey now, what gives?"

"You trust us, right?" Kaitlin asked.

I shook my head. "No, absolutely not. Would you like me to remind you what I just went through?"

She shrugged. "Either way, your reveal is going to be a surprise. Just sit back and think happy Logan-filled thoughts."

I made a mocking noise deep in my throat. I loved her, but she was a pain sometimes.

"Don't worry. You're going to look lovely." Romona took my hand, and waves of calm comfort filtered through the empathy link. Underneath that was a bubble of excitement I rarely picked up from her. Whatever the end game was, she was looking forward to it. I might not trust Kaitlin not to put me in clown makeup for the fun of it, but I trusted Romona.

I nodded once. "Okay, ladies," I said to everyone still in the tent with us, "do your worst." I closed my eyes before snapping my lids back open. "No, I didn't mean that. I meant do your best. Your absolute best."

There was a chorus of light laughs around me.

24

THE REVEAL

I held my breath as the stylist did her work. The anticipation was killing me.

"You're really not going to let me look?"

"No way, no how," Kaitlin answered.

"You look beyond beautiful." Romona's eyes once again misted over. "Trust me, just a few more minutes and we'll let you take a look at the finished product. You're going to want to see this all at once."

I blew out an annoyed breath of air. My makeup was done, and my hair was mostly ready, but these two bullies were sticking to their word and wouldn't let me see what had been done. All I knew was that my hair was half up and half down, and that was it. I tried to touch my head once to get a feel of what was going on back there, and Romona slapped my hand away. My own grandmother!

Romona took both my shoulders in her hands and looked me in the eyes, her face a mixture of pride and something else. "Okay, now for this next part, you're going to have to keep your eyes closed while we dress you."

"Oh, come on. Don't you think you're taking this a little too far? I get it's all fun and games to treat me like makeover Barbie for the afternoon, but really, you want me to let a stranger dress me?"

Her smile was radiant. "No strangers. This will be Kaitlin and me. Just this final step and then no more surprises. I promise."

"Do I have to change my underwear?"

Kaitlin burst out laughing behind me.

"What?" I twisted to look at her over my shoulder. "It's a legit question. At least let me have that privacy."

I turned my attention back to Romona, who pressed her lips together and then finally spoke. "That's not unreasonable. Kaitlin, will you please go grab her undergarments and we'll all turn around while she changes into them?"

They were taking whatever was going on way too seriously.

Kaitlin slipped behind mystery curtain number two and came back out holding some very tiny panties and what could only be described as a modern torture device parading as delicate silk and white lace lingerie.

I checked behind me. All the women who were still in the tent with us were currently facing away, and Kaitlin was holding the garments out to me with a grin.

"What?" I looked at Romona for help, but her face was peacefully blank. "This is a joke, right?"

"No-*pe*." Kaitlin answered.

With my thumb and one finger, I picked up what I'd thought were supposed to be underwear from Kaitlin and held them in front of my face.

"This is missing a butt."

Kaitlin burst out laughing.

"Go find me one with a butt, and I'll consider putting it on."

"Audrey, all the cool kids are wearing them these days."

"Oh shut it, you." I narrowed my eyes. "Like you'd wear these."

She lifted a perfectly plucked eyebrow at me.

"Oh, I'm definitely wearing something similar. Care to see?" She turned and started lifting the back of her robe.

"Stop," I yelled and yanked her robe back in place. "I definitely do not want to see that."

"I'm just messing with you. You're right. I wouldn't be caught dead in one of those, but they aren't really for you anyway. Just think of—"

"No, she's right," Romona cut in. "If she's uncomfortable with what she's wearing, she's going to be distracted from . . . you know, the important stuff."

She eyed Kaitlin, who huffed and said, "Oh fine," under her breath.

With a twirl of her hand, she materialized a bit more substance to the panties I held. They no longer resembled dental floss but covered all the important bits—even if they were still made of silk and lace and had some see-through parts. I would take this win . . . however small it was.

"Thank you," I said rather magnanimously. "Now I'll just slip back here to put these on." I started toward the curtained-off area, and both Romona and Kaitlin sprang for me, yelling no at the same time.

"Whoa there," I said and froze in place.

"You can put them on out here," Romona said, recovering from her momentary panic. "Your . . . outfit is back there, and we don't want to ruin the surprise. We won't even look. Although if you need help with the corset top, let me know."

"You mean the torture device? Yeah, sure." I rolled my eyes.

This was getting ridiculous.

After Romona and Kaitlin turned to give me privacy, I slipped out of my clothes and pulled on the underwear before giving the corset-like top piece a valiant effort. In the end, I did need their help getting into it. There was a whole bunch of lace-up hooks in the back I couldn't reach. But at least I was mostly covered when they helped me, even if I was now having trouble breathing.

After that they somehow talked me into closing my eyes as I went behind the curtain with them. I followed all their instructions to lift my leg, bend my arm, suck in my stomach and whatever else they threw at me. Getting me into this contraption of a dress must have taken them at least half an hour. When I tried to touch any of the material, I got my hands slapped again. They were dress ninjas who knew every time I tried to figure anything out.

At the end of the dressing session, the only thing I knew was that I now wore something long and strapless . . . and heavy. They could have just stuffed me into a cupcake-shaped gown for all I knew. But if they thought I was going to take one step out of this tent without getting a look at myself, they were in for a rude awakening.

"Okay,"—Romona held my left hand—"just a few more steps. Then I want you to lift your foot. You're going to be stepping onto a short pedestal."

A pedestal? "We are still in the tent though, right?"

"Absolutely." That was from Romona, so I believed her.

As Romona guided me, Kaitlin was somewhere behind me, lifting up my dress to make walking easier. She better not be showing my rear end to a tent full of people.

"Okay, now one small step up."

I followed their directions. Kaitlin asked me to lift one foot up at a time, and some tall yet still comfortable shoes were slipped on my feet as Romona steadied me.

Excited and nervous energy bounced off both girls. I didn't feel malice or even humor through their empathy links, so that relaxed me a bit. If this was some elaborate joke, Kaitlin would have been throwing off some major vibes by now.

"It's just perfect, isn't it?" Kaitlin swooned.

"She's more lovely than I ever imagined," Romona answered.

"Okay, people, are you done making me your dress-up doll yet? Am I allowed to open my eyes?"

"Yes," breathed Romona, almost too quietly to hear. "Open your eyes."

Finally.

I let out a lungful of air and opened my eyes. I blinked a second before I realized I was actually looking at myself. The tent had been transformed while I got dressed, and most of the stations had been cleared, and in front of the pedestal I stood on were three floor-to-ceiling mirror panels. They were tilted in just the right way for me to see myself from several angles.

I gasped, not sure what to look at first. My dress was white. I stuck on that for a moment. The gown was the most beautiful one I'd ever seen. It hugged my chest and torso to perfection and then flowed in soft layers to the floor, allowing just the end of my shoes to poke out.

But it also showcased the ugly black-and-green veins that snaked over my shoulder. Thank goodness they were invisible to everyone but me—my own personal reminder. I forced my attention back on the dress.

The part that hugged my body was an intricate interlacing of several different materials—lace and silk and a tulle-like covering I didn't quite recognize.

I touched it with my fingers. So soft.

"It's called orneza," Romona said. "It's a material not yet invented on Earth. It's a little like tulle, but it floats a bit more when you walk." She indicated the semi-full skirt that was made up entirely of layers of the magical substance.

"It's . . . white," I replied dumbly.

She smiled and nodded.

"What do you think of the rest?" She indicated my hair and makeup. I hadn't even looked at my face yet.

Too shocked by the wedding dress they'd put me in.

What exactly was going on here?

My eyes lifted to the mirror once again, and my breath caught. They'd turned me into a fairy princess. Minus the pointy ears and iridescent wings. My skin glowed. I turned my head each way and realized they'd applied a thin layer of shimmery powder. I pivoted so I could appreciate the unblemished side of my body.

The deep chocolate of my eyes was accentuated by shades of gold, brown, and pink. My lashes looked impossibly long and dark. A brush of color made it look like a faint blush kissed my cheeks at all times. And my skin was like fine porcelain.

I lifted my gaze to the top of my head where a delicate band of twisted metals sat. Intricate braids weaved in, out, and around the band, giving it a peek-a-boo look as well as making it appear the band and my hair together created a delicate diadem atop my head. The rest of my hair flowed in loose waves nearly to my waist—a silky, smooth river. Each loose curl brought out the natural highlights in my hair.

Had my hair grown that long without my realizing it? I'd spent so much time with it up during training, and I'd been so distracted these last few weeks, the locks must have grown without me taking note.

I was . . . overwhelmed. I'd never felt so beautiful. I'd never been so beautiful. Heavenly makeovers were magical.

But this dress. What was happening couldn't actually be happening . . . could it?

I turned to ask them, only to find that my dress had a train that was several feet long. Romona and Kaitlin had both changed into dresses of their own. Both were the same light shade of lavender, flattering to each of them, but differing styles. Romona's was cap-sleeved and flared at the waist to end right above her knees. Kaitlin's was one-shouldered and flowed to the same spot without the flare. But the material and shade were exactly the same.

They looked an awful lot like bridesmaid dresses.

"You tell me right now: What's going on?" But didn't I already know?

Romona stepped forward. "All of this was Logan's plan."

Kaitlin cleared her throat loudly.

Romona rolled her eyes. "Okay, it was Logan's idea, but he didn't plan out all the details. You're having your bonding ceremony today, Audrey."

"But why am I dressed like a bride? You told me this wasn't a wedding? And that I don't get bridesmaids. And how did you all pull this off? And when? And . . . what?"

Do not hyperventilate.

I took a shaky step off the short pedestal and finished with a choked-up, "And I can't." I caught a glimpse of my shoes, which were just as gorgeous as the rest of my transformation. Light lavender to match the girls' dresses with a decorative crystal broach that sent a rainbow of colors everywhere when it caught the light. "You don't understand. This can't happen. Logan knows why. He knows."

I wasn't making sense to them, but how could I? They didn't know what was hanging over my head.

Romona took hold of my upper arms. She gave me a light shake and forced my attention. When I looked up, she was crying, ruining her perfect makeup.

"Audrey, stop. Do you love Logan?" Her voice was strong regardless of the tears pouring down her cheeks.

"Wh—well, yes. Of course I do."

"Would you travel to Hell and back again, literally, to save him?"

"Yes, absolutely. I mean, I already did. Why are you asking me this?"

"Then that's all that matters. You both love each other and have each other's backs, no matter what."

"But, Romona, you don't fully understand. There are things—"

"Yes. I do understand. I understand everything."

I was struck speechless. She couldn't possibly know. I shook my head . . . but then I noticed her emotions leaking through the empathy link. A great sorrow lay in her heart. One she must have been covering up all day. Her devastation matched mine.

She knew.

"How?"

"Logan told all of us."

I gasped, my head snapping in Kaitlin's direction. Tears tracked down her face as well.

"How long have you known?" I asked.

Romona pressed her lips together. "Not as long as we should have. You should have told me yourself."

I opened my mouth to say something but stopped when I came up short. She was right. "But I understand why you didn't," she continued. "The point is we love you. All of us. We're going to fight this together. But today is your day. Yours and Logan's. And if you think for one moment that man wouldn't storm the gates of Hell or any other realm to be with you, then perhaps you don't deserve him to begin with."

I sucked in a breath. Conflicted. Bonding with Logan for eternity when all we had was maybe today was selfish, wasn't it? The ugly mark and its tendrils didn't let me forget I was running short on time. But bonding with me was his decision as much as mine.

"I don't know what to do."

"You do what you know is right." Romona squeezed my arms to keep me in the present. "And the right person is out there right now, waiting for you to walk down the aisle and promise your forever to him."

I gulped and glanced at Kaitlin. She was one of Logan's oldest friends. We were close, but I knew deep down she'd always have his best interests in mind. She nodded at me once. "You need to go out there and make an honest man out of that guy."

"Hey now, we haven't done a single thing that would imply we haven't been completely honorable these last . . ."

I stopped when I realized she was laughing at me.

Rolling my eyes I took a deep breath and looked at myself in the ginormous mirrors. But really I was trying to look inside. What was the right thing to do? Did I want to complete the bond with Logan? Absolutely. What held me back was the desire to do right by him. I was looking out for his own good.

I knew who I really needed to talk to about this. But I hadn't approached Him since returning from Hell. Too worried He'd turn away from me. Too afraid He'd send me back to Hell immediately. But this decision couldn't be made without consulting Him. I had to know I wouldn't be hurting Logan even more than I already had. I had to know that I wouldn't be putting his eternity in jeopardy.

I turned to my friends. "Okay, at the very least you two need to go get yourselves cleaned up. You're both hot messes right now." I gestured at their faces. "Like I'd let any bridesmaids of mine walk down the aisle looking like that."

Kaitlin let out a short burst of laughter, and Romona smiled.

"Like I'd go out in public with running mascara," Kaitlin scoffed. "It's like you don't know me at all."

"Thattagirl." Romona gave my arms one final squeeze before heading to the opposite corner of the tent where a makeup station was still set up. How did I miss that before? I guess they'd planned for a possible makeup malfunction before the ceremony. I'd bet they thought they'd be fixing me instead of them.

I stepped back up on the pedestal, but instead of looking at myself, I bowed my head. It was time.

25

CEREMONY

*K*aitlin and Romona chattered happily across the tent. I tuned them out. My hands shook, so I squeezed them into fists. I needed a moment to collect myself. A moment to gather all the courage I had and focus it on one singular goal. I wanted to shadow box to pump myself up, but considering the circumstances and my amazing but gigantic gown, that didn't seem practical.

Okay, Audrey, you can do this.

But that wasn't actually the truth. The truth was that I couldn't do this. I couldn't do anything apart from the Creator. Apart from Hugo's wisdom and Joe's guidance. I'd been running myself ragged for the last two weeks trying to exist without them. Ashamed of my own mistakes but unwilling to do what needed to be done because of fear.

"Father," I whispered. And waited.

And nothing happened.

I cracked an eyelid. I was still in the tent. I didn't realize until then that I'd expected to be transported somewhere else like the first time I spoke with the Creator in the afterlife. But I was in exactly the same spot. Was it because He hadn't heard me? Or didn't want to listen?

I closed my eyes and continued, "Father, I'm not sure if you can hear me or not. In fact, I'm not sure I want you to hear me, which I feel really bad about, but I need to confess something. And I need to ask for your forgiveness . . . and I need to ask for your advice." I paused for a heartbeat. "If not for myself, for Logan, who I know you love."

I sucked in a cleansing breath and then released it slowly. "I've been hiding from You. But I guess You already know that. I've been . . . scared to come to You because I'm ashamed, and I'm afraid You'll cast me out." There, I'd gotten the first part out. "I made a terrible mistake, and it's all my fault Satan was released. Then I lied to everyone I care about . . . about the whole thing. I've been plagued with guilt. And I know that what I've done is too big to really ask for forgiveness. But You deserve to know, straight from my mouth, how sorry I am. For all of it, but especially for hiding from You . . . and of course, for freeing Satan . . . That was really bad."

I hung my head even lower. This wasn't making me feel any better. If anything, my gut tightened. Emotions I hadn't even realized were there were coming to the surface.

"But I guess I wanted You to know how sorry I am for all of it, and I want to ask for direction. Is it all right to go forward with this when it will only mean heartbreak for Logan?"

I waited. And waited. And waited.

And I never heard an answer.

My friends finished their makeup, and I never received an answer from the Creator. At least not one I could interpret. My heartfelt pleas were met with silence.

When I told them, my friends, who now knew all the horrible details, told me this was okay and that I could move forward. And of course, I wanted to complete the bond with Logan. So I did what I could to pump myself up.

Bring the soul-fusing on. Wait, I still didn't really know what that was.

I supposed I was so far away from the Creator that He couldn't be bothered to listen to me anymore, even if I petitioned for Logan and not myself. My heart was heavy, but for Romona and Kaitlin, I put on a brave face.

"Okay, someone, please explain to me why I look like a bride and you both are dressed as bridesmaids. I've been told repeatedly that this isn't a wedding. So what gives?"

"Ah, well, yes, that was Logan again," Romona explained. "He put a lot of thought into this, and he wanted it to be special for you. So we threw some of the less important details of soul-fusing out the window and replaced them with things you are familiar with."

My heart melted. That man. There wasn't anyone better.

"And that," Romona interrupted my thoughts, "that look right there is why I'm okay with all of this."

Her words sobered me. I stood up a bit straighter.

"We all know nothing is certain right now, Audrey." Kaitlin picked up the conversation. "Logan has been working like a madman to try to figure out how to change your fate. Maybe he'll be able to . . ." She visibly sobered, pulling her shoulders back and boring her eyes into mine. "And maybe he won't. But you have the most determined person I know in your corner, so if anyone can figure out how to get you out of this mess, it's him."

"Great pep talk," I said dryly.

"Oh, and make sure you give him at least one really awesome night to remember."

"Kaitlin!" I shrieked.

"Too easy, girl." She jerked her chin up. "You might want to change that back before we head out of this tent. Because the minute we do, it's show time."

Of course my hair had gone wacky.

"So, who all is out there?"

"Oh, like half this part of the realm."

"What? You're kidding, right?"

"Nope. I took a peek already. They've all been sitting out there for the last half hour, waiting for you to pull yourself together. It's not every day you see a wedding-slash-bonding ceremony up here."

"Oh my gosh! Why didn't you tell me?" I stopped my impending rant. "Wait, why can't I hear anything? You're messing with me, aren't you?"

Her eyes widened, and she pointed to herself. "Who, me? I'd never do that."

"Romona?"

A slight grimace flitted across Romona's face. "Kaitlin's only exaggerating a bit. There is quite a crowd. And you can't hear anything because we've had a sound barrier around the tent since the moment we walked in. They've been setting up out there all day."

"You can put sound barriers up?"

She started to answer, and I waved her off.

"Sorry, never mind. That's not important. Tell me everything I need to know. Then let's do this thing."

A bouquet of exotic purple, blue, and fuchsia flowers was shoved into my sweaty hands. The colorful blooms stood out against the whiteness of my dress. Romona and Kaitlin held smaller versions of my bouquet and were lined up in front of me. Kaitlin bounced on her six-inch heels in excitement and turned to give me the thumbs up. Romona smiled at me serenely.

"I'm so very glad to be able to be part of this, Audrey. I know your parents —" Her words caught, and she cleared her throat. "Your parents would be so proud of you right now."

"Oh yeah, I'm sure. Getting hitched at eighteen and on the brink of being dragged into Hell for eternity. I'm sure they'd be thrilled."

Romona frowned. "Nothing is certain yet, Audrey. Nothing. You enjoy this day, and put your trust where it always should have been. I understand how you must have been shaken from what happened. But you forgot one very important detail along the way."

I cocked my head at her.

"The Creator is bigger than any mess you can make. Hold on to that with everything you have."

"But I betrayed Him," I argued.

"You aren't the first one," she said sadly before facing forward.

The drape had been opened, and Kaitlin was just about to step out of the tent. Soft harp music floated through the gap. I snorted. If Logan had arranged for that, he didn't know as much about me as he thought.

I craned my neck to the left, but I couldn't see much beyond Romona and Kaitlin—only the beginning of a gold aisle runner covered in light pink-and-gold-tipped rose petals.

Pretty.

The fabric drape swished closed behind Kaitlin, and it was eerily silent again.

Romona turned and squeezed my forearm. "You got this," she said before turning back around and marching her way toward the same spot Kaitlin had just vacated. After several beats, she winked at me over her shoulder and slipped out of the tent as well. Leaving me completely alone. Something I didn't want to be at the moment.

I was doing the right thing here, wasn't I? Was I being selfish? And oh my gosh, I didn't even have anyone to walk me down the aisle. That was messed up. *I shouldn't be making this walk alone.* I dropped my hand, still clenching my flowers in a death grip, and brought the other up to my face.

I was alone.

Something nudged my backside, and I yelped. Bear trotted around me and sat at my right side. Watching me expectantly, he tilted his head as if to ask what the holdup was.

"You're right. Alone or not, the man I love is waiting for me down that aisle. I think I've let him wait long enough, don't you?"

Bear answered with a thump of his tail, and his tongue rolled out of his mouth. I'd take that as an agreement.

"Let's go, buddy," I said.

Bear walked with me to the tent exit. The moment I opened the flap, he took off without a backward glance.

Wait, what?

I'd thought he was going to walk with me. The furry booger trotted down what I now saw was a very long aisle with his head held high, soaking in all the excited murmurs sent his way.

"There goes not doing this alone," I said under my breath.

I took my first step out of the tent, and a sea of bodies got to their feet, obstructing my view of the end of the aisle, where my groom—er, future bonded-for-eternity mate—waited for me. If I could just see Logan, everything would be all right. But I couldn't, and I was alone.

So I froze.

My ears buzzed, so I couldn't even hear the music playing. Was I on the verge of a panic attack? Oh no, not now.

A soft touch to my elbow drew my attention to my left. I looked over to find the Creator, clothed in brilliant light, standing by my side.

He once told me He had many different faces, but He looked exactly as I remembered. Dressed in a linen robe with a gold sash, tall by anyone's standards, and radiating strength and compassion from an ageless face full of grace and mercy. Beauty personified.

"May I?" He asked, indicating my arm.

I stared open mouthed at the being I'd betrayed. The one I loved. I nodded.

The Father slipped his arm through mine and led me down the petal-strewn path. My eyes didn't leave His face or the radiance that emanated from it as we walked down the aisle. At some point we stopped, but my eyes remained glued on Him.

"Audrey," He said to me in a gentle voice, "you've never been alone. And you'll never be forgotten. You are my daughter, purchased with the blood of my Son. You'll understand soon enough."

A soft gasp escaped my lips. His smile reached his eyes, crinkling the corners.

"I've been looking forward to this moment. It's time to look up, princess. Your groom is waiting."

How had I forgotten where I was? I hadn't even searched for Logan.

Snapping my eyes up, I met his gaze. He was standing in front of me with his hand extended. And as I lost myself in a cobalt-blue ocean, the hand at my elbow melted away, and I knew the Creator was no longer visible.

I wasn't even sure if He'd appeared to anyone but me—but a phantom kiss was pressed on my cheek before the evidence of His physical presence fully dissipated.

I took Logan's outstretched hand, and he pulled me forward. I finally snapped out of my daze to take everything in. We were standing under a portico of purple wisteria. Checking behind me, I spotted Romona standing back a ways with Kaitlin next to her. Bear had plopped himself in front of Logan and was sprawled on the ground.

Was the furry mutt asleep?

Behind Logan stood . . .

I gasped and took several steps back. Logan moved forward with me and captured me around the waist, halting my retreat. He deftly plucked the flowers from my hands and handed them to someone behind me.

Standing up directly behind Logan was Joe. Not in hunters' garb, or in faded jeans and a smudged white t-shirt, but in a stylish black tux.

"Shh." Logan had bent to whisper in my ear. "This is how it was always meant to be."

Joe gave me a reassuring nod. Kevin stood next to him with a broad grin, and behind him was Morgan.

This was getting more bizarre by the moment.

I locked eyes with Logan. "This is a weird dream, isn't it?"

He grinned and then pinched my backside . . . hard.

I yelped.

"Not a dream, love. At least not the type you're talking about."

"That was cheesy . . . and it hurt." I resisted the urge to rub the sore spot. I was still aware we had an audience.

"Are you ready yet? I've been waiting a lifetime for this moment, and I don't want to wait a second longer."

Any remaining doubts I might have had fled. "I may not fully understand what's happening, or what all this means for our future, but I'm one hundred percent ready to commit all that I am to you forever."

"Then let's do this."

At my nod, he pulled back to a proper distance. "Don't freak out again, okay?"

I rolled my eyes at his warning. What else could they throw at me today?

"Thank you all for attending this sacred ceremony." That voice was familiar.

I looked beyond Logan and thought I might faint.

Hugo is officiating our ceremony?

I cast my stricken gaze at Logan. He smiled and squeezed my hands. His hair was as wild as usual but just the way I liked it. He was clean-shaven and filling out an elegant black tux and tie in a way that should be sinful. What had been distracting me? Oh right . . . the Holy Trinity showing up at our ceremony.

I glanced at Hugo, and he winked at me before going on. I made the mistake of looking at Logan again, and I was a goner.

The shock of everything had finally subsided, and he was all I saw. Hugo was talking, but rather than hearing words, I only felt love. It poured in waves from Logan and overwhelmed my senses.

This was it. This was my one perfect day of existence.

And with that thought, my world exploded.

26

NEW WORLD

*S*ulfuric smoke stung my eyes, and the world was eerily silent. Wait, no, I was deaf.

I was sprawled on my side with bits of the wisteria arbor littered over my once pristine white dress. The skirt was now ripped in several places, and I was covered in grass stains and dirt smudges.

I blinked several times, but my vision was still a thick cloud of smoke. Human-like shapes darted in and out of view.

Logan, where was he?

I sat up and shook my head. *Whoa, bad idea.* I pressed both hands against my skull to make sure my brain stayed put. For a moment, it had felt like it was going to fall out.

My hearing was slowly returning. Screams echoed in the mist, and then shouted commands filtered through until I could hear the clash of battle. My name might have been shouted as well, but in the chaos, I couldn't tell.

I shoved myself to my legs, shaky at first but steady after a few steps. The clouds of smoke or mist or whatever blinded me to what was really happening. I swatted at it, but the substance didn't dissipate.

A familiar roar followed by a blast of fire about thirty feet to my left froze my steps and chilled my heart.

The dragon.

Satan was here.

It was happening.

Something . . . I needed something to fight with. Preferably something long, pointy, and very sharp.

I turned in a circle, like an idiot. I needed to materialize a weapon, fast.

Oh gosh, where's Logan?

NEW WORLD | 701

Something soared over my head and hit the ground to my right, hard. I heard the crunch of bones and a groan.

I sprinted toward where I thought the person had landed and found Kaitlin lying twisted on the grass. She wore full body armor, her beautiful dress long gone. I thought she was unconscious until she managed to flip herself over, eyes tightly closed, cradling her wrist to her chest.

I hovered above her.

"That. Sucked."

"Kaitlin, oh my gosh. What can I do?"

Her eyes snapped open. "Audrey?" She gasped. "You need to get out of here, immediately. He'll come for you."

There was a spooked look on Kaitlin's face I'd never seen before. Her eyes were open so wide I could see the whites all around her sky-blue irises. She tried to shove herself to a sitting position but cried out and wrapped her uninjured arm around her middle. A few ribs must have been broken as well. She sucked in a few pain-filled breaths and then shot me another frantic look. "Audrey, run."

Panic really started to sink in at her command. I wasn't going to leave my friend here at the site of my bonding ceremony turned battleground, but her words made me want to do just that.

I dropped to my knees. "No, I'm not leaving you. Tell me exactly what's going on. Do you still have your sword on you? Materializing things under pressure isn't really my thing."

She shook her head. "No. It flew out of my hand when that red dragon backhanded me. But here." She closed her eyes, and a moment later a short sword appeared on the ground next to me.

"Thanks. Now what else is out there? I can't see anything through this smoke."

"It's just that giant dragon."

I sat back on my heels and blinked at her. "Just the dragon?"

"Isn't that enough? He's huge."

"You know that's Satan, right?"

"Yeah, I kinda assumed so."

But why was he alone? Why hadn't he stormed our realm with a legion of demons as well?

"What's going through that head of yours?" she asked.

I waved her off. "Nothing. I'm just surprised he came alone."

She snorted. "Yeah, I wouldn't mind a run-in with Alrik. I have a giant bone to pick with him."

Not knowing how to respond, I took my ruined dress in my hands and started to rip strips of fabric from the skirt to bind up her wounds.

Shouts and roars from the battle had increased, but the screams had ceased. The civilians must have escaped while the hunters went up against the evil being that had no place in our home.

Guilt hammered my chest, and my heart was split on what to do. I should have been helping them. I should have been the only one bearing this pain. But leaving Kaitlin's battered body wasn't an option.

I helped her to a sitting position and started to wrap her injured arm to her ribs. I knew the fabric was only a temporary bandage, but it would have to do. Thank goodness my skirt had so many layers. She grunted and gritted her teeth during the process but didn't cry out in pain.

"Have you seen Logan?" I asked.

She shook her head.

Do not panic.

A shadowy figure appeared as I was putting the final wrapping on Kaitlin's wrist and broken ribs. I snapped my gaze up, and he solidified.

"You"—Morgan pointed at me—"go. I've got her."

"Me? Go where?"

Morgan was wearing traditional hunter armor, which threw me for a moment. I'd only ever seen him in his bulkier demon-scaled battle gear.

"Go anywhere," he snarled at me. "Just get out of here. Whatever else he's after right now, he's sure to be after you too."

In a fluid motion, he bent and picked up Kaitlin.

"Put me down, you overgrown gorilla," Kaitlin spat.

"Overgrown gorilla? Hmm, I like it. Thanks."

"It wasn't meant as a compliment."

He winked at her. "I'll take it just the same, luv."

He stalked off with Kaitlin still grumbling insults at him. He glanced over his shoulder at me before being swallowed by the smoke. "Get far away from here, Audrey. This isn't your fight."

When they were gone, I was left alone with an unseen battle raging around me. This one was most definitely my fight.

I picked up the sword Kaitlin had materialized for me and strode straight toward the threat.

27

THE CHASE

*S*talking through the smoke, I caught my breath at the sight that unveiled itself before my eyes. The red-scaled dragon—Satan in beast form—was twice the size of his previous incarnation. I wasn't sure if he was more powerful without his chains or if he'd always been able to manifest into any size he wanted.

Red-hot burning lava shot out of his unhinged, snake-like mouth toward a group of hunters who banded their shields together as a barrier. I swallowed a cry until the fire cleared and I saw the hunters were unscathed. Breathing a sigh of relief, I tightened my grip on the sword.

Show time.

"Hey you! Big ugly! Yo, slime bucket!" I gritted my teeth. Seriously, that was all I could come up with? But my insults did garner his attention. "You want me? Here I am!"

The scaled monster twisted his neck in my direction. Slitted pupils dilated and then returned to straight lines. What might have been a chuckle bounced around the dragon's chest.

"And there she issss," he hissed. "The one who made all thisss desstruction posssssible."

"You don't belong here," I yelled.

Satan turned his massive body toward me, using his tail to bat away the hunters he'd been trying to barbeque—mowing them over like he'd swept his hand across a chessboard and scattered all the pieces. I winced but couldn't spare them a glance. Hunters were made of tough stock; they'd bounce back.

Satan lowered his oversized head to my level, his snout almost touching the ground, and I stared into the face of pure evil.

"I belong wherever I want, little lamb. A large part of that isss due to you." His scorching breath washed over me and blew my hair back over my shoulders.

I hid a shudder.

"I'll sssee you in a bit. I have to grab sssomething before we leave." Leathery wings pumped, and he lifted off the ground.

Wait, what?

"Don't look so forlorn. I'll be back for you. Promissse." His forked tongue drew out the last word.

His wings continued to flap as he hovered in the air a moment longer, clearing out the area of mist and smoke. Then he shot into the sky and headed toward the marbled city.

No.

There were people in that city. Non-hunter people that wouldn't know how to defend themselves let alone fight off the beast.

I did a speedy assessment of the area now that the smoke had cleared. Remnants of our ceremony lay like carnage across a battlefield. Broken chairs were everywhere. The gold aisle runner I'd walked down was shredded to ribbons and scattered like ash. I still couldn't find Logan. The only people present were armor-clad hunters . . . and me, in my torn, dirty dress, gripping a short sword with stringy clumps of red-white-and-brown-streaked hair hanging in my face.

I glanced back at the sky to watch Satan fly toward the city. His form grew smaller by the moment. I sprinted in his direction but skidded to a halt when a mass of golden fur cut me off.

Battle Bear stood in front of me on his hind legs, razor-sharp claws out and fanged teeth bared. He wasn't going to let me pass. I tensed to fight my way past him. Unreasonable animal.

He growled at me once before dropping to all fours and presenting me with his side, crouching on the ground to give me access to his back. *Huh?*

He turned his head as if waiting on me.

"Was that growl because you were mad I left you behind when we went to rescue Logan?"

He huffed and actually nodded at me, and my eyes widened.

"Am I forgiven then?"

He stuck his tongue out at me. *Double huh.* It slowly dawned on me that he understood everything I said.

"You are a lot smarter than I've been giving you credit for, aren't you?"

Another nod. Well then, I wasn't about to turn down the free ride. I fisted some of Bear's fur and pulled myself to sit astride him. I grasped his pelt with both hands, anticipating the bumpy ride to come.

Bear pushed up, readying for our sprint when my name was yelled.

I twisted to look, and Logan was running toward me. He was safe. The knot in my chest loosened a notch.

"Audrey, no. You'll be taken," he yelled. "The bond, it wasn't completed."

And thank goodness for that. Logan and I had run out of time. I didn't have to look at the veins wrapped around my body to know that. He wouldn't be shackled to me for the rest of eternity. He'd be free to love someone else. It stabbed my heart to even think that, but leaving was the right thing.

Logan would never allow me to get in the middle of the battle I had every intention of fighting. Water threatened to fill my eyes, but I stomped the sentiment down. This could very well be the last time I saw his face—the face I loved so much, currently twisted in anguish as if he already knew I wouldn't heed his warning.

He knew me pretty well after all.

When he was only feet away, I spurred Bear on.

"I love you," I shouted and faced forward. I left a broken man in my wake. My last image of Logan was of him falling to his knees—anguish etched on every part of his face.

Some signal must have gone out to the citizens of the city to take cover, because the streets were empty—not a soul in sight as we barreled past the pristine white buildings.

Thank goodness.

Like the last time I'd ridden Bear in search of Satan, my friend seemed to know exactly where he was going.

The trip was short. Bear was headed full steam for a building I recognized. The Archives Building. The closer we got, the faster Bear's pace became.

"Whoa there, buddy. I think you may want to slow down a bit."

He half turned his head and snorted at me. O-kay then.

I looked up—we were headed straight for the entrance. As in straight for the glass revolving doors.

"Bear," I cried and hunched over, flattening my body as much as I could to his side with my face buried in his fur. There was no stopping him now. He was going to go straight through the entrance without stopping—straight through several sheets of glass.

I screamed as we hit the first wall of glass and hung on until the jarring noises stopped, along with the jolting ride.

I looked up. We were in the solarium, covered in shards of glass, yet both amazingly free of injury. I slid off Bear's back and landed on legs of jelly. I leaned against him until I was able to stand without help.

After I gained my bearings, I marched in front of him and grabbed the fur of his cheeks in my fists. "What were you thinking? We could have stopped outside and entered like normal, non-insane beings."

He snuffed as though he were laughing. I backed up a step, and he shook his body like he was shaking off water. I covered my face as glass flew off in all directions like droplets of liquid.

I pointed a finger at him. "You know, you can be a real pain sometimes."

Another maybe Bear chuckle.

I sighed. "But yes, I still love you."

Something shattered in a different part of the building, and I jumped at the noise.

Apparently we'd found the dragon. I looked down at my ruined outfit. This wouldn't do.

Closing my eyes, I concentrated to change my disaster dress into body armor. I waited until the change was complete to open my eyes and then just stared down at myself. I'd managed to materialize all my armor, including a baldric to hold my sword on my back for comfort and ease of use, but the armor was all white.

What the what?

Whatever, close enough.

I set off on the same path Logan had taken me down only a week before. The loud thumping behind me said I wasn't alone. "Bear," I shot over my shoulder, "you stay here. It's too dangerous for you."

He growled and then head-butted my back, sending me stumbling several steps forward before I righted myself.

"Was that really necessary?" I asked

He issued another growl.

"Ugh, fine. You can come."

We crept forward along the tree-lined path—well, I crept, Bear lumbered. I didn't spy a single creature and hoped they'd found hiding places.

We passed through a second set of doors, which Bear barely fit through, and entered the library. Completely vacant, the room was eerily quiet.

Quickly moving through the center aisle, we reached the end of the room, and I grasped the handle that led to the next part of the building.

The dragon wasn't here—but a roar from somewhere beyond the room shook the walls in the library. Books rained down from all six stories of shelves, creating a tidal wave of sound when they smacked the floor. I surveyed the wreckage of the once pristine room with my heart in my throat. Those books were priceless. They contained the histories of all the living humans on Earth. And now piles of records lay in scattered heaps on the chairs, desks, and floor of the grand room. Something about that was very wrong.

This whole situation was wrong. Those fallen books represented the consequences of my actions. They represented lives that would be disrupted, broken and ruined by my moment of anger. The burden of my transgressions weighed me down.

Another ear-piercing roar made the earth tremble beneath my feet. Maybe

I couldn't right my wrong, but I could do everything in my power to stop further damage. My soul might have already been damned, but if I was going to spend the rest of my existence in Hell, I was bringing that dragon back down with me.

I blew out a lungful of air and pushed through the door in front of me.

ARTIFACTS ROOM

*B*ear shrank to his normal dog size to fit through the doorway this time. Just as I remembered from my visit with Logan, we entered a small room with two doors. The one on the left led to the room full of beautiful pictures. The other door led to what Logan had called the Artifacts Room. That was the one place I hadn't been before, and the place I expected Satan to be. Although why, I had no idea.

"Bear, you're staying here."

He huffed at me and took a few steps forward. I curled my hands in his fur and forced him to stop.

"Seriously, I mean it. You are not to go in there. He'll rip you to shreds."

Bear let out a low growl, and the hair on his back stood on end.

"Don't even think about pulling an attitude with me. Stay." I pointed a finger at him.

He let out another low growl but plopped his butt on the smooth floor. I pressed my lips together. He could be as mad at me as he wanted, but I wanted him safe.

I placed a quick kiss on Bear's head before sprinting to the door. Glass shattered on the other side and I sped up, stretching for the knob . . . and then slammed right into the smooth surface.

Ouch.

The stupid thing was locked.

Rubbing a hand under my nose, my glove came back bloodied. Great, I'd probably just broken my face.

I stepped back and put my body weight into a few solid kicks. The door didn't so much as groan, but I did.

I turned to look at Bear, who was sitting with what looked suspiciously like a smile on his furry face.

"A little help?"

He cocked his head at me.

"Seriously?"

He got up and trotted over to me. More glass smashed behind the unopened door. A vicious roar shook the building. This wasn't the time for games. Whatever Satan was doing in there, I was running out of time to deal with him before more hunters showed up. I didn't want anyone else getting hurt because of me. Logan was most definitely searching for me and could appear at any time. He had to be flipping out, knowing my intention was to face Satan alone.

I rolled my eyes. "Bear, will you please help me get past this door?"

He inclined his head, and then before my eyes, my sweet, goofy, lazy dog transformed. He let out a bark that turned into a thunderous growl as his teeth elongated and his head expanded. His ears shortened, but everything else grew in length and girth. After a few blinks, Bear was no longer just Bear. He was now Battle Bear.

I patted his oversized belly. "We gotta get you some armor, buddy. You'd look good in it."

Bear shoved me to the side with his massive head. Once I was out of the way, he backed up several steps before ramming the door and the wall around it. He tore at the barrier with his razor claws and sharp teeth. When he backed up, the door wasn't just open; there was a full-on hole in the wall three times larger than the previous entrance had been

"You are truly frightening. Okay, thanks. Now stay here."

I ran through the opening, followed by the sound of claws clicking against the floor. Why did I think he'd obey?

After several steps, brightness blinded me.

What the what?

I threw a hand up to shield my eyes and skidded to a halt. Bear rammed into my back, sending me sprawling.

That did not tickle.

I struggled to my feet and shot a scolding look over my shoulder. Bear was up on two legs, towering over me . . . He shrugged.

How did he know how to do that? Whatever, not important.

With momentary blindness abated, I tilted my head up and saw . . . the sky? Most of the ceiling in this part of the building had been ripped clean off, and light shone straight in. The museum-like open room where I stood might once have been beautiful but was currently in a state of complete disarray. Debris from the hole in the roof littered the area, along with smashed display cases. Glass, wood, chunks of marble, sheet rock . . . pieces of the room were everywhere. Interspersed in the mess were books, artwork, ancient weaponry, weird contraptions I didn't recognize—all the things that must have held some sort of value. If the Creator was all-powerful, why was He allowing this destruction?

Another angry roar sounded to my left, shaking the room and forcing my attention. Satan. He was over there somewhere, still in his gigantic dragon form.

I had no idea what he was looking for. I only knew my mission now was to keep it from him. But what could Satan possibly want? What could be so important to have gone through all this trouble to obtain?

I glanced back at Battle Bear and motioned for him to drop to all fours. At least that way he was a little less conspicuous. The Artifacts Room was just one large room the size of a small warehouse. The only places to hide were behind the artifacts or cases holding them.

The element of surprise was the only thing I had going for me. This was a flimsy plan—scratch that, this wasn't a plan at all. I'd followed the monster to this place with the blind determination to stop him, but what could I really do against him? I didn't have a magic sword anymore. I was just me. And there was no way I was going to be enough.

Crouching down, I peered around a fallen bookshelf. A giant membranous wing snapped out from the far side of the room and tossed what looked to be a wooden trebuchet against the wall. Satan was about a hundred feet away. My gosh, that ancient weapon had to weigh a ton, and he'd flung it out of the way as if it were no more than a tin can.

I sat down with my back against the bookshelf and buried my face in my hands. All I had to go up against him with was a burning desire to right my wrong and protect my loved ones. I was going to fail.

But I steeled my resolve. I would give whatever I could. It would never be enough, but it was all I had.

I bowed my head in a silent prayer of thanks to the Creator for what I'd been given and asked for His forgiveness of my part in releasing this abomination.

When I lifted my gaze, I was ready. Ready for the fight I was sure to lose. Ready to do whatever I could—even if I only managed to weaken the beast for my fellow hunters. Ready to face the embodiment of pure evil. And most of all, ready to face my end.

FACE OFF

*W*hat I wasn't ready for was a fight with my overgrown bear-dog. I'd commanded him to stay put. The big, stupid, lovable, terrifying butthead would not stop tailing me as I tried to creep closer to where Satan was searching in the back of the Artifact Room.

"For the last time, you overgrown ball of fur, will you please stay put?"

Bear growled low and shook his head at me. At this point, I liked him better when he didn't understand English. He had been way more obedient on Earth.

Grabbing the fur on the sides of his giant head, I looked into his big chocolate eyes. "Listen, buddy, you know I love you. And I know you are one fierce fighter. But right now, you are too big to be following me around. That crazy unhinged dragon over there is gonna discover us any minute if you keep trying to follow me. And now that you're here, you're too vulnerable to shrink back to regular Bear size. So I need you to just stay put, okay?"

He blinked at me twice. What did that mean?

"When the other hunters arrive, you can join the fight, okay?"

Another blink. Geez, was this how Logan felt when he was trying to keep me from danger? Because if so, it explained his general grouchy attitude those first few months of training.

"Listen, boy, you are so important to me, and I can't stand the thought of you getting hurt. That dragon over there could seriously injure you. So I need you to obey me and wait for the rest of the hunters to arrive . . . please." I wasn't above begging at this point.

His furry head dipped and dropped to my shoulder. The move was so like what he used to do when he'd give me hugs on Earth. I felt a prickle behind my eyes. I was going to miss him so much, but he was letting me go. I breathed a sigh of relief. When he lifted his head, there was a strange shininess to his eyes. Almost human-like.

He nudged me with his giant snout. I had to go, and I couldn't tell him everything would be all right and that I'd see him soon, because I didn't know how the next few minutes would play out. So I placed a gentle kiss on his furry nose and whispered my love to him before scurrying over to an overturned bookcase I could hide behind.

Pushing Bear out of my thoughts, I refocused my attention on my enemy with one goal in mind: Keep him from obtaining whatever artifact he was looking for, at any cost.

Sneaking up on Satan was surprisingly easy. Avoiding the flying debris was the hard part. He thrashed through display after display of artifacts in his dragon form, tearing apart everything in his path, and then flinging it out of his way. He was making so much noise and so hyper focused on his task that I didn't have to worry much about being super stealthy. I reached an overturned display case not fifteen feet from him in a matter of minutes.

My heart beat so hard I heard the rush of blood pumping through my veins. My arms were shaking, so I grasped my borrowed sword with two hands. This was going to be like going up against a giant with a steel toothpick, but it was what I had to work with.

Audrey, please stop.

Logan.

His desperate plea echoed in my head as if he was very far away, but the desperation in the tone still shook me to my core. The look on his face as I'd raced off with Bear would forever haunt me. Running from Logan wasn't the farewell that I imagined, but knowing Logan, he would have forcefully removed me from this fight. Hearing his voice in my head right now was like a dagger twisting in my already bleeding heart.

Logan, I love you, I whispered back to him, putting as much concentration as I could into the words and hoping he received them.

His thoughts again: *Love, please. Just wait. We're almost there.* Even if his words hadn't been dripping with desperation, I would have still picked up on his fear through the bond.

I can't. This is my fight.

Before he could answer, I threw up mental shields I didn't even know existed. I couldn't afford to be distracted right now.

I stood to my full height and stepped right behind the creature from my nightmares. Every fiber of my being screamed at me to run the other direction, but instead, I bent over to pick up a heavy chunk of white marble. I hurled it at the scarlet dragon with all the strength I had.

The hunk landed with a thud and slid harmlessly off his scaly back. But the rock did its job of garnering his attention. He whipped around to face me, all teeth and talons and a mouth full of fire.

The stupidity of my plan practically smacked me in the face. I still had a lot to learn in the art of war, but right now my primary goal was to distract him long enough for greater forces to arrive—and if possible inflict some injury that made it easier for other hunters to take him down.

If this red-scaled dragon and I were both going to be thrown back to the pit today, I wanted to make sure he returned to his fiery domain empty handed.

The dragon's mouth opened, and a strange hiss-like laugh echoed off the walls. He folded his wings in front of him and slowly transformed, wings turning into a swirl of black mist and smoke, his figure shrinking and distorting until what had once stood stories high in front of me now only towered above me at the height of an angel. The blackness snapped back and folded behind him, revealing the face of the false angel.

"Oh, little weakling. Finally dressed like the helpless sheep you truly are."

I glanced down at my white body armor and steeled my expression. Who cared what color I wore?

"Throwing pebbles at a giant has only worked one time in history, and you, my stupid sheep, are no blessed shepherd boy. You're a damned soul who turned against her maker, and whose time has officially just run out."

My blood ran cold at his words, but I didn't flinch. Distraction was the name of the game right now. And if he wanted to hear himself speak, well that was fine with me if it kept him from searching for whatever he was trying to find.

"Why do you hide behind that fake mask? Are you really so ugly you can't stand to show anyone your true form?" I asked. My weapon of choice . . . kindergarten insults.

He raised an eyebrow. "In a rush to see my true form, are you?"

I shrugged, probably looking a little odd with my sword at the ready. "Just seems silly to keep up a façade. It seems rather . . . weak to me. Why constantly pretend to be something you're not?" I only half-thought through my speech—I was word vomiting to keep his attention. A trickle of sweat slid down the side of my face. "Unless you're wearing the costume to relive the glory days or something. Hoping to get back into the God-club, are you?"

He cocked his head in that creepy birdlike manner and then let out a roar of laughter. "Are you trying to bait me into a fight? Or simply trying to distract me from my task? You really think I'm that stupid?"

"More like hoping you were that stupid."

A slow smile spread over Satan's false face. Something about the way it bunched the flesh seemed very off. "I'd be happy to show you my true form. You'll be spending enough time with me that you may as well get used to it."

I thought I was prepared for what was to come, but I so wasn't.

The flesh on Satan's face started to fall off in bloody chunks. With that creepy smile still in place, holes stretched to reveal the blackened flesh of the demon beneath. His body grew in size, which caused his angelic . . . casing . . . to stretch and burst apart like an overstuffed sausage.

Spikes jutted out from his elbow joints, and the end of each finger turned into a razor-sharp claw. He snapped his hands open and closed several times, and sparks flew from the points of contact.

His wings, which were creepy enough as shadow and mist, solidified into flesh-toned patchwork, as if he'd sewn them together using strips of human's skin. My stomach rebelled, and I fought to control my nausea.

His knees cracked backward, and an extra joint appeared near where his shins used to be. As his hair fell, multiple pointed barbs punched through his skull, turning his head into a weapon. Each pointed barb oozed onyx-colored liquid.

His face was most disturbing of all. He still had pits for eyes, but a red dot had appeared in their depths. There were only a few pieces of flesh still dripping off his face, but everything underneath was charred and scaly, like every other demon I'd seen. His nose was now completely gone, and in its place were two slits, very reptilian in nature. His cheekbones were cut sharply and over exaggerated, and his smile was downright horrifying. His lips of flesh were still in place, but the lower portion of his face was now pushed out like an animal's jaws. And behind that stretched, fleshy smile were rows of jagged, triangular teeth.

His chuckle, deeper than before, bounced around in my ears, creating a stabbing sensation. I gritted my teeth to keep from squeezing my head between my hands. I got the impression he had purposefully slowed down this change so I could take in each horrifying moment, a fear tactic that was extremely effective.

Despite myself, the tip of the sword I held trembled.

"You have every reason to fear me. I am the lion that prowls in the night, seeking to devour you. I am the death everyone fears. I am destruction, despair, and the desperation that claws at your chest. I am power." The floor shook on his last word, as if the power he claimed was manifesting in the very room where we stood.

"You are not the most powerful being in the world." Dread locked in my chest, but I fought him with truth.

"From this moment on, I'm the most powerful being in your world."

I didn't even register the hit until my back slammed against the hard surface, creating an Audrey-sized dent in the marble wall. Small pebbles and fine chalk dust rained down on me as I slid to the ground.

My chest throbbed—presumably at the point of impact. The assault had happened so fast I didn't see a thing. I rubbed the sore spot and struggled to my feet. I was searching for my weapon when I was lifted off the ground by my throat and slammed back into the wall. Gasping for air, I scratched at the hand that held me in place.

Satan's grotesque face filled my vision. The slits that were his nose expanded and contracted, and sulfur breath washed over my face. I choked on the stench as I struggled for air. Bile bubbled in my stomach, screaming to be released.

The skin on my throat where the vile creature held me burned as if his hand leaked acid. Sharp claws bit into the back of my neck, and blood trickled down my spine from the split flesh.

One strong squeeze and he could easily separate my head from the rest of my body.

I kicked and thrashed, but the efforts were no more effective than a fish flailing at the end of a hook.

Black ooze from the barbs on Satan's head dripped down his face and onto the ground. I couldn't see where they landed, but I heard a sizzle below after each drop.

He leaned in, and his stretched lips of flesh and rows of pointed teeth filled my waning vision. "That's right. Squirm like the worm you are. It amuses me."

He punctuated his words with a squeeze to my neck; the burning and bloodletting intensified. My airway was completely restricted. I couldn't even gasp for air.

My limbs became heavy and my movements sluggish. My mind screamed to continue to fight, but my body wouldn't comply.

The vise around my neck released, and as I fell as if in slow motion, I watched the monster's arm whip around and strike a blur of golden fur, sending it smashing to the other side of the enormous room.

"No!" I tried to scream as Bear's body lay motionless on the ground, but all that escaped was a weak wheezing noise.

Red blood dripped off the foot long spike that protruded from Satan's right arm-like appendage.

Bear wasn't moving, but Satan didn't give my friend a second glance as he refocused, pinning his red glare on me.

"You don't know it, but you've already failed." He reached into the folds of his stretched and torn garment and pulled out an object I was wholly unfamiliar with. The gold orb he held was semi-translucent with a green mist-like substance swirling lazily in its depths. "I already have what I came here to get." His eyes narrowed as he looked down at me, lying on my back on the floor. "But it's time I stopped toying with my dinner and took it home to devour. I'm looking forward to painting that armor a lovely shade of red."

THE END

I'd failed. Failed on a scale so epic I couldn't even wrap my brain around it. There would be no more cherished moments; there would be no more goodbyes. This was it. And in the end, I had done nothing except provide Satan with a bit of sport for his own twisted enjoyment.

Even in the face of hopelessness, something inside screamed at me to fight, to never give in. I crab-walked backward and then turned to stumble away from the monster who claimed ownership of my fate.

He followed. I broke into a sloppy run, throwing glances over my shoulder as he steadily shadowed me. I'd already born witness to his otherworldly speed, so I knew he was allowing this pathetic attempt to flee—no doubt another amusement.

Tripping over debris, I fell face first onto the unforgiving floor—bruising a good portion of my face—but scrambled to keep moving, even if that meant on my hands and knees. I imagined Satan got some sick enjoyment out of watching me scurry along the ground like the disgusting bug he already perceived me to be.

My anger reached a boiling point, and as I attempted to stand, my hand brushed over a familiar object.

The pommel of a sword. It could have been mine, or it might have been one of the artifacts from this room, but I wrapped my hand around the hilt. Historic relic or not, I didn't care. I was going to use it against my enemy. Causing even one drop of his blackened blood to shed would be a victory at this point. I didn't have much left to hope for. But that voice inside urged me to keep fighting.

I went to stand, but what felt like a cinder block landed on my sword hand, crushing the delicate bones and trapping me on the ground. I cried out

—soundlessly. Something in my vocal cords must have been damaged when Satan squeezed my throat.

A black hoof—three times the size of any Earthly beast's—pinned my hand in place and twisted to ratchet up the pain and damage. Spears of agony shot through my hand and up into my arm then radiated throughout my chest and the rest of my extremities. I wanted to pass out, but I couldn't. Acid burned up my esophagus, gathering at the back of my throat. I tipped my head upward and silently screamed the name of my God.

In a flash of blue light, Satan flew off me. I watched, half-detached because of my pain, as he was blown into a set of bookshelves. Struggling to a sitting position, I cradled my broken hand to my chest, not looking at my mangled limb for fear the damage would be more than my mind could handle.

The blast had originated to my right, but I kept my eyes fixed on my tormentor as he roared and shoved himself to his cloven feet. Chucking the remains of the shelves he'd crashed into behind him, his rage stirred the atoms in the air and affronted me from every angle.

Warmth radiated from behind me, but I didn't dare take my eyes off the monster.

"This one is not yours."

Joe.

Satan opened his mouth, but instead of letting out a bellow, he loosed a stream of fire that shot straight for me. I ducked in a pathetic attempt to protect myself, but the scorching fire never reached me.

I lowered my arm to find a shield of crackling blue electricity blocking the flames from touching me. Twisting to my left, I found Logan standing with his arms stretched out in my direction, a bolt of his familiar blue lightning coursing from his palms to the electric field hovering in front of me.

A hand landed on my shoulder, and healing warmth rushed through my body, knitting together the broken flesh and bones that Satan had mangled. I flexed my hand against my chest without pain. Joe gave my shoulder one more squeeze and took a step back, eyes fixed on Satan.

"This one is mine. You cannot have her."

"No!" Satan bellowed. Black spittle shot from his mouth. "The chain's curse was set by your very word. A price has to be paid."

"I'll pay it instead," Logan said.

What? No!

Logan's words were spoken with conviction. He strode forward with confidence and determination, his eyes capturing my gaze.

My heart jackhammered in my chest.

What are you doing? I sent the message to Logan without speaking.

Loving you, he sent back.

Rather than melt at his misguided romantic gesture, I crossed over the freaked-out threshold. His intent was there in his eyes. He would do this. He would try to trade places with me without my permission.

No.

I jumped to my feet and ran at the monster who masqueraded as an angel. Satan's mouth twisted, and a sound emerged that may have been a laugh. I didn't know what my end game was here, but I had to reach Satan before he had the chance to take Logan away.

I sprinted toward my horrific future.

Audrey, Joe's voice whispered in my mind, *trust that you are mine and follow me.*

I froze, as did the world around me.

The snapping of a single set of fingers echoed off the walls, and I was free. I pitched to the side to keep from running into the immobile Satan-statue in front of me and then took three steps before I regained my balanced.

Turning in a slow circle, I saw everything suspended in time, including the spittle flying off Satan's chin. I poked at hovering goo expecting it to be hard, but it stuck to my gloved fingers like slime.

Nasty.

Logan was mid-step about twenty feet away, immobile as well. I was about to rush to him when a voice cracked the silence.

"How is it that after everything, you still doubt Me?"

I spun to find the Creator, Hugo, and Joe standing in the middle of the room.

I gasped for words. "Whoa, yeah, of course you did this. It's the whole control of time and space thing you've got going on, right?"

The Creator's face wasn't harsh, but it wasn't soft either. Lightning flashed in His eyes when I spoke. Someone was a little peeved at me. I'd thought that whole walk down the aisle thing meant things were smoothed over between us, but obviously not.

Hugo gave me a small shake of the head that let me know I was treading on thin ice right now.

I winced. The weight of my shame forced my gaze down.

"Sorry," I whispered.

"I asked you a question, child." The Creator's voice boomed in my mind as well as throughout the room. Only a fraction of His power released, and before I knew it, I was on my knees.

"What . . . what do you mean?" I squeaked out.

A warm hand lifted my chin, and I looked into Joe's pain-filled eyes. "You know Satan is the Father of Lies, dear one. Yet you've existed these past weeks in fear rather than seeking my face. I've been waiting for you to come to me, yet you haven't."

I sat back on my knees and hung my head once again. When I looked back up, it was into the denim-washed eyes of my former trainer, Hugo.

He enclosed me in a hug and whispered in my ear, "Tell me why you didn't come to me."

He rubbed my back, soothing my fears.

"Because . . ." This was an ugly truth to reveal. "I thought you would send me to Hell for what I did, and so I hid from you."

He set me back, and it was now the face of my Creator staring at me. "Hell can never have you, dear one. You are Mine, now and forever. You were bought with My Son's blood long ago, and nothing can take you from My hand."

Several beats passed as I pieced together the meaning of His words.

"You will not be spending an eternity in Hell, dear one."

Was this a dream?

"My blood covers all your transgressions, great and small." Joe was now standing behind the Creator and next to Hugo. One of each of their hands rested on the Creator.

Tears welled in my eyes; the floodgates had opened and relief washed through my body.

"But what about this mess? I mean, he's free"—I pointed at Satan's still form behind me—"and he has . . . whatever artifact he was looking for." It hit me suddenly that Satan was stuck in suspended animation. "Wait, we can just take it back now."

Springing up, I went to search his shredded garment for the round contraption he'd showed me before but was stopped when Hugo appeared in front of me. "What?"

He shook his head and herded me away from the fallen angel.

"I have a plan and a purpose for everything." The Creator nodded toward Satan. "Even this."

"You planned to have Satan released from Hell so he could break into our realm and steal something?" This made no sense.

"The plan for the end times was set in motion a very long time ago, yet no one knows the date or the time but Me. This is but another way the Deceiver continues to unknowingly play his role. The device he sought will transfer his power to another, as it has been written and foreordained. The device was created for that very purpose, and now it will find its home with him until the day is right for him to use it. The day of My choosing."

I took a step back, shocked. "But . . . then you just . . ." Where to even begin? I hardly even knew what I wanted to say. "Are we all just chess pieces to You?"

I slapped a hand over my mouth and squeezed my eyes shut at my outburst. Surely I was due for a bolt of lightning right about now.

When I finally cracked one of my eyelids open, Joe was standing alone. The look on his face was not one of anger or condemnation but sadness.

"Audrey, is that really how you think I see you?"

I opened my mouth to reply, but the words caught in my throat. I didn't think he felt that way, but if I was interpreting what he said correctly, that meant I had been used to free Satan on purpose. I'd suffered so much because of what I'd done. Logan had suffered. This didn't make sense.

"You would not have suffered at all had you sought me out, but you chose to turn away from me."

But Logan—

Joe cut off my train of thought and answered my question before I could even ask it. "Did Logan not come away from his ordeal a stronger person? Free from the chains that he'd shackled himself to for so long?"

I opened my mouth to protest, but I couldn't. He was right. Logan did return from Hell a healed man, and had I sought out Joe, I wouldn't have feared an eternity of torment.

"My deepest desire is for you to know me better. I petition my Father on your behalf daily. My love for you is immeasurable. And all I ask is for you to trust in me. To let me help you with your burdens. My heart is full of love for you, not malice. It is not my desire to lose a single human being, and you have and will always have a part in that plan."

Sadness filled my heart, for I realized my transgression against Joe had not been the mistake I'd made in Hell—as awful as plunging the blade into him had been, doing so had been unintentional. No, my true offense had been when I tried to hide from him rather than run to him for forgiveness.

"You were forgiven before you even thought to ask." He spoke softly to me, knowing my mind without me having to verbalize the words. "That mark you bore, it was intended to send you running to me, not away. It was never a representation of your curse, but your refusal to seek my face, to seek forgiveness."

I'd completely forgotten about the black stain on my skin.

"Just like the physical scars that don't heal properly represent your internal struggle, your refusal to turn to me was like a poison in your veins, spreading every day. You no longer bear that mark."

My eyes began to fill with the heaviness of that news. I had jumped to the exact wrong conclusion. Logan had been right all along. The answer was always to seek the Son; nothing good would ever come from hiding. I wanted to say something, to thank him for this act of forgiveness, but words failed me.

He smiled and nodded. Walking forward, he placed a hand on my shoulder. "Audrey, the Father knows all things. His ways are not your own. The path you are on may look dark, but you must hold tight to the truth that He is good and works all things for good."

"I won't forget again."

His eyebrows rose.

"All right, I'll *try* not to forget again. Better?"

He smiled. "How about we put the beast back in his cage . . . together?"

"We can do that?"

"Yes." He pressed a sword into my hand and stepped back. "You've always had the power of my Spirit inside you. Let's see you set it ablaze."

As seeds of doubt took root in my soul, Joe's smile fell.

"I . . . can do that?" I questioned.

"With faith the size of a mustard seed, you can do that and so much more."

"So I should just, like, tell it to flame? Is there a manual?"

The corners of Joe's mouth ticked up, but he quickly pinched his lips together to cover the action. "What do you think is the source of your power?"

"Faith?"

"So use that now, and tell the flame to appear."

I closed my eyes. *I can do this. I can do this. I can do this,* I chanted.

Hugo's words boomed in my mind. *You can only do this through my power.*

Right, not my power but the Spirit's power in me. With renewed vigor, I imagined the flames as they used to be, burning bright blue with intense holy fire. Licking only the blade. Hungry for enemy blood.

When I cracked one eyelid open, the sword was blazing. Exactly how I'd imagined it to be.

Joe's face was lit by the flicker. He smiled broadly as he lifted his hand and pierced it on the tip of the weapon.

"Whoa, what are you doing?" I swung the sword out of his reach, but trickles of blood rolled down from the end of the blade.

"My blood was used to break Satan's chains, and along with the sword of the Spirit"—he nodded at the weapon I held—"my blood will form new ones."

"Oh my gosh, give a girl a heads up next time." I pressed a palm to my overexerted heart.

"Audrey, I'm fine. Look." Joe shoved his hand in front of my face, and there was no gash. Only a round scar marred the center of his palm. "Would you like a heads up on what we're about to do?"

"Yes, please." I smiled broadly and bounced on the balls of my feet, more than a little ready to watch Joe kick Satan's butt.

He chuckled. "Then let me tell you."

In a blink, the world around us was set back in motion. I stood shoulder to shoulder with Joe, rather than a hair's breadth away from Satan where I'd been when time stood still. I grasped the sword of the Spirit in my hand, and the blade flamed with holy fire.

"I said," Joe began, "that you cannot have her. She's been purchased with my blood. The price was paid long before the deed was done. But you"—Joe pointed a finger at Satan, authority ringing from the Son's voice—"no longer belong here."

I flicked my gaze to the side to see Logan staring at Joe and me in awe. A small army of hunters surrounded us, but they all held their positions, waiting for orders from Joe.

Satan let out a rage-filled bellow and charged us. Joe turned to me and, with a nod, sped right back at him.

The two collided with a force that sent a wave of power crashing into everyone. Some of my fellow hunters stumbled and fell from the quakes.

I stood strong with my feet planted despite the blast and waited for my moment.

DEFEAT

*T*he battle raged: Joe versus our ancient enemy. But after only a few short minutes, it was obvious Joe was toying with Satan. Anyone could see it. There wasn't a scratch on Joe, yet Satan's black blood was splattered and smeared all over the floor where they fought.

And now I knew the truth. Joe wasn't just more powerful than Satan in this realm; Joe was more powerful in any realm. And despite all of Satan's well-laid plans, he had unknowingly been following the Creator's script all along. The mighty red dragon was a puppet in this game, and his strings were about to be reattached.

Joe released a blast of power from his hands, and Satan flew back into the wall.

Well, that was a cool trick.

"Audrey." Logan was at my side. He squeezed my shoulder to get my attention. "What's happening?"

My gaze remained glued to the conflict in front of me as I waited with my blood-tipped blade for Joe's signal. I replied to Logan without turning his way, "Something amazing."

"Are you hurt? Are you okay?" No doubt the blood smeared on my white body armor from my previous injuries hadn't gone unnoticed.

The unveiled anxiety in Logan's voice forced my attention. His other hand was fisted, surrounded by a crackling ball of blue electricity. His face looked carved from granite except for the muscle that twitched in his jaw. His full lips were tight, and his blue eyes blazed.

I covered the gloved hand on my shoulder with mine and matched the intensity in his eyes. I didn't have time to explain everything that had happened, but he needed some small assurance. We'd have time—all the time in the world—to catch up later.

And with that thought, I smiled—a full, heartfelt smile. No longer was my eternity uncertain. I would spend it with the man I loved. I was certain of it.

"Everything is fine. Everything's going to work out." I squeezed his hand. "I promise."

He nodded once to let me know he believed me, even if he didn't fully understand. I snapped my focus back to the main event, putting aside my celebratory mood for later.

Joe stood with his foot on Satan's chest. Satan hissed and spat at Joe and squirmed on the ground like an overturned bug.

"Gotta go, babe," I said with a wink. "That's my cue."

"Wait, what?" Logan yelled after me as I ran forward with the sword at the ready. The power of the Spirit flowed through my limbs and into the blade.

As I reached the pair, Joe lifted his foot. Satan sprang up and extended his jaws. His roar of anger was cut off by the sword I shoved into his gut. The injury wouldn't kill him, but the holy blood mixed with the power of the Spirit and Creator would do its job.

Satan's jaw opened for a different reason this time. His strangled words of disbelief were followed by his frantic attempts to pull the blade from his body.

Taking several steps back, I watched his frenzied movements as he registered the horror of what was about to happen.

"This can't be done!" he yelled. His voice pierced my eardrums like razors, but I refused to do so much as flinch.

"It has been done. It's time for you to leave and for me to make repairs to my kingdom." Joe turned his back on Satan as if he were no more than a passing nuisance rather than the Prince of Darkness.

I watched in morbid fascination as a chain appeared from the entry point of the sword. The binding twisted and grew, snaking itself around the now thrashing beast and constricting his movements until finally a shackle appeared and clamped onto the lower part of his leg, right above the hoof that had crushed my hand not so long ago.

The bellow that followed shattered all the remaining glass in the room. I was forced to cover my ears this time, as did my fellow hunters.

"Enough!" Joe commanded, his voice booming above the noise and echoing across the room. Then all was quiet.

Something pushed against my leg, and I saw Bear, back to his regular size. I took a brief second to be thankful he was okay, laid a hand on his unusually stoic muzzle, and gave it a scratch.

"It's finished." Joe's voice carried in the silence.

A crack appeared in the floor beneath Satan. The chain that bound him grew and slithered into the ground.

Satan renewed his struggles in silent defiance, for the Son had restricted his speech. The chain pulled taut and brought the beast down, dragging him across the floor in front of me.

I stared at him. The thing that once haunted my nightmares but whom I now understood had no hold over me.

The red glow in the pits of Satan's eyes latched on to me. The hatred emanating from him was palpable, creating an itchy, restless feeling across my skin.

I wanted him gone.

The fissure in the ground opened wide enough to fit his horrid body. I turned away. It was done. I didn't need to see the end.

Before I took my first step, a thud on my back brought me to my knees.

I blinked down to see a black spike protruding from my chest. Reaching a hand back, I felt the thick barb lodged in my back.

The object that had impaled me dragged me back several feet before being pulled from my body with a sucking sound. Freed, I lay on my side, unable to move, but numb to pain.

When Bear's frantic barking assaulted my ears, spears of agony sliced across my chest. Something warm and sticky soaked my cheek. The flow of red spread across the white marble floor, and warmth drained from my body. Fluid pooled underneath where I lay.

Logan was running to me, the color draining from his face. Sound snapped back into its rightful place when he reached me, gently arranging me so he could press his hands on the holes on my back and chest.

"Audrey, it's going to be all right," he was saying to me. "Joe's still here; he'll fix you right up."

"Wh—" I wanted to ask what happened, but my strength was fleeing as quickly as the blood gushed from my wounds.

"Satan managed a partial transformation before he was sucked back to Hell. He struck you with his spiked tail. But it's going to be all right."

He'd already said that, but his voice shook this time. The slickness of my blood made his dark armor shine.

I couldn't die since I was already dead, but I was bleeding out so fast. Something didn't seem right.

Logan looked in the other direction.

"Please," he pleaded with someone.

"On her back," Joe commanded. He slipped a hand beneath me, and I felt the entry wound knit together. The thought that I'd been struck exactly where my mark had first appeared drifted lazily through my mind and then blew away.

The wound on my chest still bled freely. Joe held my head in his hands as Logan moved both hands to cover the hole on my front. "It's time for you to go too, dear one."

Wait, what?

"Your journey here has ended for the time. It needs to be picked back up where it left off."

I tried to shake my head or ask for an explanation, but my body was numbing, and I was incapable of speech.

Joe leaned over and kissed my forehead. *Trust in me.* The words whispered through my mind.

"What's happening?" Logan all but shouted the words I wanted to scream.

Joe said something to Logan. My hearing was dimming by the second, so I only saw Joe's lips move. When they stopped, Logan gazed down at me with fear-filled eyes.

Dread pooled in my stomach and curdled.

Vaguely aware of other hands on me, I looked down the length of my body, and the faces of my friends swam in and out of my blinking vision. Romona held vigil at my other side. Kaitlin and Kevin knelt on either side of my legs, and Bear was on his belly with his head rested on one of my ankles.

I couldn't feel him. I couldn't feel anything.

Tears flowed freely down Romona's and Kaitlin's cheeks. I caught a quick glance of Morgan's somber face behind Kaitlin before I focused on Kevin's red-rimmed eyes. And Logan . . .

With hands still pressed to my chest that I could no longer feel, he was red faced and yelling at Joe, who stayed stationary at my head, keeping me steady.

I could no longer hear nor feel my body. In that there was some mercy, for the pool of my blood had grown past the circle of my friends. I vaguely wondered how much blood one person had in their body to spill. If I could grimace at my gruesome thoughts, I would have. But I was paralyzed except for the movement of my eyes.

My vision blinked out for more than a second, and when it returned, I looked into Logan's face.

The world had changed. I was no longer in the Artifact Room but instead somewhere in the foothills of the mountain range I loved so much.

Feeling and hearing had returned but not movement. Soft grass pillowed my body, and Logan no longer held his hands to my chest to staunch a crimson flow.

My friends and Joe stood off to the side.

A soft summer breeze kissed my cheeks, and I felt no pain, but I saw it reflected back at me in Logan's eyes.

He bent down and pressed a gentle kiss to my lips, and pulling back slightly, he whispered, "I love you."

I smiled up at him. Of course, I already knew that. My eyes grew heavy, and I was helpless to keep them open. As they closed for the last time, I was able to whisper back, "Always and forever."

REALMS

*B*eep . . . beep . . . beep . . . beep . . . the sound went on at a steady cadence of about a beep per second. It was both familiar and offensive. The rooms of the Healing Center were usually peaceful. This incessant beeping was downright annoying.

I tried to peel open my eyes, which were dry and filled with crusty goop, and only managed to open my lids a sliver. Florescent lights blinded me, and I pressed my eyes shut once again.

Florescent lights? What?

Had the Healing Center gone back to the dark ages?

Lights off, I thought, but nothing happened. The same unpleasant brightness remained, and I squeezed my lids even tighter.

I expanded my senses. My body ached. I needed to do some serious stretches, but when I tried to move, to bring my hand up to cover my eyes, nothing happened.

The beeping noise increased its pace.

Forcing my eyes open, I looked around without moving my head. I was lying in a scratchy and uncomfortable bed, covered only by a thin white blanket that had seen many washes. Several machines were stationed around me, one of which I recognized as the source of the beeping. Its screen showed a peak every time a beep sounded, and I recognized it as a heart rate machine. Next to it stood a pole that held several bags of liquid.

The beeping grew faster.

My mouth was dry. I went to lick my lips. They were chapped and peeling.

A whiteboard hung on the wall in front of me. Unfamiliar names were written on it, along with times of the day. A TV was suspended from a mount near the ceiling, and a muted soap opera was playing.

My breathing increased, and the beeping grew frantic.

What was happening? Where was I?

A stout woman dressed in mint-green hospital scrubs walked into the room, mumbling about faulty equipment. She went straight to the heart monitor and turned it off without even glancing at me.

Was I invisible? Somehow transported and trapped in an Earthly hospital?

Nothing about this made sense.

I tried to talk to the lady, but my voice failed me. Instead of coherent words, a weak wheezing noise emerged. If the woman could hear me, she was too focused on checking the various machines around her to notice. She checked each one, talking to herself about this or that, medical jargon that made zero sense.

Had that heart monitor still been on, it would have been flipping out right now, because my heartbeat was so fast and strong I could feel it thumping in my chest. One beat swallowing up the next.

I made another attempt to grab the woman's attention, not caring what noise came out of my mouth. I just needed to let her know I was here.

The only thing I knew was that I was in some sort of medical facility that wasn't the Healing Center. That meant I was either in a medical ward in another and more primitive section of the realm, or I was somehow trapped on Earth. If the latter was true, this woman couldn't see me. The living couldn't see the dead.

There was a crash at the end of my bed—the sound of someone tripping. My gaze snapped to the source.

My mother stood shock still. And she was looking straight at me.

The fist pressed to her mouth shook, and the tears that filled her eyes spilled down her cheeks.

I blinked back the wetness that filled my parched eyes.

She could see me. Something was very wrong . . . or very right.

"Oh, Mrs. Lyons." The woman in the mint-green scrubs hustled to my mom's side. "Is everything all right? I know it's hard to see your baby like this. Let me help you clean up this mess. Take a seat. I'm sure your husband can get some more food."

My mom didn't look away from me, not for a moment, her body a living statue where she stood. When the lady tried to usher her into a seat, Mom finally moved. Her hand snapped down and grabbed the woman's wrist.

"Linda, she's awake."

The woman, Linda, gasped and finally looked at me. Her mouth opened and closed several times without making a noise, until she uttered, "Thank the Lord." She jerked her gaze back to my mother.

"I'll find a doctor." Linda ran from the room.

"Baby." Mom sobbed and stumbled to the edge of my bed. She gingerly sat on the side of the mattress, in one of the few places free of tubes and wires.

Grasping my hand, she offered a brilliant smile as tears flowed from her eyes. "Can you hear me, sweetheart?"

I tried to squeeze her hand but didn't have any strength. Tears leaked from my eyes and spilled down the sides of my face.

"You were in an accident, baby. You were asleep for a very long time. We didn't know if . . . That doesn't matter now. You're back with us, and everything is going to be okay. I promise, it's all going to be better now."

My mom's face was so full of hope and joy. But my mind was a mix of disbelief and horror.

I had no idea how this was possible. I was truly back on Earth. Back in the body I thought I'd lost so long ago. Somehow I'd been given a second chance at life . . . and it was cracking my soul in two. For as unbelievable and miraculous as this was, this meant that I had unknowingly . . . unwillingly . . . left my other half in the heavenly realm.

And there was only one way I was ever going to be able to return.

Being alive was torture. My body hurt everywhere, and it didn't feel like my body anymore. I'd been lying sedate for almost a full year, so my muscles had atrophied. Weakened and shrunk from disuse—now that I wanted to use them again—they rebelled.

I'd apparently spent most of that time at some fancy center for coma patients thousands of miles from my hometown. The financial strain I'd seen my parents suffering when I took part in the battle at their house made a lot more sense now. They hadn't been given any guarantees, and the longer I remained in a coma, the lower my chances of ever waking up had grown, but my brain activity had stumped the doctors. According to their machines, my mind was functioning in a way they hadn't expected, and so my family had trudged on with the hope that some day I'd wake up—and that 'some day' had finally come.

A physical therapist came in twice a day to move my body for me while I basically just watched her and tried not to cry when she twisted one of my limbs in a way it didn't want to go.

A week after I woke up, I was finally able to move some parts of my body on my own, and I no longer felt quite so claustrophobic in my skin. I was told that next week I'd be taken to the in-house rehabilitation center twice a day for my physical and occupational therapy.

I wanted to explain everything to my family. Where I'd truly been all this time, but I was unable to communicate properly. My muscles weren't the only parts of my body that had turned against me; my vocal cords and part of my mind had followed suit.

I could barely get a word out, both because my voice had been unused so long and also because parts of my brain were scrambled. At least, that was what my doctor said, but in a more sensitive way. Even though I could think relatively clearly—yeah, I suffered little glitches now and then when I'd temporarily forget a name with a face and things like that—I was told I was going to have to re-learn how to speak and read and write.

All of that news blew . . . big time. It meant I was stuck lying in this bed, feeling like a geriatric patient rather than the healthy eighteen-year-old I should have been, struggling out a word here and there, unable to explain what had happened to me.

I saved my tears for the dead of night when I knew the only people who might see them were the nurses. My family was beyond overjoyed to have me back. My parents had both been visiting me the day I 'miraculously awoke,' and so they made plans to stay with me for a few weeks and then switch off and on until I could go home. I had video calls with my sisters and brother that basically consisted of them talking at me while I just attempted to smile.

Everything was hard. Everything hurt. And I was a conflicted mess of emotions. Thankful to have my life returned, bitter to have lost the new existence I was building. I didn't know whether to be angry at the Creator for sending me back or grateful.

My heart—my poor, shriveled, beat-up heart—hurt, big time.

Even thinking Logan's name brought a fresh onslaught of tears to my eyes. Picking one existence over the other would have been a near-impossible choice. But I hadn't been given that choice.

Was I relieved about that? Or angry? I didn't know.

My opinion changed hourly. I'd spend time with my parents, listen to their stories from the last year—how much they had missed me and how happy they were to have me back—and think that despite the pain of leaving all I had built in the afterlife, being back on Earth was the right thing. But then in the dead of night I'd lie awake wondering what my friends, what Romona and Bear, were doing and how they were going on without me.

And I'd ache.

Then him.

I would have given up the world to be with him. How could I for one second think this Earthly life was preferable to an eternity with the other half of my heart?

The cycle went on and on, around and around, back and forth.

Did he know where I was, what had happened to me? Did he visit me when I wasn't aware? Now that I had a living future . . . what should I do with my second chance at life? But what kind of life could I have without him? I would wait for him, but would he do the same?

What my family had gone through was a nightmare . . . one they were finally waking up from. Did I feel the same or not?

And I prayed. I prayed long and hard, beseeching the Creator for answers. But I didn't receive any. It felt as if my lifeline to Him had been cut off, and all I was left with was my knowledge of Him.

And therein lay my choice.

Would I choose to believe what I knew to be true, that the Creator, my God, was a good God who wanted good things for me, or would I rely on how I felt in the moment?

Abandoned, betrayed, and broken.

I knew all of that to be untrue. I knew He was with me, even now in this bed, day and night. I knew my God wouldn't leave my side.

The day on the mountain He'd showed me the many times He'd carried me through life's trials. But this was so much bigger than those incidences. And the desire to give in to my feelings, rather than grasp the truth with both hands like a lifeline and hold tight, was strong.

I knew now that even if I did let go and rail at Him, He wouldn't leave me. But that didn't mean I felt any better.

"Honey, are you crying?"

Shoot.

I attempted to lift a wobbly hand to my face but didn't have the strength.

My dad turned in the chair he occupied near my bed and pulled a tissue from a box. He quickly dabbed under my eyes and soaked up the moisture that had unwillingly collected.

"There you go." His lips were smiling, but the emotion didn't reach his eyes. He knew I was in pain; he just didn't understand the extent of it. "Audrey, I promise things will get better. You're growing stronger every day. We'll be out of this place and back home in no time. You'll get back to your old life, I promise."

I tried to give him a reassuring smile, but I'm pretty sure the expression was crooked at best. I nodded slowly to indicate I understood. Getting out even a word took an exhausting amount of effort, and I didn't feel up to it. A great deal of my mental strength went toward not thinking about a few key things and trying to live in the moment again. Pretending I wasn't this broken shell of a person.

If I kept this up, I might never talk again. But I didn't know how to process and move through the pain of what I'd lost to keep on living. I didn't even know if I wanted to process it, because it meant I'd have to move on, and I wasn't ready for that.

For the very first time, I could appreciate not having had my memories immediately returned when I arrived in the afterlife.

This was beyond overwhelming.

"Baby," my dad went on, oblivious of the true cause of my inner turmoil, "I know life seems impossibly hard right now, but you're a fighter. You. Are. A. Fighter." The fierceness in my father's eyes told me he truly believed that. That he desperately wanted me to believe that as well.

The prickle behind my eyes warned of more tears to come. I blinked them away. My parents needed strength from me right now.

"My sweet Audrey, you *will* fight your way back to us." My dad gripped my hand tightly. "And you will go on to have a beautiful life. Full of laughter and joy and someday a love and family of your own."

There was no holding back the tide of tears after those words. They welled up and spilled over onto my face unfettered. For what my dad didn't know, couldn't know because I couldn't yet express it myself, was that I would never have a love in this life because I'd already given away my heart, and I refused to take it back. Part of myself belonged to someone I most likely wouldn't see again for many years—for a lifetime.

So this life, this future, he spoke of, would never be a reality.

Yes, I'd go on. I'd live my life. And not only for my family, but for myself and for the Creator who gave it to me. I'd even live it for the people I knew who had moved on to their eternal existence, for life was truly a precious blessing. But I would never have love and a family. For there was one thing I'd resolved.

My heart belonged now and forever to Logan, and I wasn't ever going to be whole again until the day I found myself back in his arms.

TRAINING

"Just one more step. That's great. Now just one more, and I promise that will be it. That one was so good I'm sure you can do another."

"Hate . . . you," I pushed out through clenched teeth as my pathetic muscles shook with fatigue. Sweat dripped down my face and soaked the back of my t-shirt as I forced one foot in front of the other again . . . and then again.

Lying jerk-face.

"Yeah, I know. You say that every time." He chuckled. "I'm over it. You're not my grumpiest patient by far."

"Something . . . else . . . I can work on," I puffed out. A chunk of wet hair fell in my face. They'd shaved my head after the accident, and the shortened grown out length was always getting in the way.

Jared just laughed at me again.

You won't be laughing when I throat-punch you with one of these crazy cane contraptions.

But I'd never do that. Jared was my regular physical therapist at the hospital, and even though there were times I truly hated him, the truth of the matter was he was just here to help me. We'd been working together for almost a month now, and according to him I was making 'amazing improvements.'

Pfft.

Being able to feed myself and walk a few incredibly slow laps around what I called the "baby loop"—imagine a track and field circle for toddlers—didn't feel super amazing to me. The grueling work left me sore every day. I felt like I was training for the Olympics rather than simply getting back to a normal range of motion.

Jared was a cheerful taskmaster. He was quick to smile, and I'd yet been able to get under his skin in an irritating way. He basically ignored my sour moods, pretending I was talking pleasantly with him instead.

He was one of the younger therapists, probably in his mid-twenties. He had a mop of sandy-brown hair and hazel eyes with slight laugh lines running from the corners. His broad smile always reminded me of Kevin, which used to rub me the wrong way because I didn't like to be reminded of my friends from the afterlife, but I'd gotten used to it over time.

He was certainly attractive, but I only noticed it in a detached way. Like I would notice the attractiveness of a stranger, not someone I spent time with on a daily basis. I wondered more than once if they'd assigned me the young 'hot' trainer, thinking it would be more motivating for me. It probably would have made a difference to the girl I'd once been, but it didn't matter in the least to the warrior I'd become.

Throwing insults aside, I was determined to move on with my life. And in order to do so, I had to push myself to the limits. In the past month, I'd regained my ability to read almost completely. My writing was a bit sloppy, and that tied my mental and physical therapy together. Speech was the most frustrating. All the words were in my head, but I struggled to get them out. The doctors and therapist were very optimistic that it would come along as well and were quick to remind me how far I'd come in what they considered a short period of time, but my inability to communicate normally was still super frustrating.

In the days when I could hardly communicate at all, I'd decided not to tell my family about what had happened to me while my body wasted away without my knowledge. I debated it, but I couldn't find a reason to unload that burden on them. At best, they'd believe I dreamed it all up. At worst, they'd think I had more severe mental issues than had already been identified.

And in a weird way, keeping the secret meant I could keep all of it. I didn't want someone to tell me I had to give it up.

I would move on with my life because there had to be a reason I hadn't died when I was struck by that car—some purpose the Creator had for me here on Earth in a living body—but I'd always carry those loved ones with me. I didn't want to talk to someone who would try to force them from my thoughts in a futile attempt to make me forget and live a "happier, healthier life." If the Creator had wanted me to forget, then I would have woken up without any memories of my year as a demon hunter or the relationships I had built during that time.

There was a reason for the remembering.

So instead of telling anyone about the afterlife, I spent time silently beseeching the Creator, Hugo, and Joe for wisdom, guidance, and a break from the soul-wrenching pain of loss I hid from all others. I knew they were with me and were the help I needed. It took supernatural effort to keep from being angry at my situation. Every day, I had to intentionally choose to believe there was a plan and purpose in all of this.

Some days were harder than others.

"All right, I think that's good for today, Audrey. Up high for the amazing work."

Jared held his hand so high that under normal circumstances I would have had to jump to reach it. I rolled my eyes and halfheartedly swiped at him with my high-tech crutch. He deftly stepped out of the way. "Close enough."

I wrinkled my nose and stuck my tongue out at him. He had hints of Kaitlin in his personality too. I mentally slapped myself. I wasn't ever going to let go of my friends, but I had to stop constantly comparing people to them.

Jared was just Jared. He was his own person, just as each of my friends in the heavenly realm were their own person and could never be replaced.

"Oh, maybe I shouldn't have taken you out of the running for the grumpiest patient after all."

I flopped into my wheelchair and shook my head. "Sorry, am I a . . ." *No, that wasn't right.* "I am in"—*there we go*—"a"—*get the word out, Audrey*—"ju-junky mood today."

I sighed. Having to concentrate so much on something that used to be so easy was wearisome.

Jared's smile didn't quite reach his eyes. Like most people around me—lots of brave faces hiding their pity for me. Maybe someone else would be annoyed by their insincerity, but frankly, I'd rather have their poorly veiled pity than anything more forthcoming. If they wanted to believe I was buying what they were selling, that was fine with me.

In truth, I was doing a lot of play-acting myself. My parents now switched weeks flying back and forth from the hospital to stay with me, and for their sakes I made an effort to look happy. I wasn't fooling them any more than they were fooling me. It was a charade we all played that I was happy to keep up.

Things would change, I told myself over and over again. Life wouldn't always be this hard; it wouldn't always hurt this much.

But a little voice in the back of my mind mocked me and told me that I was fooling myself if I thought I could go on without him. When that voice popped up, I locked it away into the far recesses of my mind—for my sanity.

I was barely paying attention as Jared wheeled me back to my room.

"You know, soon you'll be able to start taking short walks on your own in-between our sessions."

I barked out a laugh. Awesome. More pain for more of the day.

"Cool, right?" He purposefully ignored my mocking response. "Okay, here we are. Temporary home sweet home."

"Yay," I weakly replied.

He stopped before he wheeled me into the room. I looked up at him with a question in my eyes, and he came around the front of my chair. He crouched down until he was level with me, his gaze intense and his lips pressed into a hard line.

A serious look from Jared? Uh-oh, these were few and far between. Someone was channeling a little Shannon right now.

Oh, shoot. I did it again. I batted thoughts of the prickly angel away.

"You're a fighter, Audrey. You'll get through this and be stronger because of it."

I wanted to laugh in his face, but that word popped up again—fighter—it got me every time. These people didn't know that I had been a hunter. They didn't know how appropriate the term was.

Who knew that battling with fists and weapons would be one of the easier ways to fight?

"You want me to do . . . wh-what?" It had taken a few months, but I was finally able to get a full sentence out. Yeah, I usually had a break and often a stutter, but I finally felt like I could communicate with people again.

Jared bounced up and down like an excited puppy. "We're gonna go for a jog . . . on the 'big kids' track.'"

He pointed his thumb behind him. I didn't have to look, but I did anyway. In the west wing of the hospital was a full gym. It had all the bells and whistles: not only a full-sized running track, but also a climbing wall and a bunch of fancy machines. The gym sat in the very center of the wing. All the rooms on this side of the hospital looked down on it, reminding me of a hotel atrium. Maybe the architect of this place had thought the view would be inspiring for the patients, but in reality it just made anyone using it feel like they were on display.

I shook my head. "Noo. Definitely not ready for that."

He nodded, a maniacal smile on his face. "Oh, yeah, you are."

"I ju-just got com-fortable slow walking. I only d-ditched my wheelchair las-st week. What makes you th-think I'm ready for that?" I pointed out the windows that looked down to what patients called the coliseum.

It didn't just feel like people were on display down there—that they were being judged—it was a fact. Sometimes when patients got bored, they'd sit on the sixth floor and watch the action. Cringing whenever someone wiped out . . . which always happened. I should know. I'd spent enough time as one of those quiet observers.

One truly delightful ten-year-old always tried to take bets on how long it would take for someone to bite it. I ignored him because I found that to be extremely disrespectful, but I never said anything because he was just a little kid. He was missing an eye from an accident, and his head was shaved bald with a bunch of stitches visible on his patched eye side. I felt bad for him, but I also thought he was a little punk.

Kids . . . shudder . . . at least I wasn't lamenting the loss of never having to have them. The booger eaters here drove me a little batty. But the circumstances that landed them here made me entirely depressed, so I basically ignored them when I could.

"This is happening, Audrey. Embrace it. Seize the day. Run free and all that."

"What?"

Jared was weird.

"Come on." He grabbed my hand and all but hauled me to the elevator that brought us to the ground floor.

I reluctantly followed him out when we arrived because I didn't want to be dragged again.

Upon stepping into the training space, I was immediately both intimidated and swamped with nostalgia. The hospital's atrium-like rehab training area in no way looked like the training gyms I'd spent so many hours in with both Hugo and . . . him, but something about the atmosphere brought back a wave of familiarity. And with it a swell of emotions, both good and bad.

Jared led me around the large open space, pointing out different areas and activities and letting me know when he thought I may be ready for each. He was completely oblivious to my near emotional overload.

"All right, now that tour time is over, let's talk about the training plan for the day."

Jared turned to me, and his expression instantly dropped. "Audrey, I'm so sorry. We can just have this be a tour today and start tomorrow if you need time to work up to this. I know sometimes I push you a little hard, but it's because I always know you'll rise to the challenge."

"Huh? What?" I didn't understand his one-eighty degree change. He did a quick search around and then took off, pulling a fresh hand towel from a rack.

"Here." He handed me the white piece of cloth and shifted on his feet, looking extremely uncomfortable.

I looked up at him with knitted brows. Why had he given this to me?

"It's for . . . you know, your face."

My face?

I reached up and touched a hand to my cheek to find it wet. The other cheek was also covered. I'd been crying without even knowing. Since when was that a thing I did?

I quickly scrubbed my face with the abrasive towel, wiping away the evidence of my weakness.

Geez, who cried like that without even realizing it had happened? I was turning into a total spaz.

"All right, so we'll just go back upstairs and do some similar exercises to yesterday's and—"

"No," I interrupted his nervous jabber. I knew a lot of patients leaked out tears during physical therapy. The sessions were often extremely painful. I could only assume he was acting so weird because tears weren't something he'd ever seen from *me* before. Sure, witty comebacks and playground insults, but never tears.

"Let's do . . . th-this. You were right. I c-an handle it."

Jared placed a brotherly hand on my shoulder. "Really, Audrey, we can start tomorrow."

I shook my head. "It's really okay. I-I would like to . . . move forward."

Jared pressed his lips together and searched my face. After several beats, he gave a sharp nod. "All right then. Step up to the starting line. I'm expecting four laps from you today."

I swallowed a groan. I should have taken the out. This was gonna suck.

REVELATIONS

*T*elling Jared yes was a mistake—a big, fat, huge mistake.

I leaned heavily on the railings as I limped back to my room. I was taking a detour through a part of the hospital I rarely traveled simply because I knew there would be railings for me to use. I'd refused to be wheeled back out of sheer stubbornness. A decision I regretted at the moment.

I hadn't even made it four laps. After two and a half speed-walked laps, I was on the verge of collapsing. Jared called it quits with his usual cheerfulness, telling me how great I'd done even though I knew I was a failure.

One step in front of the other.

Keeping my head bent, I focused entirely on my forward momentum. I was like the Little Engine That Could. *I think I can. I think I can. I think I can.*

There was a break in the railing in front of a patient's door. Sucking in a fortifying breath of air, I took several slow shuffle steps until I reached the other side. I happened to glance up and see the patient's name scrolled across the plate next to the door.

For some reason, I found the name sobering. This was the section of the hospital that housed the more critical and long-term coma patients. The ones who weren't expected to ever wake.

In some ways, this wing was more like a nursing home than a hospital. Each patient had their own room. They were usually decorated by family and friends, even though the patient most likely would never appreciate their efforts. People visited on a regular basis but hardly ever spent the night. Sometimes patients' families would bring in their own furniture to place around the room. Things that made them comfortable and probably humanized their loved ones.

L. London was printed on the removable sign.

I stopped and just stared at the name. *A. Lyons* could just have easily been affixed to that spot, or any of the rooms along this hall.

A shiver ran down my spine. As much as I ached for the afterlife, how would I have felt if I'd known my body was withering away in this realm? My family in limbo, hoping for a day that might never come. They'd lived like that for almost a year, and I'd had no idea.

I was about to move on when the sound of waves tickled my ears. The door to the patient's room was open a few inches, and soothing notes were coming from within.

I knew better. I knew I shouldn't. But the ocean had a hold on my heart.

So I gently pushed the door open wider and poked my head through. With a sense of awe, I stepped inside, closing the door behind me without rational thought. Someone had transformed this room into an ocean paradise. The rhythmic lull of the surf was only part of the illusion. A mural of blended blues completely overtook the wall to the right. It looked like I was standing in the curl of a wave right on the cusp of breaking. It was breathtaking.

Several large glass jars filled with shells and sea glass sat on the windowsill. In front of the open window was a wind chime made of rope and shells gently tinkling in the breeze.

Other than the hospital bed, the furniture in the room was a stylish mix of whites and creams. It reminded me of colorful shades of sand. I glanced past the pictures on a small bookshelf, somehow feeling like it would be an invasion of privacy to look too closely—but who was I kidding? I'd already invaded this family's privacy when I walked in the room. My gaze landed on a large surfboard that was mounted to the wall above the patient's head.

That's odd.

The board wasn't shiny and new but rather faded in places and on the brink of overuse. A pain twisted inside my chest.

The ocean was *our* place, but knowing this patient had loved his sport as well hit a little too close to home.

I finally let myself look at the form lying in bed—almost unrecognizable as a human being under the machines keeping him or her alive. Ignoring all the machines that littered the room had been easy at first—with the beautiful harmony someone had taken great care to transform this space—but they jumped out in stark contrast when I stared at the patient. They beeped and wheezed, keeping the person before me alive.

Out of a strange sense of curiosity, I took a step forward. I could now tell the patient was a male. Tubes came out of him everywhere, running out from under his blankets. His head was shaved, and sensors were attached to different points on his skull, most likely monitoring brain function that wasn't even there . . . but I didn't know enough about these severe cases to do more than guess.

His hair might have been light brown, but the cut was shorn so close to his scalp I could only go by the color of his eyebrows. His eyelids were taped shut, which I found a little disturbing. A flexible plastic tube ran from his mouth. His features were hollow and gaunt. Guessing his age would have been a shot in the dark. I didn't see evidence of wrinkles, which would suggest he was incredibly old, yet his body had that withered look that one often associates with the elderly.

Then again, I thought, *so did mine before I started physical therapy.*

His shoulder bones stuck out under his hospital gown—evidence that he'd once had a large build. His right hand peeked out from his thin blanket. He had long, thin fingers that, like the rest of him, were most likely leaner than normal due to whatever time he'd spent here.

I didn't know what made me scrutinize this poor soul so closely. Perhaps because I sympathized with him? Perhaps because I felt like he could easily be me?

His chest rose and fell to the cadence of the machine that was breathing for him. I was transfixed by that motion, and I honestly didn't know how long I stood there, just watching him breathe.

"Excuse me, what are you doing in my son's room?"

I startled and jumped away from the bed. Something on the shelf behind me fell over. I had been so busy with my creeper behavior that I'd missed someone entering the room.

"Oh, g-gosh. I'm sorry." My mind short-circuited on me, and I just stood there like a complete idiot, looking at a well-dressed lady. She was probably around my mother's age, but with blonde hair pulled back in a stylish twist. Her heels clicked on the floor as she walked farther into the room . . . her son's room that I had totally trespassed into.

A small frown pulled the corners of her lips down, and her brows pinched in a way that made me believe she was deciding between confusion and anger. I really hoped for the former.

But then she stepped closer, and I saw her eyes.

I took a step back. For a minute, I couldn't breathe.

She had his eyes. His exact same eyes.

She said something, but I missed it, transfixed by her cobalt-blue gaze.

Lots of people had blue eyes, I reminded myself, trying to shake off the unnerving recognition. She tilted her head, waiting for an answer to a question I hadn't even heard.

"I . . . I'm sorry. Wh-what?"

"I asked if you know a patient here."

"Oh. No. I am a pa-tient. I'm st-ill in re-hab." That one took a while to spit out. I pointed at my mouth and let out a quiet, self-deprecating laugh. "See?"

Her features softened at that, as if my hardships excused my bad behavior. Hey, I would take whatever I could get. I wasn't allowed in her son's room.

"I'll j-ust go now." I went to make a speedy exit, but then I remembered I'd knocked something over on the shelf. I quickly turned to straighten what looked to be a picture frame before retreating, but I stopped once I had repositioned it.

There were several people in the shot. Teenagers. And in the middle, with his arm draped over a beautiful blonde, was a younger version of Logan.

My vision blurred for a moment before snapping back to normal. I clutched the shelf of the bookcase to stay upright, my knuckles turning white with the grip.

"Do you know him, my son . . . Logan?" The woman was right next to me, pointing to his image.

I gaped and floundered for more than a few seconds. How was this possible? He was dead. I knew he was.

But so was I—and here I was.

Reality slammed into me—hard.

I stumbled back a step, and the woman—Logan's mother—took a hold of my elbow to steady me.

"Are you all right, dear? Do you need to take a seat?"

A distant part of my mind wondered why she was being so nice to me. She had walked in to find a stranger lurking around her son's hospital room. She should be shooing me away, but she was treating me with kindness instead. Maybe because of my condition?

She steered me toward the loveseat opposite his bed, the one facing his feet.

"I . . . ah." My hands were shaking and my breathing erratic. I had to get this under control.

I glanced up into her deep-blue eyes and almost lost it again.

This was Logan's mother. Sitting right next to me. And that meant the gaunt figure lying on the bed was . . . it was Logan.

He was here, with me . . . yet he wasn't here. I knew that better than anyone.

Did he know he wasn't actually dead, or was he just as much in the dark about it as I was? A memory tickled my mind, of when we were in the Archives Building and I asked if he'd checked up on his loved ones. *I've been avoiding this place. I probably should have at least checked in on my parents, but I'd been too . . .* If Logan had checked on his parents even once, he would have figured out where they spent their time—but by his own admission, he hadn't. So there was a chance he had no idea, just like I hadn't known.

His mother stared at me with her brow furrowed. "Maybe I should get some help?"

She went to stand, but I grabbed her wrist. She looked back at me with surprise splashed across her face. I had to say something.

"Uh . . . please no. I'm-I'm s-o sorry." I swallowed to wet my dry throat. "Your—ur son, Lo-gan. He ta-ught me how to . . . surf. Di-didn't know h-e was here."

"Oh, I see." She sat back down on the sandy-colored loveseat. "That must have been a while ago. He's been here for almost four years now."

A tear leaked out of my eye. "I'm . . . so sorry."

"Oh dear, please don't say that. It looks like you've had your own struggles. Logan will come back to us . . . someday."

She patted my hand, but I heard the hopelessness that betrayed her words. He wouldn't be in this wing of the hospital if they thought he was going to come back to them. This wasn't where they housed the patients they expected would wake up.

But I had, so why couldn't Logan?

That wasn't a realistic expectation, I told myself.

But miracles happened every day.

Two sides of my mind warred. I was on overload.

How could he be here? How was it we were both in the same place? Was it because he was going to come back to me, or was it so I could find closure to move on with my life?

I didn't know, but I wasn't going to figure it out in this short visit. My world had just been blown apart . . . again. I needed some time.

"Wo-uld you mi-mind telling me wh-at happened?"

"Oh." The color drained from her face. I shouldn't have asked.

"Never mind. That was insensitive." I was able to get it all out at once.

She patted my hand and gave me a weak smile, her eyes filling up with water. "No, it's all right. It's supposed to be good for his father and me to talk about this. Can I ask your name, dear?"

"My name is Audrey." Another full sentence.

"Well, Audrey, I'm Mrs. London. But you can call me by my first name, Celeste."

35

HOPE

I was scaring my mom, I know I was, but it couldn't be helped. After our brief talk, I'd asked Mrs. London—Celeste—if it would be okay if I visited Logan again. She'd smiled and said that would be nice and promised to add me to the list of allowed visitors. I'd then asked for a nurse to take me back to my room—more from mental exhaustion than physical.

I'd hardly said two words since.

My mother wasn't dumb. She knew something was up, and in true Mom-fashion, she was trying to shove food down my throat to make whatever was bothering me better. I'd only been able to eat a few bites of the feast she'd bought at a local eatery. After months of complaining about hospital cuisine, I should have been shoveling the food in my mouth, but now eating was like trying to swallow ash. Anything that made it down just soured in my stomach.

I finally pushed the food away, claiming to have a headache and needing sleep, which only worried my mom even more. I faintly heard her in the background trying to track down my doctor and checking up on my physical therapy sessions. I knew I should be putting her mind at ease, but I needed some time.

Logan's mom had told the story of a car crash. He'd been in the backseat of a car that had rolled off the highway and then several hundred feet down a steep embankment.

Logan had been rushed into surgery for several broken and shattered bones, but though he had healed from those injuries, he'd never woken up. He'd sustained a major head injury during the accident.

Three others had been in the same car. The driver, one of Logan's childhood friends, was now a quadriplegic. The front passenger had escaped with only minor injuries, which was a miracle considering the damage to the car.

And the fourth passenger had lost her life. The fourth passenger had been Kaitlin, the girl whom Logan had his arm around in the picture where I first recognized him.

Kaitlin was in fact dead, not in a state of limbo like Logan and me. Or had been in. Or rather, that he was still in, and I no longer was.

My head ached with the desire to make sense of it all. How was it Logan and I had been in the afterlife even as our bodies remained anchored to Earth?

I spent the late afternoon and into the evening replaying all I could remember about the heavenly realm. When I'd first arrived, Joe had never confirmed that I had died. I came to that conclusion myself. Now I found myself wondering about my memories—questioning them. How much of it had been real? Any of it? Some of it had to be, how else would I have known Logan and Kaitlin at all?

And there were little details that made sense now. Like why the zombie trees had reached for me . . . they'd recognized the Earthly life still in me where the rest had none. The revelation was small, but being able to make sense of anything right now was a comfort.

But what did this mean for Logan? Was this the real reason why the two of us seemed to have extraordinary supernatural powers? Him with his electric lightning and me with the flaming sword. Had we been singled out because we were living in the land of the dead?

I put two hands to my head and pressed against the raging headache. I might never know the answer to these questions. Most of all, I wanted to know if Logan knew now, or if he'd known then, that he was lying prone in a hospital bed.

My instincts said he didn't know. But I couldn't just ask him. Our ability to communicate was completely gone.

I knew nothing.

A ball of anger swirled in my gut. I contained the churning emotion to that space, but I wasn't sure how long I would be able to ward it off. Why was none of this explained? Why was I left in the dark? If the Creator was good and cared for me, why was He putting me through this second heartbreak?

Logan was in one way so close to me, but in another, he was just as far as he'd been since I'd woken up back on Earth.

After several minutes of talking, Celeste had finally confessed that the doctors hadn't given any hope of Logan waking, but she didn't believe that to be true.

I knew miracles could happen, but I also knew that just because the Creator had the power to wield them didn't mean he was going to.

In this case, I didn't even know what to hope for.

But I knew that I'd visit Logan again. Or the shell that used to be him. I knew he wasn't really inside there anymore . . . but maybe, one day, he would be again.

"I made four laps around the track today. And I stink pretty bad right now, but it's not like you haven't seen me look worse." Three weeks had passed, and his condition had stayed the same.

I held Logan's warm but listless hand in mine and prayed he'd show some sign of recognition. If I could command his soul to his body by sheer will alone, he'd already be back with me.

"No throwing up so far though, so I guess I have it easier here than . . . the other place."

My speech had drastically improved over the last several weeks. I spent at least two hours a day visiting and talking to Logan. Some days Celeste would be there and I'd talk to her instead. I was pretty sure my one-sided conversations with her son would freak her out. There was a part of me that believed I could talk him awake.

So far I'd been proven wrong, but I was willing to spend the rest of my life trying if that's what it took.

"But there's no one here taking bets on whether or not I'm going to toss my breakfast, so it doesn't quite feel the same . . . well, except this one kid, but he really annoys me. There's a makeshift viewing gallery on the sixth floor, and you know how I hate to make a fool of myself in front of others, so that pushes me more than Jared probably realizes. If I tell you how handsome Jared is, will it make you jealous enough to wake up?" I imagined pressure on my hand that wasn't there. "Yeah, I didn't think so, but it was worth a try. How about I tell you a little about my plans?"

Unbeknownst to my parents, I'd already started to scheme ways I could stay in the area. I knew they expected me to go home with them next month. The current plan was to keep up some of my therapy at home and also finish high school. I was a year behind, but I was a good student and only needed a few classes to actually graduate. We'd already worked out an agreement with my old school that I would take those few classes at home and then officially graduate after the first semester. The school was bending over backward to help me out, and I appreciated it, I did, but things had changed.

Whether he was conscious or not, there was no way I was leaving Logan's side. Not when I'd found him again.

So I'd been working on an alternative plan my parents didn't know about. One that they absolutely weren't going to like, but considering I was legally an adult, they couldn't do anything to stop me.

The only thing I hadn't worked out was money. I was going to need it if I was going to stay on the West Coast instead of flying back to the Midwest with my family. I still wanted to graduate high school and then eventually go to college, but if I was going to stay in the area, I needed to find a place to live. And apartments required rent. I was going to have to find a job and work.

I could do it, I knew I could. Living out here would be hard, but I would make it work. I was determined. I would live on my own, finish high school, apply to nearby colleges, and spend all my spare time with Logan.

This was going to happen.

If he ever opened his eyes, I was going to be one of the first faces he saw. And if he didn't, I would still be here to grow old with him.

I knew he would be willing to make the same sacrifices for me . . . even though I wouldn't want him to. I'd want him to live out a long and happy life. He'd probably want the same for me, but if that was the case, he was going to have to open those beautiful blue eyes and tell me himself. Otherwise, I was going to be sitting by his side for a long time to come.

"So basically, if you don't want me getting butt sores from sitting in this chair so long, you're going to have to come back to me." I sighed and shifted in the chair, running a hand through my shortened locks.

Watching Logan lie motionless was only marginally easier than when I first learned whose room I'd trespassed into. Now that I knew the figure was him, I saw the Logan I knew through the gaunt features of the person in front of me. His appearance was vastly different than my memory, but if I looked hard enough, I could find him.

"Audrey, it's so nice to see you again."

I looked up to see Celeste stroll elegantly into the room. She sat on the couch to my left.

"Oh, I'm so sorry, Celeste. Here, you can switch with me." I moved to stand, but she waved me off.

"Don't be silly. We both know he'd rather have a pretty girl holding his hand than his mother."

We both chuckled as I resettled in my seat. We chit-chatted for a while as I worked up the courage to ask the question that had been scratching at the back of my mind. I should have just let go of my curiosity, but it nagged at me.

When we hit a natural break in our conversation, I took a deep breath and went with it.

"Celeste, I know this isn't my place to ask, but . . ." *Oh, I should really just leave this be.*

I chewed my lip in indecision.

"It's all right, sweetie." She turned her head to the side. "What do you want to ask?"

I bunched my eyebrows and released my lip. "I was just wondering if Mr. London ever visited. I know I'm not here all the time, so maybe I just keep missing him, but . . ." I took a breath; all of that came out really quickly. "I was just wondering, I guess."

Logan had mentioned that his parents were together, but perhaps something had changed since his accident. It so wasn't my business, but the absence of his father nagged at me.

"Oh." She sat back against the couch, her body sagging in on itself. Her face fell, and she suddenly looked extremely tired.

"I'm so sorry. I shouldn't have asked. It's none of my business." But I still wanted to know. I looked down at where I gently clasped Logan's hand, embarrassed that I'd brought up what was obviously a touchy subject. Now my mind was going wild with possibilities.

"No, it's all right, Audrey. Logan's father . . ." I glanced up.

She was visibly trying to compose herself.

Oh my gosh, they were divorced now. That must be it. This was so awkward. I should have just done some internet research instead.

She took a deep breath before continuing, "Logan's father and I don't agree on Logan's care."

I snapped my head up to watch her more closely. That was not where I'd thought this conversation was going.

"He doesn't think that Logan should be cared for in this way, so he refuses to visit." Celeste's eyes started to tear.

I became lightheaded as the blood drained from my face.

Logan's father didn't want his son on life support. Logan's father wanted his son to die. His mother kept him alive, hoping that he'd come around someday despite what the doctors said.

"You have to understand," she went on quickly. "Richard, Logan's father, loved—loves Logan very much. But seeing him like this is just too much for him. And we just have vastly different opinions on Logan's treatment. It's just too hard for him to visit because whenever he does and he sees Logan, the way he is now, it just . . ." She let the sentence drop.

"He wants to let him die," I quietly mumbled.

"He doesn't see it that way. He thinks Logan is already gone." She sounded incredibly weary. As if this were an argument they'd had often. The beat-down tone in her voice scared me. They couldn't do it. I'd lose him all over again. I couldn't survive that.

"No"—the strength and volume of my voice startled her—"you can't let him do that. You can't. You have to fight for him. He can wake up. I know it."

Celeste's eyes opened wide. I knew the conviction in my voice did not match the story of a girl who had just gotten a few surfing lessons from her son and now visited out of a sense of kinship. But I couldn't stop the words tumbling from my lips.

"You have to keep him alive. Look at me. I woke up. He can too."

She blinked at me. "I know, dear. I believe that too. Despite what everyone says, miracles happen every day. But I do have to wonder . . ." That pause scared me. "What if keeping him like this is the wrong thing to do? What if he's suffering?"

"He's not." I was quick to answer.

Her brow furrowed and then smoothed out again. A small, albeit sad, smile graced her lovely face. Logan had definitely picked up some of her features, just in a more masculine form. "It's all right Audrey. I understand." She understood nothing. "But not everyone is as fortunate as you. Don't worry yourself about it. You have a bright future ahead of you."

Don't worry about it? Now it would be the only thing I *did* worry about.

Should I try to explain to her what had happened to me while I was in a coma? What had happened to Logan? Would she even believe me?

Probably not. Who would believe such a story?

I squeezed Logan's hand and closed my eyes, silently pleading with the Creator not to take him from me a second time.

CHANGED PLANS

"*A*udrey, this makes no sense." My dad's eyebrows bunched together in concern and confusion. He paced back and forth on the linoleum floor of my small room. I sat patiently in a chair by the window, waiting for him to calm down. My mother stood on the side of my bed, wringing her hands as she watched my father.

I'd royally botched breaking the news that I had no plans to leave the area. Or maybe there was no good way to drop that bomb? They knew I'd been regularly visiting one of the other patients, but they thought I was just doing so out of a sense of kindness. An assumption I didn't bother to correct them about.

How was I supposed to explain that I knew a patient who had lived on the other side of the country from us and spent the last four years in a coma?

They'd never believe me.

Now they just thought I'd developed a weird—and unhealthy—obsession. I can't say I blamed them. They didn't have all the information, so my actions did seem rash and nonsensical.

"I'm so sorry. I know this doesn't make any sense to you guys. But I need . . ." I struggled to find the right words. What could I possibly say to make them understand?

"Audrey"—my mom rounded the bed and took my hand—"we're so close to getting you back again. Your father and I are both here to bring you home. Sweetie, you still have therapy to undergo, classes. We have everything set up for you at home. Not to mention the fact that we want you back with us. We almost lost you once." Her eyes filled with tears. "This feels like we're losing you a second time."

Her response broke my heart. "Oh, Mom, you'll never lose me. I'll always be your daughter. This is just . . . It's just something I have to do. I promise I've thought it through. I'm still going to keep up with classes and physical therapy, but I need to stay here. I know it doesn't make sense to you. I get it, I really do."

An idea came to me. I wasn't sure if it would make a difference, but maybe it would help a little. "What if you come with me to visit Logan today? You've not met him yet."

"What do you think that will accomplish?" my father asked.

I turned to look at him, chewing my bottom lip. "Don't you want to meet him?"

"Audrey, we wouldn't really be meeting him. We'd be—"

"Honey"—my mother squeezed my hand and shot my father a wide-eyed look—"I think that would be a good idea. Let's meet this boy you're willing to turn your life upside-down for."

I sucked in a huge breath of air. "Yeah, let's do this."

It was visiting hours, but that didn't explain why Logan's room was packed full of medical professionals. A wall of them hovered around his body, and several others were milling around the room with their heads down, writing on charts or tablets. What was happening? My heart jumped in my chest.

Is he finally—

"Audrey." My thoughts were cut off by Celeste's surprised voice. Her eyes were red rimmed, but she was clearly trying to keep her composure. "I didn't think you'd visit until later today."

"Um." A million questions ran through my head. "I wanted my parents to meet Logan. I hope that's okay." I glanced around the room again. People were talking in hushed voices, and I couldn't pick up any of the conversations. "What's . . . what's going on?"

Celeste wrung her hands, and her gaze darted left and right. "Maybe it would be better if you came back later today. Then we can talk."

"Is Logan okay? Why are all these people here?"

"I can tell you about that—"

"Is this the young lady you spoke to me about?" A man dressed in a grey business suit laid a hand on Celeste's lower back. He had brown hair that was sprinkled with salt-and-pepper patches around his ears. Logan's mother was already a tall woman, but this man towered over her by several inches, even in her signature heels. She looked up at him with worried eyes and then nodded. His expression was stern but not uncaring.

"Yes, Richard, this is Audrey. She's been visiting Logan for the last few months. He gave her surfing lessons . . . before the accident."

Logan's father? What was he doing here?

"What?" I heard my dad ask behind me.

Oh, shoot. He knew I'd never been to this side of the country before. I hadn't lied to anyone, but I certainly hadn't thought this meeting through very well.

I took a closer look at Logan's father and started to see bits of his son in him. The slant of their eyebrows were the same. His eyes were green rather than Logan's blue, but the shape was similar. They had broad shoulders and a tapered waist as well as that impressive height. He looked to be in his late forties, but he obviously still took care of himself. I had a wave of longing to know what Logan would look like at his father's age. Healthy, whole, and living life together with me.

Logan's dad stepped forward and extended his hand to me. I clasped it and received a firm handshake. There was an upturn to the corners of his mouth, but so slight, I wouldn't call it a true smile.

"Audrey, I'm Richard, Logan's father."

I nodded.

"Thank you for taking the time to visit my son. That was very kind of you."

"You're welcome?"

"And these are your parents?"

I nodded mutely and stared while our parents introduced themselves. I never would have expected this was the way they'd all meet, but the introductions needed to be made one way or another. Might as well get the formalities out of the way since I was going to be a fixture in Logan's life moving forward.

"Celeste tells me Audrey will be leaving to go home shortly." The words snapped me out of my reflective daze.

"Well, that's what we were hoping for, but Audrey seems to have made some plans of her own."

Four heads swiveled in my direction. The urge to start backing away slowly was strong, but I held my ground. The scrutiny of four sets of eyes on me was no joke.

"Could someone please tell me what's going on in here?" I asked, again. "Is Logan okay? Has there been a change? Is he waking up?" There was no way to hide the hopeful note in my voice, but one look at his mother said I had gone down the wrong rabbit hole. Her eyes started to fill, and she brought a tissue to the corners to keep the tears from spilling over.

Panic welled inside my gut, churning at a fevered pace and making it feel like I was going to vomit my lunch all over the floor.

"He's not getting better." It wasn't a question. "He's getting worse? How could he get any worse?"

I looked back and forth between his parents. Celeste's eyes continued to well with tears. Richard's face was a stoic mask—so reminiscent of Logan's go-to when he hid his feelings.

My heart pinched as Logan's parents shared a look, seemingly communicating without words. My gaze ping-ponged between the two of them until finally Richard stepped away from his wife and faced me.

"I know Celeste wanted to tell you this herself later today, but I think considering the circumstances, now is probably the best time. As you know, my son is brain dead."

I flinched at the matter-of-fact way he used the perfectly acceptable medical term.

I hated those words. Celeste and I never used them to describe Logan.

"I'm sure you know that means that although we can keep his body alive, he's not really with us anymore."

I had a very bad feeling about where this conversation was going.

"You don't really know—"

"We do. We do know that's what it means."

I was too shocked at being railroaded to continue.

Richard went on, "We have two choices here. We can continue to keep up this charade of him returning to us someday, or we can bring some good to this awful situation, which will also bring some closure to his mother and myself."

I shook my head. Celeste wouldn't let this happen. She wouldn't let Logan's father take him off life support.

I looked to her for confirmation that what her husband was saying was just a review of what they considered to be the situation, not a decision that had already been made. But tears were free flowing down her cheeks now. No amount of tissues could hold the tide back.

They had decided.

"No. No you can't seriously be thinking of doing this."

"It's what's—"

Celeste laid a hand on her husband's arm, silencing him with her touch and a soft look in his direction. He nodded and took a step back.

"Audrey, you have to understand this wasn't an easy decision to make. But Logan can help a lot of people."

No, what? Logan already did help a lot of people. I'd been by his side as he defended humanity. He was owed the chance to return to us . . . to return to me.

"Help a lot of people?" My voice came out high pitched and shrill. I was half numb and half hysterical.

She nodded.

"We've decided to take him off life support and donate his organs to people who need them. This way his death won't be in vain." Her eyes begged me to understand.

I stood shell-shocked for several moments. They were going to let him die. I didn't think or care about anything else they said. My chance to live a life with Logan in it was slipping through my fingers.

I'd made a terrible mistake by not telling Celeste the whole truth. If she just knew that Logan was out there and could possibly wake up like I did, she wouldn't be allowing this. She wouldn't be giving up.

I had to make her understand. I had to make them all understand.

"No." My whole body vibrated with pent-up anger and fear. "No, you can't do this." My voice rose over the low din of voices conversing around us. "You don't understand what you're doing!"

The room became eerily quiet except for the noise from the machines as I garnered the attention of everyone present—people who were here to either oversee the process of taking Logan off life support or to harvest his organs afterward.

Logan's parents gawked at me with wide eyes. I didn't even spare my parents a glance but rather beseeched the ones who were moving this process forward.

"You don't understand because I haven't told you the full story."

Logan's father snapped out of the shock caused by my outburst first. His tone wasn't cruel, but it was unyielding. "I'm truly sorry, dear. I understand you've formed some sort of . . . mild attachment to my son, but that doesn't give you any right—"

"Attachment?" I let out a hysterical laugh. I'd formed more than just a mild attachment to Logan.

"Look"—his voice hardened to steel—"this is obviously not a healthy attachment. A few surfing lessons and spending some time with my son while he is completely unresponsive doesn't give you any right to tell his mother and I what's best for him or our family."

How could I explain this without sounding completely insane? My mind scrambled to come up with a plausible way of making them understand . . . without getting myself committed. I was truly worried someone would force a psychiatric assessment on me. The last thing I needed was to see another therapist. But that was a small price to pay if anything I said could sway their minds.

"Listen, I know Logan better than what you think. I know he can still wake up. He can come back to us, just like I did."

"Sweetheart"—my mother stepped up and put her hand on my arm—"your situation was very different than this young man's. You can't say things like that. It's not fair to his loved ones. It's not—"

"I'm one of his loved ones," I practically yelled in my mom's face and pounded a fist to my chest.

She blinked and took a step back. My father wrapped his arm around her shoulder. Their faces were twin masks of shock and concern. I couldn't hold back the tide anymore. Everyone was against me, and no one was fighting for Logan. I'd fight for him until my last breath.

"Out!" I yelled to all the medical professionals in the room. "Everybody, out! This whole thing has been canceled." I pushed my way past Logan's parents and started shoving doctors away from Logan's body. There were plenty of gasps around the room, but I ignored them all.

Keeping Logan safe was my top priority. I'd fought through Hell and back for him; I wasn't going to lose him now.

Nobody left the room. They all just stared at me. I'd taken a position at Logan's head and growled at anyone who tried to touch him.

"Tell them to leave!" I shouted at his parents.

Fresh tears poured down his mother's face, and a look of stubborn resolve came over his father's.

I didn't like that. His expression was too similar to the look Logan got when he was determined to get his way.

Now I knew where that stubborn streak came from.

"We most certainly will not." Richard looked at my parents. "Go control your daughter. She's not welcome here anymore."

"Hey"—my dad stepped forward—"my daughter has been through an incredibly trying ordeal over the last year. Let's all take a beat for a moment."

Yeah, way to go, Dad.

"Your daughter's been through an ordeal?" Richard barked a humorless laugh. "You get to leave here in a few days with your child. You get to go and resume a perfectly normal life. We've been living in a nightmare that started four years ago that we can't wake up from. Whatever infatuation your daughter has with our son"—Celeste reached for her husband, probably to stop his words, but he pulled away from her grasp and glanced at her—"yes Celeste, it is most certainly an infatuation. From what you've told me, I'd say this girl is borderline obsessed with Logan."

I sucked in a painful breath of air and reminded myself they didn't know how well I knew Logan—but that barb still hurt.

And Richard wasn't finished with his rant. "My son has been lying here, day after day, with no hope of waking up. To come in here and question our decision, one that was unimaginably hard to come to, is insensitive at best. I want you all out of here, for good. If you cared at all for us, if you cared at all for Logan, you'd leave us to grieve in peace."

My dad nodded. "I apologize, Mr. London. You're right. We were all out of line. Regardless of what Audrey's been through, this is a family matter."

Wait, what? No. I tensed, ready to fight anyone who tried to make me move.

"Audrey, come on. It's time to leave." Dad held his hand out toward me from across the room.

My breathing picked up as I eyed all four parents.

I didn't have a magical sword to protect my loved one in this situation. I couldn't physically fight my way to a victory. All I had was a story no one was likely to believe.

The shell chimes in the corner of the room started to softly move back and forth, even though the window wasn't open. The sounds reminded me that I didn't just have a story. I had the God of the universe listening, the Holy Spirit living inside me, and the Savior of mankind protecting me.

I took a deep breath to steady myself. Time to lay it all out on the table. Time to trust that I wasn't the one in control.

I'd fight for Logan in the only way I could—by trusting his future to the One who created it.

MY STORY

"*W*ait, please." I held a hand out as if the gesture alone could stop the momentum of what had already been set in motion. "There's something I need to tell you all. I haven't been completely forthright about how I know Logan."

My gaze swept the room. Everyone was staring at me. From my parents, to the doctors, nurses, medical technicians, and finally Logan's parents. That was where my focus landed. That was who I needed to convince I wasn't lying. I'd deal with the fallout from my parents after.

Richard's face was still hard. His arm was wrapped possessively around his wife's waist. His lips pressed together in a tight line as if it took effort not to talk. His brow was pulled low over eyes that blazed.

I wasn't too proud to admit I was intimidated.

Celeste was a hot mess, and I realized the arm around her waist might be there to help her remain standing. Her eyes were bloodshot from crying. Tear tracks ran down her face, and her normally perfectly coiffed hair was in disarray—the bun was half out and off-centered. She held her hands to her chest, and her shoulders were slumped as if she was protecting herself.

With a stabbing pain, I realized she was protecting herself from me.

This was not how I wanted to explain my experience in the afterlife. Under duress with at least twenty people staring at me.

But I was out of choices. I took in a fortifying breath and started my tale.

"When I got hit by that car, I thought I had died. And not because I realized the severity of my injuries on the road; I knew something monumental had happened because when I closed my eyes here on Earth, I opened them again in a whole different world. And in that place—that whole different world—I met and I fell in love with your son."

Miraculously, they listened—maybe because I didn't give them an option. I talked and talked and talked some more.

I went back to the beginning and explained how disoriented I'd been when I first woke up in a different realm, without my memories. I retold my first meeting with Logan and how contentious our relationship as mentor and mentee had been. And then how things had slowly changed. I left out a lot of private details because—awkward—who wants to talk about their first kiss with someone to their parents? But I revealed most of what had happened to me, especially the parts relating to Logan, in the months my body had been lying in a coma in this very building.

I poured my heart and my soul out in a desperate hope that something I said would give them a reason to hold on, at least a little bit longer, to the possibility that their son could come back to us.

And then when I was finished with my tale, I waited.

My cheeks were wet with the tears I'd spilled.

This whole time my attention had been on Logan's parents, but now I took a moment to survey the room. The medical staff gaped at me. My parents appeared shell shocked. Their hands intertwined, eyes wide, and silent. And finally I took a good look at Logan's parents—not just to tell my story but to gauge their reaction. I'd confessed the truth as if I were on trial, and they were the judges.

Richard's face hadn't softened, but the anger that had brewed there seemed to have morphed into confusion. Celeste brought a shaky hand up to cover her mouth. Fresh tears dripped down her cheeks.

"You really saw our baby?" she asked, her voice trembling and muffled by the hand she held in front of her face.

I nodded. "Yes, I truly did. He is . . . amazing, and . . . I love him. I know if there is any way he can come back to us, he'll move heaven and earth to do so."

Celeste turned into her husband's chest and sobbed.

"Oh, sweetheart." My father lifted his arm and offered his hand. There was a suspicious shine to his eyes. His silent invitation was clear, and I was too raw to turn it down. I rushed into his embrace. He squeezed me tightly while my mom rubbed her hand up and down my back.

They knew the truth, and they weren't rejecting me.

"Please, leave now." Richard's voice was cold and commanding.

I jerked my head up in response.

"Wh-what?"

He was still holding his crying wife in his arms, but his face was unmistakably hostile.

"You've said your piece. I think it's clear your delusions go deeper than any of us expected. Now I want you to leave us alone. You've done enough damage." He said the last part with a pointed look at Celeste.

"No. I told you the truth. I *do* know your son. He can come back—"

"Stop!"

I took a step back at the sharpness in his tone. Even Celeste went rigid in his arms. "I will protect what's left of my family." His focus transferred over my head. "I think your daughter needs some serious help, but that's up for you to decide. For right now, you need to remove her from this room."

It hadn't worked.

Despite everything I'd told them, they were going to go forward with it. They thought I was delusional. Or that I'd made it all up. Or . . . it didn't matter really what they thought, except they didn't believe me. They didn't believe I'd met their son. They didn't believe that my love for him was real. They didn't believe he would ever come back to us.

My body felt like a giant ice cube.

How could it have come to this? How was it even possible that I'd found him, alive, on Earth, only to lose him again? It was . . . too cruel to be true.

I vaguely registered my father coming to my defense and my mother soothing his temper. He gently clasped my arm and tried to pull me toward the door. I took an obedient step in his direction before what was happening really and truly sunk in.

Logan.

They were going to let him die, and I was just going to walk out that door and let them?

No way, no how.

I ripped my arm from my father's grasp, hearing my mother gasp in surprise.

"You can't do this," I yelled, and tried to push my way past people to reach Logan again. But this time, arms caught me—restraining me from going any farther.

"No, let go." I fought against people I didn't even know or see. I didn't bother to take in their appearance, as my gaze was fixed on Logan's prone form.

It didn't end like this. It couldn't.

I maneuvered out of one person's grasp, just to be caught by another. Frustration churned deep in my gut. My muscles retained the memory of their training, but I was so weak, all of my defensive techniques were useless. It was like trying to restrain a bunny.

"No." Tears streamed down my face. "Don't do this," I begged. Begged.

I heard voices behind me, but the entirety of my conscious focus was on Logan.

"Audrey, please stop fighting." My mom's pleading voice broke through my hurt-filled haze.

I spotted her to my right. She wrung her hands, and tears fell from her eyes as well.

"Baby, please. Just let it go. We need to leave the Londons to make this decision. This isn't your fight."

Isn't my fight?

I amped up my struggles.

This was the most important fight of my life. If the situation were reversed, Logan wouldn't have let me go. He would have stood guard over me night and day if he had to. He would give anything to make sure I was protected.

And I was going to fail him.

Premature grief crushed my lungs.

"You have to stop, Audrey," my mother pleaded, but I wasn't paying attention to her anymore. I'd defeated countless creatures of darkness. I'd gone up against Satan himself. I couldn't let a couple medical technicians take me down.

I could kick one in the shins and duck under his grip. From there I'd have a straight shot to run—something sharp bit into my backside. I yelled out in pain.

Did someone just stab me?

I twisted my head to see a giant syringe depressed all the way and sticking out of my right butt cheek.

What?

Someone in a white lab coat quickly removed the ridiculously long needle from my backside.

I tried to renew my struggle, but my vision suddenly blurred around the edges.

No!

I'd been drugged.

I fought like a rabid beast to reach Logan, but my movements were becoming uncoordinated and sloppy, until they turned sluggish and my vision winked in and out.

"Please," I think I pleaded out loud, but it may have been in my head. I no longer knew.

The last thing that went through my mind before I succumbed to whatever drug they just pumped into my system was *I failed you. I'm so sorry.*

And then all was quiet.

My skull was stuffed with bricks and cotton. A strange combination, but one that made it impossible to lift my head because of the weight. The world seemed strangely muted.

I groaned at the uncomfortable sensation and tried to lift an arm to my head, but something prevented me from moving. I blinked several times to bring the room into focus. It blurred for a while before my eyesight cooperated.

"Oh, honey, she's waking up."

Okay, so my mom was somewhere around here.

With a great deal of effort, I turned my head to see her sitting by my bed. My dad walked from the window to join her. Both of them wore grave looks. Pinched brows, pressed together lips, their skin leeched of color.

"What happened?" I croaked out. "Why can't I move?" My legs were straight, and although I could bend my knee slightly, something was preventing full mobility—and it wasn't the bricks and cotton.

Was I restrained?

"Oh, Audrey." My mom's hand covered her mouth as her eyes filled with tears.

I looked to my dad for an explanation.

"Sweetie, how much do you remember?"

I blinked up at him. The cotton made it hard to understand his question. "Remember?"

"Baby, you were hysterical. The hospital staff had to sedate you. You're being restrained at the moment to make sure you won't hurt yourself. Someone is going to be in later to evaluate you."

"Evaluate what?" I asked

Several heartbeats passed before he answered. "Your mental state. We think all of this has been harder on you than we realized. We, your mother and I, believe getting you home as quickly as possible is the best course of action."

I wanted to shake my head, but the heaviness prevented the movement. I squeezed my eyes shut. I knew I should be more alarmed by what my father was saying and the fact that I was strapped to my bed like a criminal, but the fog hadn't fully cleared. There was a reason I didn't want to leave, but I needed to dig for it, because I couldn't remember why I cared.

I attempted to lift my hand again, wanting to press it to my eyes, but was stopped by the soft restraint.

"Can you . . ." I swallowed. My throat was beyond dry. "Take these off of me?"

I opened my eyes to see my parents share a look.

"Audrey, why don't you go back to sleep and let the drugs wear off a little? We'll get a doctor to come in and assess you so we can get these removed. We think that, considering the circumstances, we should play by the rules right now."

What circumstances?

My mind tried to push past the fog, but the effort left me exhausted. My rapid blinking wasn't doing much to keep me awake, so I succumbed to sleep once again.

I woke up some time later to soft voices. The heaviness no longer weighed me down, but my memory was a bit hazy.

My parents were talking to my primary doctor off in the corner of my room, their voices too low for me to overhear.

"Excuse me," I asked to get their attention. "May I have some water?"

"Oh, sweetheart." My mom broke off from the small group and rushed to my side. She grabbed something from a table and brought it into view. It was a cup with a straw. She propped a few pillows up behind my head so I could drink.

The liquid coated my scratchy throat in a soothing balm. My throat was raw and painful as if I'd been screaming for a long period of time.

I nodded my thanks to her.

She stood, and the doctor took her place by my side. "Audrey, I'd like to remove these restraints, but I need your word before I do that you won't try to get out of bed."

Restraints?

I glanced down my body to see my wrists and ankles secured to the bed with some kind of padded handcuffs. I had a vague recollection of waking up like this before, but I couldn't push past the block in my memory to remember why.

"Okay, I'll stay here."

He smiled warmly and unlocked all the cuffs then helped me into a seated position.

My body was sore all over, but I didn't know why. I hadn't woken up this weak in months.

"I've been talking with your parents, and we all agree that the best thing for you physically and emotionally is to return home with them. Your physical therapy has progressed to a point where you can continue with outpatient treatment." He paused for a moment, and I knew there was something important about that pause. "And you can also seek treatment for your emotional trauma in your home state as well. We want to make sure you're on board with this plan."

Wait, I was remembering important things now. I wasn't planning on going home with my parents. I wanted to stay here. Stay here and be with . . . Logan. That was it. Had I not talked to them about my plans yet? I thought I had.

I glanced at my parents standing near the foot of my bed. "But I wanted to stay in this area. I thought"—yes, I'd definitely had this conversation with them already—"we already had this talk."

There was silence in the room as the three adults traded looks.

"Audrey," my father finally began, "I'm so sorry, sweetie, but there's nothing left for you here."

"But there is, Dad. I already told you I wanted to stay near Logan. I was—"

I gasped, remembering the trip to Logan's room to introduce him to my parents when they pushed back about me staying.

I'd wanted them to understand, at least in part, why I had made the decision.

I remembered Logan's parents being there along with all the medical personnel. And I remembered my desperate fight to reach him at the end when my confession fell on deaf ears.

I brought a shaky hand to my mouth.

My vision swam.

"Tell me he's not gone. Tell me they didn't go through with it while I slept. Tell me you didn't let them do this to me." The last few words ended on a sob.

My mom rushed around the other side of the bed to pull me in her arms. I didn't want to be comforted at the moment. I wanted information. I wanted someone to tell me everything was all right and that what I thought had happened had not.

My father's face twisted in regret.

"I'm so sorry, baby girl, but there's nothing left for you here," he repeated.

Burying my face in my mom's shoulder, I let out body-racking sobs.

I didn't try to hide my anguish like I had when I first woke up and realized all I'd lost. There was no use. I was completely undone, and the weight of losing Logan was compounded by the weight of all the other losses I'd repressed.

I cried for Logan. And I cried for Romona and Kaitlin and Kevin and Bear. I might have even cried a little for Jonathon. But most of all, I cried for myself.

And the silent cry I lifted to the Lord was only this: *Why?*

HOME

I wasn't even allowed to go to his funeral. My parents said the Londons had asked that I stay away and not contact them. I wondered how much of that "request" was Richard and how much was Celeste. I thought I'd formed something of a friendship with Logan's mom in the time we'd spent together at her son's bedside, but I suppose thinking that I was delusional and had made up a relationship with her son was reason enough for her to want to keep some distance.

Yet another name to add to the list of people I'd lost, but in this case she was also my last Earthly connection to Logan.

His mother had been telling me stories of his childhood as we sat vigil, and I loved hearing about them. I'd cherished every scrap I was given, and I mourned every tale that would now remain untold.

I lay on my side and stared at the blank white wall. It wasn't the fresh bright white I'd become used to in the afterlife, but the dull white that came with time. I hated both colors equally.

Squeezing my eyes shut, I remembered the beautiful mural painted on the wall in Logan's room. The swirls of blue and aqua that were reminiscent of the ocean and the color of his eyes.

I think he would have loved to see that painting.

By now a fresh coat of white paint was probably drying on the wall as the staff readied the room for the next patient.

"Audrey, sweetheart, everything is ready. It's time to go." My mom laid a gentle hand on my back.

I'd hardly said anything in the few days since "the event." I didn't realize how much pain and loss I hadn't processed when I woke up back on Earth until I lost Logan for the second time.

I'd created a house of cards that came crashing down that day.

The real work of rebuilding my life was just beginning. And even I knew I wasn't handling it well.

I'd briefly been forced into talking to one of the hospital's grief counselors, but I only answered the questions I absolutely had to, and I stonewalled everything else. I refused to talk about my time in the afterlife anymore, having already poured my heart out and been rejected.

My own parents now looked at me strangely, but they hadn't forced any more treatment on me. When my doctor thought I was asleep, he'd recommended I seek counseling for my "issues" when we returned home.

My parents hadn't brought the subject up to me yet. Perhaps they'd let me settle in at home first? Maybe they'd bring it up on the long plane ride home? I wasn't sure, but I knew that it was only a matter of time. They did think I was delusional. What parent wouldn't want their child to seek help in that situation?

"Audrey." My mom ran her hand up and down my back. Something she used to do when I was little and she was waking me up from a nap. "You have to wake up. We need to get going so we can catch our plane."

Nodding, I rolled over and slipped out of bed. I pulled a pair of my favorite boots on over my jeans. I'd dressed for the cooler mid-western weather this time of year rather than the sunny temperate California weather I'd unknowingly become accustomed to. I grabbed an oversized purse and walked to the door without a word. I'd forgone any long goodbyes with my trainers and doctors, not wanting to have to fake a levity I didn't feel.

I walked down the hall to the elevators that would lead to the main floor exit with my head down, listening to my mom's quiet steps behind me.

My parents had handled me with kid gloves the last several days. I wasn't trying to punish them, but I couldn't help feeling betrayed.

They hadn't believed me.

I knew that my story seemed implausible, but I still wanted them to back me up. But when I'd laid all my chips on the table, they'd let me be drugged and taken from the man I loved.

I tried not to be angry with them, I truly did, but I was.

I'd forgiven them for their betrayal in my mind, but my heart still hurt.

One minute, one hour, one day at a time. Baby steps. I could only hope that one day I'd wake up and time would pass at a normal pace.

I pushed at the revolving doors and within a few steps was standing in the sun. It warmed my head, neck, and shoulders as I sat in the car my father had rented that would take us to the airport.

I never looked up. It didn't seem fair that the sun could shine so brightly when on the inside I lived in a land of eternal rain and darkness.

A stack of papers dropped in front of me with a loud smack, shocking me out of my daydream. I yelped and put a hand to my chest, then swatted at James, who was already jumping out of hitting range.

"You're a punk." I loved the kid hardcore, and I had a new respect for him after what I'd witnessed when Satan's legion had attacked our house, but my little brother could still be an annoying jerk.

"I don't know, sis. You think you can keep up with all this work? At this rate, maybe I'll graduate before you will."

Rolling my eyes at him, I ignored the rib just like he ignored my comment.

Once a week, he collected a stack of assignments for me from my teachers at school so that I could graduate at the end of the semester. The arrangement was unconventional, but it would work. I was taking some additional advanced courses to get ahead in college. Also, the extra work kept my mind off of . . . things.

Staying busy helped me get through each day. And as much as I feigned annoyance, seeing James so alive and vibrant pulled me out of my shell.

My little brother had grown since I last saw him. Even though he was several years younger, he was now almost a half-foot taller than me, and if I had to guess from the way he was starting to fill out and his outgoing personality, getting to be popular with the ladies—but he still had a great head on his shoulders. I was proud of him . . . not that I planned on telling him that anytime soon. The last thing the boy needed was an ego boost.

He plopped down in the chair next to me. "So," he began, "you planning on going to the Homecoming dance next week?"

I laughed out loud. "Um, yeah, no. Not in a million years."

"Aw, come on. It's what all the cool kids are doing these days." James's cheesy pout was way overdone, and he knew it.

I shoved him lightly.

"You're weird, you know that?"

"Yep. Proud of it," he quipped.

"Yeah, I can tell. So, which lucky lady are you escorting this year?"

He tapped a finger on his lips as if considering. "So many choices. Maybe I'll keep my options open and go stag."

"Maybe I'll go after all . . . as a chaperone."

His face puckered as if he sucked on a lemon. "Way not cool, sis. I can't be seen consorting with the enemy. I've got a rep to uphold."

I shook my head. I knew James didn't care about any of that. This was just his way of trying to get a smile on my face . . . and his antics were working.

"I didn't realize it was so hard to convince people you're a dork. It's super obvious to me."

"Ouch, that really hurt."

"I'm sure it did."

James tilted his head and considered me for a moment. The scrutiny made me uncomfortable. "You know," he finally began, "there will probably be a lot of your old friends home that weekend. Why don't you see if one of them wants to go with you?"

"You're actually serious."

He shrugged. "Who doesn't want to relive the high school glory years?"

Most people, I thought.

"Who knows, it may be fun for you, even if for a laugh."

Oh gosh, he was serious.

"Which parent put you up to this?" I'd been home several months, and although I'd been doing better—I only cried myself to sleep most nights now —I wasn't the same Audrey my family was used to. They'd brought up counseling and I'd refused, but I knew they were worried about me. We also never talked about everything I'd confessed to Logan's family and half the hospital that day. I wasn't sure if they were just hoping it had been an isolated moment of insanity or if they were worried that bringing it up would break me. They handled me like I was made of china these days.

If they only knew. I'd been to Hell and back. I was made from tougher stuff than that.

But at the same time, I recognized the dark edges of depression that threatened to crush me every day. I just wasn't ready to admit it to anyone besides myself.

"Neither," James went on. "This was 100 percent my brilliant idea."

"Well, in that case . . . the answer is still no."

"I guess I should take down that Instagram pic of your face announcing that you're looking for a hot date then."

My breath caught. "You wouldn't."

Oh, but he would. That's why I was suddenly very nervous.

"Wouldn't I?" He jumped out of his seat and started to run for the stairs, yelling as he went, "If I take it down fast enough, I guess you'll never know either way."

"You're a brat," I screamed at him.

"I know," he yelled back.

I was too old to be fighting with my brother like we were five-year-olds. I grabbed my phone off the table and opened my Instagram app. That brat had like 4,000 followers. I was going to kill him if he had really plastered a pic of me on there.

I tapped my finger on the side of the phone while I waited for the app to open and then quickly went to his page. I didn't see any pictures of me, and I didn't really want to know if he'd just deleted me a moment before I jumped. Not many things humiliated me these days, but that would probably do it.

But . . . he was right. For the first time since I'd arrived home, a lot of my old friends and former classmates probably would be in town. Most had left home this past fall to go to college, but homecoming was a big deal in my town and often attracted a good number of alumni to watch the game.

I'd hardly talked to anyone from my old life since waking up in the hospital out west. At first it was because my motor skills didn't really allow me to communicate well, and then after a while, I kind of lost interest. I had a few girlfriends I still kept up with to some extent, but the effort was half-hearted on all sides.

People had moved on while I lay in a bed on the other side of the country. They'd finished their senior year of high school, graduated, and prepared to go to college. And I was stuck in a weird time bubble. Moving forward was like trying to walk while being immersed in a mud pit all the way up to my neck.

Slow and messy. There was progression, but every step was hard earned.

I had to carve out a new normal. I was just a little stuck on how to do that.

How was it that moving on in the afterlife had somehow been easier than moving on with my real life? It didn't make sense.

The eternal existence I had expected to experience was still there. I could still have it someday. Logan would wait for me—I told myself that daily. But now life, this life, stretched out in front of me like a purgatory I had to get through rather than cherish.

My thinking was all messed up, I knew it was, but I didn't know how to snap out of it. Probably at least in part because I didn't want to.

DREAMS

*D*reams are funny things. While asleep, somehow your brain can convince you that riding a giant banana like a broomstick over your house is perfectly normal, but when you wake up, your mind knows that it's not normal and that your super weird experience wasn't rooted in any type of reality.

Everything makes sense until you wake up.

This wasn't one of those dreams. This was altogether different.

When I opened my eyes, I knew three things to be true: I was in my room, I was conscious, and I was still asleep.

My dream self sat up and looked around. Everything was the same in my dream as in reality—no flying bananas.

When my gaze moved back to my bed, I was startled by a figure sitting at the foot. He was just like I remembered, and letting off a faint brightness that allowed me to see every one of his facial features.

My heart instantly lifted. I'd missed him.

"Joe?" I tentatively asked.

He smiled at me, the laugh lines at the corners of his eyes crinkling, but sadness still sat in the depth of his gaze.

"Why have you missed me, Audrey? I never left you."

I sucked in a breath. In the months since I'd awakened, I'd cried out to him numerous times, but the comfort I'd felt in his presence while in his realm was absent.

"It felt like you had," I admitted.

"But that's not what you know to be true. You know I promised never to leave or abandon you. With everything you have experienced, why have you doubted that? Why have you doubted me? Why have you doubted my goodness?"

Joe cut straight to the heart of the matter, because even before I lost Logan for the second time, I'd been riddled with doubts. I'd just stuffed them down deep.

"I don't know. This life . . . It's just so hard."

"I never promised it would be easy, only that I'd be with you every step."

"I know, but when I can't feel you . . ." I let the statement hang in the air between us. I wasn't sure what to say.

"Did my Spirit not teach you to push past what you feel to hold on to the truth instead?"

I hung my head. "Yes."

His finger touched my chin and brought my gaze back to his. "Then choose to believe. I know your heart is heavy. Let me carry your burdens for you."

"But you've already done so much for me."

"And you believe I've also taken much from you." It wasn't a question. He knew my heart better than I did.

I chewed on my lip.

"I don't know how to go forward. I don't know if I want to." Big fat dream-tears slid down my face.

Joe pulled me into his arms. I curled up in his lap like a small child and let the sadness and loss wash over me.

"But you must, my precious one. You have a plan and a purpose here, and it's not to hide yourself away from the world but to be a light unto it."

Why? Why did you take him?

I never would have spoken the words out loud, but they echoed in my head on a repeat loop I was unable to stop. And of course, he heard my silent question.

"I work all things together for good."

"This doesn't feel good to me. I miss him so much my heart aches every minute of every day. I miss them all. It's too much."

"I know it's too much. That's why you must share your burden with me. The answer is so simple, Audrey. Simply let go and trust that I am good. Blessed are those who do not see yet still believe."

I sobbed harder. And he rubbed my back like my mother used to.

"You are to run the race before you with endurance but never alone."

I lifted my tear-stained face and looked into his ageless eyes. "Will you let him know I love him and that I'm waiting for him?"

"He already knows." Joe wiped the wetness from my face. "It's time for you to live the life you've been given. And remember that your sadness is my sadness, your pain is my pain. You have not and will never be forgotten. Your prize is waiting for you at the end of this leg of your journey."

I sucked in a cleansing breath of air. Joe set me back down on the bed and coaxed me to lie down. He leaned over me and pressed a kiss to my forehead. From the point of contact, warmth radiated throughout my whole body. I closed my eyes to hang onto the feeling. When I opened them again, I was awake and Joe was no longer sitting on my bed, but I knew I wasn't alone.

The semester ended, and I graduated with honors. I wish I could say that I cared, but I didn't really—except for the fact that it gave me broader options in terms of universities.

I spent the winter months applying to an array of colleges, but I secretly had my eye on one in particular.

After my dream visit with Joe, I put real effort into changing the way I was living my life. Things didn't change overnight, but months later, my slow progress could be seen.

My relationship with my parents had improved. I focused on their love for me and not what I perceived as a betrayal. I reached out to a few of my closer friends and made an effort to stay in touch. I found that I missed exerting myself physically, so I started taking a few martial arts classes—much to my parents' surprise. I even started seeing a counselor. That was tricky, because there was only so much I could talk to her about, but it still helped.

I wasn't okay with Logan's parents' decision, but she helped me see the good in it, especially the lives that were most likely saved or improved because of the sacrifice made.

When I took a step back, I realized Logan would have wanted exactly what his parents had decided rather than to just waste away in a bed for the rest of his life. If it wasn't for the nagging what if questions that haunted me, I might even have been able to get over it.

I couldn't completely let go. What if he had woken up someday? But at least now I was trying to get past it.

My parents had heavily hinted that I should get out and start dating. My answer to them was always the same. I'd smile and tell them maybe, but I knew in my gut that wasn't for me. I'd already given my heart away, and I wasn't interested in getting it back.

My heart was exactly where it belonged.

There was an existence after this life, and so one day I'd receive my happily ever after. I'd just have to be patient and wait for it.

But that didn't mean there still wasn't a tremendous amount of life to experience in the meantime. I didn't think the pangs of longing every time I thought of Logan would ever go away, but I was learning to live with them, and to live a full life rather than the half one I had settled for when I woke up.

The conversation I wasn't sure would ever happen came up the day I announced to my parents where I would be going to college. They sat and listened while I outlined my detailed plan—because I hadn't chosen an in-state school to save money. No, I'd picked an expensive private school on the other side of the country. But I'd been smart about it. I'd received several scholarships and grants, and I'd planned out the rest in financial aid to make it almost as affordable as if I'd stayed closer to home.

I also insisted that my parents use the money they'd originally saved up for my education to help pay off my medical bills. I hadn't forgotten what I over-heard in our kitchen when I was a hunter—what it had been like for them to struggle under the financial burden of my care.

They were shocked into silence by my announcement until I got to that last part about how I wanted them to use my college savings. At that point they launched into their own argument: that money had been set aside for my schooling for a long time. I argued back that I'd figured out a way I wouldn't need it so they could get back in a better situation—if not for me, then for James.

A few months back, they'd nearly lost the house. They had tried to down-play the situation, but I knew they needed the money. In the end, my carefully explained financial plan was what finally convinced them.

"Audrey"—my mom's cautionary use of my name had me sitting up a little straighter—"are you sure it's a healthy decision for you to go to a school in California?"

And that began the conversation I had been waiting for.

"Yes," my dad chimed in, taking my mom's hand in a show of support, "we're obviously a little caught off guard by this choice, but it's clear you've put a responsible amount of thought into it. You're nineteen now, so your mother and I won't try to stop you from moving on with your life in what-ever direction you choose to go. But can we have an open conversation about this?"

I pressed my lips together and put a cap on the irritation that threatened to bubble up from my gut. I'd already had this discussion in my head a thou-sand times, and I knew where my parents were coming from. If I was in their shoes, I'd bring it up too.

Taking a moment to compose myself, I glanced back and forth between them. My parents. The two people who loved me most in this world.

A genuine and gentle smile settled on my face and calmed my emotions. I silently sent up a word of thanks for the extra measure of patience.

"I understand your concerns. I really do. I can give you a long list of reasons why this is a great place for me to get a degree. And if I did, that would probably put your mind at ease. But I know what you're really worried about is my underlying motive for going to a school in that location."

I paused. This next part was going to be hard for my parents, but I wasn't going to lie to them. "I could go to a number of different universities that would be a great fit for me, but I did choose this one because of Logan, and I know that's not what you want to hear. And before you ask, no, I don't plan on seeking out the Londons. I want to respect their decision to be left alone.

And I do realize you think that I'm hanging on to a strange delusion that I invented, and I understand why you'd think that. The story I told that day does sound impossible, but it doesn't matter if you believe me or not. Everything I said happened."

"But, Audrey," my father interjected, "we told you about so many of those events while you were in your coma. About the shooter at your school, about your Grandfather's stroke. Do you not think there's a possibility that maybe your mind just created that world you spoke of while you were asleep?"

Okay, we were going there.

"No, Dad. I know you don't believe me, but even if my mind invented some fantastical dream world when I was out based on the stories you and Mom told me, it still doesn't account for Logan. It's okay that you don't believe me. If our situations were reversed, I might not believe me either, but that's really not the point. I'm not moving out there to obsess over him but rather because I really do enjoy California. I think I can be happy there for four years. I like the sun and the beach. And things that remind me of him . . . help."

Mom's eyes were a little dewy. "Honey, real or not, how can you ever move on completely if you don't let go of him?"

That was a valid point.

"I have faith that it will work out, Mom. I don't need it, because I'm an adult, but I'd like your blessing on this decision. And I realize you're going to need a measure of faith in me to do so."

I waited while my parents exchanged worried looks. After what felt like forever, my mom gave my dad a small nod. He huffed and ran a hand through his hair before leaning forward and kissing her cheek. There were a few whispered words between them, and I waited patiently for their response.

"All right, Audrey, your mother and I may never truly understand what happened to you during those months we lost you, but if this is what you want to do, we'll stand behind you."

I let the hot breath of air I'd been holding leak from my lungs. "Thank you."

"Audrey, no matter what, we're always behind you."

BEGINNINGS

*S*alty wind slapped me in the face and sent my hair flying in all directions. I was letting it grow out, and it fell just below my shoulders. Thank goodness, I was finally able to get it into a proper ponytail—but today I'd let it free. I would pay for that decision with a bundle of knots later, but at the moment, I didn't care.

I closed my eyes to soak in the day. Tipping my head back, I absorbed the warmth of the sun. The gritty sand softly exfoliated the skin between my wiggling toes. The repetitive beating of the surf against the beach matched the tempo of my heartbeat.

I was more at home here than anywhere else. This had been a good decision.

I'd started summer courses at a college in Malibu, California. I'd already taken a semester off, so what was the point of waiting until the fall to start? My dad had flown in with me to help me get settled. I met and moved in with my bubbly new roommate, Ashlynn. I already knew things were going to be interesting with that one. She had a thirst for life and a carefree demeanor that was contagious. Classes had started mid-week, and it took me a few more days to get oriented. But the song of the ocean had called to me the whole time, and now I was finally here.

A full week passed before I could break away and soak it all in.

The sun hung heavily toward the sea, telling me it was late in the afternoon. I didn't care. That meant if I stayed out long enough, I could catch the sunset. I loved sunsets.

I laid out a towel and sank down onto it, forgetting my textbook for the time being and just lazily enjoying all the free vitamin D. Eventually I fell asleep to the lull of the lapping waves.

The chilling air woke me slowly, and I lifted my arms above my head and cat-stretched on my towel. I froze mid-stretch with the overwhelming feeling of a presence hovering near me.

Oh gosh, I hope it's not a creeper checking me out in my bikini.

With my eyes still closed, I brought my arms down to my side and cracked my eyelids open. I was right . . . there was someone seated at the foot of my towel, just off to the right. Thankfully he wasn't watching me. Instead he was staring at the ocean in front of us.

The sun was sitting right on the horizon, making it difficult to make out any of his features. Through squinted eyes, I could really only make out that this was a guy in board shorts, knees pulled up and arms draped over them. I couldn't even guess at his age.

I quietly slid my arms behind me so I rested on my forearms, giving me a better view. I tilted my head. He wasn't quite as close to my towel as I'd thought, but this was a big beach. He definitely didn't need to be sitting here.

His behavior was kind of unnerving.

How in the world was I supposed to tell this stranger that he was invading my personal bubble?

I almost laughed to myself. Who was I kidding? This was me. I was the queen of blunt. I was going to say it exactly like that. But I wanted a moment to study this weirdo before I shooed him away.

He didn't have any tan lines on his back, but his skin was a little too white for him to be a local. I'd quickly learned to pick out the people who lived in the area from the tourists based on level of tan alone. I, for instance, stuck out like a sore thumb, even with my somewhat naturally darker skin tone due to my heritage. There wasn't the telltale evidence of natural coloring across my cheeks and nose yet, or a tan line circling my neck from my suit strings. That actually reminded me that I should probably reapply my sunscreen.

Premature aging . . . no thank you.

I sat up and extended my hand toward my bottle of sunblock but stopped mid-reach.

His hair.

There was probably only an inch of growth on his head, but the color. Even though the halo the sunset cast on him . . . I knew that color.

My breath caught in my throat.

There was no way. Lots of guys had light hair in the beachy areas of Southern California. It had to be just a coincidence.

I forced a normal cadence to my breathing. Inhale, then exhale. Then repeat.

I could control my breaths, but I couldn't control my rapidly beating heart.

This dude needed to turn around so I could see he wasn't Logan and stop freaking out.

I was going to have to get used to this, I told myself. The sun bleached out people's hair fairly easy, and with all the surfers in this area, there were going to be people who looked like him. I needed to learn to desensitize myself.

Time to rip off the bandage.

"Yo, dude, you want to find somewhere else on the beach to plop it? You're blocking my sun." Leaning forward, I waved my hand in front of me in a shooing motion. A motion that froze the moment the guy twisted around.

My arms suspended awkwardly in the air as I took in his familiar face.

Eyes as blue as the ocean on a sunny day, brows several shades darker than the hair on his head, straight nose, strong jaw, and lips I could still remember the peppermint taste of.

And just as I was drinking in the sight of him, he was doing the same to me—his gaze searching every feature of my face before colliding with mine. And when it did, I swear a field of electricity pulled us together.

"You're awake." His deep voice was the final piece.

It was really him.

I was up on my knees, reaching for him, and I didn't even remember moving. Reality clicked in right before my fingers touched him, and I snatched my hand back.

"Oh my gosh. I can see the dead." *Wait, that doesn't make sense.* I shook my head once, my mouth spilling words as soon as I thought them. "No, *I* must be dead."

How could I bask in the miracle that was seeing Logan again when I couldn't remember how I'd died?

My breathing changed to short bursts in and out. I was going into some type of shock.

"Oh no, not this time," Logan said before he shifted his body to press his weight into me, causing us both to tumble to the towel. "Just look at me and breathe, Audrey."

The warmth of his body in contrast to the chill of the closing day caused goosebumps to break out all over my skin. Taking my face between his hands, he forced my attention.

My breathing picked up a notch.

"Not helping," I puffed out.

A smile broke free on his face. "Then we'll do things the fun way. Less talking, more kissing."

His mouth covered mine before I even had a chance to process his words.

His lips were as soft as I remembered, and they moved over mine with skill. He gave my bottom lip a teasing nip to ensure he had my full attention.

It worked.

The next moment, I didn't care that I was dead or how it had happened, but only that we were back together again.

My hands snaked up his arms and buried themselves in his hair—shorter than I remembered, but just as soft.

Who cared what realm we were in as long as we had each other?

I was lost in the feel of him . . . until water slapped me in the face and along the side of my body, and a familiar voice yelled, "Get a room, you two!"

Ashlynn?

Logan pulled away, and I tilted my head back to see an upside-down view of my new roommate.

"You can see us?" I asked.

She shot me a funny look. "The whole beach can see you two, you goofball."

Huh?

"Are you dead too?"

"You have an odd sense of humor, you know that?" She tilted her head. "I see you found her after all."

"Yep, thanks for the help," Logan said. "She was asleep when I came by, so I waited until she woke up."

"Well, that was chivalrous of you. I probably would have poured water on her," she said with a twinkle in her eye.

"Isn't that pretty much what you just did?" Logan asked with a brow hiked up.

She smirked. "Hey, Audrey, I'll see you back at the dorm later, yeah? You won't get lost, right?"

I shook my head, still watching her from my horizontal position as she jogged away.

What was going on? She could see us. I could see him. They'd met.

My head was about to explode.

The only way I could be with Logan was if I were dead. Unless he wasn't dead.

But he'd died.

Hadn't he?

"What's happening right now?" I whispered to Logan. His face hovered just above mine, and half his body pressed me into the sand.

His eyes swept my face. "I'll never get tired of looking at you," he whispered back. "You're not dead, Audrey. I'm not dead either. We're both here, on Earth, now. Alive. Together."

Moisture gathered in my eyes and spilled over. "But how? I was there. I tried to fight for you, but no one believed me. Your parents . . ." my voice gave out. That horrible, awful day. The worst of my life. And that included the day I got hit by a car.

That day I'd fought for him in every way I could, and I'd lost.

He murmured words of encouragement and sympathy over and over again. "It's all right; I'm truly here."

Finally he sat up, pulled me to him, and guided my head to his chest. He buried his face in my hair and kept talking to me until my tears were spent, and even though I still didn't know how this was possible, I was just happy that he was real.

This was real. It was happening.

I pushed back against him, and he let me go. I finally took an objective look at him.

He was clearly Logan. I recognized everything about him. But he wasn't the Logan I'd seen lying in that bed . . . and neither was he exactly the Logan I'd first met.

His shorter hair was only one of the changes about him. He wasn't emaciated like he'd been at the hospital, but neither was his build as large as it'd been before. His skin was several shades lighter than I was used to, his face a little thinner.

They were all slight changes, but each one told a story.

"Please, tell me what happened. How are you here?" I touched his face to reassure myself, and he captured my hand and held it to his cheek, closing his eyes to soak something indiscernible in.

When he opened them again, I noticed they were the one thing about him that had not changed a single bit. His cobalt eyes, and the look in them when he gazed at me was exactly how I remembered.

"I'm here because of you. I'm here because you helped save me."

"Your dad said I was delusional. They kicked me out of your room, out of their lives. I wasn't even allowed to go to your funeral. Um . . . er . . . I guess there wasn't a funeral."

"Yeah"—he scratched his head and ducked it—"you certainly made an impression on my parents that day." He chuckled softly.

"This's not funny. I was led to believe you'd died. They were going to take you off life support. What happened?" I all but yelled the last part at him.

He held his hands up in front of himself to pacify me.

"Don't try that with me, mister. Start talking."

"Okay, all right." He took my hands, and any levity in his voice completely disappeared. "It's just a long story. And if I'm going to explain properly, I have to start at the beginning."

I nodded for him to continue.

"So, after the battle with Satan, you just disappeared. As in, your body literally vanished from the pool of blood you'd been lying in. As you can imagine, I didn't handle that well."

I could imagine. In fact, I imagined that even more things in that Artifacts Room got broken real fast. I kept my thoughts to myself as he continued.

"At first I thought you'd been transported to Hell, but that's when the Son explained to us that you were still alive. None of us knew, Audrey. We had no idea that you weren't actually dead."

"Ha, you're one to talk."

"Yeah, I'll get to that in a moment." He squeezed my hand and flashed a quick grin before continuing. "I calmed down marginally when I found out what had happened to you, but if you were alive, that meant we were separated. At the same time, I couldn't begrudge you a life on Earth. I *wanted* you to live. I wanted to be happy you were alive. But I wanted to be with you too, and if we were in separate realms, that wasn't going to happen for a long time. You can't imagine how hard that time was on me."

"You're kidding, right?" I lifted my eyebrows.

He nodded slowly. "You're right. If anyone can imagine how I felt, it's you. As much as I wanted to be content with you having a full life on Earth, the thought of you having it without me gutted me. I didn't last long before I started sneaking trips down to see you."

"You visited me when I was recovering? You were there?"

He nodded. "Some of the time."

"Hold up, you broke the rules to see me?"

He quirked an eyebrow at me. "Someday you'll realize the depths of what I would do to be with you."

My insides melted, and my cheeks warmed. He brushed his thumb over one of them before speaking again.

"Whenever I could sneak away, I'd come and visit you. I'd talk to you, but you couldn't see or hear me. Being there but not able to interact with you was its own form of torture. I watched you struggle to recover . . . but I watched you slowly move on as well."

I was shaking my head before he even completed the sentence. "That's not what was happening. I just stuffed all my emotions down. I wasn't dealing with anything during that time. Were you ever with me when I visited you? If so, that had to be super weird for you."

He took a deep breath. "I didn't know I was in a coma either, Audrey. I didn't know until the day you found me. When we walked into that room, I didn't even recognize myself in that bed. It wasn't until I started looking around and seeing familiar objects that the pieces started to fit together. And then of course when my mom walked in, I knew right away."

He chuckled, but how he found any of this funny, I didn't know. "I was so surprised I actually knocked over a picture when she walked in." Oh, so that was him, not me.

"I went straight back to the realm when you left my room and demanded I be put back in my body. I'll bet you can imagine how well that went over."

"Well, seeing as I spent weeks by your side without you waking up, I'm gonna guess not well."

"Right. When I was denied my demands, I went a little"—he held up his thumb and pointer finger about a millimeter apart—"ballistic for a while. I was there, you were there, we could actually be together again in the same realm, but for some reason I wasn't allowed back."

"Is that . . . normal? Does what happened to us happen to everyone in a coma?"

He shook his head. "No, we were the exception. That's why no one would have even thought to guess it. Audrey, it's also why we had powers others didn't. It's because part of us was still alive, and in the spiritual realm, that made us extra powerful."

"I just . . . I can't wrap my brain around all this information. I have a million questions, but I don't know if I can process it all right now."

"Okay, that makes sense. You tell me what you want to know." He leaned back on his arms and pressed his lips together, his gaze steadily holding mine.

"I guess I want to know how you're alive. Your parents were going to take you off life support. Did they? How long have you been awake?"

Looking him up and down, something occurred to me. He might be leaner than the Logan I knew in the afterlife, but he was a far cry from the one I'd spent time with in the hospital. To work his way back this far after four years in a coma, he must have been awake for months.

Months where someone could have told me, but they didn't.

I jumped up. My legs were shaky. "How long, Logan? How long have you been awake while you left me to mourn your death?"

A frown marred his handsome face, but he didn't make a move toward me. "Audrey, you may not like this."

"How long, Logan?"

He sighed and ran a hand down his face and back up into his short hair before meeting my gaze. "Seven months."

I gasped. Not long after I'd left the hospital. He'd been awake almost since the time I went home. And he was just now making himself known.

I took an unsteady step backward.

"Audrey, please let me explain."

But I didn't. Instead, I turned and ran.

BETTER TOGETHER

I forgot about the chill of the evening as I bolted from Logan. His voice was swallowed by the sound of the waves crashing, but he was no doubt giving chase. The ocean wind sent my hair flying into my face. Only after several minutes of sprinting did it occur to me that I hadn't been caught.

He'd let me go. Or maybe something else had happened.

I whipped around, sweat dripping down my face, but I couldn't see much in the failing light. The sun had descended below the horizon, and only the leftover brightness lit the beach.

I turned in a circle and realized I had no idea where I was. There were no people around. A chill of fear skated up my spine.

I'd run from Logan, but in the back of my mind I'd assumed he would catch me. He always had before.

Darting my gaze left and right, I jogged back the way I'd come. I was still upset beyond reason that he'd been awake for so long without me knowing, but I'd been foolish to not let him explain. I also was incredibly stupid for having run so far.

Nothing looked familiar. I swiveled my head back and forth as an irrational fear of being attacked overtook me. I was on the verge of hysterics when I slammed into a hard chest.

We both went down in a tangle of limbs.

"Don't do that ever again." There was a strong note of desperation in his voice. "Please, promise me you won't do that again."

I pushed hair out of my face and stared down at Logan. Something to his left caught my eye, and I turned my head to see a plain silver cane lying discarded on the sand.

Logan had come after me; he'd just been unable to catch up with me.

"We don't run from each other anymore, Audrey. Even when things get hard." My attention snapped back to him, and I took in what he was saying. "Aren't you tired of always running? I know I am."

He was so right. We'd run from each other for too long. We should have always been walking together.

"Yeah, I am."

I clumsily shimmied off him and stood, watching as Logan glanced around before spotting the cane. He snuck a peek at me before grasping it and struggling to his feet.

"As you can see, I'm not quite the same man I was before." The lighting was so dim I might have misread it, but I caught something akin to shame in his eyes before he diverted his gaze.

"Will you let me explain this time?"

I nodded, and we started a slow trek back.

A brisk pace was difficult for Logan, so I slowed my steps. I wasn't sure if this was a regular thing for him or if my crashing into him exacerbated whatever physical limitations he was already dealing with.

"I watched you during those weeks at my bedside. I saw you make the decision to stay there and keep vigil over that shell of mine, and I knew you'd do it for the rest of your life . . . and I didn't want that for you. I would be ruining your life. I didn't want to realize that at first, but it became clear to me eventually. So I went to the Creator . . . and asked him to end my mortal life."

My gasp was stolen by the wind, and Logan plowed on. "Of course, He was aware of the trips I'd made to see you. I knew He would be, it's not like anything escapes His notice, but at the time I was making them, I honestly didn't care. But He allowed them just the same."

I tried to catch Logan's eye as we walked, but he remained focused on some unseen point in the distance. His jaw was clenched, and a muscle twitched on his cheek.

Was the walk that painful for him? Perhaps he was angry at me? Or was rehashing these events just difficult?

If the latter, I would have spared him from the pain if possible, but I needed to know. There was no way we could move forward without an explanation of how this was even possible. Especially now that he'd dropped the bomb on me of asking to die.

My insides churned at the thought. Why would he do that? What had happened to his promise to be with me, no matter what? I needed to know it all.

"What happened next?" I asked when the silence stretched and I was no longer sure Logan would continue.

"You were there. You saw what happened next."

"You mean . . . that day?"

He glossed over his conversation with the Creator. I almost pressed for details, but I realized that was Logan's story. I'd hear it someday when he was ready—or not at all. But I didn't have a right to force it out of him, no matter how badly I wanted to.

"Yeah, that day." He stopped walking and turned to me, grasping my upper arms gently but firmly. "Audrey, you were fierce that day. I know that will always be a horrible memory for you. And the way you were treated"—he looked over my shoulder before recapturing my gaze—"it took three hunters to keep me from throwing those people off you."

My eyes widened. It had never occurred to me that there might have been an unseen audience.

"You . . . fought?"

He cupped my cheek. "The first moment someone laid a hand on you, I couldn't stay complacent anymore. I fought for you. But you . . . you not only fought for me, you fought for us."

"You were right there in front of me, even if I couldn't reach you. From the first moment I realized it, I had hope. I thought it had to be for a reason."

I stepped forward and reached for him. The gusting wind had turned into an early evening breeze, balmy but cooling. His skin was chilled until the heat from my hands warmed him.

"I had hope . . . until the moment I was told you were gone."

Pain lanced through my heart at the memory of the crushing agony I'd felt all those months ago and a little bit every day since. My pain-filled emotions must have reflected on my face because Logan pulled me toward him with both arms.

"I'm so sorry. Everything I did . . . everything I've done . . . I thought every decision was to protect you. But so many of those choices just added to your suffering. I'm not perfect, Audrey."

I huffed a weak laugh with my face buried in his chest.

Turning to lay a cheek on him, I asked, "What happened next?"

He leaned forward and nuzzled the hair hanging over my neck, inhaling my scent.

After that sprint, I was a little worried I was veering on the ripe side, even though the sweat had already dried from my body.

"They changed their minds."

"Your parents?"

"Yeah. I mean they still thought you were completely insane."

I pressed a fist into his gut, and he let out a lighthearted laugh.

"Don't worry, that was more my dad than my mom; she thinks you're great."

"Even now?"

"Especially now." He pushed my hair behind my ear and pressed a kiss to my neck.

"Are you trying to distract me?" If so, it was kind of working.

"You're the distraction, love." He placed another kiss to the spot and then picked me up and set me away from him.

I might have pouted a little.

"Don't give me that look. Do you want to hear the rest or not?"

I nodded.

"Then let's get back to your stuff."

I started walking and realized he wasn't following. I turned to see him slowly bending and then remembered his cane. Rushing back, I picked it up and offered it to him.

"This is part of the story, I take it?"

He nodded, and we continued back. This time in silence.

Not long after, we seated ourselves back at my towel. I slipped a sundress over my bathing suit, which made the slight chill in the air the perfect temperature. Logan had—to my disappointment—brought a t-shirt, which he shrugged on before carefully lowering down next to me.

While he did, I examined his legs. One looked slightly thinner than the other, but I probably wouldn't have noticed if I wasn't trying to find the reason for his slight limp.

I turned my body so I could watch his face but made sure part of my leg was pressed against him. I needed the physical reminder that he was here to keep me grounded. Part of my brain still screamed that this was just a cruel trick or a dream I was going to wake up from.

"So, your parents changed their minds?" I prodded him to continue.

"Yes and no. They were pretty shook up from everything you said that day, even though they didn't believe you. My dad went into protective mode and did everything he could to make sure you wouldn't be allowed near me anymore." He picked up and squeezed my hand. "That's why your parents never knew the truth. They weren't given any additional information and had no reason to believe my parents had altered their course of action.

"With the stress of that day, my mom convinced my dad to let a few days pass before they went through with taking me off life support. She was never all about it anyway, but she had resigned herself to the course of action.

"I went back to being a hunter, resigned that I'd wait a lifetime to be with you. What I didn't know was that a few days turned into a few weeks, and then a month, and then two. And my father was visiting me again."

He looked at me with such vulnerability in his eyes. "Did you know that beside the day you saw him, he hadn't been to visit me since the first year I was in the hospital?"

I shook my head. "I knew he didn't come regularly like your mother, but she didn't give me those specifics. I'm sorry, Logan."

He smiled at me. "You have nothing to be sorry for."

"I'm sorry for any pain that comes your way. And learning that your dad hadn't been to see you in years had to hurt."

"He had his reasons, and he's apologized for it."

I sensed there was a story there, but I'd leave that for another time. We still had so much to catch up on.

"I had just returned from a hunt when the Savior came to see me."

"You talked with Joe? He came to me too, in a dream. He told me to have faith and move forward. That's what I've been trying to do ever since."

"You've been doing a great job. At times, maybe a little too good." He chuckled, but his eyes darkened for a moment. "Yes, we talked. My existence had started to become . . . a dark place. He pulled me back and set me on the right path. And he told me I would be returning. I was . . . shocked. I didn't even know there was still a 'me' to return to . . . again. I got over the initial shock quickly and wanted to rush back right away, but instead I was told to wait. Which gave me time to give a proper goodbye to people."

I instantly wanted to know how everyone was doing, but I pushed the desire aside. We'd have time to catch up on that later.

"I didn't start to have doubts until I woke up, captive in my own body. And that, ultimately, is what kept me from you until now."

"I don't understand."

Logan's lips flat-lined. His features were only discernible by moonlight now. He faced the ocean rather than me.

"You'll understand part of it. When I woke up, I had to relearn everything. I wasn't able to speak a word until two weeks had passed. I could hardly even stay awake. I wasn't able to move my body because of my deteriorated muscles. I was a shell of the man you knew, and because my case was so unusual, the doctors couldn't make any promises. I might have progressed to a certain point and then just stopped."

"Do you mean to tell me you let me go months"—I threw up a hand to stop Logan from interrupting—"months without knowing you were alive because . . . you were . . . embarrassed?" An angry mound of hot lava churned in my gut as I spoke, demanding to be spewed. "Days and weeks and months of depression. Of anger at the Creator, of questioning everything I thought to be true."

"And that's the part you won't understand. I was only part of a man, and I didn't want you to be shackled to that any more than I wanted you to be tied to the empty shell you'd been ready to throw your life away for."

"You had no right—"

His eyes flashed. "I did. I did have a right to make that decision. There was a point they weren't even sure I'd ever be able to go to the bathroom on my own. Do you know how that made me feel?"

I lunged and grabbed Logan's face, forcing him to look me in the eyes. He could easily have pulled away but didn't.

"You listen here. Believing I would care about any of that—any of it—is beyond insulting. Had you lain in that bed for the rest of your days, awake, I would still have been happy to spend my life with you. Since when did you start to believe I cared for you, that I loved you, for how much you could bench press? It was you, it will always be you, in whatever shape I can have you. It's you I will love."

I jerked out of my rant when something wet dropped on my left hand. I glanced up at the cloudless night, thinking it had started to rain, only to look back and realize that a tear had slid from Logan's eye and down his cheek.

I'd never seen Logan cry before.

"I don't deserve you," he whispered.

"That's not true." I leaned forward and kissed the wetness from his cheek, sliding my hands to rest on his shoulders. "It's not about what we deserve. Frankly, what we both deserve is a million times worse than what we've been given. It's that we're better together than apart . . . at least when we're on the same side."

The corner of his lips quirked at that.

"We're better together, Logan. Don't let your pride get in the way of that."

He brought a hand up and rubbed his face. "I almost did," he confessed. "Even coming to you like this"—he swept a hand out to indicate his body—"was hard for me."

"Were you scared I'd reject you?"

"I was scared of a lot of things."

"If our situations were reversed, would you have hesitated a moment to be with me?"

"No, never. Even if I had to take care of you for the rest of our lives, I would have been happy to do so."

"Then you shouldn't have deprived me of that same joy."

Logan hung his head, but he brought his hand up to draw me closer. "You're right. My pride kept me away from you. Will you forgive me?"

"Always."

Our foreheads rested against each other, and we breathed the same air.

"What do we do now?" I asked.

"Whatever we want," Logan answered with a smile. "We have a lifetime to figure it out. You game?"

"Yeah, let's do this thing."

The lips that brushed mine were soft and tender and tasted of peppermint. I knew this beautiful moment—the one I'd given up believing we'd be able to share in this lifetime—was as close to perfect as anything in this world could be.

And I silently lifted my thanks.

EPILOGUE

KAITLIN

$\mathcal{I}$ lifted my face to the sun and took in the perfect California day: a slight breeze in the air, tinged with salty brine; clear blue skies; and a temperature that was warm but not yet on the verge of crossing over to hot.

"Everything seems to be in order." Romona scanned the crowd of people rather than perimeter around them. But who could blame her? This was her family, and today was the day she'd watch her granddaughter wed.

The huntress's words were even and professional, but not even the amazing Romona could contain the shining excitement in her eyes.

Her face radiated joy.

"You know, I still think we would all fit in better if we were wearing formal attire. All this black makes it look like we're going to a funeral." I nudged Romona playfully with my hip.

"We're not supposed to be blending in. You know that. We're supposed to be sending a message that this event is not to be interrupted."

I faked annoyance and crossed my arms. "But I look so much better in strapless gowns."

"I would disagree with that," a smooth accented voice spoke behind me. My spine straightened as a zing of awareness ran down it. I shook it off with real annoyance as he went on. "This look has always had a certain . . . appeal to me."

"Do you really have to be here?" I asked Morgan without turning to address him.

He stepped up next to me, refusing to be ignored. "Probably not. I don't think there's ever been a more fortified wedding in all of history. Bloody He—"

"Watch it," I warned. I purposely kept my gaze fixed on anything but the handsome Brit to my right.

I gave myself an internal shake. Not handsome. Evil is not handsome. Ugly. He's very ugly.

Romona huffed on the other side of me. She didn't tolerate Morgan's presence much better than I did.

"Feel free to leave anytime," she added.

"And miss my best mate's big day. Never." The mocking tone to Morgan's voice covered whatever his true feelings were. That had always been the issue with Morgan, even before his betrayal and redemption I never trusted what came out of his mouth. There were layers to him that concealed his true self, and I didn't have a desire to peel them back.

Liar, a whispered voice mocked in the back of my mind.

"I'm going to do a perimeter check." I fled the tension-filled moment, quickly moving to the outskirts of our protective border.

Morgan wasn't wrong. Perhaps we'd gone a little overboard with the security today, but besides this being a highly anticipated event for us all, I knew there was one supremely evil being gunning for the stars of today's show.

The consensus was it was better to be safe than sorry. So several dozen hunters as well as a handful of angels were stationed at various points around the grounds of the beautiful garden where our friends would recite their vows.

After making sure everyone was where they were supposed to be, I stopped to take in the moment.

The ceremony was to be held in the private gardens of the Hillstead Mansion, which was situated on a cliff high above the churning sea. The reception would take place in the mansion afterward.

The garden was in full bloom, mixing the sweet scents of the flowers with the salty sea below. Red roses, blue iris, and pink azaleas created a secret garden experience that was breathtaking.

Rows of white chairs were set up in an open space in the wooden gazebo. Wisteria vines wrapped around the structure, and delicate bunches of purple blooms hung down like clumps of grapes from the rafters.

The event was going to be lovely—although bittersweet. My heart warmed at being able to share this moment with my dear friend, even though he didn't know I was here, but a prick of sadness welled inside.

I'd never have a day like this. I didn't get a second chance.

A soft melody started from the string quartet, announcing the ceremony was about to start and that people should take their seats.

As if signaled as well, a chorus of shrieks rent the air. I jerked my gaze up to watch the spot of darkness in the faraway sky grow into a churning cloud.

We should have brought more reinforcements.

THE END

Thank you for reading *Dominion*!
If you loved it, please write a review at
http://review.DominionBook.com

BONUS SCENE

*B*lack ooze and candy-apple-red blood slid down the edge of my sharpened blade. The dagger I held in my other hand was equally coated in sticky substances. Sweat prickled my brow as I picked my way through the dead and gnarled trees of this long-forgotten forest.

To my right, my comrade-in-arms crept along with me. He cast me a glance, determination written into every tense crease on his face.

This was our last chance.

We'd been battling our foe since yesterday and were both weary from the effort.

The landscape mirrored our mood. Splashed in front of us was a canvas of grays. Mist crawled along the burnt ground at our feet, weaving in and out of the bleached and broken limbs that littered the ground. I was fairly certain there were more than just tree branches crunching under our shoes, but I chose not to focus on it.

The air was too still, too silent. The broken things shifting and cracking underfoot echoed. The sky was blanketed in a steely sheet of clouds, each one tangled into the next, effectively blocking our view of whatever energy source lit this desolate place.

"Man, I sure hope we have enough juice to put this beast down."

Talon voiced the concern I'd already been turning over in my mind.

"I hear ya. I think we have enough ammo. It's big, but if we manage to move quickly and avoid getting hit, we'll be able to recharge after it's defeated."

"That's a big *if*, Logan."

"Let me know if you'd like to hide behind me again."

Talon's eye roll was accompanied by a creative hand gesture meant to insult. "Just for that, I'm going to take this next one on my own."

Sure, he was.

Talon was good . . . but not *that* good. He hadn't leveled up to where I was, yet.

I chuckled as we proceeded forward.

My ears picked up on a crackle, and the air shimmered a half-second before the vortex opened behind Talon. By the time I opened my mouth to yell a warning, he had already dived and rolled out of the way.

The creature that stepped through the maelstrom of dark magic was at least eight feet tall—and ugly. And not just your everyday-garden-variety ugly. This dude was next level. It looked like someone had put a bunch of body parts in a blender, hit 'frappe', waited for the mixture to get nice and chunky, and then dumped it out on the table and tried to reassemble it with super-glue.

Its skin was the color of bile-rich vomit and only covered the creature in patches. Fibrous tissue and bright orange fat leaked out of round pits that littered its body. One of its eyes was popped out of the socket and hanging by only a string of purple veins.

The monster's bloated arms hung to the ground. Its knuckles scraped against the rough surface, bleeding whenever one caught a jagged edge, but it didn't seem to notice. It looked like a few of his fingers and toes had been chewed off as well.

Did it eat its own digits off? And if so, I wondered what they tasted like.

It was a shame the disgusting mess was the only hint of color against the bleak backdrop of the wasted world that surrounded us.

It opened its mouth to bellow, exposing rows of jagged shark-like teeth. The war cry it made was loud enough to make me flinch.

"I get first shot!" Talon called before rushing Big Ugly.

I watched in amusement as he tried to circle the creature and come at it from behind. A beefy arm caught Talon in the mid-section and sent him crashing into the trunk of a tree.

Ouch, that looked like it hurt.

After shaking himself off, Talon rushed the beast. Sliding to the ground baseball-style, he carved a nice slice across the monster's distended belly.

"Nice move."

The creature roared as loud as before and went after Talon with a vengeance.

"Want some help?" I asked.

"No, I'm almost—ahhhh."

Big Ugly managed to get a hold of Talon's arm and yanked him into the air.

"You sure you don't want some assistance?"

"No! I've got everything under control."

No sooner had the words left my friend's mouth before the creature grabbed his leg and pulled—literally ripping Talon in two.

Ohhhh. That sucks. My turn now.

With a grin, I stepped forward. This was the moment I'd been waiting for.

"Bring it on, Big Fella. Let's see what you've got."

When I stepped out of the bathroom after my shower, Talon was still sitting on our couch, moping. Yeah, he was watching Red Bull TV now, but his arms were folded over his chest. His back was hunched, and his lips pressed into a scowl.

"Don't worry, man. You'll get it next time." I patted him on the shoulder as I walked to my room in the small two-bedroom apartment we shared.

I was on the road most of the time these days so I didn't see the point in wasting money on a fancy apartment.

Rooming with Talon suited me just fine—at least for the moment. Sure, he was an overgrown man-child hiding in the body of a professional surfer, but I'd been there once myself. It was a clean-ish place to crash and save money for the future. I did have a plan, after all.

"We could finish the next level today if you would sit your butt down for another thirty minutes with me." His eyes never left the snowboarder on the screen carving back and forth down a snowy cliff.

"No-can-do, Bro. You know today's important. Keep practicing and you won't need to beg for my help with that game anymore." I pulled on a pair of shorts.

"You know you're freakishly good at Diablo III?" he called from the other room.

"When you're lying in a hospital bed for months on end, you have a lot of time on your hands. Practice makes perfect," I shouted back.

I was buttoning up my shirt when Talon appeared in the doorway. The soundtrack for the boarding clip was still playing on the TV behind him.

"You sure this is what you want to do?"

"There's nothing I'm more sure of," I answered without hesitation and with a lightness of heart that always came when I thought about my girl.

Talon heaved a sigh and shook his head. "I mean, Audrey is hot and all, but . . ."

He let his statement hang in the air.

"She's more than good-looking, and you know it."

Audrey was beautiful.

That wasn't a point up for dispute.

When she walked into a room, heads would turn and eyes would sweep from her shiny brunette head all the way down to her brightly-painted toes. I didn't always like it—the caveman inside me wanted to throw her over my shoulder and steal her away from prying eyes—but it couldn't be helped. People were always going to notice her. The girl didn't know how to do ugly.

But she was so much more than just another pretty face. When I looked at Audrey, her soul shined back and warmed every dark corner inside me.

After grabbing my wallet and shoving it in my back pocket, I pointed a finger at Talon.

"And don't disrespect my girl." The warning was clear in my tone, and Talon put his hands up in surrender.

"Hey, as long as this is what you really want, I'm behind you. I had to make sure. Bro-code and all." He clapped a hand on my shoulder good-naturedly before loping back to the couch and plopping down.

I'd bet money he was only going to move from that spot today to eat and use the bathroom.

I laughed under my breath. I remembered those days. Talon had a rare day off from training, so if he wanted to waste it binging extreme sports and drinking a case of Red Bull, I wasn't going to get on him for it.

"See ya," I called over my shoulder as I opened the front door. "I won't be back 'til late."

"You'd better not be!" he yelled as I left.

Pulling the door shut, I closed my eyes and lifted my face, taking a moment to thank the Creator for the beautiful day as well as the ability to enjoy it. I wouldn't soon forget where my blessings came from.

Flipping the keys in my hand, I set off for my car. It was time to surprise my soulmate.

Audrey

The sun was bright and high in the sky, the music on fleek, and I was channeling my inner Kaitlin by turning my dorm room into a personal dance club.

My suitemates—all six of them—were momentarily gone so I could turn the radio up as loud as I wanted without drawing a small crowd. There was just something about a solo dance party that could put me in a good mood.

Singing at the top of my lungs and shaking my booty, I threw beach necessities into my bag.

That was three things at once; I was *so* multitasking.

I mentally patted myself on the back for being super efficient. That's how I got things done these days. If I was going to crush this college thing in only three years—two-and-a-half if I really busted my butt—I had to do more than one thing at a time.

Taking classes over the summer was definitely going to help me earn my degree faster, but I still had to overload the credits each semester to finish early.

It was the worst.

Opening the window, I let the warm ocean breeze in. A touch of brine tickled my nose, and the repetitive slap of waves against the water-soaked sand caressed my ears.

I loved it. I had easily fallen in love with the Pacific coast. The ocean was a part of me now.

Grabbing my lavender cover-up, I pulled it over my head. The silky material slid over my bikini-clad body and swished around my calves. After almost two full semesters at a school that sat right on the beach, I'd finally mastered the art of beach attire. Which was to say, I learned not to be at all concerned with what I wore for a day in the sun. There was only one person on this planet I was looking to impress, and he was halfway around the world right now.

My lips curved into a light smile even as my heart pinched at the thought of how far away Logan was. Just then, a line of lyrics from the song playing caught my attention.

You light me up inside, like the fourth of July, whenever you're around, I always seem to smile, and people ask me how, well you're the reason why, I'm dancing in the mirror and singing in the shower . . .

Ah, how perfect. That was exactly how I felt about my surfer-boy.

Throwing my hands up above my head, I belted the words while shimmying and shaking. Closing my eyes, I conjured an image of Logan in my mind.

Attacking his rehabilitation with the passion of a rookie demon hunter, Logan had made leaps and bounds in his recovery during the last year. I was so proud of how far he'd come. His limp was barely noticeable these days, and his muscled form had filled back out.

Could I just say, 'yum'?

When we were together, I was constantly stealing glances at myself in mirrored surfaces. If Logan knew how often I did that, he'd probably think I was vain, but in reality, I was just making sure there wasn't a string of drool hanging from my mouth.

My guy was extremely hard not to ogle.

With the strengthening of his body, he was back doing his favorite activity in the world—surfing. Of course, it was only recreationally, but he'd found a way to keep the sport he loved in his life. And in more than just one way.

Three months ago he'd been picked up as a commentator for the World Surfing League. He traveled to commentate at surfing competitions all around the globe. When he wasn't working an event, he was helping to produce extreme videos of athletes for their sponsors.

He loved what he did, and I couldn't be happier for him—but we both hated the distance. FaceTiming was all well and good, but it wasn't the same as seeing him in the flesh. Technology would never replace having him hold me in his arms, replicate his smell, or duplicate the feel of his fingers combing through my hair.

It was just another reason to finish up my degree as quickly as possible. Wherever Logan was, the only place I wanted to be was at his side.

And when the times get rough, there ain't no given up, 'cause it just feels so right . . .

Singing the peppy lyrics caused a melancholy to drape over my spirit. I tried to shake it off, but my heart wasn't feeling it anymore.

With a sigh, I stopped dancing and refocused on finishing my packing. Ashlynn was expecting to meet me out front in a few minutes for our girls-only beach day.

"Please, don't stop on my behalf."

The smooth voice penetrated my head-fog and caused my heart to skip a beat.

Twisting around, I spotted a large body slouched against the doorframe. A zap of electricity shot from my feet all the way to my throat, and I dropped the bottle of sunscreen in my hand.

"Wha . . . huh? Logan? You're supposed to be in Australia!"

Logan shoved off the door jam and prowled toward me. Within no time, I was folded in his arms.

Leaning forward, Logan placed a soft kiss on my neck before nuzzling the spot with his nose. Saying it was distracting was too mild of a description. The world fell away whenever he was close.

I loved it.

"I miss the colors," he murmured into my hair.

"Hmm?" Why were words coming out of his mouth? This wasn't talking-time, this was snuggle-time.

Logan's chest shook as he released a deep chuckle, jostling me. After squeezing me tight, he put several inches of space between us. He held me back by my arms when my body swayed toward him. When he was sure I wouldn't suction myself back against him like an octopus, he brought a hand up and twisted a lock of my hair around his index finger.

"This always told me when I'd successfully unsettled you."

Narrowing my eyes, I batted his hand away.

"That was the worst superpower in the history of ever . . . or the afterlife."

"Oh, I beg to differ."

"Yeah, you would."

Brushing a strand of hair behind my ear, Logan laid his hand on my cheek. I closed my eyes and pressed into his touch.

"Mmmmm," I murmured.

"Does this mean you're happy to see me?"

I lazily blinked my eyes open, an easy smile blossomed across my face.

"I'm always happy to see you. I'm just a tad confused about how I'm seeing you *right now*. You're supposed to be halfway across the world." I lifted my eyebrows expectantly.

Stepping back, Logan brought a hand to his head to run through his hair. It was shorter on the sides than it used to be and a bit longer on top. That, paired with the scruff he sported, made him look a bit like a Viking.

The look worked for him. It worked *really* well for him.

I discretely ran the back of my hand over my mouth.

Phew. No drool.

"Well, that was a bit of a lie. The competition isn't until next week. I wanted to surprise you. To take you on a special date today."

The twinkle in his eyes drew me in, and I momentarily forgot what we were talking about again.

Gah!

With a shake of my head, I snapped back into reality. The cheese factor on that brief moony-eyed moment was even a little high for me.

"I would love to spend the day with you. I'm always game for a little—Oh, no!" I snapped my front teeth together and grimaced. "I planned a day with my roommate. I'd be a horrible person if I canceled."

I placed a hand on my forehead and rubbed. I so badly wanted to spend time with Logan, but Ashlynn and I had actually set this day apart for some bonding over a month ago. I couldn't be *that* girl.

Logan's easy smile caught me off guard.

"Ashlynn was actually my accomplice today. She helped me make sure that your day was free and clear."

"Ohhhh, sneaky! But I'll take it!"

"This is *not* the same beach . . . is it?"

After an hour drive down the coast, Logan had pulled his car over in a municipal parking lot in a small beach-town. The familiarity of the location rubbed at me, but it wasn't until this moment—while we were standing with our boards tucked under our arms—that it clicked.

Logan's blue eyes danced with merriment. He shot me a wink before taking off for the surf. I took a moment to watch him slice through the water atop his board before following his lead. Once I caught up to him, we paddled past the break so we could bob along the smooth surface.

"You brought me to the place you taught me to surf!" The smile on my face couldn't have been larger.

"I did." His eyes scanned the horizon before settling back on me. "Remember me telling you I used to come here when I was growing up? We haven't come back since we . . . reunited. I wanted us to experience this place together, on this side of the veil." A smile quirked his lips, and he tilted his head. "Now, let's see if your form has improved at all since our last lesson."

With a splash aimed at his face I took off paddling.

"Prepare to be amazed."

Several hours later, we were lounging on the sand. Me in a low-rise beach chair and Logan lounging across a towel. An umbrella pierced the sand behind us, shielding the remnants of the late-lunch picnic we'd just wolfed down. I sipped chilled lemonade and glanced over at Logan as he finished off the remains of an energy drink from a blue and silver can. His Adam's apple bobbed up and down as the liquid slid down his throat. Turning toward me a moment later, he caught me staring.

Clearing my throat, I adjusted the brim of my large floppy hat and felt the heat rise to my already-warm cheeks.

It was silly. I had nothing to be ashamed of. I'd caught Logan staring at me at least a dozen times today, but I could still get embarrassed when I got caught checking him out.

Time to get my mind out of the gutter.

"I can't believe I'm saying this, but a solid workout feels good." I reached my arms high above my head, enjoying the stretch. "The ache in my muscles reminds me I'm alive."

Logan jack-knifed to a sitting position and draped his arms over his bent knees.

"I did not just hear you say that." His jaw comically unhinged.

"Oh, come on. It's not that out of character."

"Woman, I spent weeks pushing, prodding, and cajoling you to do physical activity and all I received for my trouble were complaints."

I discreetly pinched my side to keep from laughing.

"Did you seriously just call me 'woman'?"

The smile in Logan's eyes told me he was having fun with this.

"You know there's only one punishment fit for this crime."

"Crime? Admitting I don't mind a tiny bit of exercise at a time? That's hardly a crime, Babe."

Standing in one fluid motion, his arms shot out and he hauled me from my chair.

"Wait, Logan. Don't even think it!" I squealed as he threw me over his shoulder, fireman style.

"It has to be done," he said as he jogged toward the water; his broad shoulder was nice to look at, but cut into my middle.

"You promised me there would never be another dunking incident!" My screeching and squirming were doing nothing to crumble Logan's resolve. Maybe because I couldn't stop giggling?

"Desperate times, My Love."

Logan bounded into the surf, with my forehead bouncing off his back.

"Ack!" The cold water smacked me in the face and splashed on my thighs. "Alright, you've had your fun. Care to—"

I didn't have a chance to spit out any more words before Logan plunged me into the chilly ocean. An oncoming wave twisted my body underwater, but arms reached behind my back and knees and lifted me to the surface before I had a chance to panic.

My long hair flopped over my face in a soggy sheet. I'm sure I looked like a drowned rat. Crossing my arms across my chest, I huffed out a breath of air.

"Am I *so* pretty right now?" I sarcastically asked.

Keeping one arm looped around my waist, Logan folded my mop of hair back and off my face. It sat funny on my head, but I forgot all about the mess when he repositioned me. Sliding the hand around my back to my waist, he pressed me closer and wrapped his other hand around the back of my neck.

"I'm sorry, Audrey." Leaning forward, he pressed a wet kiss to my nose. "You looked entirely too comfortable in that chair."

"Oh, is that the reason you broke your promise to me and tossed me in the water again?" I asked on a whisper, bringing my face close to Logan's and my lips a hair's breadth away. "Because I looked too comfortable?"

My lips barely brushed his on the last sentence. I tasted the salt water as I brought my hand to his shoulder.

"Umm, something like that," Logan distractedly answered, his focus less on talking and more on the body part we used to form words.

"Well, in that case . . ." I only just brought my mouth in contact with his before using my strength to shove away from him. Kicking my feet up, I splashed water right in his face as I darted away.

I heard Logan hacking as I used my swimming skills to get as far away from him as possible. I knew Logan well, and he wouldn't let an attack like that go unchallenged. I could practically feel his body gaining on mine. A spurt of adrenaline pushed me to swim faster.

"If that's how you want to play it," he yelled from behind me. "Game on!"

"Logan, this is just how I remember it."

I'd thought about this boardwalk many times since the day we raced down it, searching for a refuge from the demon chasing us. That day had been charged with many emotions—not all of them bad.

"It's *just* how you remember it?" Logan asked. His hand squeezed mine as he tilted his head to the side. The upward tilt of his lips morphed into a full smile, one that was filled with contentment. I loved that look on him.

"Perhaps not *just* how I remember. I'm definitely taking in more of the sights this time."

A small Ferris wheel circled to our right. The heavy-bellied sun sat on the water's horizon behind it, shooting evening rays of orange, pink, and purple light in our direction. Vendors selling funnel cakes, hot dogs, popcorn, and cotton candy dotted the perimeter of the planked pathway. The spiced scent of roasted almonds wafted around us in a hazy fog.

As we walked by the smattering of kiddie rides, squeals of delight filled our ears. Further down the path, booths lined the left side of the boardwalk. I laughed as a family of five took turns throwing darts at a board filled with multicolored balloons. They jeered at each other and took fake bets on who would pop the most.

Logan tugged on my hand. When I glanced at him, the setting sun only illuminated half his face. The side it lit was bathed in warm light and set his blue eye ablaze, reminding me of the azure sea we played in earlier.

"Come on," he tugged gently again, coaxing me to move forward. "There's something I want you to see."

I people-watched as we meandered. The evening was filled with an assortment of different characters. Along with families, couples of all ages ambled up and down the boardwalk, teenagers moved in herds, and we even spotted the occasional solo patron.

Sucking in a large breath of fresh ocean air, I took a moment to just enjoy being alive. To cherish the feel of Logan's hand in mine. To experience the cooling of the air as night approached. To soak in the blessing of life itself.

Everything about today was just so perfect . . . that was until I was jerked sharply to the left.

"Yikes!" Tripping on my own feet, I fell hard against Logan's chest. "Logan, what are you—"

My words cut off when Logan firmly pressed me back against the wood wall of one of the rickety booths and covered my mouth with a soul-searing kiss.

His warm lips moved over mine like only his could, completely claiming me as his own.

I didn't hesitate to bury my hand in his silky hair. The short strands tickled my palm and felt like velvet.

One of his hands was wrapped around the back of my head, holding me to him while also cushioning it against the rough wood. The other was fastened to my hip, his thumb torturing the sliver of exposed skin at my side.

The kiss went on and on, and I never wanted it to stop.

In fact, the first few times Logan did try to cool things down, I pressed into him further and enticed his compliance.

He may have started this, but who said that meant he got to say when it was over?

Logan pulled back another time, and I went up on my toes and kissed the underside of his jaw.

Groaning, he captured my hands and entwined our fingers, forcing space between us.

"You're not making this easy on me, Audrey."

I giggled and nipped at him again. "Since when have I ever made anything easy for you?"

With a quick peck on my mouth, he set me back. One dark blond eyebrow arched. "You have a point."

I licked the corner of my lips and considered diving back in for another taste.

"Don't look at me like that, Audrey," Logan warned.

"Like what?" I asked, full of fake innocence.

Shaking his head, he muttered, "You *are* going to make this difficult."

What was he going on about?

From the moment he pulled me into this space, my vision had been filled with him, but my eye caught on something sparkly.

Tilting my head, I caught my breath.

In the time we'd been "preoccupied," full night had fallen. Suspended above our heads, on what must have been dozens of strings, were hundreds of mini-twinkle lights. They lit the space above us and cast a warm glow down to the ground.

Speaking of the ground, under our feet, delicate purple petals covered the packed earth. A sweet aroma wafted up, heightening the romance factor.

It was magical.

And I didn't understand what was going on.

"Logan?" I questioned.

"Do you really not recognize where we are?"

Taking a closer look at our surroundings, I saw past the lights and flowers.

How could I for one moment have not realized where we were?

The whole day had been a hat-tip to that fate-filled day, so of course Logan would take me to the place we shared our first kiss. The one that shoved our relationship in a direction neither of us thought we wanted.

The kiss had been the spark that ignited us, and from that point on, as hard as we tried, we couldn't deny what we felt for each other.

"Is this," I pointed at the ground, "the exact place it happened?"

Bringing my hands to his face, he kissed my knuckles.

"Yes. I wanted a do-over. A chance to show you how that night should have gone."

"Babe, that's very romantic, but you do realize if you had been the one to kiss me, I would have given you a black eye."

"I would have let you. And it would have been worth it."

Swoon. That was smooth.

I couldn't control the silly grin on my face. I only half-wanted to.

"This day has been amazing. Thank you."

I meant it. I cherished every day I spent with Logan, but today was special.

"This isn't the only thing I wanted a do-over for, Love. There's something else I don't think I did properly the first time."

It was then I watched Logan go down on one knee.

My stomach jumped into my chest, and my heart—I think—beat right out of it. I didn't want to take my eyes off him to check, though. One of my organs could be laying on the ground right now for all I cared. There wasn't a force in any realm that was going to cause me to miss this moment.

Keeping my hands in his, Logan looked up at me. My arms shook with nerves, and I was pretty sure my palms were sweaty.

"Audrey," Logan began, "you are more than the love of my life. You are the one I want to spend this lifetime, and our existence afterward, with. You mean—"

"YES!"

Oops, the word just popped out of my mouth. Stupid mouth. He wasn't done.

"Whoops, sorry! Keep going. I didn't mean it."

Logan's brow pinched, and he cocked his head.

"You didn't mean it?"

"No! I mean, yes! I mean—" Oh, wow, I was royally botching this one up. "Keep going. I want to hear the whole thing before making up my mind."

Welp, that was a big fat lie.

Logan's brow relaxed, and the corner of his mouth quirked up. "Do you really? Because this ground is rather hard, so this isn't the most comfortable position. If I already know your answer . . ."

He started to rise from the ground and I pulled my hands free and shoved his shoulders. "Logan London, don't you dare try to get off that knee until you've done this properly. Just like you said."

Logan couldn't hold back the laugh that burst from his chest. He tried to rub it away with his hand, but it wasn't helping. I started tapping my foot.

"Anytime now."

Clearing his throat, he finally composed himself. Holding out his hand, he silently asked for mine. I offered him my left hand, knowing that was the important one.

Logan pressed his lips together tightly. I was going to deck him if he started to laugh again.

"Audrey," he continued, "you brought me back to life when I thought part of my soul was gone forever."

Okay, it was getting good again.

"I know with my whole being that our Creator knit you together to be mine, and formed me to be yours in return. It seems as if I have loved you since the first moment I laid eyes on you, and I will love you until the very end of time."

Without me noticing, Logan had pulled a delicate piece of jewelry out of his pocket. In that moment, the only thing I registered was that it was sparkly. But it could have been a piece of knotted string, and my answer would have been the same.

"Audrey Lyons, will you be my wife?"

KAITLIN

I watched my friends embrace after Audrey's heartfelt—and very vocal—"yes" to Logan's marriage proposal.

Audrey might not have been crying, but a tear slipped down my face that I quickly wiped away. Ninety percent of that tear was joy-filled. The other ten percent was full of self-pity.

Logan and Audrey had fought for their happily-ever-after. Fought for it tooth and nail. Believed in it even when they both thought they'd have to wait a lifetime to be together. For all the heartache that went into their romance, I should have been able to squeeze out a tear that was a hundred percent for them . . . but I hadn't.

"Well, that was disgustingly syrupy." The heavily-accented British brogue drifted out of the shadows before the rest of Morgan's dark form did. "I may have to take Logan's man-card away for that sugary display of romantic rubbish."

My heart swelled before I scrunched it back to a normal size. I hated my body's reaction to the deceitful hunter-turned-traitor-turned-returned prodigal son. Half of me wished he wasn't accepted back into the fold. The other half . . . well, that half couldn't be trusted. That half was a bit of a hussy.

"Argh. What are you even doing here, Morgan?"

He leaned up against the wood planks of one of the carnival structures flanking us, the twinkle lights from above only doing so much to expose his face. There were always some shadows clinging to the dark hunter that light hadn't yet been able to chase away.

Pulling out a dagger, Morgan did some fancy move where he flipped it in the air, caught it, and chucked it at the opposite wall where it embedded to the hilt. The whole movement was smooth, practiced, and executed in half a blink. Most likely something he picked up while serving The Dark Lord.

Was I supposed to be impressed?

Folding my arms in front of myself, I did my best to look uninterested.

"I'm back-up, Luv. Haven't you heard? This area is crawling with evil beasts."

"Right. I happen to be looking at one right now." Turning my back on the insufferable annoyance, I scanned for Logan and Audrey. Spotting them, I rushed to keep up.

"Ouch, that hurts," he complained when he appeared at my side a moment later. "So, should we take bets on how long those two last? I'd say three years, tops. And that's me being generous."

I squeezed my fists tight and told myself not to rise to his bait. I quickly lost the war with myself.

"Seriously, Morgan." Cutting my gaze to him, I tossed him the stink-eye before gluing my sight back on my marks. "Those two are as close to soul-mates as they come."

"Perhaps, but you know what they say. The candle that burns twice as bright, burns half as long." He shot me a meaning-filled side-eye as we trailed behind the newly-engaged couple. "You and I? We know that better than most."

The not-so-veiled reminder of our history cut deep, but I hid my reaction behind a mask of impassivity. The only way to shake Morgan was going to be to convince him I didn't have feelings for him—positive or negative. I hadn't done a great job with that task since he returned. Morgan could get my blood boiling like no one ever had. The more I lashed out at him, the harder he tried to provoke a reaction from me. It was twisted, but I hadn't been able to restrain myself.

One thing was for sure, I needed to try harder.

MORGAN

I watched her blonde ponytail bounce as she stomped away, not breathing until she intermingled with the crowd. Only then did I let my guard down.

What are you doing, mate?

I scrubbed a hand down my face, feeling the scars that laced my forehead and cheeks—a parting gift from Satan himself.

Watching Kaitlin weave through the crowd, careful to skirt the people walking unknowingly in her path, I questioned myself again.

The ship with that particular bird attached to it had sailed the moment I turned dark. She'd done nothing but try to prove that to me since I returned to the heavenly realm.

Perhaps it was time to throw in the towel, to admit nothing was left of our candle that had once burned so passionately. After all, there was a large after-life to explore. Why was I wasting my time mooning over one girl?

But then she turned, checking to see where I was, even though when she spotted me she played it off like she was scanning for danger.

Aye, there's the rub.

Those baby-blue eyes sparked something in me I almost wished they didn't . . . hope.

PLEASE WRITE A REVIEW

Reviews are the lifeblood of authors and your opinion will help others decide to read my books. If you want to see more from me, please leave a review.

Will you please write a review?
http://review.lifeafterbooks.com

Thank you for your help!

~ *Julie*

GET UPDATES FROM JULIE

JOIN MY NEWSLETTER

Please consider joining my exclusive email newsletter. You'll be notified as new books are available, get exclusive bonus scenes, previews, ridiculous videos, and you'll be eligible for special giveaways. Occasionally, you will see puppies. 🐶

Sign up for snarky funsies:
JulieHallAuthor.com/newsletter

I respect your privacy. No spam.
Unsubscribe anytime. 🖤

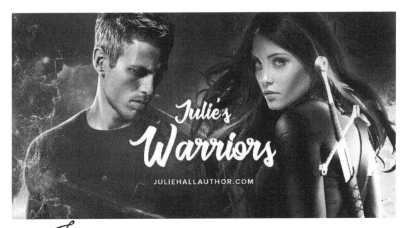

*J*oin the fan club - we're a crazy fun bunch! We love reading, puppies, and Red Bull. Okay, the Red Bull is all me.

If you love my books, get involved and get exclusive sneak peeks before anyone else. Sometimes I even give out free puppies (#joking-notjoking).

You'll get to know other passionate fans just like you, and you'll get to know me better too! It'll be fun!

See you in there!

~ *Julie*

ABOUT THE AUTHOR

JULIE HALL

My name is Julie Hall and I'm a USA TODAY bestselling, multiple award-winning author. I read and write YA paranormal / fantasy novels, love doodle dogs and drink Red Bull, but not necessarily in that order.

My daughter says my super power is sleeping all day and writing all night . . . and well, she wouldn't be wrong.

I believe novels are best enjoyed in community. As such, I want to hear from you! Please connect with me as I regularly give out sneak peeks, deleted scenes, prizes, and other freebies to my friends and newsletter subscribers.

Visit my website:
JulieHallAuthor.com

Get my other books:
amazon.com/author/julieghall

Join the Fan Club:
facebook.com/groups/juliehall

Get exclusive updates by email:
JulieHallAuthor.com/newsletter

Find me on:

amazon.com/author/julieghall

facebook.com/JulieHallAuthor

bookbub.com/authors/julie-hall-7c80af95-5dda-449a-8130-3e219d5b00ee

goodreads.com/JulieHallAuthor

instagram.com/Julie.Hall.Author

BOOKS BY JULIE HALL

Start Julie's new YA series - *Fallen Legacies*!

Stealing Embers (Fallen Legacies Book 1)

www.StealingEmbers.com

AUDIOBOOKS BY JULIE HALL

The *Life After* series is available on Audiobook!

Hear Audrey, Logan, and the entire *Life After* cast come to life, and experience the story like never before! **Relive the experience, download the audiobooks today:**

http://Audio.LifeAfterBooks.com

Made in the USA
Coppell, TX
31 March 2022

75794301R00446